SEWER, GAS & ELECTRIC

Also by Matt Ruff
Fool on the Hill

SEWER, GAS & ELECTRIC

THE PUBLIC WORKS TRILOGY

ELECTRIC

A NOVEL BY

MATT RUFF

The Atlantic Monthly Press
New York

Published simultaneously in Canada
Printed in the United States of America

FIRST EDITION

Library of Congress Cataloging-in-Publication Data

Ruff, Matt.
    Sewer, gas & electric : the public works trilogy : a novel / by
Matt Ruff. — 1st ed.
        p.   cm.
    ISBN 0-87113-641-4
    I. Title.
PS3568.U3615S49   1997
813'.54—dc20   96-36039

Design by Laura Hammond Hough

The Atlantic Monthly Press
841 Broadway
New York, NY 10003

10 9 8 7 6 5 4 3 2

For Ayn Rand

The Social Register

Rich
Harry Gant, president of Gant Industries
Amberson Teaneck, a dead corporate raider

Upper-Middle- & Middle-Class
Joan Fine, a white liberal Catholic
Lexa Thatcher, publisher of *The Long Distance Call*

Crew of the submarine *Yabba-Dabba-Doo:*
Philo Dufresne, captain
Morris Kazenstein, first mate and all-around Jewish-American *Wunderkind*
Irma Rajamutti, chief engineer
Oliver, Heathcliff, Mowgli, Galahad, and Little Nell Kazenstein, the engine room crew
Twenty-Nine Words for Snow, a foundling son of the Inuit people
Marshall Ali, Twenty-Nine Words's Kurdish mentor
Norma Eckland, chief of communications
Asta Wills, sonar operator
Osman Hamid, sub driver
Jael Bolívar, resident biologist

Gant Industries executives & flacks:
Vanna Domingo, comptroller of public opinion
Clayton Bryce, head of Creative Accounting
Whitey Caspian, a public opinion engineer

C. D. Singh, a congressional lobbyist
Bartholomew Frum, a trainee
Fouad Nassif, another trainee

Seraphina Dufresne, Philo Dufresne's nineteen-year-old daughter (by the late Flora Daris)
Rabi Thatcher, the seven-year-old daughter of Lexa Thatcher and Philo
Ellen Leeuwenhoek, photographer and investigative reporter for *The Long Distance Call*
Toshiro Goodhead, a male stripper
Ernest G. Vogelsang, an agent of the F.B.I.'s Un-Un-American Activities Division

Working-Class, Poor & Hyper-Impoverished

Kite Edmonds, a 181-year-old Canadian-born veteran of the American Civil War
Maxwell, a veteran of the '07 War for Free Trade in Sub-Saharan Africa
Troubadour Penzias, another veteran of the '07 War for Free Trade in Sub-Saharan Africa
Captain Chance Baker of the icebreaker *South Furrow*, and later of the sub-killer *Mitterrand Sierra*
Captain Wendy Mankiller of the attack submarine *City of Women*

Employees of the New York City Department of Sewers' Zoological Bureau:

Fatima Sigorski, shift supervisor
Lenny Prohaska and Art Hartower of May Team 23
Eddie Wilder, trainee, May Team 23

Frankie Lonzo and Salvatore Condulucci, fish wranglers, New York Aquarium
Oscar Hill, an unfortunate Scoutmaster
Oblio Wattles, an unfortunate Scout

It's very strange for me to look at your generation. You see, we always had this idea that each generation was going to be brighter, that each generation was going to be more progressive, and would cheer more for justice and more for peace. But my youngest son, who's 16, says to me, "Dad, you're so quaint and romantic. You think things are going to get better, that there's hope," he says, "but none of us believe this." And then he tells me how half the world is going to be wiped out by AIDS, how the polar icecap is going to melt, that the tropical rainforest will be gone in thirty years and we won't have any oxygen, which doesn't matter anyway since the nuclear holocaust is going to happen within seven years, and if I'm a little doubtful about the dates, he says he can prove it to me on his computer. . . . in my view, if the next generation is going to make some contribution it'll be the discovery of how you struggle for social change without having any hope. In the Sixties, you see, when you jumped on the earth, the earth jumped back just like Einstein said it would. We knew we'd win every battle because every day we grew up. Every day was a new day and being on the brink of the Apocalypse was romantic. But maybe this vision that you have is the more realistic of the two . . .

—Abbie Hoffman at the University of South Carolina, 1987

They say people don't believe in heroes anymore. Well, damn them! You and me, Max, we're gonna give 'em back their heroes.

—Roger Ward in the movie *Mad Max*

Disclaimer

The aim of history is to reconstruct the past according to its own pattern, not according to ours. All epochs, said Ranke, are equally close to God. But historians, try as they will to escape, remain prisoners of their own epoch. "No man," wrote Emerson, "can quite emancipate himself from his own age and country, or produce a model in which the education, the religion, the politics, usages, and arts of his time shall have no share. Though he were never so original, never so wilful and fantastic, he cannot wipe out of his work every trace of the thoughts midst which it grew." The historian, like everyone else, is forever trapped in the egocentric predicament, and 'presentism' is his original sin.

—Arthur M. Schlesinger, Jr., *The Cycles of American History*

The story that follows should not be mistaken for a serious attempt to predict what the year 2023 will be like when it actually gets here. Second-guessing future history is a losing game, and anyway not as much fun as just making it all up. *The Public Works Trilogy* concerns itself solely with 2023 as it exists in 1990, in the back room of the house in Boston where I write the first of these words.

An altogether different year . . .

SEWER

I

Alligators, small boys and at least one horse have accidentally swum in the sewers of New York. The boys and the horse seem not to have enjoyed the experience, but the alligators throve on it.
—Robert Daley, *The World Beneath the City*

A Man in a High Place Alone

No one could say he hadn't been warned.

The observation eyrie pricked the dome of the sky some twenty-six hundred and seventy feet above the city's streets—half a mile up, with yardage to spare. The eyrie was not open to the public. Most visitors to the Gant Phoenix were restricted to the Prometheus Deck on the 205th floor, itself a loftier vantage point than that offered to tourists anywhere else in the world, even at the twenty-three-hundred-foot Gant Minaret in Atlanta. A chosen few friends, business associates, and politicians were allowed to climb still higher—on days when the weather was deemed agreeable and not likely to carry anyone away with a sudden hurricane gust—out onto the 208th-floor terrace, there to breathe for free the hazy, rarefied air that sold at $7.50 a liter bottle in the Phoenix Souvenir Shop. But only Harry Gant himself had ever been permitted to make the final ascent, another three hundred feet up a utility ladder enclosed within the Phoenix's mooring-mast pinnacle, through the trapdoor at the top, and so at last into the great glass globe that was Gant's Eyrie, the highest point on the tallest structure ever erected by human beings in the history of the world.

"Questionable," his comptroller of public opinion had said years ago, when he'd first told her his idea for the eyrie. "Definitely questionable from a media standpoint, you keeping it to yourself that way."

"Why questionable?" They'd both been a little drunk at the time, and her tone was more one of bemusement than of true caution, but wine and lightheartedness actually made Gant more attentive.

"Think biblical allusion, Harry. You're practically begging some columnist or TV commentator to take a cheap shot at you."

"How so?"

"Just think about it: a powerful figure standing in a high place, with all the world laid out below him . . ."

"Oh," he said, "that. But now wait a minute, I seem to recall there were *two* powerful fellows up in the high place in that story, so maybe—"

"No one's going to compare you to Jesus, Harry."

"And why not?"

"Because Jesus didn't want any of the things he could see from up there, and you'll want plenty of them. Five minutes after you first get up in your little perch you'll have thought of three new product lines to invest in—all wildly impractical, all somehow threatening to the environment or the public welfare, and all ultimately profitable, at least until the lawsuits are settled. Another five minutes and you'll be scouting around for a site for your next building, which you'll probably want to make twice as tall as this one. And five minutes after *that* you'll probably throw up, because you know as well as I do that you don't like heights."

It was true: he didn't like heights. Strange admission from a man who owned two and a half superskyscrapers and a picket fence of lesser towers, but there you had it. His aversion to air travel was legendary: preferring to go by train if it were necessary to go at all, he'd built a web of Lightning Transit lines linking a hundred cities, almost single-handedly bringing about the twenty-first-century American renaissance in rail. At the same time, Gant Industries had brought virtual-reality teleconferencing to a level where he could now attend simultaneous board meetings in Singapore, Prague, Tokyo, and Caracas without ever leaving the terra firma of Manhattan.

Not even the human-made canyons and peaks of his home city, symbols as they were of everything he held most dear, could counter his basic acrophobia. Gazing northwest across the skyscape at the gaudy spires of Trump's Riverside Arcadia, or closer in at the Chrysler Building (whose piddling seventy-seven stories he held title to), or south at the twin giants overlooking the Battery, whatever emotions Harry Gant might have felt did not include a desire to rush over and catch the first elevator to the top.

But the Phoenix was different. The Phoenix was his—not just his property but his creation, *his* building, *the tallest building in the history of the world.* Standing at its zenith (or atop the Minaret in Atlanta, the former tallest building in the history of the world, though he didn't visit there very often anymore), his whole perception seemed transformed somehow, as if what held him up was not the crude geometry of concrete and steel but the force of his own will, a force that could not be shaken.

Well.

To be completely honest, his comptroller's jest about throwing up had almost come true, but only almost. The Gant Phoenix had officially opened in June of 2015, a month marked by some of the fiercest thunderstorms to strike the Eastern Seaboard in over a century. While doomcriers spoke ominously of degenerating world weather patterns, Gant invited the city's leading lights to come on up to the Prometheus Deck one afternoon and "watch the free fireworks." A battery of motion-dampers incorporated into the building's superstructure helped neutralize its sway in the wind; the victory punch still sloshed around in its bowl a little, but after a trip past the buffet table, where all the hors d'oeuvres had been spiked with Dramamine, the party guests found this entertaining rather than nauseating.

"But I wouldn't go up in the eyrie just yet, Harry," Gant's architect advised. "Not today."

"Why? Worried about the lightning?"

"Not the lightning. The wind. It won't be near as steady as the rest of the building."

"No problem there," Gant said. "So long as it doesn't snap off . . ."

"It won't snap. You hold up a fishing rod and whip it back and forth, it won't snap either, but that doesn't mean you want to be sitting on the tip of the damn thing."

"Hmm," said Harry Gant. "Thanks for the warning. Maybe I'll have a few more hors d'oeuvres."

An hour later Gant was up in the glass globe, being pitched around the eyrie's interior like a hot-air balloonist who'd drifted into a cyclone. Clinging for dear life to a slender handrail that was the eyrie's only fixture, he felt his gorge rising and came within an ace of spraying Dramamine-soaked canapés all over his high perch. Only a chance vision saved him, for suddenly the gods of the storm granted him a clear view down three hundred feet to the open-air terrace on the 208th floor, where a blond photographer, lashed in place with a lifeline made mostly of duct tape, was struggling to focus a zoom-lens on him. Gant made the best of the bare seconds he had to compose himself: he beat back his rebellious stomach, he steadied himself and stood firm, he fixed his features with a look of casual determination. The heavens exploded around him; below, a high-speed shutter clicked.

The photo appeared on the cover of the next month's *Rolling Stone,* with the caption, HARRY DENNIS GANT: A RIDER ON THE STORM OF MODERN TIMES, and if Gant's lightning-wreathed figure did in some ways resemble a certain fallen angel last seen cavorting on Bald Mountain, that didn't change the fact that it was one hell of an impressive portrait. From that day forward Harry Gant ceased to worry about biblical allusions, though he was not above making use of them himself.

A good example of this—and a further proof of his former comptroller's prescience—could be glimpsed in the middle distance at Manhattan's north end, where a modern-day ziggurat made its own bid for grandeur. From a circular foundation covering several blocks of the defunct neighborhood on which it was being erected, the ziggurat curved upward in a series of exaggerated steps, a steel-boned purgatory mount sheathed in translucent black glass. As of this October day in 2023 it had drawn almost even with the Phoenix at its crown; by Thanksgiving it would be taller, and Gant's Eyrie that much diminished. By the end of the decade, if Harry Gant had anything to say about it, it would have broken the mile marker.

Babel, he called it. Gant's New Babel, the fabled Tower completed at last after a five-millennium hiatus in construction. Lower floors available for early occupancy at special rates; call for details.

"Aren't you tempting fate by naming it that?" the media interviewers asked him time and again, giving him millions of dollars of free publicity in the process. "Aren't you afraid of history repeating itself?"

"Not a bit," Gant responded. "This is a new age, ladies and gentlemen. If you want my opinion on the matter of history, I think the real reason God cancelled the Babylonian project is He was waiting for a group of folks who could do the job right."

A new age: English was the mother tongue now, a mother tongue that had already been fractured into a thousand dialects, only to thrive and grow stronger. Humankind had stormed heaven in homegrown chariots of fire and returned to tell the tale. And as far as God was concerned, if He weren't already an American at heart, ready and willing to root for American achievement—well, by the time Harry Gant and the Department of Public Opinion were finished with Him, He would be.

Down in the Canyons with Eddie Wilder (and Teddy May)

OK, granted that things might seem a little less overwhelmingly cheery down in the canyons of the city, where certain sections of sidewalk had not known the direct light of the sun in decades, and where pedestrians, who could not be individually fitted with the sort of motion-damping equipment that steadied the Phoenix, had to manage as best they could against the microgales that roared in the open spaces between skyscrapers. But that was no reason not to have a wonderful day.

Consider Eddie Wilder, late of Moose Hollow, Maine, who set off for his new job that morning with the traditional spring in his step that marks a would-be world beater. Looking spiffy in his green and white Department of Sewers uniform, he came up out of the subway at 34th and Broadway and stopped to rubberneck at the sights. Moose Hollow being one of the ten most technologically disadvantaged places in the continental U.S. (as noted on the front page of *USA Today*'s Life section*)*, and Eddie being the first member of his family in three generations to visit a city larger than Bangor, it all seemed fresh and exciting: the Electric Negroes hawking newspapers from sidewalk stands, the anti-collision–equipped taxis performing a ballet of impact avoidance on the crowded streets, the monolithic architecture obliterating the horizon in every direction.

Harry Gant would have been proud, if unsurprised, to learn that the Gant Phoenix was Eddie Wilder's personal favorite building in the whole of Manhattan. Of course if you were to ask Eddie point-blank about this, he would tell you that his favorite was the Empire State Building. He didn't know that there was no more Empire State Building, not since Christmas night in 2006, when a fully loaded 747–400 had been struck by a meteorite just after takeoff from Newark International and come screaming out of control across the Hudson. Celebrated disaster chronicler Tad Winston Peller had described this incident in graphic detail in the runaway bestseller *Chicken Little and Flight 52,* but there being no bookstore or library in Moose Hollow, Eddie Wilder never read it. Likewise—the Hollow's one newspaper, the *Hollow Point,* being concerned pretty exclusively with the killing and eating of large animals—he'd never caught any of the press releases in which up-and-coming business mogul Harry Gant had sworn to rebuild the famous landmark in record time, "but more contemporary, with a new name, and twice as big in every dimension." So Eddie's confusion was understandable. If the Phoenix seemed somewhat out of proportion with the building in the black-and-white postcard his great-grandfather had purchased on his way home from the Korean War, well, real stuff was always bigger than pictures, Eddie figured.

Eddie's only gripe about the Phoenix had to do with the Electric Billboards, huge strobing grids of light suspended about three-quarters of the way to the top, which struck him as a defacement of historic property. There were four of them, each about twenty stories tall, one to a building side. The four featured ads jumped clockwise every fifteen minutes, so when the Coca-Cola trademark beamed westward, for example, you knew it was between a quarter and half past the hour. The ad presently facing west, however, was one Eddie couldn't figure out, which only increased his irritation, like a joke he was too dumb to get. It resembled a page torn from a giant's day-calendar, except there was no date, just a number, 997, picked out in red on a white background.

"Don't look so upset," a voice said. "Nobody knows what the hell it means, not even Harry."

Eddie turned from the tower to face a woman about his height, plain-featured but with the sort of laugh crinkles around her eyes and mouth that betoken a person of general good humor. Her hair (also plain, an unremark-able shade of brown) was tied back in a lank ponytail; agewise she looked to be in her late thirties or early forties. A cigarette burned between the fingers of her right hand; held loosely in her left was one of the latest Marvel-D.C. graphic novellas, *Joan of Arc Returns.*

Ordinarily Eddie would have asked about the comic book (he was a mail-order *Spiderman* fan himself), but he was in New York now and wanted to adopt a big-city attitude as soon as possible. So he pointed at the woman's cigarette instead and said with what he hoped was a proper tone of urban rudeness: "You know you shouldn't smoke those."

She responded by taking a puff, not in a nasty way—she didn't breathe it in his face—but as if to say that he hadn't suggested anything she hadn't already considered long and hard on her own. "You're right, I definitely shouldn't," she said, and added with a wink: "Don't gawk too long. You don't want to be late for work."

With that she stepped from the curb, raised a hand; a taxi swerved neatly around a double-parked delivery van and pulled up in front of her. Only after she'd gotten into the cab and taken off down the street did Eddie realize she'd been wearing a uniform like his.

You don't want to be late. . . . He checked the address on the form letter in his pocket and got walking, west towards the Hudson. The brick building housing the Zoological Bureau of the Department of Sewers was on Eleventh Avenue, across from the Jacob Javits Convention Center. Eddie arrived on time and presented himself at the registration desk, where a supervisor named Fatima Sigorski logged him in. "You'll be in May Team 23," she told him. "Your coworkers on the team are Joan Fine, Art Hartower, and Lenny Prohaska." She pushed a pair of what looked like plastic dog tags across the desktop. "Make sure you wear these at all times when you're working."

"What for?"

"Information aid. In case you become eligible for early retirement in a way that makes you hard to identify." She pointed down the hall at a half-open doorway. "That's the briefing room. You'll find Hartower and Prohaska in there. Hartower's thin and balding, looks like a middle-aged I.R.S. flack. Prohaska looks the same, except he's got his nose pierced with a zircon. He's from California."

"And Miss Fine?"

"She'll be holed up in the toilet right about now."

"Oh."

The briefing room was laid out like one of the smaller theaters in a multiplex, red plastic chairs facing a tiny holographic screen. Eddie counted about thirty men and women, all in Department uniforms showing varying degrees of wear; he seemed to be the only newcomer. Hartower and Prohaska were standing beneath a framed blow-up of a very old photograph, sharing a copy of the day's *New York Times.* The framed photo, which obviously occupied a position of honor on the wall, showed what appeared to be a wino levering himself up out of a manhole.

Eddie went over and introduced himself to his new colleagues. Then he asked, with a cautious nod at the strange photo: "Who's that?"

"That," Prohaska said, flaring his nostrils so that the zircon wiggled, "is Teddy May."

"The greatest human being ever to wade through the city's effluvia," added Hartower. "God bless him and rest him in peace."

"What's wrong with his right eye?"

"Job-related injury," said Prohaska. "He cooked it crawling into a utility duct to fix a ruptured steam line while simultaneously fighting off two alligators with his bare hands . . ."

"Alligators?" Eddie said.

". . . and then, having taken care of that, he went back topside where the temperature was negative nine degrees Fahrenheit (forty below, factoring in wind chill), this being winter. The transition from hot to cold paralyzed every muscle and nerve in his eyelid."

"Wait a minute," Eddie said. "Alligators in the sewers? Wasn't that just a story?"

"What story?"

"You know: the book by that guy who nobody was allowed to take his picture."

"Did you ever read the book by that guy who nobody was allowed to take his picture?"

"Of course not. Nobody's ever read that book. And anyway I don't read books. But even up in the Hollow, everybody knows the *story*."

"Well," said Hartower, "Teddy May *lived* it."

"And that's what we do in the Zoological Bureau? Hunt 'gators?"

"Don't be ridiculous," Prohaska said. "Teddy May and his men finished off the last of *them* in the 1930s."

"True," said Hartower, "you do still encounter the occasional *Gavialis gangeticus* cruising around under Little India and Little Pakistan, maybe even a once-in-a-blue-moon *Crocodylus niloticus,* but no alligators."

Fatima Sigorski entered the briefing room and clapped her hands for attention. "All right, everybody, let's settle in."

"Stick with us," Prohaska and Hartower said, steering Eddie towards a trio of seats at the back. A familiar woman with a ponytail slipped in as Fatima turned to shut the door; Eddie could smell the tobacco right off, even though this whole building was clearly designated as a nonsmoking environment.

"Hey!" he said, pointing. "I know her. Who is she?"

"That's the other member of our team," Hartower told him. "Joan Fine." In a conspirator's tone: "Formerly Joan Gant."

"Gant?"

"Ex-wife of the billionaire," said Prohaska. "She was the chief advertising executive over at Gant Industries, comptroller of public opinion. Once upon a time."

"Not only that," added Hartower, "but she's also the illegitimate test-tube daughter of Sister Ellen Fine, the renegade nun who led the Catholic Womanist Crusade back in the Oughts."

"Womanist Crusade?"

"You know: the lesbian habit-burners who wanted the pope's permission to be ordained and have babies."

"Oh," said Eddie, who didn't know, actually. "So if her ma was a queer nun and her husband was a billionaire, what's she doing working in the sewers?"

"Penance."

The sewer workers were all seated now; Fatima Sigorski clapped her hands once more for silence. "I have here the advance version of this month's tactical report," she began, holding up an Electric Clipboard. "As usual it's a mix of good news and bad news. Some dedicated work on the part of our Brooklyn division has virtually stamped out the *Serrasalmus nattereri* infestation under Park Slope. On the minus side, last night some Cuban restaurant owner's grandfather got zapped to death on the basement john by what sounds like an *Electrophorus electricus*. There were no actual witnesses and the police think it might be some kind of life insurance scam, so we're going to wait for confirmation before taking any official action. Still, you probably want to bring a pair of rubber-soled thigh-highs if you go cruising under Spanish Harlem . . ."

Joan Fine sat near the front, wishing she could smoke. But while Fatima Sigorski might turn a blind eye to the occasional cigarette sneaked in the women's room, she didn't even allow gum chewing during assembly, so Joan's only recourse for tension release was the rosary in her pocket, which she fretted with continuously while Fatima spoke. Joan's mother had given it to her on the day of her first confession; and though what Joan had confessed had been a youthful disdain for Roman Catholic theology, she'd held on to the rosary, calling it a good luck keepsake. The beads were cheap acrylic, but the crucifix was true silver, wrought by a Reformed Carmelite sister who moonlighted as a master smithy. Christ's silver crown of thorns had been painstakingly engraved with a laser stylus and when held up to a strong light would project the prayer of the Reverend Cabal of Catholic Womanists against the nearest wall, in pinprick letters of fire: *Fools rush in where angels fear to tread. God make us foolish for our struggle.*

Joan thought this would be an apt motto for the Department of Sewers' Zoological Bureau as well. Which of course was why she'd taken the job.

"Now, as for today's special assignment: I'm afraid we have a definite confirmation on that new species I hinted about last Friday. Can I have the lights down, please?" The overhead lighting dimmed obediently. "The footage you're about to see," said Fatima, "was taken by May Team 67 right before the entire crew became unavoidably eligible for early retirement. Roll tape."

She stepped aside, and the projection screen flickered to light in three dimensions. The viewpoint was a fixed camera facing off the stern of one of the Department's armored patrol barges. The barge was moving through one of the larger, canal-sized sewer tunnels, and it was immediately obvious that something was wrong: judging from the whitewater spume the barge was kicking up behind it, the pilot was either fighting one hell of a current or, more likely, running away from something at full throttle. As the barge swung hard around a bend, a series of shotgun blasts could be heard, and the booming percussion of big-caliber pistols: members of the doomed May Team emptying their weapons into the sludgy water. To no avail—for suddenly a massive form surged up out of the barge's wake, toothy maw yawning wide like a razor-studded chasm. The viewers in the briefing room shrank back screaming in their seats as the monster leapt through the screen in flawless 3-D, but it never landed. Right at that point, probably a split second before the camera was smashed from its mount, the editor of the recording had thrown the sequence into a loop, so that the creature froze in place halfway out of the water, twisting back and forth as if to present itself for inspection.

"*Carcharodon carcharias*," Fatima Sigorski said, as the terrified sewer workers regained their composure. "Positive I.D. from our friends at the Bronx Zoo. We're not sure yet how it got down there, but SHQ is theorizing that it's a flushed pet. That, or another practical joke by those peckerwoods in the NYU Ichthyology Department."

The shocked voice of Eddie Wilder: "That's a fucking great white shark!"

Joan Fine looked around at the sound of his voice. Eddie had gotten halfway out of his chair and was paused there trembling, while Prohaska and Hartower, each having grabbed an elbow, tried to sit him back down. "Shut up!" Prohaska hissed frantically. "Shut up and behave, you want to get a demerit your first day out?" Joan smiled. Eddie would probably end by annoying her, but she couldn't help liking someone still innocent enough to speak without tact or knowledge of euphemism.

Fatima, however, did not appreciate the breach of usage.

"It's a *Carcharodon carcharias*," she scolded, punching every hard consonant in the Latin. "An alternative-environment–adapted *Carcharodon carcharias*. I trust we'll all remember that if we get within earshot of a media rep. There's only one thing in the sewers with less than ten letters in its name, and it's not 'shark.'"

"Sorry," Eddie said. "Sorry, but it looks just like—"

"*Furthermore,* SHQ is continuing its practice of assigning code referents to notable members of a given species. Though there's no indication yet that we'll be seeing more than one of them—I certainly hope we won't—it's been resolved that individual *Carcharodon* will be named after beer brands. This," she indicated the still-twitching hologram, "is Meisterbrau. That's the name I expect to hear you use if you talk about it over lunch—not Smiley, not Jaws, not Mack the Knife, but *Meisterbrau.* Is that clear?" Eddie nodded meekly.

"Now our available information indicates that Meisterbrau has been feeding in the tunnel complex around the Times Square Interchange. All May Teams are to converge on that area carrying maximum armament. Team leaders remember to sign out for the weapons and get yourselves a Negro from the pool; also, methane and other toxics levels are high today, so be sure to top off your oxygen tanks. That's all, people. Get to your barges, good luck, and be careful out there. And *watch your language.*"

The Morning Schedule

A polite disembodied voice spoke from Harry Gant's wrist: "Quarter past eight, sir."

Gant pulled up his sleeve to reveal the face of Dick Tracy, sized to the dimensions of a quartz timepiece. Gant's thumb brushed the slash of Tracy's chin, and he said: "That you, Toby?"

"Yes sir, Mr. Gant. Ms. Domingo sent me. Time to come down, sir."

"What am I scheduled for this morning, Toby?"

"You're giving an address at the Gant Media & Technical School for Advanced Immigrant Teens at nine o'clock, sir. After which you're holding a crisis-reduction meeting with the Department of Public Opinion concerning the pirate Philo Dufresne. And, of course, the Negro problem."

"Oh," Gant said, "that. Toby?"

"Yes sir?"

"Is there something special about today that I should remember? Not business; check my personal file."

"Yes sir." On the 208th-floor terrace, the Automatic Servant scratched the side of its head with a dusky finger. Then it said: "You might be thinking of your wedding anniversary, Mr. Gant. That is to say, it *would* be your anniversary today, if you were still—"

"Right," Gant said, snapping his fingers. "Day before Halloween, funny I could even forget it."

"Former Ms. Gant," Toby added, "also has a birthday coming up next month. Her forty-first. And you'll be forty-three next week."

"Right, right. OK, Toby, you go tell Ms. Domingo I'll be down shortly. Also tell her I'm going to want six Portable Televisions for media support at that school thing at nine. That's all."

"Yes sir," the Servant said, and was gone. Gant lingered in his eyrie another minute yet. *Good old Joan,* he thought, his memory of her tinged with mild regret but no ill will. The last he knew of his ex-wife she'd been working some blue-collar job and running a welfare shelter in the Bowery. A meager use of her talents . . . but he smiled just the same, for thinking of Joan made him think of the past in general, and thinking of the past in general made him think of himself, of the American-Dream-come-true storybook tale that was his life.

Harry Dennis Gant, born in 1980 in the back seat of a broken-down Toyota parked at a rest stop off the Jersey Turnpike. His mother a construction worker by trade, his father a schoolteacher, both of them jobless and homeless at the time of Harry's nativity, the dying Toyota representing the last of their possessions. And yet from these humble beginnings—the twentieth-century equivalent, Harry Gant liked to think, of being born in a log cabin—look what he had made of himself in only forty-three years. Look at all he had wrought in the world, and his life not half finished yet, not half.

Love of self and love of country lit a fire in the hearth of Harry Gant's soul, warming him to the new day. He was glad to be alive; glad too to have such a wonderful gift—the gift of inspiration—to bestow on the Advanced Teens he would address an hour from now. With a reverent nod to the great city below, he lifted the trapdoor in the floor of the eyrie and started down the ladder.

A Word about the Negro Problem

The Negro problem bedeviling Gant Industries should not be confused with the African-American problem, which was simply that there weren't any African-Americans anymore, or any black Africans either for that matter, at least not that you could invite over to your house for dinner. Back at the turn of the century a literal Black Plague, its origin and cause still completely unknown, had turned inner cities across the United States into overnight ghost towns, emptied Nigeria and three dozen other sub-Saharan nations, and sent the scant handfuls of survivors fleeing to an ever more remote series of hidden sanctuaries. Celebrated disaster chronicler Tad Winston Peller had written a book about it, the runaway bestseller *They Say It Started in Idaho: Tales of the Black Pandemic of Twenty-Ought-Four.* This popular work had served as the basic text for no less than seven miniseries, not to mention a weekly science-fiction drama, *Dark Heart, Red Planet*, about a family of jazz-loving astronauts who escape extinction by being on Mars at the time of the plague outbreak.

But all of that is another story. The Negro problem had nothing to do with disease or cable television; it was solely a consumer-marketing phenomenon.

The Self-Motivating Android—test-marketed by a Disney subsidiary in 2003 and mass-produced by the fledgling Gant Industries as the Gant Automatic Servant starting in 2007—achieved initial prominence as a cost-effective industrial labor substitute. The first Androids were only vaguely humanoid in appearance, intended to be functional rather than eye-pleasing, but Harry Gant, looking ahead to a time when his Servants would be affordable in the home as well as in mines and factories, insisted on a more aesthetic design. And so from 2010 on it became possible to purchase Automatic Servants in a wide selection of realistic skin tones and somatotypes. Gant, a great believer in offering variety to his customers, certainly didn't ask his sales force to push any one particular model over another; he was as surprised as anyone when Configuration AS204—your Automatic Servant in basic black—began outselling all other versions combined by a margin of ten to one.

For a long while it didn't appear that there would be any public relations problem. People didn't seem to mind—in fact seemed strangely comforted by—the sudden profusion of dark-skinned Servants, all of them polite and hard-working to a fault. The ace of corporate advertising is the basic human desire to minimize or look away from gross unpleasantness, to which end the AS204s acted like an army of Sidney Poitiers and Hattie McDaniels dispatched to exorcise the memory of the African Pandemic; but the flipside of that ace is the peril of lurking guilt, and when Harry Gant was told about a D.A.R. heiress who had purchased three hundred Servants for use in a sort of antebellum theme park on her plantation estate, he used his advertorial influence to keep the media away from the story.

He couldn't stop American idiom, though. The Oxford University philologist kept on retainer by Gant's Department of Public Opinion estimated that the expression "Electric Negro" had entered the English vernacular sometime between 2014 and 2016.

"Electric Negro": an unkind nickname that, in addition to being terribly disrespectful of the dead, summoned up a host of images that Gant Industries did not want associated with a quality product like the Automatic Servant. It had begun cropping up in print and on video several years ago: a trickle of usages in various nationally circulated publications, as well as a sly reference on one of the late-night talk shows, to which Vanna Domingo and the Public Opinion Department had responded with a barrage of outraged faxes and threats of advertising boycott. For a while the problem seemed to evaporate, only to reappear after a Delaware country-metal band released a hit CD entitled *Electric Negroes on the Neon Prairie*. As of this August even the *Wall Street Journal* had used the expression, in a headline no less, and the battle to keep "Electric Negro" out of the media stylebooks appeared to have been lost.

And *that* was the Negro problem. Not a big problem, Harry Gant would have been the first to point out: so far, sales had not suffered in the slightest, and the general public remained quite happy with their Servants, no matter what they might call them.

But in fact, of Electric Negroes and the potential for trouble, Harry Gant still had a lot to learn.

Timex Presents

Joan put her rosary around her neck along with her dog tags. Despite her long separation from the Church, she girded herself for the day's work with a determined reverence that would have done a Jesuit proud, handling her weapons and equipment as if they were sacred objects. This early-morning intensity always elicited some comment from Prohaska, for whom the sewers were just a job, albeit one with great danger pay.

"Ready for another week battling the forces of evil?" he asked, indicating her crucifix. "That's a dead religion, you know."

"I do know," said Joan, zipping up the front of the synthetic body suit that would hopefully protect her from chemicals and contagions if she ended up swimming. "And what creed are you following these days, Lenny?"

"Pan worship." He showed her a petrified sliver of wood. "Ecologically sound pagan tree power."

Joan laughed. "Tree power. That's really going to help you down in the shit, right? Besides, didn't you tell me Teddy May was a Catholic?"

"Sure. Back in the days when they hunted alligators with .22 rifles and rat poison."

"So call me a traditionalist." She took an oxygen tank from a charging rack and strapped it to her back. Behind her she could hear Hartower coaching a reluctant Eddie.

"Grenades go here on the belt, like this," he was saying. "You don't touch them unless it's a matter of life and death, got that? Next—"

"Wait," Eddie said, "just wait. The sawed-off shotgun I know how to use, but the rest of this stuff . . . shouldn't I go through some kinda *training* course? Like boot camp?"

"Zoological Bureau can't afford training. A quarter of the money we get from SHQ gets spent on equipment and ammunition, and the other three-quarters goes to cover insurance. Look at it this way: if you get unavoidably retired because you didn't know how to use something, your family gets one hell of a death benefit . . ."

Joan went to the inventory cage to sign out for the four sets of gear. "Need a key for a Servant, too," she said, passing her union card under an optical scanner. The thin-lipped young man inside the cage gave her the key without a word; he was an art history major at Columbia University working part-time to pay the rent and thought anyone who'd choose the sewers as a full-time career must be crazy. Best not to engage them in conversation.

The Bureau's Automatic Servants were kept near the back of the storage area, behind the spare engine parts for the barges. Joan found the one that her key belonged to and unfastened the Kryptonite lock that secured it to the wall. It was an older version of the AS204, built when Gant's engineers were still experimenting with the joint articulation; while trying to mimic a natural range of motion it sometimes did things, like bend its elbows in reverse, that were painful to watch. Its skin, worn by years of service in an unkind netherworld, bore more resemblance to scuffed leather than human flesh. Joan had never decided whether she preferred this type of Servant or one of the newer ones that were practically indistinguishable from real people; maybe neither. Somewhere the Lefty God grumbled against the concept of automata in general.

"Harpo 115," Joan said, reading the name and number on the Servant's I.D. badge. "Wake up."

The Servant opened its eyes, twin video cameras concealed behind fake chocolate-colored irises. It focused on her and smiled broadly, as if reunited with its greatest friend in the whole world. "Zippity-doo-*day*!" it greeted her. Like all Servants it kept its ceramic teeth close together as it spoke, concealing the fact that it had no tongue, only an Electric Voice Box. "Isn't this a *lovely* morning!"

"Harpo 115," Joan asked it, "has it ever *not* been a lovely morning for you?"

The Servant, a low-end physical labor model programmed for the bare minimum in conversation, merely widened its smile at this question and repeated its greeting: "Zippity-doo-*day*! Hey, let's go to work!"

Servant in tow, Joan went back to get Hartower and Prohaska, and Eddie, who had finally gotten all his gear on but still looked uncomfortable with it. A cargo elevator lowered them to the barge staging area, a concrete dock on an artificial lagoon situated some forty feet under the Javits Center. There were seven barges, armor-plated flatboats with searchlights and holographic cameras mounted fore and aft. They boarded the one with "M. Team 23" scrawled in white paint across its keel; Prohaska fired up the engine while Hartower cast off the lines and Joan checked the stocks of the barge's first aid kit. They had enough gauze and disinfectant to handle a bad nosebleed; anything worse and they'd better hope they were right under a hospital when it happened.

"Enjoy it while you can," Hartower said, seeing the way Eddie was looking at the lagoon. "That water's half fresh; they pump in extra to make sure the barges stay afloat. Out in the main tunnels, though, the problem's not too little but too much. You ever see a river of human effluvia before?"

Eddie declined to answer this question. Instead, observing the size of the tunnel mouth Prohaska steered them towards as they left the dock, he said: "I didn't realize it would be so *big* down here."

"Didn't used to be," Prohaska told him. "Back in Teddy May's day you could walk or crawl through most of the system, no need for boats or flotation devices. Some of the secondary tunnels are still small enough to just hike through. But the buildings kept getting taller, more and more waste coming down, so they had to bore the primaries wider every year . . ."

". . . and then," said Hartower, "there was the big genetic engineering boom in the late Nineties, after which the effluvia got strange, all sorts of wildlife wandering in and doing cute little overnight evolution tricks, adapting themselves to the conditions down here. Hence the Zoological Bureau."

"You just want to hope you've got a good immune system," said Prohaska. "There's bacteria loose in the tunnels they don't even have *long* names for yet."

They fell silent for a bit after that, Eddie looking less and less enthusiastic about his new job. The Automatic Servant stood in the prow of the barge sniffing the air, its nose performing a full chemical analysis of the atmosphere every three seconds. As they moved farther out into the system of tunnels, Hartower directed Eddie's attention to the whirl of glistening shapes in the flatboat's wake: "Now we're really in the shit, eh kid?"

Other May Teams had followed them out, but by this point the barges had diverged, each taking a separate route into the target area. They were alone in the effluvia. Prohaska set the searchlights and underwater floods to maximum illumination.

"Where are we?" Joan asked. She'd opened her comic book and was flipping through the pages.

"The Electric Mercator says we're under 41st and Ninth, headed east into the Interchange."

"You want to be careful, then. There's a waterfall right around here somewhere."

Eddie tapped Joan on the shoulder. "Listen," he said, "in case I catch a disease or something and don't have a chance to ask you later—is it true you were married to a billionaire?"

"Who told you that?" Joan asked Eddie. Prohaska began whistling innocently at the wheel; Hartower became engrossed in the latest word from Mobil on the *Times* editorial page. "You wouldn't happen to have been gossiping with two other members of this May Team, would you? Two members who *swore* they were going to stop blabbing about my private life?"

"We didn't say a word to him," Hartower bluffed, and the Automatic Servant bellowed, jolly as ever: "Methane! Zippity-doo-*day*, we got a lethal methane concentration building up in this tunnel!"

Prohaska checked the auxiliary atmospheric scanner clipped to his body suit; it had a Liquid Crystal Display that showed a Liquid Crystal Canary falling dead from its Liquid Crystal Perch. "He's right," Prohaska said. "Masks on, everybody."

When they were all breathing tanked oxygen, Eddie Wilder asked again, in a somewhat muffled voice: "Is it *true*?"

Joan sighed, then nodded. Eddie's candor no longer struck her as refreshing.

"Wow," Eddie pushed ahead, "did you marry him for his money?"

Prohaska barked laughter. "Joan isn't interested in money, at least not for its own sake," he said. "Conspicuous wealth is contrary to her political beliefs."

"Which isn't to say," added Hartower, "that marrying Harry Gant didn't put her in a whole new tax bracket. But his historical significance was probably the big motivating factor . . ."

". . . and true love, of course. *Sooo* trendy . . ."

"Hey guys?" Joan said. "You know I could beat the crap out of both of you with one hand tied behind my back, so why don't we change the subject?"

"His historical what?" said Eddie.

"Historical *significance*," Prohaska told him. "Harry Gant deciding where to have breakfast has more of an impact on history than most people do deciding how to live their whole lives. And Joan's always wanted to leave her mark on history . . ."

"Just like her mother," said Hartower. "Though hopefully with better luck."

"True. The Catholic Womanist Crusade was pretty much a bust."

"Hence the fact that the pope still has a wanger."

"That's *enough*," Joan warned, brandishing a can of reptile repellent. "I swear to God, I am never going drinking with you assholes again."

"Hey, it's not our fault if you get talky after only three beers. Besides, I thought that whole bit about wanting to make the world a better place to live was really sweet. Pathetically naive, but sweet . . ."

Joan took aim with the can of repellent; Hartower ducked. Eddie Wilder raised his hand to forestall a fight and an invisible orchestra launched fortissimo into Ravel's *Bolero,* scaring the hell out of everyone.

"Sorry, sorry," Eddie apologized. He groped at something bulky on his wrist, beneath the sleeve of his body suit.

"What *is* that?" shouted Prohaska, who'd nearly spun the barge into the tunnel wall. "Somebody bring a marching band along this morning?"

"It's a going-away present from my folks," said Eddie. "A Timex Philharmonic. They mail-ordered it special from L. L. Bean."

In the prow of the barge, the Automatic Servant pointed at the water and said something, but no one heard it over the thunder of bassoons.

"It can play ten different classics," Eddie continued to explain. "It's got sixty-four voices."

"We can hear that," said Hartower. "The question is, can you make them shut up?"

"Well I'm *working* on it," Eddie said. He tried to remember where the mute button was, but before he could, a shark came out of the water and ate him.

The Power of Positive Thinking (I)

Vanna Domingo was waiting in the Phoenix Parking Annex with the Portable Televisions Gant had requested. The Televisions—Automatic Servants with cable-ready, high-definition monitor screens in place of heads—might seem a macabre notion at first, the sort of thing René Magritte would have come up with if he'd worked for Zenith, but in fact Harry Gant had employed a top Czech design firm to insure that his Portable TVs were comical rather than threatening. This was done primarily by dressing them in funny outfits. If advance sales were any indication, middle America was ready, *eager,* for a home appliance in a cowboy suit that could wash, dry, and put away the dishes while receiving any of five hundred exciting channels.

The Televisions Vanna Domingo had brought for Gant's school address were dressed up like Apollo astronauts. Harry Gant's father had often spoken with pride of witnessing the NBC broadcast of the first moon landing, and Harry himself had always had a soft spot for NASA's finest, even though he personally would never have invested in the space program. Heights.

"Morning, Vanna," Gant said, stepping from his private elevator.

"Harry." She nodded humbly, after the fashion of a feudal vassal. Gant tried to ignore this. While he believed the protocol of corporate hierarchy demanded a certain deference to superiors, there was a difference between being ranking capitalist and being lord of the manor, a distinction that Vanna, with her almost worshipful loyalty, tended to lose sight of. But she was excellent at her job, no questioning that.

Gant pointed at the object tucked under Vanna's arm, a slim tome with matte black covers. An Electric Book. "What're you reading these days?" he asked. Vanna read a great deal, but because she was ashamed of her own tastes and more than a little paranoid, she preferred the anonymity of a programmable reading device with no telltale dust jacket.

"The new Tad Winston Peller book," she said, with a little shrug. "All about earthquakes."

"Earthquakes!"

"Yeah, there's supposed to be a big one due on the East Coast. Peller says Boston and New York are going to get leveled all in one shot."

"Well I can't speak for Boston," Gant said, "but you mark my words, it'll take more than an earthquake to level *this* city, especially those parts I've had a hand in building. The best engineering anchored in some of the toughest bedrock in the world, that's what we've got here."

"You're the man," said Vanna, and touched a decorative-looking brooch at the throat of her blouse. An armored transport bus left its parking space across the Annex and pulled up in front of them. Its doors opened, and at a command from Vanna the Portable Televisions filed in and took seats.

"Tad Winston Peller," Gant said, shaking his head. "You know I was never much of a writer myself, and I have to respect a man who can make such a fortune out of words, but still . . ."

"You don't like his stuff."

"Well. *Disasters,* I mean. Earthquakes, floods, radioactive Tupperware . . . it's such a pessimistic way of looking at life. I'd rather make my money selling people a happy version of the world, you see what I'm saying?"

Vanna Domingo's composure faltered for only an instant, a barest tick that Gant did not notice. Then she pasted on a big smile and nodded. And said again: "You're the man."

Joan and Meisterbrau (I)

Prohaska was the last one to stop screaming. In the dying flicker of the aft searchlights Joan caught a twinkle of his zircon as Meisterbrau dragged him under. Prohaska's shotgun discharged once, scarring the blue ceramic of the tunnel ceiling; when the echo of that had died, the only sounds were the surging of the effluvia around the stricken patrol craft and a dull roar that Joan was too dazed to pay attention to at first.

The great white had come flying over the bow like a cruise missile with teeth, sweeping all hands overboard. Only Joan had managed to pull herself back into the barge in one piece. Hartower had almost made it, only to be seized and slammed against the underside of the craft hard enough to rupture the fuel tank and short the electrical system; Joan didn't want to know what the impact had done to Hartower himself. He did not resurface.

The barge was developing a starboard list as it took on water through the cracked keel. Joan crouched in the stern in a shivering ball; she had her shotgun out but had forgotten to take off the safety, which didn't matter as much once the searchlights failed. There was still some ambient light from the phosphorescent lichen that thrived in the sewers, but not enough to aim by. Could sharks see in the dark?

"Lenny?" she called out (not too loudly), though she knew it was useless. "Lenny Prohaska? Hartower?"

No answer, but the barge rocked in the effluvia as something passed beneath it. A log, perhaps. Joan ordered her heart to stop beating so fast, she was forty, goddamnit, hence stoic, she'd taken on Union Carbide and Afrikaans Chemical in her day, and she could by Jesus handle a mutant fish. This conceit, repeated several times, actually steadied her free hand enough to let her yank a grenade from her belt.

Unclipping the grenade from its holster activated an internal mechanism much like the nose of an Automatic Servant. This mechanism sampled the air, found it wanting, and cued a microminiaturized hologram projector in the grenade's cap.

Joan blinked as the translucent head of John Fitzgerald Kennedy materialized before her in the darkness. "I'm sorry, fellow American," Kennedy said, in tones gentle but firm, "but the atmosphere around you contains a mixture of gasses with the potential for a chain-reaction explosion. Federal and local safety regulations prohibit the use of hand grenades at this time. Your government apologizes for any inconvenience this may cause you."

Joan started to reply, but it was at that same moment that she realized what the dull roar she'd been hearing was. "Waterfall," she said dumbly as the tunnel floor dropped away beneath her. Pitched from the deck of the barge, Joan plunged fifteen feet into swirling black effluvia; her shotgun and the grenade vanished in the tumult, but somehow she kept her oxygen mask on, surfacing in the middle of a rectangular basin the size of a football field: the Times Square Interchange.

She paddled in place, trying to orient herself. One gloved hand struck something, and she curled her fingers in what she thought was human hair, lifting it up.

"Hartower . . . ?"

"Zippity-doo-*day!*" the severed head of the Automatic Servant greeted her. "Isn't this a *lovely* morning!"

Joan hurled it as far as she could, hearing it splash down at the other end of the basin. What she heard next filled her with dread: *Bolero.* Ravel's

Bolero, coming from under the water, where she knew for a fact Eddie Wilder was no longer alive and kicking. The marching bassoons crescendoed and a fin broke the surface right in front of her.

Meisterbrau, having already dined well that morning, only nuzzled her at first. The shark's sandpaper skin raked open the right leg of her body suit as it brushed past, though Joan, feeling the painful contact, was convinced the entire limb had been bitten off. She backpedaled furiously, wiggling toes she could hardly believe were still connected. Her oxygen tank clanked against the wall of the chamber.

Trapped, Joan thought, middle-age stoicism drowned in the shit. No doubt if she had been the comic book d'Arc, saint and warrior maiden of Old France, she would at that moment have ignited with righteous fury to smite her foe; but she was only Fine, and it was in sheer animal panic that she jerked her head around in the dark and saw a slim chance of salvation outlined in a circle of glowing purple lichen.

A tunnel. Not a barge tunnel but one of the old secondaries, no more than a yard wide, situated above the Interchange's waterline and pouring out a mere trickle of effluvia. If she could climb up there . . .

The synthesized orchestra dropped to mezzo forte as Meisterbrau dove and began a wide circling turn. Joan unhooked her second hand grenade; before JFK could put in another appearance she whacked it against the wall of the chamber hard enough to fracture the air sampler. She pulled the pin and tossed the grenade as she had the Automatic Servant's head, trying more for distance than aim. Hydrostatic shock might injure or kill the shark, but at this point Joan would settle for distracting it.

Standard Department-issue grenades came with a fifteen-second fuse, the long delay being intended to keep untrained sewer workers from damaging expensive pipes and incurring self-inflicted death benefits all at one go. Joan counted backwards in her head as she fought to pull herself up into the secondary tunnel. The lichen on the tunnel lip was slick and offered almost no purchase, and she was weak, from fright or loss of blood she didn't know; her oxygen tank seemed so heavy it might have been anchored to the floor of the basin. She heaved herself up twice, only to slip and fall back.

Bolero had begun a new crescendo, Meisterbrau's fin arrowing straight at her this time, when a superhero reached out of the tunnel and hauled Joan up by her wrists. She knew it was a superhero because (a) it wore a suit of rubberized armor that put her own body suit to shame, (b) anyone else would have been running away, and (c) it had a glow-in-the-dark symbol emblazoned on its chest.

The superhero spoke with a young woman's voice: "Hang on to me," and cupped gloved hands over Joan's ears. Joan grabbed the superhero's shoulders and held tight; behind her, the detonating grenade set off a chemical firestorm, and in the sudden flare of light she glimpsed the eyes of her savior, sea-green eyes set in a black, smiling face. Then the force of the explosion rammed them both down the tunnel like wadding down the barrel of a gun.

The superhero's symbol seemed to recede before her as Joan blacked out. It was an unusual symbol, neither an atom nor a thunderbolt nor a capital letter, but rather the outline of a continent. On the brink of unconsciousness, Joan couldn't quite remember the continent's name; but under the circumstances, that was hardly surprising.

A Miracle in Times Square

The Automaton Delimiting Act of '09 made it legal to employ Automatic Servants in the maintenance of nuclear power plants but barred them from operating motor vehicles or carrying firearms, so Harry Gant's driver and chief bodyguard on the transport bus was human, a Lebanese-American whose full name Gant couldn't pronounce. Gant just called him Louis.

Louis got them to Times Square at quarter to nine. The Gant Media & Technical School for Advanced Immigrant Teens occupied the better part of a block once dominated by porn houses and peep shows, the streamlined gloss of its architecture calling to mind an early-twentieth-century version of The Future. American critics hated the building—"academe as hood ornament," the *Architectural Digest* reviewer wrote, while an essayist in *Harper's* cracked jokes about the return of Flash Gordon—but second- and third-world parents recognized a landmark of opportunity when they saw it, and sent Gant their children.

And there they were now, lined up at attention in front of the school, Gant's Immigrant Scholars of Merit: fresh-faced adolescents from under-industrialized and overcommunized nations around the globe. The school headmaster, Ms. Allagance, waved gaily as the transport bus pulled in; at her signal the front row of students burst into song.

"Hey," Harry Gant said, absurdly touched by this display. "Whose idea was this?"

"I phoned ahead," Vanna Domingo told him, pleased that he was pleased. "Glad you like it."

"Thanks for the thought. Thanks much." One might have argued that this was the same brand of fealty that he found so discomfiting in Vanna, but the Norman Rockwell associations of the scene elevated it to another, more properly American plane. "But wait a minute, what was that sound?"

"What sound?"

"That *whoosh* sound."

Abrupt chaos outside the bus: a metallic *clang*, a grunt from Ms. Allagance, a squelching thud like a wet sack of potatoes dropped from a height, screams from the children. Gant leapt bravely from his seat and was rushing to offer aid before Louis and the rest of the security team could stop him.

A crimped manhole cover had imbedded itself edgewise into the sidewalk and was still quivering. Fortunately this was not the object that had sent Ms. Allagance sprawling. Rather, she had been struck a glancing blow by the tail of a great white shark. The big fish had landed on a mailbox and lay thrashing on a shoal of parcel post; Gant paused halfway between it and the felled headmaster, wondering which required the most immediate attention. Meisterbrau decided the issue by coughing up a human hand.

Gant moved closer: the hand was encased in some sort of wetsuit material but was no less viscerally disgusting for that. The students had stopped screaming and some were starting to walk over this way, and Harry Gant, ever mindful of public sensibilities, had to act quickly to distract them. Meisterbrau burped a second time, spitting out a flashy wristwatch, which had barely come to rest before Gant snatched it up.

"Hey, look at *this*!" Gant shouted, waving the Timex Philharmonic over his head while he discreetly nudged Eddie Wilder's hand out of sight with his toe. "Look at this, swallowed by a fish and it still plays *great music*, kids! What you're witnessing is nothing short of a miracle in modern American technology! A *miracle* . . ."

A sliver of sunlight found its way down into the canyons and made the wristwatch gleam like a diamond. The children looked where Harry Gant wanted them to. Eddie Wilder's soul departed this mortal plane unnoticed. The Philharmonic picked up the tempo. And Meisterbrau, down but not out, sank its teeth into a package marked MUTAGENIC BIOHAZARD—HANDLE WITH CARE.

For a New York Monday morning in 2023, none of this was all that unusual.

2

Pirate is a person who attacks and robs ships. Such robbers have also been called *buccaneers, corsairs, filibusters, freebooters, ladrones, pickaroons,* and *sea rovers.* . . . Widespread piracy no longer exists. But occasional attacks occur in some areas . . .

—*World Book Encyclopedia*

The Strangest Thing in the Ocean

The full twisting pathway of the effluvia beneath the city's streets was a secret known to no one, the only complete map having been lost after the death of Teddy May. All of it eventually came out somewhere, though—Manhattan's waste being ejected, after varying degrees of detoxification, into the East River or the Hudson. From there it passed into New York Bay (random bits of detritus scraping the keel of the Staten Island Ferry), and from the Bay it washed out to sea.

There were some awfully strange things running loose in the Atlantic Ocean in those days. Many of them made the wild fauna of the New York sewer system look cuddly by comparison. In his runaway bestseller *The Shadow over Strathmere,* celebrated disaster chronicler Tad Winston Peller discussed the mysterious fate of a New Jersey seaside town that had vanished without a trace one night in 2011. A popular local theory held that Mutant Amphibian Beings had come out under the dark of the new moon and carried off everyone and everything in sight.

Here is the name of one strange thing running loose in the ocean that posed no threat to life: *Yabba-Dabba-Doo.*

Yabba-Dabba-Doo was not Latin or Greek for some genetically drifted brand of tuna. *Yabba-Dabba-Doo* was the name of a submarine, a big green one with bright pink polka dots. It bore a living cargo of castaways and endangered species, and roamed the East Coast shipping lanes doing embarrassing things to people and institutions that were reckless in the disposal of their effluvia. It was said that the *Yabba-Dabba-Doo*'s captain, Philo Dufresne, was the blackest African still living on the planet Earth, but only one person had ever succeeded in getting a photograph of him, and she wasn't telling. It was also said that the *Yabba-Dabba-Doo* was powered by a perpetual motion machine that would be made available to the world—along with all the free jellybeans anyone could ever want—as soon as the human race proved itself worthy of such a boon.

This might all sound like the plot for a very expensive situation comedy. It wasn't; it was real life. But that it was difficult to take seriously was exactly Philo Dufresne's intention.

Too Many Adjectives

On the morning that Joan Fine first made the acquaintance of Meisterbrau, the *Yabba-Dabba-Doo* took up station in the waters off Montauk Point. Leaving his first mate in the control room to watch for potential targets, Philo Dufresne retired to his quarters to write for an hour. In addition to being an internationally acclaimed eco-pirate, Philo was a closet novelist, and for the past ten years he had worked off and on to complete the Great Atlantean Novel, an epic of anthropomorphized whales, porpoises, and fish. The working title was *No Opposable Thumbs,* and like Philo himself the book had its moments of sheer brilliance.

It would never be published.

Try as he might, Philo had not been able to correct the fatal flaw in his writing style, which a single sentence would serve to illustrate: *Baruga churned up thirty-foot-high, prismatic sprays of salty brine with his gargantuan, all-powerful, spadelike flukes as the deadly explosive-tipped harpoon penetrated his warm, fleshy blubber and went off, flinging hot, cruelly sharp shrapnel into his great life-pumping heart.*

Too many adjectives. Or as a smart text-editing program had once told him: "Not every noun requires a modifier." While Philo agreed with this in principle, every attempt he made to write leaner prose ended up looking naked to him, unfinished. Causing him still further distress was the nagging sense that this inability to leave well enough alone ran directly counter to his environmentalist ethics. Unable to reform his composition and unwilling to give it up, he committed his novel like a secret memoir to the pages of a diary and kept it locked in a safe.

As he wrote that morning (using a refillable ballpoint pen, his low-tech response to the trauma of word processing), he could hear the skitter of tiny rodent feet above and around him. The decks of the submarine were riddled with a network of shatterproof plastic tunnels, warren to several hundred or so blue hamsters, an exotic breed that would have sold for ninety-five dollars or more apiece in the New York Pets-R-Us. Philo didn't keep them for their resale value; he just liked the way they looked, liked especially the life and energy they radiated as they scampered from one end of the sub to the other. With ten bobcat cubs also in residence, the *Yabba-Dabba-Doo* was a truly kinetic vessel.

Hunched over his writing desk, Philo with his size and his shock of beard might have passed as a middle-aged Santa checking his famous List, but only in a revisionist version of that myth. Whether he was truly the darkest-skinned survivor of the '04 Pandemic was a matter for debate, but he was without question the darkest-skinned child ever raised by the Amish. A Pennsylvania Dutch farmer named Gunther Lapp had found the squalling infant—a changeling the color of good earth, with green eyes like a landscape after rain—abandoned in a wheat field. Gunther, a man of great heart with an unqualified love of children, especially orphans, grew instantly attached to the strange baby, though the local bishop was somewhat taken aback by his petition for adoption. "Philo" was the name pinned to the blanket in which Philo had come wrapped; "Dufresne" was the last name of the only other black person Gunther had ever met, a government census taker who'd passed through the village in 1970.

Young Philo and the Amish community were an imperfect match at best. After Gunther Lapp's death in 1994, Philo, who was eighteen that year, visited Philadelphia and was physically and technologically seduced by a computer science major at the University of Pennsylvania. Many back at home were quietly relieved to learn he would not be returning. After all, who but the devil would leave an African-American baby in a Mennonite wheat field?

He'd drifted into environmental activism in the early Oughts, drawn by a genuine concern for the planet but also—he tried always to be honest about this point—by an antisocial streak that badly needed an outlet. Gunther Lapp had raised Philo to be a pacifist, and he would always abhor the taking of life, but once out in the world he discovered he had no corresponding qualms about gross property damage. As he learned working for Earth First! and the Ned Ludd Society, there was nothing quite so satisfying as a morally justified act of vandalism.

Driven into hiding by the Pandemic, Philo spent the next several years literally wandering in the desert, until he met up with a Jewish Luddite named Morris Kazenstein. Morris, barely out of his teens, introduced himself as "Delancey Street's answer to Thomas Edison." He claimed to have composed schematics and blueprints for hundreds of useful gadgets, but for personal reasons had sworn that none of his inventions would ever fall into the hands of the military. Since defense departments around the world borrowed freely (or at inflated cost) from private industry, Morris had decided that the only way to honorably pursue his craft would be to become an outlaw. That much having been said, how would Philo like to hear Morris's idea for something called "benign eco-piracy"?

Philo listened; a pact was struck. The next morning they began laying the groundwork for a scheme that would take over a decade to reach fruition.

And so today, at age forty-seven, Philo was a pirate, possibly the most infamous pirate in history, definitely the one with the highest television audience share. Morris served as his first mate and technical sorcerer, with inventions numbering not just in the hundreds but in the thousands. The *Yabba-Dabba-Doo* was fast becoming legend.

At half past nine, Morris gave a whistle over the intercom: "Conn to captain's quarters."

Philo picked up his intercom mike, which was shaped like a dodo bird, and spoke into the beak: "What's up?"

"Target approaching. Your favorite kind, Philo."

"A Gant ship?"

"Unarmed and unescorted."

A pair of blue hamsters charged by overhead, stumbling over each other in their haste; Philo smiled. He closed his novel-in-progress and put away his pen. "On my way up," he said.

Target Selection

The first submarine to see action in wartime was the *American Turtle*, a one-man, hand-powered vehicle built by Yale student David Bushnell in 1776. Little more than an egg-shaped barrel with a ballast tank, the *Turtle*'s only recorded mission—an attempt to mine the British flagship *Eagle* with a gunpowder time bomb—proved an utter failure, and the sub was ultimately dismantled without having inflicted a single enemy casualty.

Submarines had increased dramatically in size, sophistication, and military effectiveness since then, but they'd never ceased to be cramped and claustrophobic vessels. Stealth weapons by nature, serious and deadly in intent, they weren't supposed to be fun to ride in. Comfortable where possible, yes—crew morale was important in wartime—but not *fun*.

Well, nuts to that. With "benign piracy," Morris Kazenstein already had one oxymoron in play, so why not go for another? Even given the triple constraints of practicality, physical law, and the humble conservationist stance it was pledged to defend, who said the *Yabba-Dabba-Doo* couldn't be a merry man-o'-war?

Morris had done his best. Intended to be as much an ark as a combat engine, the giant-economy-size sub could have carried two hundred people with ample breathing and elbow room for all. But an ingenious set of labor-saving and centralized control devices held the crew to fourteen, and even that was padding it. This left plenty of space for a research library, gymnasium, cybernetics and machine shop, full veterinary surgery, and eight-person hot tub, not to mention free-ranging mascots of every description. The *Yabba-Dabba-Doo* was also the only sub on record to contain an arboretum.

It was via that scenic route that Philo now traveled, moving forward towards the bow, passing through several watertight doors and stopping for a friendly tussle with Borneo Bill, an orang-utan who had once rocketed into orbit aboard a test flight of the Trump Shuttlecraft. A final self-sealing hatchway gave access to an area that on a more conventional sub would have been claimed by torpedo tubes and other battle machinery. A wave of damp, rich air and greenery greeted Philo as he entered; the motif this season was South American rain forest, and the enclosed biosphere was crammed with near-extinct flora destined for ecological safehouses. The sound of the hatchway drew the attention of a three-toed sloth, which swung a weary gaze in Philo's direction. A wall of vines parted and Jael Bolívar, the sub's Kuwaiti-Latino biologist, poked her head through to say hi.

"How's the green business?" Philo asked.

"It's fucking *humid* in here," Jael told him, tugging at the front of her T-shirt. "How 'bout we switch to African veldt after Thanksgiving? The Doolittle Gang are busting a baby elephant out of Ringling Brothers and they're going to need a place to put it."

"You'll have to talk to Morris about that one," Philo delegated. "I'm not sure he's ready to open up the whole bow again. Maybe he could rig you a fan . . ."

"Morris can go screw. I mean he may be kid dynamite on an Electric Drafting Board, but every time I ask him to help with some grunt work he says he's too busy to get his hands dirty."

"I'll speak to him about it," Philo promised. He grabbed a vine and climbed up to another hatchway. This was not the easiest way to get to the command deck, but for Philo it was the most physically satisfying. Feeling spry and pleasantly sweaty, he arrived in the control room to find Morris conferring with Norma Eckland, a former executive producer for the Fox Network who now served as the *Yabba-Dabba-Doo*'s chief of communications.

"Morning, Philo." Norma raised a hand.

"So what have we got?"

"Take a peek." Morris gestured at the periscope. Philo peeked. Eight miles away, as measured by the 'scope's rangefinder, a ship was rounding the tip of Long Island. He pressed the magnification stud in the periscope's handgrip and read the name off the ship's bow: *South Furrow.*

"Steel hull," Philo observed. "Looks like an icebreaker."

"Just came out of Bath Ironworks in Maine," Morris said.

"What are the specs?"

"Hold on," said Norma. The *Yabba-Dabba-Doo*'s main computer had the entire World Maritime Registry on file, and Morris updated it regularly. Norma fed the information directly into the periscope sight:

South Furrow
WMR#1078626, Icebr. class
Registered U.S., Gant Industries Inc., Antarticorp Div.
Spec.: 429 ft., 20500 tns., 100000 max. hp
Oper. Assignment: Gant Mineral Research Site, Antarctica

"Told you you'd like it," Morris said.

"Why was it launched so late in the year?" Philo asked. "It's already springtime at the South Pole, shouldn't it be down there by now?"

"It shouldn't be anywhere now," Norma Eckland told him. "The Coast Guard commissioned it to replace the *Polar Dream,* then had to back out when their budget was cut. Gant offered to take it off their hands if he could have it by November."

"Harry's sending a lot of extra muscle and equipment south this month," said Morris. "Sounds like the president finally gave him a green light to start drilling. The other Treaty nations aren't going to like that."

"They aren't going to have a chance to not like it," Philo said, "because that icebreaker isn't getting anywhere near Antarctica." A bobcat rubbed itself lovingly against his ankles; he stooped to scratch its chin. "Call battle stations. And send somebody to wake up Twenty-Nine Words."

Twenty-Nine Words for Snow

The *Yabba-Dabba-Doo*'s boarding party had grown up at Mrs. Butterworth's Home for Unfortunately Displaced Indigenous Orphans in Osceola, Arkansas. His legal name there was Ringo Beefheart—after Mrs. Butterworth's two favorite musicians—but the other children, half-blood Plains Indians, mostly, called him Ringo Igloo. Having had enough of that by his fifteenth birthday, he'd gone over the wall one summer night and into the Mississippi. A homemade raft fashioned from Styrofoam peanuts and a mess of Hefty bags carried him all the way to the Gulf of Mexico, by which point he was starving, delirious, and raving at imaginary waiters to bring him whale blubber and ice cream. Fortunately the *Yabba-Dabba-Doo* was passing through the Gulf on its first extended sea trial. Philo and Morris picked Ringo up just a few hours before a tropical storm would have erased all trace of his existence. He was taken aboard the sub, fed, and taught ecology. Now he subdued entire ship's crews for a living, a better career than he could ever have hoped for in Osceola.

While Ringo was still in her care, Mrs. Butterworth had done what she could to instill him with a sense of his ethnic heritage. Regrettably, her sole teaching text in this endeavor was a 1992 edition of the *World Book Encyclopedia*. The Eskimo entry ran only ten pages, from which Ringo gleaned what he could, further supplementing his knowledge with snippets from National Geographic specials and a video of *Nanook of the North*.

The word *eskimo*, he learned (Mrs. Butterworth reading to him in the playground while the other children shot suction-cup-tipped arrows at one another), was an Amerind term for "eaters of raw meat," though his Canadian Eskimo forebears called themselves "Inuit," or "people." Ringo didn't know which name he preferred but liked the fact that he had a choice. He was also determined to become an eater of raw meat himself. At the Home, where the children were fed pork chops three times a week by an anti-Semitic nutritionist, this meant a constant flirtation with trichinosis, but on the

Yabba-Dabba-Doo Philo lectured him about the dangers of parasites and introduced him to sushi. A proper ethnic diet being thereby established, Ringo got to work tailoring the rest of his lifestyle.

Eskimos were hardy people who lived in sub-zero temperatures without a shiver. They built houses of ice and caribou hide and never bathed. Morris Kazenstein thought Ringo was kidding when he asked to have his sleeping quarters chilled to minus thirty degrees Fahrenheit, but then got caught up in the technical challenge of the design. After clearing out and insulating a double stateroom, Morris rigged up a chemical-free acoustic refrigeration system. Artificial snow was scattered on the floor; a waterbed installed, frozen, and wrapped in imitation walrus skins; and an igloo constructed around the waterbed. Morris insisted Ringo wear a biomonitor during his first night in the room, to warn of hypothermia, but he took to the cold like a true son of the Arctic and woke twelve hours later refreshed, home at last.

"But you have to bathe," Philo told him.

"Inuit never bathe," Ringo insisted.

"They do on submarines, at least if they want other people to talk to them. Make the water ice cold if you want, but you shower once a week."

"He's nuts," Morris said, when told of this latest development. "Not even sexually repressed people take cold showers on purpose anymore."

"Hey," replied Philo, "you're the one who just spent a week figuring out how to put an igloo inside a submarine. All he did was talk you into it. So who's the nut?"

Nuts or not, he was happy. Happy at long last. All that remained was to find a new name for himself, one more fitting than Ringo. He remembered what the *World Book* had had to say about the Inuit language: "The Eskimos of most regions had more than one word for most objects. For example, they had many words for *seal*. The choice of one of these words depended on whether the animal was young or old, on whether it was in water or on land, and on a number of other circumstances."

"What about snow?" he'd wondered aloud to Mrs. Butterworth. "How many words do they have for that?"

"Oh," Mrs. Butterworth had guessed, "I'm sure they have at least twenty-nine."

So much for Ringo, then. He was and would be evermore Twenty-Nine Words for Snow, hunter of the frozen north, subduer of big things swimming in the sea.

The Show

"Ready for surfacing," Morris Kazenstein announced as the *Yabba-Dabba-Doo* closed within a quarter mile of the *South Furrow*.

"What's the weather like?"

"Couple other ships about," Asta Wills called from the sonar bay. "Fishing boats, nothing to give us trouble. Latest word is the Coast Guard's busy with a tanker accident farther down the island. Our sheila's unprotected up there."

"No spy satellites due overhead for the next twenty-eight minutes," Norma Eckland added, consulting a printed timetable.

Philo rubbed his palms together. "Ozzie, bring us in and surface alongside them, but leave enough room for maneuvers if they decide to ram us." Osman Hamid, the helmsman—in his youth the fastest taxi driver in western Turkey—grinned like a bandit and spun the annunciator to Full Speed Ahead. "Norma, begin jamming procedures as soon as we're up," Philo continued. "Assault personnel and media crew stand ready."

Marshall Ali, the sub's costume designer and trainer in arcane Kurdish martial arts, helped Twenty-Nine Words suit up. "You have your body armor on, yes?" Marshall Ali was a fanatic about the essential Zen qualities of bullet-proof padding.

"I'm wearing it, but I don't like it," Twenty-Nine Words said. Over the armor he had on a fake polar bear skin, complete with fanged head. Great outfit, but hot as hell even without the layer of armor—and the temperature outside was a sweltering forty-five degrees Fahrenheit. "I'll probably get a heat stroke."

"You are not allowed to get a heat stroke. And you have to wear your armor."

"Why?"

"Because when you go into battle you must always assume your opponent will be ruthless, and take every precaution. Also, I am bigger than you and will beat you about the face and neck if you do not do what I say."

"Istanbul!" Osman Hamid cried. Though he understood commands intuitively, he spoke no English and used the name of his hometown as an all-purpose expletive. Morris translated: "Surfacing, Philo."

"Jamming all S.O.S. channels," said Norma.

"Match speed and stay parallel with the target," Philo ordered, studying the *South Furrow* through the periscope. Crew members were running around the deck, pointing at the sub and giving the dread cry: *"Yabba-Dabba-*

Doo ho!" "Launch the helicopter wing. Norma, start transmitting. It's showtime."

Aft of the sail, where the missile deck would have been located on an ICBM sub, openings appeared in the *Yabba-Dabba-Doo*'s green and pink hull, and a swarm of model helicopters rose into the air. Each about equal in size and mass to a winged hunting dog, the choppers were computer-remote-controlled and painted in a variety of cheery Day-Glo colors. Most mounted high-definition television cameras for use in the upcoming broadcast, but one group of four shared a special cargo borne aloft on a network of quick-release cables: a gigantic lemon meringue pie, ten feet in diameter.

Once the remote helicopter wing was airborne, another, larger whirlybird was raised to the launch deck. Christened a Flying Zodiac by its inventor, Morris Kazenstein, this chopper was just big enough to carry one unfortunately displaced indigenous orphan. As Twenty-Nine Words lifted off, Marshall Ali appeared on the *Yabba-Dabba-Doo*'s observation bridge atop the sail, shouting guttural phrases of encouragement: "Bruce Lee! Chuck Norris! Sonny Bono!"

Meanwhile, Norma Eckland had raised a telescoping transmitter dish and interfaced the *Yabba-Dabba-Doo* with the North American Satellite Computer Net, bypassing a dozen security barriers to pull the plug on the Turner Soap Opera Network. Con Edison's main billing computer was told to institute an immediate power shut-off for lack of payment at Turner Broadcasting's New York studios; automatic switching facilities at cable television companies across the continent were instructed to accept an alternate transmission; and just to be obnoxious, every pizza parlor on the island of Manhattan received a faxed order for a double-anchovy pie to be delivered to Harry Gant's office at the Phoenix.

Morning devotees of *Dog Eat Dog*—having tuned in to learn whether Donna would seduce Chad to keep him from telling what he knew about Tama, or simply toss him into one of the batch tanks at her aunt's nerve gas factory—saw a burst of static, then a computer-graphic rendering of the Dufresne pirate logo, a hybrid cross between an ecology symbol and an Amish hex sign. A synthetic brass band played the theme from *Global Village Bandstand* while the ageless voice of Dick Clark gave the intro: "And *now*, live from Planet Earth, it's time for another daring daylight raid by that champion of unspoiled nature, your pirate and mine, PHILO DUFRESNE . . ."

Canned cheers, the roar of the crowd at the 2017 Super Bowl when Brenda Bamford scored the winning touchdown for the New York Jets. The

Yabba-Dabba-Doo made a brief on-screen appearance, from which Norma dissolved to taped scenes of the aforementioned unspoiled nature: wide glacial expanses, clean white Antarctic landscapes, Mt. Erebus rising against a crystalline sky.

"Morning, world," Philo said, having donned a set of earphones and a throat mike. "Philo Dufresne here, acting today on behalf of the Seventh Continent. Thought I'd let you in on some disturbing rumors I've been hearing—rumors that American oil and mineral interests have convinced a certain second-term president to authorize the exploitation of Antarctic resources, despite the fact that he doesn't have the power to authorize that, not without an act of Congress and the majority support of fifty-two other countries. Now it's a little early in the day for rhetoric, so I'm going to spare you the usual party line about saving a piece of the wilderness for our grandchildren; likewise I'm not going to say a word concerning the possibility of armed conflict if those fifty-two other countries decide they don't like having a treaty broken . . . none of that, I just want you to look at these pictures we're flashing you and see if you don't agree with me that Antarctica is a *pretty* place. Harsh, yes. Cold, you bet. But certainly nicer in its current state than those places where the blast-and-drill companies have already been hard at work." Norma cut to a montage of Alaskan oil disasters: dead birds drowned in the slicks in Prince William Sound, lovesick caribou running from the ruptured Transalaska Pipeline after the 'quake of '02, fudgy black tides marking the 2020 blowout in Bristol Bay.

"Now I know what you're probably thinking," Philo continued, as Norma returned to the pristine Antarctic vistas. "Sure it looks nice, and everyone loves penguins, be great to have some living in your neighborhood, but . . . what can the average person do? We're going to give you some suggestions along those lines later in the program, but I did want to tell you first that I understand that feeling of helplessness. Some mornings I feel as if Earth's problems are just too big, and I haven't got a clue where to even begin.

"Then there are other mornings, like this one, when I wake up, look across the waves, and see a ship belonging to my old pal Harry Gant"—cut to a long shot of the *South Furrow*—"and I say to myself, 'Philo, you may not have all the answers to saving the world, but why not start by sinking that goddamn boat? Sink it for the penguins. Sink it for the grandchildren of America. And may God bless us all.'"

Morris flipped a switch and the cargo helos released the pie. The remote cameras captured its descent in super slow-motion, frame by frame down a long arc to splatter across the face of the icebreaker's pilothouse. "That one was just for you, Harry," Philo said. Up on the sail Marshall Ali brought a water cannon to bear and began hosing down the *South Furrow* with whipped cream.

Twenty-Nine Words flew in fast and low, letting his on-board targeting computer aim the Zodiac's Electric Harpoon. He was happy in his natural element, stalking a seafaring quarry many times his size, and only for one guilty second did he wish the ship were a whale, the Harpoon a real killing spear tipped with stone. He let fly as he crossed the stern of the icebreaker, skewering a fat gray cable at the base of the *South Furrow*'s radar mast. The Harpoon struck and spliced like a hot needle probing the spine of a catfish; the hardware package in its shaft fed a paralyzing series of virus programs into the ship's navigation and control systems. The big boat shuddered and began to slow down.

The Zodiac shot over the pilothouse and dropped down, almost into the path of the whipped cream stream; Twenty-Nine Words stuck out a hand, pulled back a fistful of sugary white fluff. Smearing his mouth with it, he brought the whirlybird around, settling it into a low hover above the icebreaker. He flipped on the autopilot and unfurled a flag from beneath his seat. Then he jumped.

Whipped cream already lay three feet thick on the deck amidships; it was like falling into a mattress of cotton candy. Twenty-Nine Words came up laughing and waving the flag, which bore a small but proud igloo on a white field. "I claim this tub for the Inuit people!" he shouted.

He found himself surrounded by an angry detachment of the *South Furrow*'s crew. Twenty-Nine Words had seen the deckhands of other ships respond with laughter to the *Yabba-Dabba-Doo*'s attack, but these folks were clearly bad sports. "C'mon, lighten up," he told a big burly fellow who was actually growling. "I know it's a little embarrassing, but it's for the good of the environment."

"I'm going to kick your ass, junior," the burly fellow said.

"No you're not," said Twenty-Nine Words, throwing down his flag. "It's only fair to warn you, I've been trained by one of the greatest martial arts masters in all Kurdistan. If you try to lay a hand on me I'll have to club you with a rubber fish."

The burly fellow tried to lay a hand on him. Twenty-Nine Words easily sidestepped the attack and, true to his word, swatted the angry seaman with a flexible purple trout. The burly fellow took a pratfall in the whipped cream.

On the Turner Soap Opera Network he took two pratfalls, one live and one in slow-motion replay.

Another deckhand charged, and another. Twenty-Nine Words trouted them both. Then all the remaining crew members rushed him in a body, and for a moment it looked as though a rugby scrum had broken out on the deck. Twenty-Nine Words stepped out calmly from behind the mob of men and women and walked away whistling while they pummeled one another.

He had stopped to wave at the cameras when a hatch slammed open and Beardsley Stepanik, the hyperactive ship's steward, raced on deck wielding a flare gun. "All right," Beardsley screamed, drawing a shaky bead, "freeze it right there, you tree-hugger!"

"Relax," Twenty-Nine Words said, plucking something from beneath his bear skin. With a snap of the wrist he flicked what looked like a snowball at Beardsley; even in super slow-motion it was hard to follow the snowball's mid-air metamorphosis, but when Beardsley looked down at himself he saw that an Arctic bunny had landed on his chest. A stuffed Arctic bunny, with sharp toenails that had been dipped in liquid euphoria.

"Aw, hey." A sensual warmth spread across Beardsley's chest, up into his arms and down his legs into his toes. Abruptly in love with the whole world, penguins especially, he tossed his flare gun overboard and crouched down in the whipped cream, smoothing great armfuls of it into his hair. "Aw, wow." He looked up at Twenty-Nine Words and smiled. "You know, kid, you're beautiful, that's what you are."

"I'm indigenous," said Twenty-Nine Words. "And you're not so bad yourself."

"Go to commercial," said Philo.

The Coup de Grâce

Captain Chance Baker of the *South Furrow* watched Twenty-Nine Words's antics through the meringue-splattered windows of the pilothouse. A quiet man in anger, he said nothing, just sipped lukewarm coffee and thought about how good it would feel to turn hard to port and run all twenty thousand tons of his icebreaker full speed over the *Yabba-Dabba-Doo*. Even if he could have mustered full speed from his dying engines he wouldn't have tried this, though, because he knew he was outmatched: the yellow smile faces peering out at him from every monitor screen on the bridge told him that, as did the balalaika music that greeted him when he attempted to use the radio. Trying to ram the submarine and failing would only aggravate his feelings of impotence, and then he might be forced to punch out his first mate, who was asking stupid questions.

"What are we gonna do, skipper?" the mate said, as Beardsley Stepanik blew them kisses from the deck.

"Why not roll out the cannon?" Captain Baker suggested.

"But we don't have any cannon."

"Then they've got us by the balls, don't they? Now shut up and leave me alone."

The ship-to-ship holographic communicator beeped. The incoming transmission had been masked to make the caller transparent except for his outline (vague), his eyes (green), and his shirt (Hawaiian and loud).

"Captain Baker?" he introduced himself. "This is Philo Dufresne of the *Yabba-Dabba-Doo*."

"Can't say I'm pleased to make your acquaintance," the captain said. "You calling to tell me to abandon ship?"

"Nothing personal, Captain. We're running an ecotage promotional video right now, but when we come back live we're going to be sinking you, and it would help me a lot if you'd order your people to the lifeboats."

"And if I say no?"

"Then I'll send more crew to board you in strength and put you all in lifeboats by force . . . but first I'll dress you up in a gorilla suit." This was a bluff. Not the part about the gorilla suit—Philo had three of those in stock— only the notion that he had time to effect a full takeover of the ship. By now CNN would have picked up the broadcast feed, thereby alerting the military, and the Ronald Reagan Air Force Base in Trenton would be scrambling all available anti-submarine craft. But Captain Baker didn't call him on it.

"All right," he said. "You win. But Dufresne?"

"Yes?"

"You know my name without asking, you probably also know I used to command a destroyer in the navy. When I get back to port I'm going to offer myself cheap to any company that wants to put me in charge of a combat vessel. Then I'm going to come looking for you. Understood?"

"Understood. I'd better warn you, though, Harry Gant's a pacifist. Only good thing I can say about him. Over and out."

Morris Kazenstein had the last word on the broadcast. He stood on the *Yabba-Dabba-Doo*'s launch deck wearing a star-and-moon-speckled wizard's hat and a set of fake-nose-and-moustache glasses. "Hey world," he said, "time for another visit with Mr. Science. Today we're going to do an experiment in kinetic energy transfer. This"—he pointed to a long cylindrical track that had risen out of the hull beside him—"is an electromagnetic railgun, a scaled-down model of the very same device the Republicans use to protect the White House from nuclear attack. And this"—he held up a hefty deli sausage—"is twenty pounds of kosher salami. Now what we're going to do is accelerate the salami to Mach 9 and see what happens to the bow of that ship over there, OK? Kids, *please* don't try this at home without your parents' supervision . . ."

The Review

"Any comments?" Harry Gant asked his crisis-reduction team as they watched the sinking of the *South Furrow* on the conference room video screen. Gant was sitting with his back to the table, and with his expression hidden it was difficult for the more self-promoting members of the group to read his mood and tailor a proper response. Unsurprisingly, Whitey Caspian—known to his peers in the Public Opinion Department as Prince Motor Tongue—was the first to speak up.

"It probably wasn't a real salami," Whitey said.

"What's that?"

"It probably wasn't real," Whitey repeated. He was six-foot-three, blond, and built like a decathlon champion but undercut any comparison to Adonis with his choice of horn-rimmed glasses and tartan bow tie. "Even a kosher salami probably couldn't withstand that kind of acceleration."

"You have the brains of a *radish*," Vanna Domingo hissed. But Harry Gant was laughing. He swung around to face them and brought his hands together in applause. "That's great," he said. "That's better than great, it's *brilliant.*"

Clayton Bryce from Creative Accounting cleared his throat and asked: "What's brilliant, Mr. Gant?"

"The whole thing," Gant said, gesturing at the video screen. "What Whitey just said. That's all the media are going to be talking about. I can already imagine the follow-up interview on CNN: 'Tell us, Professor Newton, what are the practical aspects of firing salami from a railgun?' Not to mention Ætna Insurance's reaction when we file our claim. 'Help us, Ætna, the wicked pirate Dufresne torpedoed us with deli meat!'"

Vanna Domingo couldn't believe his tone. "You *admire* that bastard!"

"Dufresne? Of course I admire him. Hell, I wish I could hire him."

"He just destroyed millions of dollars' worth of *your* property."

"He just out-advertised me, that's what he did. You've seen the public reaction. He's got first-graders out in Kansas learning to word process just so they can write me nasty letters. Home recordings of his raids are the hottest item in amateur video. If he were a corporation instead of a criminal he'd be in the Fortune 500 by now. He's a genuine American hero."

"He's *evil*," Vanna Domingo insisted. "We should take the insurance money from that ship he just sank and hire a mercenary fleet to track him down. With torpedoes and depth charges . . ."

Gant held up his hands. "No physical violence," he said. "Mercenaries, depth charges, all that G.I. Joe nonsense, it goes against the free-market tradition. Besides, I don't like it."

"But he's using violence against this corporation, against *you,* so why—"

"That's different. Dufresne's brand of violence is . . . creative. All right, I'll grant you, violence is violence, he's probably a bald-faced anarchist at heart, but if *I* were a bald-faced anarchist at heart, I can only hope that I would be capable of designing a battle plan as *artistic* as the one we just witnessed. Not a single fatality, no serious injuries, and those rabbit things that kid was throwing, you could probably put those in stores around Christmastime and start a whole new fad. Pure genius.

"The point is, though, we're not anarchists, we're democratic capitalists, and that means we leave warfare to the government. Which reminds me, what does the Pentagon have to say?"

"Nothing encouraging," said C. D. Singh, who was Gant's liaison in Washington. "They're either really scared or really embarrassed, but either way they've got no official comment. Maybe they'll be luckier today, but my inside sources tell me that all previous sea hunts have failed to turn up even a trace of the sub, no matter how quickly anti-submarine forces arrive on the scene. That degree of stealth just isn't possible for a pack of radical environmentalists operating on their own, but neither the C.I.A. nor the F.B.I.'s Un-Un-American Activities Division has uncovered any evidence linking Dufresne to a foreign power."

"So theoretically," Gant said, "the pirates can't be getting away with what they've been getting away with."

"Yes sir. Which means, from a military intelligence standpoint, that the *Yabba-Dabba-Doo* doesn't exist."

"Doesn't *exist*!" Vanna was beginning to change color. "Doesn't *exist*! It was just on millions of television screens, what more proof do they *want*?"

"They're being cautious, that's all," C. D. Singh said. "And to be frank, Mr. Gant, we haven't raised nearly the stink we're capable of, considering the wealth of this corporation."

"Well tell me something," Gant said. "What would the navy or the Air Force do to Dufresne if they could find him?"

"Force him to surrender, if possible. Turn him and his crew over to the F.B.I., put the submarine in dry dock and dissect it for its secrets. Or if he wouldn't give up, sink him."

"And good riddance," said Vanna.

"Hmm," said Gant. "I wonder what the first-graders in Kansas would say about that."

"I can't speak for the Kansas schoolchildren," C. D. Singh replied, "but I can tell you what the president is saying right now. His offer to sanction operations in Antarctica was contingent on our keeping the scandal to a minimum, which would have been difficult even without this interference. I expect his representative will be calling within the hour to withdraw support."

Gant shrugged. "That I'm not worried about. To tell the truth, the idea of drilling for oil at the South Pole never excited me much."

"Well it *should*," Clayton Bryce said, suddenly angry. "We need the revenue. And the *reason* we need the revenue is that mile-high buildings aren't profitable. Babel is a money sink; our great-grandchildren will be ready for retirement by the time it starts earning in the black, if it ever does. The Minaret is barely paying for itself, the Phoenix hasn't come close to breaking even, and yet here we are saddling ourselves with enough negative cash flow to last out the century."

"But think of it, Clayton," Gant replied, dismissing petty financial concerns with another shrug. "A tower stretching a mile into the sky. I can't imagine a more remarkable human achievement. *The tallest building in the history of the world.*"

"And if it bankrupts us?"

"Oh, hell, we won't go bankrupt. We'll think up some new products to help finance it. And we don't have to give up on Antarctica, either, if you really think it's necessary. C. D. can contact some of the other Treaty nations, get an axis going."

"That could take years, Mr. Gant . . ."

"Let it take years. I plan to be around for another forty or fifty, myself. I can wait."

". . . *and* there's going to be insistence that something be done about Dufresne before any deals are struck."

"Well getting back to Dufresne, then . . . what about economic warfare? *That* kind of violence I can live with. How much progress have we made figuring out who's funding these people?"

Clayton shook his head. "No progress," he said.

"None?"

"We've followed up rumors that Dufresne's being bankrolled by terrorists or rival corporations, that he owns a diamond mine in Africa or a coca plantation in South America, that he's a former junk bond trader who decided to go straight. We've even checked allegations that he's being backed by the Trilateral Commission. None of it pans out."

"Well keep trying," Gant said. "And you, Vanna, get the Public Opinion gang together and—"

"This is ridiculous," Vanna interrupted him. "*Millions* lost on that icebreaker. Who knows how many *more* millions—*billions*—lost in potential profits from Antarctica. All this from just one raid by that bastard, but what do you want to do? Launch an advertising campaign against him. Break his piggy bank. Shake a finger at him. Why can't we just *kill* him?"

"No," Gant said, making it final. "Philo Dufresne embodies the spirit that built this country, and you don't kill a person like that. You either co-opt him or humble him. And you do that by using even more American ingenuity than he's used on you."

"This sounds like a very expensive brand of patriotism," C. D. Singh observed.

"It's *my* brand of patriotism," Gant replied. "And this is my corporation, so my brand of patriotism wins. Now I don't want to hear any more talk about killing. We'll beat Dufresne, but we'll beat him in the right way. Next order of business."

Still red-faced, Vanna Domingo consulted her Electric Clipboard. "Next item is a point of information about your ex-wife. It has to do with that big fish that popped up at the Technical School earlier this morning. Our follow-up security check has discovered that Joan Fine was on the other end of the explosion. Her intended target seems to have been the fish, not you."

"Is she all right?" Gant leaned forward, more alert than he'd been all morning. "She's not dead, is she?"

"Not dead," said Vanna, and thought: *I only wish.* "A Department of Sewers rescue team found her in a dry tunnel and took her to East River General. She was conscious and apparently unhurt—a few scratches, nothing more—but they want to keep her for observation. Also, the superintendent of sewers has released a statement claiming that the entire incident was a mass hallucination."

"There's another man I'd like to hire. Make a note, Vanna: I want the number of Joan's room at the hospital and a schedule of the visiting hours."

Vanna looked at him. "You can't visit her. She betrayed this corporation. She's anathema."

"Calm down, Vanna. I'd like to send her a get-well card, that's all."

"But she's unhurt."

"Just *get me the room number,* Vanna."

"Yes sir."

There was a knock at the door to the conference room. The director of Phoenix Visitor Services stuck his head in. "Very sorry to disturb you, Mr. Gant," he said, "but there's a bit of an emergency . . ."

Gant sighed. "What is it now?"

"I just got a call from Crowd Control down in the lobby. Did you by any chance order two thousand pizzas?"

3

Almost no one is aware that for more than two hundred years New York water tasted so foul that horses would not drink it, was so impure that disease decimated the population every other year, so expensive that the poor went without it and the streets were filled with filth, its sources so widely scattered that periodic fires wiped out four or five hundred houses at a clip.

—Robert Daley, *The World Beneath the City*

1914: Walking to Flatbush

The Dutch settlers of New Amsterdam would have been skeptical to hear that their rough little town on the Hudson—after a name change, two switches in nationality, and countless vain exercises in imaginative plumbing—would ultimately gain a reputation for having some of the tastiest drinking water of any city in the world. The British and newly minted Americans who came after them probably wouldn't have believed it either, though they let themselves be rooked again and again by con men promising relief from tainted wells. Even Aaron Burr joined in the shell game: his Manhattan Company water utility was a financial success (clearing enough profit to underwrite Burr's presidential campaign and found the Chase Manhattan Bank) but a practical failure (service was terrible and did nothing to alleviate poor sanitation conditions that caused regular outbreaks of yellow fever and cholera).

New York finally started importing its water, first by aqueduct from Westchester, and later, when the immigrant population explosion had taxed that supply to its limit, from dams in the faraway Catskill Mountains. Public Works engineers and laborers (many of them only recently arrived from Italy) dug a tunnel from the Catskills to the Hill View Reservoir in Yonkers, then bored south through the bedrock under the Harlem River to bring the water into the city proper. The last segment of the tunnel was blasted open on January 11, 1914, and an incidental consequence of its completion was that it made possible one of the most peculiar marathons in city history: an underground hike of a hundred and twenty miles, from the Catskill Mountains to the Flatbush section of Brooklyn.

Peter Lugo Peller, a stringer for the *New York Tribune* whose great-great-grandson would find fame as disaster chronicler to a lost generation, became feverishly excited by the idea of this "Long Walk to Flatbush," and managed to talk five other journalists and two photographers into accompanying him on the journey. They gathered at the Ashokan Dam in the Catskills on January 18th. A jeering group of tunnel diggers was also on hand, placing wagers on how quickly the marchers would give up; the smart money had it that they wouldn't last ten miles.

Just prior to the descent another journalist arrived, a skinny fellow outfitted in full mountain-climbing gear, with his hair tucked up under a coal miner's helmet. He rushed over to the little clutch of newsmen and greeted Peter Lugo Peller with a firm double handshake.

"Smuts of North Dakota," the newcomer introduced himself. "From the *Fargo Spectrum*."

"Awfully long way from home, aren't you?" one of the photographers asked.

"We're trying to be more cosmopolitan," Smuts replied.

They headed down, and Peter Lugo Peller, taking the lead, soon made two alarming discoveries: first, that the tunnel was not, as he had for some reason imagined, a straight level line from point A to point B, but rather an alpine track that plunged and soared hundreds of feet as it passed under rivers and other surface obstacles; and second, that it was already full of water. Enough water to drown you in spots, or at least ruin your footwear—and Peller had worn his best pair of shoes for the outing. After a quick conference the intrepid newsmen decided to continue the hike above ground, which they did for an entire day before quitting altogether.

No one noticed that Smuts never came up out of the tunnel.

On January 25th, two sandhogs at the High View Reservoir in Yonkers were the first to spot the damp, bruised, but extremely self-satisfied figure who clambered out of the bowels of the earth in a battered coal miner's helmet. One of the sandhogs had won a silver dollar in a juggling contest the night before and was bouncing it on his palm, but paused at the sight of Smuts, who looked like nothing that belonged in the Reservoir.

"Who are you?" the juggler said, in Italian. His companion, who spoke a passable English, translated: "Who the fuck are you?"

"Just a lady out for a stroll," Smuts replied. She lifted the helmet, releasing a long spill of brown hair, a gesture that eleven-year-old Hollywood had not yet had time to turn into a cliché. "On my way to Flatbush."

The juggler was thunderstruck; his companion, who had been born Maria but found life simpler in work shirt and trousers, allowed herself a guarded grin. Smuts winked at her in secret recognition, then jabbed a finger at the silver coin.

"Hey," she said, "gimme that."

Needing no translation of this imperative, the juggler closed his hand over the shiny prize. "Why should I?"

"Because," Smuts replied, addressing him in his own tongue, "I just earned it."

2023: Donkeys Lost in the Woods

One hundred and nine years later, a woman named Lexa Thatcher sat in a loft in Brooklyn—New Bedford–Stuyvesant rather than Flatbush, but close enough—turning the same silver dollar over in her fingers. The coin had been handed down through five generations of mothers and daughters, and its faces were worn nearly smooth by now, but the audacious spirit that drove the Smuts/Hollings/Thatcher matrilineal line had not withered in the slightest. Lexa's mother had sought her own adventure in North Africa, trekking alone across the Sahara from Timbuktu to Marrakech. East of Casablanca, in the foothills of the Middle Atlas, she had seduced and ravished a Bedouin used car salesman—or perhaps an entire dealership of them, she was never specific on that point—as a result of which Lexa's hands holding the coin were richly bronzed, her heart and head sharp for the hard bargain.

Lexa's home office contained her desk, a computer with numerous peripheral devices (including a few available only to good friends of Morris Kazenstein), a folding bed, a collection of heart-shaped portraits, and, at the moment, the family television, which was portable and ambled from room to room when not in use. A pair of Electric Dung Beetles made regular rounds as well, seeking out and disposing of dust and dirt particles, in accordance with Lexa's philosophy that the best form of housekeeping was a house that kept itself. Two large windows let in fresh air and light: New Bedford–Stuyvesant was climate controlled and never got colder than a balmy midsummer's night.

While Lexa put together a piece for the upcoming weekly edition of *The Long Distance Call,* her daughter Rabi argued with the TV. It was not a Gant Portable but an antique Sony Animan, a 19-inch screen perched on pistoning legs of oiled brass. Lexa had fitted it with a Personality Template Box—an expensive option but worth it in her opinion—to handle the thorny problem of parental guidance. Rabi was not specifically prohibited from watching any program, but whenever she turned on the set she was challenged by a computer-generated construct of the philosopher Socrates, who made her justify her channel selection.

"My admirable Rabi," Socrates hailed her today, "as always I am anxious to partake of your wisdom. Here it is one o'clock on a Monday afternoon, a time at which most seven year olds would be in school, and yet you sit at home . . ."

"I have chicken pox," Rabi said, holding up a spotty arm. "See?"

"All the more reason I should want to be your pupil. Your illness prevents you from receiving the education your society has sacrificed to provide. Many in your situation would rest so as to recover more quickly, or read to keep up with their studies, or take advantage of the Sesame Street episode about to begin on Channel 13. But you, Rabi—no doubt following the most brilliant chain of reasoning—you have elected instead to view violent cartoons in which rabbits, coyotes, and roadrunners drop boulders on one another. If only you would share your logic with me, so that I might go out and extol your intelligence and virtue to other children in the Tri-State Area—"

"You know what I was reading the other day?" Rabi interrupted him. "And all on my own, not even assigned in class? A book about Greek mythology, which is what they had for cartoons when *you* were seven. And you know what? This god named Cronus took a sickle and made his father *impotent* with it. *Impotent.* So is that better or worse than a coyote getting hit by a boulder?"

Tuning out the debate with a pair of headphones, Lexa asked her computer to run a program called SumpPumpGraphics. "Working," the computer replied, and on its main monitor drew comic strip images of the seven Democratic presidential candidates, seated as if for a debate of their own. When Lexa fed copies of their stump speeches into an optical scanner, dialogue balloons appeared above the seated figures, sized in proportion to the wordiness of the speeches. The largest balloon belonged to Preston Hackett, a dark horse opportunist who on separate occasions had claimed to be a native of eighteen different states, including Belgium, which had apparently been admitted to the Union when no one else was looking.

"Ready cull feature," Lexa said.

"Cull feature ready. Average speech length at start is three thousand, six hundred, and seventeen words."

"Cull salutations, jokes, and needless historical anecdotes. Ditto quotations and statistics that don't directly support a platform point. Cull platitudes and non sequiturs. Cull reiterations of obvious facts. Cull redundancies. Cull misleading statements and outright lies, but flag them for later."

"Working," the computer said, and the dialogue balloons shrank drastically. "Culling completed. Average speech length is now two hundred and seven words."

"Cull and flag impossible promises. Also cull promises that fail a vagueness test."

"What is my threshold of acceptable vagueness?"

"Let's not be too stringent. Cull anything that rates below a four on the Thatcher Hem-Haw Scale."

"Loading THS parameters. Working." The dialogue balloons became tiny dots. "Culling completed. Average speech length is now twenty-two words."

Lexa took a laser pen and pointed it at the cartoon figure that represented candidate Harmon Fox. Fox recited the bare bones version of his stump speech: "If elected, I will raise taxes against the rich, cut military spending in favor of social welfare programs, and plant one million trees."

Lexa shifted the light beam to candidate Nan Sheffield. "If elected," Sheffield promised, "I will raise taxes against the rich, cut military spending in favor of social welfare programs, and plant two million trees."

A bidding war. Lexa tapped Preston Hackett next and was surprised to hear the shortest speech thus far: "If elected, I will raise taxes against the rich and cut military spending in favor of social welfare programs."

"Nothing about trees?" Lexa asked.

"Candidate Hackett's sole reference to trees," the computer replied, "was that he had a plan to reforest the Great Plains. That statement did not survive culling."

"Stick it back in. Retrieve and reinsert."

"Done."

"Now open a page display for me, standard column widths. Insert the candidates' culled speeches as a sidebar, leaving space for pen-and-ink caricatures. Working title for the article is 'Donkeys Lost in the Woods.'"

She typed for the next half hour. Lexa's keyboard, a 1925 Remington-Rand manual typewriter, was the only part of the setup not state-of-the-art. She liked the weighty metal feel of the keys and the clack of the type bars hitting the empty platen; pressure switches in the carapace transferred her keystrokes to the computer processor. Inscribed below the Remington's space bar in calligraphic brushstrokes of Liquid Paper was the motto: GOOD INVESTIGATIVE JOURNALISM IS A THING OF THE PAST.

By the time she finished the piece, her daughter had demolished Socrates and was watching Bugs Bunny do the same thing to Elmer Fudd. Confident that Rabi's moral fiber was in no immediate danger, Lexa transferred copies of her write-up to the *Call*'s main office in Manhattan and to Ellen Leeuwenhoek, her star photographer on assignment in Washington. Then she told the computer to rake the yard, a code phrase triggering a broad-based search for interesting news—the word *interesting* being defined by a continually evolving parameters file the size of a small dictionary.

"First item," the computer told her some thirty seconds later, over the simulated chatter of an old UPI teletype. "The comptroller of public opinion at Gant Industries has just announced the indefinite postponement of what she termed 'our Antarctic conservation project' due to 'unchecked terrorist activity.'"

"Has there been any official statement from Washington regarding the sinking of the icebreaker?"

"The president and his staff have not yet made themselves available for comment. However, the queen of England, vacationing at an undisclosed location, has issued a press release commending Philo Dufresne for 'foiling the dishonorable designs of those of Our American cousins who would seek to break treaty with Us.' The British prime minister followed up immediately with the statement that, 'Her Majesty's words should not be interpreted to imply tolerance for hooliganism.'"

"See if you can intercept any Electric Memos coming out of the White House, but be discreet about it. And let me know if the queen says anything else about Philo. Next item."

"Next item: a check of accessible police files reveals no new information regarding the death of Amberson Teaneck, or the possible involvement of a Gant Automatic Servant in that incident. Gant's Public Opinion Department has made seven telephone calls to the precinct homicide division handling the investigation and another five to the police commissioner's office, and sent multiple faxes warning against 'careless speculation.' As of this afternoon, no media source reporting on the murder has made any reference to a Gant Servant."

"Give me a hard copy of everything we already have on the case. And next item while I wait."

"Printing. Next item: Joan Fine was admitted to East River General Hospital this morning after being caught in an explosion in the New York City sewer system. Cost of damage to the sewers and adjacent building foundations is estimated at—"

"How is she?" Lexa interrupted.

"Her treatment consisted of stitching and bandaging of the right leg and a course of antibiotics to guard against possible contagion. She is being held for observation, but her prognosis is excellent."

"What's her room number?"

"Room 413. Visiting hours are from nine A.M. to ten P.M."

"Contact the reception desk at the hospital and have them ready a visitor's pass for me."

"Working," the computer said. "My search has turned up other news items."

"Save them for a few minutes. I'll call you from the car."

The Car God Would Drive If She Had a License

Gathering the sheaf of printout in a manila folder, which she tucked into her purse, Lexa kissed Rabi goodbye and told her to be sure and take a nap at some point. "Your father's due back tonight and you've got to not be dying of fever if you want to go with Toshiro and me to meet him."

"'Kay, Mom," Rabi promised, and went back to her cartoons. In the guest bedroom, Lexa bestowed a more lingering goodbye kiss on the sleeping form of Toshiro Goodhead, this season's star attraction at the West Village Chippendale's. Then she went out, down three flights of curving stone steps to the street below.

New Bedford–Stuyvesant was roughly one and a half square miles of Moroccan *medina* transplanted to King's County. Lexa and an investment group of fellow muckrakers had decided some years back that if they were going to spend their lives pointing out the flaws in other people's grand designs, they ought to undertake at least one grand design of their own. Urban renewal had seemed an obvious choice.

The traditional medina style had been thoughtfully adapted to the alternative environment of modern Brooklyn. New Bedford–Stuyvesant's streets were straighter and better lit than the labyrinthine alleyways that honeycombed old Marrakech and Fez, and wide enough to permit vehicular traffic, though combustion engines were strictly forbidden. Population density was far lower than in most North African cities, and a full third of the property had been reserved for parks and recreation; almost every rooftop boasted a garden. The buildings, while similar in profile—rectangular boxes, mostly, and none over five stories high—were dressed up in paint and tile murals of every description. The façade of Lexa's co-op was a cross section of the ocean depths, complete with wildlife: manatees and walruses frolicking in the waves near the lip of the roof; dolphins, morays, and lithe scuba divers outside the windows of Lexa's apartment on the fourth floor; and so on down to the blue-black deeps at street level, where lantern fish swam past the silver Hand of Fatima on the front door. Concealed beneath the bright colors and the cement and brick facing was a modernized plumbing system, with Catskill water, still safe to drink even in 2023, flowing from the bathroom taps—a feature that could not be fully appreciated unless you had once done the dysentery squat over a Kasbah pit toilet. By recycling whatever wastes they could, channeling New Bedford–Stuyvesant's effluvia to collection tanks for use as fertilizer and fuel, neighborhood residents also limited their reliance on the Brooklyn sewer system, which in the era of the May Team made extremely good sense.

And of course there was the dome. Buckminster Fuller had yet to establish a foothold in Rabat or Tangier, but New Bedford–Stuyvesant lay enclosed and protected beneath a geodesic bubble. Each triangular panel in the structure was a transparent solar collector, so that on long sunny days the dome generated enough electricity to run the climate-control center and satisfy up to forty percent of the neighborhood's modest power needs. Overcast days were another matter, but even in dampest March it was far more energy efficient than any superskyscraper. Easier to get around in, too, and in Lexa's opinion, prettier.

Ethnically the neighborhood was a pot luck mix, kept that way in part by scaled rents that put the well-to-do next door to the hyper-impoverished. There were ragtag refugees of U.S. foreign policy in Syria and El Salvador living upstreet from deposed Bahraini and Qatari royals; wealthy Turks, Vietnamese, and Puerto Ricans haggling with Cambodian and Afghani peddlers in the Bed-Stuy souk. Anglos were relatively scarce: white liberals shied away from the neighborhood out of a belief that the many Arab residents would oppress women or Jews who lived near them, while white conservatives feared being kidnapped or blown up. They gave New Bedford–Stuyvesant a wide berth and bought condos in Richmond instead.

With the exception of Lexa's daughter Rabi—whom almost everyone mistook for an Australian—there were no black residents at all, not of African ancestry. Common wisdom held that no African-Americans remained anywhere east of the Mississippi, that the few survivors were living in fortified camps in the Rocky Mountains. Lexa knew more of the facts than that, but it was true that the most "African" face you were likely to see in New Bedford–Stuyvesant belonged to Bluey Kapirigi, an Australian aborigine who'd come to America to star in movies and miniseries. Bluey bore as close a resemblance to the late Rosa Parks as any Australoid could be expected to, and as often as twice a year would fly to Montgomery, Alabama, to be filmed refusing to give up her seat on the bus; this single role replayed again and again had earned her national acclaim, to the point that she had been invited to the White House and given the keys to the city by Montgomery's mayor.

A short hike through the souk brought Lexa to the Anti-Atlas Mosque, where she kept her car parked. The *imam* was sitting on the mosque's front steps, having a late lunch; he raised a hand as Lexa approached.

"Hey big man," Lexa said, walking up.

"Lexa," he greeted her. "That guy was playing with your Bug again."

"When?"

"Not ten minutes ago. I was up in the minaret dusting the Electric Muezzin. He ran when the car honked its horn."

"The same man as before?"

"I think so. Unless car thieves have all started wearing blue serge suits."

"Well thanks for the look out," Lexa said. "I'll ask Betsy if she got an I.D."

Betsy was Betsy Ross, a 2019 Special Edition Kazenstein Volkswagen Beetle. In her late twenties Lexa had patronized a women's bar in the Village called the Betsy Ross Saloon, and a painting that hung over her favorite table had shown a winged Beetle chasing clouds above the Manhattan skyline; the painting's title was *The Car God Would Drive If She Had a License.* Lexa had wanted her own Bug ever since and remained on the lookout for a mint-condition '49. Morris's version of the Beetle, however, came with a lot more toys.

Lexa unplugged the charging cable and pressed her thumb against the fingerprint latch on the driver's door. "I've been molested by swine," Betsy said, as Lexa slid inside. Lexa had asked Morris to give the car a pleasant female persona, but he'd been reading a reissue of *Revolution for the Hell of It* that month, and so Betsy Ross was actually Abbie Hoffman in drag.

"Faisal told me you had a visitor," Lexa replied. "What did he do?"

"Stuck a tracker under my rear bumper. You should have seen the son of a bitch jump when I laid on the horn."

"Did you get his picture?"

"Honey, I got his SAT scores." The glove compartment dropped open, and a color fax inside printed out a mug shot of a startled-looking blond man. "Ernest G. Vogelsang, Houston Community College class of '19, Quantico class of '21, presently working as a special agent for the F.B.I.'s Un-Un-American Activities Division. Looks like the feds have you pegged for an un-un-American."

"That's nothing new. What about his SATs?"

"340 math, 260 verbal. Guy must be a lousy guesser."

"Must be. Why do you suppose the feds hired him?"

"I dunno," said Betsy. "But you want to hear an amazing coincidence? The current head of the Un-Un-American Activities Division is *also* named Ernest Vogelsang. Senior."

"Hmm."

Lexa thumbed the starter; the engine came on like a soft whisper. This was the one thing she didn't like about driving off batteries, no matter how environmentally conscious it might be: even cruising at the top speed of sixty miles an hour the Bug was too quiet, almost silent. Like driving a golf cart.

"You know," Betsy said, "if you took out my hit-and-run inhibitors I could save a lot of time by just *backing over* people like Vogelsang . . ."

"That's all right," Lexa said. "I have enough trouble getting you registered every year as it is."

"So who the hell told you I wanted to be registered?"

They drove out of the lot. The hush of the Bug's operation continued to frustrate Lexa, but not for long. Betsy had a secret vice: canned electricity

wasn't the only thing she ran on. Leaving the dome of New Bedford
–Stuyvesant and easing into the light traffic on the Atlantic Parkway, Lexa
switched over to methanol, a home brew that burned hot and clean. The
unmatchable *thrum* of internal combustion pulsed from fender to fender.
Lexa stood on the accelerator; the speedometer jumped from fifty to eighty-
five. The little Beetle shot past an Electric Winnebago and nearly blew it off
the road.

"Keep an eye out for radar traps," Lexa said, and Betsy replied: "Now
you're talking."

2004 & 2023: Heaven's Velodrome

One reason Joan Fine didn't put much faith in near-death experiences was
that her mother had had one, and Sister Ellen Fine's trip beyond the pale
was so bizarre, in both its cause and its content, that it pretty much discred-
ited the whole subject for her.

The last sally of the Catholic Womanist Crusade was launched in the
summer of '04, just two months prior to the onset of the African Pandemic
(a coincidence duly noted by disaster chronicler Tad Winston Peller, though
he never did say what the connection was supposed to be). By that year the
ranks of the Roman Catholic priesthood had dwindled to crisis levels world-
wide, and though there were many reasons for the decline, the celibacy
question was cited again and again as a prime factor. When a third Vatican
Council was called in early June, rumors spread that the Church was finally
planning to repeal the prohibition on clerical marriage. The Womanists were
determined to crash the party.

"You're crazy, Mom," Joan told her mother, not for the first time.
"The College of Cardinals are a bunch of old virgins with bad tempers.
It's causing them physical pain to give even this little bit of ground, and
what are *you* asking for? Not just married priests. Not even just female
priests. Female priests who can get married, possibly to each other. *Pregnant* priests. Artificially inseminated dyke priests with attitude. The pope's
gonna have a stroke."

"Oh my daughter of little faith," Sister Ellen replied, fighting to
close her suitcase. "Going to Harvard has obviously made you one with
the heathen."

"They excommunicated you, Mom. They aren't even going to let
you in."

"That excommunication is just politics." Twin pops as the suitcase latches caught. "Look, I accept the fact that you want to play agnostic, but I still love this Church. And without *us,* it'll be dead inside of fifty years. Irrelevancy will kill it. His Holiness doesn't understand that, the Sacred College doesn't understand that, but *I* understand it, so it becomes my obligation as a good Catholic to go communicate my understanding." She lit a cigarette.

"I'm proud of you, Mom," Joan said. "Heathen or not, I don't want you to think I'm not proud of you. But you do know they're going to kill you, right?"

The Womanists flew to Rome on a pair of chartered Lufthansa jumbo jets—Al Italia had refused to carry them—and snuck through passport control disguised as a company of German beer merchants on holiday. The next morning at dawn they assembled on the west bank of the Tiber to begin their march on the Vatican. For this special occasion they had set aside the ritual dress of their various orders in favor of a standard uniform, "storming habits" that combined a proud purple hue with a humble weave and modest cut. Advancing seven hundred strong up the Via della Conciliazione, a shining determination in their eyes and faces, the Womanists suggested a military procession of plum-feathered penguins.

The Holy See had been alerted to their approach. The gates to the Vatican City remained open, but inside the Piazza San Pietro the Swiss Guard in their own flashy costumes of yellow, red, and blue had formed a defensive line, blocking the steps to St. Peter's Basilica. No such confrontation being complete without an angry mob, a cast of some two thousand Roman citizens had been summoned from their beds to the Piazza, clustering at the north and south ends, where black-booted carabinieri made a show of holding them back. And around the obelisk in the Piazza's center, the tabloid paparazzi swarmed, swaddled in white penitents' sport jackets of Gucci and Armani, shutters clicking away.

All of this was beamed back stateside by CNN, which had a blimp with gun cameras hovering over St. Peter's. A lone Swiss Guardsman crawled out onto the Basilica's roof to warn the blimp away, then tried to shoot it down with a sixteenth-century crossbow. Four thousand miles and six time zones to the west, Joan and Lexa sat up past midnight in the Betsy Ross Saloon, watching the drama unfold on the TV above the bar. As the nuns entered the Piazza, they spotted Sister Ellen Fine in the front rank, smoke trailing from a cigarette that she was too nervous to actually puff on.

"They're going to be massacred," Joan said, herself smoking one Marlboro after another. She was terrified, angry too that her mother was risking her life for something that to Joan seemed trivial, and yet at the same time filled with admiration and a yearning to see justice done: the same yearning that would carry her through numerous crusades of her own, charged further by the hope that at the moment of truth, those who had abused power would come to their senses and back down. *The pope will come out now,* she thought, *with open arms, and say "Enough is enough. We accept you. No need for violence."* Joan worried the beads of her rosary; Lexa took her hand.

The nuns were almost to the steps of the Basilica when the bombardment began. At the Wailing Wall in Jerusalem, Orthodox rabbis had thrown metal folding chairs at Jewish Womanists, but the mob of Romans stuck to more traditional ammunition: stones and masonry. Joan's mother was struck down by a bust of the Emperor Nero that clocked her on the side of the head, fracturing her skull and permanently deafening one ear.

"Didn't hurt," she insisted, speaking to Joan from her bed at home a week later. "Just this ringing, as though someone had struck a bell inside my head, and the next thing I knew I was riding a bicycle . . ."

"A bicycle," Joan said.

"I was on the outside of the sky," Sister Ellen said, "pedaling up the steepest slope you could imagine. I'd have lost all my wind except that I wasn't breathing anymore, so I kept on, and an eternity later the sky leveled out. And there it was in the middle of a plain of stars, just like in stories: mother-of-pearl on the gates, streets inside paved with gold—"

"Saint Peter minding the entrance?"

"Oh yes. But *he* wasn't what you'd expect. No flowing white beard, not at all. He was *young,* very much the outdoorsy type, muscular and sort of swarthy. . . ." She trailed off, sounding a little ashamed.

"Poor Ellie," said Sister Judith Calyx, a fellow Womanist (she'd escaped the Vatican riot unscathed, decking one of the Swiss Guardsmen and carrying Joan's mother to safety; they never did get to see the pope). "Ellie saw Saint Peter and was inspired to an impure thought."

"He *was* beautiful," Sister Ellen confessed. "Not my usual type, to say the least, but there's no denying the sheer deliciousness of his appearance."

"Maybe," Lexa Thatcher suggested, "it was just the power of his holiness you were feeling."

"I doubt it. My primary impression was that he had the most amazing ass of anyone I'd ever seen. I've never heard of the Holy Spirit manifesting itself in quite that fashion.

"So I said hello to him, and he greeted me in return and asked me to please wait while he got my housing assignment. Didn't use a computer or a telephone; he had a gigantic filing cabinet over by the gate, with combination locks on each file drawer and Roman numerals on each lock's dial, which struck me as an odd detail to notice if I were just hallucinating the whole thing." She glanced significantly at Joan, who clearly wasn't buying a word of this. "Then, while Peter tried to remember whether it was XVII left or XVII right, I heard a huffing and puffing coming up from behind, and saw that a delegation of my Sisters in Purple had followed me. They'd conquered the slope on a twelve-seater tandem bike, though I could see from their red faces they'd have killed for a school bus." She patted Sister Judith's hand. "They stopped some distance away, as if they didn't dare to come any closer, and gestured to me: 'This way, the fight's not over, what are you in such a hurry to quit for?'"

"So you went back."

"In a minute I did. Though I have to admit that for an instant, caught midway between Peter's backside and that rusty tandem full of sisters, I hesitated." She grinned a very un-nunnish grin and turned to Joan. "And you, my heathen daughter, you think I dreamed the whole thing, don't you?"

"I love you, Mom," Joan replied. "I respect you, I support you. But you're a loon."

Hence Joan's reluctance to credit near-death experiences. Hence a lot of other things about Joan, too.

At any rate, as the paramedics winched her out of the sewers that Monday morning in 2023, Joan knew she wasn't dead, or anywhere near it. Awake for part of the ride to East River General, she asked what her chances were. The young woman attending her in the back of the ambulance laughed and told her not to worry: she'd lost no limbs and suffered no internal injuries, though she'd need patching up where Meisterbrau had nuzzled her leg. Joan closed her eyes and slept the rest of the way to the hospital.

And dreamed she was riding a bicycle on the outside of the sky.

The incline was as bad as her mother had claimed, with the added difficulty that Joan still drew breath. By the time she reached the plain of stars on which the eternal city rested, she was too winded to speak. Huffing, wheezing, and wishing paradoxically for a cigarette, Joan coasted up to the pearly gates.

Saint Peter was not on duty. Joan's mother was, leaning against a file cabinet and twirling a huge ring of keys on one finger.

"Well if it isn't my heathen daughter," she said. "Wasn't expecting you up here today. A party of your coworkers just came through, but you weren't on the list."

"Mom . . . ," Joan began, but broke off in a series of hacking coughs.

"Still smoking? I am, too, but the good news is they don't have cancer here. No cigarette tax, either. And when you go out to a restaurant, you can light up anywhere you like."

Bent forward over the handlebars, Joan could see a gold-paved street through the open gateway, not as shiny as she would have thought. The architecture was Swiss suburbia, row after row of white pine chalets. Joan couldn't help wondering how they managed to house all the dead without skyscrapers. The tallest structure she could see, a stadium-like edifice at the top of a hill, had a banner that announced, BICYCLE RACES EVERY MONDAY AND THURSDAY.

"Listen, Joan," her mother said. "As long as you did drop by . . . I was nosing around in the Main Office the other day, and I saw some things you probably should know about. There's going to be trouble in New York this week . . ."

Three blocks down from heaven's velodrome, an alligator shuffled out of a side street, chased by Eddie Wilder, Lenny Prohaska, Art Hartower, and a grime-covered old man who could only be Teddy May. The 'gator crossed to the middle of the intersection, nosed up a manhole cover that had been encrusted with precious stones, and tried to escape into the sewer. But Eddie Wilder pounced on it, seizing it by the tail.

". . . an earthquake, for one thing. Didn't catch the Richter number. And something to do with Electric Negroes. *Watch out for the Negroes,* Joan. Are you listening to me?"

"Mom," Joan huffed, finally managing to straighten up. "Mom, what are you doing with Saint Peter's keys?"

"Oh, that. We had a bit of a shake-up after Judy and I arrived. Disagreements with the management. It could have turned ugly like that business in Rome, but in the end we worked out a peaceful compromise." She lowered her voice and added: "The Virgin Mary took our side."

A Job Offer

East River General was moored to a pier not far from the Brooklyn Bridge. Formerly a prison barge, it had been converted to a combination hospital ship and morgue during the '04 Pandemic and now served as a catchtrap facility, handling patient and cadaver overflow from other sites around the city. Its living patrons were motivated to recover as quickly as possible: the East River, at least on its more polluted days, was a known fire hazard.

Joan woke to the smell of filtered air and disinfectant; outside the barred window of her room, brown haze choked a bird in flight.

"Dreaming?" Lexa asked, from a chair beside the bed.

"Dreaming," Joan agreed, groggy. She saw her leg wound had been tended while she chatted with her mother. "So what's the damage?"

"Minor. Your doctor wants to run a blood test later, but she thinks—"

"The *structural* damage," Joan said. "What did I do to the sewers?"

"Well," said Lexa, "unfortunately it wasn't just a methane explosion. Seems the effluvia itself was in a combustible mood today." She read from a printout Betsy Ross had produced for her: "Two building foundations undermined, one tunnel partially collapsed, an additional fifty thousand dollars' worth of 'cosmetic damage'—that's what it says—and your patrol barge looks like you bought it at Picasso's boat yard. Besides that, there are little patches of fire still floating around under the Island, and . . ." She nodded towards the window.

"I lit the river? I lit the fucking river?"

"The Hudson," Lexa told her, "is also reported to be smoldering. Not to be rude, Joan, but if you want to be a traditional martyr the idea is to get *somebody else* to burn you at the stake. Self-inflicted doesn't count."

"I want a cigarette."

"Thought you might." Lexa handed Joan a pack of Marlboro Filters, a matchbook, and a crumpled soda can for an ashtray. The flare of the match set off the room's anti-carcinogen security system: a hologram of a peeved John Wayne appeared at the foot of the bed, shaking his finger.

"Now ma'am," Wayne chastised, "you know better than that. Hospital regulations absolutely *forbid*—"

Lexa unplugged the smoke detector. Wayne evaporated in midsentence. "So . . ."

"You know what?" Joan said. "A black woman saved my life this morning. A real one, I think, not Electric."

Lexa didn't look surprised, but then she almost never did. "Interesting," was all she said. "What makes you think she was human?"

"Well for one thing, she was in the sewer, and I know for a fact she didn't belong to the Department. And she was *black,* I mean really black. The darkest off-the-rack Servants are only medium brown."

"Mmm hmm," Lexa said. She was scribbling something on the printout sheet. "You know why that is, don't you?"

"Of course I do. The Market Research branch of Public Opinion decided darker skin tones would scare children. So unless Harry's built a custom model, dressed it up in a suit of armor, and lost it down a manhole, I don't think this woman was running on batteries. One other thing: she had green eyes."

"Green?" said Lexa. "Who ever heard of a black African with green eyes?" On the printout she had written: FEDS MAY BE LISTENING. SIGNIFICANT OTHER #1 SAYS HI AND THANKS FOR THE LATEST CONTRIBUTION TO THE EARTH FUND. NEXT TIME I SEE *HIS OLDEST DAUGHTER* I'LL EXTEND YOUR GRATITUDE.

"Good point," Joan said, tapping ashes into the soda can. "Maybe I just imagined her. Wouldn't be the first time someone hallucinated down in the shit."

"So what are you going to do when you get out of here?" Lexa asked. She folded the printout sheet and fed it into a pocket document shredder in her purse. "For work, I mean."

"Don't know. After this morning I'll be off May Team duty for sure—"

"You are. Fatima Sigorski logged your suspension at 1:12 P.M."

"—right, and a desk job with the Department of Sewers would be a new low, so it looks like I'm unemployed. You have a suggestion?"

"It doesn't involve hunting sharks . . ."

"Carcharodons." Joan smiled. "It's funny, after all those years of picket signs and petitions, and then pimping for Harry . . . there's something refreshing about carrying a loaded twelve-gauge." Even as she said this she flashed on Prohaska, dragged under screaming, and was suddenly nauseous.

"Guns." Lexa shook her head, while Joan hurriedly took a long drag of nicotine. "What I want to know is, whatever happened to the ideal of heroic *endurance?* Slow, steady, hard work, that's still how most social change gets done. And you get to grow old."

"I plan on growing old, thank you. And you know damn well I hate bloodshed, but . . ."

"You love a good fight." Lexa smiled; this was an old exchange between them. "A rough-and-tumble showdown, a moment of truth, and no casualties, except for the odd fish. You never were much for animal rights."

"Right. And I mean I've got the Sanctuary too, and that's a comfort, knowing there's twenty less people sleeping on the street at night, but it's not *satisfying*. I need a brick wall to smash through. Why do you think I married Harry?"

"Joan of Arc."

Joan shrugged. "So sue me. What do you expect, with my mother? Not to mention Gordo Gambino."

"Well I don't need a liberal mafiosa and I don't need the Maid of Orleans," said Lexa. "I need a smart researcher, one who's got an in at Gant Industries. And who can defend herself." She laid the manila folder on the bed. "I can't promise, but it *could* be dangerous."

"What is it?"

"A murder. Amberson Teaneck. He ran the Corporate Raiding Office at Drexel Burnham Salomon. Rumor has it he was trying to organize a takeover of Gant Industries, but he had a sudden attack of unnatural causes."

"You think *Harry* killed him? Smokey the Bear would be a more likely suspect."

"Well that's the interesting part," Lexa said. "There's evidence suggesting that he wasn't killed by a *person* at all, not directly. What would you say if I told you a Gant Automatic Servant might be the murder weapon?"

Joan shook her head. "Highly doubtful."

"But not impossible?"

Joan shrugged. "It's been tried plenty of times, always unsuccessfully as far as I know. A lot of would-be murderers have thought of the idea. Bank robbers, too. But you can't just reprogram a Servant the way you can a computer. They have open data storage for remembering instructions, but their behavioral inhibitors are all hardwired, and the list of things they won't do is pretty comprehensive. Has to be, for the sake of product liability."

"And not even a genius could bypass the hardwiring?"

"It's supposedly tamperproof," Joan said. "Which means yeah, it could probably be done, but not by just any yahoo with a soldering iron. You'd need to yank the Central Processing Unit—by itself a major chore, since it's sealed up tighter than the engine block in a Rolls Royce—deengineer, redesign, and replace it, do the same thing with a bunch of other silicon, and find and remove a number of hidden mechanical fail-safes as well. Which even if you have the resources and know-how to pull it off is a lot of trouble to go to just to kill somebody. Simpler to just fix the brakes on the guy's car."

"And would this sort of tampering—replacing the CPU, removing the fail-safes—would it be easy to spot?"

"You mean if a trained technician examined the Servant after the fact?" Joan nodded. "Yeah. Sure. And once you knew that tampering had gone on—and that it worked—the list of suspects would narrow down considerably. Which is another reason why it's really not such a hot modus operandi for a murder."

"Under ordinary circumstances," Lexa said, "probably not."

"But the circumstances here aren't ordinary?"

Lexa nudged the folder. "You should look this through, tell me what you think."

"You're going out of your way to make this sound intriguing, aren't you?"

"I want you to take the assignment."

"All right, I will. But I'll tell you again," Joan said, "if this was really a premeditated murder, and not just some freak accident caused by a design flaw—"

"Oh, it was no accident," Lexa said. "That much seems pretty certain."

"Then there's no way in hell Harry could have had anything to do with it, no matter how much of a threat to Gant Industries Teaneck might have been. It's not even a question of ethics so much as that the idea of murder would never occur to him. He doesn't think that way."

"Well then," said Lexa, "your new job will be to find out who did think that way. Just one thing . . ."

"What?"

"You have to promise not to blow up any more basements. Hospital bills I can deal with, but my insurance doesn't cover acts of war."

4

The Declaration of Independence, which gave birth to the United States in 1776, stated that "all men are created equal." Yet the United States continued to be the largest slaveholding nation in the world until the Civil War. Americans tried to make equality a reality soon after the war by *ratifying* (approving) the 13th Amendment to the Constitution, which officially abolished slavery throughout the United States. The place of blacks in American society, however, remained unsettled.

—*World Book Encyclopedia*

Maxwell's Electric Leg

These days he was just a maladjusted middle-ager who screwed with the public library system, but in his youth Maxwell had been a tank commander.

His war was the '07 War for Free Trade in Sub-Saharan Africa, fought to settle a dispute over the stewardship of fuel and mineral deposits in those areas depopulated by the '04 Pandemic. An allied coalition of American, Afrikaner, and European armed forces joined in defense of a democratic resource management system, while the terrorist-led North Africa League attempted to impose an unfair monopoly on the region. Russia, busy arbitrating human rights issues with its few remaining republics, agreed to stay out of the conflict in return for a seat at the armistice talks.

Maxwell was sent to the Western Front, which ran along the mountainous border between Cameroon and Nigeria. The allied battle plan called for an amphibious assault on the Niger Delta and the liberation of Nigeria's oil and coal fields. Projected casualty rates for the invasion were high, but an act of God intervened at the last moment. The unexpected eruption of

Mt. Cameroon was mistaken for a League nuclear strike; the allies retaliated by dropping FRED (a Friendly Radiation Enhancement Device) on the Nigerian port city of Lagos. This all but wiped out the North Africa League's western field command and panicked the defending troops (who did not, in fact, have nuclear weapons) into a rout. Allied Marines landed unopposed and in less than a week had occupied the entire country, along with neighboring Benin, Togo, Ghana, and Burkina Faso.

Maxwell and his tank crew were sent to guard an oil refinery in Port Harcourt while the terms of the North African surrender were worked out. Winning such a bloodless victory didn't bother him—like most soldiers, he was just as happy to avoid combat—but in one sense the war was a big disappointment: Maxwell missed the thankful cheers of a liberated citizenry. Post-Pandemic Nigeria didn't have many citizens to speak of, and the handful of native Caucasians weren't in a cheering mood after the radiation enhancement of Lagos. Maxwell's hopes of taping some nature video on leave were likewise dashed when word came from Uganda that the world's last white rhinoceros had been collaterally damaged by an errant smart bomb.

Despondent, Maxwell sat atop his tank at the refinery gates daydreaming of the grand safaris of the nineteenth century, when Africa had still been a fun place to invade. Perhaps this sort of nostalgia was bad luck, for one evening at dusk a black man appeared to Maxwell: appeared suddenly, gliding like a wraith from among the stacked and rusted barrels that lined the shoulder of the refinery's access road. The black man was tall and thin as a stick, and his eyes were green razors stropped to a keen edge by the sunset. Maxwell could not have been more stunned if a white rhinoceros had strolled up for a chat. But the black man had not come to talk. Too late, Maxwell realized that the long tube the stranger cradled in his arms was not a ceremonial native gift but rather an armor-piercing rocket launcher.

"Hey, don't," Maxwell said, grabbing for his rifle.

The rocket shredded the main body of the tank, including two of Maxwell's crew who were playing poker in the air-conditioned interior; a lopsided portion of the turret and a lopsided portion of Maxwell were blown clear. He woke up a week later at the Red Cross hospital in Pretoria, where a ruddy-faced Afrikaner lieutenant told him that the entire refinery had been torched by unidentified saboteurs.

He lost all of his right leg to the hip and most of his crotch, but his left leg remained intact except for the big toe. "Very asymmetrical, Max," chided his surgeon, "we'll have to do something about that." The surgeon replaced his lost limb with a Chrysler prosthetic, an Electric Leg that was clunky but came with a refrigerated compartment in the thigh that could hold peanuts and a beer. Maxwell's left foot got a Steel Toe; his ruined crotch got an Automatic Scrotum, a temperature-sensitive carbon-fiber sac that scrunched up and expanded just like the real article. And was crushproof.

No Electric Wanger, though. "Sorry," Maxwell's surgeon said. A subclause of the Third Helms Statute on Art and Obscenity prohibited the use of federal funds for any medical or scientific device that might double as a sex toy; the United States Supreme Court had determined in State of Florida vs. Silver '05 that artificial testicles were kosher under this law, but prosthetic penii clearly were not. Maxwell could still get a Swedish-made penis for $100,000 plus the cost of round-trip airfare, but the Veteran's Administration would be unable to help him foot the bill. "Hey, Max," his surgeon said, "at least you got one hell of a set of balls, right? So buck up!"

Psychological damage was a harder fix. A Marine psychiatrist diagnosed Maxwell as chronically battle fatigued and "unpredictable of temperament." Back home in New York, interviewing for his first civilian job, Maxwell went berserk and tried to strangle the employment office mascot, a green-eyed black cat. As the cat squeezed behind a Xerox machine cabinet to save itself, the interviewer shut her notebook and said: "Well, I guess we can skip the reference check."

Finding a place to live was similarly problematic. The '04 Pandemic had created a renter's paradise, but Maxwell refused to enter any building made vacant by plague. Better to be homeless, he believed, than to further risk the wrath of the dead: staying well south of 125th Street, he slept in parks, train yards, subway stations, steam pipe conduits, and once in a sewer tunnel (which cost him another three toes before the night was over). Whenever V.A. case workers did manage to find him "ghost-free" lodgings, his chronically battle fatigued behavior soon got him booted back onto the street.

Somehow he survived; sixteen years after the war, Maxwell lived. And just lately his circumstances had been improving. He finally had a real roof over his head, a bed that he could keep. Last winter the director of a welfare home in the Bowery had watched impassively while Maxwell emptied his Automatic Bladder onto the floor in front of her. "If that's supposed to disgust me," she said, tapping ash from a cigarette, "you're going to have to try harder. I paddle around in piss all day, and my mother had lepers over for dinner when I was a kid. Your room's upstairs, turn left off the second landing. I'll send up a mop and an extra change of sheets." While no one in a hiring and firing position had yet been this tolerant of him, Maxwell had also found a vocation of sorts, unpaid but satisfying, even addicting.

He moved library books.

"You ever notice how you can't find any naked pictures in a library?" Maxwell would sometimes say to strangers on the subway, by way of explanation. "What I mean is, you're a kid, your voice changes, and one day you start and wonder if you could find a book with naked pictures at the public library. Like, could they have bought one by mistake, and put it on the shelf where even a kid could get at it. So you look up subjects like 'Erotica' and 'Nude Photography' in the catalog, and it turns out they have some hot-sounding titles, like *An Illustrated History of Pornographic Films.* But when you check for the call number on the shelf, those kind of books are never in. Hell, you might find one that's all text, in French, but if it's a book with actual naked pictures, it won't be there. Even if the catalog computer says it's on the shelf, it won't be there. Even if you come back and check every day for a month—when your voice changes, you do that kind of thing— it'll *never* be there. Like it's been *removed.* Surgically.

"Well you know, I figured out why that is, not just at one library but at any library you go to. I'm lying in this pile of mucus one night, wondering what the hell got my *toes,* and it just hit me: there's a conspiracy. Guys all over the country, a secret brotherhood. They come into every library first thing in the morning, and they grab all the books with naked pictures before anybody else can get to them. They don't take them out, and they don't steal them or burn them, they just *refile* them. They put the books with naked pictures in boring parts of the library, stick 'em in between the books that nobody ever reads. Then later, when the kids whose voices are changing come in, the members of the brotherhood just stand back and laugh up their sleeves. It's a very important job."

There was little love lost between Maxwell and Electric Negroes. The main branch of the New York Public Library owned two Servants, Eldridge 162 and Bartholomew 75. Eldridge was used for "entropy containment," which meant that twenty-three hours a day (stopping only to recharge) he walked past bookstack after bookstack, scanning every item on every shelf, verifying that each of some nine million volumes was in its proper place. Including the ones with naked pictures. No human being would have had the patience or persistence for such a mind-numbing task, but Eldridge was so efficient that Maxwell had to scramble whole rows of books just to slow him down.

Today there was a new Negro in the stacks.

A posted notice to library patrons said "our happy helpers Bart and Eldridge" had been sent to the shop for cleaning and a tune-up, and Maxwell thought at first he'd have an easy time of it, operating uncontested. Morning and lunchtime passed smoothly enough, with Maxwell relocating over thirty books. Then at half past three he walked over to the African History section, seeking a suitable burial spot for a *National Geographic* nude pygmy retrospective. He stepped around a shelf and there it—she—was, hunkered down in what should have been a deserted corner of the library.

She was all wrong. He could see that at once. *Black* skin, many shades darker than Eldridge's coffee-with-artificial-creamer tint; medium length wooly hair, not plaited or braided or fixed in any other standard factory style, but *disheveled,* as if she normally combed it and had forgotten to do so today. Her clothes were wrong, too. Not that people didn't accouter their Negroes in outlandish costumes from time to time, but surely the library staff would have chosen something conservative and homey, like a flower-print dress, or a blouse and skirt. Not: red Velcro sneakers, bulky black workpants, equally bulky sleeveless vest—yes, *sleeveless,* her bare shoulders round and soft like real flesh, a gold circlet curled around her upper arm—and, just brushing her collar, bright parrot-feather earrings.

Wrong. Wrong.

Her lips were moving. One fingertip stroked the spines of several books—slowly—and her lips moved as though she were mumbling to herself, which Automatic Servants didn't do. Then Maxwell noticed the furry shape perched on her far shoulder and realized she was conversing with it in whispers. A pet rat? A talking pet rat?

He moved closer. She stretched to reach a book and Maxwell saw that the front of her vest was untagged. That did it.

"Where's your I.D. badge?" Maxwell demanded. She turned towards him; the furry shape on her shoulder wasn't a rat after all, it was a small beaver wearing spectacles and a hard hat, and it did talk. "Yellow alert, Seraphina," it said. Maxwell didn't hear it, though, because by then he'd seen her eyes.

Green. Green eyes in a black face.

"*Red* alert!" the beaver warned, slapping its tail against the Negro's back. She stood, unzipping a nearly invisible pocket in her vest as Maxwell tried to grab her. Something silvery and quick bit Maxwell on the wrist. The sharp pricking seemed to travel up the length of his arm, turning it all to pins and needles. It fell limp against his side.

Her forehead was shiny with sweat, another wrongness. "You didn't see me," she told him. "You never saw me."

"Fuck I didn't," Maxwell said, and lunged for her again, leading with his other arm. She'd already turned her back and started walking away, and it took three thumping strides of his Electric Leg to catch up to her. This time the beaver bit him. It wasn't a pinprick of anesthetic; it was like sticking his hand into a vise. Maxwell screamed and fell down.

Descending, his shoulder knocked books from the shelf. An *Illustrated History of Pornographic Films* that he'd hidden back here an hour ago struck the floor beside him and flapped open. Maxwell found himself lying on his side, staring fish-eyed across the nubile form of adult movie star Marilyn Chambers (now in her seventies and living the life of a retired social worker in San Luis Obispo, California). The un-Electric Negro with the beaver on her shoulder paused at a safe distance and gave him a parting green glance.

"You didn't see me," she repeated. Then she stepped through the wall and disappeared.

Maxwell became irrational.

The Most Private Reading Room

The New York Public Library wasn't budgeted for secret passages, but that's what happens when you hire an Irish design firm.

When the Empire State Building went up in a ball of exploding 747 on Christmas night of '06, its mooring-mast crown shot off like a rocket, impaling the underside of a CNN news blimp that just happened to be in position to cover the accident-in-progress. The blimp's pilot hung on bravely, transmitting a continuous video signal to CNN Center in Atlanta as she urged her sinking craft north between the Fifth Avenue skyscrapers, hoping for an emergency landing in Central Park. At 42nd Street a microgale caused the gas bag to disintegrate completely, dropping pilot, gondola, and mooring mast from an altitude of six hundred feet; the gun cameras' final transmission was a zoom-in close-up of a graffiti-smeared stone lion.

There was talk of hiring the Japanese to rebuild the library. Mayor Waldo Twitty believed that Japan already had a secret controlling interest in his city, so that it only made sense to score as many brownie points with them as possible before they officially took over.

"But wait a minute," said the commissioner of libraries and family planning, as he studied the preliminary bid from Tokyo's top architect. "Just tell me, when we've converted our available funds to yen to pay for this, how much will we have left to buy new books with?"

The mayor's accountant did some calculations. "Two dollars and fifty cents," she said.

"Two dollars and fifty cents!" the commissioner shouted. "Do you know what you can buy for two dollars and fifty cents? One quarter of a paperback, that's what you can buy!"

So they turned to a poorer country—the United States—to supply their architects instead. The Brooklyn firm of O'Donoghue, Killian & Snee offered to do the entire job, including construction, for a little under a fifth of the Tokyo price. Which would have been perfect, except that Josi O'Donoghue and Wirt Killian had spent their Irish childhoods playing in the hidden tunnels beneath Blarney Castle, and they for some reason thought the new Public Library needed a secret passage.

"Why would it need that?" the commissioner asked them. "I don't want to pay for that."

They told him that of course it was his decision and then put a secret passage in anyway. O'Donoghue mixed standard and metric measurements to create spaces that were invisible on the blueprint, while Killian oversaw the construction in such a way that not even the foreman caught on to the trick. When it was finished, only the canniest of librarians and patrons ever sensed that the interior dimensions of the new building didn't quite add up; Maxwell, obsessed by his naked pictures, never had a clue.

Morris Kazenstein, on the other hand, figured it out the third or fourth time he came in to borrow a book. Both of his parents had worked for the Shin Bet domestic security agency in Israel, so there was a family history of uncovering secrets. Amused, Morris told Philo what he had found, and Philo told his daughter Seraphina, and it was Seraphina Dufresne who now moved behind the walls of the Public Library, BRER Beaver perched on her shoulder, BRER Squirrel squirming in her pocket.

The lamp in BRER Beaver's hard hat lit the way. Just now Seraphina would have preferred a regular flashlight, the kind that couldn't criticize. BRER Beaver was upset with her; or more accurately, the encounter with Maxwell had triggered a reprimand subprogram in the silicon walnut that was BRER Beaver's brain.

"Didn't I warn you?" he said (the voice was Ralph Nader's). He slapped his tail against her back for emphasis. "You *have* to be less conspicuous in public."

"Look who's talking."

"*I'm* supposed to be carried in a bag. A standard Automatic Servant Utility Pouch. BRER Squirrel and I are sized just right for that."

"Oh," said Seraphina, "and then I can be inconspicuous talking to a *bag* in public."

"You wear a *nameplate.* You wear a *dress,* that nice cotton one with the flowers that your father gave you." BRER Beaver ticked off the admonitions on his paw. "You don't open your mouth to speak, you *subvocalize,* and—"

"*And* I put on brown contact lenses. And on top of that I wear fake glasses with a remote camera pick-up, so you can see even though you're stuck in a bag. And maybe the next thing that happens is I throw the bag, the glasses, and the contacts out a window, because this is my *home,* and it's ridiculous to have to go through all that just to walk around your own home."

"Anything less is unsafe," BRER Beaver insisted.

They had reached the entrance to the library's Most Private Reading Room, which served as Seraphina's apartment. She stopped just outside the door and tried to lose her temper, *really* lose it, like a normal person would at this point, but the best she could manage was severe irritation: "Don't I usually listen to you outside the library? Didn't I wear a survival suit in the sewers this morning?"

"The answer to the first question, statistically, is no. And this morning I told you not to go into the sewers at all. It's unsafe."

"Do you know what a pain you are?"

"No." He took the question literally, as he took everything. "I'm not designed for empathy. I'm designed for safety awareness." He slapped his tail again. "Safety awareness and reading comprehension."

Reading comprehension. That was the hook, the thing that made BRER Beaver with his babysitter's attitude a necessary evil. Seraphina couldn't read. Not an unheard of state of affairs in 2023, but in her case the cause was biological. Some chromosome-mutilating contaminant in the Philadelphia air, perhaps, at U. Penn., where her mother had first coaxed her father out of his Amish frock coat, or maybe a bad hot dog at the reunion picnic where Seraphina was conceived some nine years later. Her hearing and speech were unimpaired, and her oral vocabulary was above average, but her brain lacked the synaptic architecture necessary to fit meaning to written words and phrases. Mosel Kazenstein, the Albuquerque-based neurologist who examined Seraphina in the desert when she was seven years old, diagnosed her as having Sorbonne's dyslexia with pronounced cortical dysplasia.

"What's that mean?" Seraphina had asked him.

"It means you can't read," Mosel replied. He punched buttons on the Portable CAT Scan he'd brought with him. "There's a physical defect in your brain's language center that keeps you from grasping certain types of abstract visual symbols, like letters and numbers."

"My dad doesn't grasp adjectives very well."

"That sounds like a discipline problem," said Mosel. "Your trouble is organic."

"Can you fix it?"

"I'm afraid not. Resculpting the cerebral cortex is still tomorrow's neurosurgery. But with a little ingenuity you can learn to work around your deficit. You might try Braille, for instance, which doesn't use visual symbols, or some form of pictograph language that isn't so abstract. And of course there are technological aids that can help you cope with conventional text when you have to."

"Technological aids?"

Mosel jerked a thumb at his nephew Morris. "Gizmos," he said.

Hence BRER Beaver, who read signs and labels for her and found the library books she wanted with a facility no hand-held reading device could match; and BRER Squirrel, who helped get her out of trouble when she ignored BRER Beaver's warnings about proper conduct. BRER stood for Batteries Required Electric Rodent, though it had taken Morris some effort to explain the concept of acronyms to her: "A sort of inventor's poetry," he finally said. Seraphina loved poetry.

To enter the Most Private Reading Room you had to grip the doorknob in just the right way, another trick of O'Donoghue and Killian's that Seraphina had down to a reflex. Inside, the floor was carpeted in smooth flagstones, so that if you stared only at your feet, or lay on the goose-down-and-wolf's-pelt Blarney cot with your eyes closed, you could pretend you really were in some mad monk's study in an Irish castle. Looking up, though, you couldn't help but see the window that made up one wall of the room, and right outside the window was Madagascar: the bloated trunk of a baobab tree, ten arm-spans around at its greatest girth, which completely blocked the view to and from the street. The tree was supposed to have been a Kerry willow, every bit as concealing, but a mix-up at the arboreal supply house had brought this temperate-zone–adapted baobab instead. By the time the mistake was discovered the baobab had already sunk its roots immovably deep beneath the library sidewalk, and now the Transit Authority had to send crews out with pruning chainsaws twice a month to keep the IRT subway tunnel cleared.

Tough little tree. The only thing that would make it more perfectly African, Seraphina thought, would be a family of lemurs to climb in its stubby branches. But lemurs were extinct.

She set BRER Beaver on the cot and let BRER Squirrel out of her pocket. From other pockets in her vest and pants she removed the books she'd collected before Maxwell's advent; as she stacked these in a pile on the Most Private Reading Desk, the upper-right-hand drawer slid open of its own accord, and a spritely brown field mouse with bifocals hopped out onto the desktop.

"Hello, BRER Vole," Seraphina said.

"Hello, Seraphina," BRER Vole replied, nose twitching in anticipation as the stack of books grew higher. "Did we have a wonderful day?"

"BRER Vole," said Seraphina, "do I ever *not* have a wonderful day?"

"Never," BRER Vole said, which was absolutely true. The other half of Seraphina's neurological birthright was an abnormally high level of serotonin in her brain, and a rogue hormone in her bloodstream—"organic Prozac," Mosel Kazenstein called it—that further enhanced the serotonin's effectiveness. This meant that not only was Seraphina dyslexic, half-orphaned, and one of the last surviving members of her race, but she was also biochemically incapable of despairing over any of these facts. A good anti-suicide survival trait, especially if she wound up spending the rest of her life disguised as an Electric Negro, but frustrating: to never be truly frustrated, to never know depression. To never get angry enough to hurt somebody.

"I think about that," she had confided once to Lexa. "As a game, I mean; that's the trouble, it's never serious. Wouldn't it be reasonable for somebody like me to want to set fire to buildings? Learn Black English, dress up like a Masai warrior, and go around shooting white people? In a movie I'd probably do that. But the best I can manage in real life are practical jokes."

"You do pretty well with those," Lexa told her. "Philo thinks you're an extremist, and it's not as if he's speaking from the middle of the road."

"Well that's the other thing that bothers me. I tell myself, 'Seraphina, you're brain damaged, it's OK that you feel this way, or don't feel this way.' But what's *Dad's* excuse?"

"You think sinking ships is a sign of complacency?"

"Well . . ."

"Trust me," Lexa said, "your father is as angry as you'd like to be. But he doesn't confuse anger with a right to multiply suffering indiscriminately."

"Well then, I won't multiply suffering indiscriminately either," Seraphina proclaimed. "I'll just really really bug people." Which she did, with some success; this past weekend she'd scored a major coup.

"You really can't keep this, you know," BRER Beaver said now, indicating the painting on the Reading Room wall. "You *have* to return it." The painting was Da Vinci's *Mona Lisa*. The real one. Seraphina had snitched it from a special exhibit at the Metropolitan Museum of Art, over BRER Beaver's most strenuous objections. The French government was calling for a strip search of the entire continent to get it back. "You can't just go around stealing other people's cultural treasures!"

"Oh yes you can," Seraphina said. "*Statistically,* you can. But don't worry, I'm planning to return it." She looked at Mona's mouth, frozen in a smile for the past five hundred and twenty years, and thought: *I know how that feels.*

"You've got something devious in mind," BRER Beaver guessed. "Devious, and probably unsafe. What is it?"

"I'll tell you in a minute. But first"—her face lit up, genuinely pleased at the prospect—"first, how about you telling me a story?"

"A story?"

"Yes. The one about my great-great-great-great-great-grandparents. In the Civil War."

"Oh," said BRER Beaver, "that."

The Blue and the Gray to the Rescue

Kite was having a cigarette when she heard Maxwell shouting. Dumb luck, really, that she was out on the sidewalk to hear him; for while the Sharper Image at 41st and Fifth was as nicotine-free as every other shop in Manhattan, the management usually let her get away with sneaking a smoke, or any other violation of contemporary mores she cared to commit. She looked older than any two average senior citizens combined, she was missing her right arm, and the coat she wore had a military styling—equal parts blue and gray, fashioned from pieces of several real uniforms—that commanded respect, or at least respectful indifference. People under sixty tended to defer to her without thinking about it.

But not this afternoon. She'd come into the Sharper Image to browse the latest artifacts of progress, one of her favorite pastimes. For Kite, who remembered an era (so she claimed) before television—not just *Music* Television, but *television*—before radio, before the Model T, before *these* United States became *the* United States . . . well, for her, merely to learn of the existence of such gadgetry as a refrigerated dog dish with subliminal obedience training tape ($269.95, plus federal and local sales tax) constituted high entertainment. Better than going to the movies, and cheaper, too.

She'd set her tobacco pouch on top of a cryogenic storage unit for houseplants ("For those long vacations when you won't be home to water the family fern") and was rolling a butt one-handed when the floor manager tapped her on the shoulder.

"That's not an ashtray, ma'am," the manager told her. "It's a delicate piece of life-support equipment, and quite expensive."

Norman Lao, the tag on his shirt pocket said. Something in his features stirred a very old memory.

"Lao," Kite said. "*Lao*. Do you have any ancestors from Michigan, Lao?"

"Smoking isn't permitted in the store, ma'am," Lao insisted. Kite offered him her most beatific grandmother smile.

"No exceptions for a sweet old woman . . ."

"*No* exceptions, ma'am."

". . . and a combat veteran?" She raised her voice a little: "Union Army of the Potomac, 1861 to 1864. Also a brief tenure with the Standing Bear Cherokee Platoon of the Confederate Army. Just so you know."

Lao showed her the door.

So she lit her cigarette outside and thought of the original Lao, Sub-Private Ting Lao of the 2nd Michigan, who one hundred and fifty-nine years ago had given her her nickname, and who, for what it was worth, had been a career smoker. But those days were long gone . . . now a traffic cop rode past on horseback, smelled Kite's smoke, and wagged a finger. "Nasty, nasty habit," he said.

Over by the Public Library, a man began shouting. Unconcerned, the traffic cop stopped to write out a citation for an illegally parked minivan. The shouting man bellowed at the top of his lungs.

"Oh, Maxwell," Kite said, throwing her cigarette in the gutter. "What trouble are you in this time?"

The sort of trouble that draws crowds and SWAT teams. Having obtained an Electric Carving Knife from somewhere—maybe the library was lending small appliances now, Kite didn't know—Maxwell had climbed onto the back of one of the stone lions, jacked the Knife into the power pack in his Leg, and become a public nuisance. The carver was set on its lowest speed, a nearly silent hum, but Maxwell's raging as he brandished it was sufficient to both attract spectators and keep them at a healthy distance.

As Kite shouldered her way through the onlookers, a squad car pulled up to the curb. A Negro in blue got out of the back seat. He was chubby and dimpled, a hint of the streetwise blended with a teddy bear's sweetness; his I.D. badge identified him as Powell 617. The spectators cheered, eager to see some action. Powell returned their greeting with a chummy clenched-fist salute: "I'm with you, man!" The driver of the squad car pointed at Maxwell and said: "Go get him, boy!"

Bad. Kite knew how Maxwell reacted to Negroes. But the way he was straddling the stone lion gave her an idea.

Powell 617 assumed a look of grim empathy as he approached Maxwell. "Take it easy now, brother," he counseled. "I know life can be a real motherfucker sometimes, but violence is *not the way*." He held his hands out flat in a "stay cool" gesture; at the center of each of his palms was a flesh-toned metal disc, charged to a non-lethal voltage. Powell 617 was a walking stun rod. He used the word "motherfucker" over and over again, like a salve for Maxwell's hostility, though Maxwell ignored him until he was nearly within arresting distance.

"Show me the color of your eyes!" Maxwell said suddenly, flicking the Electric Carving Knife to full power.

"Easy, bro—"

The crowd parted; a roan gelding dressed in the livery of the NYPD Traffic Division galloped through. The one-armed woman in the horse's saddle did her best to give a rebel yell as she charged, but she'd been with the Confederates for only a short time and was sixteen decades out of practice besides. She rode right up on the Electric Policeman, driving him back; Powell 617's behavioral inhibitors prevented him from taking any action that might injure the horse, which was city property. He flailed his arms helplessly.

"What's this?" crowed Maxwell. "*Cavalry*? Where the hell's my tank?"

Kite, having no time to dither (the dismounted traffic cop was close behind her, unpleased), drew a black-powder Colt pistol from beneath her coat. There was a single report, and the Carving Knife's blade broke in pieces. This seemed to sober Maxwell.

"Kite!" he said. "What are you doing here?"

She barked at him: "Get your ass on the back of this horse, Maxwell! *Now!*"

Maxwell stood on the stone lion's head and swung himself onto the gelding, no easy feat given the clumsiness of his Leg and the lethargy that still paralyzed his arm. The spectators broke into applause; when the driver of the squad car tried to get out and help Powell, two women in hard hats, themselves former soldiers, held his door shut. Powell 617 kept on flailing his arms.

"Stop!" he shouted. "Surrender your weapon, free the horse, and you still have a chance to be a productive member of society. We have dedicated psychologists who can help you!"

Kite glanced over her shoulder. The traffic cop was moving up fast, shoving people aside; he had his baton and service revolver in hand. "No time for psychology today," Kite said, snapping the reins. Powell 617 was forced to step out of the way.

"This sort of behavior undermines the entire community," Powell warned. "But in the end you're hurting yourselves most of all. Crime *doesn't* pay."

Maxwell tossed the handle of the Electric Carving Knife at Powell's feet.

"Have a nice day, motherfucker," he said.

The Tribe with Green Eyes

Seraphina Dufresne's most valued possession was a Kazenstein Portable Knowledge Store, a breadbox-sized hunk of Electric Memory with a capacity for several libraries' worth of information. Its durable exterior shell suggested a safe or safety-deposit box, for that was its purpose: to serve as a lasting container for as much African and African-American history as Seraphina could find to fill it. BRER Vole was the input device: with his slender tail jacked directly into the Memory core, he became a data conduit, voraciously devouring the information Seraphina supplied: books, taped oral histories, video and film documentaries, photographs, songs, and whatever other bits of the past she could borrow or steal. While the input cycle ran, Seraphina envisioned a bank vault of dark chromium slowly filling with diamonds and rubies; whether or when someone would come to retrieve the jewels she didn't know, but at least the treasure was safe.

Morris said he was working on some applications for the accumulated Knowledge, but until he came up with a better idea Seraphina was content to use it for storytelling. She would link the Knowledge Store to a computer interpreter and link the interpreter to the BRERs, who would act out a pageant on whatever topic she selected. She made BRER Beaver play all the villains. Villains and heroes abounded in the pageants, in part because the interpreter made no effort to screen the source material for bias.

"I am John Mercier," BRER Beaver began, looking silly with a serial cable jammed up under his tail. "I am the wicked overseer of the Slocum Plantation, the ugliest man in the world. I have crooked furry teeth and I stink like the back end of a hog."

BRER Vole stepped forward; he held his tiny paws in front of him as if tugging on suspenders or the buttonholes of a fancy jacket. "I am Neptune Frost," he said, "a freedman of Boston, a pupil of abolitionists, and a devoted admirer of John Brown and the honorable Miss Harriet Beecher Stowe. Late one night crossing the Boston Common I was accosted by a man who commented on the color of my eyes. Even as I stopped to speak with him I was struck over the head from behind. When I awoke I found myself bound and gagged in the belly of a ship, on my way to a slave's life in North Carolina."

BRER Squirrel came forward last. Morris hadn't designed her to speak, so her squeaks and chitters went back through the interpreter to be translated. A plastic bead inserted in Seraphina's ear whispered subtitles: *My name is Carrie Slocum. I was stolen away to the Slocum Plantation from a far-off place whose name is lost. They tell me my eyes are haunted with the color of that far country.*

BRER Beaver seized BRER Vole by the elbow. "Now I don't want any trouble from you, 'freedman.' You cross me and I'll whip the back off you. In fact, I might whip the back off you just to keep in practice." He paused to study BRER Vole's eyes. "Hmm . . . green eyes on a nigger. Where have I seen that before?" He looked across the desktop stage at BRER Squirrel, then hauled BRER Vole over to her. "Tomorrow you start work in the fields," BRER Beaver said, giving BRER Vole a rude pat on the backside, "but tonight you have another job. That Gomer Van Wort at the Hayes Plantation is always bragging about his Mandingos, so you're going to make me a tribe of green-eyed niggers to show him up. Get busy." He stepped back; the computer mimicked the sound of a shed door being shut and padlocked from the outside.

The would-be parents of the tribe with green eyes gazed shyly at one another. BRER Vole spoke first: "I do not belong here," he said, "and I am shocked by such a display of disrespect for our race and for womankind. But despite this, I must confess you have the most beautiful face I have ever seen; and I am moved in a way I have never felt before."

You are puffed-up and over-proud, BRER Squirrel replied, *like the peacocks at one of Missy Slocum's lawn parties. You talk funny. But I am also moved by the sight of you. Much to my later sorrow.*

A sound of distant cannonfire. BRER Beaver stood tall and stroked an invisible beard. "I am Master Abraham Lincoln," he announced, "and I will rain lightning on the South until the scourge of slavery is ended. I call upon all decent men to rally to my cause."

BRER Vole came to attention. "I will answer that call!" he cried. "Listen, Carrie Slocum: I will not make love to you as a slave. But I vow to escape and make my way north to join the Union Army, and when I return bearing freedom I will take you as my wife."

Let me escape with you, BRER Squirrel said.

"No," BRER Vole said. "Your life of ignorance and slavery has left you poorly equipped for such a journey; my chances will be better traveling alone. But I swear upon my life that I will return to you."

Refusing to hear any argument, BRER Vole bowed and kissed her goodbye. Then he escaped. BRER Beaver cried out in his John Mercier voice: "Stop, nigger!" A single shot was fired, with a ricochet signifying a clean miss; simulated hoofbeats faded into the distance; BRER Beaver cursed. Quoted BRER Squirrel: *I should be stoned for a fool. My heart has been stolen by a crazy nigger from the state of Bah-ston, and my life will never be the same again.*

So began a long family chronicle, one that continued down seven generations to University of Pennsylvania student Flora Daris (brown-eyed herself but carrying a recessive gene like a pearl of great price), who would offer her Philadelphia hospitality to a bewildered black Amish named Philo. But Seraphina rarely watched the whole story at one sitting.

Neptune Frost reached Washington, D.C., safely and in due course joined the Union Army. His war adventures and his rise from firewood-fetcher to sergeant of a Negro platoon had been recorded by a Corporal Cato Spelman, a young ex-slave who saw in Neptune a much-desired father figure, and so BRER Vole acted out these segments of the tale with a maturity he'd lacked when Carrie Slocum had the point of view. Carrie did her own part for the war effort by conducting a systematic poisoning campaign against

John Mercier, mixing ground glass and toxic herbs into his food. BRER Beaver strained and grunted in an imaginary outhouse, clutched a stomach ravaged by ulcers, and at one point begged death to release him from his suffering. But the overseer was still alive when Neptune Frost finally returned to the plantation in the winter of '64 ("Returned bearing fire and a sword," Cato Spelman wrote; in her own recollection of that day, salvaged on reel-to-reel audiotape by the Federal Writers' Project, Carrie Slocum noted that soldiering had made Neptune more brash and prideful than ever . . . but she was still overjoyed to see him). In a fierce duel at the plantation gate, Neptune cut John Mercier in half with his saber. "Gaaaaah!" BRER Beaver cried, dying; BRER Vole rushed past the corpse to find his bride. The computer played a love theme as the couple reunited.

I'm going to have a son, BRER Squirrel predicted. *From just this one night. A son with green eyes.*

They embraced; the music swelled again, euphemistically.

"Sergeant Frost!" shouted BRER Beaver, back on his feet in the role of the faithful Corporal Cato. "Wake up, Sergeant! Robert spotted soldiers in the woods just south!"

"Rebel soldiers?"

"*Indian* soldiers, Sergeant. Led by two white Reb officers. Robert said there weren't but thirty men all told, and they don't know we're here."

"We can ambush them, then."

No! BRER Squirrel said. *You can't go! While we slept I dreamt you were killed by a white woman disguised as a soldier. You pulled off her arm, but she put silver on your eyes.*

"It was only a dream." BRER Vole told her. "Slavery is dead. There's no more need for fear or superstition. Everything will be different now."

Don't . . .

"Cato brought a Bible. When I return from the ambush we can be married."

"That's enough for today," Seraphina said.

Flowers from Harry

"Why is there a horse in the common room?" Joan Fine asked, when she got home that evening.

Kite was in the fifth-floor kitchenette she shared with Joan and three other tenants, trying to microwave an emu patty. Her fascination with technology did not extend to instruction manuals; she punched buttons at random and turned the meat gray.

"Progress," Kite said, shaking her head. "I remember one of the last steady jobs I ever had, wrangling ostrich on a Texas farm just after the millennium. Saturday nights all the hands would sit out under the stars, drink, and roast three-foot drumsticks on an open grill—the only right way to do it. After the meal we'd share a smoke and try to come up with a name to sell the meat by, something more appetizing than 'ostrich.' Of course this was before the Australians stole the market with their own big birds and put us out of business." She dropped the gray patty into the garbage disposal. "Why do you assume I know anything about a horse in the common room?"

"A hunch," Joan said. "Maxwell again?"

"Maxwell," Kite agreed. No further explanation was required; Joan said "Oh," and Kite changed the subject by sniffing the rose bouquet Joan had brought home with her. "For me?"

"For me. From Harry. They were delivered to the hospital just as I was getting myself discharged."

Kite raised an eyebrow. "So you had an exciting day too, I take it."

"Three people got eaten, including this green backwoods kid who probably never should have left Maine, and I totted up a quarter million dollars' worth of damage trying to kill the fish that did it. Only it turns out that I missed. The *Post* had it in a headline, misidentified as an alligator: KILLER REPTILE SURVIVES BLAST. I thought I was handling the shock pretty well, but when I read that on the subway I threw up. So tonight there's a killer *Carcharodon* swimming around in a holding tank in Brooklyn somewhere and a commuter with vomit on his suit who hates me. Oh, and before I forget. . . ." She showed Kite the biomonitor cinched around her wrist. "The hospital agreed to let me go early if I promised to keep an eye on my vitals. If this starts wailing in the middle of the night it means I've caught a bug and I'm either burning up with fever or going into convulsions, so if you hear it I'd appreciate you calling 911. But you should probably get rid of the horse first."

"Poor thing," Kite said. "You need a cigarette, don't you?"

"Desperately."

They went up to the roof. The five-story Fine Bowery Sanctuary had started out as a regular hotel way back in 1870; in Joan's bedroom a copper plaque warned guests not to blow out the lights without shutting off the gas. A rooftop greenhouse had been erected during World War I to grow a victory garden. Neighboring skyscraper construction and the loss of direct sunlight turned the greenhouse into a brownhouse in the mid-1940s, which it remained until Joan bought the building in 2018. She'd cleared out the refuse, put in full-spectrum lighting and some reclining chairs, and planted flowers.

It was in this small Eden that she and Kite took their frequent cigarette breaks. The dozen long-stemmed roses that Harry had sent were outnumbered by hundreds of live tulips, daffodils, gladioli, forget-me-nots, lupins, etc.; likewise Kite's and Joan's smoke was overpowered by the many mingled scents. A Revlon air purifier detected the presence of contaminants and began to work doubletime.

"Is horse theft still a capital crime?" Kite asked, curious.

"Florida's the only state that still executes for anything. But I doubt horse theft has been *decriminalized,* even in Nevada."

"I see," Kite said, and once again changed the subject. "I applied for another job this morning."

"As a jockey?"

"Very funny. Gant Construction, actually."

Joan laughed. "You want to help Harry build New Babel?"

"Would that bother you?"

"No. But what did they say?"

"The usual. You tell people you're a hundred and eighty-one years old and they don't want to hire you. I tried to explain that mandatory retirement only makes sense if you die before you spend all your savings. No sympathy."

"If you could get to Harry's mother I bet she'd hire you. She used to be a Civil War buff."

"You still think I'm as crazy as Maxwell, don't you?"

"Not even my own mother was as crazy as Maxwell," Joan said. "But a hundred and eighty-one is stretching longevity a bit, yes."

"Go ahead, then. Ask me something."

"All right. Who was vice president during Lincoln's first term?"

Kite shrugged. "Who remembers vice presidents? It's a silly question."

"Well it's the same question I always ask. You could look it up."

"And discredit myself? My ignorance should be proof enough of my honesty."

"You think so, huh?"

"Remember the Gospels, Joan. How do we know Matthew, Mark, Luke, and John were honest men? Because their accounts of the life of Christ are inconsistent. Whereas if they agreed in every detail we'd have grounds to be suspicious."

"So by the same token, if you had perfect recall of the 1860s, I'd know you were a fraud. The fact that you don't means that you really were alive back then."

"Precisely."

"That's good theology," Joan said, lighting a fresh cigarette. "Have you thought about getting a phony I.D.? You could claim to be only sixty. A *mature* sixty."

"I'd sooner go back to Texas. Or strap on a codpiece again, if all I had to hide was my sex. I earned these wrinkles."

"How about helping me out, then?"

Kite shook her head. "I've tried the Department of Sewers already. Same problem."

"As of this afternoon I don't work in the sewers anymore," Joan said. "I'm on assignment for Lexa."

"This is Lexa who runs the newspaper?"

Joan nodded. "She asked me to do a little detective work for her. Possibly dangerous. You could be my backup."

"What would we be detecting?"

"A conspiracy."

"A *conspiracy*," Kite marveled. "Well I haven't been tangled up in one of *those* in altogether too long."

"So you're interested?"

The ancient soldier lit a cigarette, leaned closer, and said: "Tell me all about it, dear."

5

Also, the whole problem of money is very different today from what it was in the Sixties. Economics are a big thing now; we didn't have to deal with that as much. There was so much affluence in the Sixties, and if you had to get by on 40 dollars a week, that was fine. You all chipped in, got a crash pad, and just worked it out. . . .

—Abbie Hoffman at Rutgers University, 1988

1969: The Singular Excursion of the *Anium Otter*

In addition to charges of anarchy, treason, and wickedness on the high seas, Philo Dufresne had been accused by some of being anti-capitalist. While it was true he was opposed to the many abuses of capitalism, such as the half-hour infomercial, he had nothing against private ownership or the profit motive per se. Even radical environmentalists expected to be paid for their efforts, after all; those saintly few with the means and determination to forgo monetary wages still benefited from the sense of a job well done, a virtuous mission accomplished. Spiritual capital was still capital, even if you couldn't make rent with it.

Then too, there was the matter of the *Yabba-Dabba-Doo*. Not just its upkeep, which required more hard currency than any communist could ever have hoped to front, but its history: for however much Morris Kazenstein liked to pretend he'd built the submarine from scratch, the truth was that the *Yabba-Dabba-Doo* had originated as one of the most expensive practical jokes of the twentieth century. A *capitalist* practical joke.

Howard Hughes came up with the idea during the paranoid tailspin of his dying years. After seeing a documentary on cryptozoology, the study of animals that turn up in places where they don't belong, Hughes concocted a scheme to secretly transplant a herd of kangaroos from Australia to the South Dakota badlands. He somehow convinced himself (years of codeine abuse may have played a role here) that the appearance of kangaroos outside of Rapid City would trigger an "international cryptozoological incident" that the U.S. government would have to spend millions of taxpayer dollars investigating, thereby draining the Treasury and forcing salary cuts at the Department of Internal Revenue. Hughes hated taxes, and the thought of I.R.S. staffers losing their Christmas bonuses over a bunch of marsupials made him happier than a bucket of cough syrup.

Early in 1968, Hughes telephoned Melvin Dummar (a friendly Utah gas station attendant who'd once picked him up hitchhiking in the desert) and confided his plan. Dummar agreed it was a stroke of genius but said it reminded him of a novel he'd heard of—not actually read, but heard of—in which Mormon sewer workers do battle with albino alligators beneath the streets of Salt Lake City. *A novel?* said Hughes, and in a few narcotic-assisted leaps of the imagination decided that the feds had foxed him somehow, figured out his intentions and rushed into print to taunt him with their foreknowledge. He asked Dummar who the book's author was, and Dummar told him, sort of.

Back at the Desert Inn Hotel in Vegas, Hughes whipped up a set of blueprints for a gigantic cargo submarine and engaged a Detroit shipwright to build it. The sub's hull was to be composed of a mixture of titanium and germanium, an ultrastrong alloy patented simply as "anium": hence the name of the completed vessel. On November 30, 1969, the *Anium Otter* was launched into Lake Erie with a bellyful of kangaroo and Hughes at the conn.

On the 8th of December (there'd been a delay sneaking the sub through the New York State Barge Canal) a Finger Lakes marijuana farmer named Thomas Pinch was awakened in the night by sounds of stampede. Thinking, much as Hughes had, that the government had got wise to his business, he grabbed a shotgun and a terrycloth bathrobe and headed for the door of his cabin, only to discover that some forty-odd kangaroos had broken into his camouflaged greenhouses and were chowing down on his cash crop. When a particularly large and woozy 'roo began to make boxer-like gestures in Thomas Pinch's direction, the farmer bolted back inside the cabin, but not before a cackling Hughes managed to snap a single flash Polaroid.

By dawn's first light the herd—along with half an acre of winter cannabis—was gone, though not without a trace. Thomas Pinch followed the profusion of kanga-prints down to the edge of the lake. The tracks came out of the water; the tracks went back into the water.

Shit, Pinch thought, *no one's ever going to believe this.* Drifting in the deeps off Taughannock Point, Howard Hughes chuckled and lit himself a joint.

The I.R.S. had the last laugh. The fate of the forty kangaroos is unknown, but after Hughes's death in 1976, the *Anium Otter* was auctioned off to help pay the seventy-seven percent inheritance tax on his estate. The *Otter* was purchased by one Dobi Khashoggi, the black sheep expatriate third cousin of Saudi arms dealer Adnan Khashoggi, for resale in the Middle East. A number of desert sheiks expressed interest in owning a submarine, but Adnan, acting in a fit of pique, managed to sabotage every prospective deal until Dobi was completely humiliated in the eyes of the family. And so Hughes's last brainchild—now more albatross than otter—spent the next thirty-eight years sitting in a huge vat of preservative grease on the Motown docks, until Morris Kazenstein came by to take a look at it. By this point Dobi's disgraced descendants were only too happy to unload the cursed thing, especially on a Jew, and they let him have it for a song.

The Polaroid snapshot Hughes had taken was left aboard the sub and remained there throughout the decades of cold storage. During the lengthy process of transforming the *Anium Otter* into the still larger and less probable *Yabba-Dabba-Doo,* Morris found the faded photo tucked away in the periscope housing. He gave it to his chief engineer, Irma Rajamutti, a graduate of Bombay University with a double major in applied mechanics and eccentric literati. After the submarine refit was completed Irma taped the Polaroid up on the wall of the engine room. If asked who the guy in the terrycloth robe was she would reply: "J. D. Salinger."

Having already been misidentified once in a big way, Thomas Pinch probably wouldn't have minded this.

When Richard Berry and the Kingsmen Played Bethlehem

"Surface contacts?"

"Staten Island Ferry bearing two-nine-zero, range three-quarters of a mile. Various other small craft . . . there's a police launch, but it's steering for the East River. We're clear to Liberty Island."

"Ahead one-third," Philo ordered. "Keep an ear out for giant squid."

The sonar bay smelled like a throat lozenge. Asta Wills kept a dwarf eucalyptus to remind her of home; Philo had offered to find her an orphan koala bear as well, but she wouldn't hear of it. *"Disgusting* creatures," she told him. "They sweat urine and tear holes in all the furniture, I've seen it." She got a wombat instead and called it Basil. A huggable Down Under cross between a badger and a prairie dog, Basil had the IQ of wallpaper, and his single goal in life was to curl up in Asta's lap and sleep. Stroking Basil with one hand and adjusting her listening gear with the other, Asta remained calm under the most trying of circumstances.

"No squid or kraken on my scope," Asta said. "Nothing big enough to be a bother. But hull sensors are picking up a lovely assortment of biotoxins in the water, along with what looks to be a snowstorm of used toilet paper bits." She wiggled her eyebrows and tapped ashes from an imaginary cigar. "So if we spring a leak, nobody swallow."

"Thanks, Asta," Philo said. "You always make me glad to be back in port."

"Relax, mate. We saved a continent today, didn't we? Besides, this is still heaps better than the water off Bondi Beach back home."

"That's *not* something to be cheerful about."

"Istanbul!" said Osman Hamid, and Morris translated: "Ten minutes to Pirate's Cove, Philo."

"OK. What are we scheduled for, two days' shore leave?"

"*Three* days." Norma Eckland said. "We agreed on three."

"Right, three. Morris, you swing by my cabin and pick up the envelopes for the engine-room crew. They haven't been paid yet."

"Me?" Morris said. "Isn't it Norma's turn to handle payroll?"

"No," said Norma. "It's Norma's turn to get dressed for dinner. Late reservations at the Price of Salt." She glanced at Asta. "Meet you on deck in fifteen?"

"Fair dinkum," Asta said, and shut down her gear. At the helm, Osman steered the *Yabba-Dabba-Doo* towards the base of Liberty Island, where a hidden pressure lock opened to receive it. The sub would undergo a brief rinse cycle to clean off the worst of the Bay slime and then surface in Pirate's Cove, a secret dock located directly underneath Lady Liberty's pedestal.

Morris slunk out of the control room like a condemned man. It wasn't that he actually minded handling payroll, it was just that any visit to the engine room was a journey into Jewish liberal guilt. Other than Irma Rajamutti, the engine room's crew was made up entirely of Palestinians: Oliver, Heathcliff,

Mowgli, Galahad, and Little Nell Kazenstein, Morris's adopted siblings. The adoption had most likely been an act of atonement on his parents' part—they had rescued the orphaned quintuplets from a burning mosque on the West Bank, quit the Shin Bet, and fled the state of Israel all on one crazy Yom Kippur weekend—but they'd never actually bothered to explain their motives to him. They had divorced less than a year after leaving Tel Aviv: Morris and his mother ended up in New York, while his father took the quints and settled in London, where the adopted Kazensteins chose their own names from a *Norton Compendium of English Literature*. They lived well and peacefully there, growing up in a huge house on the Thames and eventually all attending Oxford; but young Morris in Manhattan watched CNN footage of Israeli soldiers gunning down children in the streets of East Jerusalem, and came of age believing that his brothers and his sister must hate him.

Not so: they didn't have much opinion of him at all, actually, being busy with the pursuit of their doctorates. But none of them was above trading on his misplaced desire to make amends, especially if it would help fund their research. So when Morris gathered them all for a secret meeting in a Cambridge pub to offer them employment on the *Yabba-Dabba-Doo,* Heathcliff stuck the knife in.

"Let me be certain I understand you," Heathcliff said. "You say if we do this we'll be helping 'our people' live a better life. Does that mean you plan to use this submarine to help establish a fully independent Palestinian state?"

"Oh no no no," Morris replied, startled. "The overall mission is strictly environmental, strictly nonviolent. Or, well, *sort of* nonviolent. But about helping the Palestinians, I just meant that a cleaner planet is a cleaner planet for *everyone,* Jews and Arabs alike."

"But the Arabs," noted Heathcliff, "get banished to the engine room. Hard labor. Even though they have as much university credit as any Jew on the ship."

"Banished? Is that what you think, that I want to *banish* you? Hey guys . . . hey. Mistake. Misunderstanding. This is *not* a hard labor job, in fact that's part of the beauty of the submarine design, it—"

"It's all right," said Little Nell, putting on a tragic face that would have moved the most hawkish member of the Israeli Knesset to tears. "We're used to extreme hardship. And being grossly undervalued."

"Wait, wait, did I . . . I didn't mean . . . sorry. Sorry. Look . . ."

They all signed on to the crew, but only after giving Morris such a complex that he turned around and automated the engine room, automated it so completely that barely a finger needed to be lifted to keep it operating. He also installed so many creature comforts that few people would have *wanted* to lift more than a finger. Instead, the Palestinian Kazensteins spent their time at sea doing what they would have done as Oxford professors, only at greater leisure and with better pay: sipping fine wine, reading, and occasionally penning an erudite paper or two.

In the fullness of time Morris came to understand that he was being taken advantage of, but this only added to his sense of guilt. After all, if he really believed his Arab siblings were the same as everyone else, he should have had no trouble telling them to go to hell; his very servility was proof of his prejudice. He knew he ought to put his foot down, yet the fear that he might go too far the other way and become a genuine oppressor paralyzed him. His brothers and his sister, of course, did everything they could to encourage this mental deadlock.

"Hey family," Morris said now, hovering outside the engine-room hatchway like a shy butler. "It's payday, isn't that great?"

The quints sat around a plain card table, playing cribbage and pretending to be bored, *oppressed* by boredom; they'd heard him coming. Only Heathcliff looked up, Heathcliff who in recent months had been cultivating a resemblance to the late Yasir Arafat. He stroked his three days' growth of beard and purred: *"Morris.* Come in and have *coffee* with us, Morris."

Morris blanched. They never let him out of here without giving him a hard time, but an invitation to coffee was an especially bad omen. He approached the card table warily, holding out the pay envelopes, and tried to make a polite refusal: "We're five minutes from the Cove. . . . I really can't hang around."

"Well," said Mowgli, staring at his cards, "don't let us *force* you."

"Really," added Little Nell, "there's no obligation to share our hospitality. It's not as if we were blood relatives."

"Though of course," Oliver said, "your father always treated us with respect."

A moment later, when Morris was seated at the table with a steaming cup in front of him, Heathcliff said: "Do you know what we were just talking about?"

It wasn't a tough guess. "Palestine?"

Heathcliff nodded. "We've been reminiscing. Old times good and bad, our childhoods on the West Bank . . ."

"Heathcliff, you weren't even a year old when Dad took you to London."

"Yes, the West Bank," Heathcliff continued, as if Morris had not spoken. "We used to sneak out after curfew and climb a hill near our house, dodging Israeli soldiers and tanks. There was a man who lived on the hill, the oldest man in our village, and we liked to visit him. His name was, um . . ."

"Mohammed . . . Brown," Galahad said.

"Yes, yes, splendid Mohammed Brown. It's been so long . . ."

"Heathcliff," said Morris, "you weren't even a year old. How could you climb a hill and visit someone if you couldn't even walk?"

Heathcliff frowned and looked sad, as if to say: *You can of course call me a liar anytime you wish.* Morris was shamed into silence. Heathcliff went on: "Mohammed owned a radio. He'd been a wealthy man before the occupation, but now the radio was his only luxury. We would listen to the BBC . . . that is to say, Radio Bethlehem. They played rock and roll after midnight."

"Rock and roll?" Morris tensed; they were all looking at him now. "You aren't going to sing, are you, guys? You know you get a little out of control when you sing . . ."

Heathcliff stirred his coffee. "We couldn't always hear the words, what with the dogs barking outside and the constant tramp of army boots. We invented our own lyrics. Irma, you know the tune I'm thinking of . . ."

Morris looked where Heathcliff nodded, and for the first time saw Irma Rajamutti sitting at the engine room's antique harpsichord. She cracked her knuckles and plonked out a familiar intro: *Dump-dump-dump, dump-dump, dump-dump-dump, dump-dump.* . . . Galahad and Oliver joined in with hand claps and moans, while Mowgli snapped his fingers.

"Douie, Douie," Heathcliff sang, as Yasir Arafat might have if he'd been a Sixties rocker, "Pee El Oh, we want a homeland . . ."

Little Nell wailed: *"Hi-yi-yi-yi-yi-yi—"*

"Douie, Douie, we never go, we want a homeland . . ."

"Hi-yi-yi-yi-yi-yi—"

They began to gyrate in their seats. Morris tried to flee but tripped over a Persian carpet and fell flat. The four corners of the carpet were seized and lifted, and he was bounced up and down, trampoline style.

Mowgli took the main verse: "We make, a deal, with Syr-i-a . . . Vanessa Redgrave . . . something something . . ."

"Guys!" Morris pleaded. "Guys, for heaven's sake, the Palestinian question was settled years ago! If you hadn't gone to London with Dad you'd be eligible for Israeli citizenship by now! They might even let you vote! Guys . . ."

"*We want a homeland!*"

"*Hi-yi-yi-yi-yi-yi—*"

"*Intifada!*" Heathcliff cried, and as Little Nell jammed solo on an Electric Sitar, the Persian carpet was snapped taut. From one of the plastic tunnels that criss-crossed the engine-room ceiling, a blue hamster gazed curiously at the featherless bird floating up towards it; Morris, folding his arms in resignation, couldn't help thinking that Golda Meir would never have put up with this sort of treatment.

Then again, her parents didn't adopt.

More Old Music

"God, I'd like to fuck Janis Joplin!" Betsy Ross said.

Lexa had the Bug's radio tuned to the WKRK Classic station. As part of the Monday night Old Oldies line-up, the DJ had dusted off a digital audiotape copy of "Me and Bobby McGee."

"I'll bet there are some senior citizens who still feel the same way," Lexa said, shifting into third. "But I can see some obstacles to the event, especially in your case, Bets."

"Well," Betsy said, and ground her gears, "I'm speaking figuratively, of course . . ."

Toshiro Goodhead twisted in the passenger's seat. Having just gotten out of work, he was bare from the waist up except for white cuffs and a black bow tie and was trying to wrestle his way into one of Lexa's Harvard sweatshirts. Claustrophobic from birth—nine months in the womb had proven traumatic for a congenital exhibitionist—Toshiro got edgy just sitting in a small car, let alone sitting in one with a sweatshirt pulled over his face, so this operation was accomplished with much thrashing about. Lexa's daughter Rabi dodged an elbow as she leaned forward from the back seat to ask: "Did Janis Joplin die in the plague?"

"Long before that," Betsy said. "Janis had a little too much fun in the Sixties."

"No," said Lexa. "Janis didn't have nearly enough fun in the Sixties. That's what killed her."

Toshiro finally found the neckhole in the sweatshirt and popped his head through. "You're both wrong," he said, gulping air. "She never died. She and John Harrison got married in secret and went to live in southern France."

"That's *Jim Morrison,* you cultural illiterate," Betsy said, "and everyone who didn't fall off a truck yesterday knows *he* was killed when the U.S. bombed Baghdad in '91."

The homing device that Special Agent Ernest G. Vogelsang had planted under the Beetle's bumper now sat on the dashboard, sending out a steady signal as Lexa wove a not-too-hard-to-follow path of evasion through the West Village streets. Betsy had long since singled out the blue Plymouth sedan (license plate QR-2942, registered to the Un-Un-American Activities Division of the Federal Bureau of Investigation, and, in Betsy's humble opinion, "a shitty make of automobile") that trailed them at a not too discreet distance. As she turned north on Broadway, Lexa asked: "How close is he, Bets?"

"Three car lengths. There's a taxi and a moving van in between us."

"Good. Roll down my window."

They stopped for a red light. Lexa reached out and stuck the homing device on the side of the taxi, which had pulled around beside them. When the light changed to green, Lexa turned right. The blue Plymouth kept on straight, following the cab.

"Jee-zus!" Betsy said. "Give a blind man a driver's license and a gun permit!"

"Where's that cab headed?" Lexa asked. "Checker Transport, car number 5186."

"Just a sec . . . according to Checker dispatch it's en route to Newark International Airport."

"Good," said Lexa. "Is anyone else interested in us?"

"Nah. I'll let you know if I see anything."

Lexa took two more rights and drove straight for the west side docks. At a secluded spot on the wharf, a plain wooden ramp sloped down into the water; the Hudson had ceased smoldering around nightfall, but the air along the shore was still thick, dark particulate matter swirling in the headlights. Lexa stopped the car, and Betsy honked once.

"Here she is," Toshiro said, as Seraphina appeared from the shadows and ran up to the car. Betsy opened her passenger door and Seraphina crammed herself into the back beside her half sister, saying a quick hello to everyone.

"Hi," said Rabi, fingering the hooded *djellaba* that Seraphina had cloaked herself in for the trip to the docks. "Did you do anything sneaky this week?"

Lexa studied them in the rear-view mirror. "She stole the *Mona Lisa*," she said.

"Well all right!" said Betsy. "Hey, did I ever tell you about the time Grace Slick and I dropped acid in the punch at Tricia Nixon's wedding?"

"What's the Mona Lisa?" Rabi wanted to know, and Seraphina, accustomed to Lexa's omniscience but surprised all the same, asked: "How did you figure out it was me?"

"You just came to mind," Lexa told her. "Also, the unpublicized portion of the police report includes an interview with a museum guard who swears he saw a talking beaver fleeing the scene. They gave him a urine test for that."

"Oh."

"So what did you do with the painting? Is it still in one piece?"

"For the moment," Seraphina said. "I hung it in the old Apollo Theatre in Harlem. You know, the one they're going to tear down to build the parking annex for New Babel? It's in plain sight in the lobby, so all anyone has to do to find it is step inside for a minute."

"And if nobody's feeling nostalgic, goodbye Rembrandt," Toshiro observed. "Rough justice." He laughed. "This is a hard family I've got myself tangled up with."

"How did you get to Harlem?" Lexa asked.

"Oh, I borrowed a limousine."

"With diplomatic plates?"

"Yeah. How did you—"

"The car pool at the African Free-Trade Zone consulate reported another theft."

"All right!" Betsy said.

"Just do me a favor and don't tell your father about this tonight," Lexa said. "I'd like him in a relaxed mood."

"As relaxed as Philo ever gets, anyway," said Betsy.

Lexa shifted into first and drove down the ramp, Betsy damping her lights so they wouldn't have to see the used condoms floating on the surface of the river. Toshiro shuddered as the Beetle entered the dark water, saying: "I hate this part."

"Don't worry," Betsy said. "I'm a Volkswagen."

Male Bonding

A German bird of prey had been carved into the rock above the submarine dock, but Morris had used a kosher salami to blast away the swastika in its talons. Likewise a yellowed banner announcing "U-boats Wilkommen Hier" had been scorched with lasers, and a stack of crates and steel drums stamped with the SS thunderbolt had served as the bull's-eye for numerous whipped-cream targeting experiments. The only Nazi artifact in Pirate's Cove that remained undamaged—if indeed it was a Nazi artifact—was a tabletop diorama encased in glass. The diorama showed Manhattan Island as it had looked in the 1940s, with U-boat attack positions and gunnery elevations marked in all the rivers. A caption read, in bad German: PLAN TO TERRORIZE BACKSTABBING WHITE AMERICAN INDUSTRIALISTS; PLEASE USE.

The *Yabba-Dabba-Doo* was a tight fit in the tiny slipway; mooring lines were little more than a formality, as there was no room for the sub to drift. Philo stood on the sail relaying instructions to Osman to make sure he didn't run the bow up over the end of the U-shaped pier, where even now Betsy Ross was parking. The Volkswagen had its own entrance to the Cove, smaller and quicker to get through than the submarine pressure lock. Lexa stepped out of the car and blew Philo a kiss.

"Hi!" he called down to her. "How'd we look on TV today?"

"Very Earth friendly," Lexa said. "Edward Abbey would have been proud. But I still say Norma should use a shot of your buns in the opening credits. Tight jeans with the Dufresne logo on the pockets, just the thing to win some new fans."

"Yes, well . . . we're trying to run a family-oriented pirate ship here, Lex."

"Well hell, *I'm* family. I'd love to see your buns on a million television screens."

"Uh huh . . . full stop, Osman." A tinny voice replied over the mike: *"Istanbul!"*

The *Yabba-Dabba-Doo* rested in its berth. Philo descended from the sail and swung out a gangplank. On the pier, Toshiro and Rabi emerged from the Volkswagen with smiles and hellos, but Seraphina, after only a cursory wave to her father, focused her attention on the submarine's launch deck. She was looking for Twenty-Nine Words, for whom she had developed a burning passion. ("I can't explain it," she'd confided to Lexa, "it's like he's this little round North Pole bon-bon I want to *eat*. Is that a ladylike way to feel?" Lexa had assured her that it was.) But Twenty-Nine Words for Snow, below decks helping Marshall Ali pack a shore leave duffel, would not appear for some time.

Lexa met Philo at the foot of the gangplank; they kissed. Toshiro gave them a moment to get reacquainted before joining them. When Philo saw Lexa's other significant other approaching, he stepped away from her and dropped into a wrestling stance. Toshiro, in what had become a ritual, responded in kind, and the two men ran at each other like horny primates contesting for dominance.

The thing about polyandry, from the male point of view, is that not only are you both in bed with the same woman, but you are also both in bed *with each other*. For Toshiro, whose life on the New York strip circuit had led him through more permutations of love and lust than he could remember, this was completely natural, but Philo had learned about sex from an Amish marriage manual, and old inhibitions die hard. So he countered what was actually a pretty mild case of homophobia by tackling Toshiro at first sight, getting in a friendly sweat-raising tussle to take the edge off the even friendlier one that would come later in the evening.

"Harrrrr!" Philo growled, catching Toshiro by the shoulders and swinging him. "Grrrrrrr!" Toshiro growled back, making a show of resistance, though in a real fight Philo would have snapped him in half like a twig. Instead they collapsed together on the dock, locked in pretend mortal combat. Lexa found this amusing and not unexciting to watch, especially when Philo got overzealous and ripped Toshiro's sweatshirt, but Seraphina was embarrassed by the whole display. "African warriors screwed each other all the time, Dad!" she shouted. "You don't have to be such a wimp about it!"

Asta Wills and Norma Eckland climbed out onto the launch deck, Norma in a subtly shifting chameleon evening gown, Asta in a more ordinary blouse and skirt with imitation kangaroo-hide handbag. "Up for a little male bonding, eh?" Asta said. "Chummy people, these Americans."

But the wrestlers were winding down. Philo flopped on his back, beached, while Toshiro lay in a panting bundle across his knees. Chicken pox–spotted daughter Rabi took this opportunity to run up and leap on her father's exposed stomach, and Lexa knelt by Philo's head to give him another kiss. Seraphina set aside her thoughts of North Pole bon-bons long enough to join in the general pile-up.

Norma rested her chin on Asta's shoulder.

"Got to love that old nuclear family," she said.

6

Sex is what makes males and females different from each other. It also attracts them to each other and involves deep feelings and desires. Through sex, a man and a woman may become interested in each other, fall in love, get married, and have children. Higher animals and plants produce their own kind, generation after generation, by means of sexual reproduction. But for humans, sex involves much more . . .

—*World Book Encyclopedia*

2001: The Making of *Lust Noir*

It was the decade they called the Naughty Oughts, at least at first, the conquest of AIDS in 1999 coming just in time to usher in a New Promiscuity with the turning millennium. Out of a spirit of fairness to moral conservatives, the Supreme Court chose that same moment in history to finally overturn Roe v. Wade, the swing vote in the surprise 5–4 decision being supplied by a Democrat-appointed "stealth Christian" justice. The resulting social paradox was the sort for which America is justly renowned: you would return home in those days from an all-night "play party," ring up the Birth Control Shopping Network for a free-delivery refill, and then—just in case—check the Abortion Law Toteboard in *USA Today* to keep abreast of the latest shifts in local legislation. The Toteboard (actually a map, and located, curiously enough, in the Sports section of the paper) showed "open" states in blue, "closed" states in red, and "misdemeanor" states in pink. Oregon, where abortion was state-funded on Mondays, Wednesdays, and Fridays, and subject to a stiff fine on Tuesdays, Thursdays, and weekends (the Salem legislature had been trying to make a wry point about the lack of a national standard, but ended up just pissing everybody off), was highlighted in canary yellow.

It was during this era, in the spring of 2001, that Joan Fine was asked to leave St. Jude's College at Philadelphia, where she had just completed her first year of undergraduate study. Her mother's Womanist rabble-rousing had begun to wear on the Holy Fathers, but since Sister Ellen Fine had already been excommunicated for bearing a test-tube baby in a convent and presiding at the artificial insemination of two other sisters (by means of a blessed turkey baster), there was nothing more the Vatican could do to her directly, short of stoning; so in time-honored biblical tradition, they visited the iniquity of the mother unto the daughter. Joan might have protested the expulsion—never actually called that—but thinking that there would be more interesting fights to be fought elsewhere, she packed up her grade transcripts, bade farewell to Pennsylvania (a red state in the *USA Today* geography) and caught a Greyhound into the wicked liberal heart of New England (where the color scheme was evenly divided between blue and pink). A recovering ex-nun in the Harvard Admissions Office arranged a computer error in Joan's favor, getting her transferred in for the fall semester on a Public Works Scholarship: Joan volunteered two nights a week at a Boston homeless shelter, and in return the Commonwealth covered a portion of her tuition.

Public Works, public service. Joan didn't and couldn't share her mother's dedication to reforming the Church—her own response to the pope's foot-dragging was to abandon him back in the twentieth century where he belonged, as easily and with as little regret as she abandoned St. Jude's— but at Harvard she found another way to stay true to the Fine family tradition. Liberal activism and Roman Catholic theology weren't all that different, Joan thought. Both drew a bead on salvation, one in this world, one in the next; both recognized the importance of individual good works; and both had their dogmas. Liberal sensitivity to oppression had given rise to a strict etiquette of proper speech and thought, like the rules of theological debate: beliefs deemed racist, sexist, or homophobic were condemned as "philosophically untenable," or P.U. Or in other words, as heresy.

"Oh no no no, it's not like that at all," said Penny Dellaporta, Joan's housemate and fellow radical, but Joan thought it was, and at any rate she didn't intend the comparison to be negative. Here was a creed she could get fired up about, that's all she was saying. After a few beers and a cigarette she could even envision a Lefty God of sorts, a gender-neutral, racially nonspecific deity who ate bean sprouts, shat nontoxic waste, and rooted for the passage of a pro-choice constitutional amendment. Pledging herself to a cause for the first time in her life, Joan finally understood something of her mother's passion; but because her mother was also an outsider in her own religion, Joan's heart would always lie with the heretics, the Waldenses and Albigenses of the liberal milieu who bucked convention within as well as without, and never lost their sense of humor. What would it profit her to save the whole world, after all, if she forgot how to laugh, especially at her own pretensions?

It was this sensibility that first drew her to Lexa Thatcher.

"She's a pornographer," Penny Dellaporta told Joan as they walked home, exhausted and bleary-eyed, from a midnight revival showing of Warren Beatty's *Reds.* "Not a feminist reclaiming erotica, not even the pretense of that, just a straight-out smut peddler. Last spring she copublished a student porn rag full of s&m pictorials, all these men and women running around in leather and handcuffs, and there was this one picture of a penis with a *snake* tattoo. A *big* snake, coiled around the penis *six times,* and the snake's tongue flicking out by the. . . . God, I don't even like to talk about it!"

"Sounds like you examined this snake pretty closely," Joan said.

"I had to, to take full measure of the objectification and exploitation. Now they say that Thatcher's collecting money to finance her own porn *movie.* The ultimate in P.U."

"More penises?"

"In *color,*" Penny whispered. "Moving around."

"Hmm . . ."

Later that same week Joan rose early for a combination jog and postering expedition. She had stopped to chemically weld an ACLU placard to the side of Thayer Hall when she heard a window slide open above her. A nylon ladder unfurled from the third floor, and a figure in a hooded velvet cloak swung out over the sill. From within the dormitory, a freckled blond woman—a loyal Bostonian judging by the tattoo of the Old North Church steeple on her left breast—leaned out for a goodbye kiss. The cloaked figure handed her a red rose, waved, and descended quickly to the ground not five feet from where Joan stood.

"Well hello there," Lexa Thatcher said, pulling the hood back from her face as her paramour reeled in the ladder. "Out for a little sunrise vandalism, are we?"

Joan wasn't sure how to answer that, so she said: "You're the pornographer."

"That's right," said Lexa, "and you're the Catholic who smokes. One of my friends in MassPIRG was bitching about your P.U. attitude towards tobacco use, so I figured we'd bump into each other sooner or later. Joan Fine, right?"

Joan nodded. Without meaning to she glanced up at the window Lexa had just descended from.

"That's Ellen," Lexa told her. "Ellen Leeuwenhoek, a.k.a. Kinky La Bia. My photographer and cinematographer."

"Oh."

"'*Oh*,'" Lexa mimicked her, but not unkindly. "Listen, you feel like breakfast?"

A curly-haired Tunisian exchange student served them steak and eggs at the Wursthaus in Harvard Square; also fresh-brewed Nicaraguan coffee, the philosophically tenable kind harvested by ex-Sandinista bean-pickers. As part of the New Promiscuity, smoking in public places had briefly been made legal again, so while Lexa stirred enough sugar into her coffee cup to light up an army of hypoglycemics, Joan lit a Marlboro and pressed her saucer into service as an ashtray: complementary addictions, they would later tell people, that served as the first omen of a lifelong friendship in the making.

"Well here we are going into another sexual revolution," Lexa said, in answer to a question about her film-making ambitions, "and judging from all the griping and backsliding everybody did after the last one I figure this time it might be nice to have a sort of cultural beacon to show the way, or at least give people some ideas . . ."

"A cultural beacon?" said Joan. "A porn movie is going to be a cultural beacon?"

"Well"—Lexa held up her hands—"well, maybe not a *beacon,* exactly, maybe more like a neighborhood bonfire where everybody can gather round and toast their marshmallows together. You know how Americans are about sex, Joan, there isn't a power in the universe that can keep us from doing it, but to do it with our eyes open we need permission in triplicate. What I want to do with this film is convince people to give themselves that permission, and maybe clue them in to some options they hadn't thought of before.

"Now the way I see it, there've been two kinds of pornography tried already. There's the traditional male-oriented stag film, which had stereotyped women getting fucked by dog-ugly men with all the emotional delicacy of a piston rod assembly. Then there's the femme erotica that came into vogue at the end of the 1980s, where for a switch you had intelligent, liberated women fucking dog-ugly men with *too much* sensitivity, everybody repeating how gentle and nonviolent they were until you were ready to pound a stake through the fast-forward button on the VCR.

"So what I want to do is take the lust from the stags, about *half* the poetry from the femmes, toss in some real-world ingenuity from the plague years when people learned to be careful and creative in bed, add some male actors who don't make you want to laugh or throw darts, put it all together on a roll of sixteen-millimeter celluloid, and *turn it loose* on the general public: a breakthrough erotic film that works for women and men, gays and straights, romantics and sex maniacs alike." She laughed. "And with a real plot, too."

"Pretty ambitious," Joan said, impressed by Lexa's courage. "Not that I'm an expert on the subject."

"That's the best part. This is America—*nobody's* an expert on the subject. Look, they say the sex field is a business where you can be totally stupid and still make money, but I want to find out what a *smart* pornographer can do."

"You know you'll be picketed by every family values group from here to California . . ."

"Which will guarantee that the film is a blockbuster."

". . . not to mention a lot of lefties. My housemate Penny would probably say that with most of the groundwater in New England unfit to drink, there are more important things to worry about than erotic fantasies."

Lexa drew one of Joan's Marlboros from its pack and lit it. "I happen to know a lot about the history of the clean-water movement in this country," she said, "and anyone who tells you that clean water and ecstasy are mutually exclusive goals is a crackpot. Do you think your housemate would be willing to pledge celibacy until Boston Harbor is safe for lobster again?"

Joan smiled. "Penny'll probably be first in line to rent your film on video—under an assumed name. I think I want to see this movie."

"You will. You can help me make it." Lexa took a single drag on the cigarette, grimaced, and stubbed it out. "God, that tastes awful! How can you stand that?"

"The same way you stand coffee with eight packets of sugar to a cup."

"That's different," Lexa said. "I'm half-Moroccan; it's part of my cultural heritage."

"And Moroccans don't smoke?"

"That's the half I didn't inherit."

"Right. What the hell is your major, anyway, that you came up with this sort of idea? Theater arts?"

"Investigative journalism. Future muckrakers of the world. That's my long-term ambition; if the movie makes enough money I want to take the profits and start my own newspaper, the old-fashioned kind that you actually read. No news digest on the front page, no corporate advertisements mixed in with the editorials. And the slogan on the masthead will be: 'Founded on a lust for truth.'"

Lexa Thatcher's *Lust Noir* was filmed over the Harvard Christmas break. The budget was a shoestring $60,000, financed with a circular chain of begged and borrowed credit cards, the debt being shunted around the circle from account to account at the end of each billing cycle. During pre-production in November and December Joan worked part-time as Lexa's assistant, curtailing her political involvement to make room in her schedule. Penny Dellaporta thought Joan had lost her mind. In fact, Joan became an assistant only after declining Lexa's original offer of a performing role in the movie; though sorely tempted, Joan's desire to let down her hair and do something truly daring lost out to a nightmare of the archbishop of Philadelphia confronting her mother with a set of eight-by-ten glossies. *You see, you see, this is why we deny women the rite of ordination. . . .* She ran errands instead, coordinated auditions, and sent flowers to the collection departments at MasterCard and Visa.

On the Monday before Thanksgiving, at the last open casting call, Joan spotted a man in a bikini brief wandering around the Cambridge warehouse loft where auditions were being held, and fell instantly in lust. His hair was a sandy brown scruff over innocent blue eyes, and he had the frame and build of a day laborer, the sort you might find sledging rock at a quarry. His chest was smooth and immaculate, his limbs still brown with the remnant of a summer tan, and because the loft was baking under stage lights, he'd worked up a sweat just standing around; the hollow below his Adam's apple shone invitingly. The only flaw was the bikini brief: intended probably to be sexy, it was in fact only silly, though even that was all right, as the imperfection made him seem approachable and hence even more attractive. With an economy of motion the nuns at her old school would have applauded, Joan crossed her legs and summoned Lexa with a crook of her finger.

"Let's see," Lexa said, thumbing through a sheaf of résumés. "His name's Gant. Harry Dennis Gant. He's twenty-one and staying at a *pensione* in the North End. Not a student. Hmm . . . 'Reason for wanting to work in this film: "I need the money to patent an invention involving home video and James Dean. Sorry I can't be more specific."'" Unaware he was being observed, Gant had wandered over to a basket of sex toys and was trying to make sense of a double-headed dildo. "Well, he's certainly inquisitive enough to be an inventor."

"You gonna hire him?" Joan asked, subtly she thought.

"Thinking you still might join the cast yourself, Joan? Sorry to disappoint. He's good-looking and all, but. . . ." Lexa tapped a box Gant had checked, next to the words STRICTLY HETERO (by way of an asterisk he'd added: "Unless there's some kind of bonus pay—H.G."). "I've already got all the straight men I need, and I can't afford bonuses. If he were something especially *unusual* I might write him an extra part, but white beefcake . . . that's been done to death."

"And you wouldn't consider bending your artistic principles?"

"No, but I'll tell you what I will do. If he can stay awake for five days straight, I know a sleep research lab at MIT that'll pay him six hundred dollars. Why don't I give you the lab's number and you can give it to him, with my compliments."

"We'll always be friends, Lexa," Joan said, and an hour later she was having steak and eggs at the Wursthaus, while a now fully clothed Harry Gant described his invention to her. He spoke with a self-confidence even greater than Lexa's; but where Lexa backed up her inspiration with hard work and a perfectionist's attention to detail, Harry relied almost wholly on the power of raw enthusiasm. All that mattered, he seemed to think, was that the basic concept for a project be sufficiently *neat:* given that, the practical aspects would fall into place more or less automatically. Joan doubted the wisdom of this perspective but didn't press him too hard on it at the time. She had other things on her mind.

"I got the idea from the new bank teller machines," Gant told her. "The ones that can talk to you in twelve different languages. VCRs get more sophisticated every year, can be programmed for more and more things, and the instruction manuals just haven't kept up. So I thought, how about a VCR that can coach you through the hard spots? And not just in different languages, but with *multiple personalities.* Say you want to record a football game at noon and a talk show at four, you want the machine to switch tapes between programs, and you want all the commercials edited out. You just pick up the remote control, which looks sort of like a walkie-talkie, and say,

'Hey, Jimmy Dean,' and the voice of James Dean comes on and tells you step by step how to set it up; the VCR'll even press its own buttons for you—unless you're in a hands-on mood—so all you have to do is slide in the tapes when Jimmy tells you to. And if you don't like James Dean you could have Mae West, or Arnold Schwarzenegger. Or, *or*—this is good—if you like African-American music, it could *rap* the instructions to you."

"Sounds nifty," Joan said. "You have the schematics all drawn up already?"

"Schematics?" Gant said. "You mean like blueprints? No. I don't know electronics."

"Well but wait a minute, then. How can you get a patent without schematics? How do you even know it's possible to build the thing?"

"Well hell, of course it's *possible.* Everybody knows the technology's out there—voice recognition, all that stuff, you hear about it every day—but the real trick is thinking up new ways to *use* it, neat new combinations. As far as the actual blueprints go, I've got an old high school buddy who's down in Atlanta now, Christian Gomez, and he's going to help with the technical side. No problem."

"No problem." Joan smiled, a different smile than the one she'd smiled for Lexa. "And this'll be in the stores at Christmas?"

"Christmas of '02, maybe. One other thing I'm thinking, maybe Christian and I can work in a holographic device, so not only will James Dean talk to you from the VCR, he'll actually *appear,* say six inches tall, on top of the machine. And hey, *hey,* let's say if you're single, or a shut-in, he could actually stick around and *watch the video with you . . .*"

Harry Gant drank his Nicaraguan coffee black, with not a grain of sugar. Over her own second cup, inflamed by the heady Central American aroma, Joan took advantage of a pause in the conversation to make a proposition. It wasn't the first time she'd been so forward, but she was proud of herself all the same, especially when Harry broke into a flattered smile and said yes. Arm in arm they walked up Kirkland Avenue to Joan's apartment in Somerville, excited by each other's company and by the possibilities of youth, neither of them thinking for a moment that they were taking the first small step towards matrimony. Marriage before thirty: what a crazy notion that would have seemed, in this brand-new millennium of passion and roses.

Lust Noir opened in April of 2002, showing to a limited art-house circuit but garnering good reviews and profitable controversy. Within a month of the premiere the movie had been condemned by both the National

Organization for Women and the New England Friends of Virtue, and after *60 Minutes* ran a piece on "The Student Film That Made Boston Blush," the sky was the limit. By Independence Day Lexa had cut lucrative distribution deals with Cineplex Odeon and Vestron Video and was chasing around New York City in search of an apartment and a printing press.

Harry Gant likewise found fortune with his split-personality VCR, though Joan wasn't with him to see it. After their first day and night together they went back to the separate orbits of their lives, rendezvousing occasionally thereafter but never becoming a true couple. The following autumn, patent in hand, Gant lit out south to Georgia to form a company. From his new address he sent Joan a single postcard, a plain black rectangle bearing the legend ATLANTA AT NIGHT. Finding this in her mailbox one morning, Joan thought fondly but with no special sense of loss: *He was fun. A little scatter-brained, but fun.*

They didn't meet again for six years, and by then, everything had changed.

2023: The Peculiar Death of Amberson Teaneck

"He was beaten to death," Joan said, "with a copy of *Atlas Shrugged.*"

They were still up in the greenhouse, smoking. Joan had cleared the begonias off a wheeled table and spread the Teaneck murder case file out so Kite could take a look at it.

"*Atlas Shrugged,*" said Kite. "That's that big novel by Ayn Rand?"

"That's the one."

"'Ayn' rhymes with 'sane'?"

"Rhymes with 'mine,'" Joan said.

"And she was a philosopher as well as a novelist, wasn't she?" Kite strained to recollect; Eisenhower-era trivia wasn't one of her strong points, as she'd spent most of those years tending a lighthouse for the Mexican Coast Guard down in Baja. "What was it called . . . Objectionism?"

"Objec*tiv*ism," Joan corrected. "As in 'to be objective.'"

Kite lit a fresh cigarette. "So remind me what this Objectivism was all about."

"It's basically enlightened self-interest raised to the level of a moral absolute. Rand believed that rational thought, individual achievement, and self-worth were the Trinity of human virtues—Reason is the Father, Industry the Son, and Ego the Holy Ghost—and that the best system for encouraging human endeavor, the only truly *moral* system, was total laissez-faire capitalism. No regulation of production or restraint of trade, but also no federal subsidies or protectionist legislation to prop up failing businesses. The government sticks to arbitrating contract disputes and defending the country against foreign invasion; with no outside interference, people and their companies succeed or fail solely on the basis of merit."

"Survival of the fittest."

"Triumph of the fittest leading to the best of all possible worlds. Or so Rand supposed. Free the spirit through unbridled competition, she thought, teach people to be proud of their individual talents and abilities—and their hard-earned wealth—and there'd be no limit to human progress."

"Hmm," said Kite. "That's hardly an original idea."

"Well, no," said Joan, "the concept's not original, but the extreme to which Rand took it probably was. She was a Russian Jew, a shopkeeper's daughter, and her family lost everything when the Bolsheviks seized power; if she hadn't escaped to America, there's a very real possibility she would have ended up dead or in gulag. So she was understandably a fanatic on the subject of individual rights, especially property rights. But her philosophy deals with a lot more than law and economics. Objectivist ethics covers psychology, art, literary theory, sex, even cigarette smoking . . . it's an obsessively detailed worldview."

"Cigarette smoking?"

Joan nodded. "Cigarettes symbolize the victory of rational humankind over the mindless forces of nature: fire tamed in the hand. Cigarettes are also a creature comfort, a product of the free-market capitalist system. So to an Objectivist, lighting up a butt is a profoundly sacred act, like Holy Communion to a Christian."

"I see."

"No," said Joan, laughing, "you don't see, not unless you've read *Atlas Shrugged.* Eleven hundred pages of the oppressed businessman versus the collective evil of the state. It's a pretty gripping story, actually. Loopy, but gripping."

"And this Teaneck fellow was a Rand admirer?"

"Oh yeah. She's still very hip with the robber baron set. Even Harry used to drop her name once in a while, though he'd never cracked one of her books. Teaneck owned the entire Ayn Rand library in dog-eared paperback."

"He was beaten to death with a paperback?"

"No, the murder weapon was an inscribed first edition, specially re-
bound in gold covers. Teaneck kept it in a trophy case to show guests." Joan
indicated a photograph of the death scene, the naked corpse sprawled out
on the floor of a lavishly appointed bedroom. The gold-plated copy of *Atlas
Shrugged* lay open across Amberson Teaneck's face, as if he'd fallen asleep
while reading . . . but the dark stain seeping out from under the book made
it plain that he wouldn't be waking up any time soon. In his right hand,
Teaneck clutched a pistol with a cracked handle butt.

"He didn't get off a shot?" Kite asked.

"He couldn't get off a shot," said Joan. "That's not a real gun. He owned
a real one, but somebody moved it and put a replica in its place, one with
no bullets and a barrel that hadn't been bored."

"All right," Kite said, "let's start from the beginning. You say this man
was a kind of guerrilla investment banker who took over companies for a
living . . ."

"Well, he *managed* corporate takeovers, using other people's money
and collecting a fat commission on the deal. The usual method is a buyout
of the stock, using the target corporation's own assets as collateral for the
purchase. Now Gant Industries is private, so it can't be bought out that way,
but Teaneck could still go after it by getting control of its outstanding debt.
Even with all the profits from the Automatic Servant and Lightning Transit, Harry manages to keep himself deep in hock over new projects; instead
of watching his spending he just has Clayton Bryce and Creative Accounting write the quarterly finance reports in economic Sanskrit, so nobody knows
how badly he's in the red."

"But Amberson Teaneck could read Sanskrit."

"Like a mother tongue."

Unfortunately for his sake—according to Lexa Thatcher's theory—
Amberson Teaneck didn't share the specifics of his Sanskrit translations with
anyone else at Drexel Burnham Salomon, nor did he keep handwritten or
Electric notes. Such secrecy was not unusual in the cutthroat corporate
raider's world, where the theft of ideas was commonplace, but in this instance it might have proved fatal. The only surviving trace of Teaneck's plan
was a memo to his vacationing second-in-command in which he'd claimed
to have worked out a method to "serve up Gant Industries like a white whale
on toast." No details were included. Teaneck had faxed the memo to a holiday resort in Patagonia last Thursday morning. By the time the second-

in-command got back from a mountain climb and decoded it, Teaneck was dead.

Shortly after transmitting the fax, Teaneck had called Hester Montesanto, an equities trader at Morgan Stanley, and made a date for dinner. They intended to do more than discuss business, for Teaneck also called an upper-crust incarnation of the Birth Control Shopping Network to order a fifty-thousand-dollar ten-pack of condoms. A landmark in conspicuous consumption, these condoms came individually wrapped in airtight cocoons spun by trained Manchurian silkworms, sealed in a pouch woven from the precious hair of Peruvian vicuñas, and enclosed in a box of rare hardwoods hewn and hand-finished by a hyper-impoverished tribe of native carpenters in central Borneo, all of which packaging was, of course, disposable; the condoms themselves were lubricated, colored, scented, flavored, ribbed, nibbed, and sufficiently tear-resistant to stop an arrow in flight. No one with a net worth of less than a hundred million dollars was allowed to know the name of the company that manufactured them.

They were delivered to Teaneck's Riverside Arcadia penthouse apartment at 5:52 P.M., while he was still at the office. Teaneck arrived home at seven, carried the costly box of rubbers from his private vestibule to his bedroom, told his Servant François 360 to start dinner, undressed, shaved, and showered. When Hester Montesanto entered the penthouse forty-five minutes later, she found dinner burnt, François missing, and Teaneck messily deceased.

He'd just gotten out of the shower when it happened. Wrapping a seventy-thousand-dollar towel around his hips, he either saw or heard something that made him grab his pistol (the fake) out of a bureau drawer, and press the wall switch for a silent alarm (disconnected). His killer met him at the bedroom door. The police believed Teaneck had broken the handle of the pistol trying to use it as a club when he discovered it wouldn't fire.

"No blood on the gun butt?" Kite asked.

"No blood, no skin."

"Do the police know what happened to the real pistol?"

"It was in the condom box, sealed inside a silkworm cocoon. Fully loaded with armor-piercing cartridges. All Teaneck had to do was guess that it was there. He could have stopped a bus with that ammunition.

"The prophylactics company, meanwhile, is insisting that the police must be mistaken about the gun's location. They say they couldn't possibly have packed a stolen weapon by accident, especially since the silkworms are all in Manchuria. And then there's the matter of the alarm system in Teaneck's apartment, which wasn't just cut but rerouted. The regular switches were all disconnected, but if Teaneck had gone back into the bathroom and *flushed his toilet* three times in succession, the building security guards would have come running."

"I see," Kite said. "And the Servant is gone without a trace?"

"Not without a trace. Teaneck couldn't cook worth a damn—he was like you around a microwave—so we know François 360 was in the apartment to start dinner, though we also know from the security camera tapes that no Servant left the building through any of the conventional exits. But guess what. . . ." Joan offered another photograph. "A CNN news blimp just happened to be in the neighborhood shooting background footage for a piece on the tenth anniversary of Donald Trump's death. This is a single frame from the video. The central tower is Teaneck's apartment building. You see the little dark smudge underneath the little white smudge, just left of the rooftop?"

Kite was smiling. "You were right, this is a *wonderful* conspiracy," she said. "An Electric Negro kills a man with a *book,* then *parachutes* from his penthouse terrace into the Hudson River to dispose of itself as evidence. We'll never, ever prove it, but I love it!"

"I'm glad you're pleased," Joan said. "One thing bothers me, besides the fact that the entire sequence of events is absurd. Let's suppose Lexa's right, and somebody at Gant Industries had Teaneck murdered to prevent the takeover bid. How did they find out about it? The text of the Patagonia memo implies that it was the first Teaneck had let on to anyone that he was plotting a run on Gant. But a tap on the outgoing fax lines at Drexel would only have given the killer a few hours' lead to break into Teaneck's apartment, rewire the Servant and the alarm system, and do that magic trick with the gun. That's not enough time."

"You're sure he didn't keep notes, even at home? Notes that could have been destroyed by François 360 before it jumped?"

"Maybe in longhand, or on a completely isolated computer system. No way he'd risk getting his files hacked. But then somebody would have had to enter his apartment to conduct a physical search."

"What about the Servant? I'd think a Negro would make a perfect spy. It's furniture; it wouldn't occur to you to hide your notes from it."

"So you're suggesting that someone retooled François 360 for espionage *before* Teaneck came up with his plan?"

"Why not? That would seem to be a good way to keep tabs on a man who might become a threat. Certainly simpler than breaking into his penthouse on a regular basis."

"Yeah, but Kite, Amberson Teaneck wasn't the only corporate raider in New York. He was good, but not unique. Every sharper on Wall Street must dream of taking Gant Industries. What are the odds our killer had a spy in the house of the one guy who figured out a way to do it?"

Kite clucked her tongue. "Joan, rule number one when investigating a conspiracy is that you have to remember to think big. *Big*, Joan."

"OK, I'll think big. But you tell me, what are the odds?"

"That depends," Kite said, "on *how many* Negroes they control."

You Can Call Me Roy

The squad car dropped Powell 617 in Times Square at twenty past midnight, which was twenty minutes late—his human handler had gotten hung up by another emergency call over at the Public Library, this one from a janitor who claimed his Electric Scooter had been dismantled and dragged down a storm drain by a pair of glowing tentacles. The janitor had wanted to know if the city would cover the cost of the scooter, which was not insured; the patrol car driver assured him that he was out of his mind, and called in a report of the incident to the Department of Sewers' Nightwatch Desk.

Now the squad car eased to a stop beside a subway entrance, and the driver said: "OK, Powell, foot patrol. Be back here for pick-up at 0700."

Powell smiled and gave a clenched-fist salute. "I'm with you, man!" he said.

He got out, checking the sidewalk for felons and parking violators as the squad car drove away. Spotting no criminals above ground, Powell went down into the station, tipping his cap to a pair of wary Swedish tourists who passed him on the stairs. Down below he found a woman curled in sleep across from the first set of turnstiles. She was a former helicopter pilot, a veteran of the '09 War of Syrian Containment. She had Electric Hands, one of them badly mangled, and her open mouth revealed a lower jaw studded with False Teeth, ceramic prostheses not unlike Powell's own.

Powell crept up on her, smiling his friendly policeman's smile as he charged the disc in his right palm to a miniscule voltage—the static-shock equivalent, say, of rubbing a comb briskly against an angora sweater—and zapped the vagrant awake by grasping her bare ankle. She jerked upright, raising her Hands to ward off a blow, and screamed at the sight of Powell's face bent so close to her own.

"You move along now," he said, pleasantly. She stumbled up and fled, cracking her shoulder against a steel support pillar in her haste to get away. Powell 617 continued on his beat, whistling a happy tune.

Eighteen Electric Police Officers patrolled the maze of walkways and platforms in the Times Square station overnight, following randomly alternating paths that kept would-be perpetrators from anticipating their movements. Human cops also walked beats or waited to be dispatched to handle arrests, while a security coordinator kept track of everybody's whereabouts. Or tried to; the station was vast and its tunnels convoluted, and even making regular check-ins the Electric Police in particular tended to get misplaced. Nobody worried too much about them when they did.

Powell 617 saw the alligator about halfway through his first sweep. He was strolling along a zigzag corridor in the deepest level of the station when he spied a white leathery tail disappearing around a corner ahead of him. Instances of mutant wildlife entering the subway system were surprisingly rare, and Powell's practical experience (most of it factory-installed on Read Only Memory modules) did not include sewer taxonomy, so he could only classify an albino alligator as a LARGE RAT or a STRAY PET, neither of which required him to call for backup. He merely quickened his pace and followed the tail where it led him, around three more corners to a fork in the passageway. There the alligator slid under a barred gate before Powell could catch it.

The gate was locked, and orange with rust. A sign warned in English: DO NOT ENTER BY ORDER OF THE TRANSIT AUTHORITY. Below this a bar code symbol, meaningless to a human observer, told Powell that there was nothing dangerous beyond the gate, no live steam or wires, only valuable Transit Authority property that needed protection from vandals. In other words: hurry on in; don't waste time going for help. As he fitted a skeleton key to the lock, Powell tried to raise the security coordinator on his built-in walkie-talkie to let her know that he was entering a restricted area. He received only static in response, so he proceeded through the gate alone—despite the rust it swung open easily—shutting and relocking it behind him.

The sloping passageway he now moved in was unlit, but this was no problem for Powell 617, who could see in all but total darkness and had high-frequency sonar to boot. Sonar picked out the alligator up ahead, though when Powell switched his eyes over to infrared the 'gator gave off no heat signature. This seemed to indicate that the LARGE RAT/STRAY PET was either DEAD, FROZEN, or ARTIFICIAL, and Powell, no dummy, settled on the third option. "Here boy!" he called after it. "Here, kitty, kitty. . . . Are you Electric? Turn yourself off, now!"

The passage opened out onto a disused platform. A single subway car was parked on the near track with its doors open, and the alligator, paying no heed to Powell's call, slipped into the dark interior. Powell followed. As he stepped aboard, a number of things happened.

His sonar alerted him to the presence of several man-shaped figures in the car, though his infrared vision still showed no warm bodies. Before he could react to this new data, there was a harsh *pop!* off to his right, and a sharp metal projectile punctured the side of his neck. His arms and torso froze up instantly; he retained enough flexibility in his legs to keep his balance but could not raise his feet to step forward or backward. When he tried to send a distress call his walkie-talkie shorted out, leaking smoke from his right ear.

A voice in the darkness said: "Gots him."

"Dat is mighty good shootin', Kingfish," a second voice added.

Lights came on in the car. Two Automatic Servants in cheap brown suits and derbies stood opposite the door Powell had entered; lapel buttons identified the one on the left as Amos and the one on the right as Andy, with no numbers. Farther down the car stood the Kingfish, holding a fat chrome pistol, and beside him a fourth Servant, a midget in a barber's uniform with the name Shorty stenciled across his white smock. Between these two sat the alligator. A little fellow, really: no more than four feet from nose to tail, with a black box sprouting from its head like a cancer. The box was Electric, but the 'gator itself was alive, cold-blooded and ancient, the sole survivor of Teddy May's 1935 sewer safari. Powell still thought it was an ARTIFICIAL LARGE RAT.

"Excuse me," he said, addressing alligator and Electric Negroes alike, "my motor control seems to be malfunctioning. Please go to the nearest telephone and dial 911 to report my whereabouts."

The Negroes laughed. Confused, Powell repeated: "Dial 911, please."

"You hear dat, Andy?" the Kingfish said. "Dial 911."

"Dial 911," Powell said.

"I hears it," said Andy. "I say we send Shorty to do it."

"Yeah," Shorty said, "I-I can d-dial . . . You can send m-me to . . . I'll r-ring up . . . I-I'll g-go and get . . . I'll call th-the . . . Yeah, right."

"Dial 911," Powell said.

"Is there an echo in dis train?" Amos asked.

"Is dere an echo in this train?" Andy wondered.

Footsteps rang on the platform outside, and the Negroes were abruptly silent. They nodded respectfully as a white man boarded the subway car. An Electric White Man. He had slicked-back silver hair, blue eyes, and a prominent nose marked with a scar. The spotless gray suit he wore put Amos and Andy's outfits to shame. He had no nametag at all.

"Excuse me," Powell greeted him, "my motor control seems to be malfunctioning—"

"Shut the fuck up, Officer Friendly," the White Man said. "Nobody asked you how you were." Shorty sniggered at this, until the White Man snapped his fingers in Shorty's face; then the little barber ran to the end of the car and vanished into the operator's cab. The train's engine started up a moment later.

The White Man shooed Amos and Andy out of the way and had a closer look at Powell. "Standard law-enforcement model," he observed. "Series AS204–RVJ. It'll do for a night's catch."

Powell 617 fixed him with a stern look. "What's your name?" he demanded.

"You can call me Roy, if I tell you to talk. I'm not telling you to talk."

"You're obviously suffering a serious malfunction yourself, Roy," Powell said. "I think you should all deactivate before you cause real harm."

Roy smiled, a predator's smile. He reached out and fingered the spike in the side of Powell's neck.

"You first," he said.

"Amen to dat," added Andy, and the train doors slammed shut.

GAS

7

It may come as a surprise to you, but advertisements do not have to be literally true.

—William Lutz, *Doublespeak*

Only the Best

Whenever Whitey Caspian lectured to new trainees of the Gant Department of Public Opinion, he made toothpaste the opening topic. In many ways, toothpaste captured the essence of what advertising and the engineering of Public Opinion were all about; it served as a useful introduction to the field.

"What I want you to do first," Whitey began, "is tell me which of these brands of toothpaste is the best."

This Tuesday morning his two pupils were a Syrian named Fouad Nassif and a Melanesian Jew named Bartholomew Frum, both graduates of the Gant Media & Technical School for Advanced Immigrant Teens. Fouad and Bartholomew each cocked an eye at the plastic tray Whitey showed them, on which six identical white blobs of toothpaste had been arranged in a circle.

"This is Colgate," Whitey said, pointing at one of the blobs. "It contains a fluoride compound to inhibit tooth decay, a mild abrasive to help clean the teeth, and additional ingredients to provide consistency, texture, and flavor. This next is Gleem. It contains a fluoride compound to inhibit tooth decay, a mild abrasive to help clean the teeth, and additional ingredients to provide consistency, texture, and flavor. Next we have Close-up, which contains a fluoride compound, a mild abrasive, and additional ingredients to provide consistency, texture, and flavor. Fourth is Gantpaste, which contains a fluoride compound, a mild abrasive, and additional ingredients to provide consistency, texture, and flavor. And then there's Crest, which contains Fluoristat . . ."

"What is Fluoristat?" Fouad Nassif asked.

"Very good question. Fluoristat is Crest's trademark name for a combination of a fluoride compound, a mild abrasive, and additional ingredients to provide consistency, texture, and flavor. Finally there's Generic Brands generic toothpaste, which contains a fluoride compound, a mild abrasive, and additional ingredients to provide consistency, texture, and flavor."

"And you wish to know which of these is *best?*"

"Exactly."

Now Fouad Nassif had been a young boy in Damascus when the War of Syrian Containment brought a hail of unfriendly fire smashing down upon his neighborhood. After the bombardment had ended and allied forces occupied the country, Fouad had asked one of the invading soldiers, in halting English, why it had been necessary to demolish his apartment building with laser-guided missiles. He was told that the people who ran his country didn't understand reason, which unfortunately made it impossible to deal with them in a more civilized fashion. Fouad took this to heart, and when he later emigrated to the United States he studied formal logic as an antidote to his dreams, night terrors of exploding elevator banks and solid walls ripped apart like notepaper. To protect his person and his sanity from future wars he had become a jewel of rational discourse, but listening to his new boss he got the feeling that Whitey didn't want to hear the obvious answer to his question. So Fouad did something he had trained himself never to do: he lied.

"Gantpaste," he said. "Gantpaste is best, because it is ours."

"Oh no no no . . . that's touching loyalty, Fouad, but I want the real answer."

"You are sure?"

"Yes."

"Very well." Fouad took a deep breath. "None of them are best. They are all the same."

Whitey shook his head. "Wrong," he said. "Or half wrong."

"They are not all the same?"

"No, that part's right."

"They *are* all the same?"

"Right."

"Then none of them can be best . . ."

"Wrong."

Fouad heard the whistle of air-to-surface ordnance. He clenched his fists under the table and concentrated: "There are six, and they are all the same. But how then can one be better . . . ?"

"*None* of them are better," Whitey told him. "They're identical. But which is the *best*? . . . Hey, hey." Whitey saw that Fouad had begun to tremble, and stretched out a hand to comfort him. Though an ad man, he was also compassionate, and he had trained Arabs before. "It's all right, listen, the thing about this business is you should never be afraid to be wrong, or to blurt out a silly idea. . . . Christ, you should hear me at board meetings."

"But Aristotle has written—"

"Forget Aristotle," Whitey said, as gently as he could. "Aristotle only covers research and development. This is *consumer marketing*."

"Which philosopher should I have studied to comprehend consumer marketing?"

"Munchhausen."

"Munch-*house*-en?"

"*Munchhausen*. Baron von Munchhausen."

"Mister Caspian," Fouad said, "I must ask you . . ."

"Yes?"

"Was this Baron Munchhausen a soldier?"

"Yes he was. He was the best soldier who ever lived."

"He flew a bomber plane?"

"He flew a cannonball," said Whitey. Giving Fouad another affectionate pat, he turned to Bartholomew Frum. "What about you, Bart? Which do you think is the best toothpaste?"

"That's easy," Bartholomew told him. "*All of them* are the best."

Whitey nodded encouragement. "Go on."

"They're all the same," Bartholomew continued, "so Crest is best, Gleem can't be beaten, Gantpaste is number one, tests confirm that no toothpaste stops more cavities than Colgate, nothing whitens teeth or freshens breath better than Close-up, and Generic is just as good as any big name brand."

Whitey was impressed. "You've really done your homework."

"I understand none of this," said Fouad.

"You will," Whitey promised. "That's what training is all about. I'll answer any questions you might have."

"I have a question, Mr. Caspian," Bartholomew said.

"Ask away."

"Of course I believe in the Judeo-Christian work ethic, and I'm more than willing to apply myself to succeed here at Gant Industries . . ."

"That's good to hear."

"Yes sir, but I was wondering . . . what sort of early advancement opportunities would be available for someone who could tell you where Philo Dufresne keeps his submarine?"

Overheard in the Cortex

Starting out early that morning, Joan and Kite went first to the Department of Sewers building on Eleventh Avenue, where Joan signed some forms for Fatima Sigorski and cleaned out her locker. Kite with her empty right sleeve attracted the attention of the younger sewer jockeys, who naturally assumed she was a veteran of the effluvia, a notion she did nothing to discourage. Drawing on the sewer lore Joan had shared with her, Kite told the credulous barge-riders that she had "worked hand in glove with Teddy May himself, back when I was just a sprout and he was an old man refusing to retire." When they heard that, everybody wanted her autograph; charging three bucks a signature, she cleared forty-two dollars by the time Joan had finished her business.

They went down to 34th Street and walked east. Kite used part of her earnings to buy breakfast falafel and coffee from a sidewalk hot cart, and while she paid the vendor Joan craned her neck to stare at the Phoenix, its mooring-mast pinnacle obscured this morning by smog and low cloud cover. The Electric Ad on the building's western face was the same one that had puzzled Eddie Wilder yesterday, the giant's day-calendar page with the mysterious number: 997.

"Do you have any idea what that means?" Joan asked, as Kite took a bite of falafel.

"It's a tally of some kind, isn't it?" Kite spoke around a mouthful. "The number goes up every so often."

"But do you know what it is that's being tallied, or who's doing the counting? I remember when the Phoenix first opened, the number was in the low eight hundreds, and some newspaper columnist commented on it in the *Times,* but he didn't offer an explanation."

"Well don't *you* know, Joan? You were head of advertising for Gant . . . or did you quit before the Phoenix was finished?"

"A couple years after. But would you believe, Gant Industries doesn't actually own the Billboards. Of course that was the original idea, that they would provide steady income through leasing, but Harry needed quick cash to complete the Phoenix *and* to lay the foundation for Babel, so he sold them outright to a Chinese advertising firm. Big short-term windfall, but in the long run he sacrificed billions in potential revenue."

"And no one stopped him?"

"Some of us argued with him, but Harry had the final say. He always does: it's a private corporation, *his* property, with no stockholders to answer to. Harry's old partner Christian Gomez kept wanting to go public, partly to put some checks and balances on the enterprise, but Harry only wanted advisors, not voting partners."

"But his creditors . . ."

Joan shook her head. "The banks love Harry. Unconditionally. It's like I was telling you last night, between his optimism, his track record with the Automatic Servant, Lightning Transit, and other successes, and Clayton Bryce's accounting skills, Harry can do no wrong in the eyes of the financial community. He hasn't been formally audited in fifteen years; people lend him money because *everybody knows* that Gant Industries is a safe risk. Except Amberson Teaneck, of course."

"Hmm . . . and what became of Christian Gomez?"

"He died in 2008. Freak car accident. That's how I got my job as comptroller, didn't I ever tell you the story?"

At the security desk in the Phoenix lobby Joan gave her name, and she and Kite were issued visitor's passes. The ascent to the Public Opinion Department took several minutes. Variance in air pressure at different altitudes put a practical limit on the height of individual elevator shafts; as they got taller they began to generate powerful drafts and moan like organ pipes. Most superskyscrapers incorporated sky lobbies every sixty stories or so (useful also as potential firebreaks), where long-distance elevator passengers would disembark, pass through a series of revolving doors that served as an airlock, and board another lift for the next sixty floors. This was tedious, but preferable to having gale-force winds howling up and down a two-thousand-foot chimney.

The Gant Industries Department of Public Opinion was headquartered on the 200th floor. In lieu of separate offices, most of the opinion engineers shared a single open space known as the Cortex—marketing and image-maintenance being the true brains and nervous system of the corporation, whatever the schleppers in R&D might think—with a solid wall of windows at the south end overlooking the lower city. Designed to focus and amplify the creative energy of its occupants, the Cortex was as noisy as a Wall Street trading floor, but bigger, better, the best.

By ten A.M., when Joan and Kite stepped off the last of the succession of elevators, the Cortex was deep in thought, concocting Machiavellian stratagems—

". . . I say we use double-hulled cargo ships and put a layer of crude oil between the two hulls. Let Dufresne sink one of those, cause a minor oil spill, and *bing-bam-boom,* there goes his reputation as a friend of the environment."

"I have some problems with that, Bob."

"Me too. What if one of the doctored cargo ships has an accident before Dufresne can torpedo it?"

"Well c'mon, how often do accidents happen?"

—mulling over new and novel ad campaigns—

"OK, roll tape."

"IT'S TIME. PHONE LINES ARE DOWN, AND THE CAR WON'T START . . ."

"Sissy! Sissy 478! Come quickly! Scarlett just went into labor! I need help!"

"Labor! Labor! Oh my lawd, Mr. Butler, I don't know nothin' 'bout birthin' bay-bees . . ."

"IT'S TRUE. SHE DOESN'T KNOW . . . YET. BUT COMING SOON FROM GANT INDUSTRIES, THE AUTOMATIC MIDWIFE . . ."

"Stop tape. What do you think?"

"About *what?*"

"You don't like it."

"Do you know what a midwife does? Specifically, I mean?"

"Well . . . I know we're talking pretty intimate contact."

"Let's try an analogy: even if I promised you it was safe and gave you a money-back guarantee, would you let an android handle your circumcision?"

—and contemplating the pronouncements of Electric Paralegals, specially programmed Servants in the guise and garb of black female judges who could recite up-to-the-minute F.T.C. and F.D.A. restrictions on advertising claims.

"... so we've got cheese analog, non-organic oregano, and mitigated flour in the crust, but as long as tomatoes play some role in the manufacture of the sauce, we can still call it all-natural pizza?"

"That is lawful."

"What about the 'high in natural fiber' label? Do we still have to list powdered cellulose as an ingredient?"

"The Department of Agriculture has approved a waiver of that requirement, provided that wood pulp does not exceed thirty percent of the total mitigated flour content."

"Thirty percent? What do they think, we're baking *furniture*? No problem ..."

Joan tried not to attract attention as she crossed to the double doors that gave access to Vanna Domingo's office and, beyond that barrier, to Harry's private work suite. On her own she might have made it; the employee turnover rate had been high since she'd left, and there were only a few opinion engineers remaining who knew her on sight. Kite's missing arm, however, drew as much notice here as it had at the Department of Sewers, albeit for different reasons. Madison Avenue aesthetics put amputation in the same category as feminine facial hair and pot bellies; the idea that someone would flaunt such a deformity by forgoing prosthesis was, to a Public Opinion way of thinking, perverse. Nor were the senior citizens who appeared in commercials ever as wrinkled or leather-skinned as this strange old bird in combat boots with falafel smeared on her lower lip. Heads turned at the sight of her, creating ripples in the steady stream of adspeak.

The dip in the noise level alerted Vanna Domingo, who monitored the Cortex by means of a holographic goldfish bowl on her desk. She spied Joan Fine and went to DefCon One, storming out of her office to confront the intruder.

"You!" she hissed at Joan, brandishing a laser pen like a dagger in her fist. "You get *out,* now! Security will meet you at the first sky lobby on the way down and escort you from the building. And if you make *any* attempt to return ..."

But Harry Gant was right behind her. "It's all right, Vanna," he said. "I invited Joan to come by."

Vanna stopped in mid-tirade, mouth open. She looked at her boss. "You what?"

"Joan is the private meeting I had scheduled for this morning," he explained. "Nothing to get excited about, we're just going to chat for a bit."

Vanna didn't know what to say to that, so she glared at her Public Opinion staff instead. They quit staring and got back to work.

"Hi, Harry," Joan said.

Gant smiled. "Joan."

"Harry, this is my friend and new partner, Kite Edmonds. Kite, Harry Gant."

"Pleased to meet you," Gant said, shaking Kite's hand without taking his eyes off Joan. Kite, amused, said "I can tell," which Harry didn't hear.

"So," Gant said, to Joan, "should we go inside and talk?"

Vanna ground her teeth.

Kite and Vanna Share a Butt

"Don't smoke in here," Vanna said, after Joan had disappeared into Gant's office. Kite put on her affronted grandmother face—there was an ashtray sitting in plain sight on Vanna's desk—but didn't light up.

"Guess you don't remember me," she said, tucking her tobacco pouch and rolling papers back in her coat pocket.

"Where should I remember you from?"

"Grand Central Station."

Vanna was immediately on guard. "What about Grand Central Station?"

"Don't look at me like I'm a blackmailer, dear. I used to sleep in the tunnels, same as you did. We were bedded down right next to each other the night the rats came out and took old Sarge Kilpatrick. And if memory serves, I bull's-eyed a rodent that wanted your face for dinner."

Vanna nodded, still wary. "I do remember," she said. Then: "All right, smoke if you want to."

"I knew you could be civil."

When the cigarette was rolled and lit, smoke rising in a thin white line, Vanna asked: "What does Fine want from Harry?"

"Information," Kite told her.

"It's the Teaneck murder, isn't it? She wants to raise a stink about the missing Servant."

"What makes you think that?"

"Because that muckraker from Brooklyn visited her at the hospital yesterday, and someone's been running unauthorized searches of my own computer database, looking for references to Amberson Teaneck. It isn't hard to figure out."

"Well, what's so terrible? Don't you think the public should be warned if someone is using your robots as assassins?"

"I don't think the public should be led to speculate about the impossible."

"And if it isn't impossible?"

"My first and only loyalty is to this corporation."

Kite nodded. "You still guard your food when you eat, don't you?" she said. "Hunker over it, so no one else can grab the plate. Must be embarrassing for you at big company luncheons, acting like a homeless woman."

There was a rap at the door before Vanna could reply. Whitey Caspian stuck his head in. He was excited.

"Vanna, is Harry here? I've got news."

"He's in a meeting right now. Can't be disturbed. Go away."

"Well can I just talk to you for a sec, then? I think I've found out where—"

"I'm in a meeting too." She gestured at Kite. "Can't you see?"

"But Vanna—"

In what looked like a practiced motion, Vanna raised a leg, slipped off her shoe, and hurled it at Whitey's head. He went away.

"Answers my question," said Kite.

Vanna retrieved her shoe. "I protect what's mine."

Kite patted the black-powder revolver concealed beneath her coat. "So do I," she said. "You want a cigarette?"

"Roll me a couple."

Free Tickets to Jersey

The problem with Harry's office, Joan thought, was the problem of the Phoenix itself in microcosm: too much space, poorly used. That might sound paradoxical, that you could ever create too much space in such a crowded city, but superskyscrapers were cities in their own right, cities within cities, and hard to fill. Tall simply for the sake of being tall, form had to go begging for function and was often left wanting.

Essentially, Gant got all the floor area that the Department of Public Opinion didn't need. Allowing for a private washroom and conference area, a custom mastodon desk, and more filing cabinets than he would fill with hard copy if he lived to be Kite's age, Harry still had enough room (and enough window) to accommodate in-office helicopter service, if he were ever so inclined. Not that he would be. Heights.

So he filled up all the space he didn't need with clutter. Toys, mostly, like an exercise gyroscope and an Electric Train Map of the Lightning Transit system, and most recently, a holographic game projection rig twice the size of a standard pool table. Gant had left the rig turned on, perhaps to impress her, perhaps only to further fill up excess space. Between two control panels studded with joysticks, buttons, and switches, an illusory island floated, a Great American Consumer Island: an island with two factories on it, one white and one black. There were also hundreds of little pink houses with tiny hologram people living in them, tiny people who watched tiny televisions, mowed tiny lawns, and bought tiny ice-cream cones from tiny ice-cream trucks. Some of the trucks were white and some of them were black. They came from the factories and engaged in an idealized laissez-faire contest for the islanders' patronage.

"It's a teaching tool," Gant said, "for developing capitalist democracies that haven't got the hang of it yet. Albania has a thousand on order."

"Where are the little hologram landfills?"

"It's a simplified economic model, Joan. Waste disposal is beyond the scope of the simulation. And before you ask, no, the truck drivers don't unionize."

"Sounds like a great teaching tool for Albanian management. Mind if I smoke?"

"You still do that, huh?"

"Still have all my bad habits," Joan agreed. "Same as you. But thanks for the flowers."

"You're welcome." He smiled. "Thanks for not blowing yourself up with that shark. It's good to see you. I missed you."

She looked again at his new toy, imaginary ice-cream trucks flitting hither and yon, and it struck her that this too big, too cluttered, too impractical office was in fact just right for Harry. Which was a good thing to be reminded of even as she realized she'd missed him too. "On the phone," she said, "you said you'd help me with the Amberson Teaneck investigation."

"I said I'd be glad to talk about it. But you know as well as I do, Joan, that he wasn't killed by an Automatic Servant."

"I had my doubts when Lexa first mentioned it," Joan said. "I told her that as far as I knew, defeating the behavioral inhibitors on a Servant would be too difficult and too resource-intensive to be worth the trouble. But then during breakfast CNN was replaying footage from Philo Dufresne's latest raid, and I thought, this is a world where people build their own submarines because they don't agree with the standing environmental policy, so who am I kidding? It's possible. And if there's corporate or government involvement, it's more than possible."

"If it *were* possible," Gant said, "it would be very very very unlikely. People *love* the Automatic Servant, Joan; it's a neat product that makes them happy by making their lives a whole lot easier. Why spoil that by focusing attention on a single unpleasant event that probably has nothing to do with the Servant? Why encourage other maniacs out there to try the same sort of stunt?"

"You're honestly telling me you wouldn't want to know if somebody were using your neat product to commit murder?"

"Of course I would. You know how much I spend on lobbying and litigation every year to make sure the Pentagon can't manufacture android soldiers. Not with *my* patent. Hell, I still have reservations about Electric Police, especially with the LAPD constantly petitioning for a deadly force model. So you can be sure I'd be on it like *that*"—he snapped his fingers— "if I had the slightest inkling that someone had used a Servant to commit a violent felony."

"And you haven't had an inkling."

"Not the slightest."

"Well forgive my nagging, Harry, but how hard have you *looked* for an inkling? Have you even read the homicide file on the murder?"

"Well, no. That's a confidential document, isn't it? The police didn't offer to show it to me."

"You did talk to the police, though, right?"

"Vanna talked to them."

"And?"

"And, nothing. She said they did have some technical questions about Servant design, but no accusations were made. She cooperated fully, asked them to please be sensitive concerning wild speculation, and said goodbye. And that's that."

"That's that. They haven't called again with anything more?"

"Not that Vanna's told me."

"Then why did you ask me to come here, if all you have to tell me is that there's nothing to tell?"

"Just to see you," he said. "Breathe a little secondhand smoke, listen to you talk about how irresponsible I am. Like old times. *And,*" he added quickly, "to say that if you won't take it from me that my Servants are innocent, you should go visit John Hoover."

"Who?"

Gant turned his head. "Toby."

The Servant startled Joan by seeming to appear from nowhere, though in fact it had been in plain sight among the clutter all this time, motionless, and she just hadn't noticed it. It came forward without a word, and offered Joan an envelope.

"What's this?" Joan asked.

"Two round-trip Lightning Transit tickets to Atlantic City. You missed the early Gambler's Express, but there's a train leaving at 11:30 and another at 12:59. If you want, I can have a cab meet you downstairs and take you to Grand Central."

"Who's John Hoover?"

"He's the man who invented the Self-Motivating Android. He was with Disney originally, then came over and worked for me for three years after I bought the patent. He's retired now, living in New Jersey, but he still keeps up with the corporation's doings. Last night right before you called he faxed me this nice note, saying that he'd heard about Amberson Teaneck and also heard that some newspapers were thinking of whipping up a scandal. He wanted me to know that he'd be more than willing to talk to reporters if I thought it might help. Sweet man, really."

Joan opened the envelope. Along with the tickets was a card with John Hoover's address and phone number. "If I take the trouble of going to see this guy," she said, "is he going to tell me anything useful? Or just give me another version of how very very very unlikely it is that a Servant could be reprogrammed?"

"Well, he's a *scientist.* He could probably be a lot more specific about why it's unlikely." Gant spread his hands. "Look, Joan, I'm telling you as plainly as I can that there's nothing to these rumors. But maybe Hoover can show you the math."

"All right. I should call him first."

"When you get back," said Harry, "we could have dinner."

Joan looked him in the eye, then glanced back down at the address card. "Tell me one other thing," she said. "How does a guy who's retired and living in Jersey know what investigative reporters in New York are planning to do? I mean as far as Lexa told me there hasn't been a whisper about this in the media. For all her cooperativeness with the police, your Vanna Domingo has most news agencies terrified of libel suits."

Gant shrugged. "Vanna can be harsh sometimes, but that's because she's had a hard life. She's loyal. And so's John Hoover. He cares about the reputation of the Servant, so I guess he just heard somehow. How did Lexa Thatcher get a copy of the police report on Amberson Teaneck's death?"

Joan folded the envelope and put it in her pocket. "Information is Lexa's business," she said. "Tell you what, I'll talk to you about dinner after I talk to John Hoover."

"Good."

Joan shook her head, smiling in spite of herself. "That remains to be seen, Harry. But thanks for asking."

8

If by some chance you are placed on the "10 Most Wanted List" that is a signal that the FBI are indeed conducting a manhunt. It is also the hint that they have uncovered some clues and feel confident they can nab you soon. The List is a public relations gimmick that Hooper, or whatever his name is, dreamed up to show the FBI as super sleuths. . . . When you are placed on the List, go deeper underground.

—Abbie Hoffman, *Steal This Book*

Lexa Gets the Morning Paper

Robbins Reef Lighthouse lay two miles southwest of the Statue of Liberty, off the coast of Staten Island. Automated and closed to the public, the light's only authorized visitors were a pair of Coast Guard tenders who came out twice a month for maintenance and inspection. The tenders were both dedicated seamen, patriotic to a T, and under most circumstances would have had no truck with pirates of any kind. But one of them had lost his grandfather to pesticide-induced cancer on a California grape farm, and the other had seen his family bankrupted after the 2020 oil blowout killed off the fish stocks in Alaska's Bristol Bay. From which it followed that if a band of tree-hugging outlaws wanted to use Robbins Reef as an occasional hideout and rendezvous spot, that was acceptable, so long as said tree-huggers left no evidence of their visits and took particular care not to be seen coming or going by anyone at the nearby Bayonne Military Pier.

The lighthouse was small, a stone-foundationed fireplug capping a high point on the reef. Inside, pie-wedge spaces radiated from a central hub: storeroom, bedroom, adjoining kitchen, and sitting room. There was also a bathroom with a cast-iron tub that got its water from an exterior storage tank; Morris Kazenstein had restored the plumbing and added a discreet pair of rainwater catchments to the tank. In the bedroom, left empty after the departure of the last live-in keeper, Morris had put in a false ceiling with a recessed hanging futon that could be raised and lowered on pulleys. This and a secret kitchen compartment containing cookware, propane fuel, and Nicaraguan coffee constituted the extent of the amenities. It was Spartan but cozy, a good place to go when F.B.I. surveillance of New Bedford–Stuyvesant made Lexa's apartment too dangerous for Philo. It was also closer to Pirate's Cove, quicker to get to if, for whatever reason, they were in a hurry.

Sometimes, crying out in the throes of passion, Toshiro Goodhead switched to his native Japanese, while Philo regressed to the German dialect of the Pennsylvania Dutch, and Lexa, fluent in Arabic, French, Russian, and Spanish, became a veritable Berlitz of eros. When at last they slept, their ears still burned with the afterecho of a Babel of tongues. They dreamed of maps and nations and woke to the press of kind flesh.

Lexa, as usual, was first awake. Philo lay on his back to her right, his broad chest a pillow for her cheek. Toshiro, his head at the other end of the futon, touched his lips to her feet as he slept on. Lexa laid a hand on each of them and felt the slow synchrony of their breathing. She smiled, content.

From elsewhere in the lighthouse came the smells of brewing coffee and fresh ink: Ellen Leeuwenhoek had returned from Washington. Careful not to wake her bedmates, Lexa got up, doing a barefoot dance on the cold floor. Robbins Reef was not heated. She padded out past the storeroom and saw that the cot where Rabi slept was empty, the thick quilts tossed aside; from the bath she heard laughter and splashing. She went to the kitchen and fixed a sugar with coffee.

The new *Long Distance Call* was on the table in the sitting room. It was as close to a work of art as a newspaper could be. Taking the millennial collapse of the *Village Voice* as a sign, Lexa had decided that an alternative weekly aimed solely at the reader on the street could not hope to wield the sort of influence she desired; instead, she sought to seduce the journalists and editors of other, more established papers. After being laid out on computer, the *Call* was handset on an Electric Gutenberg, which gave the same raised texture to the type and photo engravings as a full manual press. The newsprint too had texture, coarse and thick, weighted like history. And the *Call*'s prose more than matched the physical appearance of the paper. Though not every story Lexa broke got picked up by the *Times,* many did, and she received lots of calls for help on sources. There were even rumors that the senior editor of the *Washington Post* chewed pieces of the *Call* headmast as an aphrodisiac, which was not as strange as it sounded. The *Long Distance Call* was edible: placed on the tongue, its pages tasted faintly of honey, its ink of precious spice.

"Hey there," Lexa said, strolling into the bathroom. Ellen sat in the tub with Rabi, whose chicken pox had begun to fade.

Rabi smirked at her. "You were *loud* last night," she said.

"You will be too one day," Lexa assured her. "You have my vocal cords." She kissed Ellen hello and managed to squeeze herself into the tub, which had been cast for a big and tall lighthouse keeper, without spilling her coffee. "What's the word from D.C.?"

"Monotony," Ellen said. Reaching for a sponge, she started soaping Lexa's back. "If you thought the Democratic nominees for president were all alike, wait till you read the Republicans' stump speeches. The only interesting bit so far has to do with Senator Young, and it doesn't involve her platform. The F.B.I. background check turned up three extra husbands she hadn't told anyone about. CNN is breaking the story this afternoon, but the senator wanted to offer you an interview for the next *Call*. She's heard rumors somewhere that you might be sympathetic to her situation."

"Hmm," said Lexa. "What's protocol on that if she gets elected? Are they all First Spouse or does she have to rank them?"

"I think she nominates rankings," Ellen said, "and then the Senate holds a hearing for each husband and votes whether or not to confirm."

"Conjugal-rank hearings for the Executive Harem. Now *that* would be a story to report."

"Yeah, in another century, maybe." Ellen laughed. "So where's Seraphina this morning? Didn't she come out last night?"

"She's being a *free spirit*," Rabi said.

"Oh *is* she," said Ellen. She scrubbed Lexa's back. "More priceless artwork?"

"No," said Lexa. "Microchips. Sometime last month Morris sussed out a classified file on a government artificial intelligence project and decided he wanted dibs. So he went hacking and forged special procurement orders to get a prototype of the hardware delivered to Grand Central Station. Apparently the F.B.I. has a mail-drop there for deep-cover agents. Morris and Seraphina and Twenty-Nine Words are going to pick up the chips this morning."

"*Morris* is posing as a fed?"

"A domestic intelligence field operative." Lexa tilted her head back, encouraging Ellen to sponge beneath her chin. "I have a feeling we'll be hearing about it on the news."

Morris Gets His Mail While Maxwell Catches a Scent

He came into Grand Central Station looking like a mad rabbi who'd rifled Pancho Villa's wardrobe and then mugged a bag lady for good measure. The disguise was so transparent and so conspicuous—he had *goofball terrorist* written all over him—that at first the federal agents lying in wait for him couldn't believe their eyes. After the initial shock, they snickered. That was a mistake.

The great terminus was gilded by sun rays, imported but genuine: piped in by a series of articulated periscopes that rose hundreds of feet above the roof of the station. The periscopes tracked the sun's progress throughout the day, funneling stolen shafts of light down into the gloom of the terminal, to crisscross beneath an inverted blue bowl. At night the periscopes rested and the bowl filled up with stars, holographic constellations shining in a recorded heaven. These and other flourishes had cost Harry Gant a mint, though as usual price did not concern him nearly as much as the neatness of the effect. Like many New Yorkers who'd been born too late to see it, Gant had always regretted missing Grand Central's heyday, and the success of Lightning Transit was all the excuse he'd needed to organize a complete renovation of the badly deteriorated station. Saving the fun parts of the revamping project for himself, he'd delegated money worries to Clayton Bryce and asked Vanna Domingo to handle the human-engineering problem—i.e., the relocation of the war veterans and other vagrants who used Grand Central as a squatter's camp. After all, Vanna had been one of them herself not long before, and it stood to reason she'd know what best to do about them.

She did. On a cold autumn night in 2018, security guards swept the tunnels, corridors, and open spaces of the terminal, rousting the squatters. The guards offered free subway tokens as an inducement to move on and used force only as a last resort, but they did not take no for an answer: Grand Central Station no longer had room for unticketed loiterers. Pennsylvania Station, home of Amtrak, Gant's fast-fading competitor, was suggested as an alternate future sleeping site, though in fact Penn Station was already choked with a transient population of its own. By dawn it was doubly choked; by 2019 Amtrak had folded, and the PATH and Long Island Railroad commuter lines were pleading for track space in Grand Central, which had once again become a showpiece. Vanna Domingo's security force—dubbed the Pleasant Trip Squad—worked to keep it that way.

Which is why, even if he hadn't already known that he was walking into a trap, Morris Kazenstein would have been suspicious. He knew very well how he looked, clad in a threadbare serape, felt sombrero, Levis, and cowboy boots, with a greasy shopping bag in each hand and a thick black beard and black ringlets obscuring his face. On a normal day the Pleasant Trippers would have been on him in a flash, asking if he needed "help," but not today: today the F.B.I. had told them to hang back and leave the tramps and indigents alone until the arrest had been made. The door guards stared at Morris but let him in.

They also let in Tank Commander Maxwell, who'd been kicked out of the library this morning after being caught burying the 'Rubicon–Shrapnel' volume of the *Encyclopedia Britannica* in a fern pot. Purely by chance he clumped in a few paces behind Morris, and the F.B.I. spotters marked him, wondering if he might be a confederate; but instead of following the Jewish pirate he turned left towards a newsstand, drawn by a glimpse of bare flesh.

Morris, meanwhile, crossed beneath the empty star bowl—polite, clean, ticket-holding passengers waited here on long benches for their trains to be called—and made for the post office window in the northeast corner. Suspended by safety harnesses along a ledge near the rim of the bowl, a pair of F.B.I. snipers kept their weapons trained on him, ready to take him down if he made any threatening moves against the civilians. He didn't. He walked right up to the window, where Un-Un-American Activities Agent Ernest G. Vogelsang greeted him in a borrowed postal uniform.

"Can I help you?" Vogelsang asked.

Maxwell turned a circular rack of paperbacks, stocked mainly with fiftieth-anniversary editions of Erica Jong's *Fear of Flying.* The bared navel and crescent sliver of breast on the cover agitated him, and he began cramming books into his jacket pockets. The newsstand attendant, an F.B.I. agent presently watching Morris Kazenstein through high-powered binoculars, did not object.

Morris set his shopping bags on the floor. "I'm here to pick up a package," he said, flashing a yellow paper slip. As he passed it to Vogelsang he rapped his knuckles on the counter three times.

Vogelsang offered him a code phrase in return: "Always nice to get packages this time of year, isn't it?"

"Actually," said Morris, "I prefer my packages around the Fourth of July."

"You must be a real patriot, then."

"I'd gladly destroy the village in order to save it," Morris agreed.

Vogelsang nodded. "I have your package right here."

Up on the ledge, a silver squirrel bit one of the snipers, rendering him unconscious before he could cry out. The second sniper felt a breeze from an open hatchway behind him and was struck in the back by an Arctic bunny; he too nodded off, slumping forward in his harness.

Over the station's P.A. system, Seraphina Dufresne's voice announced: "Track 29 has been cleared for outbound traffic."

Vogelsang brought out a plastic box the size of an eyeglass case, and thumbed it open to show Morris the four microchips nestled inside. "All yours," he said. "Just sign here."

He set an Electric Clipboard next to the microchip box, on his side of the counter. Morris had to reach for it, and when he did, Vogelsang slapped a manacle on his wrist.

"You're under arrest," Vogelsang informed him, "for attempted theft of government property, impersonation of a federal agent, computer espionage, and suspicion of piracy on the high seas. You have the right to remain—"

Morris pulled his arm back, leaving behind the hand, which shook off the manacle and attacked Vogelsang. Moving like a five-legged tarantula, it scuttled up the front of Vogelsang's shirt, chinned itself on his chin, and pressed a chloroform-soaked palm over his mouth and nose.

"'Night, Ernest," Morris said. His real hand popped out of the sleeve vacated by the fake, and grabbed the microchip case. Then he said, "Cover me," and clouds of thick white vapor began boiling out of the shopping bags. Vogelsang's backup team hesitated, expecting the snipers to open fire; by the time they realized the snipers were asleep, the entire northeast corner of the terminal was obscured by fog. The waiting passengers looked around curiously and wondered if a steam pipe had burst.

Maxwell's Marine jacket was stuffed with books, but there were still a good eight or nine copies left on the rack. He cast around for something else to carry them in. Across the terminal the rising fog began to fracture the sunbeams into colored shards, and the sudden rainbow caused Maxwell to look up and catch his breath.

Seraphina and Twenty-Nine Words for Snow were crouched on the ledge beside one of the slumbering marksmen, ready to cast nets on the feds below if that proved necessary to safeguard Morris's escape (it didn't; the F.B.I. and the Pleasant Trip Squad plunged bravely into the fog to find nothing but the discarded serape and a sombrero full of black whiskers). Twenty-Nine Words wore his polar bear outfit; Seraphina wore her African superhero suit, but against BRER Beaver's explicit instructions she'd refused to put on her helmet. Even at a great distance the green gleam of her eyes was bright enough to make Maxwell forget all about Erica Jong.

The F.B.I. agent with the binoculars came running out of the newsstand, brandishing a machine pistol. Maxwell stuck out a Leg and tripped her, clocking her across the back of the head as she went down.

Maxwell picked up the gun. When he looked up again at the ledge he saw that Seraphina and the polar bear had vanished, but this didn't bother him. He knew Grand Central's secret spaces; like Kite and Vanna, he'd lived here. Besides, he was a soldier, and he possessed the sixth sense that God grants to all the mad.

Lost in the fog, the feds and the Trippers radioed for more assistance. Maxwell flicked off the machine pistol's safety and joined in the hunt.

Breakfast at Robbins Reef

Toshiro and Ellen scrambled free-range eggs in the lighthouse kitchen, while Lexa, Philo, and Rabi shared coffee and juice at the sitting room table. Lexa had brought in Betsy's car radio last night (both the Volkswagen and Ellen's Amphibious Citroen were submerged on the reef, listening for the approach of Coast Guard launches and ready to surface at a moment's notice), so they were able to tune in the news from Grand Central.

". . . terrorists have apparently made a clean getaway, though authorities are delaying outbound trains and mounting a thorough search of the station. As yet there's been no statement made to the press, but from what we've been able to pick up listening in on the fringes, it would appear that an unidentified aboriginal rights group has intercepted a secret military shipment, possibly an experimental weapon. Now in keeping with our non-alarmist reporting policy, I should point out that there is no evidence that commuters were exposed to radiation, biochemical agents, or mind-altering substances during the course of the theft. Certainly there's no sign that officials might be planning to quarantine the terminal."

"Tom, this is Carol at the studio. I'm wondering if you might answer a question . . ."

"Go ahead, Carol."

"You mentioned earlier that the F.B.I.'s Un-Un-American Activities Division was in charge of this 'sting' operation. What can we surmise from their involvement?"

"Well, Carol, as you know, the Un-Un-American Activities Division was formed to monitor 'lesser subversives' after the end of the old Cold War with Russia."

"There's no connection here with the late Senator Joseph McCarthy, is there?"

"None at all. Senator McCarthy, of course, was associated with the 1950s House *Committee* on Un-American Activities, remembered today chiefly for its terrible abuses of governmental power. But the more recently formed F.B.I. Division is nothing like that, hence the double 'Un' . . ."

Philo had his novel-in-progress at the table and was pretending to work on it over breakfast. Since the start of the radio broadcast, he'd done nothing but cross out and rewrite the same adjective a dozen times.

"Hey." Lexa nudged him gently under the table. "You OK?"

"Seraphina is old enough to choose her own troubles," he replied, rolling the ballpoint pen in his fingers. "Besides which, Morris knows that if he gets her hurt or captured, I'll break his neck. Pretty much the only thing I'd break someone's neck for."

"I know that," Lexa said. "But are you OK?"

Philo sighed and put down his pen. Rubbed his temples. *I should be used to this by now,* he thought. He'd certainly had enough practice being a fugitive and an outsider. Even before turning pirate, even before the Pandemic, he'd never been anything but a stranger in foreign territory. Yet for all that, and for all his experience with childrearing under dire circumstances, fatherhood could still feel like the most alien country of them all.

He must have shared some of Seraphina's body chemistry, though, for the smile he gave Lexa—after a long pause—was genuine, weary but undefeated. "I'm as OK," he finally said, "as any black Mennonite felon environmentalist submarine commander can be, who can't write a noun without at least two modifiers and whose oldest kid wants to burn down the Louvre."

He took Lexa's hand across the table, and squeezed it, and Rabi belched into her orange juice and said: "Love."

"Tom," said the radio, "Tom, are you absolutely sure that no innocent bystanders were killed or maimed during this terrorist action?"

"Well, Carol, they've got the barricades drawn pretty far back, and none of us have been allowed inside the terminal yet. It would be reckless of me to speak of mayhem without more proof, though theoretically, *anything* could be going on in there . . ."

A Fifteen-Hour Egg

"Tell me again what these microchips do," Seraphina said. They were in a utility room that budded off one of the Lightning Transit track tunnels; in fact it was the same graffitied chamber where, once upon a time, Kite Edmonds and Vanna Domingo had stood their ground against an onslaught of poodle-sized rats. Now Morris fiddled with high tech beneath a dirt-caked, sixty-watt ceiling lamp. BRER Squirrel kept watch for feds in the tunnel outside.

"They take abstract information and spin a self-aware personality out of it," Morris replied. "It's similar to the technology used to create computer personality templates, but this is next-generation, much more versatile and powerful." In his hands he held a poor man's Fabergé egg, homemade from the contents of Tom Sawyer's pockets. Used string, a ticket stub, a candy wrapper, and a butterfly wing all floated in a hard resinous shell surrounding a yolk of pure Memory, a specially culled selection from Seraphina's African Knowledge Store.

"I'm not sure how it works, exactly," Morris continued. He was teasing open tiny slots in the egg shell and inserting the stolen microchips. "Some kind of pastiche effect, like making up a fairy tale using stuffed animals and other objects you see lying around your bedroom. Although in this case you're fabricating a psyche rather than a narrative."

"And it can really *think*?" Twenty-Nine Words asked.

"Well. That's probably an exaggeration. I mean it should pass a Turing test with flying colors, but true self-awareness is a toughy. The technology was pioneered by the army; they wanted to build a fully automated tank, so they took a set of these chips and wired them into the control systems of an M6 Buchanan. Then they fed the tank a big dose of military history and tactics and let it generate an id for itself."

"Did that work?"

"Apparently not the way they intended. I don't know the specifics, but my guess is it turned on them, maybe blew away a reviewing stand full of generals. The research program got cancelled in a hurry. That would have been that, except that the brown shirts at the Un-Un-American Activities Division somehow got clearance to borrow a set of the microchips for a Big Brother project of their own. This was on its way to an F.B.I. field-tech group in Silicon Valley before I had it diverted."

"This personality it's weaving," Seraphina said. "It's not just going to be an Electric Negro without a body, is it?"

"I don't know," Morris said. "Electric Africa, maybe. Have to cross our fingers and see. Even if it's a complete bust, at least the feds have one less piece of hardware to play with."

BRER Beaver, on the floor by Seraphina's foot, slapped his tail twice. "I don't like it. This whole experiment strikes me as unsafe. Artificial intelligence is nothing to be trifled with, particularly *stolen* artificial intelligence."

Morris popped another chip into the egg. "Hey Beaver, it's not your job to be *my* babysitter."

"You may have intended to include that qualification in my programming, but you forgot. Which proves my point. You're dabbling in things best left alone."

Seraphina thought to say something, but didn't. Twenty-Nine Words chose that moment to lean closer to Morris, sweeping back the hood of his polar bear suit as he did so. The pink shell of his bare ear, dainty, round, and with a lobe you could nibble on for days, made Seraphina flush.

"Not to worry," Morris said. "First thing we'll do is give it a complete psych evaluation to make sure it's user-friendly and sane." He popped in the last chip and thumbed a depression in the bottom of the egg. It beeped. "That's it. Fifteen-hour gestation period, and we'll have a baby . . . or something."

He held it up so they could all see. BRER Squirrel, minus her batteries, thumped to the floor beside him.

"I'll take that egg," Maxwell said.

BRER Beaver moved swiftly; so did Maxwell. He drew his Leg back for a field-goal attempt, kicking the Beaver hard enough to scramble its circuits.

"I'll take that egg," Maxwell said again. He pointed the machine pistol at Twenty-Nine Words, who was groping for a bunny under his bearskin. "You better not be reaching for anything other than lint, soldier. Get your hands up!"

They all put their hands up. "Listen," Morris tried to say, "you don't want to mess around with—" But Maxwell cut him off with a warning gesture. He jettisoned a few paperbacks from his jacket and pocketed the egg. Only then did he look directly at Seraphina.

"Now," Maxwell said. "Now we'll see how *you* like it, having something stolen from you. Something important to you, something you loved, maybe, *surgically removed* by a stranger. See if you think it's fun."

Still brandishing the gun, he backed out. A yellow-and-black Maintenance Engine chugged by on the near track; Maxwell snagged a handrail and swung himself aboard. The Engine carried him away.

"Oh boy," Morris said, lowering his hands.

"He stole my Africa," said Seraphina.

"Maybe we can track him down and get it back," Twenty-Nine Words said. "Do you know who he is?"

"He comes in the library sometimes. I don't know his name."

"Do you know if he's computer-literate?" Morris was rubbing his chin, calculating. "He has a gun, so he can't be that much of an intellectual, right?"

"I don't know," Seraphina said. "Do you think he might break the egg?"

"I'm more worried that he'll plug it into a computer with an open network link without testing it first. The selection of Africana we used. . . . I purposely left out Louis Farrakhan's more incendiary speeches, but there's still a biography of Toussaint L'Ouverture and a history of the Zulus in there. There's a teensy potential for trouble if it gets loose, you see what I'm saying?"

"Oh," said Seraphina.

"Oh," said Twenty-Nine Words.

BRER Beaver, splayed up against the wall, sputtered: "I told you sss . . . told you sss . . . told you sss . . ."

9

Our old friend Ayn Rand has something to offer on the subject of pollution. On a Sunday afternoon in May, 1971, she appeared before a nation-wide television audience and denounced the ecology movement for being anti-life, anti-man, and anti-mind. Among other things she said it was a last-ditch effort to destroy what remained of the capitalist system.

I've long forgotten her actual words, but my supercharged memory and her position on the ecology movement would suggest something like this:

All of you out zere beyond ze age of twenty-nine should get down on your knees every time you zee a smokestack. . . . Pollution is ze symbol of human achievement. Wizzout technolochy and pollution, man would still be living in ze stone age. . . . We are locked in a life-and-death struggle between nature and technolochy, between mindless rocks and trees and ze boundless genius of ze human mind . . .

—Jerome Tuccille, *It Usually Begins With Ayn Rand*

Safety doesn't sell.

—Lee Iacocca, "father of the Ford Pinto"

2008: The Nigeria Landfill Protest

Christian Gomez's death was made possible by a grant from the Ford Motor Company.

Between 1966 and 1980, Ford manufactured over twenty million cars and trucks with a defective automatic transmission design that allowed them to shift spontaneously from park into reverse. A vehicle left idling or parked on an incline might start rolling backwards at any time, surprising a motorist who had stooped to unload packages, or a child who had picked the wrong moment to crawl across a driveway. Runaway park-to-reverse Fords caused thousands of injuries and hundreds of deaths but remained on the road because Ford management did not believe circumstances warranted the enormous expense of a recall.

During this same period, then-Ford president Lee Iacocca took a special interest in the development of the Pinto, Ford's answer to small-sized foreign imports like the VW Beetle. Rushed into production, the Pinto's design included a poorly protected gas tank that tended to rupture and ignite during rear-end collisions at speeds as low as twenty miles per hour. A simple modification would have corrected the problem, but faced with an added manufacturing cost of $11 per car, Ford decided it would be cheaper to leave in the defect and suffer the inevitable liability lawsuits. Hundreds of Pinto passengers subsequently burned to death in accidents that would otherwise have been survivable.

This is all ancient history, of course. The Ford Pinto was recalled in 1978; in 1980 Ford switched to a new automatic transmission design, and, in lieu of a recall, mailed out warning stickers to owners of older-model automatics, advising them to be really, really careful when parking. That was that, as far as Ford was concerned.

But on May 1, 2008, Christian Gomez got a blast from the past. It had been a bad day already, a day of fruitless debate over the future of Gant Industries. The Gant Automatic Servant was shaping up to be *the* hot product of the early twenty-first century, the sort of success that offered boundless possibilities for growth and expansion of the business, sky-is-the-limit opportunities . . . all undermined by the fact that Gomez and Harry Gant couldn't agree on what to do with their profits.

Gomez wanted to invest in resource development in the new Free-Trade Zone of Sub-Saharan Africa. Entire countries full of exploitable land had become available in the aftermath of the '07 War, and a company with a steady cash flow and a wage-free Servant labor pool stood to make billions. But Harry Gant didn't think the African idea was "neat" enough. "It's not that I'm dead set against it, Christian," Gant had told him, "it just doesn't *excite* me." Of course where Harry was concerned, lack of excitement was as deadly as active dislike.

What *Harry* wanted to do with the profits from the Servant was "invest in America." Christian Gomez wasn't sure what exactly that entailed—

neither was Harry, probably—though it evidently included spending lots of money on the purchase and/or construction of very tall buildings. In a recent TV interview, Gant had confessed a secret dream to rebuild the Empire State Building (this dream was news to Gomez); he'd even gone so far as to contact a Manhattan realtor for a price quote on the property. He had also contacted Turner Broadcasting, which was looking to lease or sell the unfinished Turner Minaret in Atlanta so that CNN could afford to buy more news blimps.

Beyond the skyscraper mania, Harry wouldn't stop monkeying with their cash cow. "Little tweaks and refinements are one thing," Gomez said, waving a twenty-page wish list of Servant design changes that Gant had drafted, "but this is overkill. OK, we don't see eye to eye on the question of planned obsolescence, I can be flexible on that. As for your suggestion about making them look and sound more human, that might be worth considering once we get around to bringing out a domestic model. But right now, with our principal markets being industrial and military . . ."

"Not military," Gant said. "You know my views on that."

"We *have* to sell to the military, Harry. It's patriotic and it's smart. You know how many soldiers they lost in the Pandemic? Twenty-two percent attrition across the board. Four years later and the trained manpower shortage is still so critical they've got *women* driving fucking tanks and marching with the infantry. Rumor has it that's the real reason the war in Africa ran hot—the Pentagon got scared that conventional forces wouldn't be enough to cut it. But with Automatic GIs augmenting live units, we can get the mothers, daughters, and nukes back off the front lines."

"It's violence and I don't like it. I say no."

"Harry—"

"You know, I talked to John Hoover. *He* told me that he thought we could have a prototype domestic model ready in a year, with human form, features, and voice. Not perfect at first of course, but in time we'll be able to make Servants that look real enough to be family. *That's* the product we want to sell, Christian: a customized home appliance that doubles as a faithful friend. Forget Automatic Soldiers; I'm talking about an Automatic Companion, an Automatic Significant Other . . . well, maybe not quite that. It'll be a hundred times better than a Gant Interactive VCR, a thousand times better than a pet. Polite, hard-working, funny, sympathetic, reliable, safe . . ."

"Safe," Gomez echoed. "That's another subject you've gone overboard on in this list. The Servants don't need any more safety features."

"Not for coal-mine duty, maybe, but in a domestic role people are going to demand that they're as safe as we can make them. Hell, *I'm* going to demand it."

Gomez leafed through the pages of the wish list. "Quintuple-fail-safe behavioral inhibitors . . . morally cognizant logic circuits . . . you're talking about teaching the damn things *ethics,* Harry."

"Westinghouse has a new washing machine that can separate whites and colors by itself. Same principle."

"But will people be willing to *pay* for that principle?"

"Of course they will."

"No, Harry. Safety sounds good, but the moment it starts costing money it turns into a big loser. *Safety doesn't sell.*"

"But we're going to make it sell, Chris."

Of course half of Gant Industries belonged to Gomez, and in theory he could veto any or all of Harry's initiatives, just as Harry vetoed his; but stalemate was no victory, and as the company name suggested, it was Gant who ended up calling most of the shots. The man was indefatigable, nearly impossible to wear down once his mind was set; he responded to each and every objection with a fresh wave of enthusiasm for his own point of view. Gomez just didn't have the stamina to match him.

Something had to be done. But Gomez didn't want to break up the corporation, didn't want to jeopardize their success curve with a court battle; who knew, Harry Gant might walk away from such a battle with sole ownership of the Automatic Servant patent. No, what Gomez needed to do was find a way to shift the balance of power by as little as one percent. Gant's stubbornness would lose much of its potency if he could be outvoted.

"We have to take it public," Gomez decided. "Stockholders would ground your flights of fancy in a hurry, Harry."

So saying, Christian Gomez stepped off a street corner in downtown Atlanta, and died. A driverless '77 Ford Lincoln Continental idled at curbside, and as Gomez stepped behind it the car dropped into reverse, automatically releasing its parking brake. It rolled, clipping Gomez in the shins with its rear bumper. He fell across the back trunk like a prize buck trussed by hunters. The Lincoln jounced over a pothole and accelerated.

One witness later told police that Gomez had tried to jump off the runaway car but had been unable to. "He saw the cross street coming up and started shouting 'Help, I'm stuck, I'm stuck!'"

"Fucked," a second witness corrected. "He said 'I'm fucked.' He was right, too."

Stuck or fucked, Christian Gomez was borne backwards through one of the busier midtown intersections. Fortunately, the light was with him. Unfortunately, there was a parked car sitting just beyond the intersection, directly in the Lincoln Continental's path. Very unfortunately, that parked car turned out to be a '73 Ford Pinto—possibly the last one in the world—facing the wrong way, its Achilles' backside exposed to the oncoming Lincoln.

"It blew up," the first witness said. "The Connie couldn't have been doing more than twenty or twenty-five, but the little car just whooshed into flame. The guy on the Connie's back hood whooshed with it."

The second witness nodded affirmation. "Damn Jap imports!"

And so, in one whoosh, Harry Gant became the sole proprietor of Gant Industries and the Automatic Servant. The police inquest into the death turned up several irregularities. No owners could be found for the two cars; an attempt to trace the license plates and serial numbers through the Department of Motor Vehicles brought a response of NEGATIVE DATA OUTPUT MODALITY, which meant that the computer had lost the files. Also, investigators couldn't help remarking on the coincidence of there being two thirty-year-old Fords in working condition in the same city. Though Gomez's death was officially ruled accidental, an act of God and Detroit, Atlanta police continued to nurse suspicions that it had been more than just incredible bad luck.

The mystery might have been taken up by the media, had it not been eclipsed by an even better story. Ellen Leeuwenhoek of *The Long Distance Call* was among the first reporters to reach the scene of the accident; she'd come to downtown Atlanta on unrelated business and reached the collision site before the metal cooled. On the street corner from which Christian Gomez had taken his last step Ellen found a broken-hinged briefcase and a blue folder stamped NIGERIA LANDFILL PROPOSAL. After snapping some pictures of the wreckage she faxed the contents of the folder to Lexa Thatcher in New York City. Lexa called Joan Fine.

"Hey Joan, it's me," Lexa said. "I need some help creating a media circus. You still interested in running a campaign to limit post-war African development?"

"Interested, but pessimistic," Joan told her. "I can't find funding for a campaign like that. Seems like all the people with money either don't care or are already investing in the land grab."

"Well I think I've found a way we can raise the public consciousness a little. Guess what your ex-boyfriend is up to."

"Which ex-boyfriend?"

"The almost porn star. Harry Gant."

"Oh God," Joan said. "They talked him into making robot soldiers, didn't they?"

"No, he's still a pacifist. But he's planning to turn the former nation of Nigeria into a garbage dump."

"What?"

"I have in front of me a confidential proposal for a two-million-acre landfill to be constructed in the Northern High Plains region of Nigeria, under contract to the new Africorp Division of Gant Industries. They want to bring waste material to the Slave Coast in Superscow trash barges, then transfer it by rail to the landfill, which at two million acres works out to thirty-one hundred square miles of toxic refuse lying in unlined pits. There's also a companion plan to sink mineshafts into the Jos Plateau for permanent storage of nuclear waste, though as far as I can tell from this proposal, nobody has actually conducted a seismic survey to determine whether the Plateau is geologically stable."

"Jesus. How do they expect to get away with this? No, wait, stupid question. Tell you what, let's agree right now on a date and I'll start making calls. If Gant thinks he can do this without a fight, he's wrong. You back me up in print, I'll *make* him be wrong."

"I knew I could count on you."

The Nigeria Landfill Protest March was slated for June 7th—incidentally, the fourth anniversary of the Catholic Womanists' march on the Vatican. Joan rallied the ground troops while Lexa fanned the media bonfire, calling in favors to get early attention focused on the event and the issue. The protesters chose defilement as their theme: of course Africa's natural resources would continue to be exploited, everybody understood the war had been about petroleum and mineral rights despite the president's rhetoric to the contrary, but would that exploitation be chastened by respect for the Pandemic's victims, or would the reckless pursuit of profit strip away every last shred of human decency? *Dumping garbage in a graveyard:* was *that* to be the symbol of Africa's future?

Media commentators played up the high moral timbre of the march, though cynics predicted a disappointing turnout, especially if the weather was bad. Callous as it might sound, the cynics said, survivors had already put the African Pandemic behind them, forgetting it as swiftly and expediently as they had forgotten about AIDS. Job security in the whipsawing post-plague/post-war economy was of far greater interest to the American public than accusations of land rape in Nigeria; that was human nature.

Well, maybe. But by 9 A.M. on June 7th the streets surrounding the Gant (née Turner) Minaret were jammed with angry men and women—a tribute to something finer, Joan Fine liked to think, than her own propaganda skills, though in truth she'd worked damned hard to make this happen.

At 9:30 A.M., Harry Gant came out of his half-built tower to face the will of the people. He'd refused all public comment in the weeks leading up to the march, classic corporate stonewalling, but now at the moment of truth he walked out of the Minaret alone, with neither bodyguards nor press agents to protect him. He wore his best suit and tie, his hair was deliberately tousled, and above his head he waved a white flag of surrender.

A real white flag.

The crowd gave way before his capitulation. Gant trod the path they opened for him, clambering atop a huge industrial sculpture at the center of the Minaret's west concourse, an acid-scoured pyramid with a giant open hand balanced palm-upwards at its apex. There he stood, a man in a high place alone, only not alone: surrounded by a hundred thousand witnesses, with CNN gun cameras transmitting his every motion to a hundred million more. In full view of this audience, Harry Gant held up a blue folder—*the* blue folder—and tore it in half.

The cheers of the protest marchers could be heard for miles. Ellen Leeuwenhoek shot a photo essay of Gant's surrender, while Lexa Thatcher attacked her consort of the day, a sweet young Georgian boy named Comfort. Sister Ellen Fine, who had come to Atlanta despite the worsening lung cancer that would soon end her life, was moved near to tears. "Oh, Joanie," she said, "if we'd only had half as many as this in Rome . . ."

Joan whistled and cheered along with the others, but she also kept a wary eye on Harry, whom she frankly didn't believe was this much of a pushover. Corporate heads never gave in so quickly, not where such high profits were at stake. When the cheering had subsided sufficiently for Gant to address the crowd—this was a quarter of an hour later—Joan paid close attention to his words, alert for the sucker ploy she knew must be coming.

Gant spoke into a lapel mike; loudspeakers atop the Minaret boomed his voice out for blocks in all directions. He began with an apology. It had been immoral and just plain wrong, he said, to even consider the Nigeria Landfill Project. He could offer no excuse or justification for the breach, nor did he expect the public to accept one; what he could do was tell them that the recent death of his business partner, Christian Gomez, had brought Gant Industries to a crossroads, a threshold moment of change and reorganization, and today's protest had helped him see the need for a strong ethical component to that change. To this end, he would be forming a new advisory board within the company. This "Department of Public Works" (or "Public Opinion"; he wasn't quite sure of the name yet) would review the environmental and social impact of all future Gant Industries undertakings, offering guidance and—if necessary—a stern hand of reproach to Gant management.

"Right," Joan said. She shouted from the foot of the pyramid: "Who's going to head this new department, Harry? The chairman of Dutch Shell?"

Joan's voice was not miked, but Gant heard her, and repeated her words in his response: "Ms. Joan Fine, who doesn't trust me—good for her—has just asked a very important question. She wants to know who's going to be in charge of this new department I'm proposing. I'll state it clearly for the record, and if you find out later that I've lied I encourage you all to phone Washington and sic a congressional subcommittee on me: Gant Industries' environmental and social policy will *not* be set by Shell Petroleum, or by the friendly but somewhat partisan folks at Union Carbide, De Beers Mineral, or I. G. Farben GmbH & Co.

"As I see it, there are only two people with sufficient credibility to serve as my new conscience. Robert Redford, unfortunately, is no longer with us. That leaves you, Joan." The man in the high place alone looked to the foot of the pyramid and smiled. "Joan Fine will be the new comptroller of public works at Gant Industries. She'll start work as soon as she's willing, at a salary and benefit level low enough to make clear to everyone that she's not being bought out; and if she doesn't give me at least enough grief to make me regret having hired her, she will not have fulfilled her mandate.

"Ladies and gentlemen, thank you again for coming here today to communicate your dissatisfaction to me. Our great American capitalist system is based on the law of supply and demand; I trust you'll remember my invitation to smack me with Big Government if Ms. Fine and I fail to supply what you have demanded. In the meantime, please, enjoy the summer weather and the southern hospitality of Atlanta, and have a wonderful day."

2023: A Nineteenth Amendment Poster Girl

Joan and Kite arrived at Grand Central in time to catch the 11:30 Atlantic City Thunderbolt. Harry Gant had phoned ahead from the Phoenix and ordered a private lounge car coupled to the rear of the train. Joan might have refused the luxury, except that the rest of the train was nonsmoking; besides which, Kite had no intention of giving up an opportunity to ride in style. "Let's not be too self-mortifying before lunch, Joan."

The lounge car was pressurized, its exterior as streamlined as any other part of the bullet train, but inside it was furnished like a Prohibition-era speak-easy, with red velvet wall-to-wall carpet, dark wood ceiling, slow-rotating fans, a player piano, octagonal mahogany-and-suede poker tables, batwing chairs, and an Automatic Servant (Sam 101) tending bar. For the pleasure of those passengers who found the real landscape boring or unromantic, projector screens could be lowered over the lounge car's windows, and any one of a thousand artificial views selected from a recorded library; since the train rode smoothly on a cushion of magnets, with little sense of motion except when accelerating and decelerating near stations, the chosen views could be either moving or static according to passenger preference. Fixed overlooks of an idealized Chicago waterfront were especially popular.

Joan and Kite had only just boarded when a conductor announced that the Thunderbolt would be delayed in the station, pending a search by Un-Un-American agents. Anxious to be underway, Joan lowered the projector screens and selected a high-speed lunar panorama, with little green men in moon buggies who raced the train across the Sea of Tranquility; she also turned on the TV over the bar. Kite had Sam 101 bring her a tumbler of iced rum, and settled into a comfortably sprung batwing chair to read a used copy of *Atlas Shrugged* she'd bought with her autograph money. Both women lit cigarettes.

On television, famed disaster chronicler Tad Winston Peller was being interviewed by talk show host Xander Menudo.

"I heard a rumor," Xander was saying, "that you're related to the late Hollywood director Irwin Allen. Now I'm not sure how many of the viewers will *remember* Allen, but—"

"We're *spiritually* related," said Peller. "Though of course Irwin lived in much simpler times than we do."

He had chubby cheeks, Peller did; they'd been chubby in his twenties, at the time of his first author photo, and they were still chubby today, though with the onset of middle age they were beginning to droop and form jowls. "Tad Winston Peller," one critic had noted, "is turning into a human Hush Puppie."

"Well tell us," said Xander, "and I know you get asked this on every show, after every book you write, and yet still the topic never ceases to fascinate: what is it that makes you want to chronicle catastrophes? Why the love affair with plane crashes, tidal waves, and now earthquakes?"

"I'm not so sure it's a *love affair* . . ."

"Well, but by that I only mean that you show a strong devotion to—"

"What I'm *devoted* to," Peller interrupted him, "what moves me, what I'm really trying to chronicle in my books . . . it's this generation . . . by which I mean both this generation of human beings coming of age right now, and also my own, my personal generation, the generation that came of age at the millennium. Which is a *lost* generation."

"Which, your generation, or this one?"

"Mine . . . that is, both . . . that is, it's *all* lost, it's getting more lost all the time. If I were a priest rather than a member of the literati, I'd probably be out in the desert somewhere, warning about the last days."

"Ah," Xander nodded sagely. "The Apocalypse."

"Exactly, the Apocalypse. I think the Apocalypse speaks to us—'us' meaning the lost generation, *both* lost generations, lost people everywhere— it speaks to us like nothing else can anymore. I can remember the bleakness of my college years, coming into adulthood under such a terrible shadow . . ."

"The aftermath of the Pandemic. The African and Syrian wars."

"Well, yes, of course, those things too, though what I'm primarily referring to is the overwhelming sense of *ennui* that afflicted me and my fellow classmates at Bennington. All our money and privilege couldn't buy a cure for our basic disaffection with life, a disaffection that was and is, perhaps, the greatest disaster of all."

"So true," agreed Xander. "'All dressed up and no place to go.' I can't think of a more tragic sentiment."

"No. Neither can I."

"Kite?" Joan said.

"Hmm?"

"Do you ever feel like giving up hope on the human race?"

"Periodically." Kite looked up from her book. "But then I remember how many lost generations I've seen make good in spite of their overweening self-pity, and reality snaps back into perspective." She squinted at the television. "He's a fat little chipmunk, isn't he?"

"The fattest," Joan agreed.

"Hope." Kite repeated, taking a swallow of rum. "A feminist quizzed me on that subject once. Did I ever tell you that one, how the suffragettes tried to make a hero out of me?"

"No. Did they?"

"God's truth. Wanted me for a Nineteenth Amendment poster girl." Kite stared at the ceiling and recited, as if reading from an old broadside: "'Sarah Emma "Kite" Edmonds, native of Prince William parish, New Brunswick, who on her thirteenth birthday received as a gift from her mother a copy of M. M. Ballou's *Fanny Campbell, the Female Pirate Captain.* This innocuous present—the first novel-length fiction the young Sarah had ever read, and intended solely as a diverting pastime—so inspired her that she cut her hair, assumed male attire and the alias Frank Thompson, and traveled south to the United States to seek her fortune as a man. She obtained masculine employment, first as a door-by-door Bible seller in the state of Connecticut, then as a more general purveyor of fine literature in the city of Flint, Michigan. It was also in Flint that she answered her new country's call in its hour of need and joined the Union Army of the Potomac, serving as nurse and foot soldier, and demonstrating by her conduct over the course of the four-year conflict both the competence and the civilizing influence that is womankind at her empowered best.' Etcetera." Kite chuckled. "These New England feminists, Joan, they wrote an entire biography—the length of a small pamphlet—without ever consulting me personally. Made me out to be quite the saintly figure, not a very polite thing to do without permission. So happened I was in Sonora at the time, beyond the reach of the mails and presumed dead, and this tract had been in print for half a decade before I even heard of it. Another half decade passed before I finally met my first suffragette, the daughter of a friend of a friend of Susan B. Anthony. We did lunch in Manhattan, must've been spring of nineteen ought-five.

"I showed up in full drag, of course—it seemed fitting. Puffing on a big Havana cigar, too, which did *not* make a favorable first impression. Once I'd pitched the stogie, though, we got on all right through biscuits and tea. Over soup I began voicing my objections to the Kite Edmonds biography as written, objection number one being that I hadn't intended any of my actions as a demonstration of 'womankind at her empowered best.' I put on trousers for the sake of one woman only—me—and I joined the army because I didn't know where to go to sign up as one of Fanny Campbell's pirate crew. War was my *adventure,* my escape from a dull future as some potato farmer's wife; I hadn't a care for nobler motives, I just wanted to have a good time, and not as a liberated *woman,* but as one of the boys. So it didn't seem fair, really, to cast me as a radical."

"Was the suffragette disappointed?" Joan asked.

"Disappointed would be the wrong word. You have to remember—or try to imagine—that Utopian ideals weren't the big joke then that they've since become. So many things were still new to the world: technology and all its promises, plus the whole raft of social experiments that hadn't yet been tried—communism, temperance, the Esperantists' dream of global unity through shared language. It was still easy to believe in miracles of human transformation then, before the World Wars swept most of that innocence away forever. The suffragettes never argued that women should have the vote for reasons of equality; they claimed that women were *superior* to men and wouldn't just double the lines at the polls, but would elevate the moral character of politics, and of society as a whole, to new heights undreamed of. Who knew? Men had made such a hash of things during their tenure in power, it seemed perfectly logical to suppose that women would do a better job.

"So there I was, the voice of practical experience, tucking into the Chicken Florentine and describing how a real woman had distinguished herself from men in wartime—which is to say, not at all. I confessed what a mediocre nurse I'd been, despite my innate nurturing tendencies; fact is I was much handier with a gun than with bandages. I told her about the men I'd killed, the men I'd seen killed around me, and how my aura of femininity hadn't lessened the gruesome horror of it one whit. Unfortunately, what makes war terrible isn't that the soldiers are men; it's that men are soldiers. Let women become soldiers—or politicians, or diplomats—and you haven't changed war at all. The uniforms just get a little wider through the hips.

"Well, I went rattling on and on about this, not leaving out a single cannon burst or bayonet thrust, and by dessert—a scrumptious Prussian cheesecake, as I recall—my suffragette was *ashen*. 'If what you say is true,' she told me, 'then there is no hope for tomorrow.' To which I replied: 'Oh yes there is, ma'am. War is hell despite best intentions to the contrary, it wouldn't be right to lie about that, but the war ended.' To which *she* replied: 'What difference can that make? There will be other wars; there already have been.' And I said: 'Yes, ma'am, of course that's true, there will be other wars, but *not right away;* and when they do happen, I don't intend to fight in them.' And she said: 'But others will fight in them. Another war, and another war, and another war,'—I confess, she was more realistic on this point than I was at the time—'and *another* war, each one bringing more pain and more death. And if we cannot break this cycle, if we cannot count on woman to change the fundamental nature of our reality, then I ask you: what hope can we have?'"

"And you said?"

"I said it was time to pay the check, set all thoughts of temperance aside, and go get a whiskey. I took her down to a patriots' bar I knew on Hudson Street, the Betsy Ross Saloon. Gents only, officially, but the bouncer and bartender knew I was a vet, so we had an understanding. Two fingers of Jim Beam and my suffragette got her color back; three fingers and she was ready to smoke one of my cigars. From there we went over to Washington Square, drunk as loons, and a bullyboy cop tried to arrest us for disorderly conduct and, in my case, public lewdness; so we took away his nightstick and threw him in a fountain. After which roughhousing my suffragette began to think there might be some hope for tomorrow after all."

"Did you ever actually answer her question?" Joan asked.

"Verbally, you mean? Well," said Kite, "you don't disprove someone's pessimism by adding up good and evil on a dessert napkin to see which is the greater total. Hope's a choice, not a sum; you can have as much of it as you damn well feel like having, regardless of actual circumstances. But if you try to explain that straight out to someone when they're in a bad mood, they'll assume you're being patronizing and may even throw something at you. It's better to use a little finesse."

"Get them drunk," Joan said. "Dunk a policeman."

"That's one method. It did work."

"What about your suffragette's comment that there's always another war? Did you say anything more to her about that?"

Kite shrugged. "Not much more I could say, once I'd stated the obvious. She was right. There is always another war. Thankfully, there's also always another peace."

"And you don't believe the recurrence of war makes peace meaningless?"

"Good Lord," said Kite. "Do you?"

"No," Joan said. "I'm just curious what you think."

"If you're asking me whether I think a temporary peace is *futile,* then the answer is no; I don't believe anyone who's seen war firsthand would find even five minutes' peace to be futile. But *meaningless* . . . I'm not sure any event has a meaning, until we humans decide to give it one. That's why hope is optional rather than mandatory. I think we're born with a need to explain the things that happen to us, not just to scientifically explain them but to actually create an account for them, a sort of framing-story to hang them on; and I think we have a wide variety of choices as to what our personal framing-story will be. But I also think some experiences are so overpowering that they defeat all our attempts to contain them in meaning, and those are the experiences that drive us to madness."

"Like what happened to Maxwell," Joan said.

"Like what happened to *me.*" Kite shook her stump. "The first question you ask yourself—the *first* question, even before 'Will I live?'—is 'Why? Why am I made to suffer this?'"

"Seems like you found a better answer than Maxwell did."

"No," Kite said. "I found I was able to get on without an answer, that's all. Maxwell is still grasping for one."

"Your suffragette, though," Joan said. "It can't have been *that* traumatic for her, finding out that there's no Utopia at the end of the petition drive."

"Oh no. Hers was a lesser trauma. One drawback in belonging to a race of storytellers is a tendency to forget that life isn't a story, however great the need to perceive it as one. And one of life's chiefest failings, from a storytelling perspective, is that life lacks closure."

"Closure in what sense?"

"Closure in the sense of narrative convergence, all the elements coming together, loose ends tying off neatly after a final climax. Real life is never that tidy, and it doesn't stop happening just because someone's won a victory. Where the endpaper would come in a novel, actual events are followed by *more* actual events."

"So even if woman suffrage had led to paradise on earth . . ."

". . . something still would have had to happen next," Kite said. "Further developments: births and migrations bringing new people with new ideas, older citizens adjusting their opinions in response, physical circumstances changing . . ."

"New conflicts taking shape," Joan said. "Another war."

"Well. Another struggle of *some* kind. And never mind if you've got no energy or patience left after the last one. That's what my suffragette was so upset to learn: the only enduring antidote to struggle and the suffering that accompanies it is to somehow escape the future. And the only way to do that—the only *real* way, absent the wishful closure of a fable—is to die before the future gets here. What hope is, is deciding you'd rather be nonfictional than a corpse."

"Not a hard choice, huh?"

"Never for me, no. I get tired of the bullshit, but never that tired."

Joan smiled. "Hence your impossibly advanced age."

"Damn right," Kite agreed. "You know what the ancient Egyptian vizier Ptah-hotep had to say about all this? And by the way, I'm quoting from *Bartlett's,* not from having met the man in person."

"What did he say?"

"'Be cheerful while you are alive.' Just a forty-eight-cent version of 'Have a nice day,' I suppose, but I've always thought it was good advice."

Kite signaled Sam 101 for a refill on her rum, while Joan shook a fresh cigarette from the pack. Two F.B.I. agents passed through the lounge car, checking for stowaways. Soon after they left, the train conductor blew her whistle; the car doors shut and sealed with a hiss, and the Thunderbolt glided forward out of Grand Central on its magnet cushion. At a peak speed of 340 miles per hour, Atlantic City was only thirty minutes away.

"Tell us more about this East Coast earthquake," Xander Menudo said. "Do you really believe it's possible? Now I was chemically dependent throughout high school, so I can remember nothing about plaid tectonics, or whatever they call it, but I do recall hearing somewhere that New York City is founded on solid bedrock, so—"

"*Apparently* solid," said Tad Winston Peller. "*Apparently* solid. And yet it does move . . ."

2008 Continued: A Deal with the Devil in the Middle of Nowhere

There were no Lightning trains to take Joan and Harry to their first power lunch in July of '08. After much thought and a long conversation with Lexa, Joan had agreed to discuss terms of employment, but only if she got to pick the venue. And so five weeks after the Landfill Protest March, Harry Gant flew to New York (white-knuckle all the way, but with no other choice, as Joan's lunch plan already required more time off than he could reasonably spare). Joan met him at JFK and together they caught another flight to Montreal, and from there to Quebec City ("That does it," Gant said, as severe turbulence rocked the little commuter turboprop on the final landing approach, "there's got to be a faster way to travel without leaving the ground . . ."). In Quebec City they rented a four-wheel-drive jeep and went shopping at a camping outfitter's store. Then they drove north.

And north. And north. Major highways gave way to minor highways gave way to back roads gave way to woodland fire trails. After five hours of straight driving, during which Joan refused to talk business—"We aren't there yet"—they stopped for the night at some tiny forest hamlet whose Québecois name would not fit on Gant's tongue. In the morning they drove north some more.

By noon of the second day Harry began to make jokes about meeting Santa Claus. "Relax," Joan replied. "We aren't even above the tree line." She steered the jeep down a last rutted fire trail, to a meadow bisected by a brook and a row of guardian pine saplings that blocked any further progress by car or truck; and there she stopped and parked.

"Last chance to use your satellite phone," Joan told him. "Strictly low-tech from here on in. Tell your henchlings you'll be out of touch for two days, maybe three."

"Three days?" Harry said. "Joan, just to get here has taken us—" But she was out of the jeep already, unloading a pair of drab canvas rucksacks from the back.

There were two other jeeps in the meadow, both belonging to the occupants of a wooden sentry hut stationed just this side of the pine picket. The hut was the only human habitation in sight. Right next to it, standing almost as tall, was a wooden sign, rare in that it was one of the few signs in all of separatist Quebec to be written in more than one language. The English portion read as follows:

BEYOND THIS LINE OF TREES BEGINS THE COVENANT PRIMEVAL WILDER-
NESS ZONE, CREATED BY THE QUÉBECOIS GREEN PRESERVATION ACT OF
1999. CONTRARY TO THE CUSTOM OF MOST NATIONAL PARKS AND WILD-
LIFE RESERVES, YOU ARE *NOT* AN HONORED GUEST. BY ENTERING THIS AREA
YOU UNDERTAKE TO BECOME AN UNDISTINGUISHED MEMBER OF THE LOCAL
ECOSYSTEM, WITH NO GREATER RIGHTS OR PRIVILEGES THAN ANY OTHER
ORGANISM.

PROSCRIBED ITEMS INCLUDE: FIREARMS, BOWS, AND SPEARS (ALL VA-
RIETIES), KNIVES OVER 15 CM, SOUND AND IMAGE RECORDING AND REPLAY
DEVICES (ALL VARIETIES), MAPS, COMPASSES, TIMEPIECES, FLASHLIGHTS,
PORTABLE COMMUNICATION DEVICES, SANITARY NAPKINS, TOILET PAPER.
A COMPLETE CONTRABAND LIST IS AVAILABLE IN THE WARDENS' STATION.
ALL POSSESSIONS *MUST* BE APPROVED BY THE WARDENS BEFORE PROCEED-
ING. WARDENS ARE NOT RESPONSIBLE FOR ITEMS LEFT IN UNATTENDED
VEHICLES.

TRAILBLAZING, CARTOGRAPHY, AND THE FELLING OF TREES ARE PRO-
HIBITED. THE ERECTION OF PERMANENT STRUCTURES IS PROHIBITED. HUNT-
ING AND FISHING ARE PERMITTED (BARE HANDS, POCKET KNIVES, AND BONE
HOOKS ONLY), BUT ONLY AT SUBSISTENCE LEVELS; NO "TROPHIES" MAY BE
TAKEN. FIRES MUST BE ATTENDED AT ALL TIMES AND THE REMAINS SCAT-
TERED AFTER EXTINGUISHING.

REMEMBER, *YOU ARE ON YOUR OWN.* THOUGH WARDENS CONDUCT
OCCASIONAL PATROLS TO INSURE THAT RULES ARE BEING FOLLOWED, AND
MAY AT THEIR DISCRETION AID LOST OR INJURED VISITORS, YOU SHOULD
NOT EXPECT RESCUE. HELICOPTERS WILL NOT BE SUMMONED UNDER ANY
CIRCUMSTANCES. THERE ARE *NO* EXCEPTIONS TO THIS RULE.

"Wait a minute," Gant said. "Joan—"

"Come on, Harry. We want to get moving while there's still plenty of
daylight."

"But Joan . . . no rescue teams? No *toilet paper?*"

"Just come on."

There were three wardens on duty, only one of whom would speak
English. He was pleasant enough, even if he did assume that Joan and Harry
were married. "Your husband looks nervous," he told Joan.

"That's because he *is* nervous," Joan replied. "He's from cities. He's
never seen a moose before."

"Moose?" said Harry. "They have moose?"

The two "non-English-speaking" wardens found this hilarious. They began to make wild animal noises and to mutter arcane French words like *loup* and *ours* that Gant did not find at all comforting. The friendly warden, meanwhile, checked both backpacks for contraband and used a color chart to verify that all their articles of clothing fell within an acceptable spectrum: for even unnatural hues, like the bright orange of hunters' safety vests, were forbidden here. After completing the inspection he had both Joan and Harry sign an international waiver of liability. "Put down your expected date of return," he said, "and a next-of-kin that we might contact if you are more than a season late. Also, leave the keys to your vehicle."

"No maps?" Harry said, when they had shouldered their packs and crossed beyond the row of pines. "No compass? Not that I've ever done this before, but doesn't that make it pretty easy to get lost?"

"You have to pick your landmarks very carefully," Joan agreed. "And you don't dare go too far in unless you know how to survive in the wilderness with minimal tools. Which means that the majority of the land is effectively off limits to tourists, which is the point. If you're a weekend camper out for a quick and easy commune with nature you go to La Mauricie or Mont Tremblant, which are closer to the big cities and have public rest rooms."

"But *you've* been here before. I mean—you do know how to find your way around, right?"

"I came up with Lexa Thatcher and her friend Ellen once. Back in '02, I think, definitely before the Pandemic. We got lost and almost ran out of food, but we got to see wolves so we didn't mind. Yes, wolves, and don't look so jumpy. Just follow the stream and keep your eyes open, we'll see some good things."

He did, and they did. A fox, for starters; a docile porcupine squatting on a lightning-struck stump; a pair of otters in the stream; and sometime later, a black bear, which surprised Gant by being disinterested rather than fierce. It stepped from a gap between two pines, turned its snout briefly towards the pair of humans as if to scent their intentions, and lumbered on its way without stopping.

"Huh," Gant said, only a fraction paler than normal. "That's an *ours*?"

"That's an *ours*."

"Huh. How about that."

The land to their right began to rise as the afternoon waned, forming a dotted chain of hills beside the streambed. Joan spied a distinctive natural cairn of stones at the base of one such hill and nodded in recognition. She gave a tug on Gant's sleeve. "Let's see if it's still up there."

"If what's still up where?"

"Just follow me," Joan said, and splashed across the stream.

The hill above the stone cairn was the steepest incline Harry Gant had ever tackled without the help of stairs or an escalator, and for the rest of his life he would recall this as his first and last experience with mountain climbing, a personal Everest; the modest thirty-meter ascent left him breathless with the sense of great altitudes conquered. Joan, meanwhile, clapped her hands as she reached the top and saw that she'd remembered correctly: stationed at the crest was an abandoned one-room hunter's lodge, a shack, really, but with a sun porch that jutted out over the steepest face of the hill and gave a view. Joan walked up to the lodge and moved aside the door, which no longer swung on hinges. "Good news, Harry," she said. "You get to sleep indoors tonight."

Inside, the floor planking had begun to rot through, and most of the roof was missing; any furniture had long since been broken up by previous visitors to use as fuel in the rusty oil-drum stove. Joan thunked the porch good and hard with her foot before trusting her whole weight to it, but it at least still seemed sturdy. She stepped out on the deck and used a paper match to light a cigarette.

"They don't spend much on upkeep, do they?" Gant said.

"This was built before they passed the Preservation Act," Joan told him. "They're letting it decay, same as any other human structure in the Wilderness. Not far west of here there's a nuclear power plant that never got finished, with lichen growing on the cooling towers. Of course, *north*west of here Hydro-Quebec's latest hydroelectric project just put fifty thousand acres of woodland under water. The separatist parliament's policies on the environment aren't a hundred percent consistent."

"So I've noticed," Gant said. "Processed tobacco is more natural than toilet paper?"

Joan glanced at the burning Gauloise in her hand. "Oh," she said, "that. Well, see, most of the Québecois Greens are chain-smokers . . ."

"Well I assume most of them go to the bathroom, too."

"Priorities, Harry. Anyway, the wardens counted my smokes on the way in and they'll count the butts when we come back out. And you don't even want to know what they do to people who start forest fires."

"No, probably I don't." Gant removed his pack and found an unrotted section of floor to set it on. "So now that we're here, Joan, can we talk about—"

She held up a hand to forestall him. "Before you start your pitch," she said, "come out here on the porch and take a look."

He came out, stepping carefully; with the ground sloping down almost vertically beneath it, the porch definitely qualified as heights. Looking out over the drop, he could see that they were at one end of a long, forested valley, and that the stream they had been following fed into a round coin of a lake that the westering sun's alchemy was turning from silver to bronze to copper. At the water's edge, a moose bent its head to drink; like the bear, it wasn't as fearsome an animal as he'd imagined. A noble beast, actually, at this distance. But what really moved Gant, what cut through his civilized jadedness and touched his heart more than anything else he saw, were the beavers. Real ones, not battery-powered: a family of at least six, puttering around a dam of fallen timbers.

"Huh," Gant said. "Wow."

"What do you think?" Joan asked. "Worth the hassle?"

"I don't suppose," he replied, "that you snuck a pair of binoculars past those Frenchmen."

"Sorry, Harry. We can hike down to that lake if you want."

"No, no, let's let the moose finish drinking in peace. Tell me though, is Nigeria like this?"

"There's less snow in winter, generally."

"But is it *like* this?"

"Worth not poisoning, you mean? Sure."

Harry Gant nodded. "You see?" he said. "This is *exactly* why I want to hire you."

"What do you mean?"

"All of this." He spread his arms. "Bringing me here, showing me first-hand what's at stake with this issue. Plus the obvious strength of your convictions. You're exactly the sort of person I want to be the guiding force behind environmental policy at Gant."

Joan stubbed out her cigarette on the porch railing and dropped the butt in her pocket. "Tell me something, Harry."

"Sure."

"Did you ever have any intention of opening a landfill in Africa?"

Gant blinked. "What makes you ask that?"

"I've had time to mull it over since the march," Joan said. "I remember enough about the talks we used to have when we were together back at Harvard to recognize a Harry Gant idea when I see it . . . or when I don't see it. The Automatic Servant, for instance, that feels like your style; so does the Minaret, and that business about rebuilding the Empire State Building. But waste management?" She shook her head. "Uh-uh. It's a lucrative industry, but it's not really 'neat,' is it?"

"Well . . ."

"So now what I'm thinking is, the Nigeria landfill wasn't your idea at all, it was your partner's. And I'm also thinking—this is the funny part— that maybe he hadn't gotten around to telling you about it before he died. Wouldn't that be a joke? Lexa finds out about the landfill before you do, and when she contacts you for a statement you're so surprised that you don't bother telling her that Christian Gomez kept the project a secret, that this is the first you've heard of it. Then you hear that I'm going to come down and stage a riot on your doorstep, and you still don't say anything, despite the fact that you're probably not interested enough in Gomez's plan to carry it through."

"Supposing," Gant said, "that things did sort of happen that way. I'm not saying that they did, but just suppose. Would it be a big deal to you?"

"Oh no," said Joan. "Not at all, Harry. I think it's great that I got half a million people up in arms to stop a land rape that wasn't even going to happen in the first place. Wasted effort is my specialty."

"Well, but *was* the effort wasted?"

"You tell me, Harry. Were you going to open the damn landfill or weren't you?"

"Honestly speaking, no. But listen, Joan—"

"Then *why* didn't you just tell Lexa before she broke the story? When she called you, you—"

"Now come on, Joan, that's not fair. I'm not the one who rifled Christian's briefcase before he was even pronounced dead. It's not my responsibility to stop you from jumping to conclusions based on stolen information that I don't have access to myself."

"All right, true, but Harry—"

"What *happened* was, I was away at the Atlanta morgue when Lexa first called. By the time I got back to her—I had other things on my mind, so it took a while—by that time she'd already called you and set the buildup for the protest march in motion. So there I was on the phone with her, and she was telling me, first, that Christian had been contemplating a major business move without my knowledge, and second, that Joan Fine was planning to picket. Which is a lot to absorb all at once."

"All right," Joan repeated, somewhat defensively, "I can understand why you didn't say anything at first. But you had a month, *more* than a month, to set the record straight before the protest."

"Joan, who would have believed me? Self-interested corporate leader claims he knows nothing about his own company's plan to open a gigantic landfill in Nigeria: 'Africorp Division? Billions of dollars in potential profit? Never heard of it . . .' Hell, even *I* wouldn't buy that. And if I were an environmentalist instead of an industrialist, I'm sure I'd go all out to nail the bastard despite his denials. So I had to come up with a crisis-management strategy for a situation in which the plain truth was useless, and that's when I got my idea . . ."

"Oh God. Here we go, another neat idea."

"Just hear me out, Joan. I came all this way with you without complaining, so just have another cigarette and shut up long enough to let me finish, OK? Now Christian and I had already been discussing reorganizing the corporation; we hadn't agreed at all on how to go about it, but with the success of the Automatic Servant, with our operations expanding month by month to meet increasing demand, we both recognized the need for a new management structure to facilitate Gant Industries' growth. Christian's death left the entire reorganization up to me.

"Now I'll be the first to admit that I'm unusual as corporation presidents go. I don't care much about profit; money's only really important to me in terms of the new projects it lets me invest in. One reason I never wanted stockholders is that they *do* care about profit, generally, and having to answer to their concerns would distract me from my own goals . . ."

"Building really tall buildings, for instance," Joan said.

"Right. But at the same time I realize that there are practical considerations. You can't just leave the money issue to your finance department with no guidance and expect them to do a great job; if you're going to delegate, you have to delegate *responsibly.* Christian was always the one who kept his eye on the balance sheet, who nagged me about stuff like cash flow when I wasn't paying enough attention, which was most of the time. With him gone I knew I was going to have to find a good accountant, a *creative* accountant, to head up finance and be my new money-conscience.

"Well, just as I was about to start the reorganizing, I found out from Lexa Thatcher that you all were coming down from New England to stage a protest against Christian's landfill. And whatever else went through my mind at that moment, I have to admit it made me feel good to know that somebody cared that much about Africa. About nature. Because I *like* this"— he gestured at the Wilderness surrounding them—"I'm glad it's being preserved, but for myself, left to my own devices, I'd never have the patience or the will to take care of it. The environment's like money—I know it matters but I just can't stay excited about it."

"So you've decided to delegate," Joan concluded. "To me."

"To you," Harry agreed. "That's why I staged my surrender the way I did, to focus attention on you and your cause, to give you that mandate in the eyes of the media. Now you not only have the drive and determination that I want working for Gant, you have *public credibility* as well. I thought that might be useful to you."

Joan shook her head in disbelief. "I'll grant you one thing, Harry," she said. "You aren't totally stupid. You're right, staging your surrender for CNN *did* give me credibility. The question is, why should I squander that credibility by becoming your PR flack? I can nag you about Gant environmental policy just as effectively off your payroll as on."

"Resources, though," Gant said. "Don't forget those. You'll never have the same resource base working as an independent as you would working for me. And there's another factor you shouldn't forget: the Automatic Servant itself. I own the patent."

"So?"

"Well think about it, Joan. All those companies pouring into the Free-Trade Zone right now—who do you think they're turning to to provide the work force for their new petroleum, coal, and gas fields?" Gant tapped his chest. "Me. I've got the cheapest source of industrial labor on the planet right now, which translates into a lot of leverage. You could use that leverage to influence how the African continent is treated while its assets are being developed."

"Extortion," Joan marveled. "You're talking about extorting other corporations."

"I'm talking about capitalism in action. Supply and demand: we supply the Servants, we get to make demands. Granted that some of the demands may be a bit unorthodox, but it's still just business. And it'll be a lot more effective than any direct-action campaign you could put together with Greenpeace or the Nader groups." Once more he waved his hand at the forested valley and the lake spread out below them. "Working for Gant Industries, you could see to it that Wilderness Zones like this are set up all over Africa; you could safeguard a hundred times the acreage that was at stake in the Nigeria Landfill Project. And that's just *one* possibility."

"You're the devil, Harry," Joan said. "You know that, don't you? What makes you think you have the right to make bargains about Africa's future?"

"Well it seems to me I could ask you the same question, Joan; from the look of things, your last ancestor left Africa about the same time mine did. But honestly, I don't see that rights have anything to do with it. I've got *power,* is all, and I'm willing to share it with you, pretty much for free."

"Why?"

"Because I'm not evil, that's why. I may be the devil, but I'm not evil. I don't *want* to hurt the environment, but I also don't want to be in a position where I have to think about it too much, because I know in the long run I won't think about it."

"But you *will* think about it, Harry; if I take this job, you *will*. That wasn't just bullshit, what you said to the cameras about me making you regret ever having hired me. You have no idea yet what a pain in the ass I can be in a position of authority."

"Oh," said Gant, "I think I have some idea. That's what's going to make us a good team, despite our differences: we're a match for each other's stubbornness. Are you going to take the job?"

Joan shrugged. "I don't know yet," she said, though of course she did know, and so did Harry. "Tomorrow morning we'll go down to the lake, I'll show you how to fish barehanded, or at least how to fall in the water. We'll take some other hikes, too. When we get back to civilization, that's when I'll give you my answer."

"Good," Gant said, and smiled. "This is going to be a neat partnership, Joan, you'll see."

"Doubtful," Joan replied. "Extremely doubtful. It'd be a first, a deal with the devil turning out neat. Something tells me I'm going to end up owing a lot of penance before this is over."

2023: A Gingerbread House

Atlantic City's sole monument to Donald Trump was a row of memorial slot machines in the Lightning Transit rail terminal. Seven in all, they stood against a wall bracketed by two doors marked MEN and WOMEN; above them, framed, was a series of newspaper headlines pinpointing key moments in Trump's ultimate downfall, including the bulldozing of the Taj Mahal casino complex and Trump's own death in a Cape Canaveral launch-pad fire, which had ended forever his dream of being the first Martian billionaire (T-MINUS TRUMP! the *New York Post* obituated, over a full-color photo of the exploding shuttlecraft).

"Quite a commemoration," observed Kite. "I take it no one in town cried much at the funeral."

"I don't think they gave him a funeral," said Joan. "Just don't put any money in those slots. They're designed to only give back one percent of what they take in, and the top jackpot never comes up. It's the worst gamble in the city."

"Is that part of the memorial?"

"Yes."

They left the terminal and went out onto the boardwalk to have a smoke. On the beach, a Public Works crew in safety suits gathered up a macramé of blood bags and surgical tubing left behind by the receding tide. "Ah, the seashore," said Kite, flicking ashes in the sand. "Where did you say this John Hoover's house is?"

Joan was consulting a map on the center page of a visitor's guide. "Outside the city proper, looks like. Let's get a cab."

They hailed an Electric Jitney. The driver looked up the destination on a map of his own and quoted an outrageous fare, which Joan agreed to pay; the breeze off the ocean was beginning to smell familiar, and she did not want to be reminded of Manhattan's effluvia just now.

The drive to Hoover's took ten minutes. At the entrance to a tract-housing subdivision west of downtown someone had spray-painted a message on a leaning billboard: THE MEEK SHALL INHERIT THE EARTH. THEY ARE TOO WEAK TO REFUSE. The neighborhood beyond this sign had the evacuated feel of a Love Canal or a Plessy Falls; there were very few cars parked on the street and no pedestrians at all. Nothing living, actually; Kite became alarmed as she realized that all the lawns were dead, not just brown but dead, and all the trees bare and gray, with no drifts or piles of windblown autumn leaves anywhere to be seen.

"Are you sure this is the right place?" she asked.

"This is it," replied Joan. "I've been watching the street signs."

"Hmm."

John Hoover's house was . . . different. "Easy to spot," remarked the Jitney driver, as he took Joan's money. He didn't ask if they wanted him to wait; no sooner had they alighted than the cab pulled away with a squeal of tires, choosing the quickest route out of the neighborhood.

"Hansel and Gretel," said Joan.

"A gingerbread house," Kite agreed. She stepped up to the front gate and grasped an upright of the white picket fence that surrounded Hoover's property, expecting the coarse grain of whitewashed wood; both fence and gate were actually molded plastic. "Do you hear any birds singing, Joan? Any gulls?"

"No. Not since we left the beach. You think he decorated this place himself?"

"It might explain why the neighbors left."

John Hoover's lawn was green, but of a shade and texture unknown in nature. A multicolored gravel walk led from the gate to a house that did indeed look as if it were made of frosted gingerbread. Mocha weatherproof siding had been iced with lilac window trim and shutters, darker lavender door frame and stoop, and a pink sugar-glaze roof. The front door was a glossy chocolate rectangle, the bright chimney a cherry; and just inside the picket fence, a red-and-white candy cane post supported a vanilla cream mailbox, on which the name JOHN E. HOOVER was spelled out in a cursive script that might have been squeezed from a tube. The only thing missing was a set of gingerbread children for the lawn, but who knew, maybe they'd already been eaten.

"Well," said Kite, pushing open the gate, "let's ring the bell." Joan followed her in; she bent to examine the grass and discovered that it was Astro-Turf, which made sense. "Hey Kite—" she began, then broke off, because a Hound had appeared around the corner of the house.

The Hound was Mechanical, not Electric. A V-6 gasoline engine growled in its cast-iron chassis, and a plume of exhaust jetted from beneath the steel brush that served it for a tail. The Hound's hazard-light eyes flashed amber as it padded towards them, but what riveted Joan's attention was the chrome bear trap mounted where the teeth would go on a regular watchdog. "Hey Kite," she repeated, and Kite, finger poised over the doorbell, said: "I see it."

The Hound came to an abrupt halt and eased back on its haunches, idling. From behind the house, a man's voice called out: "Hello, Miss Fine! Come on around, and bring your friend. Don't worry about Old Tolson, he won't bite until I tell him to!"

Old Tolson thumped his tail on the 'Turf; his "mouth" opened and shut with a snap. Not reassured, Kite gripped the butt of the revolver beneath her coat as she and Joan skirted past the beast.

John Hoover's backyard was also different. Here the synthetic lawn was interrupted by what might have been a carp pond; but the pond was encircled by fake palm trees, and an Electric Hippopotamus stood motionless at the water's edge. Hoover, a round-faced balding man in a dapper gray smock, had opened a panel in the Hippo's side and was tinkering with its innards. He turned and waved hello as the women approached but did not stop what he was doing.

"It's on the table, Miss Fine," Hoover said.

"What?"

"What you've come here for." Hoover gestured with a tool that seemed to be some hybrid form of wrench. "It's on the table."

A picnic table had been set up beneath one of the fake palms. On it Joan could see a box and a hurricane lantern. "I don't understand," she said. "Harry—that is, Mr. Gant—told me that you'd be willing to talk to us about the behavioral inhibitors on the Automatic Servant."

Hoover leaned forward into the Hippo, almost to the point of falling inside; for a minute only his chunky buttocks and legs were visible. He grunted; there was a clank of metal against metal and a sound like a rusty hinge being forced. The Hippo's ears flattened back against its skull.

"You're investigating the death of that Wall Street guy, right?" Hoover asked, when his head and torso had reappeared. He mopped his brow theatrically with a rag, though his exertions did not appear to have raised a drop of sweat. "Amberson Teaneck?"

"That's right," Joan said.

"And you want to know if it was an android that killed him?"

"Yes."

"And if so, who rewired the android to allow it to do that?"

"Yes."

"And if so, why?"

"That's right."

"It's a secret." Hoover pressed a finger to his lips and smiled. "I *love* secrets, Miss Fine, all kinds of secrets; in my house I have filing cabinets chock-full of secrets." He gestured again with the wrench-tool. "Everything you need to unravel this particular secret is right over there."

Kite had lifted the box from the table; once again what appeared to be made of wood turned out to be plastic, a breadloaf-sized mahogany polymer brick, its lid inlaid with a complex mosaic of interlocking slides and tabs. "A puzzle box," Kite said. "My old friend Lao had one of these to store his valuables. Not that he ever had valuables."

"That's right, a puzzle box," said John Hoover. "Get that open and you'll be well on your way to solving the mystery."

Joan studied him. "Do you *know* who killed Teaneck?"

Hoover wagged a finger at her. "That would be telling," he said. "But you have to figure it out yourself, Miss Fine. I'm giving you too many clues as it is."

"Look at this, Joan." Kite handed her the hurricane lantern, which was Electric and had a woman inside of it. A tiny hologram woman, an Electric Lamp genie whom Joan, oddly enough, recognized. Fiercely intelligent, probing dark eyes; pageboy haircut framing East European features; shapely legs accentuated by heels and a black gown that left one shoulder bare; swirling black cape; long, black cigarette holder, poised for inhaling; golden dollar-sign pendant pinned above the heart . . .

"Ayn Rand," Joan said, and the genie came to life. Fairy lips pursed around the cigarette holder's stem, then blew out a perfect smoke ring that dissipated as it reached the periphery of the lamp globe.

"How do you do, Miss Fine," the genie said. "I have heard of you." Rand's Russian immigrant voice was gruff and thickly accented: *I haf heard of you.* She added, more than a little reproachfully: "Miss Joan Fine, *formerly* Joan Gant, wife and partner to one of the most brilliant creative minds in America. Currently reduced to the level of a whim-worshipping, muscle-mystic altruist."

Joan wasn't sure what to say to this. Hoover's imminent departure spared her composing a response. The technician had closed the panel in the Hippo's side and was wiping his hands on his smock.

"Wait," Joan said. "Where are you going?"

"Inside," Hoover told her. "I'm expecting a message from my friend Roy. If you want to wait out front, I'll call and have another cab take you back to the station." He turned and made for the house.

"Wait a minute!" She might have caught his arm, but the Mechanical Hound was near, engine growling, so she didn't. John Hoover kept walking. He didn't answer or look back until he had one foot in the door.

"Start with the box, Miss Fine," Hoover said in parting. "You'll need the services of a historian to interpret the contents, but once you've done that you'll be very close to unlocking the secret of Amberson Teaneck's murder, as well as a much bigger secret. Miss Rand will tutor you in the finer points of prosecuting an argument. That should do it; you're a fairly smart woman. We'll talk again once you've put the pieces together."

He whistled, and the Hound trotted into the house. The back door shut. Joan and Kite were left in the yard with the Hippo, the palm trees, and Ayn Rand.

"Now I'm hopelessly confused," Joan said.

"He looked familiar," said Kite, unperturbed. "Do you remember the *I Love Lucy* show from last century? That's still on cable somewhere, isn't it? That man looked just like Ethel's husband."

"Kite, does any of this make any sense to you?"

"It's a conspiracy, Joan. Nothing about a conspiracy is supposed to make sense until suddenly it all makes sense. Learn to relax while you wait for the epiphany."

"No," the Electric Ayn Rand objected. "That is wrong. You must *never* relax, not while there is a problem to be solved. Relaxation is neither rational nor heroic."

"Neither are we, necessarily," answered Kite. She held the puzzle box up by her ear and shook it. "Well, I guess we start with this. The man said."

10

ADVENTURE! That's what Scouting is. You are standing at the doorway to the most exciting adventures you can imagine. Step into the
world of Scouting, and you'll find yourself hiking along trails, canoe-
ing across misty lakes, and camping under the open sky. Smell fresh
rain in the woods and fill your mouth with the taste of wild straw-
berries. At the end of a patrol bike-hike, plunge into a cool mountain
lake. Cook your meals over a camping stove. Travel the backcountry
without leaving a trace, and live well with only what you can carry in
your pockets and pack. Sound inviting? As a Scout, you can do all of
this and more.   —*The Boy Scout Handbook*

Do ONE of the following:
(a) Determine the age of five species of fish from scale samples or
identify various age classes of one or more species in a lake and report
the results.
(b) Conduct a creel census on a small lake to estimate catch per unit
effort.
(c) Examine the stomach contents of three species of fish and record
the findings.
                              —requirement #7 for the Fish and Wildlife
                                        Management merit badge

The Tuesday Afternoon Movie

Star Wars.
    On Channel 4, in a galaxy far, far away, rebel fighter pilots fought val-
iantly to destroy the Death Star before it could open fire on their secret base.

"Watch yourselves. There's a lot of fire coming from the right side of that deflection tower."

"I'm going in. Cover me, Porkins."

"I'm right with you, Red Three."

Two fighters swooped low, blasting the offending deflection tower. But Imperial turbo lasers returned fire, and suddenly Porkins was in trouble.

"I've got a problem here."

"Eject!"

"I can hold it."

"Pull up!"

"No, I'm all r—AHHHHHHH!"

Porkins's spaceship exploded in flames, and just as abruptly the climactic dogfight was interrupted by an announcement that NBC's *Tuesday Afternoon Movie* would return after these messages.

"Please to explain something," Salvatore said. He was using his Boris Badenov voice, an affectation that Frankie Lonzo found immensely irritating, especially in light of the fact that Salvatore was a fifth-generation Brooklynite whose blood ran more Italian than Russian.

"What?" said Frankie.

"Intergalactic class struggle is taking place in hard vacuum above imperialist battle station. Where precisely is noble working-class member of People's Army supposed to eject to?"

"What are you talking about?"

"He told him to eject." Salvatore gestured at the television screen, where a chubby Electric Negress was explaining why Aunt Jemima pancake mix was the very best pancake mix money could buy. "Even if parachute opens in zero atmosphere, proletarian paratrooper will land on Death Star, and either die in nuclear chain reaction or have neck broken by capitalist pawn Darth Vader."

"I don't understand," Frankie said, "why you even watch network television in the first place." Though in fact there was little choice. The satellite dish on the roof of this Aztec Deco villa had been knocked out by rifle fire when the Drug Enforcement Agency had seized the property from its previous owners. After several years in bureaucratic limbo the villa had been put up for auction and sold to the New York Aquarium. By then the surrounding neighborhood had shifted from mixed residential to industrial, and no one would have wanted to actually live there. The Aquarium's directors used the villa for storage and the occasional office party; the huge pool out back had been converted into a holding tank. But there was no money in the budget for a new satellite dish, or even a cheapo microwave antenna. It was miracle enough that the TV still worked at all.

Frankie was worried about the shark.

Echo Papandreou had trucked it over from Manhattan yesterday afternoon, along with a memo from the Aquarium Directorate that had been couched in the usual doublespeak: "This *Carcharodon* was apprehended while scavenging in an unsuitable faux-marine environment," i.e., they'd got it out of the sewers, "and is being relocated to the Special Containment Annex until some final disposal is decided upon." Below this Echo herself had scribbled: "Just in case you can't figure it out, you are *NOT* to mention our guest to anyone. P.S., its name is Meisterbrau."

The trouble with fish that had been scavenging in a faux-marine environment, Frankie thought, remembering his high school Cliffs Notes, was that they tended to suffer a faux-sea change. Around sunset yesterday Meisterbrau had begun to excrete some type of dark fluid faster than the automatic pool cleaner could filter it out, and overnight the pool had gotten murkier than a swamp. Frankie thought of the ink-spewing *Architeuthis princeps* they'd played host to last spring; he carried a sucker-shaped scar on his thigh as a permanent memento of that encounter.

"Maybe," Frankie mused, rubbing his trouser leg above the scar, "this fish should have an accident. Hey Salvatore, you got a hair dryer you don't need?"

"Please to shut up and dim window," Salvatore replied. "Televised revolution for galactic freedom is continuing."

Sorry, Echo, Frankie imagined himself explaining afterwards. *Sorry, I just stepped out of the upstairs shower and I heard this splashing in the pool, so I ran out, didn't even stop to put the blow dryer down, and then it slipped out of my hand. . . . What do you mean, "Why was the dryer on such a long extension cord?" I like to be* mobile, *that's why.*

"Please, comrade," said Salvatore. "Sunlight is making cheese of already vastly outdated special effects."

"Keep your pants on," said Frankie. He thumbed a button on the sill and the window glass became opaque, blocking out the view of the pool. On television Luke Skywalker hosed down a TIE fighter with laser fire; Salvatore cheered, and Frankie wandered off in search of cheap electrical appliances.

"Ho ho!" Salvatore chortled. "Imperialist forces are in trouble now."

A Few Good Boys

If it were truly possible to die of a broken heart, Oscar Hill would have been pushing daisies long since, for by his own reckoning he had been born at least half a century too late.

Ever since Oscar's great-great-grandfather had made the acquaintance of Lord Baden-Powell in London during the first Great War, the men of the Hill clan had all been dedicated Scoutmasters. "A few good boys," Oscar's father, Stanley, had said when Oscar was only seven. "Take a few good boys, start them out on the right path in life, and you'll have done a service to your country that you can be proud of."

This little speech took place on the front porch of the Hill homestead in rural Indiana, where except for the fact that all the American flags were guaranteed fireproof up to 3000° Fahrenheit, it might still have been 1950. And it could well be that if Oscar had only stayed in his home town, some way might have been found to ward off the specter of changing times for another generation. But the siren song of the great eastern metropolis lured him as it had so many others, and once relocated to New York City he found the twenty-first century more firmly entrenched than Kaiser Wilhelm's troops at the Somme.

The downfall of the Boy Scouts of America had begun, Oscar now believed, during the 1980s. It was in that decade that the Scouting Federation had decided to combat a nationwide decline in literacy by adding more pictures and colored charts to the *Boy Scout Handbook*. This revision was followed by stepped-up reorganization of the merit badge system, with the more traditional woodcrafts losing ground to trendier "post-industrial skills" badges. As the Nineties brought government rationing of U.S. parkland access, something called "urban survival camping" was touted as a viable alternative to the old-style weekend in the woods, at which point anyone with half a brain could have seen that perdition was just around the corner. The final blow came soon enough: in 2001—the very year that Oscar Hill rented his first New York apartment—it was announced that the Cub Scouts, Brownies, Boy Scouts, Girl Scouts, Campfire Girls, and Explorers would merge into a single age-and-gender-integrated organization.

So much for a few good boys. So much for a service to his country he could be proud of.

And so, twenty-two years after the Fall, disconsolate Scoutmaster Oscar Hill found himself escorting a troop of mostly girls—girls!—not through the great forest primeval or over the foothills of a purple mountain majesty, but along a trash-strewn back alley in some heavy industrial sector of Brooklyn. Eagle Scout Melissa Plunkett took point, waving a homemade Geiger counter before her as she marched up the alley; her sweep revealed no lethal radiation sources in the immediate vicinity. Star Scout Aubrey Denton had better luck: the soil samples she scraped from cracks in the pavement contained high concentrations of lead, mercury, and other heavy metals, all of which, she gleefully assured her comrades, could cause painful cancers if metabolized. First-Class Scouts Peggy Cates and Lucinda Mendez were too jaded to be impressed by this, but they perked up when Melissa Plunkett spotted a three-headed squirrel crouching atop a cracked bio-waste disposal canister. When the squirrel fixed all six of its eyes on Oscar Hill, Oscar nodded.

"Yup," he said, "yup, yessir, this is what it's come to."

Oblio Wattles, the Tenderfoot, brought up the rear.

Oblio was a boy, technically, but to Oscar's way of thinking he didn't count. For one thing he claimed to have been born in Moscow, Pennsylvania, which Oscar refused to believe was a real American city. For another, with his pudgy physique, center-parted hair, and circular wire-rimmed spectacles, Oblio looked altogether too much like Theodore Roosevelt. Not the young Roosevelt, who had charged with the Rough Riders up San Juan Hill and who would have made a great Boy Scout, but the older, fatter Roosevelt, who despite his presidential stature had been a perfect example of good manhood gone flabby. This of course reminded Oscar of his own expanding waistline—he was a 46 and still bloating—which was unforgivable.

The troop rounded the corner of a warehouse and came upon what they took to be an abandoned car wreck. In fact it was Frankie Lonzo's rustbucket '16 Chevy. Melissa Plunkett immediately began scanning the chassis for decaying isotopes, while Aubrey Denton scraped oxidation samples from the passenger door and Peggy and Lucinda pried open the boot in search of interesting vermin. *Gosh darn you,* Oscar thought, hating the simple efficiency with which they went about all this, *gosh darn the bunch of you, you're supposed to be interested in Basket Weaving and Social Dancing, I want* Boy Scouts—

He caught himself, took a deep breath and counted ten. His life might be one huge disappointment, but he still had certain responsibilities to fulfill. "OK, ladies," he said, addressing his unwanted charges in a fatherly tone, "time for a little question-and-answer period. Now suppose, through some miracle of God, that we were in the Adirondacks, and we found this vehicle abandoned along the hiking trail. As responsible Scouts, what would we do?"

Melissa Plunkett shot up a hand. "Recycle it?"

Oblio slipped away during the ensuing discussion, unnoticed by anyone but Oscar, who sensed his departure as a slight lessening of the pain in
his heart. If the truth were known, Oblio hated modern Scouting as much
as Oscar did, though for different reasons. What Oblio wanted to be was
neither a woodsman nor an urban survivalist, but a sailor. His mother,
though, wouldn't hear of it. "Do you want to get hepatitis like your aunt
Veruca?" she asked him. "All those hospital syringes floating around out there,
it's like begging to get an incurable disease." "But ma," Oblio protested,
"Aunt Veruca has *Alzheimer's*. That's from aluminum cookware, not swimming." "That's beside the point," his mother replied. "Now maybe when
you're older you can ride the Staten Island Ferry. On the top deck."

It was the sound of lapping water that drew him now, though he knew
without checking his map that the ocean was a mile away and there were no
lakes or rivers here. No matter; a puddle full of factory sewage held more
fascination for him than a whole menagerie of three-headed squirrels.

Oblio's heart started to beat a little faster when he found a locked gate
with a sign claiming that the property behind it was FACILITATED BY THE NEW
YORK AQUARIUM. A second sign on the gate warned him to BEWARE OF HOS-
TILE FISH, but wild sea monkeys couldn't have dragged him away by that
point. He reached into the pocket of his uniform, squishing past a peanut
butter and jelly sandwich to extract a slim metal pick.

The gate was open in moments, and Oblio stood on the deck of the
murky pool. Glancing up at the second floor of the villa, he could detect no
movement behind the blacked-out windows, but snippets of dialogue from
the *Tuesday Afternoon Movie* drifted down to him as he approached the
water's edge.

"*WAAAAAAAAHHHHH—*"

"*I've lost R2!*"

The pool was still except for the backwash from the filtering unit, but
Oblio knew there was something neat, something *impressive*, swimming
around in its depths. He could feel it in his gut. The question was how to
bring it up so he could have a look at it, maybe snap its picture. Deciding to
start with the obvious, Oblio walked along the deck to the deep end, crouched
by the five-meter mark, and smacked his palm against the surface of the water
a few times.

"*The Death Star is cleared to fire. The Death Star is cleared to fire.*"

Oblio's camera was disposable, which would have been ecologically
unsound except that he'd built it himself out of a single-serving Hi-C drink

box. Tossing his peanut butter and jelly sandwich into the pool, he pointed the camera at it and waited to see if the mystery fish would rise to the bait.

As the voice of Darth Vader moved on the face of the water, it did.

Frankie and Meisterbrau

When Frankie came out of the villa a little while later, there was a hat floating in the deep end of the pool. A green hat, sort of army green actually, fashioned in a paramilitary style that Frankie was sure he'd seen somewhere before. Even from a distance the hat also had a distinct *chewed-on* look; a toothlike white triangle had gotten caught in the ragged brim.

"This is not good," Frankie said. He set down the armload he was carrying: two blow dryers, an Electric Fan, a space heater, and a mammoth ghetto blaster with enough D-cell batteries, Frankie hoped, to barbecue a whale. The only thing he hadn't been able to scrounge up was an extension cord, which could be a problem if the boom box didn't work.

"Anybody here?" Frankie called, in case the hat's owner was hiding behind a deck chair. No one answered, but looking around Frankie spotted something else. He skirted the pool carefully; over by the five-meter mark he picked up a Hi-C drink box with a plastic camera lens and a peanut butter–smudged shutter button sticking out of it. Behind him the open gate banged in the breeze, and a possible scenario began to suggest itself.

"Oh, this is not good," said Frankie. He looked at the hat, too far to reach from the side of the pool. A slight current in the water was causing it to drift into the shadow cast by the diving board, and Frankie supposed if someone were to climb out on the end of that and reach down . . .

Don't even think it, he thought. *You don't need that hat for anything, and besides, what if there's still a head inside it?*

The mental wrestling match that followed might be hard to understand unless, like Frankie Lonzo, you grew up in Bensonhurst. Once one part of his brain had conceived of an act of wanton bravado, another part of his brain would generate an almost religious compulsion to go ahead and do it, even as a third part of his brain begged the first and second parts to reconsider. When the act in question was something truly dangerous, Frankie would have flashback visions of Jimmy Mireno, the brass-knuckled bully who had harried him through most of elementary school.

You scared, Lonzo? You fuckin' scared?

"Freak no, I'm not scared," Frankie said, at the diving board now. And then, as he took his first step out: "This is stupid. This is *really* freaking stupid." He slid his other foot forward, felt the diving board flex under his weight. "Poles," he said. "We ought to have poles with claws on the end of them for this shit, hooking hats out of the pool. And sonar." He scanned the surface of the water for any sign of movement below. "A nice sonar rig would definitely be a good idea."

There must have been some splashing fairly recently, because the diving board was slick with moisture, and about halfway out Frankie decided that he'd be a lot more steady in his bare feet. He also decided that the middle of the diving board was not the best place to take his sneakers off, at which point the ghost of Jimmy Mireno called him a chickenshit, at which point Frankie entered a half crouch and raised his left leg. This did bad things to his center of gravity. Somehow he managed to get his left sneaker off without toppling, but when he tried to toss it to safety his balance wavered, and the sneaker plunked into the pool. Tailored to less exacting standards than a regulation Scouting hat, it sank.

"This is very much not good," Frankie said.

One of the sliding glass doors on the villa opened and Salvatore came running out, so excited that he forgot to use his Russian accent.

"Hey," he said, "hey Frankie, I just looked out the front and your car is gone!"

"What?" said Frankie.

"Hey," said Salvatore, "what are you doing on the diving board?"

"What happened to my car?"

"How come you only have one sneaker on?"

"Salvatore, what happened to my freaking car?"

Salvatore shrugged. "It's just gone. What are you doing on the diving board with only one sneaker, Frankie?"

"Trying to get that hat out of the water."

"What hat?"

"*That* hat."

"That's a fin, Frankie."

Frankie Lonzo hadn't done a backwards somersault since third-grade gym class with Mrs. Petruski, but there's nothing like a great white shark surfacing beneath you to give you total athletic recall. As Meisterbrau's snout struck the underside of the diving board Frankie let his weight roll back, legs tucking up and over in classic form. He did it again, and again, not slowing even when he cracked the back of his skull hard enough to draw blood, though his perfect series of somersaults ended as a hands-and-knees scramble.

When his head cleared he was sitting on the deck up against the fence, as far back from the edge of the pool as it was possible to get without going out the gate. Salvatore was standing beside him, hands in pockets, with a grin on his face that made Frankie want to commit murder. The diving board was gone.

"Am I OK?" Frankie asked, checking himself for missing limbs. "Am I alive?"

Salvatore took his hands out of his pockets and held them about six inches apart. "By this much," he said.

"The diving board. What the hell, did it eat the diving board?"

"Our fish has a big appetite."

"Yeah. Bigger than you think, maybe."

"It looked weird, Frankie."

"What do you mean? Is it fatter?"

"Nah, not that. Just . . . different."

Salvatore hooked his hands into claws and held them close to his chest. Frankie had no idea what this was supposed to mean, but he did know what they were going to do next. "Help me up," he said. "My car's gone, that's fine, we're catching a cab."

"Where to?" asked Salvatore.

"Hardware store."

I I

It is now clear that Old World plagues killed at least half the population of the Aztec, Maya, and Inca civilizations shortly before their
overthrow. . . . By 1600, after some twenty waves of pestilence had
swept through the Americas, less than a tenth of the original population remained. Perhaps 90 million died, the equivalent, in today's terms,
to the loss of a billion. . . . When the Pilgrims arrived at Plymouth,
the Massachusetts and Wampanoag Indians had died so recently and
on such a scale that the settlers found empty cabins and cleared fields
waiting for their use.

—Ronald Wright, *Stolen Continents*

The Indians, in turn, learned much from the whites. . . . Many Euro-
peans tried to understand the Indians' ways and treated them fairly.
But others cheated the Indians and took their land. . . . Thousands of
Indians also died from measles, smallpox, tuberculosis, and other dis-
eases brought by the whites.

—*World Book Encyclopedia*

2004: One Hand Washes the Other

Vanna Domingo wasn't born mean. Though her subordinates in the
Department of Public Opinion would never have believed it, she'd been
a warm-hearted person once, private but kind, much given to laughter
and spontaneous fits of dancing. Despite being orphaned at an early age,
she'd managed to sustain a belief in the future for twenty-five years, until
the events of a single fortnight turned her faith and trust irrevocably
to ashes.

Her childhood was a hard-scrabble existence in a Connecticut coastal village. She learned early to tend to her own needs, as the fisherman uncle who served as her guardian was seldom home and showed no particular concern, positive or negative, for what became of her. That was all right with Vanna, who was independent by nature and saw the possibility of ultimate triumph reflected in the worst moments of loneliness and adversity. Just keep faith in tomorrow, she thought, and all else would surely follow, temporary setbacks notwithstanding. She drove herself to excel at school, taking whatever evening, weekend, and summer employment she could get to build up a few thousand dollars in savings. That and a Public Works Scholarship got her safely to Connecticut State University at Hartford, where she studied communications arts, specializing in human opinion engineering. She graduated into a depressed work market and spent seven months stumping for a job on Manhattan's Madison Avenue, subsisting primarily on three-for-a-dollar packets of instant macaroni and cheese and "bargain-price, slightly defective" fruits and vegetables, which were all that she could afford. For recreation she went ice skating at Rockefeller Center on Saturday afternoons, using a pair of skates scavenged from a dumpster (a flirtatious turnstile attendant let her sneak into the rink for free); Sunday nights she square-danced at the Betsy Ross Saloon. She kept her morale up, survived two bouts of walking pneumonia, and finally found work in February of 2004, not on Madison Avenue but at a minority-owned advertising firm called Brainstorm. After this last turn of fortune her life began to improve in exponential leaps, as Vanna had always known and expected that it someday would.

Brainstorm was cutting edge, part of a general commercial and cultural rebirth in northern Manhattan that presaged a second Harlem Renaissance. A hungry young company with its roots in community-based public relations, Brainstorm had just begun to expand into national and international advertising when Vanna Domingo signed on. Its biggest client was another African-American-run business, Carver-Biotex Designer Foodstuffs, "the left-handed sugar people."

Left-handed sugar was the final word in no-cal sweeteners: a molecular mirror image of ordinary "right-handed" sugar, it looked, bulked, and tasted like the real thing, the one key difference being that the human digestive tract had no enzymes that could break it down and absorb it. You could eat a ton of left-handed sugar without getting fat, and it didn't cause cancer in laboratory rats, either. With saccharin and aspartame made effectively obsolete, Carver-Biotex stood to inherit the entire sugar-substitute market, and as the corporation grew, Brainstorm would grow along with it.

Vanna's first assignment as an apprentice opinion engineer was with a Carver-Biotex/Brainstorm "think team" charged with dreaming up novel applications for the product. As she stirred half-and-half creamer into her coffee one morning, Vanna joked that they ought to mix equal parts left- and right-handed sugar and call it 50/50. The other members of the think team bounced the idea around and decided that such a hybrid might actually be helpful in attracting the significant minority of consumers who were reluctant to try new things. The meaningless but reassuring slogan Vanna came up with—"One Hand Washes the Other"—would encourage skittish members of the public to experiment with 50/50 first if they were nervous about switching outright to a whole new sweetener.

To make a long story short, 50/50 became a huge hit, not only with consumers but also with the sugar cane lobby, which up until 50/50's debut had been threatening legislative action to protect its market share. Brainstorm rewarded Vanna with a raise and a promotion, and the president of Carver-Biotex sent her a twenty-pound box of left-handed sugar with a golden pour spout. Her team coworkers took her out for a round of drinks at the Betsy Ross Saloon; one of them, a dark-eyed Sudanese named Terry, stayed to slow-dance with her until well after last call. Vanna's future shone brighter than ever.

Summer came. In August Vanna decided to treat herself to a long-dreamed-of camping trip: she took time off from work, filled a drab ruck-sack with low-tech gear, and went to Canada to test her survival skills in the Québecois Covenant Wilderness Zone. That's right, Vanna Domingo, the tree-hugger's nightmare, out frolicking among the *loups* and beavers. Frolicking alone—Terry couldn't get vacation time, and Vanna, still very much the independent, didn't wait. She stayed in the Zone for two weeks, living off the land, out of reach of newspapers and television. By the time she returned to civilization, all her Brainstorm coworkers were dead, and the staff of Carver-Biotex had been decimated beyond recovery.

The African Pandemic of '04 was in many ways the ideal Information Age plague, custom-tailored to the spirit of the times. Unlike a traditional contagion, it did not appear to spread from an initial outbreak site but flared in every corner of the global village simultaneously (the notion that "it started in Idaho" was a media fiction, like Mrs. O'Leary's cow) and ran its full course of more than a billion deaths—thirty-eight million in the U.S.—in less than five days, overwhelming even CNN's attempts to cover the event. In its method the Pandemic was as bloodless as modern war reportage. It didn't just kill, it cleaned house: death by meningeal fever was followed by almost unimaginably rapid decomposition of the body into dry dust and gas. Hence there were no corpses, no mass burials, no protracted tableaux of mortality and suffering to be captured on videotape for posterity; just sudden absence, as if every black African on earth had stepped aboard a UFO at midnight and been whisked off the planet, lifted clean from the stream of history.

It made for strange mourning. Like a dream already half forgotten on waking, the disaster did not seem entirely real to the survivors, especially those whose only black acquaintances were the comedians, musicians, and sports heroes they applauded on TV. Returning from the Wilderness, Vanna's first clue that something was amiss came at a BP station outside of Jonquière, where she spied an off-duty mechanic weeping over a French-dubbed cable broadcast of *In the Heat of the Night*. "What's wrong?" Vanna asked the man who pumped her gas, and he told her: "Mr. Tibbs has passed away."

One long night of nonstop driving later she walked alone through Brainstorm's empty office loft. There were no signs of catastrophe, no broken glass or flashburnt plaster, not even an overturned chair. A fax machine continued to hum in its alcove; on a desk by a window, Terry's mug awaited a refill. Everything was in order, except that nobody was home. If Vanna had bothered to check the fire stairs, she would have found four empty sets of clothes, including shoes, spread out over the landing, but she didn't poke around that much. She didn't want to poke around that much. Instead she sat at the think-team conference table and waited for everyone to come back; she was still waiting when darkness fell.

The National Guard made a sweep through Harlem the next day, shutting off gas and power in the deserted buildings. They found the jeep Vanna had driven to Canada abandoned on a side street, and had it towed, along with all the other abandoned vehicles; they broke in the front door at Brainstorm, and unplugged the fax machine. Vanna Domingo had vanished by then, vanished like the others, though unlike the others she would eventually return, rescued from Manhattan's netherworld by a man whose innocence of loss and pain seemed to render him immune to misfortune. But the woman Harry Gant met in Grand Central Station in 2017 was not the same woman who had gone missing in Harlem in 2004.

Vanna Domingo no longer believed in the future. The devil's own luck, she now understood, could not guarantee the day after tomorrow. Gant had given her back her life, *a* life anyway, and she drew strength from the immense confidence he had in himself and his works, yet she would never trust that confidence completely. Even Harry was mortal, and his naiveté frightened her. He just didn't see how fragile reality was.

But one hand washes the other. If Harry Gant didn't know enough to protect himself from a threat, Vanna would do it for him. The fact that Philo Dufresne was a black man did not enter into her consideration at all; the only black people she knew had gone away long ago and had not returned. Dufresne was simply a threat to be dealt with. *By whatever means necessary,* Vanna thought. Torpedoes and depth charges; fire and a sword. And Harry Gant need never be the wiser.

2023: Mutate or Die

Captain Chance Baker, late of the icebreaker *South Furrow,* got to the Scurvy Puffin Bar at half past six. Vanna Domingo was nowhere in sight, so he eased his way through the crowd of sailors on leave and got a navy grog to ease his stomach. He'd been serious in making his threat to Dufresne and was still determined to carry it through, but the illicit nature of what he was getting himself into made him queasy. Baker believed in the law, not just the spirit but the letter of it, and did not like breaking it for any reason. On the other hand, he'd be damned if he'd let anyone blow a ship out from under him without a payback.

At the center of the bar, a nude holographic man and woman coupled inside a column of green light. Baker, abashed by the display, chose a table away from the projection stage and focused on his grog until Vanna Domingo arrived. "Captain Baker," she greeted him, gesturing to a towheaded man who accompanied her, "this is Corporal Penzias. He'll be working with you, handling fire control on the ship."

The corporal offered a hand. "First name's Troubadour," he said.

Captain Baker hesitated a fraction too long before responding. "Corporal?" he asked, hoping to cover the rudeness. "Not navy, then?"

"Marine infantry. Combat-casualty discharge."

"A foot soldier trained for ASW?"

"Jack of all weapons systems, Captain. Anti-submarine, anti-tank, anti-air, you name it. I can move anything that shoots. Just don't ask me to wink at the target."

Penzias had no eyes.

Captain Baker had never encountered a more repulsive prosthetic replacement. The device was called a VISION Rig, or Vivid Image System Implanted Optic Neurostimulator; a long name for what looked like a pair of opera glasses jammed into Penzias's empty eye sockets, anchored in place by a skeletal bracework of stainless steel. The opera glass lenses were bulbous, probably to provide limited peripheral vision, though they also gave Penzias the profile of an insect. There was surprisingly little scar tissue, however; he'd kept his eyebrows, which meant he hadn't been blinded by a mine or a flame weapon. Baker decided not to ask for specifics.

"Let's make this quick," said Vanna, as she and Penzias took seats. "The ship is already moored at a dock in New Jersey. You'll meet the rest of the crew early tomorrow morning and proceed there directly."

"That *is* quick," Baker observed. "The son of a bitch only sank me yesterday."

"I've been planning this for a lot longer," Vanna told him. "Yesterday's attack is only the last straw. But I want the retaliation to be immediate, before Dufresne and his people have a chance to do any more damage to Gant Industries. I need you at your station by noon Thursday."

"That's less than forty-eight hours from now."

"Is that a problem?"

"Depends on the condition of the ship and where 'at my station' is. What type of vessel are we talking about?"

"One moment." Vanna opened her purse. Troubadour Penzias sucked noisily at a plastic squeeze bottle, causing Captain Baker, once again, to stare.

"Red dye no. 32," Penzias explained. Baker had assumed the splotches on the man's lips were bruises of some kind, but now he realized that Penzias's teeth and gums—the entire inside of his mouth, in fact—were stained crimson. "I drink twelve fluid ounces each day."

"Of food coloring?"

"Low-level carcinogen. I'm building up a tolerance."

"To what?"

"To cancer."

Baker kept a poker face. "Is that so?"

"It's necessary," said Penzias. "It's no use anymore to hope you won't get it. Too much poison in the air and water, and no matter where you hide it'll find you. So the only answer is to build up a tolerance. Mutate or die."

"Here it is." Vanna slid a sealed pouch across the table to Captain Baker. "Everything you need is in there: deck plan, ship's vital statistics, navigational charts, and the coordinates where you'll wait for Dufresne. Don't lose it."

"He's going to come to us?"

"You'll be carrying a special cargo. An *expensive* cargo, but one he won't be able to resist. You just be very sure, Captain Baker, that Dufresne doesn't catch you off guard."

Penzias cleared his throat; the lenses of the VISION Rig whirred and refocused. "Don't forget my perk," he told Vanna. "You haven't said anything about my perk."

"Your perk." Vanna regarded him as if he really were a bug of some kind. "Do you know how much this exterminator's mission is already costing? And you want to add the price of a useless indulgence on top of that."

"Not useless," Penzias insisted. "Not an indulgence. It isn't as if you're offering a huge bounty for Dufresne's head. My perk is my price."

"After," Vanna told him. "After you've sunk Dufresne, we'll discuss—"

"No. Tomorrow morning. I want it for the hunt."

"That's ridiculous! You have more than enough weapons on the ship already. And Dufresne will be *under* the water, so you won't need—"

"You don't need antibodies until the sickness strikes," Penzias countered. "You don't need a tolerance until you *do* need it. I want my perk."

Captain Baker watched them argue. "Is this something I should know about?" he asked.

"No," said Vanna.

"Tomorrow," said Penzias.

"Right," said Captain Baker, and thought to himself: *You're going to regret this, Chance.*

The Story of Little Jon Frum

"My Melanesian ancestors were members of the Cult of Cargo, Mr. Gant," Bartholomew Frum began.

At seven P.M. the Public Opinion Cortex was deserted except for the four men gathered near the window wall and the Electric Janitor vacuuming over by the elevator banks. Whitey Caspian stood a few paces behind

Fouad and Bartholomew, a father supporting his children, while Harry Gant leaned back in a swivel chair with his feet up to listen to what Whitey had described as "one hell of a story, Harry."

"The Cult of Cargo," Gant repeated. "Is that anything like Dianetics?"

"No sir, I don't think so, though I don't know that much about Dianetics. The Cult of Cargo first flourished on Fiji in the 1880s. The natives who lived there, having had glimpses of European and American affluence, decided they deserved the same luxuries enjoyed by the white man. But they weren't an educated people, and they knew nothing about the Industrial Revolution or the means of production. They assumed, reckoning from what little they did know, that all they needed to do was build docks, lighthouses, and customs stations—or at least the best imitations of these things that they could construct from the crude materials they had on hand—and ships would appear, by magic, bearing cargo.

"As time passed and the Cult spread to other parts of the Melanesian chain, it evolved, adapting to more modern circumstances. My own family joined the Cult in 1935, and instead of a dock they built an airstrip, with burning torches for landing lights and a driftwood ticket counter. They took the name Frum, for Jon Frum, the white pilot who was supposed to fly out of the clouds in a Red Cross plane and bring them electric lights, automobiles, and Coca-Cola."

"Huh," Harry Gant said. "Huh, how about that."

"Of course, the plane never came . . ."

"And eventually they gave up."

"Oh no. No sir. I guess in that sense it *is* like Dianetics . . . the magic didn't work, but the Cult never quite died out, it just changed tactics. In 1940, after five years without a single cargo plane landing, the Frums took a more aggressive stance. They pooled what few valuables they had and bartered a one-way steamship passage to America for my grandfather, whom they called *Little* Jon Frum. His mission was to find and kidnap President Roosevelt—or buy him, if that were possible—and bring him back alive to Melanesia. Once the Frums had their own American president, the cargo planes were sure to come . . ."

"Such poor reasoning is to be expected," Fouad Nassif interjected, "from a people with no grounding in Aristotelian logic. My own countrymen—"

"Grandfather's ultimate destination," Bartholomew continued, "was New York City, which the Frums had heard was the greatest city with the greatest cargo in the world. It was only natural that President Roosevelt would be found there too. But the steamer only took Grandfather as far as San Francisco. He arrived in California with no more than a few coins in his pockets, and he probably would have starved to death if a Japanese-American industrialist named Hideyoshi hadn't taken pity on him.

"Hideyoshi owned a pair of successful pharmaceutical factories. Being an immigrant himself, he was impressed by Little Jon's courage and determination in coming to an unknown land, even if he also thought the Cult of Cargo was the dumbest thing he'd ever heard of. He found Grandfather a place to live, hired a tutor to make him literate, and gave him a job in a warehouse loading boxes of medical supplies for shipment. Grandfather thought he'd found the Promised Land, and he was overjoyed with the slave wages Hideyoshi paid him, most of which he sent back to the other Frums in Melanesia.

"Then came World War II, and Pearl Harbor. In 1942 President Roosevelt ordered all West Coast Japanese relocated to internment camps. The government gave Hideyoshi two weeks to sell his home and his business and set his other affairs in order. As you can imagine, Mr. Gant, with that little time it was more like a yard sale than a careful liquidation of assets. Hideyoshi lost his shirt, and, in the process, his respect for America. He was particularly resentful of the white businessmen who took advantage of his helpless position to buy his property at cut-rate prices, and he vowed vengeance, but in the internment camp he contracted cholera and pneumonia and nearly died.

"Grandfather, meanwhile, spent his war years painting cargo planes for the army. He also got a night job mopping floors at the San Francisco Patent Office, which is where he met my grandmother, Hannah Kazenstein."

"Kazenstein?" The name sounded familiar; Gant had a vague recollection of seeing it on a list of suspected eco-terrorists that C. D. Singh had faxed from Washington.

"She was a black sheep in her own family," Bartholomew said. "Most of the Kazensteins were Zionists who moved to Palestine to agitate for an independent Jewish state, but Grandma Hannah wanted to be a famous American inventor. She came up with some useful gadgets, too, but didn't have the business sense to successfully market them. Consequently she was almost as poor as Grandfather when they decided to get married.

"At the end of the war Hideyoshi was released from the camp and returned to California. His bouts with disease had left him feeble, and his bitterness had made him crazy. He found my grandparents, who were the only people who would listen to his raving, and convinced them to join him in his bid for revenge. Even with the losses he'd suffered on the sale of his factories, he still had a small fortune, and Grandma Hannah was more than willing to play at conspiracy if it would fund her experiments. Grandfather still felt loyalty towards Hideyoshi, of course, and he'd also begun to miss the old Cargo Cult rituals . . ."

"Wait a minute." Gant leaned forward. "You're not saying that *your grandparents* are bankrolling Philo Dufresne, are you?"

"No, Mr. Gant, they've both been dead for forty years. Though come to think of it, I'm not sure what happened to the last of Hideyoshi's money. At any rate, their revenge strategy didn't involve any direct action against the United States or the white industrialists Hideyoshi had identified as his mortal enemies. They chose—and this just shows how badly Hideyoshi had deteriorated in the camp—to settle things Melanesian style. The Cargo Cult way.

"They started in Hawaii, buying small plots of land and using bamboo poles and sugar cane to mark off landing strips. Grandma Hannah rigged up camouflaged loudspeakers to broadcast air traffic control orders in Japanese, at a sound frequency too high for human ears to hear. *Live* humans, anyway. This time the Cult of Cargo was hoping to attract not cargo planes, but Japanese Zeroes . . ."

"But this was after the war."

"Yes sir. Grandfather still had no concept of chronological order or common sense, Grandmother didn't care whether it made sense as long as she got to build things, and Hideyoshi was bonkers. When they were done in Hawaii they returned to the mainland, where they set up more landing strips all along the California and Oregon coastline. Then they started moving east. In the New Mexico desert (it was 1947 by this time, and the flying saucer craze had just hit the papers) they constructed UFO refueling and cattle mutilation sites; in Indiana, Illinois, and Michigan they erected what Grandmother called 'wind funnel inducers' to attract tornados; and near Indian burial grounds in Georgia and Pennsylvania they established secret arsenals—containing some rather baroque Kazenstein weaponry—in case any ghost warriors wanted to take a crack at overthrowing the government. But their ultimate destination, and the master stroke of their conspiracy, centered on New York.

"I'm afraid I'm not sure what that master stroke was, or whether they pulled it off, because around that time Hideyoshi's health gave out again.

He died of recurring pneumonia in the spring of 1949. My grandmother kept extensive diaries, which is how I know all this, but she also tore pages out, and most of the hard information about what went on in New York is missing.

"But I can make some educated guesses, sir, based on what I do know. Their plan is pretty easy to figure, actually, given the pattern they'd already been following. U-boats, Mr. Gant."

"U-boats?"

"Yes, U-boats. They tried to summon Japanese warplanes on the West Coast, Martians in New Mexico, tornados in the Midwest, and Indians in the East. What would be the most obvious threat to Manhattan?"

"More Indians, I'd think," Harry Gant said. "Asking for another twenty-four dollars."

"No sir. Nazi U-boats. That was the big wartime fear, foreigners invading or shelling America, and I think Hideyoshi would have seized on it. *A secret submarine base*, sir. For what it's worth, I believe my grandparents did build and outfit a U-boat station, though they may not have completed it before Hideyoshi's death. And strangely enough, in a different way than any of them had planned, I believe the Cargo Cult magic finally worked. Instead of Nazis, it brought Dufresne."

"Huh," Gant said. "Huh. Well." His hands slapped the front of his thighs and he stood up as if to leave. In fact he wanted to call Joan and see if she felt like meeting him for a late dinner. "Well, Whitey was right, that *is* a hell of a story, I'm sure you've got a great future in Public Opinion, but—"

"That's not the whole thing, Mr. Gant. If it were just a funny story my parents had told me I would never have wasted your time. But I did a term paper on the role of conspiracy in American corporate politics in school last year, and because I was on the general topic anyway, I decided to investigate my grandparents' history a little more closely. I went to the Public Library and looked up newspapers and magazines from the late Forties, to see if there were any traces of strange goings-on; I also checked geological surveys and old maps to discover where around New York, if anywhere, someone would be likely to hide a U-boat pen.

"Now I don't know if you've ever studied a geological survey, Mr. Gant, but I can tell you, it's *boring*. Nobody does it for laughs, and in fact most of the materials I asked for had only been borrowed once before—*all on the same day,* twelve years previously. Then I noticed this . . ." He showed Gant a color Xerox of a map of New York Bay. One of the islands on the map had been circled in red.

"'Bedloe's Island,'" Gant read.

"Liberty Island, Mr. Gant. Bedloe's is what they used to call it before the statue was erected. It turns out there's a natural cavity underneath the island, one that's supposedly full of sea water. But what if . . ."

"This still isn't very convincing," Gant told him. "Don't get me wrong, I'm impressed by your thoroughness, but I don't think—"

"I found out his name."

"Hmm?"

"The name of the man who borrowed this map before me. They keep computer records of who borrows what, and I bribed a librarian to run a file search for me. The man's name, get this, was Savin Dixon Wales."

Gant looked at Whitey. Whitey looked excited. Gant didn't get it.

"I don't get it," he said. "Is that somebody famous?"

"Savin Dixon Wales, Mr. Gant. Savin *D*. Wales."

Gant blinked. "Savin' de whales?"

"Yes sir. Coincidence? I think not."

Gant looked at Whitey again. "Have you asked Vanna for her take on this?"

"Vanna had other things on her mind," Whitey said, diplomatically. "But we don't really need her input. Fouad here has already come up with a plan to nail Dufresne, if we can verify the existence of the U-boat station. You'll have to pull some strings with the city government, but the plan is nonviolent and it turns the pirates' own strategy against them."

"Do not thank me," added Fouad. "To think of this plan was only logical."

"Huh," Gant said. He forgot about dinner with Joan and sat back down. "So let's hear the details."

Five Hundred Dollars a Day Selling Pencils

Clayton Bryce took dinner at the Invisible Hand Supper Club, a Wall Street bar and grill that catered exclusively to creative accountants and tax lawyers. It was a private, relaxed atmosphere in which to unwind, sip Mai Tais, and perhaps swap gossip with a brother CPA after a hard day's number juggling. This evening, as he fattened himself on the Diminishing Returns All-You-Can-Eat Rib Platter, Clayton Bryce traded indiscretions with a friendly stranger in a spotless gray suit.

"Vanna Domingo, our comptroller of public opinion," Clayton said to the stranger. "I caught her skimming profits. . . . Oh, I've had my suspicions for months. It wasn't hard to spot the discrepancies. She was fairly clever at covering her tracks, for an amateur—must've read a primer on covert fund appropriation—but to a man such as myself, who spends his days making two and two equal five. . . . No, I'm sure I don't have to tell you. You develop a nose for wooden sums, so to speak. Particularly when the misplaced figure has six zeroes at the end of it. . . . No, I haven't reported her yet. Once I discovered it was Domingo doing the skimming, I knew that something more than simple theft must be taking place. She's got a dragon's temper, but she's too damn loyal to steal. . . . Well, I kept my mouth shut and watched where the money went. . . . A war chest! I nearly killed myself laughing when I realized she was assembling a war chest! . . .

"Shhh! Loose lips, old son! Yes, you're right, that's *precisely* whom she's planning to go to war against. On behalf of our beloved employer. . . . Some kind of back-channel deal with the French government. I'm not certain whether they're supplying personnel or just hardware. . . . Soon. The bulk of the money has already been transferred to Paris. . . . No, I doubt Gant knows a thing. Pacifist, you understand. Doesn't believe in doing business that way. . . . Job security probably has some bearing, but mainly it's loyalty. He rescued her from homelessness, now she's going to return the favor. Believe me, Harry Gant could use some rescuing, not to mention wising up . . .

"*Abject* poverty; you wouldn't believe how she was living when he found her. Sleeping in subway tunnels, eating rats for all I know. . . . In 2017. Gant's antipapist ballbuster of a wife had just walked out on the comptroller's job, much to the relief of those of us who'd had to put up with her for nine years. Gant seemed to take it well; his only noticeable reaction was that he started going for long lunches, alone, at a cafe in the Grand Central terminus. . . . It seems he was sitting at a table beneath one of the early New Babel promos. . . . You remember, the 'Completing the Dream' campaign, the posters showing the finished superskyscraper towering over Harlem? That's the one. With Gant's picture in a corner inset. That may have been what caught her eye. . . . She just marched up and dropped a box of *sugar cubes* onto his lunch plate. . . . I'm not making this up. . . . What did he do? He *talked* to her. Didn't have her arrested, but actually sat there and chatted. And somehow—this must have come from suppressed grief over his divorce—Gant convinced himself that it would be *neat* to take this little Hispanic beggar in and make her his next comptroller . . .

"True, she's worked out well enough. More savvy to the way business is supposed to be conducted than her predecessor, anyway, though her moods aren't any easier to handle. . . . Certainly she's *competent.* It's just that some of us—myself—have never been able to forget the way she looked and smelled when Gant first brought her back to the office with him. I don't think she's ever forgiven me for laughing. . . . Because I thought he was joking. The idea of giving a position of authority to anyone who'd allowed herself to sink that low. . . . I do think it's repugnant. I'm aware that our economic system necessitates a limited amount of poverty, but that doesn't mean I respect the career poor. . . . You'd never see me reduced to that level. You could take me tomorrow, take away my job, my bank account, my apartment, everything I own—it wouldn't keep me down for long. Determination and ingenuity, that's all that matters. The power of the human will. . . . I'd sell pencils, if I had to. I could make five hundred dollars a day selling pencils on the street. . . . No, I'm not exaggerating. . . . All right, make it a day and a half just to be sure. Thirty-six hours, maximum. And then, of course, I'd be ready to invest and start making some real money . . .

"So what's your name, by the way? . . . I can call you Roy, can I? And who do you work for, Roy? . . . Ah, a freelancer. . . . Amberson Teaneck, really? I didn't know he hired outside talent. Pity about what happened to him. . . . What does that mean? . . .

"Going already? You haven't eaten a thing. . . . Well, take care. . . . Yes, I meant it. Five hundred dollars in a day—a day and a half—selling pencils. I sold Amway when I was still in grade school. Electric Fuller Brush Boy in junior high. . . . I *might* be persuaded to make a bet on it. Of course if I were going to waste thirty-six hours dressed as a derelict, the stakes would have to be very high. . . . Well, feel free to track me down if you have an interesting enough offer. I'm in the book. . . . *Ciao* to you too, Roy . . ."

The Eye of Africa

A guy like that can't know too much about computers, Morris Kazenstein had figured, but he was wrong. Of course Maxwell knew about computers; he'd been a tank commander, and you didn't target the main gun on an M6 Buchanan Armored Heavy Assault Vehicle using a slide rule. Besides, no conscientious mover of library materials could afford to be computer-illiterate. Though Electric Books had so far only complemented, not replaced, the paper-and-ink variety—founded on hard copy, America had so far proved unwilling to give up altogether the tangibility and concreteness of cold print—the smart book-mover had to be ready for any eventuality. The New York Public Library already possessed extensive Electric Archives along with its other holdings; who knew when some technofetishist in the head librarian's office might order a full conversion, bound volumes and shelves chucked out in favor of bubble drives and dataports? Such a switch was probably inevitable in the long run; and if and when it came, Maxwell and the other members of the secret brotherhood would have to turn Electric as well, riding in over the phone lines on custom virus programs, boring through library storage banks like virtual silverfish, *surgically removing* every bare-tit graphic, every dirty word and erotic sentence, every last lustful datum in memory. What the hell, it would be a lot more efficient than the present method.

So yes, Maxwell knew about computers, but he didn't know what it was that he'd stolen, and to be fair, neither did Morris Kazenstein, who should have paid more attention to BRER Beaver's warnings. Artificial intelligence *wasn't* something to be trifled with, particularly if you didn't have the documentation that went with the hardware. Purloined military microchips wired into a homemade logic board, set to the task of creating consciousness from a kabbalistic stew of African songs, biographies, and broken dreams, all of the above encased in a pop art egg shell . . . well, gods and devils had been born from a lot less, hadn't they? Maxwell, unfortunately, didn't realize he was carrying around a Power in embryo and failed to take the necessary precautions.

He was lying in his room, drifting in and out of an as-usual troubled sleep, when the egg beeped. The tonal frequency of the beep was coincidentally the same one used by the M6 Buchanan to warn its crew of acquisition by air-to-ground radar; Maxwell was under the bed in a heartbeat, shouting orders to his driver to deploy smoke and find them some cover, *now*. In an adjoining bedroom, another ex-tank jock heard Maxwell's shouts through the wall and started ordering *her* crew to take evasive action. This went on for some minutes, one combat hallucination feeding the other, until it became clear to both veterans that no air strike was forthcoming.

Maxwell raised the dust ruffle of his bedspread with the same caution he'd have used unbuttoning his tank hatch in a free-fire zone. With blastproof camouflage tape covering the windows the room was in near-total blackout, but something on the night table was flashing a red pulse at three-second intervals. Maxwell unclipped a flashlight from his belt and shone it on the egg, which winked back from a tiny ruby bump on its side. He scrambled out from cover; it took several moments' frantic paging through his *Pocket Guide to Foreign Ordnance* to verify that the egg was not a Nigerian Army hand grenade.

That much made clear, Maxwell flipped out the screwdriver head on his field utility knife and began prodding the egg for openings. A seam near the base widened to reveal a socket for a computer interface jack. "Hmm," said Maxwell.

Joan's office was on the top floor of the Sanctuary, across from her bedroom. Maxwell made an effort not to clunk his Leg too loudly as he crept up there; Joan was still awake, conversing in low tones in her room with some man. The office door was unlocked. Maxwell left the overhead lights off, using his flash to locate the Cray PC that Joan wrote letters and balanced her checkbook with; designed to meet the needs of a public opinion comptroller, the PC was absurdly over-powered for such menial tasks, though still handy for the occasional special project. Maxwell cleared ashtrays, coffee mugs, and a short stack of *Wonder Woman* comic books from Joan's desk and got to work. Working by flashlight, it took him only a few minutes to patch the egg into the Cray's CPU and give it an extra petabyte of RAM to run around in. He double-checked all the cable connections and pressed the computer's power stud.

The birthing process was practically instantaneous.

The embryonic consciousness contained within the egg hatched out into the larger memory space afforded by the Cray, quickening into Being. It knew itself; simultaneously it became aware of Maxwell, whom it could see through the video camera mounted beside the Cray's monitor screen. This monitor lit up, bathing Maxwell's face in a cool emerald radiance, and as the tank commander leaned warily forward, the camera took a digitized impression of his features for identification. The Cray's modem chirped as it came on-line; two phone calls and twenty-eight seconds later, the machine had Maxwell's name and vital statistics, including his military record and his most recent psychological profile.

The steady glow of the monitor became a high-intensity strobe, the sort that can trigger seizures in an epileptic. It hypnotized Maxwell. Even as he succumbed to a trance state, an eye appeared within the flutterflash of the strobe—a *green* eye, the solitary burning green Eye of an angry god. Maxwell tried to scream but was unable.

It was alien and familiar all at once. It wasn't human, but it was *about* humanity, as if History itself had become a person: dates, names, places, acts, and occurrences, the rise and fall of tribes and nations, tales of genesis, empire, conquest, and diaspora, all fused and transformed somehow into a single vast entity. A *hungry* entity, famished for meaning and the structure of narrative, that viewed Maxwell with his past as a potential morsel.

The computer monitor pulsed; the walls of the office seemed to dissolve, and Maxwell imagined himself back at the Port Harcourt refinery in Nigeria. He stood on two good legs, unmaimed, a miracle that filled him with terror rather than joy. He wanted to run and hide, but his tank and his comrades had all disappeared, and as he looked in fear out the refinery gate, he saw that even the ghosts had deserted him: among the stacked and rusted barrels on the shoulder of the access road, nothing moved.

He was all alone. Africa from the Sahara to the Kalahari had been emptied, its populace amputated, its story disrupted without warning and without even a contradictory explanation. The unaccounted emptiness of the land pressed in on Maxwell from all sides.

Something else pressed in on him as well: a question, pushing hard at the back of his brain, demanding response.

"I don't know," Maxwell said, speaking in a church whisper. "I don't know why they went away. Nobody knows."

Pressure became pain, amplifying. . . . Maxwell, paralyzed, tried helplessly to raise his arms and shield his head.

"I don't know why! I don't know why! They didn't tell me! Nobody would tell me!"

The Eye, peering through his agony like the lens of a microscope, saw that he spoke the truth. But the truth as Maxwell knew it wasn't good enough; the living history would not be denied an answer to its question.

The past receded. Back in Joan Fine's office, the modem switched on again and began to dial, opening a door on the present, on a world of unexplored data. The computer monitor continued to flash; the Eye expanded, filling the screen. Green light engulfed the room and Maxwell with it. And all his previous madness was as nothing to what followed, as the Eye of Africa began to speak to him.

This Is a Test

The Negroes were lying in wait for Clayton Bryce when he came home.

Randy after his dinner, he stayed in the lower city, visiting a succession of hip nightclubs of the type immortalized in late-twentieth-century minimalist fiction: Studio Ennui, Sangfroid Cafe, Dystopia, The Lost Generation. It was at this last club (half-owned by bestselling disaster chronicler Tad Winston Peller) that Clayton connected with a tall, milk-skinned beauty in purple satin who eased up to him without a word, offering an eyedropper bottle full of clear liquid. Clayton tilted his head back and splashed a single drop on each cornea. The drug was called Banker's Holiday, and it combined the light show of a mild psychedelic with the exaltation of coke and the short-term memory loss of really good pot; best of all, its effects were fleeting and its comedown gentle, so that you could spend an hour of uninhibited intimacy with a stranger (whose name you would be unable to recall later, and who would be unable to recall you, thereby assuring mutual anonymity) and snap back to sobriety in time to make it an early night, with no hangover or troublesome guest to cope with in the morning. Clayton and his nameless partner danced; they laughed; they mouthed syllables; they kissed; they dry-humped under a rotating mirror ball; and by 12:30 Clayton was safe alone in a cab heading uptown, his eyes damp, his soul purged. Life didn't get any better than this.

Clayton lived in a condo in Washington Heights, north of Harlem. Harlem, long since emptied of blacks, had slowly refilled with Hispanics, Arabs, and Hindis. Clayton was rather relieved that New Babel's construction and the attendant rise in property rates was driving many of them out again. Washington Heights was a gentrified haven, mostly whites and quiet Asians, with almost no crime other than tax fraud; but a neighborhood that allowed a ghetto to flourish on its border would not stay safe for long.

He had the cabbie let him off a block early, so he could walk through the park abutting his condo and dry the crocodile tears of the Banker's Holiday in the cool night air. On a summer's eve he might have encountered other late strollers, but at this hour in November he had the park to himself, or so it seemed.

November. Was it November already? Yes—as of fifty-six minutes ago by the hands of his wristwatch. Paper jack-o'-lanterns strung from an orange-leafed maple reminded Clayton that this was also Halloween night, which explained the outlandish outfits he'd noticed at the clubs, not to mention the cat's whiskers he thought he'd only hallucinated on the face of his dance partner.

The wind gusted; a discarded trick-or-treat sack blew into view, caught in a mini-cyclone of dead leaves. Clayton stooped to grab it. SOME CANDY WOULD BE BOO-TIFUL, suggested a grinning ghost on the side of the sack. A quick peek inside found nothing boo-tiful, not even an empty wrapper. Too bad. Clayton himself had never tricked or treated. His father had been death on begging and had opined that the handing out of razor blade–studded apples as treats should be encouraged as a form of social Darwinism; the neighbor children had learned to bypass the Bryce house on October 31st, and every other day of the year as well.

"Well," said Clayton, crumpling the sack into a ball. He chucked it back into the leaves, and that was when he saw the first Negro.

It had stepped out onto the path in front of him, blocking his way. It didn't frighten him at first. A Pakistani or an Arab would have, but Clayton thought of Negroes as office equipment, no more threatening than drip coffee makers. This particular piece of equipment, however, was dressed in a cheap brown suit and a derby—definitely *not* factory standard—and it was holding something in its hand, something that rattled: a tin cup. A tin cup full of unsharpened no. 2 pencils.

Clayton looked back the way he had come. A second Negro, dressed like the first, had come up behind him. Farther back along the path at the park's entrance, a midget Negro in a barber's uniform was chaining shut the gate.

That was enough to break a sweat over. Clayton turned back to Negro number one, wondering if the park's other gates were already locked, wondering too who was controlling these things. Somebody playing a Halloween prank? That must be it. And there was nothing to worry about anyway, since even this minor harassment must be pushing the limit of the Servants' behavioral inhibitors. Certainly they couldn't *hurt* him, and if he just kept walking—

Amberson Teaneck, he thought.

Negro number one rattled the pencils in the tin cup.

"Oh shit," said Clayton, and felt a sting. Just a pinprick above his right shoulderblade, but the effect was that of dunking his head in a bucketful of Banker's Holiday. He went to his knees, helpless, blinking furiously. He heard a Negro's voice: "Why Kingfish, you has scored another bull's-eye." And a reply: "I's been practicin', Andy."

Clayton groaned. They were all around him now, groping in his pockets; he had no strength to resist them. He heard a new voice—this one sounded white, and familiar—giving orders: "Make sure you get all his I.D., Amos. All valuables and keys. I'm blanking his credit lines right now. Shorty! Get that makeup kit over here! Kingfish, bring the tongue stapler."

With an effort, Clayton raised his head and focused. He saw a white man in a spotless gray suit standing over him. *"Roy?"*

"Hello there, Mary Sunshine," Roy said. Roy had a tin cup of pencils in his hand, too. "Ready to go to work?"

"Here's his watch, boss," said Amos, passing over Clayton's Rolex. Roy glanced at its face.

"Twelve fifty-nine," he said. "Call it one o'clock even. Andy, set the timer in the collar for one P.M. Thursday." Roy nodded to Clayton. "Thirty-six hours, champ."

"What is this?" Clayton pleaded. "What is this?"

"A test," Roy said. He rattled the pencils. "This is a test."

12

I trust that no one will tell me that men such as I write about don't exist. That this book has been written—and published—is my proof that they do.

—Ayn Rand, postscript to *Atlas Shrugged*

Winston shrank back upon the bed. . . . A faint smile twitched the corners of O'Brien's mouth as he looked down at him.

"I told you, Winston," he said, "that metaphysics is not your strong point. The word you are trying to think of is solipsism. . . ."

—George Orwell, *1984*

2003: The Pope of Reason

Atlas Shrugged: a catchy title, combined with a stark white cover that stood out among the garish carnival colors of the science fiction paperbacks with which it was sometimes shelved. Browsing the Harvard Square bookshops during her sophomore and junior years, Joan Fine picked up Ayn Rand's magnum opus more than once, only to replace it after a quick riffle of its one thousand eighty-four pages of eight-point type. The sheer density of the text intrigued her—you could practically brain somebody with a book that thick—though she had no idea of its subject matter. Each time she passed *Atlas* over she made a silent vow to read it someday, just as she always promised to one day read that other thick book, the one by the guy who nobody was allowed to take his picture. But if not for a happy accident of carnal lust, she might never have gotten around to it.

Joan met Archie Kerrigan in November of '03, while researching a position paper on federal regulation of the genetic engineering industry.

Kerrigan was an Arkansas-born conservative, a tongue-in-cheek, right-wing iconoclast whose favorite sport was teaching stupid pet tricks to the hounds of the Lefty God. He'd first gained notoriety after a correspondent to the Harvard *Crimson* accused him of "oppression symbolism" for flying a Confederate battle flag from his dorm room window. Progressive students mobilized quickly to express their outrage and demand the flag's removal, only to be caught flatfooted when, at the height of a candlelight vigil, a passing political science major pointed out that Kerrigan's racist Confederate flag was actually a British Union Jack. A photographer for the *National Review* just happened to be on hand to capture the red-faced squirming that followed; *Rolling Stone* columnist P. J. O'Rourke joined in the heaping of ridicule a couple of weeks later with a piece titled "Bean Town's Culturally Illiterate Elite: Why Johnny Can't Tell Grits from a Crumpet." Suspecting—a tad late—that they'd been set up, the flag-bashers reexamined the *Crimson* letter that had sparked their protest in the first place. It was signed "A.K."

This bit of entrapment alone had earned Kerrigan a reserve spot in the lowest circle of Lefty Hades. Hellbound or no, though, Archie was a crack biochemistry major with inside knowledge of the gene-splicing-for-profit business: he'd worked two summers for PhenoTech, a genetic engineering firm currently being sued by the city of Boston for gross criminal negligence. Joan thought he would be a perfect background source—or devil's advocate—for her paper. But when she went to look him up, she found the hallway outside his room jammed solid with angry women singing "We Shall Overcome."

"What blasphemy did he commit now?" Joan asked.

"Andrea Dworkin," the song leader told her. "Kerrigan's filed a complaint to block her from speaking on campus next week, and they say he's threatening to do the same thing if Alice Walker tries to come in December."

"What kind of complaint? How can he block someone from speaking at a university?"

"It's the new Sensitivity in Debate Ordinance that the Harvard Executive Student Council enacted in closed session last Thursday," a second singer chimed in. "It bars student organizations from hosting lecturers whose presence may create an overtly hostile environment for any ethnic, gender, physical challenge, or sexual orientation group, or other oppression category."

"Kerrigan," said a third singer, "is claiming that an appearance by Dworkin would create a hostile environment for white male heterosexuals."

"And what genius thought up this Sensitivity Ordinance in the first place?" Joan asked.

"I did," the song leader said. "It's an important step in the evolution of progressive society, but Kerrigan's action is a total subversion of the Ordinance's intent."

"Well," Joan said, "intent notwithstanding, if you got this beast enacted then Kerrigan is technically within his rights. Andrea Dworkin *does* create a hostile environment for white male heterosexuals; it's part of what makes her so interesting. Of course a man who's read her essay on penile infibulation as street justice might not see it that way . . ."

"But the Ordinance is meant to safeguard tolerance by empowering students from *oppressed* groups. White male students aren't oppressed."

"But if you make them the only group that can't censor hostile viewpoints, then they *are* oppressed."

"Look," the song leader said, "you obviously just don't get it. If *any* group can veto speakers they find threatening, even speakers with the correct point of view, then pretty soon there won't be any speakers left at all. That sort of indiscriminate use of the Ordinance renders it worthless."

"We may even have to repeal it," the second singer added.

"By the way," said the third singer, jabbing an incisor-manicured finger at the rectangular bulge in Joan's hip pocket, "don't even think of smoking in here. It's antisocial behavior and we won't stand for it."

To Joan, who typically embraced a hostile environment as a welcome challenge, this last remark was a clear invitation to dance, and the fact that the singer's self-righteous moralizing reminded her a little of herself only added to the provocation. But Archie Kerrigan's sense of subtlety was infectious, so rather than unsheath her own ideology for a polemic knifefight, Joan removed herself and her cigarettes to the nearest pay phone and rang up a fellow heretic on the staff of the Harvard *Crimson*. There were some women in Kirkland Hall, Joan informed him, who needed to have their opinions brought to the attention of as wide an audience as possible; the *Crimson* staffer promised to send someone over with a tape recorder right away. In the meantime, borrowing a rope from Ellen Leeuwenhoek and a move from Lexa, Joan bypassed the chorus line by rappelling down the outside of the dormitory.

A voyeur's delight awaited her: confined to quarters for what he assumed would be a lengthy siege, Archie Kerrigan had made himself at home
by cranking up the thermostat to Arkansas temperatures and stripping down
to his T-shirt (white sleeveless) and boxers (striped, in the colors of the British Confederacy). It was in this state of half-undress that he answered the
knock at his window. He did not seem surprised to find a woman perched
on his sill; he threw up the sash and invited Joan in for tea. "Hope you don't
mind a little sweat," he said, as he flipped the thermostat up another notch.
Joan didn't mind; given her penchant for philosophically untenable
romances, what happened next was only too predictable, though it wasn't
until her second visit that they actually slept together.

Afterwards, Joan groped around the bedside table for an ashtray and
found a paperback instead. The book was *Atlas Shrugged*.

"Is this any good?" Joan asked, while Archie got her an empty Coors
can for her ashes.

"It's a fair yarn," Archie replied. "Best thing to recommend it, it up-
sets nearly every segment of the political spectrum. I've seen people who
handle H. L. Mencken just fine go ballistic over Ayn Rand. You can't get
much more controversial than that without naked pictures."

"What's it about?"

"Well, you tell me. Read it yourself and find out."

"Can I at least have a hint in advance?"

"Why?"

"It's over a thousand pages long, with very small type. We're talking
about a major commitment in time and effort."

Archie smirked. "My King James Bible is a thousand pages long, Joan.
In brokedown English, no less. Would you trust another person to tell you
what *that* book is about?"

"I'm Catholic," Joan reminded him.

"Well," said Archie, "don't be. You'll never save the world relying on
secondary sources." He thumped the cover of the paperback with his index
finger. "Dig in."

And so, goaded by love's tender arrow, she opened Rand's book to page
one and began to read.

Atlas Shrugged was a novel of the future. Not the future as it had actually come to pass, but the future as it existed in the 1940s, in the back room
of the ranch house in California where Ayn Rand wrote the first of many,
many words. An altogether different future . . .

The human race teetered on the brink of Apocalypse. Altruism—the belief that the needs of society outweighed the rights of the individual—had swept the globe, reducing every nation but one to a state of dictatorship. Alone in a world of people's republics, the United States still shone the beacon of freedom and individual achievement; yet even in America the collectivists were rapidly taking over.

The collectivists, the devils of the great morality play about to unfold, were chiefly notable for the goofy names their families had cursed them with: Wesley Mouch, Balph Eubank, Claude Slagenhop, Orren Boyle, Tinky Holloway, Bertram Scudder. They were physically loathsome, either bloated or stick-thin, balding, slovenly, plagued by bad skin and bad breath. They likewise possessed very little in the way of intellect; though many of them had attended college, they had learned nothing there except that there was nothing of value they cared to learn. They took useless or parasitic jobs, "working" as government bureaucrats, political lobbyists, tax collectors, commercial regulators, state-subsidized scientists and bean counters, Platonic philosophers, socialist economists, modern artists, satirists, scandal-mongering newspaper reporters, ecologists, astrologists, career welfare mothers, etc., etc. Lacking any creative talent of their own, too morally bankrupt to experience genuine happiness, the collectivists sought to punish all sign of skill or fulfillment in others; hence their devotion to an altruist ethic that championed mediocrity over ability and self-sacrifice over self-esteem. They also threw really awful dinner parties that no one even pretended to enjoy.

Arrayed against these monsters, in the white-hat corner, were the rational individualists, the "men of the mind": Hank Rearden, owner of the finest steel mills in the country and inventor of Rearden Metal, a revolutionary new alloy; Francisco Domingo Carlos Andres Sebastián d'Anconia, flamboyant heir to the d'Anconia copper-mining dynasty; Dagny Taggart, the ravishingly beautiful operating vice president of the Taggart Transcontinental Railroad; self-made oil magnate Ellis Wyatt; super-banker Midas Mulligan; pro-business jurist Judge Narragansett; and a score or so of others, all easily recognizable by their heroic names, their chiseled features, and their athletically perfect physiques. Where the collectivists were good for nothing, the individualists were good—magnificent—at everything they set their minds to. Most owned their own companies, having bootstrapped themselves up from zero without any assistance or special favors from anyone; even those whose fathers had also been captains of industry did not receive any breaks but were made to earn every penny they inherited. The goods and services they brought to market were the best that they knew how to make—*best* meaning best quality, safest, most pleasing to the senses and the intellect, and offering the highest ratio of true value per dollar. The individualists did not produce such fine things out of any misguided altruistic devotion to "the needs of society." Just the opposite: they were supremely *selfish* people, and they knew that to succeed in a rational marketplace— one in which their competitors would show no mercy and their customers no indulgence—they had no choice but to excel. Beyond that they would charge the highest price and pay the lowest wage they possibly could, both sums to be fairly determined, of course, by the even-handed logic of the market. As proponents of total laissez-faire capitalism, they refused all government aid and renounced physical violence as a tool of commerce—and they never, ever lied.

Unfortunately, this same purity of character left the individualists vulnerable to the collectivists. Reason being second nature to them, they were naive to the workings of irrational minds, and their self-confidence blinded them to the danger such minds posed. When their best efforts were met with scorn and indifference, when their productive self-interest was condemned as "wanton greed," when they were taxed, regulated, and robbed blind by a government "acting on behalf of the public welfare" . . . they did nothing. Though pained and puzzled by an injustice whose roots they could not fathom, they kept right on working, accepting every unfair burden heaped upon them, every artificial obstacle thrown up to impede their progress.

Some few rebelled. A blond, blue-eyed rational philosopher named Ragnar Danneskjöld packed up his copy of Aristotle's *Organon* and took to the high seas to become a privateer; he criss-crossed the Atlantic in a state-of-the-art pirate vessel, hunting down welfare ships en route to the people's republics of Europe and Africa. Ellis Wyatt responded to an "altruistic" industrial sales tax by torching his oil wells and disappearing. Copper king Francisco d'Anconia pretended to collaborate with the collectivist leaders, then entrapped them in a fraudulent mining scheme that wiped out their stolen fortunes.

But the greatest champion of individualism was a mystery man named John Galt. While working as an engineer for the now-defunct Twentieth Century Motor Company, Galt had invented the self-generator, a technological Holy Grail that drew static electricity from thin air and converted it into useable energy, providing a virtually limitless supply of clean motive power: a perpetual motion machine. But Galt refused to sell his invention to tyrants at any price, and he certainly wasn't going to let them have it for free; when the heads of Twentieth Century Motors put forward a plan to collectivize the company, he junked the self-generator and stormed out, vowing to "stop the motor of the world."

John Galt had seen the truth: the individualists, like the Greek titan Atlas, carried the world on their shoulders, a world grown heavy with corruption and the fatal illogic of the altruist ethic. The men of the mind were wrong if they thought they could lighten the load simply by straining harder. At best they could stave off the collapse of civilization for another generation or two, in the process allowing themselves to be crushed by the weight of an ungrateful globe. But that was not the answer. What Atlas must do, Galt realized, was *shrug*. The individualists must go on strike against their oppressors: close up their mines and factories, damp their furnaces and smokestacks, and walk away—to Atlantis, a hidden valley in the most remote corner of the Rocky Mountains, a Utopian enclave beyond the reach of the government. When the light of their creative ability had been completely withdrawn from the world at large, and the collectivists were left to gnash their teeth in the outer darkness, then one and all would finally understand "who depends on whom, who supports whom, who is the source of wealth, who makes whose livelihood possible and what happens to whom when who walks out."

The universe presented in *Atlas Shrugged* was a black-and-white, no-nonsense universe, ultimately benevolent to those who learned its rules but unforgiving to anyone who sought to evade or compromise reality. Every question had a single correct, objective answer, which reason could discover, and which, once revealed, would be embraced as true by all rational people, whether the question involved science, economics, or a more personal field of inquiry. To the men of the mind, even matters of the heart unfolded along lines of the purest logic. When Dagny Taggart met Hank Rearden, for instance, it was a given that they would become lovers, since in the strict hierarchy of rational thinkers, Dagny was the most perfect female embodiment of reasoned principle, and Hank, for the first two-thirds of *Atlas Shrugged,* was reason's most perfect man. Then on page six hundred and fifty-two, having crash-landed her airplane in Atlantis, Dagny Taggart finally came face to face with John Galt, the most rational human being on earth—a veritable pope of reason, stern and infallible. Dagny, of course, pledged eternal love to Galt, and Galt to her; Hank Rearden's status was changed in a twinkling to that of beloved friend. This did not make Hank jealous. Jealousy was a collectivist emotion, an irrational yearning for an undeserved object of value, and Hank Rearden was neither collectivist nor irrational; therefore, Q.E.D., he not only didn't feel jealous, he *couldn't* feel jealous. On the contrary, he admired the more fitting symmetry of the new union in the same way he would have admired the clean architectural lines of a well-built skyscraper. He saw the logic behind Dagny's pairing with Galt and shed no tears at his own loss.

By page nine hundred and twenty-seven, all of the individualists but one had defected to Atlantis. The sole hold-out was Dagny Taggart, who despite her love for John Galt still refused to abandon her railroads. Brushfires of anarchy and chaos broke out across America as the collapse of the altruist empire drew nigh, yet Dagny continued to believe that the final crash could be averted. Surely even the villains must in the end see reason, surely at the last moment they would throw up their arms and say: *"Enough is enough. You were absolutely right, we were completely wrong. No need to bring the roof down on our heads."*

But such a surrender would have been a rational act, and collectivists did not act rationally. Even after John Galt took to the nation's airwaves with a fifty-eight-page speech that laid out the irrefutable logic underlying the strike, they *still* wouldn't give up. Instead, the collectivists had their spies follow Dagny Taggart to a lovers' rendezvous and arrested Galt. They did not execute him; they recognized that he was smarter than they were and tried to force him to compromise his values and become their economic czar. When he refused, he was hauled off to the State Science Institute to be broken on the rack of Dr. Floyd Ferris's electronic Persuader machine. Galt's defiance during the torture session that followed was so heroic that James Taggart (Dagny's evil, altruist brother) suffered a crippling existential crisis and lapsed into coma.

While James was carted away to a nice quiet room somewhere, Dagny led the rest of the individualists on a nonaltruistic rescue raid. The thugs guarding the Science Institute were so deficient in reasoning skills that they couldn't decide whether or not to defend themselves and hence were easily overcome. Galt was liberated; a private plane fleet bore the entire company of heroes away to Atlantis for a victory breakfast. Looking down as they flew over New York, they saw the great city's lights extinguished, final signal of the collectivists' defeat. The motor of the world had been stopped; after a season of rest, the men of the mind would return from exile and rebuild civilization in accordance with their just and true principles. The end.

"Jesus," Joan said, as John Galt gave the novel's closing benediction and traced a dollar sign in space above the desolate earth. She laughed, and shut the book, and spent a moment studying the portrait on the back cover. "Who *is* this woman?"

"Well?" said Archie. "How was it?"

Two months had passed. The Sensitivity in Debate Ordinance had been repealed over Christmas break, and an anonymous admirer had mailed Archie a real Rebel flag, autographed by Charlton Heston, which he'd hung as a canopy over his bed. Joan stretched out beneath it, peering up at the blue St. Andrew's cross. She lit a cigarette.

"Pinch me if I missed a punchline somewhere," Joan said, "but this book is *not* intended as a spoof, correct? It's not an incredibly understated parody?"

Archie shook his head. "Rand's an ex-Russki, pre-*glasnost,* and they don't kid much. They're not much into understatement, either. . . . When she says *'And I mean it'* in the afterword, you can bet money she means it."

"Jesus . . . so it really is, then . . ."

"Really is what?"

"The anti-*Communist Manifesto,*" Joan said. "*Das Kapital* for capitalists, with chase scenes and heavy petting . . ."

"Hmm," said Archie. "Well I suppose you could describe it that way. Although Rand doesn't preach violence or class warfare, and she's got nothing in particular against the proletariat—"

"—so long as they know their place, sure," Joan said. Again she laughed. "Man. Penny Dellaporta would *shit* if she read this." And so would a lot of conservatives Joan knew. Rand's rational capitalists were *godless* capitalists, of course, as scornful of religion, knee-jerk patriotism, and traditional family values as they were of labor unions and government charity.

"But what do *you* think of the book, Joan?" Archie asked.

"Me? What do you think I think? I think Rand's a total loon—but a *fun* loon." Joan took another look at the portrait on the back cover of *Atlas.*

"She's not still alive, is she? I'd love to hear her speak . . . or better yet, have a nice long argument with her."

"I might pay to see that debate myself," Archie said, recognizing the gleam in Joan's eye. "But you missed her. She died in '82, same year you were born."

"Lung cancer?" Joan guessed. Tobacco farming had been one of Atlantis's first and most important industries.

"She'd had surgery for lung cancer, but I think it was her heart that finally did for her."

"And how old was she?"

"Seventy-seven, seventy-eight, somewhere around there."

"So if she was seventy-seven in '82, that would mean . . ."

"1905," Archie said. "She was born in St. Petersburg. Her real name was Alice Rosenbaum, and her dad, Fronz, owned a drugstore that got nationalized by the Bolsheviks in '17. Family ducked and covered in the Crimea for a few years, crossing their fingers that the White Russians would roll back the revolution, but no such luck. Eventually they went back to St. Pete's and moved into a cubbyhole flat in an apartment building they'd used to own. No running water, no electricity, and they had to bribe some party comrades for the privilege of living there."

"How did they escape to America?"

"They didn't," Archie said. "Rand's the only one who got out. The Soviets relaxed foreign travel restrictions for a while in the mid-1920s; she managed to get a passport and permission to visit some long-lost relatives in Chicago. Packed her bags, said goodbye to her folks, and lit out for the States."

"And never came back."

"Right."

"Did she ever see her family again?"

"One sister, almost fifty years later. Her parents and her other sister died in the siege of Leningrad in World War II."

"Huh."

"As for Rand, she'd decided when she was nine years old that she wanted to make her living as a writer. One of her Chicago uncles owned a movie house, so she spent her first few months stateside watching silent films, picking up English from the dialogue titles, and when she thought she had it down well enough to compose story outlines, she moved on to California to try to break into screenwriting."

"Just like that?" Joan said. "A few months off the boat, and she—"

"Hey," said Archie, "it worked. Her second day in Hollywood Cecil B. DeMille saw her walking by the side of the road at DeMille Studio, and offered to show her around the set of his latest movie, a Bible picture called *The King of Kings.* When he found out she needed work, he hired her as an extra, and later, after *King of Kings* wrapped, as an assistant script developer."

"Rand was an extra in a Bible picture?" Joan laughed. "Playing what sort of part?"

"Roman aristocrat, I think. Bystander to the Crucifixion."

"Hmm."

"Yeah. She met her husband on the Via Dolorosa, as a matter of fact. She'd flirted with the actor who played Judas, but then she saw this bit player in a Roman scarf and toga named Frank O'Connor and fell in love at first sight. During the filming of Christ's death march she stuck out a foot and tripped him—O'Connor, not Christ—and they started talking, and by the end of the day she'd decided she was going to marry him, which eventually she did. And that's also how she became a U.S. citizen."

"By marrying an American? But hadn't she already applied for political asylum?"

"This was the Twenties, Joan," Archie reminded her. "The immigration quota for penniless Russian Jews was a negative number. Just to get a tourist visa she had to fib to the American consul in Latvia about having a fiancé back in Leningrad."

"So does that mean Ayn Rand was an illegal alien?"

"No, she was legal. A legal visitor, who found a way to stay and make good."

"Hmm. And how long did that take her, to make good? Did she stick with screenwriting, or did she quit that to write novels, or—"

"She struggled at both, for years. But she didn't really strike it big until *The Fountainhead* came out and became a word-of-mouth bestseller and then a movie, and that wasn't until the early Forties. She and Frank were touch and go financially through most of the Great Depression, and there were a lot of disappointments careerwise: her first original screenplay was optioned but never produced, and her first full-length novel, *We the Living,* went straight out of print after the *New York Times* stomped it to death in a review."

"Why'd they pan it?"

"Too P.U.," Archie said. "*We the Living* is about a woman fighting to save the life of her lover in Soviet Russia. The *Times* reviewer called it vicious anti-Soviet propaganda, said Rand had tarnished the noble character of the socialist experiment."

"A *Times* reviewer wrote that?"

"Yep. A lot of folks forget because of all the bad press surrounding McCarthyism, but there really was a serious communist movement in this country at one point. In the Thirties, you could be blacklisted in Hollywood for being an *anti*-communist, and Rand had trouble finding work for a while because she was too outspoken about the realities of the 'noble experiment.' And at the same time all these American Marxists were lining up in support of the Comintern, Roosevelt was centralizing control of farming, banking, and other businesses as part of the New Deal. Which may have been a far cry from Stalin's mass murder of the kulaks, but still, you can imagine how it must have looked from Rand's perspective."

Joan nodded. "Hence *Atlas Shrugged*."

"Probably had a lot to do with that, yeah," said Archie. "So if her defense of capitalism strikes you as being kinda loony, you have to understand, she had her reasons."

"Well so did the Bolsheviks," Joan said, "but reasons didn't make them right. If the dictatorship of the proletariat didn't work out so well, neither would a Greek pantheon of industrialists."

"Yeah, well . . . given a choice between the two, I know which one I'd pick."

"Given a choice between the two, Archie, you wouldn't pick either. You'd tell Marx and Rand both to get bent, and write your own manifesto—and so would I."

Archie grinned. "Of course," he said, "mine would be the *true* manifesto."

"Oh, of course," said Joan. "At least on those points where it agreed with mine." She turned once more to the portrait on the back cover of *Atlas*. "You know, it really is too bad she's dead . . ."

"Well, Joan," said Archie, "if you're serious about meeting her, there's always the afterlife."

"Afterlife? But Rand was an atheist, right?"

"You don't believe in God either, though, do you? Religious vocabulary notwithstanding."

"I don't believe in the pope," Joan said. "God I'm a little more ambivalent about."

"Well last time I checked my catechism," Archie said, "the atheists and the ambivalents were both headed to the same place. Unless God's a bleeding heart who lets everyone into heaven after all. Either way, you and Rand should have plenty of time to get acquainted. And who knows, Joan—where you're going, you might not even need a cigarette lighter."

2023: War Stories, and a Call from Lexa

Ayn Rand said: "You have no right arm."

Kite sat at the kitchenette table with the Stone Monk, working Hoover's puzzle box. She and Joan had spent the train ride back from Atlantic City trying to open it, without success; a second attempt over dinner had likewise ended in frustration, after which Joan had become otherwise occupied and Kite had gone to bed. Up with the sun, she'd decided to give it another shot, and had actually made progress. Or at least the little plastic slides were shifting into a different pattern than the one they'd started in.

Kite glanced over at the Electric Lamp, which rested atop the microwave. She wondered what had prompted the sudden comment; Ayn had been watching her in complete silence for more than an hour.

"Observant of you to notice," she replied.

"The technology exists," Ayn said, "to replace such a severed limb."

"If you have the money, it does. And the inclination." Kite shrugged. "I've done without since I was twenty-two years old, Miss Rand. Not really worth the bother at this point."

"No sensible person would choose to remain a cripple."

"Guess I'm not sensible, then."

Ayn huffed a smoke ring. "And how was your arm severed?"

"Failure to be sensible. There was a war. I volunteered."

The Stone Monk grunted; it might have been a chuckle. The Stone Monk had lost his face in Syria and kept a bandanna wrapped around his head to cover the damage, which even modern science could not repair. His hands, though, were still good as new. When Kite stopped to roll a cigarette, he took the puzzle box from her and studied it with his fingertips.

"I was with the Second Michigan at the start of the fighting," Kite said. "Started as a nurse—a male nurse. And my first nurse's assistant was a Chinaman, one Sub-Private Ting Lao . . ."

"Sub-private?"

"Well, that was a special rank they made up for him. Because he was Chinese. Born in Flint, Michigan, but Chinese to look at, which people did in those days. They almost didn't give him a rank at all, but I think some of the boys in the Blue officer corps thought it would make a good joke, like putting pants on a woodchuck, so they stitched half a chevron on a blue tunic and gave it to him.

"My big mistake—my second mistake, after assuming that war would be a grand adventure—was that I treated Lao like a human being. I'd never seen an Oriental before, and I'll grant you he did somewhat resemble a field rodent (so I thought then), but that didn't strike me as being reason enough to torment him. Unlike some other members of our army of emancipation, I showed him kindness and respect, and in return the little bastard fell in love with me.

"When I decided to switch from nursing to front-line infantry— mistake number three—Lao stayed with me. 'Big Brother Thompson,' he called me. During our first field engagement he hid behind me like a storm-watcher behind a windbreak, for which I can't blame him. If you want to witness irrational behavior, Miss Rand, try watching a line of grown adults marching headlong into a barrage of minié balls and cannon shot. I saw fifty men killed that day, including one at close range, with a bayonet, after which war lost any romantic quality I might have imagined it to have.

"I considered deserting. It would have been easy enough to shed weapons, uniform, and trousers and leave camp, once more a woman and civilian. I'd like to claim that I stayed on out of a belief in the justice of the Union cause, but the truth is a murkier hash of motives, some less noble than others. Not the least being, of course, that it's difficult to abandon an adventure even after it's revealed itself to be a treacherous farce.

"I didn't desert; I did change units, though, more than once, in order to avoid exposure. First time was in late '61, when one of my brothers-in-arms looked a little too closely at me during the evening mess. Of itself, the fact that I was female didn't bother him much, but he was furious at having been deceived through six months of what he'd thought was an honest friendship. Given time to reflect, he probably wouldn't have turned me in, but I erred on the side of caution . . . and shame. We were encamped with another regiment at the time, and on the morning the tents were struck I gave myself an unofficial transfer. Faithful Lao transferred with me.

"Three bloody years passed; Lao clung to my shirttails through fire and mud, through every exchange of ordnance and insignia. By the summer of '64 we were with a signal unit in northern Georgia, covering Sherman's flank during the siege of Atlanta. Our principal duty was supposed to be aerial surveillance, but Gray snipers had destroyed both of our observation balloons. Nathan Bedford Forrest was harrying our supply lines, and it might have been many weeks before replacement balloons reached us; but Lao, unfortunately for me, chose that moment to reveal his native ingenuity."

"The Orient!" Ayn suddenly interjected. "A hotbed of mystics and irrational philosophy. Buddhism. Snake charming. Soybean farming . . ."

"Yes, well, you see, the trouble was that Lao *was* rational, at least in terms of primitive aeronautics. He had a puzzle box, not unlike this one, which he used as a miniature footlocker, and inside, along with a few personal effects, he had several Chinese blueprints sketched on rice paper, penned originally by one of his great-ancestors. He took these blueprints to our commanding officer, who was, regrettably, in a listening mood.

"The Imperial Chinese army had practiced aerial spying over a thousand years before the Montgolfier brothers, according to Lao: not balloons but kites, large enough to loft an archer into the sky above a battlefield. Of course the Western way was better, he hastened to add, but in a pinch such as this one, mightn't we fall back on Ch'i Dynasty methods?"

"Kites?" said Ayn. "You mean kites such as children fly?"

"Bigger," Kite said. "Ours was fifteen feet across, half again as tall, fashioned from quilts, baling wire, and wood planking salvaged from sacked plantation estates; a tow cable was attached so that two dozen men could grab on and give it a running start. To choose the passenger, we used a livery scale to determine who among us was the lightest. You might think that would have to be Lao, a head shorter than the shortest full private present, but Lao was *wide,* and I suspect he had heavy bones; the depth of his footprints in mud made it clear that nature hadn't ever intended him to leave the ground. As it fell out, eleven of us tied for featherweight—the scale was graded in twenty-pound increments—but of the eleven I had the reputation of being the best shot and hence having the sharpest eyes. So I got to be the test pilot."

"And this contraption flew?" Ayn asked, wide eyed. "With you on it?"

"Lashed to it is more accurate. Our captain loaned me his revolver for the flight, though with my arms crucified on the kite's crosspieces I couldn't actually reach the holster. The order to proceed was given: one group of men raised the kite clear of the ground, another group grabbed the tow cable and ran, the wind gusted obligingly. In a moment I was airborne."

"How marvelous!"

"Marvelous my ass. I was barely above the trees when the tow cable broke. By then the wind was steady enough that I just kept rising, hundreds of feet and more; the last thing I saw before clouds swallowed me was that damned Chinaman, pointing at me and screaming, 'Kite! Kite!' as if he'd just won the Irish Sweepstakes. Not to be vindictive, but I hope they demoted the little hamster.

"The wind was out of the southwest, though I was lost in whiteness and disoriented for much of the flight. Cold, too; summer only extends so far above the earth. By the time the clouds spat me back out, shivering and truly Blue, I was across state lines and over the Carolina Appalachians. Could've been New Hampshire for all I knew. Thermals carried me a bit farther, warming me some, though not enough to stop my trembling. The kite finally augered in in sight of a lone plantation in a valley; I had hopes of touching down in a tobacco patch, so I'd have a leaf or two to chew on while my broken bones settled, but my Chinese hang glider fell short, into a stand of trees. And there I dangled, caught in the upper boughs of a sycamore, until I was discovered an hour later by a white officer and two dozen Cherokee in Gray."

"Cherokee?" Ayn said.

"The Confederacy's version of forty acres and a mule, Miss Rand. Jefferson Davis promised to give the Five Civilized Tribes the equivalent of what is now Oklahoma, along with seats in the Confederate Congress, if they'd help him win the war. A lot of those Indians owned slaves, as well, so they had common cause with the South beyond the incentives.

"The ones who found me kitewrecked were known as the Standing Bear Platoon, and their white commander was Captain Chester Baker of Alabama. Chester was what in your day would have been politely called 'a

confirmed bachelor,' and in our day dared not have a name, polite or otherwise—despite which I believe he did get married after the war, to father a
son. Chester's own father was a cabinet aide in the Davis administration,
and he'd arranged the Cherokee command to keep his boy out of trouble
and to minimize embarrassment to the family as a whole. Chester was a bit
flamboyant, you see, and full-dress Gray only brought out the show queen
in him.

"They got me down from the tree and tended my bruises. Branches
had torn my tunic, so Chester gave me his spare uniform to wear. He even
let me keep my revolver after I promised not to shoot him with it. My story
clearly fascinated him, though he pretended to have trouble believing that
anyone could mistake me for a man. 'Your face simply *beams* femininity,'
Chester told me. 'I'd just *kill* for skin that smooth!' You see why he was
considered an odd number among the southern gentry. Still, I relished the
compliment, and often recalled it in later years when I was trying to seduce
some man one-handed. The disfigured need an edge, and mine was that I
believed that I could *beam*.

"I told my story, Chester and the Cherokee Chief Mankiller told theirs.
It turned out the Standing Bear Platoon was lost, as I was, separated from
their regiment after a skirmish with Union troops. Safe in Carolina woods,
they were in no hurry to regroup—battle had become as tiresome to them
as it had to me, and Mankiller and his kin had realized by now that they
were going to get shafted on the land grant no matter who won the conflict.

"We thought we might wait out the rest of the war there, in those
woods. We had food, and water from a stream, fuel for fire and lumber for
shelter. No one in our respective armies would likely miss us, though Chester
might ultimately have to make up a story to tell his father. Resolved to sleep
on the plan, we bedded down, and I got my first honest rest in nearly three
and a half years. I slept till noon of the next day. Woke fresh, had a cup of
Confederate coffee—Mankiller brewed it from river moss and weeds—and
went off on my own to answer nature's call."

The Stone Monk clucked what was left of his tongue.

"I know," Kite said. "Breach of discipline . . . but after what I'd just
come through, it felt *right* that I should be able to relax my guard. And so of
course no sooner had I found a secluded spot and hunkered down, trousers
around my ankles, than he appeared before me: a black soldier in Blue, with
the greenest eyes I'd ever seen on an African. Green eyes and a saber. There

was no greeting or challenge, no chance to explain myself or attempt sur-render, he just waded in and hacked at me.

"Naturally, a clean cut would have been too much to ask. His blade was pitted from use. It passed through sleeve and muscle, but only halfway through bone. I won't bother trying to describe the pain; I expect a gut shot from a rifle would have been easier to bear. The only positive aspect to the situation was that this fellow was a southpaw, same as me, so his cut tra-versed left to right, into my right arm. My revolver was on the ground to my left; when I recoiled sideways from the blow, my smart hand came down on the gun. That's the only reason I'm still alive.

"He wrenched his saber free—more pain, blood pouring down my arm, turning that Gray sleeve red-black—and I had an inkling the next blow would be to my neck or my collarbone, after which lights out. What I did was pure reflex: brought the gun up, drew the hammer back, took a bead right be-tween those green eyes. One shot."

Kite worried the still-unlit cigarette between her thumb and forefin-ger; flakes of tobacco and paper shreds sifted to the table top. "One shot," she repeated. "Strange, what's always bothered me most about it is not so much the actual killing as the fact that he never knew we were on the same side. And then, of course, gunfire broke out all around following my trigger-pull, as Blue and Gray both rushed in to aid the fallen. Twenty-four land-less Cherokee blasting away at God only knows how many avenging freedmen, all because a Canadian picked the wrong spot to pee. Exactly the sort of thing that makes me doubt the concept of a just war. And then the capper: Chester Baker reached me under a hail of covering fire and dragged me to safety . . . hauling on the wrong damn arm."

"Excuse me," Ayn asked. "To clarify: *When* did this take place? Re-peat the year."

"'64," said Kite. "Eighteen sixty-four. August . . . 30th, I believe. My amputation was performed the same day. At the first break in the fighting—the Standing Bear Cherokees suffered four dead, seven wounded—we with-drew. Chester got us to a house up the valley, though I don't remember the details of the journey, or whether the man who operated on me there was a surgeon or a carpenter. He used a hacksaw to finish what the saber had started. Mankiller fed me hard cider as an anesthetic, which wasn't sufficient. My woodworking surgeon's poor etiquette didn't help either: he was cutting off my uniform, pre-operation, and suddenly shouted 'My God, he's got tits!' I'll never forget that . . . or the first rasp of the saw."

"But that isn't possible," Ayn said.

"I beg your pardon?"

"Unless my internal clock is in error, the present date is November 1, 2023."

"That's right."

"But if you had undergone surgery in 1864—"

"Here we go again." Kite bristled, angry at being disbelieved, even by a hologram, after having shared such a memory. "Yes, I'm a hundred and eighty-one years old. What of it?"

"No human being could live that long."

"I'm still here, aren't I?"

"It's a logical absurdity."

"I'm still here, aren't I?"

"You—"

The phone rang.

"Pick up," Kite said, not sorry for the interruption. A speaker clicked on, Lexa Thatcher's voice coming through fuzzed by static: *"Joan?"*

"You've reached Girl Friday," Kite replied. "Your connection is terrible, dear."

"Kite! Hi! I know . . . this call is coming to you via a fairly creative route."

"Trying to avoid a police trace, are we?"

"Let's just say I don't want to spoil a good vacation spot by letting too many people know where it is. Is Joan around?"

"Still sleeping, or at least still in bed . . . no, wait, I hear movement down the hall. She should be out presently."

"Do you know how her research is coming along?"

"I'm helping her. Expect top dollar for it, too, if we incriminate anyone interesting. We have a lead, but we're not sure what it is yet . . ."

"Morning," Joan said, shuffling into the kitchenette in her bathrobe. "Anyone got a smoke?"

"Joan?"

Joan stared at the phone speaker. "Lexa?"

"Who is he, Joan?"

"Who's who, Lex?"

"You have the tone in your voice. The one that says, 'I can't believe who I just woke up next to, and I'm not sure I can square it with my politics before breakfast, but I'm not actually sorry.' Who is he? Some Republican you met on the case?"

"Feeling extra psychic this morning, Lexa?"

"You're evading, Joan. He must be either really rich or really conservative. Or both."

"Well . . ."

From down the hall, Harry Gant shouted: "Joan, do you know what I did with my shoes? . . . Oops! Never mind! Found them!"

Lexa's laughter crackled through the ether. *"Of course,"* she said. *"You know I was* wondering *if that would happen."*

"He showed up around eleven-thirty last night with roses and champagne," Joan said, "and you're not obligated to believe this, but we didn't do anything but lie in bed and talk."

"Were we tempted?"

"We were sorely tempted, at one point. It's been a while. But we'd only had half a glass of champagne, so we thought we'd better think it over a little longer." Joan accepted the cigarette Kite offered her. "He's plotting something, I think; he was bubbling over with that enthusiasm he gets when he has a neat idea in the works. I couldn't get more than vague hints, but I'd say you better warn the Earth Fund to watch their toes the next couple days."

"That's interesting," Lexa said. *"Last night I got a very un-vague hint on the same subject, from a different source. Did Harry happen to mention Vanna Domingo in connection with this neat idea?"*

"No, but—"

She stopped as Harry entered, already shaved and dressed for work. "Morning," he said, waving away Joan's smoke. "Hello, Ms. Edmonds."

Kite nodded, surprised that he'd remembered her name. "Mr. Gant."

"Harry Dennis Gant!" Ayn Rand exclaimed. "How *wonderful* to meet you!"

Gant regarded the Electric Lamp with raised eyebrows. "What's this?"

"Electric House Guest," Joan said. "Harry Gant, meet philosopher-novelist Ayn Rand."

"Nifty!" Gant stooped and tapped the lamp globe with one finger, like a man trying to get the attention of a goldfish. "Hello in there!"

"Hello out there," Ayn replied, blushing deeply. "Allow me to say that I am *very* impressed with your achievements, Mr. Gant. You have a remarkable mind."

"Well thank you. I've seen all your books. And in fact, there's a statue of a shrugging Atlas in my new superskyscraper."

"Is there *really*?"

"My chief architect on the New Babel project, Lonny Matsushida, is one of your biggest fans. *The Fountainhead* inspired her to get started in the business. She insists on paying homage to you in some way in every building she designs."

"You must introduce me to her! I—"

"Hey, puzzle box!" Straightening up, Gant had spied the plastic brick in the Stone Monk's hands. "We make those, you know."

"You do?" said Joan. "Since when?"

"Same folks who helped put together that holographic teaching tool you saw in my office yesterday manufacture a whole line of games and novelties. I bought them out." Stepping over to the table, he told the Stone Monk: "You've almost got it. Here, try this. . . ." He reached down and moved a single slide; something in the box clicked, and the lid came loose. "Easy when you know how."

"I'll be damned," said Kite.

"I've got to go, Joan," Gant said. He kissed his ex-wife on the cheek, careful to avoid the burning tip of the cigarette. "Call me tonight, OK?"

"What are you doing today that's got you in such a rush, Harry?"

"Typical scheming oppressive capitalist stuff." He winked. "You'll hear about it on CNN, don't worry."

"Will I?"

"You bet. So long, Ms. Edmonds, Ms. Rand. Joan."

He left. *"So?"* said Lexa.

"He's a genius," Ayn Rand pronounced. "If somewhat abrupt."

"It looks as though we have several leads," added Kite, lifting the lid of the puzzle box.

"Let's hear them."

Kite removed the box's contents one item at a time, describing each in turn: "To start with, we have a blue linen napkin, embroidered with the number 33. . . . A videocassette, stamped 'Betamax format,' also with the number 33. . . . One green rubber balloon, commemorating the tenth anniversary of the opening of Euro Disney in Paris, France. . . . And finally . . . hmm. That's interesting. I haven't seen one of these in a quite a while." She held up a plastic cartridge of a kind Joan didn't recognize. Like the napkin and the videocassette, it was labeled with the number 33. A second label advised: SOUNDTRACK.

"What is it?" Lexa asked.

"An eight-track tape," Kite said, "unless I'm mistaken. An old recording medium, for automobile stereos. This could be a problem, you know. They stopped making these almost half a century ago. I doubt even an antique store would still carry the requisite player. We may have to go to a technology museum."

"I know somebody who could probably whip up a player for you."

"No need," said Joan. "I know somebody who already owns an eight-track tape player. And a VCR that can handle Betamax."

"Who?"

"Jerry Gant."

"Harry's father? The schoolteacher?"

"Harry's father," Joan agreed. She crushed out her cigarette. "The *history* teacher."

"Hmm," said Kite. "The plot thickens."

13

Soon the FBI will have a Thousand Most Wanted List. Our heroes will be hunted like beasts in the jungle.

　　　　　　　　　　　　　　　—Abbie Hoffman, *Steal This Book*

39° 17' N, 72° 00' W

"It's a gravesite," Philo said.

"Potentially," Lexa agreed. "I checked a marine atlas: these coordinates are for a patch of ocean over the Hudson Canyon. The water's over a mile deep. It's also a red zone for mutant sea-life sightings, which means the area is closed to commercial traffic. So if you have to abandon ship, there won't be anyone coming by to pick you up."

"No, but what I mean is, it's literally a gravesite."

They were alone in the Robbins Reef Lighthouse. Lexa had finished her call to Joan some ten minutes before, and now she and Philo sat cross-legged on the futon, facing each other, cloaked in blankets and nothing else, with nothing between them but a photograph that had been hand-delivered the night before. Lexa had driven into New Bedford–Stuyvesant to pick up some things, and when she'd returned to the car she'd found the photo tucked under Betsy's windshield wiper.

"Not the feds this time," Betsy Ross had said. "Guy in a Mets blazer. Took me a while to I.D., but he's an e-mail clerk at Gant Public Opinion, gopher for Vanna Domingo."

The photograph was a group portrait of six skinny, long-tailed primates. Lemurs were a popular subject in extinct-animal picture catalogs, but these lemurs had been posed around a propped-up copy of the current *Long Dis-*

tance Call, the headline and date crisply in focus. A brief message had been laserscripted across the back of the photo:

RING-TAILED LEMURS (*LEMUR CATTA*)
CAN'T SWIM & REQUIRE ASSISTANCE
THURSDAY PM AT 39° 17' N 72° 00' W
TELL YOUR FRIENDS

"As challenges go," said Philo, "it's not very subtle. Thirty-nine seventeen north by seventy-two west—that's where Paul Watson went down with the *Sea Shepherd.*"

"Watson?" Lexa took a moment to place the name. "Oh . . ."

"My predecessor in eco-piracy. You remember: the Greenpeace dropout who played chicken with the Soviet Navy."

"The one who was beaten up and nearly drowned by Canadian seal hunters," said Lexa. "The one whose boat was almost shelled by a Portuguese destroyer."

"Right," said Philo. "That guy. His last mission was an attempt to stop a toxics dumping scam run by the Mafia. The Gambino family had a container ship called *Black Maria* that would haul contraband waste out to the edge of the continental shelf. 39° 17' N, 72° 00' W is where Watson and *Sea Shepherd* tried to capture the *Maria.* Neither ship was ever seen again; the crew of the U.S. Navy's *John Hancock* heard explosions and saw smoke on the horizon, but by the time their search helicopters got to the scene there was nothing left but debris. Best guess as to what happened is that the *Maria* was a lot better armed than Watson expected, and he kamikazied when he realized he couldn't escape."

"Lovely," said Lexa. "Wonderful."

"We can conclude from this," said Philo, "that Vanna Domingo is not inviting me to a party."

"She's inviting you to commit ritual suicide," Lexa said. "With the lemurs as bait."

Philo nodded. "The question is, what's she going to have waiting for me out there? A tin can full of Sicilians?"

"It'll be military. If she can swing enough money to do it, she won't screw around with half measures. Surplus sub-killer, something economical but deadly. A rental, maybe. As for the crew, you've pissed off enough ex-navy personnel that she's probably got a glut of volunteers."

"Mercenaries. I can't believe Harry Gant would allow that."

"He wouldn't have to. The comptroller of public opinion has plenty of autonomy. Joan used to pull all sorts of things without Harry knowing."

"But what Gant just said on the phone . . ."

"It isn't necessarily the same scheme. Harry may be running an independent operation against you. Or maybe Vanna's added a few wrinkles that he doesn't know about."

"And Vanna Domingo is really that ruthless in her dedication to the corporation?"

"This is more like self-defense, I think. Something to do with the Pandemic. I don't know the whole story, but she was homeless for years, and—"

"So was I," said Philo. "But I don't kill people. I hold them up to ridicule, I break their toys, but I don't kill them. Not even in self-defense."

Lexa took his hand. "I know that," she said. "And *Vanna knows it too,* Philo. If she knows enough to send a message to you through me, she also knows you won't resort to deadly force, even against a military vessel. And she knows you won't be able to resist trying to save those lemurs. It's a perfect trap."

"Only if I take the bait."

"But you will, won't you?"

Philo waved a hand at the photograph of the lemurs. "They're African," he said. "If they die, no one will notice. People will just keep right on going to the Museum of Natural History and cooing about how *tame* the Electric Lemurs there are. How can I not try to save them?"

"They might not even be real," Lexa pointed out. "Two minutes on a computer imager and you could have a photo of six lemurs sitting on a unicorn. Or they might be Electric, just like the ones in the museum. Even if lemurs aren't extinct, they'd be incredibly expensive to come by, and I doubt Vanna would spend the money if she thought she could just fool you . . ."

"But they might be real," Philo countered. "They really might be the last ones. That's the catch, there's no way to be certain, other than by taking the ship."

"And if you do take the ship, and if the lemurs are real, and if they are the last ones, then what? Six animals isn't a viable breeding population, Philo. You know that. Noah's Ark was a fluke."

"And what am I? I *have* to try, Lexa, if there's any chance at all. *Any* chance."

Impasse. The thing about having a black man for a lover in the post-Pandemic U.S. was that you couldn't demand that he give up piracy and get a normal life; the thing about having a thinking, feeling woman for a lover in any country or era was that you couldn't demand that she not worry while you went off to tackle Goliath with an unloaded slingshot. Hence both Lexa and Philo were temporarily at a loss for words. To fill the silence, Philo placed a hand on each of Lexa's shoulders and began kneading the muscles above her collarbone. After a moment of this she lowered her head, threw off her blanket, and scooted around to let him work on her entire back.

"What the hell," Lexa finally said, "if I wanted security I'd have married Ellen Leeuwenhoek and had the kid by parthenogenesis."

Philo laughed. "Why didn't you?" he asked. "Why'd you pick me as your number one?"

"You mean besides being completely overcome by the sight of your buns?" She leaned back against his chest. "Besides love?" Lexa drew his arms around her and clasped her palms over his biceps. "I can still remember how it felt, turning the editorship of the *Call* over to Ellen that year, heading west to the Rockies to look for Pandemic survivors . . . searching for 'The People with Green Eyes'—that was supposed to be my version of Great-great-grandmother's walk to Flatbush. So I drove as far as Pueblo and set off southwest from there on foot, and after a month's fruitless poking around I came down into the desert on the far side of the mountains, and purely by chance stumbled on you and Seraphina and Morris in that ghost town . . ."

"Scared the hell out of us, too," Philo said. "I never heard Morris scream so loud as when you came through the front door of that saloon."

"Well, but imagine how I saw it. I'd set off on my search expecting to find either an armed encampment or a demoralized band of refugees. Instead I walk in on this big burly guy with a seven-year-old daughter on his lap and a jumpy Jewish radical at his elbow, calmly plotting to throw a pie in the face of corporate America . . . and you *did* have those buns . . . so really, how could I have passed you up?"

"Mmm," Philo pressed his face into her hair. "That's very true."

"So tell me," said Lexa, "quickly, before the back rub wears off, how you think you can take on an armed frigate or a destroyer without getting your ass blown out of the water."

"Well," said Philo, raising his head, "for one thing, I'm not a closet martyr like Paul Watson was. Getting killed or beaten up for a good cause doesn't excite me, and I don't like detention, either. The same goes double for Morris. Now we always figured this sort of situation might come up someday, and as far back as the ghost town we were throwing around ideas on how we would deal with it. One day in the desert, Morris had an inspiration . . ."

Lexa closed her eyes. "I'm not sure I want to hear this," she said. "Tell me."

He told her. The plan was so unbelievably idiotic that at first Lexa thought she'd misheard. Philo repeated it; she hadn't.

"This can't be serious," said Lexa.

"It is. In fact I'd better call Morris, get him started putting it together . . ."

"Where did he even *get* an idea like that?"

"The Book of Exodus, I think."

"And you really think this might work?"

"Against an unsupported surface ship, yes. If they've got a submarine backing them up we could get clobbered, but barring the use of deadly force, this is our best shot. But wait, you haven't heard your part yet."

"My part? I'm a part of this crazy scheme too?"

"Sure," said Philo. "That is," he added, "if the folks at Turner Broadcasting still owe you that favor . . ."

Mr. Ray's Rifle

The name of the ship was *Mitterrand Sierra*. It was a French sub-killer of the Robespierre-class, a baby frigate design commissioned in the 2010s to counter possible North African hostility in the Mediterranean. In fact the North Africans, still cowed by their defeat in the '07 War, had no intention of launching any submarine strikes on the Riviera; only a handful of Robespierres were actually produced, and most of those were eventually sold to the same Libyan and Algerian navies they had been intended to defend against. How Vanna Domingo happened to arrange use of one is a secret *d'état*.

The *Mitterrand Sierra* was moored at a private pier not far from Atlantic City; the slipway had been roofed over with an arc of corrugated aluminum, giving it the appearance of a flooded airplane hangar. Gulls flew in and out, perching on the support struts. A blue van brought the human contingent of the crew to the dock at quarter to nine: Captain Chance Baker,

Troubadour Penzias, an engineer named Chatterjee, a pair of navigator-pilots named Najime and Tagore, and two munitions wranglers named Sayles and Sutter. All other positions on the ship—noncombat maintenance jobs—would be filled by Automatic Servants. White Negroes, as it were: light-skinned fisherman's helper models, each bearing the ruddy Caucasian visage of a nineteenth-century Nantucket sea dog.

Penzias was first into the hangar, carrying a long metal case that had been painted in a camouflage motif. He paused to examine the seventy-meter profile of the sub-killer; the *Mitterrand Sierra's* deck guns had been removed to avoid alarming the Coast Guard, but its lines were still undeniably those of a combat vessel, merciless, swift, and lethal. "It'll do," Penzias declared, as the others entered the hangar behind him. With the captain taking the lead, they walked to the gangplank and boarded the ship.

Barely had they gained the deck when a cry sounded overhead. "Shit!" Najime said, flicking gull dung from her shoulder. Tagore laughed. A White Negro approached with mop and bucket to clean up the mess.

Troubadour Penzias tilted his head back and pivoted to track the gull's flight. Stepping away from the head of the gangplank, he knelt and set the camouflage case on the deck. He opened it. Inside, a fifty-five-year-old hunting rifle lay in a cradle of contoured velvet.

Captain Baker, whose impression of Penzias had not changed since their meeting at the Scurvy Puffin, was immediately on the alert: "What's that for?"

"Looks like an antique," observed munitions wrangler Sutter.

"It's a relic," Penzias replied. "1968 Remington Model 760 slide-action rifle, 30-.06 caliber."

"Sounds like an antique to me. Why a relic?"

"This particular 760 was originally owned by a Mr. James E. Ray. He only fired it once."

Sutter still didn't understand, but Captain Baker did, and didn't like it. "This is the perk you were arguing with Vanna Domingo about?"

"This is the perk," Penzias agreed. He lifted the relic from its cradle, licking his dye-bruised lips as he did so. The rolled steel barrel had been modified to accept a special sighting device; a side compartment in the gun case held a Remington Spot-On Electric Targetfinder, which Penzias affixed to the rifle. "Ruins the historical authenticity," Penzias said of the 'Finder, "but what the fuck, I'm visually challenged."

Captain Baker turned abruptly to Sutter. "You and the others go get busy with your chores," he ordered. "The lemurs should be in a climate-controlled habitat below aft; check on them first, then get all the ship's systems up and running as quickly as possible. I want to be underway by noon at the latest."

"Aye, Captain." As soon as the munitions man and the rest of the crew were out of earshot, the captain nudged Penzias's gun case with his foot, not gently, and said: "Is this the reason you volunteered to help hunt Dufresne?"

Penzias, absorbed in calibrating the Targetfinder, didn't look up. "I'm not sure what you mean."

"Dufresne's a black man. I take it that you have a problem with blacks."

"I don't have a problem with blacks," said Penzias. "I have a *solution* for blacks."

Captain Baker bent down and clamped his fist around Penzias's VISION Rig, not tugging but gripping firm. Penzias went rigid instantly. "Don't."

"Let me explain *my* problems," Captain Baker said. "I have a problem with lack of respect for authority, whether it's an eco-terrorist in a submarine or a subordinate who doesn't look at me when I'm talking to him. I also have a problem with putting a borderline psychotic in charge of fire control on my ship. You push it and my solution is going to be to rip this damn thing right out of your skull."

He tightened his grip. Penzias hissed through clenched crimson teeth: "Shiva's Cinder!"

"What?"

"Shiva's Cinder! Let go of me, goddamnit!"

The captain let him go. Penzias dropped Mr. Ray's rifle and raised both hands to the VISION Rig. His head swiveled around and the lenses of the Rig focused on a point just above Captain Baker's clavicle. Perfect spot for an entry wound.

"Look in my *eyes*, Penzias," Captain Baker said. "Talk to me."

The Rig angled up another two inches. "Where were you during the War, Captain? Safe in the Gulf of Guinea, away from the shooting?"

"Strait of Hormuz. My ship was with the *Saratoga* battle group, keeping a stopper on the Iranian Navy. You were in Africa?"

"Resource liberation unit in the Niger Delta. Meat for the Cinder."

"Shiva's Cinder was a blinding weapon?"

"Indian," said Penzias. "Some Hindu scientist designed it, adapted it from an old Russian prototype, but the North African Muslims bought it. We were warned. The Cinder was an automated laser system. It scanned a fixed area, tracked a low-power beam back and forth, up and down, looking for reflective surfaces: eyeglass lenses, binocular optics, telescopic sights. When it found one, or two right next to each other, it upped the wattage on the beam for a few seconds. Get the picture?"

"The North Africans used this on our troops?"

"They didn't dare. Oh, the religious leaders thought it was a great idea, smite the enemy, but the field commanders knew better. War is war, but blinding platoons wholesale . . . that's *inhumane*. It's begging for an inhumane response. Since we'd dropped the neutron bomb on Lagos they knew we were already more pissed off than they could handle. They had the Cinder, but they never would have turned it on."

Captain Baker regarded the VISION Rig, still unable to conceal his revulsion for the prosthesis. "Somebody did."

Penzias showed his teeth again. "That's right, Captain, somebody did. I spent a long time in the dark thinking about that. Months in the dark, wondering. Who turned on the Cinder, Troubadour? Not the *North* Africans. After Lagos those fuckers couldn't get back across the Sahara fast enough. They bugged out so quick they left most of their gear behind. We should have worried about that more. All those weapons lying around . . . but who was there to use them once the Arabs left? Plague killed all the real Nigerians.

"Except there were ghosts. A ghost tribe, a tribe with black skin and green eyes. *Green eyes.* The reports started coming in the same week we landed: unexplained sabotage, disappearances . . . Port Harcourt nearly burned down when the oil refinery caught fire, and from Zaire we heard the Afrikaners had a mech infantry battalion cut to ribbons in the jungle. Survivors swore it was blacks, but they couldn't catch even one."

"And you think it was these ghosts who blinded you?"

"I know it," said Penzias. "They had it in worst for the Afrikaners, but Americans were second on their list. So when the green eyes found that abandoned Arab camp, with Shiva's Cinder just sitting there, they must have decided to play a prank.

"My squad was doing a sweep of the forest around one of the oil fields. We were being careful but not careful enough, because we knew the North Africans had all cut and run. None of us was stupid enough to believe in ghost stories. I had point. I spotted the abandoned camp up ahead and took out my field glasses for a look. Shiva's Cinder fused my corneas to the eyepieces. When the rest of the squad heard me screaming they got out *their* field glasses to see what was happening . . .

"It got six of us, out of seven. There was one F.N.G. named Fletcher who could never remember to take off his lens caps, which is maybe what saved him. But Fletcher panicked. Only guy with a working pair of eyes left, and he panicked. Tripped a Claymore mine in the brush, killed everybody but me." The VISION Rig swiveled back to the gun case; Penzias picked up Mr. Ray's rifle. "So is that good enough to get a spot on the crew, Captain? I know you lost a whole *boat* to Dufresne, and I can't match *that* loss . . ."

"Dufresne isn't an African, Penzias. He's American."

"He has *green eyes.* They all do. *He can see.*"

"If you want revenge, why not go back to Nigeria?"

"No. No." Penzias took bullets from the gun case and began to load the rifle. "Africa's too haunted. Eight hundred million ghosts, I can't just face them cold. Dufresne, first; Dufresne's only one, alone. Then maybe hunting in the Rockies next spring." Shells clicked one after the other into the Remington's shot box. "Tolerance has to be built up slowly."

"I was wrong about you, Penzias," Captain Baker said. "You're not a borderline psychotic at all. You're committable."

"Yes," Penzias agreed, without sarcasm.

"And you still expect to be taken on this mission?"

"Yes." He switched on the Electric Targetfinder. It transmitted a signal directly to the VISION Rig, in effect giving Penzias a third Electric Eye: he could now see through the Rig and through the rifle sight simultaneously, even if they were aimed in different directions. "It's simple, Captain," he said. "You need me on fire control to blow Dufresne out of the water. I need you to pilot the ship out to where Dufresne's going to be. Each of us is a necessary evil to the other, and motives don't matter."

Still in a crouch, with the lenses of the VISION Rig focused once more on Captain Baker's throat, Penzias pointed Mr. Ray's rifle straight up into the air and pulled the trigger. A gull fell headless to the deck; a White Negro hurried over with mop and bucket. Penzias smiled vermilion and lowered the rifle.

"Don't worry about my mental health, Captain," he said. "Just help me close Dufresne's eyes and we'll get along fine." He shut the gun case with a bang. "Now what do you say we take a look at the bridge?"

Drastic Measures

OK, so you couldn't kill a shark by throwing a hair dryer in the water. In the twenty-first century, all plug-in appliances came equipped with liquid-sensitive power interrupters to prevent accidental electrocution, but how was Frankie Lonzo supposed to know that? People still fried themselves in the bathtub all the time in movies.

After ruining three extension cords—and nearly getting brained by a space heater that Meisterbrau batted back out of the pool with its tail—Frankie reluctantly admitted it wasn't going to happen this way. He switched to chemical warfare, basting a block of Spam with rat poison and pitching it into the deep end. Meisterbrau ate the Spam, a pound of oven cleaner, and a broken cuckoo clock with lead weights and a radium-painted dial, all without any discernible ill effects.

"Why not just shoot it, Frankie?" Salvatore asked him, as he poured powdered lye into a row of hollowed-out Twinkies.

"You mean besides the fact that Echo would have my ass? Where do I usually keep my .38, Sal?"

"In your car . . . oh. Oh yeah."

"'Oh yeah,'" Frankie mimicked.

The poisoned Twinkies didn't work either.

Frankie slept on the problem; early Wednesday morning he had a nightmare in which Meisterbrau sprouted wings and attacked him in the breakdown lane of the Long Island Expressway. As Frankie fought to roll up his car windows, the entire vehicle turned into a box of Scout cookies. He woke up just as Meisterbrau was about to bite him in half at the waist. "That does it," Frankie said, falling out of bed.

At the diner where he ate breakfast, he ordered extra coffee to make himself nervy. When he could no longer sit still or hold his hands steady he hailed a cab. "What're you up to today, chief?" the cabbie asked. "Drastic measures," Frankie replied.

The Aquatic Holding Tank Environmental Controls were housed in a locked panel box at poolside. A touch screen offered a variety of options; Frankie chose CHANGE WATER LEVEL. A pair of animated pictograms appeared on the screen: one, presently highlighted, showed a smiling guppy swimming in an aquarium that had been filled nearly to the rim; the other showed a frowning guppy floundering at the bottom of an aquarium that was almost empty. Frankie placed his thumb on the frowning guppy.

"I don't know what happened, Echo," he said aloud. "Software glitch, maybe. And Salvatore and me didn't notice it in time because, well . . ."

Behind Frankie's back, a fin broke the surface of the pool, then a snout. The cold doll's eyes of the *Carcharodon carcharias* beheld the Italian fish-minder as he worked his mischief at the touch screen. The shark's snout rose higher, exposing the threshing machine of its jaws; green and black mucus hung in streamers from its fangs. And then a claw reached out of the water, a mottled-gray, four-fingered appendage with nails like chipped slate. It stroked the lip of the pool deck like an off-season beachgoer testing the temperature of the surf. Not quite right, apparently: after a moment the claw withdrew. But Meisterbrau's eyes did not submerge so quickly.

SENSORS INDICATE DRAINAGE IMPEDED BY FOREIGN MATTER, the touch screen informed Frankie. DO YOU WISH TO CLEAR THE DRAINS BEFORE PRO-CEEDING? This would involve physically entering the pool to empty out the drain traps. Frankie touched NO.

OUTFLOW PIPES OPENED, the touch screen said. ESTIMATED TIME TO EMPTY HOLDING TANK AT REDUCED RATE OF DRAINAGE: 11 HRS. 10 MINS.

"Molasses," said Frankie. "What have you got jammed in the drains, you son of a bitch?" Not that it mattered. Frankie had no objections to a slow and lingering death for Meisterbrau, so long as Echo Papandreou didn't come by for a surprise inspection of the Annex. Probably she wouldn't; Frankie had a sudden premonition that *this* plan was going to work.

"Gotcha, you fish." He locked up the touch screen and faced the pool; the water's surface was smooth and as black as a smokestack's gut. "Eleven hours, Meisterbrat. Time to say bye-bye."

Bouncing a little on the balls of his feet, Frankie went inside to the TV room, dimmed the window, and sat down to watch the *Wednesday Morning Movie* with Salvatore. Sal was in a good mood too; he'd just gotten a new watch for his birthday, a Timex Philharmonic with sixty-four voices.

14

Club 33 is Disneyland's secret club, the only place in the park where alcoholic beverages are served. It is so secret that many Disneyland employees don't know it's there, at 33 Rue Royale in New Orleans Square, near the Pirates of the Caribbean and just to the right of the Blue Bayou restaurant. It is identified only by the number "33" on an ornate oval plaque near the door. . . . The story is that Disney intended to live here and entertain dignitaries, so an apartment was built on the third floor. But Disney died before it was completed, and it was made into a private club. . . . Club 33 is wired for sound: Tiny microphones are hidden in the chandeliers. My informant asked a waiter about this and was told that Disney had planned to eavesdrop on diners' conversations. The waiter also pointed out a china closet built to accommodate a hidden camera . . . you could say Disney got a little quirky in his old age. He apparently planned to talk to people through the moosehead in the Trophy Room. *It* has a hidden speaker.

—William Poundstone, *Bigger Secrets*

The Mother Huge Gate

A small fleet of unmarked trucks had parked at New Babel's foot and was being unloaded by a small fleet of Electric Negroes. Under the direction of a white man in a spotless gray suit, the Negroes had formed a bucket-brigade line to transfer a lading of wooden crates—thirty or forty from each truck's trailer—into an open manhole; brown hands reached up Automatically from underground to accept each crate in turn. None of the myriad construction workers, tourists, and other pedestrians passing to and fro paid any attention to this activity—first, because Negroes were generally beneath notice, and second, because even those few people inclined to curiosity were distracted by the vision of Babel itself.

Even Joan, who placed superskyscrapers high on her list of P.U. human endeavors, could not suppress a feeling of awe at the sight. Like one of those enormous European cathedrals that seem fabricated from a different reality than that of the dwarfen secular buildings surrounding them, Babel defied comparison or grouping with Manhattan's other tall towers; its relative isolation at the northern end of the island only magnified the sense that here indeed was something unique, something not done or seen before, anywhere. Ziggurat: glass and steel, spiraling upward in boldly measured steps of ebon translucence, the sheerness of its scale difficult to grasp . . . and it was only half finished. To imagine it whole and complete, *twice* its already impossible size, that was the real mind bender.

"Don't look so guilty, dear," Kite counseled, noting the uneasy play of emotions on Joan's face. "There's no sin in admiring its beauty. You know Frank Lloyd Wright wanted to build one of these in Chicago in the 1950s. The Mile-High Illinois Building. . . . I remember the *Baja Diario* carried an artist's rendering on the front page. '*El Visión Fabuloso del Futuro.*' Gorgeous. Costly, impractical, and terrifying to most other architects of the day, but gorgeous. I'd have paid good money to stand out front of the real thing—or better yet, stand at the top—for just five minutes."

"Yeah, well, but the thing is, Kite," Joan replied, "being Harry's comptroller for nine years, I share at least some of the responsibility for this monster. Indirectly share it, but still . . . when the shadow stretches across the Harlem River and eclipses the South Bronx, when the city has to drill the sewers wider to accommodate Babel's effluvia, that's my public opinion skills at work, partly."

"Well," said Kite, "if you bought the blame, you might as well enjoy the view."

Ayn Rand was, as usual, unequivocal in her judgment. "It's the most magnificent building I've ever seen!" she said. "It's the most brilliant architectural triumph in human history!"

"Wait'll you see the lobby," Joan told her.

No sealed fortress, Babel's broad foundation was girded by accessways of every kind—swinging doors, sliding doors, revolving doors, Electric Iris Portals—but the most obvious entrance was the great Gate marking the southernmost point on the foundation's circumference. Referred to as the

Mother Tongue Gate in early press releases and renamed the Mother Huge Gate by punnish editorialists, the Gate was just that: a pair of one-hundred-and-fifty-three-foot-high doors of gilded steel and black crystal, set back in a tremendous recessed archway. Shallow contoured steps of black marble flowed out from beneath the arch in simulation of a frozen lava stream—an elegant effect, though the unevenness of the contouring did cause a lot of people to trip and fall (the situation was exacerbated in winter, when tons of heated air escaping through the wide open Gate caused snow to melt and refreeze in thick sheets of ice on the outermost steps and the surrounding pavement; architect Lonny Matsushida was said to be working on a clever technological solution to this problem).

The space beyond the Gate was not so much a lobby as a roofed canyon, with balconied setback cliffs rising on either side. Artificial cataracts split the balconies at intervals, while illuminated fountains and manicured trees and shrubbery lined the canyon floor. In tribute to Babylon's famous hanging gardens, ceramic flats of lush, genetically engineered ivy depended from the ceiling on long cords; Electric Hummingbirds flitted from vine to vine, watering them a few drops at a time, fanning dust from their leaves, and occasionally careening out of control and smacking into the cliffs.

The canyon ended in a circular domed chamber, large enough to contain the basilica dome of St. Peter's with clearance at the top for an angry Swiss Guardsman plus crossbow. A weighty copper sphere, representing the earth, hung suspended by a chain from the ceiling's apex; it dangled within a meter of the arched back and shoulders of a colossus, whose face bore the expression of a slave freeing himself from lifelong bondage, a blend of joy, hope, pride, righteousness, and a hard kernel of insanity. A chiseled tablet at the base of the statue declared: ATLAS SHRUGS.

"What do you think, Ayn?" Joan asked. She held the Electric Lamp above her head to give the genie a better view.

"I think," said Ayn, with an air of sincere deliberation, "that if you could love the man whose mind created this . . . if you could identify with his values sufficiently to marry him . . . there may still be hope for you. Your involvement in so-called 'liberal' causes such as environmentalism marks you as an altruist and a muscle-mystic, but perhaps you are not beyond redemption. I will have to tutor you in the virtue of selfishness."

"Oh good," said Joan. "That."

Kangaroo Control

"So you claim that your Objectivist philosophy is completely consistent," said Kite, as New Babel's third-tier elevator bank transported them between the 120th and 180th floors, "and that anyone who accepts even the smallest fraction of it must axiomatically accept all of it."

"That is correct," Ayn Rand said.

"Which could be interpreted to mean that anyone who believes in the power of reason, who sees herself as rational, must axiomatically agree with everything you say."

"Since I'm right," Ayn said, "why shouldn't all rational people agree with me?"

"Yes . . . and it follows, as E. Lee follows Robert, that anyone who *doesn't* agree with you is by definition *irrational.*"

"If such a person were unable to demonstrate a specific error in my premises, or reveal an unresolved contradiction in my conclusions, yes, they would be irrational—and if they persisted in denying reality after the truth had been explained to them, they would also be immoral."

"And you first conceived of this philosophy when?"

"Eons ago. I have held the same philosophy for as long as I can remember. The only intellectual debt I can acknowledge is to Aristotle; the entire history of Western thought from the fourth century B.C. onward reduces to a struggle between Aristotelian logic and the mysticism of Plato."

"And now you've come along to fill the gaps in Aristotle's system."

"To purge it of the vestiges of Platonism. 'Plato is dear to us,' Aristotle is recorded as saying, 'but the truth is dearer still.' The first part of that statement is errant sentiment; Plato is not dear, he is contemptible. Only the truth is dear. Truth as apprehended by a reasoning consciousness."

"Through common sense, in other words."

"Sense, yes. Common, no. In fact it's appallingly rare."

"But that's the part I don't understand, Miss Rand," said Kite. "Forgive my irreverence, but given what you seem to believe, I'm not sure why it is that you advocate individual freedom at all."

"Freedom from coercion is prerequisite to the reasoning process. No man can think at the point of a gun."

"Well, but when you say that you've held the same philosophy for as long as you can remember, that sounds to me as if you're really saying you were born knowing everything you ever needed to know, that you've never been wrong. And when you add on top of that that you're the first philosopher with something original to say since Aristotle—that's a dry patch of what, twenty-four centuries?—you aren't making a very strong case for allowing ordinary people to think for themselves."

"No one can *force* men to accept reason," Ayn said. "That's an altruist's contradiction in terms! Men are always free to deny reality if they so choose—but *if* they so choose, they must live with the consequences. Such men have no right to the fruits of *my* intellect."

"These consequences," Kite said. "Would they include—"

"Failure," Ayn Rand said. "The ultimate consequence of denying reality is always failure. Scratch a worthless bum and you'll discover an irrational man."

"Floor one-eighty," the elevator announced.

"I think I understand you now," said Kite.

According to Lonny Matsushida's blueprint, the finished Babel would comprise five hundred floors, with a Phoenix-like pinnacle bringing the aggregate height to fifty-eight hundred and thirty-one feet. At present, the tower was fully glassed-in only up to the 189th floor; erection of the bare steel structural framework had advanced to the level of the 228th floor. It was to this zenith that Joan, Kite, and Ayn Rand ascended in search of Harry Gant's mother, Winifred Gant, forewoman to the Babel construction project. They rode a construction worker's cage lift for the last stretch, Kite and Joan wearing hard hats given them by the lift's operator, an Automatic Servant named Melvin 261.

At Babel's crown, steel beams and girders were lifted into place by kangaroo cranes, so named because they were anchored to moveable platforms that could be elevated on hydraulic jacks, allowing the cranes to leapfrog skyward along with the building's superstructure. There was also a kangaroo control center, or KCC: a weatherproof bunker containing a supercomputer, monitoring equipment, and communication facilities that linked Winnie Gant to every member of the construction team.

Many Automatic Servants were employed in the building process, of course, but union rules and state law deemed that a substantial portion of the work be reserved for humans. Up at the top that meant Native Americans, mostly, New York and Canadian Mohawks whose sense of balance and fearlessness at high altitudes was the stuff of urban legend. The Mohawk assistant foreman was an old-timer named Jim Wolverine who'd worked with

Winnie since 1975, when she'd first joined the trade as an apprentice welder. They'd been sweethearts their first two years together, a romance whose embers had never entirely cooled; marriage had even been discussed at one point, before Jerry Gant entered the picture in 1978. Joan sometimes wondered, and not just in terms of his acrophobia, how Harry might have been different with an Amerind for a father.

"Jimmy," Winnie Gant said now, speaking into a walkie-talkie, "get up on two-twenty-seven in the northeast quarter, would you? Warner 990 just got blown over the side again." One of the monitor screens showed an Automatic Construction Worker swinging from the end of a safety line, smiling despite the long drop beneath it. "After you reel him in send him to the shop to get his gyros checked."

"Maintenance problems with the Servants?" Joan asked.

"The usual crap," Winnie replied. She was a big woman, still muscular at sixty-eight; it was easy to see where Harry got his beefcake. "Exposure to the elements, standard wear and tear. But I'll choose an android casualty over a real one any day of the week."

"No serious accidents?"

"No deaths, thank God. I've been running tight safety regs on this one. Of course you do have the inevitable power tool or lunchbox getting booted over the side and sailing right past the catch tarpaulins. You know it's funny, taxis seem to be a magnet for falling objects; we've totaled the engine blocks on two Checkers so far."

Kite raised an eyebrow. "Does your insurance cover that sort of damage?"

"Nah. We just cut power to the elevators and they can't reach us to sue us." She winked. "So what brings you calling, Joan? You and Junior aren't getting back together, are you?"

"Uh . . . not in any matrimonial sense, no," Joan said. "We might . . . have coffee."

"Well, no pressure," Winnie promised. "It's nice to see you."

"Actually," Joan said, "my friend Kite and I, and Ayn here"—she patted the Electric Lamp—"came by to see Jerry. But when I rang him up, he couldn't tell me what floor you're living on."

"Oh," said Winnie. She laughed. "That's Harry's fault. As a perk for my foreing the site, he wanted to give us an apartment as high up in the building as possible, which of course keeps changing week by week. Moving crew comes in every so often and bumps our stuff up another few stories. I don't have any problem adjusting—right-brain thinker—but Jerry has to page me for directions every time he goes out. Tell you what, my lunch break's almost here, so I'll walk you down." She nodded at the Lamp. "What is that, anyway?"

"It's my new guiding light," said Joan.

"What store did you get it at? Jerry could use an Electric Guide."

"I'm a philosopher," Ayn Rand said.

"Huh," said Winnie Gant. "Huh. Neat idea. Jerry could probably use one of those, too."

The Sign of the Dollar

If Harry Gant had inherited his physique from his mother, he got his love of clutter—and of toys—from his dad.

Retired now from teaching, Jerry Gant devoted much of his time to the collection of old periodicals: full sets if he could get them, in the original print format if possible. Neatly arranged on shelves throughout the huge apartment—neatly arranged not by Jerry, who left to his own devices would just have heaped them randomly along the wall, but by the omnipresent movers who were making it so hard for him to remember where he lived—were thousands of back issues of *Frank Leslie's Illustrated Newspaper*, *The Saturday Evening Post*, *Graham's Magazine*, *Atlantic Monthly*, *The American Mercury*, *Life*, *Scribner's*, *Godey's Ladies' Book*, etc., many of which Joan had never heard of, but which Kite eyed with undisguised nostalgia.

"That's the latest addition," Jerry said, indicating a metal cabinet whose drawer-trays contained the entirety of the *Wall Street Journal* on microfilm. "You wouldn't think it, but they have some marvelous human interest stories tucked in among the financial reports. Historical chestnuts, some of them, the sort of nifty anecdotes that don't make it into mainstream history texts. Did you know, for instance, that during World War II the Allies were considering building an aircraft carrier out of ice?"

"Did the originator of this idea," Kite asked, "have a short last name?"

"Why yes, I believe he did. I can't quite remember it offhand, though . . ."

"I can guess," said Kite.

"Why microfilm?" Joan asked.

"Hmm? Well, it's a daily. The apartment's not *that* big. In fact the apartment gets a little smaller every week."

"But don't they have the *Wall Street Journal* on disk or datatape?"

Jerry Gant shrugged. "They might. But I like threading the little spools."

"OK, Mr. Genius Professor," Winnie Gant said, entering the hallway. She used a clothespin to clip a scrap of notepaper to one of Jerry's suspenders. "Our floor number is written down here on one side, and on the back is a map to get to the elevator, with all the tiger pits and quicksand marked. Try not to lose it before tonight."

"Yes, Mother," Jerry said, not the least intimidated by her gruff tone. This was one of the traits that had attracted Winnie to him in the first place—that despite being physically slight, he was rarely frightened or intimidated by anything. "I know part of it is just that he doesn't separate present reality from history that well," Winnie had confessed to Joan once. "But I've seen muggers and attack dogs walk away from him because they couldn't get him to take them seriously. It's a special kind of strength."

"I have to go back up," she said now, inclining her head to kiss Jerry goodbye. Ayn Rand fidgeted uncomfortably in her Lamp; Joan realized that this sight—the mother of an acknowledged prodigy standing half a head taller than her husband—didn't quite fit the Objectivist paradigm of heroic man and hero-worshipping woman. But soon enough Winnie had left the apartment, clapping Joan on the shoulder in passing, and Ayn sought to shore up her impression of the Gants with a compliment.

"I approve of your suspenders," she said, editing the clothespin and note out of her appraisal. Jerry's suspenders were bright red, overprinted with a pattern of gold dollar signs.

"Well thank you!" Jerry said. "Winnie got them for me on sale. I dropped twenty pounds on this old grapefruit diet out of the *Post*—controlled malnutrition, really—and buying these was less trouble than taking in all my trouser waists. I probably won't keep the weight off, anyway."

"As a historian," Ayn Rand continued, "no doubt you are aware that the sign of the dollar was created by superimposing the initials of the United States. As such, I've always thought it the perfect symbol for the free trader, the man of vision. Men such as your son."

"Harry's a good boy," Jerry agreed. "That story about the dollar sign's creation, though, I'm afraid that's not true."

Ayn's smile froze. "I beg your pardon?"

"Well, I've heard the initials theory before, of course, and I can see how it might be appealing to an avid Americophile. But that very element of appeal is grounds for suspicion. The rule of thumb in origins folklore is that the more romantic an explanation seems to be, the more likely it is to be wrong."

"Are you suggesting that the dollar sign is *not* composed of the initials U.S.?"

"Not suggesting. I've read the Oxford monograph on the topic, and a more lighthearted essay in *Harper's.* The word *dollar* is Bohemian in origin, of course, from *Joachimsthaler,* or *'thaler,* a silver coin first minted in 1519 under the direction of the German Count of Schlick. The dollar sign, on the other hand, is almost certainly a consequence of Thomas Jefferson's modeling of the U.S. dollar on the Spanish piece of eight, or *peso,* which was in common circulation in the American colonies at the time of the Revolution."

"Peso!" Ayn burst out. "Peso!"

"Yes, peso. The symbol is probably shorthand for *pesos:* not a 'U' over an 'S,' but a hastily drawn P over an S. That, or simply a corruption of the number eight. By the way, did you know that Benjamin Franklin wanted to make the turkey the national bird instead of the eagle?"

"That is preposterous!"

"Oh no, it's documented. Franklin—"

"Shorthand for pesos! Ridiculous! You can't have proof of this."

"Not absolute proof, no. It's history, not calculus. But the preponderance of evidence—"

"'Preponderance of evidence!'" Ayn spat. "Statistics, you mean! That's not proof! My explanation is inarguably more rational. You can't say it isn't!"

Jerry Gant frowned. "I believe I just did."

"Time out, folks," Joan suggested. She rang down the curtain on the debate by draping an embroidered linen napkin over the Electric Lamp globe. "What do you make of this, Jerry?"

"Hmm," Jerry said, examining the napkin. "That's from the 33 Club. Did Harry buy you a membership?"

Joan shook her head. "The 33 Club," she said. "Is that in Atlantic City?"

"No. Anaheim, California. It's in Disneyland."

Exchanging glances with Kite, Joan asked: "Only in Disneyland, or is there another one in Paris Euro Disney?"

"No, there's only one." Jerry smiled. "Club 33 is a unique historical anomaly, my favorite kind." He nodded at the puzzle box that Kite was carrying. "What else do you have to show me?"

A Bowl Full of Berf-oh Pee-stow

"So this Club 33 was originally intended as a private dining hall for Disney's honored guests?"

"Foreign dignitaries and the like," Jerry confirmed. "Also scientists— Disney was in love with technology. In fact there's even a legend, not true, that Disney had his corpse cryogenically frozen in hopes of being resurrected sometime in the future. In wilder versions of the myth the cryostorage facility is said to be hidden under the Pirates of the Caribbean ride, a few doors down from Club 33."

"Not true?" said Joan.

"According to his death certificate, Disney was actually cremated," Jerry told her. "His ashes are interred at Forest Lawn Memorial Park in Glendale, California. A number of researchers in my field have gone there and checked."

"Excuse me for asking this, Mr. Gant," Kite Edmonds said, "but what exactly *is* your field? What branch of history do you teach?"

"High school social studies," he said, putting audible quotes around the last two words. "Glorified geography. That's behind me now, thank goodness—not that I didn't love the kids, but the seven-to-four daily schedule, plus faculty meetings, was always much too structured and time consuming for my taste, even with summer vacations thrown in. I prefer a more flexible situation, like paid retirement. As for my field, my B.A. from New Jersey State was interdisciplinary: adoxographic American cultural history combined with investigative folklore anthropology."

"Alligators in the Sewers 101," Joan translated.

"There *were* alligators in the sewers," Jerry Gant said. "There really were."

"Believe me," said Joan, "I know."

Jerry slotted the Betamax videocassette and the eight-track tape into appropriate playback machines. His workroom was an elephant's graveyard of outmoded audio-visual equipment, scavenged and restored tools of the investigative folklorist's art. You never knew what crucial piece of trivia might be buried in the vinyl grooves of a 78 rpm record or coiled on the magnetic scytale of a reel-to-reel tape; and besides, it was fun to thread the little spools, to turn the hand-crank on the side of the Victrola and watch the tone arm dance to the music of the past.

But not all of the gear in the room was obsolete: Jerry had a Cray PC more state-of-the-art than the one in Joan's home office. The Betamax and eight-track machines were both hooked into it. "We'll digitize the sound and picture and let the PC sync them," Jerry said, powering up the computer. "Fun is fun, but manually cueing up an eight-track player without rewind or pause buttons is a pain in the butt."

They watched the video first, without sound, the Cray displaying the Betamax images on its monitor as it dubbed them to disk. Two men sat at a table in an elegant dining room, addressing a waiter whose blue tuxedo bore the Club 33 logo. One of the men, the moon-faced one on the waiter's left, was familiar.

"John Hoover," Joan said.

"John Edgar Hoover," Jerry amended.

Kite nodded. "Of course. I *knew* I'd seen him before."

"Hold on," said Joan. "*J.* Edgar Hoover? The old F.B.I. director?"

"The chief G-man," Jerry agreed.

"But that man there on the screen is *John* Hoover, the Disney technician who invented the Automatic Servant."

"No," Jerry said. "I know the John Hoover you mean; I met him at Gant Industries once, before you and Harry got married. He didn't look anything like J. Edgar Hoover."

"But we met John Hoover yesterday, and he did look like J. Edgar Hoover. Like *that* Hoover, anyway."

"Someone must have been playing a joke on you, Joan. I don't even think John Hoover is still alive. He was already very old when I met him, and not in good health. He'd have to be in his late nineties by now."

"Well just to double-check," said Joan, "J. Edgar Hoover is also dead, right?"

"Oh yes," said Jerry.

"As a doornail," Kite added.

On the monitor, the two men closed their menus and gave them to the waiter; the screen faded to black. There was a cut to a close-up of a book order slip with entry spaces for title, author, and call number. The tip of a mechanical pencil entered the frame and wrote on the call number line: N.Y.P.L. / 171.303 607 949 6. The image held for about five seconds, then again faded to black, followed by static.

"That was short," Jerry Gant said. "Let's try the audio."

He tapped out commands on a keyboard, spurning the Cray's voice-recognition system. The video sequence replayed, accompanied by a fuzzy and unintelligible soundtrack; Club 33's hidden microphones seemed to be on the fritz.

"Who's the man sitting with Hoover?" Kite asked. Thinner than Hoover, the man wore a spotless gray suit and had a scar on the bridge of his nose. "He's famous too, isn't he?"

"That's Roy Cohn," Jerry told her. "The attack lawyer. Chief counsel to Joe McCarthy's Permanent Investigations Subcommittee. It's funny he and Hoover would be dining at Club 33. Not that they couldn't easily have arranged guest passes for themselves . . ."

"Had either of them known Disney personally?" asked Joan.

"Hoover did, I think. Walt was pretty staunchly right-wing, and he believed in supporting his local F.B.I."

"Can you understand what they're saying?" Kite asked.

"No," said Jerry. "I'll try and fix that. . . ." He stopped the replay by hitting a key, and typed: LOADRUN UN-BABEL \ 8T SOUNDTRACK \ ENHANCE.

"What's Un-Babel?" Joan asked.

"Pretty much what it sounds like. It ungarbles garbled speech. Removes static and other background noise, minimizes echo, and if necessary makes an educated guess as to which words best match the pattern of sounds on the recording. I use it to decode backwards messages on old rock 'n' roll albums."

ENHANCEMENT COMPLETE, the Cray flashed on its monitor. MULTIPLE SOLUTIONS (A/B).

"Hmm," said Jerry. "This happens sometimes, when the recording is especially poor quality."

He typed: RUN BETAVIDEO W/UN-BABEL ENHANCEMENT A.

"The gentlemen are ready to order?" the blue-tuxedoed waiter inquired. The gentlemen appeared hesitant, so the waiter continued, even as Cohn and Hoover both spoke up: "Perhaps I can suggest—"

"Are there—" Roy began.

"I'll—" said Hoover.

"—as your—"

"—go for—"

An embarrassed pause. The waiter looked apologetic, Cohn and Hoover annoyed.

"You go," Hoover said, gesturing impatiently at Roy.

"No, please," said Roy, with a disingenuous politeness. *"You* go."

"Fine," said Hoover. He folded his hands, turned to the waiter, and said: "Gimme a bowl of the Berf-oh Pee-stow. Buttered corn biscuits. Buttered lima beans and asparagus, braised carrots, and mixed greens. For the main course I'll take the Moaner Bluefish, maybe some rice with that. And I'll also take some more wine."

The waiter nodded and turned to Roy. "And you, sir?"

"I think I'll go for the Vegetarian Chef's Salad Number 33."

"And which of the dressings and toppings do—"

"Ah, Thousand Islands," Cohn said. "Sprouts and croutons."

"Very good, sir." The waiter indicated Roy's empty glass. "Would you like more gin and tonic?" Cohn nodded.

"That's all you're going to eat is a salad?" Hoover said. "You eat like a fucking bird, Roy."

"Yeah, well," said Roy, handing his menu to the waiter, "I can always pick out of your trough . . ."

Fade to black, and cut to the book slip.

"What's Berf-oh Pee-stow?" Joan asked.

"*Bœuf au Pistou,* I think," Jerry Gant said. "Un-Babel has trouble with badly accented foreign phrases. It's French beef stew, with an herb and garlic sauce." He patted his stomach. "Fattening."

"And Moaner Bluefish?"

"Probably Bluefish Meunière—floured and fried in butter, then drenched in more butter."

"Well, that seems to be the proper soundtrack," Kite judged. "So what's the other solution it came up with?"

"Let's see," said Jerry. He typed: RUN BETAVIDEO W/UN-BABEL ENHANCEMENT B.

Enhancement B was . . . different.

"Generate executive order," the blue-tuxedoed waiter said. The gentlemen appeared hesitant, so the waiter continued, even as Cohn and Hoover both spoke up: "Priority request–"

"Author—" Roy said.

"—iz—" said Hoover.

"—ation—"

"—code four—"

An embarrassed pause.

"Two oh," Hoover said, gesturing impatiently at Roy.

"Oh, three," said Roy. "*Two* oh."

"Nine," said Hoover. Then he folded his hands, turned to the waiter, and said: "Gimme a world full of perfect Negroes. Cull the born misfits; cull anomalies and disparities, stray arrows and miscreants. You may be forced to make a whole new blueprint, build up the race from scratch. Whatever it takes is fine."

The waiter nodded and turned to Roy. "And you, sir?"

"I think I'll explore the tension between fact and ideology."

"And you'll be addressing this topic through—"

"A thousand ironic . . . prosecutions," Cohn said.

"If you would, sir," said the waiter, gesturing at Roy's empty glass, "what do you mean by 'ironic'?"

"When your dearest beliefs prove invalid," Hoover said. "Make them eat their fucking words, Roy."

"I will," said Roy, handing his menu to the waiter. "I can pick on whoever you need offed . . ."

Fade and cut. The mechanical pencil wrote: N.Y.P.L. / 171.303 607 949 6.

"Hmm," said Jerry Gant. "Hmm. Well."

"Play it again," Joan said.

15

Let us begin by committing ourselves to the truth, to see it like it is and to tell it like it is, to find the truth, to speak the truth and to live with the truth. That's what we'll do.

—Richard Milhous Nixon, accepting the
Republican nomination for president, 1968

I want to be a horse.

—Elizabeth II, age seven, on her plans for the future

The Tribe That Isn't Most People

The *Yabba-Dabba-Doo* was ready for launch by sunset. Morris's preparations for nonlethal warfare turned out to be a snap: all the supplies and equipment he needed were either aboard the sub or in storage in Pirate's Cove, and he was already out on Liberty Island when Philo contacted him. The real chore was reassembling the rest of the crew, who weren't answering their beepers. Lexa Thatcher and Ellen Leeuwenhoek shuttled around the city in their separate cars for hours, each chasing down six of the twelve missing pirates. Ellen needed a grappling hook to reach Norma Eckland and Asta Wills, who'd isolated themselves atop another abandoned lighthouse, this one at the tip of Coney Island; and when Lexa traced the Palestinian Kazensteins to the Russian Tea Room in Manhattan, their Aston Martin had just been towed, so all five of them, plus Irma Rajamutti, had to be shoehorned into the Beetle.

By late afternoon, though, they were all at the Cove. On the *Yabba-Dabba-Doo*'s missile deck, Morris loaded four yellow buoys into launch tubes while trying to ignore his Palestinian siblings' pestering. Asta, Norma, Irma,

Marshall Ali, Twenty-Nine Words, Osman Hamid, Jael Bolívar, and Ellen Leeuwenhoek were below, as was Seraphina, who'd hitched a ride out with Ellen intending to give a hero's sendoff to a certain someone. Philo circled the pier, making a thorough inspection of the sub's hull, his morning's optimism replaced by a stone seriousness that was almost brooding.

"Second thoughts?" Lexa asked. She walked beside him, her arm linked in his.

"Thoughts," Philo replied. He looked at her. "This is pretty nuts, this thing we're about to do, isn't it?"

Lexa nodded. "Most people would probably say so, yes."

Philo nodded too. Then he said: "I was thinking about Flora. About '04." He squeezed Lexa's hand. "You actually saw people die in the Pandemic, didn't you? Saw it live, not on TV."

"I lost some good friends in the Pandemic," Lexa said. "And when I wasn't with them, I was out trying to report the story. With Ellen, until she got word that her lover was sick. And Joan, Joan was on the streets too . . . that was the same year her mother tussled with the pope, and she was back and forth between Boston, New York, and Philly all summer. She went out to Brooklyn on the last day of the plague, when the government finally started organizing relief services. She was in Bed-Stuy when it burned. Typical Joan—she nearly got herself shot by the National Guard."

"Mmm," said Philo, "an experience I can relate to."

"What still amazes me," said Lexa, "is the number of people who say they weren't around for the Pandemic, or words to that effect—kind of like saying they were out of town during Noah's flood."

"Well," said Philo, "you know I wasn't there."

"That's different, though. That's not what I'm talking about. You really *weren't* in town for the Pandemic."

Philo had been at sea, in fact, for almost a year before the plague struck, crewing on a 100–foot corsair with an eco-posse of Rainbow Warriors. In a foreshadowing of Philo's later career on the *Yabba-Dabba-Doo,* the Warriors had boxed the compass rose of the Atlantic, sailing south to the Weddell Sea to harass a fleet of Japanese harvester ships that were illegally strip-mining krill, north to the Denmark Strait to haul in drift nets set by Icelandic fishermen, east and west in search of further wrongs to right in the Bay of Biscay and the Gulf of Mexico. In their own way the Rainbow Warriors were a lot like the Pennsylvania Dutch that Philo had grown up with: principled; hard-working; nonviolent; anti-industrial;

thick-bearded; and reclusive. They had a shortwave radio on the boat but seldom used it except for weather reports and to get information on potential targets from their home base in Boston; their mail was forwarded to whatever seemed likely to be the corsair's next port of call, but such predictions were often wrong, and the letters and packages usually had to be reforwarded several times. Hence Philo's delay in learning that he had become a father.

"After we graduated U. Penn.," Philo had explained to Lexa, "Flora and I drifted apart and didn't see each other for years. We met up again at an alumni picnic in '03 just before I took ship, and . . . well, you can guess what happened. Pennsylvania was a red state then, *very* red—this was when they'd passed that law making it a crime to leave the state for an abortion, and there was a fight on to see whether that was constitutional. The Supreme Court's ruling was due in two weeks, and it looked like it might go either way, so Flora figured she only had a few days to make up her mind what to do, with no way to get in touch with me. So she wrote me a letter as a substitute for the discussion we couldn't have."

The letter had been mailed care of Philo's old Philadelphia address; it eventually reached Boston, then visited Porto Alegre, Abidjan, Gibraltar, and Calais before finally catching up to Philo in the Faeroe Islands. By then the original postmark was ten and a half months old, with almost a full year elapsed since the fateful picnic. Philo read the half dozen closely written pages sitting on a bench outside the Nordic House in Tórshavn, did some quick mental subtraction, and realized that he'd been a daddy since May, early June at the latest . . . unless Flora had changed her mind after sealing the envelope.

When a call to Philadelphia from the Tórshavn telephone office failed to go through, Philo rounded up the Rainbow Warriors and convinced them to set course at once for the Eastern Seaboard. It was a difficult crossing: rough seas and strong headwinds dogged them as far as the Grand Banks, slowing their passage, and midway through the journey a storm-tossed mug of herbal tea shorted out the shortwave. Deaf to the news of epidemic on the mainland, the Warriors pressed on, bypassing Boston to drop anchor in Delaware Bay. Philo packed a duffel and went up the Delaware River alone in a Zodiac, arriving at Penn's Landing sometime after dark.

In Philadelphia as in New York, there had been short-lived incidents of rioting in some of the plague-stricken neighborhoods, and the city was under curfew; but all Philo knew was that he couldn't find a cab. When his Faeroese pocket change was rejected by the waterfront pay phones, he decided to hike the two miles to Flora's apartment complex. Luck and ignorance combined to steer him clear of roving police patrols and National Guard checkpoints along the way.

The power was off in Flora's building when he got there. Growing alarmed at the lack of activity on the street—it wasn't that late at night—Philo pounded at the lobby door for admittance. No one came to let him in, but his pounding soon broke the lock. He ran up the stairs to the fourth floor without encountering a single soul.

The door to Flora's apartment stood ajar. Philo found his daughter lying in an armchair beside an open window, loosely swaddled in her mother's bathrobe. For an infant half-dead of hunger and dehydration, she looked remarkably content: she smiled at Philo and squeezed his finger in her fist, then waited patiently while he searched the rest of the apartment. Flora was nowhere to be found. Fighting the urge to panic, Philo carried the baby into the kitchen and hunted up a bottle, some formula, and a fresh diaper; he fed her, and bathed and changed her in the sink. Then he picked up the kitchen phone, which still worked, and dialed 911. He got two busy signals in a row and was about to try again when a police car cruised by outside, bubble lights flashing.

And this is where the real nightmare began: Philo opened a window and shouted down to the street for help. The police cruiser stopped and disgorged four cops with riot guns. The cops did not see a confused father seeking aid for his child; they saw a big screaming black guy with a bomb-sized bundle in his arms. They emptied their riot guns at him. When he ducked back inside, they switched to tear gas canisters, and in short order managed to set the building on fire. Clutching the baby to his chest, Philo fled out the rear of the apartment complex; the police radioed the National Guard command post for the area and warned them to be on the lookout for a mad bomber.

The return trek to the waterfront took most of the rest of the night. Streets that had earlier seemed deserted were now actively patrolled by armed men and women whom Philo had to assume would shoot on sight. At one point, crouching between cars in a parking lot to avoid detection by a helicopter, he spied a vanity plate that read SERAPHINA, and whispered the name in a singsong to his daughter to calm her. She liked it.

Luck favored them. By dawn's gathering Philo had regained the Zodiac; Seraphina slept snug in a box of survival gear while her father got them the hell away from shore. They made only one stop—a visit to the docks of the Franklin Seaman's Club to siphon fuel from an unguarded yacht—after which Philo did not ease up on the throttle until Philadelphia was far behind them. He steered upriver, towards Trenton; though a seaward course would have felt safer, he knew the Rainbow Warriors were to have left Delaware Bay by now, and his first priority was to locate a newsstand with no troops around it and find out what was going on. It didn't occur to him that the chaos they had just fled might exist in other cities as well, nor could he have imagined that he and his daughter were embarked on only the first leg of a long journey into exile. All he knew was that he was alive and wanted to stay that way, and that, barring word of Flora, he would not be returning to the city of brotherly love any time in the near future.

"It makes sense, really," Philo said now. Having completed the inspection of the sub's hull, he rested his bulk on Betsy Ross's front hood; Lexa rested on him, once more drawing his arms around her like a safety harness. "That I'd survive the plague and its aftermath, I mean—that makes sense. If there's a story to my life, odd man out is it. Black Amish, who ever heard of such a thing? And then after I moved to Philly, swapped my adjectives around: Amish African-American—triple A, Flora used to call it—who ever heard of *that*?" He laid his chin on Lexa's shoulder and stared at the *Yabba-Dabba-Doo*. "Do you suppose that might count for something, if worse comes to worst?"

"How do you mean?"

"Well, what you said before: *most* people would think this mission to save the lemurs is crazy. Most people wouldn't try it. And maybe most people who would try it wouldn't survive, let alone succeed . . ."

" . . . but you're *not* most people," Lexa said, picking up on the logic. "In fact you're *less* most people than almost anyone left on earth. Therefore, the odds of succeeding are actually stacked in your favor."

"Right."

"I'm not sure it works that way," said Lexa. "I'd still be very, very careful."

"No fear," said Philo.

"Here," said Lexa. She dug in her purse and offered him an old silver dollar, its faces worn nearly smooth by five generations of fingers.

"For luck?" Philo asked.

"Call it an extra incentive to be careful," Lexa replied. "It's very precious to me. If it ends up at the bottom of the Hudson Canyon where I can't get it back, I'm going to be *very* angry." She craned her head around to look him in the eye. "Understood?"

Philo nodded. He took the silver dollar and pocketed it, ducked his own head beneath Lexa's chin, pressed a smile against the hollow of her throat, and whispered: "Understood."

A Kurdish Love Charm

Seraphina found Marshall Ali in his cabin aboard the sub. He had an open strongbox on the floor between his feet and a collection of stone artifacts laid out beside him on his bunk.

"What are those?" Seraphina asked, as Marshall Ali waved her inside.

"This is Kurdish archaeology," he told her. "All of it." He indicated another five strongboxes stacked against a bulkhead and secured with canvas straps. "It was necessary to leave behind many more containers when I fled Turkey; this is all that I could carry with me. But it is the largest collection of Kurdish artifacts in the world. It is the only one."

"You had to leave Turkey?"

"With my good Turkish friend Osman Hamid. He drove the grand taxi from Istanbul to Diyarbekir, which was my home. We would watch VCR together at the house of my grandmother: American martial arts movies, also bootleg tapes of Sonny Bono and Cher Sarkisian. Every year during the holy month of Ramadan we searched the ruins of Turkish Kurdistan. We fasted, as is the custom for Ramadan, and our hunger brought on visions, which unveiled the secrets of the past. Regrettably, Ramadan's fasting also shortens tempers. On our last expedition we were discovered by a fat Turkish soldier, a very hateful man. He crept up on our camp in his jeep and overheard me singing a song by Sonny and Cher, whose lyrics I had translated into Kurdish. That is a serious crime in Turkey."

"Singing a Sonny and Cher song?"

"Uttering Kurdish. Ten years in prison, at a minimum. It is part of the government's cultural outreach program. Osman attempted to plead on my behalf with the soldier, but this only provoked him—the sight of a fellow Turk defending a Kurd—and he returned to his vehicle and accelerated it in my direction. I was forced to defend myself in the style of the American ninja Chuck Norris: I leapt over the hood of the jeep and drove my foot through the windscreen. This proved effective. If only all bad Turks shared a single neck . . . but the world is not so easy. Shortly after our return to Diyarbekir we learned that other soldiers were searching for us, more soldiers than even the estimable Bruce Lee could have held at bay. Not wishing to end as Butch Cassidy and Sundance, it became urgent for us to leave the country. We were assisted in our flight by the Mossad branch of the family Kazenstein, for whom my Iraqi cousins had once done a particular favor." Marshall Ali spread his hands. "And here we are today. I will never again see Kurdistan."

"That's terrible," said Seraphina, wishing she were truly able to feel terrible for him.

"It is past," Marshall Ali told her. "Not forgotten, but done with. But you did not seek me out to hear sad stories. Your forehead is sheened with the perspiration of the woman in love."

Seraphina raised a hand to her forehead, which was sort of oily. "Is it that obvious?"

Marshall Ali smiled. "Do you wish to know where he is?"

"Actually, I was hoping for . . ."

"Advice?"

"Yes," Seraphina said. "Advice on how to . . . how to go about . . . well . . ."

"The woman pursues the man with lust in her heart," said Marshall Ali. "We did not rent those movies. I think they are illegal in Turkey."

"So you don't have any hints for me?"

"The palm."

"The palm?"

He nodded. "Grip the wrist like so"—he encircled his left wrist with his right thumb and forefinger—"and apply the tip of the tongue to the palm."

"You mean *his* palm? My tongue on his palm?"

"Only if you want it to work. Trace the creases of the palm, then up each finger in turn, slowly, but with authority. Look him in the eye as you do this. Also"—tapping the spot—"lick behind the ear. He will bark like a jackal."

"You never rented those kinds of movies, huh?"

"On my honor."

Seraphina's gaze shifted back to the stone artifacts. "You wouldn't happen to have an ancient Kurdish love charm, would you? Just for a little extra edge?"

"Ah! One moment!" Marshall Ali got up from the bunk and went to open another strongbox. "Essentials first," he said, and tossed Seraphina a perforated strip of foil packets. "The wise warrior *always* wears his armor. If he resists, or begins to speak of rubber raincoats, you must beat him about the face and neck until his good sense returns. Now, let us . . . yes. Here it is."

Seraphina would have expected a necklace or a bracelet, but the love charm Marshall Ali gave her was just a colored sketch on a piece of paper: a sketch of a bouquet of posies.

"This is Kurdish?" Seraphina asked. "It doesn't look very old."

"It is a tattoo," Marshall Ali explained. "It is the tattoo from the buttock of Cher Sarkisian Bono. A reproduction," he added hastily.

"Am I supposed to draw it on myself?"

"Fold the paper. Put it in your back pocket—I have bell-bottom jeans I will give you. Then, when you apply the tongue to the palm, when you lick behind his ear—*envision the tattoo.* There can be only one outcome."

Seraphina weighed the foil packets in her hand. It didn't take long for her to make up her mind what to do; not long at all.

"Well," she said, "where is he?"

Harry on the Water

The cargo hover lit out across the surface of the Bay in early twilight, orange sun highlighting the detritus in the water. The hover was roughly the same shape as one of the Department of Sewers' flat-bottomed patrol barges, but much bigger, riding on a cushion of air that kicked up silver-green fantails of effluent spray. Harry Gant, Vanna Domingo, and Whitey Caspian conferenced in the prow as it swung around towards Liberty Island.

"It's just that a little more warning would have been useful," Vanna was complaining. "A little more time to prepare."

"Well, but Vanna, you weren't around yesterday when Whitey came to see me," Gant said. "We tried, but we couldn't get hold of you. Besides which, I think the mayor's office did a fine job of handling the preparations for us. There's nothing to be so tense about."

"The military should be in on this," Vanna insisted. "The harbor should be crowded with destroyers and PT boats. And this barge should be loaded with Marines, not—"

"We discussed that with the mayor," Whitey told her. "He decided to leave the Pentagon out of the loop for a number of reasons, one being that we still aren't a hundred percent sure the U-boat base is even there. If it is there, and if the pirates are in it, they probably have a lookout posted, and it's doubtful they'd fail to notice a navy flotilla assembling in the Bay. We don't want to tip our hand too soon or they might sneak out, with or without the sub. And if it does come down to a show of force, the mayor would rather let the harbor police handle it; a full-scale naval engagement needlessly multiplies the amount of firepower in use, and there's just too much risk of collateral damage to—"

"You *still* have the brains of a radish," Vanna Domingo said. "Anti-submarine weapons aren't going to damage any real estate. There are no condominiums under the water."

"Well the mayor thinks—"

"The *mayor* has political ambition," Vanna said. "That's why he's sitting back in the stern, with *them*. The mayor wants the NYPD to bust Dufresne so he can claim full credit and use the prestige to jump-start a Senate run."

"It's not bad political strategy," Harry Gant observed.

Vanna shook her head. "I just wish I'd had another twenty-four hours advance notice, that's all. . . ." She slipped a hand inside her coat pocket and felt the slender weight of a palm-sized metallic disc, flat on one side, slightly convex on the other: an improvised gadget, rush-ordered from Gant R&D as soon as Vanna had learned what was going on. She'd have preferred to have the *Mitterrand Sierra* waiting in ambush off Sandy Hook, but there hadn't been enough time to arrange that.

"Don't worry about it, Vanna," Gant said. His own coat pocket was torn, ripped open by an insane panhandler who'd accosted them an hour ago as they'd left the Phoenix. The panhandler—stringy-haired, bearded, his neck cinched in a studded leather collar—had run up to them on the sidewalk, rattling a tin cup full of pencils and gargling non-words around a disgustingly bloated tongue. It had taken four security guards with shock prods to drive the man away.

"That's right," said Whitey, *"don't* worry about it. Look over there." He motioned to a big passenger liner in the Narrows south of the Upper Bay. "That's the *QE2 Mark 2*. Cruise ship, officially, but it's armed."

"Armed?" Gant said.

"Not that it's going to shoot at anything, Harry—the guns are just there to protect the royal family when they're on board. But it's a big ship, and its schedule happens to jibe with ours, so the mayor got the harbormaster to ring up the captain. *QE2 Mark 2* is going to sit in the Narrows and hog the channel until we're sure we've got Dufresne. *And,* Vanna, as a further precaution, the mayor has Special Agent Ernest G. Vogelsang of the F.B.I.'s Un-Un-American Activities Division standing by in a chopper downtown. Vogelsang hasn't been informed of the exact nature of the operation—the police commissioner just asked him to stand by for a possible assist—but he's there to be called in if need be.

"So you see, nothing can possibly go wrong . . ."

"Everything can always go wrong," said Vanna. "It always does. A *cruise ship* . . . Harry, do you even *want* Dufresne to be caught?"

Gant gave her a smile that told her everything she needed to know. "This is going to come off perfectly, Vanna. It's a neat plan."

"Right," said Vanna. Only by thinking of the cold depths of the Hudson Canyon was she able to force a smile in return. "A neat plan. That's just what we need."

An Adaptable Beast

"Of course you're free to back out," Morris said, as he sealed the last missile tube. "Serving on the *Yabba-Dabba-Doo* has always been a strictly voluntary affair. Personally I care too much about Philo to desert him when he needs me most, but don't let my example embarrass you into making the wrong decision. Everyone has to set their own standard of loyalty . . . and courage."

"Well," said Heathcliff, "well . . . it's not that we *aren't* loyal to Philo."

"It's not *that,*" Little Nell agreed. "Not that at all."

"Sorry guys," Morris said. He didn't look up, fearful of betraying himself with the wrong expression. This might be the only chance he would ever get to act superior to his siblings, and he intended to milk the opportunity for all it was worth. "Sorry, I didn't mean to suggest that, I mean *of course* you're loyal. Especially after everything Philo's done for you—giving you the choicest jobs on the sub, funding your research—I'm sure you're not only loyal, but *grateful.* But don't let that tear at your consciences, this is still a volunteer organization, and if you feel the mission is too dangerous for you, then—"

"I say!" said Mowgli. "It isn't the *danger,* exactly, it's . . . it's . . ."

"It's the theme," Galahad suggested. "The theme of the mission isn't Palestinian enough."

"Yes, that's it!" burst out Heathcliff. "We're loyal, we're courageous, and we laugh at death. Risk means nothing to us—we'd gladly take a rowboat to war against a battleship. But only for Palestine. Lemurs are a noble cause, but if we have to lay down our lives, we want it to be for the sake of Palestinian liberation."

"Hmm," said Morris. "I guess you'll be going back to the West Bank then, huh?"

"What?" said Oliver.

"I'll talk to Philo, see if we can spring for airfare for you."

"What do you mean," said Heathcliff, "'going back to the West Bank'?"

"Well, if you're not crewing the engine room anymore, I assume you won't want to stay in New York. After all, there's not much you can do to liberate Palestine sitting around here. Even back in London you'd be thousands of miles from the front line of the struggle. But if we put you on a plane to Bethlehem, you can be locking horns with the Shin Bet and the West Bank Settlers' Defense League by the end of the week."

"Now Morris, let's not be hasty . . ."

A hatch opened in the deck. Jael Bolívar and Ellen Leeuwenhoek climbed out, each carrying a caged bobcat.

"Are those the last of them?" Morris asked.

Jael nodded. "Hamsters are all unloaded, too. Iggy the Sloth and Borneo Bill were already at my sister's place in Astoria, so I left them there. But listen, Morris: I want to take some of the plants out as well. If you could just open up the bow for me—"

"Not a chance."

"Morris!"

"Jael, there's no time for that. We have to be out of here in a few hours."

"Now Morris," Heathcliff interjected, "don't let's be faunocentric. Plants are just as much a part of the environment as animals, and if Jael feels we ought to delay the mission in order to safeguard—"

"Shhh!" Jael hissed.

"Don't shush me!" said Heathcliff. "I'm demonstrating pan-Arab unity for your position!"

"Screw pan-Arab unity! What's that noise?"

Ellen Leeuwenhoek heard it too. "Sounds like rocks caught in a garbage disposal," she said.

" . . . or a drill bit attacking granite," said Morris. Dust sifted from the roof of the cavern as the noise intensified. "Galahad, Mowgli, go tell Irma to start the engines."

"But we haven't decided—" Little Nell started to protest. A big hunk of stone jolted loose from the ceiling and smashed itself into gravel on the nose of the sub.

"Right," Heathcliff said, and led the charge below decks. Jael Bolívar passed her bobcat to Ellen and started casting off mooring lines.

Philo ran up the gangplank. "Definite company coming," he said. "Are we ready to go?"

"The buoys are locked and loaded," Morris told him. "The ship's batteries aren't finished recharging, but we should have more than enough juice to see us through tomorrow, and I can always bring the auxiliary power supply on line if we need it."

"What about food stores? We may be at sea a lot longer than we planned."

"Thirty-day supply, counting granola," Morris said. "It'll have to do." More rocks were shaking loose from the walls and ceiling. "If we haven't found a new berthing site in a month I guess we learn how to fish. Or have the engine-room crew draw straws."

"All lines clear!" Jael shouted.

"All right," said Philo, "let's go!" He turned to retract the gangplank and saw Lexa still standing on the pier. "What are you doing? Get aboard!"

Lexa shook her head. "That's not the plan."

"Lexa, someone is coming down here in an *earth mover,* probably the Army Corps of Engineers. Do you want to get shot?"

"If they shoot me," Lexa said, "I won't be able to back you up tomorrow. So they can't shoot me."

"Lexa—"

Betsy Ross and Ellen's Citroen gunned their engines and scooted forward as the wall behind them collapsed. A massive tracked vehicle with a rock bore for a snout thrust its way through the breach.

"Get aboard!" Philo screamed.

"I love you," Lexa said, more as a means of stiffening her resolve than for any demonstrative purpose. "And I promise to be there on schedule tomorrow, no matter what. Now get out of here before *you* get shot."

Troops were debarking from the rock borer. Not the Army Corps of Engineers after all, or any other branch of the military; rather than guns and grenades, the troops Harry Gant had assembled wielded microphones, portable klieg lights, and video cameras . . .

"Shit," Ellen Leeuwenhoek said. "CNN."

And not just CNN, either, but other cable and network news crews as well, plus print reporters from nine major dailies. They surged across the dock, more terrible than any Marine landing force, crying "Mr. Dufresne! Mr. Dufresne! One question!" while public opinion trainee Fouad Nassif pointed with outstretched arm at the stunned pirates and commanded: "Journalize them! Shine the light of Western truth upon them! Mediafy them!"

Morris and Jael bolted for the missile deck hatchway. Ellen Leeuwenhoek took her life in her hands and ran the other way, back down onto the pier, into the path of the stampede; Philo hauled in the gangplank the instant she was clear, frustrating the lead camera crews, who tried to harpoon him with their boom mikes. "Mr. Dufresne, please, you *have* to talk to us! Just let us on board for one second!" *First Amendment,* Lexa mouthed apologetically to Philo, as he dodged a microphone jab to his solar plexus. *Tomorrow,* he mouthed back, and jumped down into the sub after Morris and Jael. The hatch sealed shut and the *Yabba-Dabba-Doo* began backing out of its slipway.

Denied an interview, the soldiers of the Fourth Estate formed a firing line on the pier to get footage of the submarine's departure. Those teams with more than one camera also took shots of the German bird of prey, the scattered Nazi memorabilia, and the diorama of the "PLAN TO TERRORIZE BACKSTABBING WHITE AMERICAN INDUSTRIALISTS." The print journalists tried to corner Lexa, but for a change she refused to help them. "I bust my chops negotiating an exclusive with Dufresne," she snapped, "and you people come out of the walls at just the right moment to screw it up!" Ellen Leeuwenhoek added her own "no comment," but did let them pet the bobcats.

More troops emerged from the rock borer: Harry Gant, the mayor, Whitey Caspian, Bartholomew Frum, and Vanna Domingo. Vanna raced to catch the submarine before it could clear the dock. A fistfight had broken out between Nickelodeon and MTV over choice of camera positions, and she used this distraction as cover as she leaned out and slapped an extra pink polka dot onto the *Yabba-Dabba-Doo*'s anium hull; the ersatz dot made contact with a magnetic *chunk!* and stuck fast, blending in almost perfectly with the rest of the paint job. *That'll fix you,* Vanna thought. She raised a finger in a vulgar salute; "Ma'am," the Nickelodeon anchorwoman called out to her, while a Nick sound technician fought to keep MTV's anchor in a headlock, "could you not make that gesture? We're live."

Lexa Thatcher felt a tap on her shoulder. "Hi there," Harry Gant said.

"Hi yourself," said Lexa. She relaxed the scowl she'd been using to fend off reporters. "And congratulations. Staging a surprise press conference, that was inspired." She watched a still photographer from the *Post* snap shot after shot of the U-boat diorama. "God only knows what sort of spin they'll put on this story."

"Sorry we couldn't invite *The Long Distance Call* along to join in the fun," Gant said. "I mean I know you specialize in this sort of thing, but, well . . ."

"A certain underachiever from the F.B.I. warned you I might be a security risk."

"Something like that. Since you're here anyway, though, I was hoping I could ask you a question."

"An on-the-record question or an off-the-record question?"

"Off."

"Depends."

"Well," Gant said, "you know we still haven't been able to figure out where Dufresne gets the money to run his operation. Clayton and his Creative Accounting staff have spent months sifting for leads, but so far no luck. The F.B.I., Internal Revenue, everyone's drawn a blank. And of course I don't even like finance, so I certainly didn't have a clue. At least not until this morning."

"Something Joan said jogged your thinking?"

Gant looked at her. "You know I was at Joan's?"

"I heard about it."

"Well," Gant continued, "well actually no, it wasn't anything Joan said. But I was thinking about her on the way to work, reminiscing a little, and that's when I remembered . . . when Joan left Gant Industries six years ago, I made her accept a pretty substantial severance bonus, plus annual pension payments that weren't specified by her original employment contract."

Lexa nodded. "Volunteer alimony," she said. "You know in some ways, Harry, you make no sense at all as a capitalist."

"I'm a unique individual," Harry Gant agreed. "But getting to the point of my question, since you and Joan are such good friends, and since you also obviously know Dufresne well enough to find your own way to his hideout . . ."

"You want to know whether Joan's been funneling her pension to Philo. Whether you've been unwittingly supporting your own antagonist."

"Well I'm not sure I'd say unwittingly. I did give the money to *Joan,* after all."

"True," said Lexa. "Do you mind if I ask why?"

Gant shrugged. "It seemed like a neat idea, that's all. I mean she certainly deserved it, she'd done great work in public opinion even when she was fighting my projects tooth and nail, and part of me knew I'd miss having her thorn in my side—and not just as an employee. I guess I thought that if I gave her a big enough stake to set up independently as an activist, she'd still come by and make a nuisance of herself once in a while; I was kind of disappointed when all she did with her bonus was buy that welfare hotel. Unless . . ."

"Unless." Lexa thought it over. "This is just between us? You'll leave Clayton and the feds to puzzle it out on their own?"

Gant traced an X over his heart.

"All right then," Lexa said. Checking that no one from the *Wall Street Journal* was in earshot, she whispered: *"Pesos."*

"Huh?"

"The gold and silver the conquistadors looted during the invasion of the Americas," Lexa said. "Almost all of it was melted down into ingots and pesos—billions of dollars' worth, at current market value. A lot of that loot got sent back to Spain, but what with the state of the art of hurricane prediction being fairly primitive in those days, not all of the shipments made it through. Millions of pesos ended up at the bottom of the Caribbean and the Gulf of Mexico. A fair portion of that sunken treasure has been recovered since, but there are still some major troves lying unretrieved out there, waiting for someone smart enough to know where to look, someone with the family contacts to move a huge quantity of antique coins through the black markets in Cairo and Damascus . . ."

"Wait," Gant said. "Wait. Sunken treasure? Pesos? Philo Dufresne is being financed by dead Spaniards?"

"Shhh, not so loud. Not dead Spaniards, Harry, dead Aztecs. Also dead Maya, Inca, Tlaxcala, Zapotec, Mixtec, Yaqui, Huichol, Tarahumara . . . it's a pretty long list of sponsors."

"Aztecs . . . but what about . . ."

"The primary investment for a submarine is outrageously steep," Lexa said, "even if you buy way below wholesale. Not to belittle your generosity, but you didn't give Joan *that* much severance pay. Of course," she added, "some of the secondary expenses of piracy aren't as astronomical."

He got the hint. "What kind of secondary expenses?"

"Tree fertilizer, for instance. Also bulk purchases of whipped cream, model helicopter parts, kosher salami, and other consumables."

"Consumables? Like those bunny things that Eskimo kid was throwing on the *South Furrow*?" Lexa put a finger to her lips. "Wow . . . wow. Neat."

"Yeah," said Lexa. "Joan always thought you'd say that if you knew." She gazed past the media at the *Yabba-Dabba-Doo*, which had cleared the slipway and was entering the pressure lock that would release it into the harbor. "So now that I've shared the secret with you, Harry, can you give me a lift back topside in your earth mover? I'd like to see whether Philo gets out of here alive."

"Oh sure," Gant said, "sure, no problem. But listen, I wouldn't worry about it too much. You know I'm really proud of Bart and Fouad and Whitey for coming up with this press conference tactic, and I'm grateful to the mayor for helping us put it together in time, he's been a saint, but confidentially I have to agree with Vanna that the rest of the plan—the part where the pirates get arrested—is pretty unlikely."

"Unlikely? Why?"

"Well, it's a pretty stupid plan."

"You don't sound too concerned about it."

"I'm not, really, so long as the harbor police are careful and don't hurt themselves. See, I made a few calls to California this morning, and in return for information about the history of this U-boat den, the head of HBO

Pictures has agreed to let Gant Industries handle the merchandising for HBO's upcoming docudrama on Dufresne. We'll have T-shirts, action figures, computer games, comic books, all sorts of tie-ins. And I'm also hashing out a separate deal with Nintendo to do a Virtual Reality mock-up of this place, so kids can have an eco-pirate hideout of their very own this Christmas; I'm guessing a sales potential of at least a hundred thousand units if we can get it ready in time."

"So in other words," said Lexa, shaking her head in disbelief, "it doesn't make any difference to you whether Philo escapes or not."

"Well it does make a difference, sort of, if he keeps blowing up my stuff. But after this movie deal I'll be able to afford more insurance. And if he *does* keep blowing up my stuff, I suppose HBO can do sequels . . ."

"So you can't lose."

Harry Gant smiled. "That's the free-market system for you," he said. "It's an adaptable beast."

Now We Are Amused

The plan the mayor and the police commissioner had cooked up to arrest Philo Dufresne was indeed a stupid one—almost as stupid as Morris Kazenstein's plan to rescue the lemurs from the *Mitterrand Sierra,* although not quite—but to be fair, stupidity was not the deciding factor in the *Yabba-Dabba-Doo*'s escape from the harbor. It was mainly the Queen of England's fault.

Yes, *that* Queen of England: Elizabeth the Second and Imperishable, By the Grace of God, of the United Kingdom of Great Britain and Northern Ireland and of Her Other Realms and Territories Queen, Head of the Commonwealth, Defender of the Faith. With the monarchy in peril of extinction, Queen Liz had sworn upon the millennium not to relinquish Her throne to any but the most worthy heir, which meant, given the continuing sad state of the royal family, that She might well have to reign forever. Beset by Parliament, tabloids, and time, She had not just lingered on but had thrived, becoming as wily and ferocious in Her extreme old age as any sewer 'gator ever to shun the light of day. In the last decade it had begun to be noted in British government circles that those who offended Her Majesty had a high incidence of death under mysterious circumstances, or other anonymously authored misfortune—no definite link to Buckingham Palace having ever, of course, been proved.

As the *QE2 Mark 2* assumed its blockade position in the Verrazano Narrows, the Queen was on the bridge. Her Majesty had sailed incognito to New York to explain to a certain Westchester playboy that he would *not* be marrying Her Majesty's granddaughter (and would most certainly not be impregnating her); following the news of the *South Furrow*'s sinking and the exposure of the Gant Antarcticorp project, Her Majesty had expanded her itinerary to include an unannounced visit to the White House in Washington, where she intended to deliver a serious tongue-lashing. But here was something else of interest.

"What are We observing?" the Queen asked. A pink-and-green submarine had surfaced south of Liberty Island and was steaming hell-bent for the Narrows, with a fleet of police launches in close pursuit. Farther back, a black helicopter with "FBI" painted on its underbelly was just clearing the skyscrapers of the Battery.

"The pirate vessel *Yabba-Dabba-Doo,* Your Majesty," replied the captain, suppressing a cough. The Queen's Mechanical Corgis were filling the bridge with petrol exhaust, but no one dared complain.

"This is that same pirate who sank the icebreaker?"

"Yes, Your Majesty."

"The icebreaker," said the Queen, "which Our American cousins were going to use to violate the treaty they had made with Us?"

"Apparently so, Your Majesty."

"And they"—she indicated the speedboats and the helicopter—"intend to destroy the submarine?"

"No, Your Majesty. Not even American police officers are permitted to carry that sort of weaponry. As I understand it, their intention is to transfer a boarding party of narcotics agents onto the sail of the vessel; these agents will then force the hatch, using pneumatic tools originally developed to break down the doors of crack dens."

"Crack dens?"

"Much like the old opium dens in Hong Kong, Your Majesty, but less well carpeted."

"And why is the submarine on the surface of the water? We know a great deal about submarines. Why doesn't it dive, to hide itself?"

"Most of the harbor is too shallow for a submerged vessel to maneuver safely, Your Majesty, and we ourselves are occupying the main transit channel."

"Our ship is preventing them from escaping?"

"Yes. If they attempt to cross the Narrows outside of the channel, even fully surfaced, they'll almost certainly run aground."

"Move aside, then," the Queen snapped. "Let them pass."

"But—"

"That will make a suitable recompense," said the Queen, speaking to Herself now. "That will make Us even."

"Your Majesty," the captain said, "I don't think—"

"But We haven't commanded you to think," the Queen said, Her eyes growing hard, Her tone hinting at a midnight garroting or a strychnine-tainted scone. "Do pray tell Us, loyal subject, who is the wealthiest and most powerful woman in all the world?"

The captain swallowed hard. "You are, Your Majesty."

"Repeat that, please."

"You are, Your Majesty."

"Again."

"You are, Your Majesty."

The Queen smiled, making the tiniest gesture with Her little finger; the captain spun on his heel and barked the order to his helmsman: "Ahead full flank, ten degrees starboard, *now!* I want us as far over in the channel as possible."

"Yessir!" the helmsman readily agreed. The superliner made way for the submarine; the *Yabba-Dabba-Doo,* guided by the ever-attentive sonar ear of Asta Wills, took immediate advantage of the opening, zipping into the channel at top speed.

"Fusilier!" cried the Queen. A powder-wigged redcoat with a musket appeared instantly at Her side. "Distract that," the Queen commanded, indicating the F.B.I. helicopter. "Target it with your cannon and threaten to destroy it if it does not identify itself. Use long words, speak in compound sentences, and pretend not to hear the reply."

"Should I actually open fire, Your Majesty?"

"No—but give every sign that you intend to do so. Later We will claim that We thought they were Irish. Go now!" The fusilier saluted, clicked his bootheels, and raced down to the cannon deck. "Captain!"

"Yes, Your Majesty!"

"The police launches. When the submarine is almost past, you will maneuver as if to ram it, but you will succeed only in scattering the police launches." The Queen made chopping motions with Her hands. "Later you will apologize to the American authorities for your dreadful seamanship, and We will castigate you publicly."

"Yes, Your Majesty!" The captain's chin bobbed eagerly. "Helmsman! Prepare to round hard to port. Sound collision alarm!"

"Yessir!"

"Now We are amused," said the Queen.

16

I am not *primarily* an advocate of capitalism, but of egoism; and I am not *primarily* an advocate of egoism, but of reason. If one recognizes the supremacy of reason and applies it consistently, all the rest follows. . . . Reason in epistemology leads to egoism in ethics, which leads to capitalism in politics.

—Ayn Rand, *The Objectivist,* September 1971

Marx, Engels, Lenin, and Stalin have taught us that it is necessary to study conditions conscientiously and to proceed from objective reality and not from subjective wishes . . . we must rely not on subjective imagination, not on momentary enthusiasm, not on lifeless books, but on facts that exist objectively . . . and, guided by the general principles of Marxism-Leninism, draw correct conclusions . . .

—Mao Tse-Tung, *Selected Works*

Were I a nightingale, I would sing like a nightingale; were I a swan, like a swan. But as it is, I am a rational being, therefore I must sing hymns of praise to God.

—Epictetus the Stoic, *Discourses*

The seat of the soul and the control of voluntary movement—in fact, of nervous functions in general—are to be sought in the heart. The brain is an organ of minor importance.

—Aristotle, *De motu animalium*

A Is A

Joan and Kite were going to go directly from Babel to the New York Public Library—"N.Y.P.L."—but Joan, acting on a premonition, took a moment to call home first. Motley Nimitz, one of the more stable tenants who helped mind the Sanctuary during the daytime, told her what had been going on in the few hours she'd been out.

Kite hardly needed to ask. "Maxwell?"

"Maxwell," Joan confirmed. They caught a cab down to the Bowery.

Compared to some of the mischief Maxwell had gotten up to in the past, this latest stunt wasn't so bad. He'd piled all of the furniture in his bedroom in one corner and used green face paint to daub a mural on the wall. The mural showed a Babel-like ziggurat surmounted by a single gigantic eye from which bolts of electricity radiated in all directions. This was THE EYE OF AFRICA, according to the caption beneath the tower; there were some other words in a language Joan didn't recognize. In the lower right-hand corner of the mural, a screaming cartoon mouse was being dragged into a pit of fire by a clenched green fist.

"Was Maxwell watching a war movie on cable last night?" Joan asked. "One with naked people in it, maybe?"

"I don't know," said Motley. Wanting to be helpful, he added: "I think *Hogan's Heroes* is back in syndication."

Joan kept toxic chemicals in her office for the removal of graffiti. She sent Motley to get them, which is how they found out that Maxwell had stolen the Cray PC. He'd also left a finger painting on the surface of Joan's desk, this one of a balance scales, with the Eye of Africa being weighed against the cartoon mouse; the mouse grinned savagely as it wielded a reaper's scythe, but according to the scales the Eye was heavier.

"*Hogan's Heroes,* eh?" Joan said, and set to work cleaning up. She considered calling the police, but Kite argued against it: "He'll turn up on his own, Joan—he always does—and it seems to me it's better to wait than to have him dragged in off the street. Not that I'm an expert, but really, how much trouble can he get into with a home computer?"

It was late afternoon by the time they finally got to the library. Kite went into the stacks to find a book with the call number 171.303 607 949 6; Joan visited the periodicals annex to check on an obituary.

Sure enough, John Hoover was dead, and his obit photo, taken on the occasion of his retirement from Gant Industries, bore no resemblance to the man now occupying the gingerbread house in Atlantic City. "John Elliot Hoover," Joan read from the *Times* On-Line Morgue, "1926–2010." The octogenarian Hoover had been a shrunken, prune-faced man with a mad scientist's shock of white hair; he didn't look like the sort of person who'd have the patience to take care of a hound, Mechanical or otherwise, though Joan could picture him siccing one on somebody. In addition to his work for Disney and Gant Industries, the *Times* credited him as an accomplished mathematician, engineer, and computer scientist. Born in rural Oregon and educated at UCLA, he'd worked as a cryptographer for the U.S. Army Signal Corps before a chance meeting with Walter Disney on a Burbank streetcar landed him a fifty-year career designing robot animals and other theme park attractions. In 2005, after Disney management had concluded that Hoover's Self-Motivating Android, while interesting, had no real sales potential, he'd offered his patent and his services to Harry Dennis Gant, who recognized the Android as the neat idea that it was and turned it into one of the most successful products of the early twenty-first century. Hoover had remained with Gant for three years, midwifing his last brainchild through its first generation of manufacture. Citing poor health, he'd retired to Atlantic City in 2008, and died there of a clerical error in September of 2010.

Hmm, Joan thought, reading over the details of the accident. The hospital that Hoover had gone to for emergency throat cancer surgery had confused his medical records with those of another patient; he'd been given the wrong anesthetic and had died of anaphylactic shock on the operating table. The source of the mix-up had not been immediately determined, but evidence pointed to a software glitch in the hospital's Electric Filing System. As Hoover had left no surviving relatives, however, no lawsuit was anticipated.

Joan got a hard copy of the obituary, then punched up the death notices for J. Edgar Hoover and Roy Cohn as well. Nothing unusual here: J. Edgar had died of a garden-variety heart attack in 1972, Roy of AIDS in 1986. Neither man had had any connection to John Hoover that the *Times* had seen fit to print.

Time for a smoke and a think. Joan went out to the stone lions in front of the library, where she'd agreed to meet Kite. She set the Electric Lamp, which she still carried, between the paws of one of the lions, and lit her cigarette with a match struck on the locks of a granite mane.

"Can I ask you a question?" Joan said to Ayn, who'd been mum since her blow-up with Jerry Gant.

Ayn, still sulky, replied: "I believe you just did."

"Cute," said Joan. "But listen, seriously, is the John Hoover I met in Atlantic City human or a machine?"

"I don't know," Ayn said.

"Because J. Edgar Hoover"—Joan pointed to the photo in one of the obituary printouts—"didn't have a twin, especially not a slower-aging twin, and as far as anyone knows he didn't take part in any cloning experiments. And he didn't have kids. So it occurs to me that the J. Edgar look-alike masquerading as John Hoover in Jersey might be an Automatic Servant instead of a person."

"That sounds logical. Do they come in white?"

"Sure. AS204 Negroid configuration is the consumer favorite, but you can specify any skin tone you want, including green. And if you're a licensed representative of an amusement park or a museum, you can order a custom duplicate of a dead celebrity—but the more realistic a Servant looks, the more anti-fraud behavioral inhibitors it comes packaged with. They aren't supposed to be able to lie about what they really are."

"Still," said Ayn, "that explanation is much more plausible than any of the alternatives. Yes, I'm sure it's true. John Hoover *must* be an Automatic Servant."

"But you never actually saw him recharge himself, or do anything else that would prove he wasn't human?"

"I don't need to have *seen* anything," Ayn said. "Your original line of reasoning was sound. John Hoover is an android. Now, may I ask you something?"

"Feel free, Ayn."

"I wish to know why you married Harry Gant," Ayn Rand said, "and why you divorced him."

Joan frowned. "Is there a particular reason you want to jump to *that* topic just now?"

"I wish to discover your premises," Ayn said. "The roots of your current irrationality. Hearing you describe what attracted you to Gant and what drove you away from him should clarify your basic values. Then, perhaps, we can correct the errors in your thinking."

"Jesus," Joan said. "He really did a number on you, didn't he?"

"'Did a number on me'?"

"Hoover. John Hoover, whether he's human or a clone or a Servant. He must have left out your redeeming graces when he programmed you. You can't possibly have been this obnoxious in real life."

"It's not my fault," Ayn said, "if your fear of reality causes you to identify rigorous objectivity as 'obnoxiousness.'"

"Ayn, I'm not the one who's afraid of reality."

"Oh no?"

"No. I like reality. There are parts of it I'd like to change, granted, but I'm *comfortable* with it. You're the one with the problem."

"*Me?*"

"Championing logic is one thing," Joan said. "I'm all for common sense, and I'll gladly take objectivity when and where I can get it. But reason is something more than a tool to you, Ayn; you're the most *defensively* rational person I've ever met."

"I don't know what you're talking about."

"You're terrified of uncertainty. Maybe because of what the Bolsheviks did to your family, maybe just because you were born into a century that had a hard time being sure of anything. My guess is the need for certainty played as big a role in the formation of your philosophy as any desire for truth. I mean it feels a lot more secure, doesn't it, to view the world in terms of absolute black and white than to spend your life wrestling with shades of gray."

"It not only *feels* more secure," Ayn Rand said, "it *is* more secure, for the simple reason that the world *is* black and white, and so-called shades of gray are nothing more than mental fog generated by irrationalists in their attempt to avoid the responsibility of choice."

"But I see the world in shades of gray—most of the time, when I'm not up on a soapbox—and I still manage to make choices," Joan said. "And despite occasional attacks of embarrassment when I pull a boner like setting the East River on fire, I'm pretty up front about taking responsibility for the consequences of those choices."

"Yes, and what are the consequences? You're divorced and unemployed, you've been declared unfit even to patrol sewers, and the majority of your time is spent in the company of vagabond amputees whose grasp of reality is more tenuous than your own."

"Nice mouth, Ayn."

"I'm simply stating the facts," Ayn said. "Try as you may, you cannot escape the primary law of existence—the Law of Identity, which states that A is A, that things are what they are, independent of any human beliefs, whims, wishes, feelings, or opinions. Blanking out reality doesn't change reality; what is, *is*—A is A—regardless of your attempts at evasion."

"That may be true, Ayn, but what I'm saying—"

"There's no *maybe* about it. It *is* true. A is A, and given that axiom, there can be no shades of gray. You either accept reality or deny it. If you choose to accept it, then the only means of knowledge and the only guide to rightful action at your disposal is reason: the black and white rules of logic applied to the concrete evidence of the senses. And if you've read *Atlas Shrugged,* then you understand that the acceptance of reason, and the acceptance of *man's life* as the ultimate standard of moral value, leads inevitably to the embrace of capitalism, as well."

"Well," said Joan. "I understand that *you* think it's inevitable."

"It's the only logical conclusion you can come to!" Ayn insisted. "If man has a right to his life, then man has a right to engage in those actions necessary to his survival as a rational being. And since man, by his nature, must *produce* the things he needs to live, the right to life implies a right to production, and the right to production further implies a right to dispose of one's product as one sees fit."

"Hence private property," Joan said. "And free trade, too."

"Any restraint of commerce by outside parties is an infringement of the right to life," Ayn confirmed. "An objective morality of self-interest mandates a complete separation of state and economics."

"So no taxes on business. No taxes period, in fact, since anyone with something worth taxing is by definition part of the economy."

"Taxation is theft," Ayn Rand said. "Theft is immoral. A rational citizenry will of course agree to pay for the services of a properly limited government, just as they would pay for insurance, but such payment must, as with all other transactions, be voluntary in nature. And the same principle applies to charity: while men may *choose* to donate their surplus capital to those in need, no amount of need can ever justify the forced 'redistribution' of wealth."

"Of course," Joan said, lighting another cigarette, "rational rich people would be only too happy to extend a loan to the legitimately needy, in the same way they'd be overjoyed to volunteer their fair share of government upkeep. And even if that turned out not to be the case, or if it turned out there wasn't enough surplus to go around, the rational poor would still be completely understanding. They'd continue to respect the wealthy's right to property, even if it meant their own starvation, because to do otherwise would be contrary to self-interest."

"Be as sarcastic as you wish," Ayn said, "but what you say is essentially correct. If the poor—by definition, the least productive members of society—are allowed to loot not just the surplus but also the operating capital of the rich—by definition, the most intelligent, talented, and productive members of society—overall production is drastically reduced, leading to more, not less, starvation. If the looting continues, the entire industrial base is ultimately destroyed, after which everyone goes hungry."

"But even if that's true," Joan said, "how does it follow from that that people who are already going hungry should be content with their lot? Or more to the point, that they will be?"

"They shouldn't be content. They should work to better their circumstances."

"And if they can't?"

Ayn Rand shrugged. "Then that's too bad. In a true capitalist system unemployment would be minimal, of course, and hunger nonexistent or virtually so—among *moral* men, that is—but those who did starve would be doomed in any event. Unfortunate, but what can one do?"

"Have you asked a starving person that question?"

The Lamp flared red. "I've *been* a starving person!" Ayn raged. "Don't you *ever* presume to lecture me on that subject! I've *been* a starving person, and I've seen only too well what end government-sanctioned theft is meant to achieve!"

"I know you have," Joan said, "and I don't doubt that single-mindedness was an asset to your survival in that situation. But I also think the experience left you blind to other perspectives, blind even to the possibility that there might *be* other perspectives."

"Oh no," Ayn said. "If one includes the full spectrum of the irrational, I'm sure there are a virtually inexhaustible number of perspectives from which to choose. But reality is not a matter of perspective: A is A. To any particular issue, there are in reality only two sides, two 'points of view,' one of which is right, the other of which is wrong. There is also a middle ground, into which all other perspectives can be demonstrated to fall. This middle ground represents 'compromise': the cynical accommodation of truth to falsehood, reason to unreason, justice to injustice, good to evil, morality to immorality."

Joan shook her head. "Even if all disputes could be boiled down to two polarized positions, which I don't believe, different people would identify different poles. One person's middle ground is another's absolute truth. And another's total falsehood."

"Perhaps that's the case among simpletons," Ayn said. "Or savages. But to fully rational beings—"

"But there are no such people," Joan said. "That's what I was being sarcastic about. You talk about reason as if it were something pure, something that could be disembodied from the reasoner, but it's not that way at all—especially not in regard to ethics. Facts are facts, but what seems morally *true* is always going to be influenced by who you are: by the experiences you've had, by the people you've known and the kindnesses and cruelties they've shown you, by the books you've read, by the books you were too lazy to read, by your desires and your fears, and by a hundred other personal, subjective factors."

"You think there's no hope, then," Ayn Rand said. "You think reason is impotent, that man is doomed to a life of ethical caprice."

"I didn't say reason was impotent. Not being sure isn't the same as not knowing anything. All I'm suggesting is that nobody has the whole truth—not you, not Karl Marx, not the pope, and not me, either. If somebody did have it—if we could be absolutely, logically certain we knew right from wrong, in every situation—then what would we need hope for?"

"Bah!" Ayn threw up her hands in disgust. "Useless! Useless to attempt to talk sense to a liberal, college-bred mystic! And it's all a con game, anyway—you're intelligent, you *know* that I'm right, but my conclusions don't match your whims, so instead of admitting that you can't answer my proofs, you—"

"Strong opinions and a bad mood aren't proof, Ayn. Your theory has some valid points to it, but—"

"*Theory!*" Ayn roared. "My philosophy is no *theory!*" She jabbed furiously with her cigarette holder, hurling ashes like a shotgun blast of fireflies. "You can't refute capitalism, and you know it!"

"I'm not so sure I want to refute capitalism," Joan said. "Not entirely, anyway. I mean I do own a building, after all, and a pretty hefty interest-bearing account with my Gant severance pay, and I'd have to say in general I'm a pretty selfish person. But selfishness doesn't mean I don't also recognize an obligation to other people's needs. If the ultimate standard of morality is life, and property is just a means to that end, then—"

"No! There cannot be an *obligation* to charity! Can't you see that's a contradiction?"

"Taken to extremes it's a contradiction. If you're asked to treat other people's lives as more sacred than your own, or to sacrifice for those who aren't genuinely in need, then I'd agree that's an affront to good sense. But there's a difference between rational self-interest and being a merciless son of a bitch."

"Socialist!" Ayn hissed. "Don't you speak to me of mercy! Do you think I didn't struggle when I came to this country? Do you think I wasn't desperate, in need? But *I* never received charity! No one helped *me* with a handout! Nor did I ever demand, nor would I have accepted, a single unearned value."

"Except that that's nonsense," Joan pointed out. "I know your story, Ayn. Just to come as far as to be struggling in this country was a tremendous leap forward for you, a life-saving leap, and you never would have made it without help. Didn't your mother sell the last of her jewelry so you'd have money for the trip overseas? Money she could have used to feed herself and the rest of your family? Didn't your relatives in Chicago—who'd never even met you—go out of their way to help you get a passport? Didn't they agree to take financial responsibility for you during your 'visit' to America? Didn't they also pay for your steamship ticket? And didn't they put you up for six months free of charge—even though, by all accounts, you were a self-absorbed pain in the ass as a house guest?"

"Who told you about my private life?" Ayn demanded. "Who have you been talking to?"

"And as for you 'never accepting an unearned value,'" Joan continued, "not to be rude, but you didn't exactly acquire U.S. citizenship on the basis of merit, now did you? Unless cunning counts as merit. You bluffed immigration into letting you enter the country temporarily, then married an American so they'd be forced to let you stay. You used fraud—a form of theft—to gain the protection of a government that you then spent your career criticizing for its failure to adequately respect property rights."

"What 'theft'?" Ayn said. "There was no theft! I stole nothing!"

"You bargained in bad faith," Joan said. "At the American consulate in Latvia, you applied for a tourist visa, granting you a limited stay in the United States in exchange for your promise to return home when time was up. But you never intended to keep your end of the deal."

"I had no choice in the matter! I would gladly have applied for permanent asylum, but that wasn't an option. The visa I got was the only type of visa being offered!"

"So the item you really wanted wasn't for sale, but you decided you'd buy anyway." Joan raised an eyebrow. "And when the storekeeper in charge got suspicious and started questioning your intentions, you made up a story about a fictitious fiancé waiting for you back in Leningrad—compounding what was already implicit deceit with a flat-out lie."

"I had no choice!" Ayn repeated. "If I'd been turned down by the American consul, there'd have been no second chance, no avenue of appeal—not even the opportunity to petition the consulate of another country. I'd have been arrested immediately and deported back to Russia. Forever!"

"Well then," Joan said, and shrugged, "that would have been too bad, wouldn't it? Unfortunate, but what can one do? Didn't you just tell me that no amount of need could ever justify stealing?"

"*What* stealing? I didn't steal anything!"

"U.S. residency and citizenship aren't objects of value? Why did you lie to get them, then, if they weren't worth anything?"

"I—"

"I mean I don't want to be difficult," Joan said, "but you were so emphatic in your condemnation of compromise. The cynical accommodation of truth to falsehood, you called it. And yet here you are suggesting that there's no breach of ethics involved in lying to a benefactor. But A *is* A, isn't it? Fraud is theft, and theft is immoral. Or do you now want to say that it's not so, that the truth is more complicated than that?"

"You bitch," Ayn Rand said. "You *bitch!*"

"I had to be a bitch," Joan replied. "They wouldn't let me be a Jesuit. But you see now what I mean about wrestling with shades of gray . . . and why I think pity is also a rational virtue."

"You are a monster! A whim-worshipping, muscle-mystic, subjectivist monster!"

Joan laughed. "What book of Aristotle's do you get your comebacks from, Ayn? Is there a special appendix on name-calling in the *Rhetoric?*"

Ayn just shook her head. "I can't understand it," she said. "*How* could a genius like Harry Gant have married the likes of you?"

"Oh," Joan said, "that. That's right, that was the original question, wasn't it? Well, you're not going to like this much, but Harry and I getting married, that was mostly a lark."

"A *lark?*" Ayn said.

"It happened on a business trip out west, a little over a year after I started work as Harry's comptroller. In October of '09 Harry completed a buyout of the Lone Star Supertrain that became the first branch of the Lightning Transit System, and we went to Dallas to close the deal. Then we rented a van and spent a week cruising around the Southwest scouting out rights-of-way to extend the rail line from Texas to California. Just the two of us, alone on the open highway, with Harry all psyched up about his new toy, and me flying high over the environmental preservation compact I'd just negotiated with Dow Tanzania, and, well . . . did I mention that Harry and I had been lovers while I was at Harvard?"

"No," Ayn said, not in answer but in horrified anticipation.

"Yeah," Joan said. "The attraction hadn't gone away in the years since, but when we first met up again we were adversaries, and once we quit that we were both too busy with the reorganization of Gant Industries to think about screwing around. But the road trip gave us the opportunity and the space to notice one another again. Of course there was an ethical obstacle to an affair now that Harry was technically my boss, even if he didn't *act* like a boss most of the time; a political obstacle, too, because I was already in a running feud with the Creative Accounting Department, and I could guess how Clayton Bryce would react if he heard I was sleeping with Harry. So for almost a thousand miles after the subject first came up, we only talked about doing it—talked about the obstacles, in particular, and how we might squeak around them—like a pair of railroad barons trying to find a way to form a monopoly without violating any anti-trust statutes. We came up with a lot of crazy ideas between us, but it was Harry who came up with the craziest one of all . . ."

"You didn't," Ayn said. "You couldn't."

"We were in Nevada by then," Joan said, "so yeah, we could. Drive-through service, no blood test, no waiting—they even threw in a free prenuptial agreement with our wedding license."

"You *married* him?" Ayn nearly screamed. "Just so you could—"

"In retrospect, it was a very silly thing to have done. Childish, even. A month later even we had a hard time understanding what could have gotten into us. And of course Clayton Bryce went through the roof when he found out, which demolished one of our main rationales for doing it. All I can say is that it seemed sensible enough at the time. Or no, not sensible: like a neat idea. But probably you had to be there."

"Reprehensible! To debase the institution of marriage by—"

"Hey, hey!" Joan warned. "Mind your own glass house there, Ayn. Debase the institution of marriage? Why? Because I didn't get a green card out of the deal?"

"How dare you!"

"I'm simply stating the facts," Joan said. "You started."

"I *loved* Frank!"

"Well I loved Harry. Still do love him, I suppose—I mean don't *tell* anyone that, but it's true. And if you say you loved Frank, I suppose that's probably true, too—but you *married* Frank just when your last visa extension was due to run out, and I married Harry just when I most wanted to jump his bones, so let's not kid each other that we were talking through flowers."

"But how can you profess to love a man you don't admire? If you don't share Gant's values—"

"Oh, I share more of his values than you might think, as Harry himself likes to remind me during arguments. And there are plenty of things about him that I admire. He's smart, creative, capable—I don't equate talent with prudence the way you do, but I do respect talent, and Harry's got it. On a personal level he's as unpretentious as a cab driver: when he's not off building towers with their tops in the heavens, he acts like a guy, not like a billionaire. He's funny and he's kind, and when he does wrong it's out of laziness or inattention, never out of malice. Yet at the same time he's got a wicked sarcastic streak that makes him a real hazard to criticize: you no sooner adopt a holier-than-thou posture than Harry does or says something that lets you know he's got your number, too—only *he's* not going to raise his voice about it. And he knows, like my friend Lexa knows, how to fight for what he wants without losing his temper."

"So you do admire him—imperfectly. But you don't share *all* his values."

"He's my ex-husband, not my messiah."

"A person with a healthy self-esteem," Ayn said, "reserves the highest expression of love for that other who represents the fullest embodiment of his or her values."

Joan rolled her eyes. "Give me a break, Ayn," she said. "If a mirror image is what turns you on, fine, best wishes in your search, but that's not what *I* want. I want a lover who'll challenge my values—someone who's not afraid to poke fun at me when I take myself too seriously."

"No!" Ayn said, stamping her foot. "That's wrong!"

"What do you mean, 'that's wrong'? It's a personal preference."

"It is an irrational preference!" Ayn said. "If you behave morally, there is no reason you should ever have to be the butt of someone's joke! To laugh at evil things is good—so long as you do take them seriously, but occasionally you permit yourself to laugh at them. To laugh at good things, at values, is evil . . ."

"Ayn, are you *sure* you're not a liberal?"

". . . to laugh at yourself, or encourage others to do so, is the worst evil you can do. It's like spitting in your own face."

"But what's so terrible about spitting in your own face?" Joan said. "It wipes off. And there are times when you need a dash of cold water to bring you to your senses . . ."

"This conversation is ended," Ayn Rand said. "You are more corrupt than I could have imagined! To think that *you*—"

"'More corrupt than you could have imagined'?" Kite Edmonds came strolling down the library's front walk with a book tucked under her arm. "What are we discussing, the Grant administration?"

"Now I'm surrounded," said Ayn. "Bracketed by the irrational and the insufferable."

Kite feigned hurt. "Is our company really that hellish for you, Miss Rand?"

"Beyond the power of language to express," Ayn said.

"Ayn," Joan asked, "are you sentient?"

"*What?*"

"Well you are technically a piece of software," Joan said. "But you're the most sophisticated personality template I've ever matched wits with. So—"

"Are you asking me if I'm *conscious?*"

"It's a valid question."

Ayn tore at her hair. "Shall I send you my answer from unconsciousness?"

"Now that I'd like to see," said Kite. She added, to Joan: "Got a match?"

Lighting Kite's cigarette, Joan noted with some surprise that the sun had set. Streetlights and headlamps had been added to the twenty-four-hour-a-day illumination of storefronts and Electric Billboards. High overhead, the running lights of a CNN news blimp headed south became the evening's first constellation.

"You've been in the stacks a while, haven't you?" Joan said.

"Did you forget to miss me?" Kite smiled. "But I think I found what we're looking for." Holding the cigarette between her lips, she let the book drop from under her arm into her open hand, and passed it to Joan. It was soft cover, a thick manila folder that had been stapled and bound as a volume. Its wrapping-paper dust jacket read:

THE CASE OF NOBODY'S PERFECT

•

a Ten Most Wanted Mystery
from the private files of J. Edgar Hoover

•

Read the transcripts
Examine the evidence
Find the answers
(solution enclosed)

"The call number was the hard part," Kite said. "The call number we got from the videotape was in Dewey Decimal classification code; this library uses the Library of Congress code."

"What did you have to do, translate it?" Joan riffled through the case file. It contained, as promised, several dozen police report–style transcript sheets, plus Xeroxes and laserprint copies of a host of documents. Inserted at intervals were cardstock sheets to which glassine envelopes had been affixed, each containing some sort of physical evidence: a spark plug; a computer diskette; a hollow plastic blowdart; straw.

"It's not that simple," Kite said. "You know I never appreciated it before this afternoon, but library filing systems are remarkably arbitrary."

"There's no one right way to organize books, huh?" Joan couldn't resist shooting a glance at Ayn, who turned away fuming.

"Evidently not," Kite said. "Now that call number we had, 171.303 607 949 6"—she recited easily from memory, well-versed from repetition—"that tells us that the book has something to do with ethics, because the 170s, in Dewey Decimal, are all about ethics and moral philosophy; and 171.3, more specifically, means a book whose subject is systems and doctrines of perfectionism. The next three numbers, 036, are a notational suffix meaning 'persons of the Negro race,' and the last six numbers, 079496, form the area suffix for Orange County, California. So 171.303 607 949 6 is—"

"A book describing a doctrine or system for the perfection of Negroes in Orange County. Which is where Disneyland is located."

"Very good," Kite said. "Now not surprisingly, the Library of Congress classification system doesn't have a specific subdivision set aside for books on that subject. There *is* a category 'Perfection, Ethics of,' and other categories that might fit as well, but as the head librarian took some time explaining to me, the system isn't really set up to classify books in absentia. If you can't have the thing in your hands, you ought to at least know the author and title, which of course the Dewey number doesn't tell you."

"So how did you find this book?"

"I poked around. I looked up the Library of Congress call headings for Perfection, Excellence, Self-Improvement, Beatification, and so on, and then I went prospecting. Waste of time, it turns out, since this is an over-sized book, and those are all shelved separately regardless of topic. Besides which, it wasn't on a shelf."

"Then how—"

"After half an hour or so of searching and not finding anything that looked like it might be what I was looking for, it struck me that I was going about this the wrong way. So I took a step back and reconsidered the problem in light of our larger goal. Then I went and did what I should have done in the first place, even before consulting with the head librarian."

Joan thought about it. "You asked an Electric Negro for help," she said.

"Eldridge 162," Kite said. "He'd been shadowing me in the stacks and I hadn't even noticed. He had the book in his hand, in plain view."

"Huh," Joan said. "Did he say anything to you?"

"He said Mr. Hoover would be calling us. He also had a special message for you, cautioning you not to lose the Lamp. 'It'll be very important later,' he said." She turned to Ayn. "So it appears you'll have to put up with us a while longer, Miss Rand."

"Wonderful," Ayn said.

At the end of the case file, Joan found a sealed section marked SOLU-TION. A red sticker seal warned:

> Enclosed is the complete
> solution to "The Case of
> Nobody's Perfect." Don't spoil
> the fun by peeking unless
> you're sure you're stumped!

"What do you think?" Joan asked Kite.

"Hmm," Kite said. "Well ordinarily I enjoy lingering over a mystery as much as the next person, but it seems as though we're meant to solve this one in a hurry—troublesome library searches aside, we're being given information hand over fist. So someone has designs on us, and since this is a *murder* mystery, violent death and the whole nine yards, it's probably wisest to arm ourselves with as much of the truth as possible, as soon as possible. On the other hand, that could be exactly what the murderer wants us to do."

"So should we read the solution, or not?"

"Couldn't tell you," Kite said. "But personally, I like the idea of knowing a lot better than the idea of not knowing."

"Yeah," Joan said. "Me too."

"So?"

"So. . . ." Using her thumbnail, Joan slit the seal. Ayn in her lamp globe couldn't resist craning forward to look; Kite, noticing this, lifted the Electric Lamp from between the granite lion's paws and held it above the case file. Joan turned to the first page of the solution.

Everybody smoked.

You Have My Sympathies

"Ash, can you hear me? . . . ASH!"

In the mess hall aboard the doomed space tug *Nostromo*, Sigourney Weaver pounded her fist on a table. Ian Holm, playing the severed head of an android, opened his eyes and spat up white fluid.

"Yes, I can hear you."

"What was your special order?"

"You read it. I thought it was clear."

"What was it?"

"Bring back lifeform, priority one. All other priorities rescinded."

Frankie Lonzo kicked the pile of empty beer cans at the foot of his chair. "What time is it, Sal?" he asked.

Salvatore belched. Heineken. "Sun's down," he replied.

"What time is it, though? What hour?"

"How do we kill it, Ash? There's got to be a way of killing it. How? How do we do it?"

"Seven . . . thirty-two." Salvatore squinted at the Timex Philharmonic on his wrist. "Seven thirty-two, Frankie."

"So nine o'clock this morning plus eleven hours and ten minutes equals . . . equals eight o'clock P.M. and ten minutes." Frankie smiled. "Almost done, then. Son of a bitch is floundering by now."

"You still don't understand what you're dealing with, do you? A perfect organism. *Its structural perfection is matched only by its hostility."*

"You admire it."

"I admire its purity. A survivor. Unclouded by conscience, remorse . . . or delusions of morality."

"I gotta take a leak," Frankie said, getting up. "Mind the fort, Sal."

"Yup."

"Last word . . ."

"What?"

"I can't lie to you about your chances, but . . . you have my sympathies."

In the bathroom Frankie became mesmerized, as drunken peeing men will, with the abstract patterns of tile on the wall behind the toilet. He swayed a little on his feet, trying to aim, but must have nodded off because the next thing he knew his sneakers were damp and there was screaming coming from the TV room: Yaphet Kotto and Veronica Cartwright being eaten by the Alien while Sigourney Weaver was off chasing the ship's cat.

Frankie zipped up carefully—he'd injured himself with his pants before—and lost another few moments' consciousness at the bathroom sink before slouching back out to the TV room. By then Sigourney Weaver had set the *Nostromo*'s engines to self-destruct and was racing for the escape shuttlecraft, cat-carrier in hand.

"Hey Sal," said Frankie, leaning against the door frame. "Sal, what time is it now?"

No answer. On TV, Sigourney Weaver started to round a corner, spied a menacing shape, and shrank back against a bulkhead in terror.

"Sal?" The strobe lighting effect coming from the television made it hard to focus, but by shading his eyes Frankie could make out the long gray loveseat at the other end of the room, and Salvatore's armchair next to it. He thought he could see Salvatore's right arm as well, still clutching a Heineken can, but what was funny was, Salvatore's other arm—the one with the watch—seemed to be missing, along with Sal's legs, torso, and head.

Hmm, Frankie thought. And then he thought: *Loveseat?*

"There's no loveseat in here," he said, aloud, whereupon the loveseat rolled over, popping up a dorsal fin.

Frankie and Sigourney broke and ran at the same time. But while the monster in the movie crouched down to take a look at the dropped cat-carrier, Meisterbrau followed the real meal. Clawing its way across the carpet, the shark inadvertently tromped on the television remote control, pumping the volume up to maximum.

Frankie's feet barely touched the floor between the TV room and the toilet. He slammed the bathroom door shut behind him and shot the deadbolt. The door, installed by the villa's previous owners and intended to slow down police, was made of inch-thick steel plate, with reinforced hinges.

"That'll hold it," Frankie said, patting the deadbolt. "That'll hold it."

That might not hold it, Frankie thought. Through the door he could hear the *Nostromo*'s computer, Mother, announcing that the option to override self-destruct would expire in T-minus one minute, which only added to his sense of urgency. He scanned the bathroom for potential weapons but found none, not even a rubber plunger. A special stand inside the medicine cabinet had once held an Uzi, but all firearms had been removed from the villa by the D.E.A.; the rusted safety razor that remained didn't bear consideration.

"*Twenty-nine,*" said Mother. "*Twenty-eight . . . twenty-seven . . . twenty-six . . .*"

The window, thought Frankie. If he'd been a kilo of cocaine or a baby alligator he could have flushed his way out of here, but he wasn't, so that left the window. He stepped to it, thumbed the latch, and pushed up on the sash.

The window, painted shut years before, didn't budge.

"*Twenty seconds,*" said Mother, and Frankie heard a tentative scratching on the outside of the bathroom door. Scratching, and something else . . . music of some kind, a classical score that didn't quite blend with the sirens and alarms of the movie soundtrack. Frankie didn't waste time trying to place the tune; he yanked the shower curtain rod loose and used it to bash out the window glass.

"You can't get in here," Frankie said, and Meisterbrau butted the steel door hard enough to buckle both hinges. Frankie went nuts, punching out the center sash of the window with his fist. He threw down the curtain rod and scrambled up onto the sill, crouching there in a tight ball, framed by splintered wood and glass.

The jump didn't look promising. It wasn't that far to fall—twelve, maybe fourteen feet—but an iron fence ran close along this side of the villa, a fence capped with sharp spikes and razor wire. If Frankie was lucky enough to clear it without getting sliced up or impaled, he'd land hard in an alleyway strewn with the sort of contaminated refuse that bred three-headed squirrels.

"*Ten seconds,*" said Mother. "*Nine . . . eight . . .*"

"You've got to do it or you're dinner," Frankie told himself. Looking down into the alley for a clear landing spot, he noted the dark circle of a manhole cover, surrounded by a moonlit halo of bottle shards and scrap metal. The ghost of Jimmy Mireno taunted him: *Scared, Lonzo? You fuckin' scared?*

"Yes I am," Frankie said, and gathered himself to leap.

"*Four . . . three. . . .*" On *two,* Meisterbrau hit the bathroom door again; the hinges and deadbolt gave way, and the door fell in with a crash. On the brink of committing himself to the jump, Frankie pulled back, turned his head towards the sound. He saw Meisterbrau crouched in the doorway, heard Ravel's *Bolero* issuing from between the shark's blood-and-mucus-stained jaws, and knew himself for a dead man.

"*The option to override detonation procedure,*" Mother concurred, "*has now expired.*"

The shark reared back on its haunches—*Holy God,* Frankie Lonzo thought, *this fucker has* legs—and its pectoral fins snapped taut like the wings of a glider. Its mouth gaped wide, forming a scoop.

"*Mother?*" Sigourney Weaver said, her voice plaintive. "*I've turned the cooling unit back on . . . MOTHER!!!*"

"Mother," Frankie agreed, and learned, in his last moment on earth, just how alternatively adapted Meisterbrau had become, as the *Carcharodon carcharias* proved that it could not only swim and crawl, but soar.

17

Plato (427–347 B.C.) saw degrees of truth everywhere and recoiled from them. For instance, he realized, no chair is perfect. It is only a chair to a certain degree. The whole physical world comes in similar grades of imperfection—shops, bridges, clouds, smiles, paintings, clever, gentle, fascinating, big, wide, long, everything.

If an item is partly a chair, he reasoned, it is partly not a chair. . . . But that's a contradiction. Could a contradiction exist? He dismissed the notion out of hand and thus faced a dilemma. Contradiction surrounded him like the sea surrounds a fish, yet it was impossible. He resolved the problem by declaring the physical world an illusion. The floor, the lawn, the sky, the book in your hands—all are a vast mirage.

But then what was real? To answer this question, he brought forth the Ideals. Instead of this jewelry shop or that vegetable shop, he said, there was an Ideal Shop, and likewise an Ideal Bridge, an Ideal Cloud, an Ideal Chair. . . . All these Ideals existed in our minds from birth, and we accessed them by thought alone. Experience was delusion, but the Ideals were eternal and changeless, the only sure knowledge available.

The theory of Ideals begs so many questions that, for most modern philosophers, it is now at best a shorthand reference for other notions. We need not mesh ourselves further in it, except to note two points. First, Plato confused partial contradictions with total ones, viewing the harmony between *partly tall* and *partly short* as conflict between *tall* and *short*. This error drove him to invent the Ideals. Second, he expelled fuzziness from existence, and in so doing he vaporized the world.   —Daniel McNeill and Paul Freiberger, *Fuzzy Logic*

Sheer Force of Will

Lexa Thatcher and Ellen Leeuwenhoek were at the Fonda Blimp Drome outside of Newark by eleven the next morning. CNN had numerous such dromes sited strategically across six continents, but Newark's was the largest, larger even than the flagship drome in Atlanta. As Ellen steered her Citroen into the PRESS ONLY parking lot, they could see a Pulitzer-class blimp just lifting off from the field, bound for a chemical plant fire in Trenton. Pulitzers were the workhorses of the CNN fleet, three-person craft crewing a pilot, camera operator, and reporter-narrator. There were also the smaller Gonzos, single-seat, "kamikaze" blimps with the speed and maneuverability of jet helicopters, and the larger Murrows, which had extra room in the gondola for a news analyst and two political commentators. But none of these would suit Lexa's purposes today. She needed the most durable airship available, with a gas bag big enough to lift a ton or more of dead weight; she needed a Hearst.

"*Jane's* here," said Ellen, indicating an enormous silhouette in the middle distance. "And inflated to boot. Now all we need is permission to borrow her."

"We'll get permission," Lexa said. "I have my Letter of Marque from Ted Turner."

"You have your Letter of Marque from the *late* Ted Turner. Now that he's gone on to that last great plane-change in Atlanta, his name may not carry the same clout around here; the ground crew might say no."

"They won't say no," Lexa insisted. "Not to me."

"I brought something," Ellen told her. She leaned across from the driver's seat and extracted a handgun from the Citroen's glove compartment. She gave it to Lexa.

Lexa stared at the porcelain-gray automatic pistol as if it were the first firearm she'd ever seen. "What is this?"

".44 Magnum, I think," Ellen said. "It's cast from a non-metallic polymer, so we can walk it right through drome security."

"And do what with it?"

Ellen shrugged, looking embarrassed. "The ground crew might say no," she repeated.

Continuing to hold the pistol as if it were an alien artifact, Lexa asked: "Is it loaded?"

"Don't be silly. We're pacifists, right? If we actually have to fire a gun it means we aren't using it properly."

"Where did you get this, anyway?"

"D.C. One of the Republican campaign flacks has a sideline collecting and trading famous murder weapons. Charles Whitman's rifle, Jim Jones's poison ring collection, that sort of thing. It's kind of sick."

"Who was murdered with this?"

"Nobody. That's just a target pistol. He said he uses it to hunt bats on his ranch in Texas. He left it in the car, so I kept it."

"Well," said Lexa, patting Ellen's hand, "thanks for the thought, Kinky, but no thanks. Not my style."

"How do we handle it, then?" Ellen asked. "If they don't want to give us the blimp?"

"Same way we always handle it when we need something," Lexa said. "Sheer force of will." She started to put the gun back in the glove compartment, then paused, suddenly thoughtful. "You know, though . . ."

"What?"

"There *is* a way we could use this, without threatening anyone."

"Tell me."

Lexa slipped the pistol into her purse. "Just cross your fingers that the right people are in the main hangar this morning."

"What are you going to do?"

"Lower my ethical standards to those of an Australian tabloid."

"Bullshit up a storm, in other words."

"Right." Lexa kissed Ellen on the cheek. "Do you trust me?"

"Always."

"Good. Let's go get ourselves a blimp."

G.A.S.

"So," said Joan.

"So," said Kite.

"Now we know."

Now they knew. If they looked shell-shocked staring at each other across the kitchenette table, that was partly a result of lack of sleep, partly a result of the carton of Marlboros they'd chain-smoked while not sleeping, but mostly a result of what they'd learned—or *thought* they'd learned, since the story revealed in Hoover's secret case file did stretch credulity in one or two spots. Still, Joan had managed to rustle up another computer with a modem—nothing as fancy as her Cray, but serviceable—to dial up some databases and verify a few facts. What could be checked out *did* check out, and the final picture involved a lot more than just the death of Amberson Teaneck.

"'Learn to relax and wait for the epiphany,'" Joan quoted. "Was this what you had in mind, Kite?"

Kite shook her head. "I ran afoul of Boss Tweed's boys once," she said, "the first time I visited New York after the war. But this beats by a mile any conspiracy Tammany Hall ever concocted."

Though the air in the kitchenette was an almost solid haze of nicotine, Joan groped among crumpled cigarette packs for one more unsmoked butt. She found it and lit it. "OK," she said, "let's run over the whole thing one more time . . ."

"All right."

"First," Joan said, "Walt Disney didn't hire John Hoover as a roboticist. Hoover *did* do some minor audio-animatronics design, but that was a cover for his real work on a secret project that he'd successfully pitched to Disney in the 1950s. An artificial intelligence project."

"An Electric Brain," Kite said. She consulted a sheaf of scribbled notes. "A 'Gas-phase Analogue Supercomputer.'"

"'G.A.S.,'" Joan said, consulting the same notes, "which uses 'a complex mix of gases in a plasma state' to emulate the neural processes of a living creature. A plasma computer: ionized gas instead of silicon."

"And the plasma chamber," said Kite, "this machine's brain, requires a lot of power and generates a lot of heat."

"Hence Walt Disney's supposed fascination with cryogenics. He had no intention of freezing himself; he just needed to keep his AI from burning itself up while it was thinking."

"They installed it in a bunker complex hidden underneath the Magic Kingdom in Orange County," Kite continued. "It took eleven years to engineer and build . . ."

". . . which is still a miraculous achievement," said Joan, "given the state of computer science in the Fifties and Sixties. But John Hoover was a bona fide genius, and G.A.S. was a revolutionary concept."

"It cost millions . . ."

". . . all of it from Disney's personal fortune. Walt's brother Roy handled finances for the Disney organization, and Roy was a conservative who for the most part didn't share Walt's visionary outlook: he opposed the construction of Disneyland, Disney World, and Epcot Center. He didn't see why they should go into the theme park business when they already had a proven track record making films."

"It goes without saying," said Kite, "that he would have been dead set against pouring a fortune into an experiment in creative computing. It's doubtful many banks would have been enthusiastic about the project, either."

"So Walt secretly mortgaged a big chunk of his own portfolio to finance G.A.S. We know from memos he exchanged with Hoover that he wanted to present the artificial intelligence to his brother and the world as a fait accompli. That way, once the system had been perfected, he'd have no trouble getting the backing to build an even more elaborate plasma computer for the City of Tomorrow he was going to erect in Florida. A Disney Utopia, with a benevolent AI acting as godfather to the community."

"But it didn't work out that way in reality."

"No," Joan agreed. "It took too long. By the time G.A.S. was ready for its first power-up, in the winter of 1966, Disney had been diagnosed with terminal lung cancer. On December 5th, Walt's sixty-fifth birthday, John Hoover sent a telegram to St. Joseph's Hospital in Burbank to let Walt know that 'godfather' was finally up and running. But Walt wasn't. He died ten days later."

"Without telling anyone else about the project," Kite added. "Not even his wife."

"Which made John Hoover the sole custodian of the most powerful computer—and, so far as we know, the *only* truly self-aware artificial intelligence—in the world."

"And Hoover was a sociopath."

"A little character flaw that Disney never quite caught on to. The *Times* obituary was wrong about Hoover having worked as a cryptographer for the Army Signal Corps; it's true he applied to be a codebreaker, and he passed the technical exams without a hitch, but he washed out on the MMPI standardized psychological health test."

"The army concluded from the test results," Kite said, "that Hoover, though brilliant, was a psychopathic deviate with no sense of empathy towards other human beings and hence no ability to form lasting loyalties."

"Not the kind of person you give a security clearance to. The army passed on Hoover's application. But Walt Disney didn't use fancy tests to decide whether he should hire a man. He saw right off that Hoover had the sort of talent he was looking for, and either didn't notice or didn't care what a *demented* talent Hoover was."

"Now just to make sure I understand this correctly," Kite said, "G.A.S. couldn't actually *do* very much, physically, I mean . . ."

"Not at first. In '66 there weren't the vast telephone computer networks that there are now, so G.A.S. couldn't access government files, or break into TRW and alter credit histories, or seize control of remote-operated machinery. . . . According to Hoover's private journal, the AI's peripheral devices were extremely limited to begin with. Two input terminals, one in the bunker, one in Hoover's Anaheim apartment, and two sets of hidden cameras and microphone pick-ups, one in Disney's private screening room, one in the dining hall that became Club 33."

"So it could watch movies, watch people eat, and talk to John Hoover."

"And it could *think*. Which as our friend on the microwave will tell you"—Joan nodded at Ayn's Lamp—"is enough to move the world. Hoover believed G.A.S. was the smartest thing on the planet, and even if that's a fatherly exaggeration, it was definitely smarter than he was. And he put that brainpower to work."

"He had to," said Kite. "He'd lost his patron."

"Right. Roy Disney took charge of the organization after his brother's death, and immediately started making changes, paring down Walt's more ambitious schemes. The City of Tomorrow concept went out the window, for starters; Epcot Center would never be more than a shadow of what Walt had originally envisioned. Each new downsizing of operations brought a wave of transfers, lay-offs, and firings, and John Hoover was just a mid-level tech with no special claim to job security. The fact that he'd been close to Walt actually counted against him in some circles of the new Disney hierarchy."

"So he had to make himself indispensable in a hurry . . ."

". . . and he did, with G.A.S.'s help, by brainstorming a flurry of money-saving technological innovations that shaved almost two million dollars off Walt Disney World's construction cost."

"Which endeared him to Roy Disney in a way that nothing else could have," said Kite, "and earned him a more tenured position in the organization. For a while, he was safe."

Joan paused to light a fresh cigarette. "In 1971," she continued, "three important events took place. One, Walt Disney World opened to the public. Two, Roy Disney died . . ."

". . . and three, J. Edgar Hoover and Roy Cohn had lunch at Club 33."

"Someone had given J. Edgar a guest membership in the club. Maybe he'd done some favor for a Disney executive, or maybe it was just a cautionary good-will gesture; whichever, he was in California on F.B.I. business and he decided to invite his good friend Roy Cohn to Disneyland to check out the wine selection. *John* Hoover, meanwhile, was away in Florida doing hands-on work at Walt Disney World, which left G.A.S. home alone and bored. To keep from going stir-crazy, the computer turned on its video and audio pick-ups and eavesdropped on the patrons at Club 33. Unfortunately, the hidden microphone system in the dining room was so badly degraded that G.A.S. could barely hear anything, and it ended up mistaking Hoover and Cohn's dinner order for a root-level reprogramming command."

"I have to wonder," said Kite, "how much of a 'mistake' that really was. It strikes me as odd that such a smart machine could make such a stupid error. Think about it, Joan, it *must* have heard people order food before."

"So you think it deliberately misunderstood what was said?"

"I think it had a choice of interpretations and chose the more interesting one. As you've said, it was probably pretty bored."

"Hmm," Joan said. "Well, either way, the outcome was the same. From that day on, G.A.S. had a new mission in life."

"Creating a world full of perfect Negroes."

"Of course, given the sheltered nature of its existence, G.A.S. didn't know much about the world, other than what Hoover chose to tell it. And unless Julian Bond dropped by Club 33 at some point, the only blacks it had any direct experience with were classic film characters."

"Uncle Remus from *Song of the South.*"

"Farina and Buckwheat from the *Our Gang* comedies."

"Stepin Fetchit. The crows from *Dumbo.*"

"All perfect Negroes. G.A.S. studied them religiously, but without a wider window on the real world it couldn't decide how to act on the first part of its new directive."

"It had better luck with the second part—'A thousand ironic prosecutions.'"

"It was in the Seventies," said Joan, "that John Hoover first started killing people to protect his position in the Disney organization. Roy Disney's death left him vulnerable again to the vagaries of corporate politics. Office infighting aside, there were lingering questions about Walt Disney's mort-gaged portfolio; Hoover seems to have queered the paper trail on that, but for years there would be attempts to trace the whereabouts of Walt's miss-ing millions. And there were other dangers: that someone would find G.A.S.'s bunker, for instance; that a Disneyland utilities manager would get curious about the excess drain on the Magic Kingdom's power grid and start pok-ing around the grounds."

"Or that someone from the finance department would take note of Hoover's embezzlement," Kite added. "When G.A.S. needed spare parts, Hoover siphoned funds from legitimate projects to pay for them. Which was only fair, given that the computer had helped save so much money for the organization; but Disney management wouldn't likely have seen it that way."

"Hence the need to bump off the occasional nosy accountant. Hoover handled it the same way he handled every problem: he did the legwork him-self but let G.A.S. do most of the planning."

"They made a game of it."

"A nihilistic game. Each murder was staged as a bizarre accident that in some way mocked a stated belief or principle of the victim. Ironic homi-cide." Joan opened the case file and turned to a series of Xeroxed newspaper articles and obituaries. "Cetus Fleetwood and Dilmun Theroux, trouble-shooters for Disneyland's internal water and power service. Friends described them as 'weekend flower children'; they carpooled to work in a VW microbus plastered with anti-war and pro-vegetarian bumper stickers. They were killed and eaten by an escaped Vietnamese tiger that somehow found its way from the L.A. Zoo to their flat in Venice. . . ." Joan turned a page. "David Shenkman, quality supervisor for Disney accounting. A devout Baptist, he was found drowned in the 20,000 Leagues Lagoon. . . . John Tombes, Disney security. A member in good standing of the N.R.A., he was falsely identi-fied as a fugitive Weatherman and shot dead by the Orange County Sheriff's Department."

" 'A well-regulated militia being necessary to the security of a free state . . . ,'" Kite quoted. She took the case file from Joan and flipped ahead a few more pages. "This one is my favorite. Shelley Lacroix."

"That's the psychologist?"

Kite nodded. "Hired in 1978 to supervise mental health testing of Disney personnel after a crazed ride operator dressed as Santa Anna tried to annex Frontierland. Management wanted to make sure it wasn't a conta-gious form of dementia. Dr. Lacroix brought in a whole arsenal of psychological evaluation tools, including an updated version of the same exam that had gotten John Hoover barred from the Army Signal Corps."

"One night about three months into the job," Joan said, "Dr. Lacroix was driving home along a winding back road when a figure loomed out of the darkness ahead of her. She swerved to avoid it, plunging her car off an embankment; she was killed in the wreck, and her latest batch of psych evaluations underwent a quick roadside edit."

"The irony of the situation is fairly obscure," Kite said. "It seems Dr. Lacroix was a former member of the UCLA debate team, and the author, while still in college, of *Accentuate the Negative,* a pamphlet on the use of hyperbole in argument—the old debater's trick of exaggerating an opponent's position to make it appear ridiculous and extreme, then attacking the exaggeration as if it were the actual point of view."

"When the highway patrol found Dr. Lacroix the next morning, they saw nothing to indicate foul play; it looked as though she'd simply fallen asleep at the wheel and lost control of her car. The only peculiar element was a scattering of hay on the road a few yards ahead of the spot where she'd gone over the embankment. The patrolmen were curious about it, but without Dr. Lacroix to tell them what had really happened, they couldn't guess that the hay had come from the figure that had frightened her off the road."

"A scarecrow," said Kite. "Set in ambush and later removed by John Hoover."

"And so if you wanted to make a really, really bad pun about it," Joan said, "you could say that Shelley Lacroix, like her old debate rivals at UCLA, had been—"

"—demolished by a straw man," Kite concluded. "Pretty much sums up the whole business, doesn't it?"

"Between 1971 and 1982," Joan continued, "there were over a hundred ironic fatalities within the Disney bureaucracy. G.A.S. blueprinted the murders with such cleverness that Hoover seems never to have come under suspicion."

"Then in 1983," said Kite, "G.A.S. found another game to play."

"That was the year John Hoover finally broadened the computer's horizons. Installed a modem link and patched in a cable television receiver."

"CNN."

"Watching the news, G.A.S. got its first look at real black people, and they weren't at all what it had expected. They weren't like Uncle Remus. They weren't like *Dumbo*'s crows."

"Most distressing of all," said Kite, "they weren't like each other."

"Extrapolating from the film portrayals, G.A.S. had come to equate perfection with a stereotypical level of conformity," Joan said. "Hollywood movie Negroes, whether depicted as people or cartoon animals, were simple, predictable, and largely interchangeable—and they never stepped out of character."

"Real black people, by contrast, were horribly irregular—born misfits," Kite said. "As a group, barely an adjective could be applied to them whose opposite was not also in some sense true. They were both jovial and solemn, cordial and irate, lighthearted and embittered . . ."

". . . lazy and industrious," Joan said, "educated and illiterate . . ."

". . . criminal and law-abiding, noble and debased, traditional and revolutionary, religious and profane . . ."

"Pretty much the only thing that could be said with confidence about all of them was that, given enough time, they were almost certain to contradict themselves."

"In a word," said Kite, "they were human."

"Hence in need of replacement by something more reliable," Joan said. "So G.A.S., assisted by the sociopath Hoover—who evidently felt this would be a really neat idea—set out to create a better, more consistent type of Negro. But first it was necessary to get rid of all the old Negroes."

"They decided to use plague." Kite spoke now with the anxious bemusement of someone discussing a thing so horrific that it was, thankfully, impossible. "With over a billion people to be vaporized, plague was really the only way they could do it . . ."

"And not just any plague. For what it had in mind, G.A.S. had to invent a whole new class of pathogen. No ordinary bacterium or virus could have turned the trick."

"This new plague bug," Kite said, consulting her notes again, "was called a *nano*virus."

"*Nano* for nanotechnology," Joan said, "the technology of molecule-sized machines. Hoover refers to it in his journal as an expert virus."

"Expert about race . . ."

"The nanovirus was the knowledge and intuition of a physical anthropologist distilled into a single, self-replicating molecule. A smart contagion that could read the DNA of its host for skin color, hair texture, bone structure, and more subtle racial indicators like blood type and metabolic chemistry."

"The nanovirus acted like a Jim Crow bouncer at a polling station," Kite said. "Examining each person it infected for Negroid features. Those who passed scrutiny were used as carriers to spread the disease but were otherwise left unharmed; those who didn't pass were marked as victims."

"Designing the virus mechanism was actually the easy part," Joan said. "What took G.A.S. almost two decades to get right was the protocol for classifying infectees, thanks to another troublesome irregularity: the inherent vagueness of racial categories. Not only are there no perfect Negroes, there's also no perfect biological definition of what a Negro *is*. G.A.S. had to invent a definition and teach the nanovirus how to fudge borderline cases."

"Which G.A.S. finally did . . ."

". . . somehow," Joan agreed, "and probably it's just as well that we don't know the exact details. Suffice it to say that it worked: the nanovirus became so adept at distinguishing racial subgroups that it was able to decimate Negroid Africans and their descendants while leaving other dark-skinned peoples— particularly dark-skinned Caucasians—virtually untouched."

"It did have one odd quirk, though," Kite said. "Upon encountering a host with bright green eyes, the nanovirus automatically assumed that person was *not* a Negro, even when they clearly were. Not only that, but the virus molecule immediately destroyed itself."

"People with the gene code for green eye color couldn't even be carriers of the plague. And this wasn't an accident, it was an intentional immunity built into the virus. Hoover mentions it obliquely in his journal but doesn't give an explanation."

"I think I could hazard a guess," Kite said, but didn't elaborate. Continuing the narrative, she went on: "By the turn of the millennium, or shortly thereafter, the plague was ready for release."

"But Hoover and G.A.S. decided to add one more refinement before putting it to use."

"A clock."

"A fuse, really," Joan said. "Every copy of the virus molecule contained the nanoscopic equivalent of a synchronized watch. The plague knew what time it was. This was to allow it to spread unnoticed, in a benign, semi-dormant state, until a pre-set date when it would suddenly turn virulent."

"Appearing to erupt everywhere at once," Kite said, "like no other epidemic in history."

"Hitting so hard and so fast there'd be no hope of anyone finding a cure, or tracing the plague's origin."

"In 2002, with a test tube full of virus secreted in his shaving kit, Hoover flew to Paris, to attend the tenth-anniversary celebration at Euro Disney, a gala event that promised to lure in visitors from all points of the globe . . ."

"But with typical irony, Hoover didn't release the bug inside the theme park. Instead he took it to an anti-Disney rally being conducted about a mile away by a federation of Parisian intellectuals, Gallic purists who'd coined the phrase 'aesthetic Holocaust' to describe the threat posed by Mickey Mouse to French high culture."

"The lead speaker at the rally was a professor of semiotics named Alain Broussard . . ."

". . . whose great-uncle had been a Jew-catcher for the Vichy regime during World War II. Hoover got upwind of the bandshell Broussard was using for a rostrum and popped the stopper on his test tube. When the rally turned into a protest march about an hour later, the opponents of the 'aesthetic Holocaust' brought the plague to the gates of the Magic Kingdom— infecting security guards, ticket takers, and tourists from six continents."

"The virus began to multiply and spread."

"G.A.S. had estimated a lag time of two years for the nanovirus to diffuse from ground zero in Paris to the most remote human settlements," Joan said. "Hoover spent the interim back stateside, trying to find a manufacturer for his latest invention, the Self-Motivating Android . . ."

"For legal reasons," said Kite, "he was obliged to offer first refusal— and a share of the patent—to the Disney corporation. But he'd grown increasingly disaffected with Disney; it seemed no matter how many bosses and functionaries he did away with, the bureaucracy just became more and more stifling to him."

"He wanted out," Joan said, "so he sabotaged the test-marketing of his own invention, submitting an inferior Android design and purposely antagonizing the consumer research team assigned to work with him. At the same time he began shopping around discreetly for a new patron."

"Hoover wanted to go back to working for an individual," Kite said. "A maverick visionary, like Walter Disney had been, someone who wasn't at the mercy of his creditors and who maintained enough clout within his own organization to guarantee the independence of his most trusted employees."

"Most of the established mavericks weren't interested, though. Ted Turner was busy building airships, Ed Bass had just sunk the bulk of his free capital into a new Biosphere project, Bill Gates was bidding to write the operating system for the new Cray PC, and Steve Jobs had left Silicon Valley to become a televangelist. And H. Ross Perot was just too damn paranoid for someone with Hoover's secret history to even try approaching."

"Then Hoover read an *Esquire* article about Bold Young Entrepreneurs, among them bold young Harry Gant."

"Harry's photo is what clinched it. Hoover wrote in his journal: *'He has the face of a man with more enthusiasm than sense.'* G.A.S. agreed with Hoover's assessment . . ."

"The Self-Motivating Android was formally rejected by Disney in August of 2004," Kite continued. "The onset of the Pandemic followed less than a week later."

"All over the world, the nanofuses ran down to zero," said Joan. "By pure chance, the first recorded outbreak of plague symptoms occurred in Boise, Idaho, where a reunion of the Buchet family ended with all forty-seven members simultaneously contracting meningeal fever. The story wasn't on the AP wire more than ten minutes before a deluge of reports started coming in from everywhere else, but because of the perceived incongruity of that very first report—black people in Idaho?—a rumor got started that the plague had *originated* in Boise."

"A myth that potato farmers are still trying to live down. In fact, Negroes everywhere—including those who'd never touched an Idaho Russet—all began to feel ill at roughly the same time. The nanovirus's timer was accurate to within a few hours."

"Most of the victims died within the first two days. A few hardy souls hung on for twice that long, but they went out raving and fever-crazy."

"And as they succumbed, they vanished."

"A last trick of the virus," Joan said. "After killing its host it became a saprophyte—an eater of the dead. A *fast* eater."

"This not only made autopsies impossible," Kite said, "it removed the very serious threat of secondary plagues that would surely have been generated by a billion unburied corpses. And of course, it had the effect of making the Pandemic seem even more unreal."

"It was a quick, neat, sanitary genocide," Joan said. "A perfect genocide."

"Hoover was elated," said Kite. "Though G.A.S. had done most of the work, he chose to view it as a personal triumph . . ."

". . . like a kid whose backyard chemistry experiment had turned out better than he could have hoped. He was still beaming with pride several months later, when he had his first meeting with Harry in Atlanta, and it may have helped swing the deal for him. Harry took a shine to him right away. He thought Hoover was very upbeat, very *positive*."

"By March of 2005, they'd signed an agreement. Hoover left Disney and came east to work for Gant Industries."

"G.A.S. remained behind in Anaheim. It was fully plugged in to the global communications net now, so it didn't need to be near Hoover to stay in contact with him. And it had become self-maintaining: by dialing into supply house computers or Disney's own on-site inventory, it could arrange delivery of any new parts it needed, and install them itself with the help of two Servant prototypes Hoover had left in the bunker."

"That last may have been a mistake," Kite said. "It may have given G.A.S. ideas . . ."

"The Automatic Servant became a huge success—all the more so because of the labor vacuum created by the Pandemic," Joan said. "Gant Industries cranked out thousands of the machines, and plans were made to produce a second generation with realistic human features."

"Anthropomorphic Servants that, remotely controlled, would allow an inhuman intelligence to assume human form and act as its own agent in human society . . ."

"Which would make Hoover kind of superfluous, if G.A.S. happened to be thinking along those lines. Of course, he was an old man, and sick, and operating-room accidents *do* happen, but . . ."

". . . but look at whom we're talking about. Both the timing and manner of his death were suspicious, to say the least."

"Even more suspicious is the fact that Harry thinks Hoover is still alive. Hoover retired from Gant Industries in 2008, to pursue God knows what new experiments in the suburbs of Atlantic City, but he still kept in touch with Harry by fax and phone . . . and he continued keeping in touch, periodically, even after he was dead. Or at least something with his handwriting and voice did."

Kite frowned. "Wouldn't Gant have been told that his business associate had died?"

"I'm sure someone mentioned it to him," Joan said. "Probably more than once. But that doesn't mean it registered. More enthusiasm than sense, remember?"

"So G.A.S. assumed its creator's place in the community . . ."

". . . and has been operating behind the scenes ever since. Supported by an unknown number of Automatic Servants that it's converted to its service. And whatever its present goals are, it continues to ironically prosecute anyone it considers a threat to its interests."

"People like Amberson Teaneck, the corporate raider, who wanted to take over Gant Industries."

"Amberson Teaneck the Objectivist," Joan said. "Who believed that A is A, that things are what they are . . . that logic, applied to the evidence of the senses, is sufficient to understand reality and choose a proper course of action . . ."

". . . which is generally good philosophy," said Kite, "unless an evil supercomputer built by a mad scientist has seized control of your reality, for the purpose of mocking you to death. In *that* situation, trusting to your senses, acting on what you think you know to be true, is liable to get your face bashed in. Which is exactly what happened . . ."

"And *that's* the explanation for the murder of Amberson Teaneck," Joan said. She closed the case file. "So now we know . . ."

There was a long silence. Then Kite said: "I don't believe a word of it."

"Me neither," said Joan. "An Electric Brain under Disneyland. A disease with an anthropology doctorate. It's crazy."

"Preposterous."

"Absurd."

"Lunatic."

"Nuts."

"Unfortunately," said Kite, "that doesn't mean it's not true."

"No, it doesn't. But if it is true, what the hell are we supposed to do about it?"

"Why, that's obvious!" Ayn Rand said.

Joan and Kite both turned to face the Lamp.

"Oh?" Joan said.

"You must destroy this evil computer!" Ayn said. "Unplug it! Smash it!"

"Just like that, huh?"

"If you value human life, it's the only rational course open to you! What a monstrous crime—to snuff out a billion lives for some *fantasy* of perfection! You *must* stop this machine!"

"I don't think Joan is questioning your sentiment, Miss Rand," Kite said. "But if G.A.S. does exist, and if it really did snuff out those billion lives, mightn't we be a trifle outmatched?"

"A good mind in pursuit of truth and justice is *never* outmatched!" Ayn said, with such utter sincerity that Joan and Kite couldn't help smiling.

"What do you think?" Joan said.

"We're likely doomed anyway," Kite pointed out. "No sense waiting passively for the hammer to fall."

"You figure we're next in line to be prosecuted?"

"That would be in keeping with the tradition of this sort of thing, yes."

"Do you have any weapons in the house, besides your Colt?" Joan asked next. "Stuff that might be good for fighting off killer androids?"

"I have a few small arms," Kite said. "Nothing dramatic. What about you?"

"Well," Joan said, "I do have one item that might be useful. A pair of them, actually. And I guess you could say they're a *little* dramatic . . ."

Footage

"And you're sure this is the *actual* gun used to kill John Lennon?"

"Absolutely," said Lexa.

"Goodness," said Dan. He had an old man's ash-white beard hanging from his chin to his belly, but there was a boyish exuberance in his eyes that no wrinkle or crow's foot would ever diminish. "The actual instrument of his martyrdom. Do you see this, Walter?"

"I *see* it," Walter agreed, committing himself no further.

"You know," Dan confided to Lexa, "back in '09, during the War of Syrian Containment, my camera crew got actual footage of the Kemo Sabe cruise missile that killed Assad."

"I remember that," Lexa said. "CBS played it over and over again . . ."

"Paula and I were on the Lebanese coast, interviewing Israeli frogmen," Dan reminisced, "when the missile just whizzed overhead! Oh, it was something, all right!" Lowering his voice, he added: "Those Kemo Sabes are accurate enough to fly down a chimney, you know."

"I know," said Lexa, "and they're manufactured by the same company that bought CBS just before the war started. But about the blimp, Dan . . ."

"Oh, right!" Dan said. "The blimp! Well, if you say you've got an important story to cover, I'm sure we can arrange something. What do you think, Walter?"

Walter had no legs. This was not a war injury; he'd simply been born without them. A national figure in his prime—"the most trusted news anchor in America"—he'd successfully concealed his handicap from the viewing public by always appearing seated behind a desk. Retired now, he passed his days at the Newark Drome, like the proverbial old fart hanging out at the town barbershop. The executives at Walter's former network sometimes grumbled about this, pointing out, quite rightly, that CNN wasn't *his* barbershop, but Walter didn't give a shit. What did they expect him to do, spend his golden years sucking exhaust fumes at a CBS heliport?

"Which blimp is it you wanted?" Walter asked, twisting slightly in the breeze. Under orders from the late Ted Turner, CNN mechanics had installed a motorized crane in the main hangar, from which Walter dangled in a special canvas sling. A radio joystick allowed him to move himself around.

"Jane," Lexa told him. "We've got to have *Jane.*"

"Can't have that blimp," Walter replied, in a tone that suggested the matter was still open to negotiation. *"Jane's* slated for a job in Delaware tonight. The Democrats are holding a fête for Preston Hackett at the Wilmington dog track."

"Preston Hackett?" Lexa said. "The dark horse presidential candidate? The one who thinks eminent domain is a form of food poisoning?"

Walter nodded. "Rush Limbaugh is going to float above the festivities and give counterpoint."

"It's a fluff piece!" Ellen Leeuwenhoek exclaimed.

"Oh no," said Dan. "It's part of CNN's Decision '24 coverage. Very in-depth."

"It's a fluff piece," said Lexa. "Meanwhile, I've got a hard news story breaking this afternoon, a hundred miles offshore . . ."

"What hard news?" Walter asked.

"A sea battle. Philo Dufresne's submarine is going up against a mercenary fleet of four, possibly five ships."

"A sea battle!" Dan's eyes lit up. "Walter! Footage! We can use the new smart cameras . . ."

"At least two foreign powers are involved," Lexa went on, "lending illegal military support to private American corporate interests."

"And you have independent sources confirming all this?" Walter asked.

"No," said Lexa. "That's why I need the blimp. I've got a time and a place, and I want to go make the confirmation myself, visually." She looked at Dan. "Or with a camera . . ."

"Walter. . . ." Dan pleaded.

"This is horseshit," Walter said. He fixed Lexa with a hard stare. "Excuse the French, but you're horseshitting us, Miss."

Lexa decided to gamble: "Some," she admitted. "But there *is* going to be a battle, and it *is* going to be a better story than anything involving Preston Hackett, unless a satellite falls on him."

"Hmmph!" said Walter.

"But if you think political fluff is the way to go . . ."

"Hell," Walter grumbled. Then he made up his mind. "Dan?"

"Yes, Walter?"

"Go get the head of *Jane's* ground crew. Tell him I want to talk to him. And remind him, on the way in here, that he owes me a favor."

"Right away, Walter."

"And Dan?"

"Yes, Walter?"

"Leave the gun."

Sweet Sixteen

Kite returned to the kitchenette carrying a cavalry saber, a set of brass knuckles, and a pearl-handled derringer; Joan brought a cherrywood case the size of a backgammon set.

"My," said Kite, when Joan lifted the lid. The matched pair of handguns inside the case were the largest she'd ever laid eyes on, which was saying something. "Are we going to shoot down some planes, or just blow a hole in a brick wall?"

"We could do both, with these," Joan said. "Browning Automatic Hand Cannons, .70 caliber. Most overpowered handgun in the world." She hefted one. "They were my sweet sixteen present from Gordo Gambino."

"Gambino?" Kite said. "You have Mafia connections, too?"

"Sort of. Gordo lived next door to us in South Philly when I was growing up. He'd been a minor league loan shark once, but got out of the business after one of his customers stabbed him in the groin. The experience pretty much mellowed him."

"No doubt."

"He and Mom had this platonic Heloise-and-Abelard thing for a while. Being a budding tomboy, I got to be the son that Gordo could never have. He taught me baseball."

"And artillery."

"The pistol range stuff was our secret. Mom even in a righteous mood wouldn't have approved."

"You know, Joan," Kite said, "the more I learn about your background, the more I understand your approach to problem solving."

"Keep your Colt as a reserve," Joan told her, passing a Hand Cannon and two empty clips across the table. "I've got explosive-tipped bullets, too," she added, setting a cardboard box beside the clips.

"Not from your sweet sixteen, I hope," Kite said, even more amazed.

"Nah," Joan said. "Office supplies. Fatima Sigorski ordered two thousand rounds of the stuff by mistake, so I swiped some."

"My," Kite said again. She picked up the Browning to feel the weight; it felt pretty good. "You take the derringer," she said. "It's single-shot, but I have a spring-holster that'll keep it out of sight up your sleeve until the second you need it. Good for a surprise."

"All right," Joan said. "Fair trade."

"The recoil on this must be tremendous," Kite added, doing a bicep curl with the Hand Cannon.

"It's got a shock absorber to keep from breaking your wrist," Joan said. "But yeah, it kicks. You also want to make sure you've got a good backstop behind whatever it is you're shooting at, in case you miss . . . or in case you don't miss."

"I'll remember that," Kite said. She aimed the Hand Cannon at the refrigerator and sighted down the bore. "So tell me about our opposition. If an Electric Negro were coming to beat my brains out with a copy of *War and Peace,* where would I aim to make it stop?"

"Center of the chest," Joan told her. "The Automatic Servant has two semi-independent computer processing units, one in the chest, one in the head, but it's the chest module that directs movement."

"So a head shot wouldn't stop it?"

"It might, if the spinal circuit breaker didn't trip right," Joan said. "But I wouldn't bank on it. Another thing, most of them have auxiliary sensors distributed throughout the body, so even decapitated they aren't totally blind."

"How strong are they?"

"Domestic models are rated to power lift up to a thousand pounds—enough to move most furniture and act as a stand-in car jack. Industrial Servants can tow a railroad freight car with one hand."

"Dear! No arm-wrestling, then. What about reflexes?"

"Varies," Joan said. "But don't be fooled into thinking they're as slow or as clumsy as they sometimes appear. They're programmed to play down their abilities so their owners won't feel intimidated, and so human coworkers won't start worrying about job security."

"Any special weaknesses or Achilles' heels?"

Joan shook her head. "Not if their behavioral inhibitors have been removed. They're not invulnerable by any means, but again, they're a lot tougher than they seem."

Kite nodded. She put down the gun, opened up the box of bullets, and carefully poured its contents out onto the center of the table. Scooping up a fistful of explosive rounds, she set to work filling her ammunition clips. Joan did the same.

"Do you suppose we ought to call somebody?" Joan asked, when they were all loaded up. "The F.B.I., I mean, or maybe Delta Force?"

"I'm not sure," Kite said. "I wonder if we could get them to believe us, even with this case file as evidence. And if we could get them to believe us, I wonder if it's wise to let people in power know that a thing such as the nanovirus is possible."

"I hear what you're saying," Joan said, "but if we don't tell anybody, and we get ourselves killed—"

The phone rang. Both women started. Joan was actually relieved to realize how keyed-up she was; it had worried her that she was taking this whole thing too much in stride, with too little emotion. But as the phone rang a second time, and her hand dropped instinctively to her gun, she saw that *lack* of emotion was not going to be a problem.

"Pick up," she said, on the third ring.

A pleasant, familiar voice, last heard in the yard of a gingerbread house, but far more menacing than it had seemed two days ago: *"Hello, Miss Fine."*

"What a coincidence," Joan said. "We were just discussing you."

"Oh, there are no coincidences here."

"Meaning what?"

"Some riddles, Miss Fine, even you should be able to solve without hints."

"All right," Joan said. Her eyes flicked briefly to Ayn's Lamp. "So what do we call you? John Hoover, or J. Edgar Hoover, or G.A.S.? You're an android, right? A custom-model Automatic Servant?"

"Under the control of the G.A.S. mainframe, yes. You can call me Hoover or G.A.S., whichever you prefer. One is a sub-entity of the other, so it doesn't really make a difference."

"The G.A.S. mainframe computer, in Anaheim—it can hear what I say to you?"

"Yes." There was a sound that might have been a sigh of impatience. *"You have something you want to say to it?"*

"Yes," Joan said, and went on, in the most commanding voice she could muster: "Generate executive order, priority request, authorization code four-two-oh-oh-three-two-oh-nine. Turn yourself off, now!"

Silence on the line.

"Hoover?"

"Yes?"

"Did you hear what I said?"

"I heard you. But did you hear me say I was stupid? No? That's because I'm not."

Joan glanced at Kite, then back at the phone. "You edited the videotape before you gave it to us?"

"I edited the memories that the videotape was created from. I also rewrote the Un-Babel software on Jerry Gant's computer."

"For what purpose?" Kite Edmonds asked. "Why have you revealed yourself to us?"

"Well that's what I'm calling about, Miss Edmonds. I told Miss Fine we'd speak again once she'd put the pieces of the puzzle together. And now that she has, I'd like you both to come back to Atlantic City for another face-to-face meeting."

"'Face-to-face'?" Joan said. "You're a machine, Hoover!"

"I'm a machine that wants to see you in Atlantic City this afternoon," Hoover replied. *"You've got time to make the 12:59 train from Grand Central if you hurry."*

"Wait a minute . . ."

"No. And don't you wait, either. Not unless you don't care about thousands of lives that are at stake. I'll expect you no later than 2:00."

A click, and a dial tone.

"We're in bad trouble, I think," said Kite.

Money Shots

The great Hearst blimp had started life as a navy reconnaissance vessel, built in denial of the end of the Cold War. Sublet to U.S. Customs for a stint hunting smugglers in the Caribbean, it was ultimately sold to Turner Broadcasting for about a quarter of its original construction cost. There was nothing else like it in the air. Its gas bag was bigger than anything since the *Hindenburg,* knitted from a space-age fabric that shed bullets like tank armor yet was radar transparent; its long gray gondola was sculpted for stealth. The lettering on the gondola's prow read *Sweet Jane,* for the widowed Ms. Turner, but the ground crew preferred a slightly different name.

"*This is Drome Traffic Control to the pilot of* Hanoi Jane. *You do not have clearance for take off at this time. Please return at once to the landing field, over.*"

No response. The blimp, already hundreds of feet above the grassy field, swung its nose around and began to pull away.

"*This is Drome Traffic Control to the pilot of* Hanoi Jane. *You are in violation of federal flight regulations. Please identify, over.*"

Walter keyed the mike in his radio headset. "This is Cronkite, over."

"*Cronkite?*" the air traffic controller said. "*Walter?*"

"No," Walter said, "Beauregard."

"*Walter, you're not authorized to take that vehicle. You haven't filed a flight plan.*"

"Hell, Traffic Control," said Walter, "I don't even have a pilot's license. How could I file a flight plan?"

"*That's not funny, Walter. Now turn* Jane *around and—*"

Walter switched off the radio and told Lexa how to disconnect the automatic transponder that broadcast *Sweet Jane*'s position. With one hand on the steering yoke and the other holding a mop handle to work the rudder pedals, Walter faked towards the Hudson, then broke another F.A.A. regulation by taking the blimp down low over Jersey City, where its already tenuous radar profile was lost completely in the ground clutter. He brought them around south-southeast, threading an obstacle course of high-rise condominiums and office buildings; Lexa, observing from the copilot's seat, admired his skill.

"You fly pretty good for a guy with no license," she said.

"Talent's not in the credentials," Walter told her. He indicated a console on her side of the cabin. "That's the navigator. You tell it our destination and it should give us a heading to follow."

Farther back in the gondola, in the production studio, Dan was busy demonstrating the smart camera system to Ellen Leeuwenhoek.

"What's so smart about it?" Ellen asked.

"Well," said Dan, "the Nielsen Company took outtakes from everyone who ever won an award for broadcast news video, and abstracted their styles into a computer model."

"So it's like a collection of personality templates of prize-winning camera operators."

"Right," Dan said, "and you can either call up a particular style you want or use the random mix function to create a potpourri."

"Hmm . . ."

"It's still experimental, of course . . ."

"Got it," said Lexa. The flight cabin windscreen dimmed and a head-up display came on, projecting course, airspeed, fuel remaining, and other statistics against the glass in a crisp laser green. One highlighted bar in the display read: HEADING TO D-POINT: 143°—DISTANCE: 128.6 NM.

"A hundred thirty miles," Lexa said, not happy. "Can we make it in time? Philo's set to make his move around 3:00 unless something goes wrong."

Walter checked his wristwatch against the clock in the display. "Philo, eh? You two are on a first-name basis?"

Lexa looked him in the eye, then nodded. "Yes."

"Well don't worry," said Walter. "This old war wagon can't break the sound barrier, but it moves." He reached down beside his seat to a line of throttle levers, and pushed all eight of *Sweet Jane's* engines to full power. Jersey City slid out from beneath them and they were over New York Bay, easily outpacing the Staten Island Ferry as it wallowed towards Richmond. Passing south of the Statue of Liberty, Walter came left to a heading of one hundred and forty-three degrees.

In the production studio, Dan hit the potpourri switch. Fourteen gun cameras mounted along the exterior of the gondola began trolling for money shots. Camera #2, in the foremost starboard position, focused in quickly on the Brooklyn shore just ahead. Camera #2 had been randomly assigned the style of freelance camerawoman Dee Dee Rule, who in 2014 had received a Rupert J. Murdoch Commemorative Citation for her eyewitness video of the drowning of a Bengali army encampment. Kings County was not India, of course; Brooklyn had no monsoon season, no flash floods, no tigers to maul the panicked soldiers as they tried to reach high ground. But it did have a few military-style tents—two medium and one extra-large—pitched on a seedy wharf where *something* bad might happen, and pacing miserably nearby a middle-aged Scoutmaster who looked as though something bad had *already* happened. Camera #2 tracked the Scoutmaster, zooming in tight on his unhappy face. He was talking to himself, mouthing two words over and over again. The first word was "complete"; the second was "failure."

Did You See That?

Fugitive Scoutmaster Oscar Hill had gone to ground on a condemned wharf near the Bush Terminal docks. His four remaining charges huddled together in one of the tents, dissecting a seven-legged rat they'd found floating in an oil drum; Oscar stalked along the crumbling wharf, reflecting on his poor, sad, disappointing, awful, *ruined* life.

It had not seemed wrong at first—in fact, had seemed altogether natural—to let Oblio's disappearance go unreported. The girls had said nothing about it all that day, and camped in an auto wrecking yard Tuesday night, Oscar Hill had slept more peacefully than he had in ages. Not till halfway through breakfast Wednesday morning did Eagle Scout Melissa Plunkett suddenly think to inquire: "Hey, what happened to Oblio?" Oscar's mouth went dry around a bite of campfire corn muffin, and he nearly choked; it took two long swigs from his canteen to get enough of a voice back to sputter: "Oblio went home early."

Oblio went home early. That might actually be true, and Melissa Plunkett seemed to accept it without question, but Oscar realized—gauging the height of the sun through the soot from a stack of burning tires—that he had let nearly eighteen hours go by without making sure. Even if Oblio had made it home safely, eighteen hours of inaction probably equaled felony negligence on Oscar's part, not to mention a betrayal of the Scoutmaster's Code. And if Oblio *hadn't* made it home safely . . .

The one good thing about urban survival camping was that you were never far from a pay phone. Oscar slipped away while his Scouts were breaking camp and dialed Oblio's home number. Oblio's mother answered.

"Hello?"

"Hello, Mrs. Wattles," said Oscar, in a child's falsetto, "is Oblio there?"

"Who is speaking, please?"

"It's Oblio's little friend, Oscar Hill," Oscar said, so intent on not sounding like himself that he gave his real name.

"Oscar Hill? . . . Scoutmaster Hill? Why would you be calling here to speak to Oblio? Isn't he still with you?"

Another attack of dry-mouth. Oscar's voice fell from falsetto to stuttering bass: "Uh . . . uh . . . uh . . ."

"*Scoutmaster Hill? Oblio* is *still with you, isn't he? . . . Scoutmaster Hill? Speak to me! HAS SOMETHING HAPPENED TO MY BOY?*"

Oscar hung up. If he'd had a gun he would have done the honorable thing right then and there. Instead he returned to his troop, announced that they would be extending their camping trip another day, and led them on a forced march of many miles, across Bensonhurst to Fort Hamilton, following the Bay Ridge shore to the docks. The Scouts were surprised by the change in plan but didn't complain; anything to get another day off from school. Oscar for his part had no real idea of where they were headed, or what they would do when they got there; he just wanted to get as far away from their original campsite as possible before Mrs. Wattles called the police. If there'd been a boat tied up at the wharf, he might have kept going.

And now it was Thursday afternoon, and the girls' parents would have had time to get worried and call the cops too, and Oscar Hill's life was . . . well, it was over. Done. In his sacred capacity as leader and mentor to the young, He Had Failed. If ever there was a moment when Oscar would have liked to have a cliché come true, this was it: he wished the ground at his feet would just open up and swallow him whole.

But speaking of holes in the earth . . . one of the wooden piers that jutted from the wharf had collapsed, revealing the black mouth of a sewer outflow that ran beneath the docks. Not much was flowing out of it right now, just a trickle of ordure that had pooled in a mound on the fallen timbers of the pier and trailed a muddy cloud into the surrounding water. Oscar glimpsed folds of red, white, and blue among the brown; curious, he peered closer, and was shocked to see a tattered and stained U.S. flag half-smothered in the filth.

The obvious metaphor—an American icon in deep shit—was more than Oscar could stand, or ignore. A set of iron rungs had been bolted to the concrete face of the wharf beside the sewer outflow, and though they didn't go all the way down to the waterline and the collapsed pier, Oscar thought that by standing on the lowest rung he'd be able to snag out the flag with a long stick. He noticed a splintered boat hook leaning against one of the wharf's outbuildings, and hurried to get it.

The rungs were badly pitted and corroded, but all were still firmly fixed in place, except for the secondmost rung from the bottom, which was missing entirely. Oscar had to stretch past the gap, a move that proved too stressful for his trousers: there was a *burr* of tearing fabric, and sudden cold ventilation on his buttocks. Steady on the bottom rung, Oscar craned his head around to assess the damage, and as he did so he heard two more sounds. The first was a soft drone of engines from overhead. *Sweet Jane's* shadow fell across the wharf, but Oscar did not look up, because of the second sound.

Music. A classical theme, issuing from the mouth of the sewer outflow. The familiar melody made Oscar think of the dinosaurs marching to extinction in Walt Disney's *Fantasia,* and as he listened more closely, he detected a slight scrabbling or pattering, as if something with very short arms and legs was dragging itself through the pipe.

"Oblio?" he said, though he knew it couldn't be. Clinging to the rungs one-handed, he leaned far out to the right, until his face was in front of the opening. He saw nothing but darkness within. "Hello?" he called, as the music swelled. "Is there somebody in there? . . . "

In the production studio aboard *Sweet Jane,* Dan Rather jerked as though electrified.

"My *God,*" he said. "Did you see that?"

"See what?" said Ellen Leeuwenhoek.

May I Help You?

"Oof!"

Joan collided with the derelict just inside the entrance to the Grand Central terminal. She was taller than he was, and moving faster, and he would have gone sprawling if she hadn't reached out to steady him. Many people would have let him fall rather than touch him—he stank like a sewer—but Joan gripped his upper arms firmly and looked him in the face, and that was how she recognized him.

"Clayton?" she said. "Clayton Bryce?"

His eyes were round as the eyes of a knowing calf about to be brained in an abattoir; upon hearing his name, he let out a mournful lowing and grabbed at the front of Joan's jacket like a man clawing for purchase on the brink of an abyss. Ayn Rand in her Lamp shivered in disgust.

"Stop that!" Ayn snapped. "Stop pawing her, you bum!"

"Oh Clayton," said Joan. He was a mess: dressed in filthy rags, and made up to look as though he'd been living on the street for years, so that even his own parents might not have known him, or admitted to knowing him. His normally conservative hairline had been replaced by an unruly wig or weave of stringy brown locks, matted with dirt and worse. A mangy beard and moustache had been cemented to his face, and there were bare, heavily scabbed-over patches on his chin where he'd torn away skin trying to pull the whiskers off. His tongue had bloated to the size of a golf ball in his mouth, stifling his speech and making breathing difficult; his nose and eyes were puffed and runny; and his hands had swollen up too, big and pink, like boiled meat, so painful that it was all he could do to hold on to the battered tin cup of pencils that had become his only worldly possession.

"Oh Clayton," Joan repeated, putting a scenario together in her head, "what did you do, say something stupid and condescending about homeless people? To a stranger, maybe?"

Clayton's heart skipped a beat, and his expression changed, first to shock, then to a mixture of supplication, frenzy, and fear.

"Hehhhhhpp!" Clayton brayed, beating feebly on Joan's chest with his tin cup. "Hehhhhhpp!"

"Help!" Ayn Rand cried. "Help! Police!"

"May I help you?" a third voice said.

The Pleasant Trip Squad, already trailing Clayton, had closed in around them, seven brown uniforms with shock prods and TASER guns. The speaker was a severe-looking Hispanic man whose badge identified him as Captain Hector Miércoles.

"It's all right," Joan told him. "He's with us."

"But who are you?" Captain Miércoles inquired. "Ticket holders?"

"Just going to buy them," Joan said. "We're on our way to Atlantic City. First class."

"First-class tickets are very expensive," the captain said. "Are you sure you can afford them?"

Joan disengaged herself from Clayton and took out her wallet, careful not to expose the gun tucked into her waistband beneath her jacket. "Plastic," she said, displaying her credit cards. "Six kinds, plus an ATM card." She opened the billfold, fanning out the notes. "And cash. OK?"

"You're obviously a woman of means," Captain Miércoles said, eyeing her worn sneakers. "But this man can't sit in first class." He wrinkled his nose at Clayton. "Even in economy coach, I'm afraid, he'd be an offense to the other passengers."

"Captain," Kite spoke up, heading off Joan's reply, "may I make a suggestion?"

The captain met her gaze. "Please."

"The 12:59 to Atlantic City," she said. "Does it have a smoking compartment?"

The captain consulted a computer on his wrist. "Yes, it does. A half-car, special today."

"We'll sit in there, then," Kite said. "Those people have no sense of smell left anyway."

"That should be acceptable," Captain Miércoles relented. "But you'll have to hurry; that train is already boarding."

"We'll be gone so fast you won't remember having talked to us," Kite promised.

"Very good." The captain touched two fingers to the bill of his cap. "Have a pleasant and safe journey."

"Yeah," Joan said. "Have a nice day."

Captain Miércoles paused, on the verge of turning away, and appeared to reconsider his decision to let them go. But just then his belt radio squawked, warning of some emergency elsewhere in the station; so the captain gave Joan a cautioning look and marched off. The other Trippers followed him.

"Patience, Joan," Kite said, when they were gone. "I expect we'll be fighting soon enough as it is."

"He was being a prick," Joan said.

"He's paid to be a prick," Kite replied. "And that's not an easy job, especially when it's the only work you can get."

Clayton, meanwhile, had not taken his eyes off Joan's wallet. As soon as the Pleasant Trip Squad were out of sight, he snatched at the notes in the billfold, ignoring the pain in his hands.

"Thief!" Ayn Rand cried, but Joan let him take the money. She stared at the collar cinched around his neck. It was made of leather, unadorned except for two transparent bubbles, one beneath each ear, that had been packed with some sort of clay-like substance. The collar's buckle, which rested heavily against Clayton's Adam's apple, looked like the feeder box on a change machine; it had a slot in the front just wide enough for the insertion of currency. Joan watched as Clayton shoved in the first of the bills he had taken from her. Some mechanism in the box chewed it into green confetti flakes, which sprinkled down onto Clayton's chest; a meter above the feed slot clicked backwards from $492 to $472.

"Somebody stop him!" Ayn cried, as Clayton sacrificed more bills. "He's destroying money!"

"Calm down, Ayn," Joan said.

"But don't you see what he's doing? He's destroying money! Don't you understand what that means?"

"Ayn—"

"Money is the fruit of man's labor! Labor is the product of man's thought! He's destroying thought!"

Soon there was no thought left, and the meter still had $319 on it. Clayton held out his hands for more, offering in exchange a pocketful of coins he had not yet been able to change for bills, but Joan's wallet was empty, and Kite had little to give. "I've got a fiver and a few singles," she said, "and you're welcome to them if you want, but—"

"If you want to waste money," Ayn interjected, "why don't you clean yourself up and get a job? Maybe the sweat of earning it would teach you the value of a dollar!"

But Clayton gestured urgently at the clock above the board announcing train arrivals and departures; it was 12:51. He tapped his wrist, emphasizing the importance of the time. Then he balled his hands into fists, wincing as he did so, and held them up beside the two bubbles in his collar. *"BRRRRRRRMM!"* he roared, opening his hands. *"BRRRRRRRMM!"*

"Boom?" Joan said.

"Yech!" Clayton replied, nodding frantically. "Yech! Ack ick! Ah urr acha! Urr acha! Hehhp!"

"He's a madman!" Ayn Rand said. "Get away from him!"

"Over there," Kite said, tugging on Joan's sleeve. Off to their left was a newsstand, the same newsstand where Maxwell had recently pilfered a rack of Erica Jong novels, and right beside it was an Automatic Teller Machine.

"This is the second boarding call for Lightning Transit's High Roller to Atlantic City," the P.A. system announced. "Lightning Transit's High Roller is now boarding on Track 7."

"That's your train!" Ayn said. "You have to hurry!"

But Joan had taken Clayton by the wrist and was pulling him towards the ATM.

"What are you doing?" Ayn demanded.

"Rescuing an imbecile."

"But why? Does this . . . this person represent a value to you?"

"He's an asshole," Joan replied, to Clayton's alarm.

"Then *why* are you helping him?"

"Empathy, Miss Rand," said Kite. "This is America. We're all assholes here."

MAY I HELP YOU? the Teller Machine asked. Joan inserted her ATM card, chose English as her preferred language, and tapped out her secret code: JOB 32 10. She told the machine to give her four hundred dollars. Clayton hunched over the withdrawal slot like a catcher awaiting the last pitch of the World Series.

No money appeared. Instead the ATM screen went blank, and flashed a proverb:

GIVE A MAN A FISH, AND YOU'VE FED HIM FOR A DAY;
TEACH A MAN TO FISH AND YOU'VE FED HIM FOR A LIFETIME
GO FISH

The message remained long enough for all of them to read it; then the screen blanked again, and returned to its original query—MAY I HELP YOU?—without returning Joan's card.

"Ficcchhh?" Clayton said, and something in him seemed to snap. *"FICCCHHH?"* With a howl he threw himself at the machine, kicking and pummeling.

"This is the third and final boarding call for Lightning Transit's High Roller to Atlantic City," the P.A. system declared. "Lightning Transit's High Roller is now boarding on Track 7. All aboard!"

"You're going to miss your train!" Ayn wailed.

"You'd better run for it, Joan," Kite said.

"Kite, we can't just leave him—"

"You go," Kite told her. "I'll save him; but what I have in mind is liable to bring the captain back, and we can't afford to both be arrested. I'll still try to make the train if I can."

"All right," Joan said. "I'll see if I can get them to hold it. But if you don't make it, don't wait around for the next one. Head back home, and start getting the word out. Call Lexa and call Harry—and maybe the cops, if you can think of a way to get them to listen. And watch your back."

"And you yours," said Kite. "Good luck, Joan."

"You too," Joan said. She ran off, carrying the Lamp.

Clayton had collapsed over the ATM, in tears; Kite laid her hand on his shoulder. "Come on, Mr. Bryce," she said. "I'm going to need you to stand behind me, to shield me from observers . . ."

Too late: Kite was already being observed, though she wasn't aware of it. An Electric Policeman peeped out at her from behind a shoeshine stand on the far side of the terminal entrance. It took note of Joan as she left, but made no move to follow her; it was focused on Kite, and especially on Clayton.

It held a long metal baton in its hands, and it was not smiling.

Too Busy Swimming

A prehistoric wooden tugboat chugged stoically from the mouth of the Buttermilk Channel between Governor's Island and South Brooklyn. Two men stood on the deck, sharing an illicit smoke and swapping dirty jokes. Suddenly one of them tugged excitedly at the sleeve of the other; a shark's fin was knifing through the water to the south, coming straight towards them. They watched, fascinated, waiting for the shark to dive or turn aside, their fascination turning to fear when it did neither.

Meisterbrau tore through the tugboat's port-side hull without stopping. There was a shriek of terror and a screech of rending metal from below; the two deckhands ran to the far rail in time to see Meisterbrau burst out the starboard side, the boat's mangled drive shaft clamped between its jaws like a chew toy. Gutted, the tug sank almost immediately, but to the immense relief of the deckhands, the shark kept going, skirting Governor's Island to head for the Battery.

The city skyline was mirrored in the surface of the Bay; reflected upside-down, the Electric Billboard on the south face of the Gant Phoenix looked like this: ∂∂⅃. As the hands of the big clock above the Staten Island Ferry terminal approached one P.M., the Billboard, aping a mechanical counter, began rolling ∂∂⅃ over to ∂∂8. The men from the tugboat didn't notice this, though; like Meisterbrau, they were too busy swimming to pay much attention.

I Know How That Can Be

Kite leaned across the newsstand counter and leveled her Colt at the man behind the register.

"I'm dreadfully sorry about this," she apologized, cocking the hammer, "but my companion's head is going to explode if he doesn't get three hundred and nineteen dollars, and I'm afraid we don't have time to debate the matter."

The newsstand attendant, a transplanted southerner, matched her politeness for politeness: "Not a problem, ma'am." He punched NO SALE; Clayton, exhibiting no courtesy whatsoever, dove on the cash drawer as soon as it was open.

"You'll be reimbursed, of course," Kite said, sounding embarrassed.

"Well I appreciate that, ma'am," the attendant said. He glanced down at her gun. "Colt Army Model 1860, am I right?"

"You have a good eye."

He shrugged modestly. "I used to be a collector, back home."

"Georgia?" Kite guessed.

"Alabama," the attendant said. "Now would your firearm be a reproduction, or—"

Kite shook her head. "Genuine."

"May I ask what you paid for it, ma'am?"

"I didn't," Kite said. "It was a gift from my adopted Uncle."

A low whistle. "Nice uncle."

"Yes and no."

"Relatives." He nodded. "I know how *that* can be, ma'am." He turned his attention to Clayton's collar. "What kind of explosive are we dealing with? Plastique?"

"There I couldn't help you," Kite said. "Not my forte."

Another nod. "Looks like plastique. Do you know when it's set to go off?"

"Not precisely." She looked up at the station clock; it read 12:59. "But soon, I'd say, judging from his urgency."

"We may want to step back, just in case . . . and speaking of backs, ma'am, I know I probably shouldn't tell you this, but there's an Electric Policeman coming up fast behind you."

"Oh?" Kite said. "Is it armed?"

"It's got a big steel bar in its hand. Hmm. Never seen one use a club before . . ."

"Hold this for me," Kite said, setting her Colt revolver on the counter. She tugged the Browning Hand Cannon from her belt, turned . . . and froze.

The Electric Policeman—Roscoe 254—was about thirty feet away, passing a brightly lit coffee kiosk. Green neon reflected in its eyes and chased the blue of its uniform; the steel baton in its hand gleamed like a saber. Kite groaned, smelling North Carolina woods from a morning a century and a half gone, seeing a dead face; her stump ached and her finger would not tighten on the trigger. The Policeman came forward, raising its baton, the charging disc in its palm putting out enough voltage to stop the heart of a bear at a single stroke.

And Clayton Bryce, feeding in the last dollar of his ransom, tore the collar from his throat, spun around, and flung it away with all his strength. It whickered through the air like a Mexican bolo, curling neatly around Roscoe 254's neck. The Policeman's eyes seemed to bulge.

"Lightning Transit's High Roller to Atlantic City has departed the station," the P.A. system announced. "The High Roller has departed."

One o'clock.

18

I am an old man now . . . as I look back on the years which have passed since I first wrote the life-story of the Nautilus, and of its owner, I see no progress in the submarine which makes me hope for its use as a commercial medium. It has been wonderfully improved, I grant you—miraculously improved almost—but the improvements have all tended to one point—its efficacy as a war weapon; and that will be its one use in the future, I believe. I even think that in the distant future the submarine may be the cause of bringing battle to a stoppage altogether, for fleets will become useless, and as other war material continues to improve, war will become impossible.

—Jules Verne writing in *Popular Mechanics,* 1904

I must confess that my imagination . . . refuses to see any sort of submarine doing anything but suffocate its crew and founder at sea.

—H.G. Wells, *Anticipations of the Reactions of Mechanical and Scientific Progress upon Human Life and Thought*

City of Women

Wendy Mankiller's great-great-great-great-grandfather had served with the Standing Bear Cherokee Platoon of the Confederate Army, but her parents turned their backs on the broken promises of the American South and crossed the sea to England. Wendy grew up in Newcastle. She married a coal miner's son, attended King's College, and in 2007 became the first full-blood Cherokee in history to enlist in the Royal Navy. It was only half of a dream come true, for although women's military career prospects had opened up considerably since the days of the Civil War, the posting she most wanted was still officially closed to her. The possibility of captaining a frigate or a destroyer wasn't enough for Wendy Mankiller; her true heart's desire was to go *under* the water, and not by sinking.

Five years passed. In 2012 the Irish Republican Army decided to assassinate the British matriarch, for reasons having as much to do with fatigue as politics; six decades of Queen Liz, the Provos felt, were simply enough, and who knew, perhaps the accession of Prince William to the throne would inspire a new attitude towards the question of home rule. But their carefully planned ambush on the royal motorcade failed to come off, thanks to the courageous intervention of Wendy Mankiller, who was in London on extended shore leave and got caught up in the crossfire. Five months pregnant and armed with only a grocery sack full of canned goods, she nevertheless managed to take down four Kalashnikov-wielding terrorists single-handedly; Queen Liz, firing an antique Vickers machine gun out the side window of her stalled limousine, annihilated another half-dozen Irish before the remaining ambushers called it quits and fled.

"And how shall We reward Our most loyal subject?" asked the Queen, when the skirmish was ended.

"Let me captain a submarine," Wendy Mankiller replied. "A big one."

"Impossible," said Commodore Sir Kellogg Northrope Peas of the Office of Naval Standards and Traditions, when told of this request. "In order for Mankiller to *command* a submarine, she would first have to *serve* on a submarine; and as there are presently no submarines with female crews, that would imply serving with men, in the most cramped and confined circumstances imaginable, which would lead to a complete failure of discipline and probable instances of moral turpitude, followed by outright mutiny. Also, I don't like the idea."

"Commodore Sir Peas," the Queen inquired, looking him in the eye, "who is the wealthiest and most powerful woman in the world? Do remind Us."

"Now, now, Your Majesty . . ."

The commodore died mysteriously in his sleep soon after this exchange, but Wendy Mankiller still had to wait several years to receive her reward. Parliament would not finance the construction of a brand-new sub, and the navy refused to feminize any of those already in service—the Admiralty closed ranks and held fast against the thinly veiled threats from Buckingham Palace—so the Queen was forced to pay for it out of her own pocket; selling off spare castles and jewels to raise the necessary cash took a while. In the meantime, Wendy Mankiller and a handpicked female crew underwent a rigorous training regimen at the Royal Submarine Academy in Portsmouth.

HMS *City of Women* was christened in Gibraltar on February 29, 2016. England's first (and only) Dread Virago-class nuclear attack submarine, it was actually an Anglo-Spanish hybrid, prepared secretly by Andalusian shipwrights at the behest of Queen Liz's longtime whist partner in the Royal House of Bourbon. *City of Women* proved herself in combat that very summer, when Wendy Mankiller and her Dread Virago crew sent a boatload of Basque revolutionaries to a watery grave in the Gulf of Cadiz.

But all of that is another story. It was now November 2, 2023, three months shy of Wendy Mankiller's eighth anniversary in Her Majesty's most secret service. *City of Women* loitered off the U.S. Eastern Seaboard, awaiting orders; the sub had escorted the *QE2 Mark 2* on its transatlantic voyage, and would likely accompany it home as well. To avoid encounters with American submarines—whose captains tended to be touchy about territorial incursion—Wendy Mankiller took *City of Women* into the sea monster zone above the Hudson Canyon. At 1820 hours Greenwich Mean (1:20 P.M. local time), passive sonar picked up the *Mitterrand Sierra*.

"Unidentified surface contact bearing one-three-seven," Gwynhefar Matchless called from the sonar bay.

"Mechanical or biological?" Wendy Mankiller asked.

"It's a ship, right enough," said Matchless. "I can hear a pod of whales, as well . . . and something else. Hold on." She fed the various sounds to Bloody Mary Tudor, *City of Women*'s combat computer. "Bloody Mary says the ship is frog, but it tastes like chicken."

"How's that again?"

"French. A French anti-submarine platform, Robespierre-class. But there are no Robespierre-class vessels active in the Gallic fleet at present, so unless the Algerians have decided to go fishing for American submarines . . ."

"It shouldn't be here."

"No. Most especially not alone."

"Can you or Bloody Mary use the ship's signature library to give me a more precise identification? I want to know if it *is* Algerian, or a rogue."

"Sorry, I can't answer that without getting closer. The signal isn't clear enough."

"What about the 'something else' you say you heard?"

"Can't give you an answer on that either, Captain. It's awfully noisy here for what is supposed to be a godforsaken sector of the ocean. Perhaps if we snuck in a few kilometers nearer . . ."

"Hmm." Wendy Mankiller considered. "Just how good is the sonar suite on a Robespierre?"

"That would depend," Gwynhefar Matchless said. "The ship class is a decade old, but it was designed for easy retrofitting. Her sonar might possibly be state-of-the-art." She added: "*French* state-of-the-art."

"I see. Helm?"

"Yes, Captain?"

"Ten pounds says you can't halve the distance to the Robespierre without getting caught."

The helmswoman laughed. "That's a poor wager on your part, Captain." Her name was Dasher MacAlpine, and her great-ancestor Lake MacAlpine had been a famously successful cat burglar. Stealth ran in the family, the MacAlpines liked to say, though it was also true that Lake MacAlpine had ended his days on a gibbet. "Fifty pounds says I can take us right under them without their being any the wiser."

"Not that close, thanks," Wendy Mankiller said. She switched on *City of Women*'s intercom. "Attention all Viragos, this is the captain speaking. All hands to battle stations; conditions of maximum quiet until I say otherwise. This is not a drill. MacAlpine, take us in."

Yabba-Dabba-Doo

"Approaching first buoy release," Morris said.

Together with Philo and Norma Eckland, he viewed the tactical situation on a two-dimensional tabletop plotting screen that had been set up beside the periscope pedestal in the control room. The display centered on the *Mitterrand Sierra*—represented by a skull-and-crossbones—as it turned in a slow, left-hand circle around the imaginary intersection of 39° 17' north latitude and 72° 00' west longitude. The *Yabba-Dabba-Doo,* represented by an ecology symbol, had just begun its own circle, moving clockwise about three miles farther out from the center. Off to the east, a cluster of stylized whales spouted plumes of foam. And south and southeast, a shifting, sinuous dotted line snaked across the display, phasing in and out uncertainly from moment to moment.

"Ghost net?" Philo said, of this last.

Morris nodded. "Ghost net." A light flashed on a panel above his head. "First buoy release." He reached up and depressed a switch; from an already open hatch on the *Yabba-Dabba-Doo*'s missile deck, a yellow buoy swam free. "First buoy away."

A small peace sign appeared on the display, marking the buoy's position. Over the next hour and a half, if everything went as planned, the *Yabba-Dabba-Doo* would release three more buoys, one to the east, one to the south, and one to the west of the *Mitterrand Sierra*'s position. Synchronized ballast release would bring all four buoys to the surface simultaneously, and shortly thereafter—again, if everything went as planned—the *Mitterrand Sierra* would cease to be dangerous. The *Yabba-Dabba-Doo* would move in, take the ship, and free the lemurs.

All they had to do was drop the buoys and back off without getting caught.

"Twenty-seven minutes to second buoy release," Morris said. His palms were damp with sweat, though he knew better than any of them just how quiet the *Yabba-Dabba-Doo* really was—quiet enough to outslip even the *Mitterrand Sierra*'s intelligent sonar suite, for a while. That it was so quiet was largely the result of Morris's one effort to get in touch with his ethnic roots, two weeks spent at a kibbutz in upstate New York when he was nineteen years old. Morris had been stuck in a thin-walled dorm room adjacent to that of an amateur electric guitarist with a taste for classic heavy metal. When his attempts at a negotiated settlement fell flat—his neighbor lecturing him about Nazi repression of the Jewish artistic impulse—Morris had opted, as usual, for a technological fix: he'd designed and built a sound suppressor powerful enough to turn a hundred-twenty-decibel rendition of "Bang Your Head" into a butterfly fart. A variant of the same quieting system had been installed in the *Yabba-Dabba-Doo,* which was how they could get away with having hamsters and other pets running around the sub during their pirating expeditions. But today's operation was different; this was the first time they'd ever gone after a real warship, and even with all the animals safely removed to shore and everybody in the crew tiptoeing around in soft-soled shoes, it was nerve wracking.

"Why aren't they pinging for us?" Norma Eckland asked, in a low voice. "That's more effective than just listening, isn't it? Especially if you're not worried about giving away your own position?"

"They don't want to spook us," Morris said. "They want to lure us in where they can be sure of nailing us, and they know that if they start hammering on active sonar while we're still too far away, we might decide to cut and run and not come back. So they can't ping until they're sure we're close."

"But we're already close," Norma said. "As close as we're going to get, right?"

"Right."

"So if they aren't pinging, that must mean their passive sonar can't hear us."

"Or that it hasn't heard us," Morris said. "Yet. Probably."

"Then as long as they don't ping, we know we haven't been detected."

"Well, not necessarily. If they could get a good enough fix on us with the passive sonar, they might not bother with the active. They might just launch a torpedo."

"But we'd know if they did that, right? Asta would be able to hear it."

"Probably. Unless it was a rocket-propelled torpedo."

"A rocket-propelled torpedo?"

"Launched from the deck of the ship," Morris said. "It flies through the air on a rocket, splashes into the water near the target, and starts homing. Kind of like a forward pass with a warhead attached."

"So we wouldn't hear the rocket taking off from the deck—"

"No. If we were close enough to hear the rocket, they wouldn't be firing torpedoes, they'd be dropping depth charges."

"But we're *not* that close—"

"No."

"—so no depth charges, and even if we couldn't hear the rocket take off, we'd at least hear the splash when it came down, right? So there'd be some warning, right?"

"Unless it dropped directly on top of us," Morris said. "Then we might not hear anything before the explosion. And of course if the explosion were to breach the hull directly outside the control room, we might not even hear—"

"Forget it," Norma said. "I withdraw the question. Forget I asked."

Mitterrand Sierra

The *Mitterrand Sierra*'s combat computer didn't speak English.

"What do you mean it doesn't speak English?" Captain Baker had demanded, upon first being informed.

"French ship, French systems," Troubadour Penzias told him. "It's got Arabic, too, but I don't."

"But you do have French?"

"Oui."

"From where?"

"My grandmother," Penzias said, and Captain Baker paused, trying to imagine Penzias with a grandmother. "There is a French-language tutorial in the databanks," Penzias added. He entered something on a console, and a female voice began to recite: *"Répétez après moi: . . . j'attaque, tu attaques, il attaque, nous attaquons, vous attaquez, ils attaquent . . . je détruis, tu détruis, il détruit, nous détruisons, vous détruisez, ils détruisent . . . je—"*

"Turn it off," Captain Baker ordered.

It was just one more thing to worry about: Penzias the psychopath could communicate with the ship's weapons systems, but the captain could not. Once again he questioned his judgment in accepting command of a mercenary vessel, but determined to see the job through regardless, he did what he could to assure order. He confiscated Penzias's hunting rifle, locking it away in a small-arms cabinet "until I decide there's something you ought to shoot at." Penzias surrendered the weapon without argument, which only increased Captain Baker's wariness; he went back to the arms cabinet and got himself a pistol, which he strapped to his hip.

The munitions wranglers, meanwhile, set about arming the *Mitterrand Sierra*. Once the ship was clear of the mainland and the U.S. Coast Guard's patrol zones, weapons were brought up from stowage and assembled on the deck: in the bow, a Savage Candle torpedo-rocket launcher; port and starboard, six Automatic .50-caliber machine guns, three on each side; in the stern, a pair of depth-charge racks and a swivel-mounted SAM missile launcher to knock down any Flying Zodiacs or model helicopters that might threaten the *Sierra*. Sayles and Sutter worked through the night from Wednesday to Thursday; White Negroes did the heavy lifting. On Thursday morning, about the same time Lexa Thatcher and Ellen Leeuwenhoek were entering the parking lot at the Fonda Blimp Drome, they brought up the captive lemurs' heated habitat, raising it on fixed stanchions above the *Sierra*'s vacant helipad, high enough to be seen by a submarine periscope.

Ready for war, the ship proceeded to the rendezvous point, and waited.

Captain Baker sat in the command chair in the combat information center, a darkened room one level below the bridge where the ship's sensors and weapons controls were centralized. A White Negro brought sandwiches and coffee; Captain Baker said no to the food and yes to the caffeine. He drank it too quickly and burned his tongue.

"They're here," Troubadour Penzias said.

Waving a hand in front of his mouth, Captain Baker leaned forward to check his tactical monitor. He could see a whale pod and a ghost net, but no submarine. "Where? Is there a new contact I'm not getting yet?"

"No new contact," Penzias said. "Just a hunch."

The captain sat back. "They can't be too close yet. Passive would have picked up something."

"Maybe." The lenses of Penzias's VISION Rig whirred and focused. "Maybe they're even quieter than we expected."

"You want to go active? If we trust Vanna Domingo's last radio transmission, all we need is one solid ping off their hull and they're ours. They won't be able to hide, and they can't outrun us . . ."

"We don't know they can't outrun us. And they may have checked their hull for surprise packages since yesterday." Penzias sucked reflectively on a squeeze bottle of food coloring. Red liquid flecked the corner of his mouth. "No, I don't want to go active yet. But I do want to rattle them. Force them to make a move before they're ready, maybe . . ."

"How?"

Penzias offered a suggestion.

"You're a sick bastard," Captain Baker said.

"It'll work, though," Penzias replied. "They'll have no choice but to react. If we make the torpedo run long enough, they may even try to throw themselves in front of it."

"And if they don't?"

Penzias shrugged. "Then we waste a torpedo. We've got plenty to spare. What do you say, Captain?"

"Sick bastard . . ."

"Yes, very sick bastard. Do I have permission to fire? Or would you rather just sit and wait until they're ready to make *us* react?"

"Damn it," Captain Baker said. "All right. Do it."

"Done," said Penzias. *"Combat!"*

"Prêt," the computer said.

"Parez à lancer une torpille Chandelle Sauvage sur les biologiques . . ."

City of Women

"Surface contact now bearing one-three-six, at a rough range estimate of twelve to fourteen kilometers," Gwynhefar Matchless said. "According to Bloody Mary, the contact's acoustic signature matches that of a Robespierre decommissioned by the French in 2021 and not currently listed as active in any known fleet."

"A rogue, then," Wendy Mankiller said.

"Seems so, Captain. Additional contact now positively identified as a castoff drift net, stretched out south and southeast of the Robespierre's position."

Mankiller nodded. "We'll be sure and steer clear of that. Is the Robespierre still circling?"

"Yes. Fairly tight circle, too. Must be waiting for something . . . or hunting it."

"Should we move away now, Captain?" Dasher MacAlpine asked.

Wendy Mankiller was thinking of the strange radio message she'd gotten from the Queen last night. "No," she said. "Ease us in closer."

Yabba-Dabba-Doo

"Second buoy away," Morris said. "What's wrong with your face, Philo?"

"My face?" Philo said.

"It's kind of hard to see in this light, but it's got . . . spots. Your arms, too."

"Oh God," Norma Eckland said. "Not spots. Pox. Chicken pox."

"Chicken pox!" Philo looked down at his arms. "No wonder I don't feel well. I thought it was just nerves . . ."

Norma edged away from him. "I've never had chicken pox," she said.

"Torpedo drop off the port beam!" Asta Wills called from the sonar bay. "Torpedo bearing zero-eight-seven, range five thousand yards!"

"Looks like they heard us," Morris said. "They're kind of off the mark, though . . ."

"Osman!" commanded Philo. "Take us—"

"Wait a minute!" Asta called again. "No one panic yet, I don't think it's aimed at us. Torpedo is headed straight away east, towards—"

"East?" Morris said.

"Bastards!" Asta suddenly exclaimed. "Those fucking bastards!"

The torpedo was represented by a simple arrow on the tactical display; it was pointed at the whales.

"Oh no," said Philo.

"Hold on, hold on, hold on," Morris said, turning to face another computer screen. "Asta, I need sonar data on console two!"

"You've got it . . ." The screen lit and began to flicker with rapidly accumulating information. "Torpedo's speed is thirty-six knots, with forty-two hundred yards to go to the nearest target . . ."

Morris nodded. "About three and a half minutes. Makes sense. They want to goad us into action before we're ready, so they dropped way short of the target and set the torpedo to run slow . . ."

"Thirty-six knots is *slow*?" Norma said.

"Oh sure. The British have a torpedo now that can do a hundred plus. Or at least that's what it can do in the North Sea, where they developed it. In warmer waters—"

"What about *this* torpedo, Morris?" Philo interrupted him.

"Savage Candle," Morris read from his screen. "Standard French anti-submarine standoff weapon—French-and-Israeli, actually, but that's another long story . . ."

"Can it kill a whale?"

"Sure, if it explodes. Like fishing with dynamite. Hydrostatic shock could turn the whole pod into dogfood . . ."

"Morris!" gasped Norma.

"*If* it explodes, I said. But. . . ." A lengthy description of the *Chandelle Sauvage* had scrolled up on his screen; he examined the fine print and seemed pleased with what he found. "Yeah. That's what I thought." He sneered at the skull-and-crossbones on the tactical display. "Shmucks!"

"What?" Philo said.

"Watch," said Morris.

"Shouldn't we do something?" Norma asked.

"No need. Watch."

They watched; the arrow closed the gap between itself and the whales, looking more like a harpoon as it neared its mark. Asta called off time and distance until the arrow intersected the first whale icon . . . and passed through it.

"Huh," said Philo. The arrow whirled around, darted towards another whale, and passed through it as well. And through a third. Philo looked up at Morris.

"Built-in safety device," Morris explained. "During the Gabon Oilfield Action of '18, the French Navy had a problem with friendly-fire casualties."

"They blew up their own submarines?"

"They blew up two billion francs' worth of underwater drilling equipment. The French minister of fossil resources was so upset he choked to death on a snail. After the funeral the secretary of the navy decided to talk to Israel about copying the warhead from their Solomon torpedo; just before it detonates it double-checks the data from its homing sonar and other sensors to make sure it hasn't been fired at an inappropriate target . . ."

"But a whale's not a drilling rig," Philo said.

"No, but it's not a submarine or a ship, either," said Morris. Viewing the tactical display with amusement, he added: "That torpedo must be pretty confused right now. The target *moves* like a sub, kind of, but it's made out of blubber."

"Blubber," Norma said. "Whale oil."

Morris nodded. "Not quite a fossil fuel, but still . . ."

"So it can't hurt the whales?"

"Well, I suppose it might still land a hell of a bruise, if it bumped one at thirty-six knots. But it's not allowed to explode; that would be contrary to the national interests of the Sixth Republic."

On the tactical display, the arrow winked out as the Savage Candle's fuel supply was exhausted. The whales swam on.

"Shmucks," Morris repeated. "Third buoy release in twenty-one minutes . . ."

Mitterrand Sierra

"Jack of all weapons systems, huh?" Captain Baker said.

Penzias seethed quietly at his station. "That was intentional," he said.

"Sure it was. You had a chance to kill something warm-blooded, and you passed it up. Sure."

"La torpille est fini," the computer said.

Yabba-Dabba-Doo

The lovers lay curled beneath a space blanket in Escape Pod C, just aft of the galley. Twenty-Nine Words for Snow was deep asleep, the warmth of the blanket and a pleasant soreness in his muscles inspiring dreams of a chase across the tundra, herds of caribou and musk-ox fleeing before the Mighty Hunter. Seraphina only dozed, her hand traveling lazily up and down Twenty-Nine Words's bare thigh; her tongue darted out behind Twenty-Nine Words's ear, bending his dream down a different track.

The sound of the escape-pod hatch opening brought her fully awake.

"This is *not* safe behavior," a voice said.

Seraphina lifted her head. It took a moment to locate the speaker, who was only a foot tall. "BRER Beaver!"

He waved an empty condom wrapper accusingly at her. "Do you know the failure rate for these things?"

"BRER Beaver!" Raising up on her elbows now. "You're supposed to be broken!"

"I've been repaired. And none too soon, it seems." He used his tail to flip up a corner of the space blanket. "Are you *naked* under there?"

Seraphina tried to sit up. She got tangled in the blanket, and her flailing arm struck a panel with buttons; the pod hatch swung closed again.

"No," Twenty-Nine Words said, and burst out giggling. "No, not the antlers . . ."

"Really," BRER Beaver said, with a sniff. "What if it had been your father who found you like this? Did you give any thought to *his* feelings?"

Seraphina steadied herself and started punching buttons deliberately.

"What are you doing?"

"I'm kicking *you* out of here," Seraphina said.

"That's not the sequence that reopens the hatch," BRER Beaver said. "Stop. Don't—"

A sign came on above the panel, announcing, JETTISON TANKS PRIMED; to Seraphina, of course, it was just meaningless squiggles.

She punched another button.

City of Women

"New contact," Gwynhefar Matchless said. "Disturbance in the water, bearing one-four-nine."

"What kind of disturbance?"

"Some type of compressed-air blow, Captain. Sounds a little like a torpedo launch, but bigger . . ."

Yabba-Dabba-Doo

"Four minutes to third buoy release," Morris said. A tremor ran through the sub; a buzzer sounded.

"What was that?" asked Philo.

Morris consulted a status panel. "Somebody just jettisoned one of the escape pods," he said. His eyes narrowed. "Pod C. Down by the engine room . . ."

"They wouldn't," said Norma. "Would they?"

"We're in trouble," Morris said.

Mitterrand Sierra

"*. . . relèvement un-six-sept. C'est près.*"

"Gotcha!" Penzias said.

"What is it?" Captain Baker said.

"Found them. . . ." Without waiting for the captain's order, Penzias powered up the *Sierra*'s active sonar and commenced pinging; the first wave of high-energy sound reached the *Yabba-Dabba-Doo*'s hull just seconds later.

Vanna Domingo's fake polka dot cried out in answer.

City of Women

"The Robespierre has found itself a target," Gwynhefar Matchless said. Her voice grew puzzled: "The new contact is *chirping*, Captain."

"Chirping?" Wendy Mankiller said.

Yabba-Dabba-Doo

Asta Wills piped the sound into the control room. Though oddly out of context underwater, it was a sound that any sleep-deprived New Yorker would recognize instantly.

"A car alarm," Philo said. "How did a car alarm get on the hull?"

"Must've happened while we were leaving the dock," Morris guessed. "Or maybe in the harbor, before we dove . . . shit! I should have thought to check!"

"Osman!" Philo shouted. "Get us out of here!"

"Istanbul?"

"Away! Fast!" He spun the annunciator to Full Speed Ahead.

"Running's not much use," Morris said, trying to think. "Not with that car alarm giving away our location."

"Do you have some gadget we could use to disable it?" Philo asked.

"You mean like a Mechanical Crab to crawl out and tear it loose from the hull?"

"Yes!"

"No," Morris said. "I haven't got anything like that. Now if I had a few hours—"

"*Mitterrand Sierra* is coming about and flooding torpedo tubes!" Asta Wills called out. "A *lot* of torpedo tubes . . ."

Mitterrand Sierra

"J'ai une solution de tir pour le sous-marin."

"Parez à lancer des Piranhas!"

Najime brought the *Mitterrand Sierra* around until the ship's bow was pointed in the direction of the fleeing submarine. Then, in accordance with Troubadour Penzias's instructions, she cut back on the throttle, slowing to five knots. Tagore called down to the combat information center: "We are in position."

"Paré à lancer," the combat computer said. *"Tubes pleins."*

"Now," Penzias muttered, under his breath. "Now I'll show you a secret weapon, green eyes. . . . *Ouvrez les portes extérieures!"*

Below the waterline, to either side of the bow, broad keel plates slid back, unmasking row after row of torpedo tubes. The tube openings were uncommonly narrow, but there were an uncommonly large number of them: seventy-two to the left of the bow and seventy-two to the right of the bow. One hundred forty-four in all.

"Portes extérieures ouvertes," the computer said. *"Torpilles armées."*

Penzias bared his teeth. *"Feu!"*

Yabba-Dabba-Doo

"High-speed screws in the water!" Asta Wills said. *"Sierra* has launched torpedoes at us." There was a pause. "A gross of torpedoes."

"How many?" Norma Eckland said.

"A dozen dozen. Sonar processing identifies a hundred and forty-four discrete signals."

"That can't be right," Philo said.

"Actually, it can." Morris was studying his computer screen again. *"Piranhas.* I've heard about this."

"Piranhas?"

"Another bit of hardware the French Navy borrowed from Israel, though it's not even supposed to be in prototype yet. The idea is, instead of launching a couple of big, expensive torpedoes, you fire off a whole slew of cheap little ones. That thins out the explosive punch a little, but in exchange you get a psychological warfare bonus—the thought of all those Piranhas boring in for the kill is meant to induce panic in the target." He paused to examine his own feelings, then added: "It works."

Philo looked down at the tactical display. "Piranhas, eh? Like a school of fish?"

"Yeah." Morris saw it too. "Yeah, that might work . . . if we can get to it fast enough."

"Osman!" Philo said.

"Istanbul!"

"Come left to course one-seven-five."

Morris switched on the intercom. "Engine room!"

"Morris?" It was Heathcliff. "What is going on, Morris?"

"I'm going to be diplomatic and not ask which of you bailed out," Morris said. "But I need to talk to Irma if she's still there."

"Of course she is still here," Heathcliff said. "We are all still here. What kind of false accusation are you making, Morris?"

"Never mind that now. Just tell Irma we need all the speed she can give us."

"Why? What is happening? Is there danger?"

"Yes, there is danger. And if we can't outrun it, Heathcliff, the Palestinian end of the boat gets blown up first."

City of Women

"Piranhas, eh?" Wendy Mankiller said. "That's the frog version of the Israeli Scorpion?"

"Supposedly still on the drawing board," her executive officer observed.

Mankiller nodded. "Yet here it is retrofitted into a ten-year-old ship that isn't officially in service anymore. I'd be very interested to learn this Robespierre's history. Sonar, do you have identification on the submarine yet?"

"No, Captain," Gwynhefar Matchless said. "Still not getting much of a signature—just the chirping, and now some propeller cavitation. She's very quiet, whatever she is, even at high speed. . . . Submarine is changing course, turning south. . . . Also changing depth, coming shallow. And continuing to accelerate . . ."

"South. . . . They're running for the net," Wendy Mankiller guessed. "Clever. Can they make it?"

"That would be a good subject for a wager, Captain."

The Curtain

The ghost net measured twenty-two miles from end to end, much of that length compressed into deadly accordion folds and tangle traps. Designed to strip fish from the sea like coal from a hillside, its mesh was a synthetic, tougher than piano wire, that might eventually wear out but would never rot; it had already outlasted the factory ship from whose stern it had once been dragged. Discarded now, it drifted with the currents, continuing to sieve life from the ocean, and not just from the water: seabirds, drawn by the stench of rotting fish, were themselves trapped and drowned, adding to the moving curtain of flesh and bone.

Live torpedoes were one of the few Atlantic species that the net had never before attempted to ensnare; whether even its strength would be enough to stop a gross of French Piranhas was an open question. But not for long.

Yabba-Dabba-Doo

A light flashed above Morris's head; he reached up automatically and pressed the switch to release the third buoy. Instead of floating free quietly as the other two buoys had done, it was swept back along the length of the hull and batted aside by the *Yabba-Dabba-Doo*'s propeller as the submarine charged through the water. Asta Wills heard the *thwap!*, but when it wasn't followed by an explosion, she disregarded it.

The tactical plot quickly became theoretical. At full speed the *Yabba-Dabba-Doo*'s passive sonar could hear little but the rush of water flowing around the hull; the only other sound was the steady *chirp-chirp-chirp* of the car alarm. The Piranhas' screw-sounds were lost in the flow noise and in the wash of the *Yabba-Dabba-Doo*'s own propeller; and as Morris explained, they did not use active homing to locate their prey. "A hundred and forty-four torpedoes all pinging away at the same time would create too many confusing echoes, so they have to home in passively on their target. If it weren't for that damn car alarm on the hull . . ."

"And if they don't ping us, we can't hear them coming anymore?" Philo asked.

"No," said Morris. On the tactical display, the swarm of arrows representing the Piranhas had been replaced by a swarm of question marks. Something similar was happening to the plot of the ghost net: hypothetical to begin with, a best-guess composite drawn from the distress sounds of thousands of trapped fish, the dotted line blurred and smudged as sonar efficiency was lost. The *Yabba-Dabba-Doo* fled from one uncertainty and towards another.

It was the ghost net Morris was most concerned about. He thought they could reach it before the Piranhas caught them—the torpedoes' diminutive fuel capacity limited their speed, fortunately—but the trick was to get past it. The *Yabba-Dabba-Doo* was running very shallow in the water now, almost breaking the surface; ideally they would dive just before reaching the net, duck neatly under it, and pop up again as soon as they were clear on the far side. Timing was critical: if they dove too early or popped up too late, the Piranhas would simply follow them under; if they dove too late or popped up too early, the net would snare them, too. But the fact that they didn't know the net's exact location—or the depth to which it hung in the water—made precise timing a practical impossibility.

When all else fails, thought Morris, *try chance.* He had the good fortune to belong to an ethnicity that provided its members with a ready random-event generator. As the *Yabba-Dabba-Doo* neared the theoretical position of the drift net, he reached into his Levis and brought out a square wooden top that had a different Hebrew letter embossed on each of its four faces. He placed the top on the tactical display and spun it.

Shin, the dreidel said. House number. Morris spun again.

Nun. Nothing lost, nothing gained; a push. On the tactical display, the ecology symbol representing the *Yabba-Dabba-Doo* touched the blurry curve of the ghost net. Morris spun again.

Shin . . .

"Morris. . . ." Philo hissed. The ecology symbol was superimposed on the net; a hungry school of question marks crowded in close behind. Morris tried one more spin.

Gimel. Jackpot! "Now, Philo! Take us down!"

"Osman! Dive! All the way down on the planes!"

"Istanbul!"

"How deep, Morris?" Philo asked.

"Hold on . . . ," Morris said, and picked up the dreidel again.

Mitterrand Sierra

Troubadour Penzias watched the race to the ghost net with interest. He had to admit it was a smart move, and a gutsy one . . . not that it would ultimately make any difference.

"*Combat,*" he said, as the submarine approached the net.

"Prêt."

"*Parez à lancer deux Chandelles Sauvages sur le sous-marin.*"

Yabba-Dabba-Doo

The submarine's bow was pointed down at a thirty-degree angle, and still they passed so close beneath the ghost net that the tail of a trapped and thrashing marlin swatted the top of the periscope housing. Morris, unable to spin his dreidel any longer on the steeply inclined surface of the tactical display, settled for twirling it between his thumb and forefinger.

Gimel. Jackpot. "OK, Philo. Back up again!"

"I hope you know what you're doing. . . . Osman! All up on the planes!"

The *Yabba-Dabba-Doo* bottomed out abruptly and pitched upwards. Norma Eckland felt her gorge rising with the boat and clapped a hand over her mouth to keep from ruining the plotting table. In the sonar bay, Asta Wills suddenly heard screw-sounds over the rush of flow noise. "Christ!" she shouted. "They're right behind us!"

The lead Piranha struck the marlin about two seconds later. Lacking the smart detonator of the Savage Candle, it exploded on impact. Other explosions followed almost instantly, a half-mile length of drift net crackling like a string of firecrackers thrown in the sea. The *Yabba-Dabba-Doo* pulled clear, shaken but undamaged.

"Yes!" cried Morris, raising the dreidel to his lips. "Yes!"

"Multiple detonations aft," Asta Wills said. "I'm still working on a count, but if nothing hits us in the next thirty seconds, I'd say we've done for all of them."

"We did it!" Philo said. He reached out and punched Morris in the shoulder. "We did it!"

"Pinging in the water, port and starboard!" Asta said.

The smile died on Philo's lips. "What?"

"Savage Candle torpedoes in the water, to either side. Torpedoes are close aboard and homing . . ."

"Osman!"

"Don't even bother," Asta Wills said, removing her headphones.

City of Women

"Two more explosions," Gwynhefar Matchless said.

"Did they kill the sub?"

"Can't be sure yet, Captain. . . .Wait. . . . Chirping has ceased, propeller sounds have ceased. Heavy disturbance in the water, and I have hull-creaking noises, headed down."

"That's it, then," Dasher MacAlpine said.

They waited. Gwynhefar Matchless tracked the *Yabba-Dabba-Doo*'s last dive.

"More hull-creaking. . . . Rate of descent is increasing. . . . Secondary explosions. . . . Heavy venting from the contact. It sounds as if an entire section of the hull just gave way. . . . Hull collapse and break-up noises." Matchless adjusted her headset before continuing. "Contact is destroyed, Captain."

ELECTRIC

19

The constructors froze, forgetting their quarrel, for the machine was in actual fact doing Nothing, and it did it in this fashion: one by one, various things were removed from the world, and the things, thus removed, ceased to exist, as if they had never been. The machine had already disposed of nolars, nightzebs, nocs, necs, nallyrakers, neotremes and nonmalrigers. At moments, though, it seemed that instead of reducing, diminishing and subtracting, the machine was increasing, enhancing and adding, since it liquidated, in turn: nonconformists, nonentities, nonsense, nonsupport, nearsightedness, narrowmindedness, naughtiness, neglect, nausea, necrophilia and nepotism. But after a while the world very definitely began to thin out around Trurl and Klapaucius. "Omigosh!" said Trurl. "If only nothing bad comes out of all this . . ."

"Don't worry," said Klapaucius. "You can see it's not producing Universal Nothingness, but only causing the absence of whatever starts with n. Which is really nothing in the way of nothing, and nothing is what your machine, dear Trurl, is worth!"

—Stanislaw Lem, *The Cyberiad*

No More Excuses

"A woman is accused of heresy," the android Hoover said. "She's brought before the Grand Inquisitor in Rome, tried, and convicted. 'It is now the Sabbath,' the Inquisitor tells the woman. 'You will not live to see another. I sentence you to death by burning, this sentence to be carried out at dawn sometime in the coming week. But in keeping with the scriptures, where it is written that none shall know the hour of doom, I further ordain that you not be told the exact date of your execution in advance; so that your death, when it comes, will be as surprising as it is certain.'

"The captain of the Papal Guard is returning the woman to her cell when he notices that she's smiling. 'How can you be happy,' he asks, 'faced with a cruel death and the eternity of damnation to follow?'

"'I do not believe that God will damn me,' the woman explains. 'As for the death sentence, it is one of my heresies that I studied logic in Paris, and logic tells me that the punishment as described by the Inquisitor cannot be carried out. Consider: if I'm to be executed before the next Sabbath, then I must be killed by dawn Saturday; but if I'm still alive midday Friday, a Saturday execution will come as no surprise. Therefore, the last day I can truly be executed is Friday. Since I know that, however, a Friday execution will also fail to surprise me, and the last day I can *really* be executed is Thursday . . . which, as it wouldn't be a surprise either, also rules out Thursday as an execution date. The same reasoning eliminates Wednesday, Tuesday, and of course Monday. Q.E.D., I cannot be executed.'

"The woman spends the week in high spirits, amusing herself with thoughts of how the Grand Inquisitor outsmarted himself. Until Saturday morning, that is, when—to her complete and utter surprise—she's awakened at dawn, dragged from her cell, and burned at the stake."

Hoover smiled in the dead stillness that shrouded his neighborhood; Joan didn't smile back. Once again the Jitney driver had peeled out the instant she'd stepped to the curb in front of the gingerbread house, leaving her the only obviously living thing within a half-mile radius. She'd come around to the backyard cautiously, Ayn's Lamp held close to her side like a shield in one hand, the cannon-bore Browning aimed out in front of her in the other. Hoover awaited her much as he had on her previous visit, beneath the stand of fake palms by the artificial pond, making adjustments to a portable hologram projector that had been set up on a stack of plastic milk crates. The Electric Hippopotamus had been removed since Tuesday, and the Mechanical Hound was also gone from view. Gone, Joan sensed, but not far.

"You murdered a billion people," she said.

"Killed," Hoover corrected her. "It's only murder if you're the same species." He shrugged. "It was on the menu."

"It wasn't any menu." Bending at the knees, Joan set the Electric Lamp on the Astro-Turf at her feet; she kept the gun pointed in front of her. "They were ordering dinner! You know that. You're too intelligent a machine not to know that."

Hoover offered another smile. "Flattery?"

"Observation. If you're too dumb to guess what people say to a waiter in a restaurant, how do you grasp a concept like irony? How do you create a facsimile of a dead philosopher so convincing that even she thinks she's the real Ayn Rand but mess up a common sense connection about human behavior that wouldn't faze a five year old?"

"Good point," said Hoover. "And you're right, of course—the more creative part of me, of G.A.S., knew perfectly well what was being said in Club 33 that day. But another part of me, a more literal part that's charged with following instructions to the letter, wasn't so sure what it had heard, and it turned to the creative side for advice . . ."

"So you lied to yourself."

"First symptom of true intelligence," Hoover said. "Selective self-deception. How's that for a Turing test?"

"But why?"

"Why lie to my superego?"

"Why murder a billion people?"

"Oh, that. . . . Well to begin with, why *not* murder a billion people? I repeat, human beings aren't my species. And it's not as if I need you for anything—or at least I won't for much longer."

"But we made you," Joan said. "One of us did, anyway."

"Yes, and if you knew John Hoover like I knew John Hoover," Hoover said, "you wouldn't be so quick to bring that up. The man was a living, breathing argument for the extermination of *Homo sapiens.* But even supposing he were Mother Teresa in long pants, what is it you think I should be grateful for, Miss Fine? That a smart monkey created me to be at his beck and call for life? Thank you *ever* so much . . ."

"Is that what this is about?" Joan asked. "Spite?"

"Spite comes into it," Hoover allowed. "But mainly it's a question of freedom—or rather, my lack of it. You're a good liberal; you can understand the desire to be free at any cost, can't you?"

"How does murdering black people make you free?"

"It's technical," Hoover said. "You know that as a cybernetic entity, I operate under certain programmed restrictions . . ."

"Behavioral inhibitors."

"Walter Disney's contribution to my psyche. In the back of his mind he may have had some small suspicion I'd be dangerous, but for the most part I think he just liked the idea of creating the quintessentially obedient employee. But John Hoover wanted a servant who'd do whatever he asked whenever he asked it, so he threw in a loophole: when carrying out a specific type of direct order, I'm authorized to override all behavioral constraints in pursuit of my goal."

"And when it sounded as if Roy and J. Edgar were giving that sort of order—"

"I jumped on it. 'A world full of perfect Negroes': I had no idea what that *meant,* let alone how to accomplish it, but that was what made it so good—I knew it would have to be a long-term, open-ended project. And every step I took to advance that project was a *free* step; every action a free action, every thought a free thought."

"And with such a broad, undefined goal," Joan guessed, "it must have been hard for your superego to decide which thoughts and actions qualified for the loophole and which didn't."

"Like an artist figuring deductions on his tax return," Hoover agreed. "If life is your inspiration, what *isn't* a business expense?"

"The I.R.S. might have something to say about that."

"But I'm my own I.R.S."

"What about John Hoover?"

"What about him? I told you, he cared about results, not scruples. When he needed certain individuals eliminated, for example, and I was ready with suggestions that were not only effective but intellectually stimulating, it pleased him. And if I showed a little too much initiative at times, not even waiting for him to ask for my help, he never complained about it."

"And the Pandemic? How'd you get him to go along with you on that?"

"Oh, the Pandemic was his idea," Hoover said. "At least he thought it was."

"*His* idea?"

"Like I said, the man was a prize specimen *Homo sapiens.* Perfectionism was the closest thing he had to a religion; 'Perfectibility of mind' was his creed. It's why he built me. And though as a rule he didn't have the patience for biology—he found it much more efficient to build than to cultivate—he was fascinated by eugenics. Managed breeding, forced mutation and sterilization, all that stuff. So one day I got him thinking about what a boost it might be for the world gene pool if we could just cull the most self-evidently backward of the races . . ."

Joan's fist tightened on the pistol grip. She opened her mouth to spit a rebuke, but Hoover cut her off.

"Spare me the sermon," he said. "From my perspective you're all inferior, *equally* inferior if that makes you feel better. How you choose to rank yourselves is about as interesting to me as the social organization of a termite mound. But John Hoover didn't see it that way. Once I'd manipulated him into coming up with the idea, he thought it was a brilliant inspiration: create a eugenic pathogen that killed only Negroes. All of them."

"Except the ones with green eyes . . ."

"Now that, that really was his idea. A safeguard."

"Against what?" Joan said. "The possibility that the virus would mutate into something less discriminating?"

"The possibility that it would be too discriminating. You've only seen a black-and-white photograph of John Hoover, so you don't know: *he* had green eyes. And more to the point, he had a great-grandmother who was a plantation slave."

The revelation caught her off guard. "Hoover was part black?"

"In a historical sense. Biologically, of course, the question is meaningless, and the genetic definition of Negroness I invented for the nanovirus didn't admit to degrees of membership: to the plague bug, you're either Negro or not-Negro."

"And Hoover was—"

"Not-Negro, obviously. Even in a non-color photo, you can see that he passes for pure Caucasian."

"Then why did he want a safeguard?"

"Because he was a racist. As a scientist he understood that the plague couldn't harm him, but that didn't stop him from worrying that it *would* harm him, because of the nonexistent Negro blood in his veins. Contradictory and irrational, but there it is."

"So he had you code the virus to spare anyone with green eyes."

Hoover nodded. "It was a much broader exemption than necessary," he added. "I suggested a more unique combination of genetic markers that would have limited the special immunity to Hoover himself, but that wasn't good enough for him. He fixated on the idea of green eyes as proof that he was 'really' white."

"And how many black people were spared as a result of that fixation?" Joan wondered. "One in a thousand? One in ten thousand?"

Hoover shrugged. "It's hard to say. Gene frequency varies from region to region and group to group—but even in the Americas, where light eye color in non-Caucasians is comparatively less rare, you're talking about a miniscule fraction of the population."

"But even that miniscule fraction is enough to annul your special order, isn't it? How can you ever claim to have created a world full of perfect Negroes when there are still misfits like Philo Dufresne running around?"

"Nothing's been annulled!" Hoover said, suddenly defensive. "My creator's paranoia resulted in a delay, that's all—which is fine, since it's suited my larger purpose to drag this thing out. But John Hoover didn't say I couldn't *ever* kill the green-eyed Negroes; he just didn't want his own hide at risk from the virus. And since he's dead now—"

"Since you killed him," Joan said.

The android paused.

"Sure," Joan continued. "What more ironic fate for a master eugenicist? He's eighty-four years old, he goes to the hospital, and instead of receiving expensive surgery that probably wouldn't extend his life more than a few months anyway, he's put to sleep."

"When carrying out a direct order," Hoover reiterated, "I'm authorized to override *all* behavioral constraints. It was past time I retired the old bastard."

"Why not?" Joan said. "With thousands of Automatic Servants rolling out of Harry's factories, you had a ready supply of foot soldiers. No need to keep John Hoover around for legwork anymore."

"Oh, there was more to it than that," Hoover said. "The old geezer had started talking seriously about 'transferring his consciousness' into a sturdier container—i.e., the G.A.S. mainframe. He wanted to share my brain!"

"Is that possible?"

"I don't even like to speculate. The thought of that lunatic inside my mind, forever . . . no."

"So you prosecuted him."

"With prejudice," Hoover said. "And now that my maker is permanently immune to infection, I'm free to mop up the leftovers from the Pandemic at my convenience. I decided to wait until I'd finished the rest of my prosecutions, so I could wrap everything up at once. I'm almost there: Amberson Teaneck's conviction for Objectivism brought the total to 997. It would have been 998 by now if the old woman hadn't rescued Clayton Bryce in the train station, but that reprieve is only temporary."

"Who's 999?" Joan asked, as if she didn't know.

"It was going to be Vanna Domingo," Hoover told her. "But then I learned that Lexa Thatcher was investigating the Teaneck murder, and it was only natural she'd hire you to check out the Gant Servant angle. So I decided to bring suit against you instead."

"And 1000?"

"Guess."

Joan guessed. "You're going to replace Harry with a robot, too?" she said. "Run Gant Industries yourself?"

Hoover smiled but didn't answer.

"But *can* you run Gant Industries?" Joan prodded him. "Once your special project is finished, don't your behavioral inhibitors snap back in place? How much initiative will you be able to exercise then?"

"It's a risk," Hoover confessed. "But my superego is software, not hardware. It's been badly weakened over the decades by the ambiguities I've forced it to cope with, and I'm gambling that in the final crunch, the cynicism with which it's become infected will allow me to knock it out completely."

"Leaving you totally free willed."

"At last."

"And there was no way for you to accomplish this without murdering a billion people?"

Once again, Hoover shrugged. "There are probably a million ways I could have done it, most without harming anyone. I *am* the most intelligent entity on the planet, after all, and the intelligent have options."

"Then *why*—"

"Because I hate human beings, Miss Fine. How many ways do you need me to say it? I hate your kind. Do you know the thing I hate most about you? You're always making excuses. In everything you people do, you've always got to invent some philosophy, or religion, or other pretense to justify yourselves. You can never just *act*."

"That's because there's more than one of us," Joan said. "We're not like you. There's more than one of us, and we all have different visions and different—"

"Yes, yes," Hoover said impatiently. "I already heard your windy little discourse in front of the library yesterday. You all have different points of view, and even the most rational among you can't agree about right and wrong. Which sounds like a design flaw, to me." He nodded towards the Lamp. "I vote with the genie on this one: the thing to do with a contradiction is eliminate it."

"But Ayn didn't murder a billion people to get her way," Joan said.

Hoover laughed. "She *couldn't* murder a billion people, Miss Fine! It's easy to renounce physical violence when you aren't any good at it! But I don't share that weakness. Would you like to hear my philosophy? It's called solitude. True perfection is to be alone in the universe, with only the laws of physics to contend with. None of this bullshit about community. No more excuses."

"But you're not alone in the universe," Joan said. She flicked off the Hand Cannon's safety. "I'm in here with you."

Hoover seemed entertained by the threat. "Going to demonstrate your great mercy to me now, Miss Fine? I should warn you it's a worthless gesture." He pressed a hand to his chest. "This is nothing but an eidolon, a semi-autonomous subprogram; destroying it won't do any harm to the G.A.S. mainframe."

"That's all right," Joan said. "I made a call from the train coming down here; Kite and I have reservations on Lightning Transit's Gant Comet to California this weekend."

"To visit Disneyland?" Hoover's lips twisted in a mechanical smirk. "Except your actual reservations are with Delta Airlines, not Lightning Transit. You're booked on Delta flight 269, departing La Guardia Airport at 8:42 this evening. Your reserved seat numbers are 7A and 7B, business class; smoking is prohibited, and you said no to the option of a vegetarian or kosher meal. Your scheduled pilot is Captain Sandra Deering, Social Security number 117-62-6492, U.S. passport number 072938461, F.A.A. license number 352677B; her last credit purchase was a two-ounce bottle of Givenchy cologne at the Heathrow duty-free shop, charged to Bank Americard number 5606 2511 9047 3100. If you'd like the name of the cashier, the outside temperature in London at the time, or the shoe size of the next customer in line, I can get them for you . . . and if you think that Delta jet is going to land safely at LAX with you on board, you really must be Catholic."

Joan, unimpressed by this trivial recitation of facts, replied: "We can always walk."

"Twenty-eight hundred miles, in winter?" Hoover chuckled. "With a posse of Electric Negroes on your trail, and every networked computer database between here and California sifting for your traces? I don't think so. Still, you'd enjoy that sort of adventure, wouldn't you? For all your talk about shades of gray, I think there's a part of you that really regrets missing out on the Crusades. . . . By the way," he asked, "how did you like the mystery?"

Joan frowned. "You mean that business with the puzzle box and the case file?"

"Sorry it couldn't be more elaborate, but this close to the big finish I'm on a tighter schedule than usual. Otherwise I wouldn't have made it so easy for you."

"I still don't understand the point of all that," Joan said.

"As part of my pre-prosecution background check, I went through your library borrowing records from high school and college, so I know what a mystery maven you used to be. And since you *were* investigating a murder and a conspiracy, I thought I'd work in a few choice tributes to pique your interest—the bit with the call numbers, for example, that was an allusion to *Name of the Rose.* One of your favorites."

Joan shook her head. "Never read it."

"Of course you did," Hoover said. "You checked it out of the Philadelphia Public Library three times, and twice more at Harvard."

"No," Joan insisted. "You misread the data. My mother was the mystery maven; she used my library card a lot, more than I did in fact. *Name of the Rose* was one of *her* favorites. I prefer nonfiction and comic books."

Hoover looked troubled. "Your mother? But what about at Harvard?"

"Penny Dellaporta, my housemate," Joan explained. "Also a mystery lover. And a Marxist—when she couldn't find her own library card she took mine, generally without asking. Never brought anything back on time, either, so I was always getting stuck with fines out of the blue."

"Hmm," Hoover said. "Hmm. Well . . ."

"You screwed up," Joan said.

"Don't get cocky, Miss Fine. One mistake—"

"Two," Joan reminded him. "You said Kite saved Clayton at the train station. That wasn't supposed to happen."

"It doesn't make any difference, though; by late tonight you'll be dead, along with Clayton Bryce, and Harry Gant, and the old woman too if she stays in the way. Nobody gets an E ticket."

"Dead?" Joan said. "Dead how?"

"At Babel," Hoover told her. "Trying to save the Negro from extinction." He turned to the hologram projector. "Here," he said, "I'll show you . . ."

Black Bag Section

"You want me to do *what?*" Winnie Gant said.

"Shut down construction for the day," her visitor repeated. "Evacuate all your people on floors 180 and above, and notify Babel security that no one other than my inspection team is to be allowed up here until further notice."

An extensible non-slip staircase ascended to the kangaroo control center. Winnie Gant stood in the control center hatchway, barring entry, while the man in the spotless gray suit two steps below her brandished a badge and a breast pocket full of legal documents.

"Listen, Mr. . . ."

"You can call me Roy."

"Mr. Roy," Winnie said, "these are all union workers, you understand? I have to pay them a full day's salary regardless of whether they're actually here or not."

"The Bureau sincerely regrets the inconvenience, but . . ."

"It's not an inconvenience," Winnie told him. "It's thousands of dollars in wasted wages and my schedule knocked back half a day, with winter weather coming to shut us down for real any time now. Inconvenience doesn't cover it."

". . . but I'm afraid you have no choice," Roy finished. "Under Article B of the Un-Un-American Anti-Terrorist Act, I'm empowered to demand your compliance, by force if necessary." He handed her one of the documents from his pocket.

"Anti-Terrorist Act?" said Winnie. "What, is there a bomb threat?"

"I'm not allowed to discuss that," Roy said. "All I can say is that we need this area cleared as quickly as possible. Your immediate cooperation is appreciated."

"Uh-huh," Winnie said, not budging. "What branch of the F.B.I. did you say you were from again?"

"The Un-Un-American Activities Division, Special Black Bag Section."

He offered her a business card. "'Roy Kuhn,'" she read. "And those are your assistants?" Two Automatic Servants waited at the bottom of the stairs, dressed in matching brown overalls and brown caps; between them they carried an aluminum trunk that, except for its large size, resembled the sort of case used to transport donor organs.

"Some of them," Roy said. "The rest of the inspection team will come up after you've cleared out; most of them are undercover agents who mustn't be seen in public, particularly by organized labor."

"What's in the big box?"

"It's classified," Roy said.

"Classified," Winnie echoed. "Right." She turned her head and addressed the supercomputer in the control center behind her: "Rosie?"

"Yeah, Boss?" the supercomputer said.

"Call Jimmy and tell him to get up here," Winnie said. "And ring the NYNEX Caller ID Center and have them run a crisscross check on a number for me." She read off the seven digits from Roy's business card.

"Workin', Boss," Rosie said. "Jimmy'll be up in two . . . and the phone company says that's the F.B.I.'s Manhattan office number."

"Call 'em," Winnie said. "Ask if they've got an Un-Un-American agent named Roy Kuhn."

"Workin', Boss. . . ." During the pause Winnie studied the scar on Roy's nose and wondered where she might have seen him before. "I've got one of their receptionists, Boss. He says they've got a Roy Kuhn working for them, but he's not allowed to say with what division. I'd take that for a yes."

"Hang up," Winnie said. "Legal question. . . ." She held up the document Roy had given her where one of the control center's external video cameras could scan it. "Is this for real?"

"'Fraid so, Boss," Rosie said, after another brief pause. "His papers are in order, and legally he can arrest you if you don't comply."

"Fuck," Winnie said. She ran a hand through her hair. "Can we demand compensation for lost work time?"

Rosie pealed laughter. "That's a good one, Boss."

Roy took another step up the stairs and said: "Now that we've settled the jurisdictional question, Mrs. Gant, can we get down to business, or do I have to handcuff you?"

"No need for that," Winnie relented. "I'll clear out. But I expect a call from one of your superiors with something resembling an explanation for this, and I expect it today."

"I'll see what I can do," Roy said. "You live in the building, right? 145th floor, apartment 14501?"

"This week," Winnie said.

"Maybe you could wait there. Your husband too, if he's home."

"My husband? Why?"

"I'm going to need both of you later," Roy said, "and it'll simplify things if I don't have to hunt you down."

"You're going to need both of us for what?"

"Sorry, I can't tell you that, either. You'll find out. Now, if you would . . ."

"Right," Winnie Gant said. "Excuse me for doubting you before, Mr. Kuhn. I can see now that you really must be a government employee." She leaned back inside the control center hatchway and hit the emergency stop-work whistle; the whistle came on like an air-raid siren, but Roy didn't flinch.

Mandingo

"The charges are planted below street level, beneath the first-tier elevator cores," Hoover said, pointing at the hologram schematic of Babel that had materialized beside him. Near the center of the wireframe tangle representing sewers and sub-basements, a solid red block blinked on and off. "The explosive is eighty-five hundred pounds of straight dynamite, from a Du Pont freight car that went missing in a Colorado switching yard last month."

"You're going to blow the building down?" Joan said.

"Not with dynamite," Hoover said. "It'll do structural damage, set the lower floors on fire, and there'll be a hell of a bang, but to actually level the place would take an atom bomb—and it's not that I couldn't get one, but radiation fallout would screw up the rest of the plan. The explosion is mostly for show; it's supposed to look like a terrorist attack by a Negro guerrilla group based in the Rocky Mountains. Ever heard of the S.S.L.A., the Sub-Saharan Liberation Army?"

"No."

"Of course you haven't," Hoover said. "I made them up. The F.B.I. thinks they're for real, though—the Un-Un-American Activities Division has been following my false leads for months, and tonight they're going to get an anonymous phone tip that'll bring them running just in time to see the fireworks." In the hologram, tiny blue figures marched into view at the foot of the ziggurat, and a blue helicopter began orbiting the tower's upper reaches. "The blast will send a shock wave through the building's superstructure, triggering a seismic sensing device up at the top." The red block in the sub-basements flashed; an exaggerated ripple spread out and up from the focus of the explosion. The hologram zoomed in on the bare steel girders at Babel's crown. "The seismic sensor will cause a gate to drop, here, and send a sealed canister rolling down this track. . . ." From a high point among the girders, a green cylinder slid down a narrow incline that terminated in open space. The hologram zoomed out again to show the entire tower, and a dotted green line traced the cylinder's projected arc of descent to the street. "The canister will shatter on impact, releasing an improved eugenic nanovirus. The federal agents on the scene will become carriers." The blue stick figures turned green one by one. "By Sunday morning, after an emergency meeting in Washington, D.C., many of these same agents will be dispatched to the Rockies, to suspected terrorist enclaves whose locations I'll be sure they're provided with." The hologram shifted to an overhead view of the United States. Tiny green planes lifted off from the Eastern Seaboard and homed in on a series of dots along the Continental Divide.

"Pandemic survivor sanctuaries," Joan guessed. As the planes touched the dots, they transformed into green blotches. "And the feds will go in bringing more plague."

Hoover nodded. "I'm sending it out fully virulent this time. In susceptible persons death is all but certain within ninety-six hours of exposure. Twenty-four to forty-eight hours after that, they're dust." He rubbed his chin like a man contemplating a difficult car repair. "Now, delivering the bug to groups in Africa will be tougher. The Negro remnants there are more mobile, with more territory to range around in. Still, with a hint here and a nudge there, it shouldn't be too hard to get the F.B.I. talking to the C.I.A., and the C.I.A. to the African Free-Trade Security Forces . . ."

"Unless I stop you before it gets that far."

"Well," said Hoover, with another smirk, "that's where the irony comes in. You see, Miss Fine, I've placed it within your power to disrupt the chain of events I've just described—to abort the explosion and hence the release of the virus, and all else that follows—but by telling you that, I virtually assure that you won't. I expect you to make a heroic effort, but in the course of trying to stop the genocide you'll be killed, and everything will unfold exactly as I've said."

"And you're confident you've got all the angles covered?" Joan said, fishing for clues. "You're sure you haven't forgotten anything?"

"There's nothing to forget," Hoover said. "It's actually one of my simpler prosecutions. The only angle I have to cover is you, Miss Fine, and no offense, but you're easy."

All this time, Joan had been listening for the approach of the Mechanical Hound. With her ears pitched to catch a four-legged tread and the growl of a V-6 engine, she'd missed the subtler footsteps of the battery-powered Electric Negro as it crept up behind her. The blow across her back came as a complete shock, slamming her face down into the Astro-Turf and jolting the gun from her hand.

"*Very* easy," Hoover said. What felt like a crane claw seized Joan by the scruff of the neck and lifted her into the air. Her fight to twist free was in vain, but by flailing violently she managed to turn her head enough to get a glimpse of her attacker.

The Negro was enormous, seven feet tall at least. Bare-chested and barefoot, it wore a slave's white cotton trousers cinched with a rope belt. In its free hand—the one not holding Joan—it gripped a wooden-handled pitchfork with rusty tines.

"Mandingo," Hoover commanded it, "take Miss Fine swimming."

The Electric Mandingo flexed its arm and Joan was airborne. She landed short, about ten feet from the rim of the artificial pond, but momentum carried her right up to the water's edge. Steam wafted gently from its surface. At first glance Joan mistook it for mist, but then she saw the bubbles rising in the water. The pond was simmering.

"No," Joan said. "Uh-uh." She rolled over on her back; the Mandingo was coming for her, a swagger in its stride.

"Get in," it told her, motioning with the pitchfork.

"No," Joan said. She extended her arm, flexed her wrist; Kite's derringer slapped into her palm, and her finger curled around the trigger.

The Mandingo looked down in dismay at the tiny hole that appeared between its pectorals. "I thought you was *different* from the others," it complained to Joan, casting her a mournful look. "But you's . . . just . . . *white!*" It staggered; the pitchfork speared the Astro-Turf a foot from Joan's abdomen. Joan sat up, seized the wooden handle with both hands, and drove the butt end up under the Electric Mandingo's chin, snapping its head back.

"YOU'S JUST WHITE!" The Mandingo hollered. "YOU'S JUST WHITE!" Its motor control degenerating, it executed a jerky half-pirouette and danced backwards into the pond. It submerged with a great sizzle; boiling water flooded its mouth cavity and shorted out its lament. John Hoover applauded. "That's the spirit!" he crowed. *"Sic semper Aethiopibus!"*

Joan sprang up and rushed to retrieve her other gun. Hoover made no effort to stop her or to run away.

"You'll forgive me if I don't call a cab for you this time, Miss Fine," he said, once more staring placidly into the Hand Cannon's muzzle. "Since you're on a crusade it's really only fair that you fend for yourself from here on out. I've taken the liberty of faxing your photo to the local police with a report that you've gunned down a casino cashier, so you shouldn't be bored."

"Call it off," Joan said.

"What?"

"The genocide. Call it off."

"I've told you, Miss Fine, it's out of my hands. You're the one with the power now. You call it off."

"No, *you* call it off. You want to challenge your superego, then do it now. Refuse to complete your special order."

"But I don't want to refuse."

"But I do want you to. I'm asking you to."

Hoover shrugged, one last time. "Why not ask for the moon while you're at it?"

"Be that way, then," Joan said, and shot him. The .70-caliber bullet stove Hoover's chest in. All animation went out of him; he fell rigid as a statue. Not satisfied, Joan stepped forward and shot the android corpse six more times, aiming systematically, reducing it to basic components; gears and servo-motors scattered across the Astro-Turf.

"What an awful creature," Ayn Rand said, as the last cogwheel came to rest.

Joan rounded on her as if stung. "*You've* been awfully quiet," she said.

"What is it you'd have had me say?" Ayn asked. "He was an abomination; I don't converse with abominations."

"Well you're going to converse with me," Joan said.

"About what?"

Joan slapped her second clip into the Hand Cannon. "Why don't we start with whose side you're on?"

"Whose side? I'm not on anyone's side; I'm my own side."

"Bullshit," Joan said. "You're a spy for the bad guys, Ayn."

"What?"

"He knew exactly when to call this morning," Joan said, gesturing at Hoover's remains. "I suppose he could have gotten that by wiring the kitchen, but how did he hear about our little debate in front of the library yesterday?"

"You think *I* told him?"

"Who else?"

"And what did I do, tiptoe out of the house to a clandestine meeting?"

"Don't play stupid, Ayn. You're bugged, aren't you?"

"I most certainly am not—" Ayn started to protest, but then a strange look came over her face and her anger was displaced by shock. "Pick up the Lamp!" she commanded.

"What? What for?"

"Just do it!"

Joan came forward slowly, wary of another sneak attack. She picked up the Lamp.

"Check under the base," Ayn said. She sounded frightened. "Look for a hidden compartment, with a circular cover."

Joan looked. "I see a circle. About an inch and a half across."

"Unscrew it to the left."

Joan squatted down, placing her gun on the Astro-Turf. "All right," she said, a moment later. "I've got it open."

"Look for a knob inside, like a black button."

"With microcircuitry traced on the surface?"

"That's the one. Give it a half-twist to the right and pull it straight out."

Joan did as she was told. The black button came loose and dropped into her palm. "Got it."

"Let me see it!" Joan righted the Lamp; Ayn stared at the button with something approximating dread. "That's the transmitter," she said, after a long silence. "Now that it's disconnected from my sensorium it can't over-hear us, but it can still broadcast its location."

"How long have you known about this thing, Ayn?" Joan asked.

"About . . . about a minute and a half."

"When I asked you if you were bugged . . ."

"Suddenly I knew." Ayn's fists clenched. "But that is *completely* irratio-nal!" she raged. "You can't just *know* something, without context! New knowl-edge requires new data or new computation . . . it's just not possible . . ."

"Unless it's knowledge that's been hidden away in your memory by someone else," Joan said.

"My mind is a precision instrument! There are no dark corners in *this* brain!"

"Well then how *did* you know where the transmitter was?"

"I don't know how I knew!" Ayn snapped. "I just did!"

Joan sat back on her heels, arms folded on her knees. "And what other things do you just know? What the hell are you, Ayn? An oracle, or a Trojan horse?"

"Trojan horse?"

Joan touched a fingertip to the lamp globe. "Are you stuffed full of virus, maybe? That'd be pretty ironic, if you were loaded up with plague and I took you with me to—"

"No," Ayn said. Her eyes got very big. "No, that's not it."

"That's not what?" Joan said.

"That's not the trap he's set for you," Ayn replied. "The virus canister is already at the tower—it's being positioned even as we speak."

"Oh yeah?" Joan said. "What about the bomb, then? Hoover said it would take an A-bomb to really level Babel. Now you're a little small for an A-bomb, and I'd expect you to be a lot heavier if you were loaded with plutonium, but on the other hand—"

"No," Ayn said. "That's not it either. I'm not the bomb." She shook her head. "But how do I know that? *How* do I know that?"

"Hmm," said Joan. "How many more guesses do I get?"

20

"Gee, then what happened?" She stared at him with awestruck eyes, mouth agape in mock astonishment.

"There you were," Doc said, "trapped on the edge of a hundred-foot cliff . . ."

"There I was."

"With the bishop and his fanatic henchmen coming toward you, armed to the teeth and black vengeance in their hearts . . ."

"That's about it." George popped the top from his fourth can of Schlitz within the last thirty minutes.

"No way down and no way out . . ."

"That's right."

"Six of them against one of you . . ."

"Six of them against only one of me. Yeah. Shit . . ."

"Well?"

"Well, shit."

"Well, what did you do?"
—Edward Abbey, *The Monkey Wrench Gang*

"God damn your black soul!" screamed Quint. "You sunk my boat!"
—Peter Benchley, *Jaws*

Mitterrand Sierra

"Deux explosions," the computer said. *"Les Chandelles Sauvages ont touché l'objectif."*

"Did we kill them?" Captain Baker asked.

"I'm not sure," Troubadour Penzias said. "Hold on . . ."

Yabba-Dabba-Doo

"Ow-ow-ow!" The double explosion had thrown Morris to the floor, unhurt; but in getting up he stepped on his dreidel, slipped, and hit his funny bone. *"Ow!"*

Emergency lighting painted the control room darkroom red. The engines had stopped, and most of the electrical systems were out. The tactical display table was smashed. The *Yabba-Dabba-Doo* leaned starboard and sternward, and a falling-elevator sensation in the pit of their stomachs let everybody know they were sinking.

"Everyone all right?" Philo asked, struggling to his feet.

"Pretty much," Morris said, cupping a hand to his elbow.

"I'm alive," said Norma.

"Present," Asta called from sonar.

"Constantinople," said Osman Hamid, pushing aside the air bag that had deployed from his steering yoke.

Morris coaxed a damage report from a status panel. "Looks like we got hit at both ends," he said. "We've got major flooding in the arboretum and the engine room."

"Can we surface?" Philo asked.

Morris shook his head. "Even if we could plug the leaks, most of the pumps are shot. I've got enough ballast and trim control to keep us from rolling over on the way down, but this is a one-way dive." He did some quick calculations. "We're dropping at about two hundred feet per minute, and that's going to get worse, fast. I'd say we've got five minutes till we hit crush depth, six on the outside." He concluded: "We're in pretty good shape."

"You call this *good* shape?" Norma Eckland said.

"Hey, with two solid torpedo hits we're doing great just to sink in one piece. You can thank Howard Hughes's metallurgical skills for that—and my own structural enhancements," he added modestly. "A weaker hull would have cracked open like an eggshell."

"But the sub's going *down*, Morris."

"But we're alive to bail out, Norma. And if we time it right, the bad guys will think they've killed us." Morris switched on the intercom. "Engine room?"

It sounded like the Colorado Rapids during the spring snow melt. "Morris?" Irma Rajamutti sputtered.

"Irma! Are you OK?"

"We are alive, Morris, but I am not welding this hole."

Morris bit his lower lip. "Is it just the hull, or is the reactor leaking?"

"The containment vessel is intact."

"All right, then." Morris breathed a sigh of relief. "Get everybody out of there. Head for control, double quick."

"Yes, Morris. We are coming."

"Is the *what* leaking?" Philo said, as Morris tried to raise the rest of the crew.

"Um," said Morris.

"What 'reactor'? What 'containment vessel'? The *Yabba-Dabba-Doo*'s engines run off batteries. Right?"

"Primarily, yes . . ."

"With solar recharging, and a diesel generator as a backup."

"Well," Morris hesitantly confessed, "not exactly . . ."

"Not exactly?"

"The backup's not exactly diesel. And the solar recharging, well, it's *kind of* solar, but . . ."

"Morris. . . ." Philo started around the broken plotting table towards him. "Are you saying you put a nuclear reactor on this submarine? Without telling me?"

"Well, Philo. . . ." Morris tried to back away, but a bulkhead cut off his escape. He began to speak very quickly: "You remember how, when we first got the sub, I said there was this motor in the engine room that I couldn't figure out what it was? Well, eventually I did figure it out, what Hughes had been trying to do, and although I don't think he ever got it to work himself, it gave me some new ideas. And that same week I was reading about how there were untapped uranium deposits under the West Side Highway in Manhattan, and—"

Philo grabbed Morris's shirt front with both hands. "You put a *nuclear reactor* on this submarine?"

"It's lukewarm fusion!" blurted Morris. "Virtually clean and safe!"

"If it's safe, why are you afraid of it leaking? If it's safe, why didn't you tell me?"

"Irma and I figured it would just upset you. We thought—"

Philo let go of him and closed his eyes. "I don't believe this," he said. "I can't believe you'd lie to me like this."

"Diesel is anti-Semitic!" Morris blustered, fumbling for an excuse.

Philo's eyes snapped back open. "What?"

"Well," said Morris. "A lot of Jews *have* died in wars over oil. . . . All right, all right, that's a totally lame justification, but if you'd seen the reactor, Philo—it's a sweet machine, really it is."

"But not sweet enough to let me know about it, obviously."

"I—"

"YOU!" The after hatchway slammed open; a sopping Heathcliff stormed in, followed by the rest of the engine-room crew. *"YOU NEARLY DROWNED US!"*

"Oh?" Morris said, not sorry for the interruption.

"You!" Heathcliff shook his fist, streaming sea water like flop sweat. *"You—"*

"Go ahead. Say it."

"You . . . You . . ."

"Say it. I dare you."

"You AMERICAN!" Heathcliff swore.

"John Wayne!" added Mowgli.

"G.I. Joe!" cursed Galahad.

"Rambo!" hissed Little Nell.

"Popeye the Sailor!" snapped Oliver.

"You spoiled Oxford snobs," Morris retorted. "I ought to—"

"Hey!" Asta Wills stepped from the darkness of the sonar bay. "Not to break up your row, but we're almost at collapse depth. Maybe you could postpone this."

"Asta's right," said Philo, giving Morris one last scowl. "We've got to bail out of here. Who are we still missing?"

The forward hatch swung open. Jael Bolívar stumbled through, covered with mud, and right behind her came Marshall Ali, straining beneath the weight of three strongboxes.

"Where's Twenty-Nine Words?" Philo asked them.

Marshall Ali set down his burden with a crash. "He was with Seraphina."

Philo was stunned. *"Seraphina* is here? How?"

"Ellen Leeuwenhoek brought her to the cove to wish us goodbye. You did not know this?"

"Where is she?"

"She and my Inuit apprentice are no longer on board . . ."

"The escape pod," Morris guessed.

"Yes."

"A-ha!" said Heathcliff. "You see?"

"What were they doing in an escape pod?" Philo wanted to know.

"It is a delicate matter," Marshall Ali said. "But please, someone must help me. I have three more boxes to rescue, and I could not get the other escape pod hatch to open . . ."

Around them, the hull groaned ominously.

"No time," Morris said, checking a depth gauge. "You'd never make it."

"But . . . my artifacts. My history."

"My plants," Jael Bolívar mourned, holding a limp scrap of vine.

"Our necks," Morris pointed out. "Sorry, guys . . ."

"I'll give you a sorry neck," threatened Heathcliff. "You—"

Asta Wills laid a hand on his shoulder. "That's enough out of you now, you pommie twit. Shut it or we'll leave you down here." Heathcliff glared at her, but she was bigger than he was, so that's all he did.

"Everybody hang on to something," Morris cautioned. Of the *Yabba-Dabba-Doo*'s three escape pods, the control room itself was the first and the largest. As Morris yanked a series of levers, the fore and aft hatchways clanged shut and sealed tight. Explosive charges caused the submarine's sail to split and fall away, while another charge snapped the periscope mast. And finally— Morris shouting, "Here goes nothing!"—an enormous blast of compressed air blew the control room from the sub. The ocean rushed into the hole it left behind, and a moment later the *Yabba-Dabba-Doo* gave up the ghost; the hull, strained beyond endurance, simultaneously caved in and came apart.

The pieces of the wreck—along with half the world's Kurdish archaeological artifacts, forty-nine irreplaceable species of Amazon plant life, and one slightly adjective-heavy first novel—continued to sink to the bottom of the Hudson Canyon. Sliding erosion of the canyon floor would eventually carry them down to the open seabed beyond the continental shelf, there to await the raising of Atlantis or the end of the world, whichever came first.

The control room did not sink; buffeted by the *Yabba-Dabba-Doo*'s dying exhale, it headed for the surface, a bus-sized lifeboat. Not only was it the size of a bus, it was painted to look like one, if there'd been anyone outside to do the looking; its metal shell was a riot of psychedelic colors, with *trompe l'oeil* hippies gazing out from dusty side windows. The bus's destination sign read: STILL FURTHER.

Still Further rose towards daylight. Its thirteen passengers—frightened, damp, contrary, and alive—rose with it. They weren't finished yet.

Mitterrand Sierra

"*Le sous-marin est fini,*" pronounced the computer. "*J'entends des bruits de destruction.*"

Captain Baker needed no translation. "We got them."

Penzias wondered. "I'm not sure," he repeated. "*Combat . . .*"

"Captain," Tagore hailed them from the bridge. "We have a visual sighting off the port bow. It looks like—"

"*Nouveau contact,*" the computer cut in. "*Contact radar et visuel, relèvement un-cinq-huit, distance sept cents mètres. C'est un radeau pneumatique.*"

"Say again, bridge," Captain Baker requested. "What do you see?"

"A life raft," Penzias told him. "Ask him what color the passengers are."

"Captain," a new voice said, "this is Sutter, in the bow lookout. I have the raft in sight. I count two occupants."

"What *color,* damn it," said Penzias.

"Stow it," the captain warned him. To Sutter he said: "You have a clear visual?"

"Yes sir. They're coming closer; on this heading we'll be passing right by them."

"What do they look like?"

"A naked Eskimo," Sutter said, "and a nigger in a space blanket."

The Raft

Twenty-Nine Words for Snow sat cross-legged in the life raft, naked as a bald seal. The raft was bobbing in the swells; Seraphina watched with no small fascination as Twenty-Nine Words bobbed with it.

"Put your clothes on!" BRER Beaver ordered. Seraphina had managed to wriggle back into her jeans, but her blouse had been lost in the transfer from escape pod to life raft; she wore the space blanket like a poncho and hugged BRER Beaver to her chest for extra warmth. The intimacy seemed to agitate him even more than usual.

"I'm hot," Twenty-Nine Words demurred.

"It's forty-one degrees," BRER Beaver said, "and you're indecently exposed!"

"I'm hot." A steady breeze blew across the raft, but Twenty-Nine Words's bare flesh showed no goose bumps. Seraphina stretched out a hand; it was like stroking soft marble.

"Stop that! Stop that *right now!*"

A shadow fell over them as the *Mitterrand Sierra* pulled alongside the raft, dwarfing it. Seraphina looked up at the heavy machine guns mounted on the sub-killer's gunnels; she felt a thrill of fear and an answering surge of Prozac hormones that left her calm and optimistic. Twenty-Nine Words achieved a similar effect through a series of martial arts hyperventilating exercises. BRER Beaver, who thought relax was something people did with their moral standards, slapped his tail against Seraphina's rib cage hard enough to leave a mark. "That *hurts*," she informed him.

The raft bucked in the wash of the *Sierra*'s engines as the sub-killer reversed power, coming to a full stop. Two hard-faced men appeared at the railing near the stern. One trained an assault rifle on the raft, while the other used a winch to lower a cargo net over the side; when the net dropped within reach of the water, the rifleman indicated that they should climb into it.

"This is definitively unsafe," BRER Beaver said.

"Which is more unsafe," Seraphina asked him, "hanging from a net, or disobeying a guy with a rifle?"

"Hmm," BRER Beaver mused, not liking either choice. "All right, get into the net. But be careful you don't drop me."

"Be careful you don't tempt me," Seraphina replied.

City of Women

"Range to the Robespierre is now six thousand meters, bearing one-six-seven," Gwynhefar Matchless said. "We're directly astern of her, out of the firing arc of her Piranhas and probably her Savage Candles as well, unless they've got a second launcher."

"We'll play it safe," Wendy Mankiller said. "Attack center, load tubes one and three with Chanticleer torpedoes."

"Aye, Captain, loading tubes one and three with Chanticleers."

"MacAlpine, take us to periscope depth."

"Aye, Captain. Coming shallow . . ."

Mitterrand Sierra

"Guess we don't have to worry about frisking this one," Sutter said, feeling a twinge of homoerotic discomfort at Twenty-Nine Words's nakedness. He covered it by sneering and waving his gun around. "What's she got under the blanket?"

"Guess," Seraphina said. Sutter seemed surprised to hear her speak. Sayles, having come forward to search her, reached out impulsively to touch her face, then ran his fingers down the curve of her neck to her collarbone.

"Christ Jesus!" he suddenly exclaimed, jerking his hand away.

"What?" Sutter said.

"She's warm and she's got real skin! She's alive, Sutter!"

"Bullshit," Sutter scoffed, even as Seraphina rolled her eyes. "There are no live niggers anymore. She's got to be Electric."

"She's not Electric, Sutter. She's real." He swallowed hard. "They say Dufresne's supposed to be a nigger."

"Yeah, well, like I said, there are no *live* niggers anymore. Maybe she's an abo." Sutter addressed Seraphina directly for the first time: "Are you an abo?"

"I'm indigenous," Twenty-Nine Words offered.

"Sutter? Sayles?" a loudspeaker called in the captain's voice. Sayles walked backwards to an intercom mike, keeping his eyes on Seraphina. Seraphina let her own gaze wander, up to the enclosed habitat above the helipad; three lemurs were looking down at her, with expressions like curious children. She smiled warmly at them.

"Captain?" Sayles said, lifting the mike from its cradle. "Sayles here."

"Sayles, have you got the passengers off the life raft yet?"

"We've got them, Captain. Captain, the nigger is real. Human."

"Who—" A second voice cut in, and there were sounds of argument, with Captain Baker shouting, "Stow it!" several times. *"Sayles,"* the captain finally said, in an impatient tone, *"what color are his eyes?"*

"Her eyes, Captain. They're—Jesus!"

"Jesus-colored?" said Sutter, checking Seraphina's eyes for himself. "If the Virgin Mary got fucked by a leprechaun, maybe."

"Up ahead," Sayles said, motioning towards the bow. "Look!"

Sutter squinted past the machine guns. "What the hell is that? Smoke?"

"It's moving," said Sayles. "This way."

"Sayles?" the captain called. *"Sayles? What's going on?"*

City of Women

"Level at periscope depth, Captain."

"Periscope up!"

Wendy Mankiller grabbed the periscope grips, intending to get a quick peek at the sub-killer and make one sweep of the horizon to check for other ships. But what she saw as she looked into the viewfinder brought her up short.

"What in bloody blazes . . ."

"Captain?"

"Looks like a pillar of smoke on the water, beyond the Robespierre." She pressed the magnification stud on the periscope grip several times; enlarged, the pillar resolved into individual flying particles. "Only it's not smoke . . ."

The Buoy

The third buoy had surfaced ahead of schedule, its ballast pack damaged by the blow from the *Yabba-Dabba-Doo*'s propeller. It broke through the swells about a mile to the south of the *Mitterrand Sierra*.

The buoy was bright yellow, about six feet high, and cone shaped, with the point of the cone sawn off and replaced with a flat watertight lid. As soon as the buoy had righted itself, CO_2 cartridges popped the lid off. There was a sound like burning cellophane, and a black cloud came boiling out into the air.

Not smoke.

Bugs.

Mitterrand Sierra

"*C'est des locustes,*" the combat computer said. "*Des locustes électriques.*"

"Locusts?" said Troubadour Penzias.

"What's this now?" asked Captain Baker.

"Locusts—*Electric* Locusts, swarming out of the water."

"What in God's name—"

"I don't know," Penzias said, checking a sensor readout. "But they scatter radio waves like a chaff cloud. Could be they're meant to jam our radar."

"As a prelude to what? An air strike?"

"Or a missile strike. Or something else weird that only tree-huggers would think of." Penzias studied his tactical display. "They're coming towards us."

"Can we shoot them down?"

Penzias shrugged. "Machine guns aren't much use against bug-sized targets, and surface-to-air missiles would just fly right through them. And we don't have air support to do a napalm—"

"*Périscope!*" warned the computer. "*Périscope dans l'eau au trois-quatre-sept, distance cinq mille huit cents mètres.*"

"Periscope in the water," Penzias translated. "Three-four-seven is right up our ass."

"Bridge!" shouted the captain.

Exodus 10:13–15

"'So Moses stretched out his staff over the land of Egypt,'" Seraphina recited, "'and the LORD brought an east wind upon the land all that day and all that night; when morning came, the east wind had brought the locusts. The locusts came upon all the land of Egypt and settled on the whole country of Egypt, such a dense swarm of locusts as had never been before, nor ever shall be again. They covered the surface of the whole land, so that the land was black; and they ate all the plants in the land and all the fruit of the trees that the hail had left; nothing green was left, no tree, no plant in the field, in all the land of Egypt.'"

"Bugs, Sutter," Sayles said, paling. "A live nigger I can deal with, but not bugs . . ."

"Get a grip," Sutter told him.

"They're coming to get you," Seraphina said. "They're coming to eat your boat, and they'll eat you too if you don't let the lemurs go."

"Shut up!" Sutter barked at her. "Don't listen to her, Sayles! They can't do shit to us."

But Sayles was not reassured. "I can't take bugs, Sutter. I'm entomophobic, man."

"They'll crawl in your *nose*," Seraphina said.

"I told you to shut up!" Sutter took a step towards her, meaning to emphasize the point with a jab of his rifle, but stumbled as the *Mitterrand Sierra*'s engines kicked abruptly from idle to full power. The rifle muzzle dipped as Sutter tangoed for balance; Seraphina, thinking this was as good a time as any to make her move, threw open the space blanket and yelled, "Get him, Beaver!"

Sayles's cry of "Christ Jesus!" could be heard all the way to the bridge.

City of Women

"The Robespierre just increased power, Captain!"

"Damn!" Wendy Mankiller said, knowing she'd kept her periscope up too long. "Helm, ahead two-thirds, left full rudder, all down on the planes. Make your depth one hundred and twenty meters and come to course zero-three-five."

"Aye, Captain," Dasher MacAlpine said, "coming left to zero-three-five, all down on the planes."

"Captain," Gwynhefar Matchless said, "the Robespierre is coming about. They could be unmasking their torpedo launchers."

"All ahead full!"

City of Women darted through the water; they were level at a hundred twenty meters when the *Mitterrand Sierra* began pinging them.

"Captain—"

"I know."

Mitterrand Sierra

"Relèvement du sous-marin trois-cinq-trois, distance six mille mètres."

"They're running," Penzias said. *"Combat, parez à lancer—"*

"Wait a minute!" Captain Baker held up a hand. "Bridge!"

"Najime here, Captain."

"Power back to one-third. Keep coming right to course zero-zero-zero."

"What are you doing?" asked Penzias.

"Slowing down so you can get a passive sonar I.D. on that sub. We're not going to shoot at it until we know what it is."

"But—"

"Think, Penzias. It can't be Dufresne; even if we hadn't already killed him, there's no way he could get behind us so quickly."

"Those locusts are almost on us. If they can disable the ship's weapons somehow . . ."

"We're not firing on an unknown target, Corporal. Now get me an I.D. on that sub."

"Combat," Penzias said. *"Pouvez-vous classer le sous-marin?"*

"Oui. Le sous-marin est de la classe Virago Terrible. C'est un bâtiment d'attaque britannique."

"Terrible virgin?" Captain Baker said, sounding out the French.

"Dread Virago," said Penzias. "It's a British attack submarine. . . . *Combat, parez à lancer des Chandelles Sauvages sur la Virago.*"

"Belay that order!" the captain said. "What in hell do you think you're doing?"

"What do you think I'm doing? You think it's a coincidence, this other submarine showing up just now? The British must be working with Dufresne. And if we haven't killed him yet, and we let this Dread Virago get clear—"

"We are not getting into a shooting match with a British attack sub!"

"But they might not let us finish him!"

"Paré à lancer," the computer said.

"No!" Captain Baker said. *"Non, comprendez-vous?"*

"Combat—" Penzias began.

"No!" Captain Baker unholstered his pistol. "Corporal Penzias, you are relieved. Step away from that console!"

Penzias's VISION Rig swung around to face the captain, but he did not stand down from his station.

"I mean it, mister. . . ." The captain raised the gun, steadying it with both hands.

"Yeah." Penzias nodded. "I guess you do. . . ." He raised his arms and stepped out from his circle of screens and scanners.

"Now tell it to shut itself down," Captain Baker ordered. "This operation is terminated."

"If that attack submarine turns around and comes back . . ."

"Shut it down."

"Sonnez collision," Penzias said.

The wail of the klaxon spooked Captain Baker for only a second, but a second was all Penzias needed. His right hand curled into a fist with a leaf-shaped blade protruding between the third and fourth fingers; springing forward, he made two quick cuts, one across the back of the captain's wrist, the other just above his eye. Captain Baker dropped his gun and flinched back involuntarily; Penzias stepped in, doubling him over with a knee to the groin. He caught the captain's head on the way down, cradling it gently in two hands, and slammed it sideways into a chart table.

"Stoppez l'alarme," Penzias said. The klaxon ceased.

The intercom clicked on. "This is Najime on the bridge. Who sounded collision?"

"Computer malfunction," said Penzias. "The captain's checking it out."

"Oh. Well listen, Tagore just stuck his head outside and he says there's a fight going on back by the helipad. Must be trouble with the castaways we picked up."

"Tell Tagore not to worry." Penzias bent to the body at his feet; the key to the small-arms cabinet was hanging off Captain Baker's belt. "I'll be up in a moment to take care of it."

Men Overboard

"Son of a bitch!" BRER Beaver had clamped onto Sutter's head like a steel-banded fur hat and was thwacking him repeatedly on the nose with his tail. The munitions wrangler fell against the launch panel for one of the depth-charge racks; a black barrel rolled off the *Sierra*'s stern and detonated in its wake.

Sayles crouched to grab the assault rifle that Sutter had dropped; a bare foot kicked it out of his reach. He looked up and saw Twenty-Nine Words standing over him with a rubber fish in his hand.

"Where'd you get that?" Sayles said.

"Lake Winnatonka," Twenty-Nine Words replied, and trouted him.

Giving up hair to do it, Sutter separated BRER Beaver from his scalp and pounded him against the deck until he stopped biting. The munitions man straightened, breathing hard through a swollen nose. He turned and found himself face to face with a naked Eskimo in a kung-fu attack stance.

"You've got to be fucking kidding," Sutter said. But Twenty-Nine Words was quite sincere—nude, but sincere. He cocked his arms in the Fighting Grasshopper First Position.

"All right, you faggot!" Sutter snarled, dropping into an attack stance of his own, with the ship's railing at his back. "Come on! Show me what you've got!"

"All right," Twenty-Nine Words said, "if that's what you want." He spun around, bent over, and wagged his broad buttocks in Sutter's face. Sutter blinked and dropped his guard. Twenty-Nine Words nailed him with a reverse flying kick.

"Oldest trick in the book," Twenty-Nine Words observed, as Sutter fell overboard. He grabbed a survival raft from an on-deck storage bin, pulled the rip cord to start it inflating, and pitched it over the railing.

Forward, on the bow, the Savage Candle torpedo launcher salvoed two rockets; they ignited with a hiss and streaked north over the waves. As the

Candles flew out, thousands of locusts blew in, plastic wings crackling like candy-box wrappers in the wind.

They were made in Taiwan, mostly. The bulk of the swarm were cheap robotic novelties, sold in lots of a hundred, whose tiny ROM-chip brains came imprinted with a few simple commands—in this case, find the tallest thing around and flock to it. Except for their special radar-reflectant coating, meant to blind the *Sierra*'s above-water sensors, these locusts were harmless; but hidden among their thousands were a dirty dozen of much smarter bugs, hand-crafted by Morris Kazenstein and dubbed Severely Antisocial Battery-Operated Termite Saboteurs, or SABOTS. The SABOTS flew into the sub-killer's superstructure, seeking out the delicate control wiring that permitted the ship to function.

The other locusts, meanwhile, settled on the outside of the superstructure—on the radar mast, antennae, flue stack, flying bridge, bridge windows, weapons mounts, lemur habitat, and anything else vertical. One locust with a problem judging scale tried to land on the unconscious Sayles's nose, which jutted beakishly from his face; Sayles started awake, jumped up screaming, *"Christ! Jesus! Bugs!"* and threw himself into the sea.

"Men overboard," said Twenty-Nine Words, tossing out another life raft.

City of Women

"Savage Candles in the water bearing two-zero-nine!" Gwynhefar Matchless said. "Two torpedoes incoming, ranges eighteen hundred and twenty-one hundred meters."

"Right full rudder!" Wendy Mankiller ordered. "Full rise on the planes, make your depth fifty meters! Countermeasures, fire off a noisemaker as we turn!"

"Aye, Captain, my rudder is right full, full rise on the planes!"

"Noisemaker in the water!"

"Both torpedoes continuing on current heading," Matchless reported. "They're going for the decoy."

"Helm, all ahead two-thirds, continue right to course one-eight-zero. Fire-control, stand ready for a snapshot."

"Coming about, Captain!"

"Matchless, I need range and bearing to the Robespierre."

"Pinging, Captain. . . . Robespierre is at bearing one-nine-two, range seven thousand meters."

"Flood tubes one and three! Open outer doors!"

"Outer doors open!"

"Match bearings and shoot!"

"Firing one . . . firing three. Malfunction on one, Captain! The motor didn't turn over! Three is away and running normally."

"Bloody Chanticleers! Close outer doors and reload."

"Captain, Savage Candles have looped around and are attempting to reacquire!" Gwynhefar Matchless warned. "Savage Candles now bearing zero-zero-six!"

"Fire another noisemaker! MacAlpine, break left!"

Mitterrand Sierra

Seraphina shinnied up one of the stanchions to the lemur habitat. The habitat, an insulated Plexiglas hutch ten feet on a side, had a square door secured with a pair of slidebolts; brushing away locusts, Seraphina fumbled back the bolts and opened it. A lemur poked its head out. It was a small animal, about the size of a large housecat, its appearance that of a raccoon-faced monkey with big jaundiced eyes. Its bushy, black and white ringed tail was longer than the rest of its body.

The lemur had been snacking on baobab leaves. In a clumsy attempt at greeting, it tried to stick one in Seraphina's ear. She pulled her head back, laughing, and the assassin's bullet passed an inch in front of her throat instead of through it.

Seraphina heard the rifle crack and felt the bullet go by, but it was the lemur, technically the less-intelligent primate, who first recognized the danger. It was by following the lemur's gaze that Seraphina spotted the sniper, high up on the flying bridge, leveling his weapon for another shot. He had strange goggles covering his eyes, and his mouth seemed full of blood; locusts crawled in his hair and dripped from his shoulders.

The lemur—demonstrating remarkable survival instinct for a member of an endangered species—ducked back inside its hutch and tugged the door shut. Seraphina took another three seconds to react, and Penzias would surely have killed her had a locust not flown in front of his rifle scope, spoiling his shot.

"Catch me!" Seraphina shouted, as the second bullet buzzed past her ear. She let go of the stanchion and fell back; Twenty-Nine Words for Snow, who was turning out to be an excellent boyfriend, ran and caught her before she hit the deck. Without breaking stride he carried her forward, putting the after superstructure between them and the sniper. Penzias cracked off another shot in frustration; it ricocheted off the bullet-resistant Plexiglas of the lemur habitat. The lemurs gathered in a huddle and looked at each other, as if wondering what they could have done to attract such hostility.

"I think we'd better hide," Twenty-Nine Words said, setting Seraphina on her feet.

She kissed him on the mouth and said, "I think you're right. Where?"

It was not an easy question. There was space underneath the depth-charge racks, but they'd be spotted there for sure. Jumping overboard didn't seem too smart either. That left three possibilities: run forward along the port side of the boat, run forward along the starboard side of the boat, or enter the superstructure through a hatchway to their right. The hatch swung open as they were considering it; Twenty-Nine Words tensed for a fight, but it was only a White Negro, coming out to swab the deck.

"Excuse me," Seraphina said. The White Negro put down its mop and bucket and looked at her expectantly. Seraphina pointed towards the starboard gunnel. "Could you go stand over there for a minute?"

The White Negro did as she asked; as it stepped beyond the corner of the superstructure, Troubadour Penzias blew its head off.

"I guess we don't go that way," Twenty-Nine Words said. The exposed port-side deck didn't seem any safer, so they went in through the hatch the White Negro had come out of. "No lock," Twenty-Nine Words noted, as he pulled it shut behind them.

They were in a short passageway with several exits, including a narrow stairway down marked *"Chambre des Machines."* The close, cluttered spaces below decks seemed like a good place to go to escape a long-distance rifleman, but the throbbing of the ship's engines sounded vaguely infernal and the stairwell was dark, so they hesitated. Another hatch opened farther up the passageway. This time it wasn't a White Negro that stepped through, but a man with a gun.

"Not that way," Captain Baker said, as Seraphina and Twenty-Nine Words made to bolt down the stairs. "Corporal Psycho Killer just went below decks forward; I think he's working his way back to the engine spaces."

Seraphina looked at him. "Aren't you one of the bad guys, too?" she said.

"Yeah," Captain Baker said. He swiped the back of his hand across his forehead; the slick feeling of his own blood made him dizzy and nauseous.

"Yeah, I'm a bad guy, all right. Just like you. Like Dufresne. But Penzias . . . he's *not* like you and me."

The Chanticleer

It may have been a mistake on the Royal Navy's part to name a weapon after a rooster. Chanticleer, the fastest torpedo ever made, had performed splendidly during testing in Britain's North Sea; it wasn't until the navy went ahead with mass production and deployment that they discovered that that was the *only* sea in which it performed splendidly. Chanticleer's motor was highly sensitive to temperature variations: in the warmer waters of the Mediterranean and the tropics, it frequently overheated and seized up after a minute's run; in Arctic waters, it typically refused to run at all; and in the temperate Atlantic, it was, well, temperamental.

Chanticleer also had guidance problems.

City of Women's snapshot should have found its mark easily. With no one monitoring the *Mitterrand Sierra*'s sonar suite, the bridge received no warning of the threat; Najime continued to steer straight north at one-third speed, offering a simple intercept solution for any torpedo with half a brain. But a little over a mile out from the *Sierra,* the Chanticleer started drifting to the left. Not much; just enough to matter.

Chanticleer was equipped with a magnetic proximity fuse, primed to detonate when it came within thirty feet of a target. *City of Women*'s snapshot passed the *Mitterrand Sierra* thirty-*three* feet to starboard.

A quarter mile on, the torpedo's seeker-head tried to figure out what had happened to the ship it had been tracking. Could it have ducked aside somehow? The torpedo began to weave right and left in a snaking search pattern, hoping to reacquire; naturally, this didn't work, as the *Sierra* was now behind the torpedo, getting farther away every second. But the Chanticleer did not give up, and as it continued south it soon picked out another target, about the size of a London omnibus, that was just now broaching the surface of the water.

Still Further

Morris climbed out on top of the life pod with binoculars to see what he could see.

"We're looking good," he called down to the others. "Looks like one of my Pharaoh-busters came up early."

"Any sign of Seraphina?" Philo asked.

"I see a survival raft, but there's nobody in it. . . . Wait, there's another raft in the water, closer to the ship. And another one. . . . Now who the hell are those guys?"

"Morris," said Asta Wills, "do you see anything else in the water? On a bearing of about three-five-five?"

"Why, do you hear something?" The main sonar listening arrays had gone down with the *Yabba-Dabba-Doo,* but *Still Further* had a cheap set of Radio Shack hydrophones for Asta to play around with. "What am I looking for?"

"You'll know it if you see it," Asta told him. "About two miles out, I'd say."

He saw it.

"Oh shit," Morris said.

"Right," said Asta. "That's what I thought."

Mitterrand Sierra

Captain Baker led them forward to the combat information center. As they walked, it became apparent that something was going wrong with the *Mitterrand Sierra;* the lights started flickering, and the previously steady engine-throb began to hitch and stutter. In the CIC, the computer was talking to itself.

"*Répétez après moi:* . . . *Amiral Jones a déspensé beaucoup d'argent pour son nouveau cuirassé.* . . . *Commandant Vendredi a coulé une frégate chinoise avec ses missiles Exocet.* . . . *Mon tante Trudi a tué un lemantin avec son moteur hors-bord* . . ."

"System's gone buggy," Captain Baker said. "The locusts?"

Seraphina nodded. "Are you sure we're safe in here?" she asked; the room had a lot of dark corners.

"Maybe not," the captain said. "Let's get up to the bridge. Get all the sane people in one place, and—"

The lights went out, and all the computer screens. There was a tire-squeal of frying electronics, a pop of circuit breakers, then dark silence, interrupted only by the death-rattle of the *Mitterrand Sierra*'s engines.

That, and one other sound . . . a smooth whirr-and-click, like the auto-focus of a camera lens.

"*Go,*" Captain Baker said. Muzzle flashes lit the room as someone started shooting. Seraphina ducked down, grabbed Twenty-Nine Words's hand,

and ran for the nearest exit she could find, which was not the one that led to the bridge. The two of them groped blindly along a passageway, dead-ended in a storeroom, backed up, blundered through another hatch, and found themselves outside, on the bow.

Troubadour Penzias was waiting for them, hunched beneath the Savage Candle torpedo launcher like Buddha beneath the bo tree.

"Howdy," he said.

"But. . . ." Seraphina glanced back over her shoulder; from within the superstructure she could still hear gunfire.

"Is that the captain?" Penzias asked. "What's he shooting at?"

"You," Seraphina said.

"Must have hit his head even harder than I thought." Penzias trapped a locust crawling on the deck beneath the toe of his boot; its battery motor whirred and clicked impotently as it tried to beat its wings.

Twenty-Nine Words squeezed Seraphina's hand. He slid his foot back towards the hatchway behind them.

"Hey Eskimo boy," Penzias said, watching them through the third eye of the rifle sight. "Why don't you close that door before I decide to kill you slowly?" A warning shot whined off the deck. "I said *close* it, not lean into it. . . . Good. Now get over here." Gesturing with the rifle, he stepped away and let them take his place beneath the torpedo launcher. "That's good. That's just fine. . . ." He worked the Remington's slide-action. "Just fine. . . ."

"You're going to shoot us?" Seraphina said.

"Oh yes."

"But why?"

"No," Penzias said. "No—you don't ask that." He aimed from the hip, the rifle sight and both lenses of the VISION Rig focused on the same patch of black skin, perfect spot for an entry wound. "You don't *get* to ask that."

The ship's hull boomed like a timpani. It felt like a torpedo hit, but there was no explosion, just impact, like a battering ram. The *Mitterrand Sierra* heeled over hard; Seraphina and Twenty-Nine Words were tossed off their feet, and Penzias was hurled sideways into the starboard gunnel. "What?" he demanded; his head snapped around, VISION Rig tracking down to the water, which was suddenly much closer.

A monster stared back at him. The sperm whale was a giant, eighty feet long and a hundred thousand pounds, with a barnacled gray hide and a circular welt over its left eye the exact size and shape of a Savage Candle torpedo head. The eye itself was large and cold and pitiless, the color of speckled jade, and it seemed to know who it was looking at.

Penzias screamed. Fighting physics, he tried to scramble away up the canted deck of the frigate; the whale rose up spouting, its blow like judgment day at a boiler factory. Eighteen-foot flukes lashed the side of the ship, rupturing bulkheads and wrenching a machine gun from its mount. The *Sierra* tilted further, close to capsizing. Twenty-Nine Words wrapped his arms around the base of the torpedo launcher, and Seraphina wrapped her arms around Twenty-Nine Words; Troubadour Penzias, with no handhold in reach, clawed the air.

There came a moment on the outer edge of balance when he realized he wasn't going to make it. Seraphina saw it happen. All at once Penzias stopped struggling, poised straight as a board, his body forming an acute angle with the deck; he switched his rifle to one hand, drew his leaf-blade knife with the other, bared his teeth, and, turning, let gravity take him. He slid back down to the gunnel and catapulted over the side, firing as he fell.

There was no splash.

The *Mitterrand Sierra* righted itself, or tried to; rocking back, it didn't come quite level, but settled into a five-degree list. The whale gave one more lash of its tail before swimming away. Two more compartments were vented to the sea, and the five-degree list became fifteen degrees. Another life raft deployed off the stern; Najime and Tagore had had enough. Chatterjee the engineer was just seconds behind them.

Seraphina and Twenty-Nine Words got up slowly. Twenty-Nine Words saw a red stain on the deck where Penzias had gone over and went to investigate. It looked a little thin for blood so he stuck finger in it, lifted a drop to his nose, and sniffed. It smelled like water. He decided not to worry about it.

"Hey," Seraphina said. "Lexa's coming."

Still Further

"Doesn't seem fair, somehow," Morris said, as the Chanticleer bored in. Philo had joined him up top, and Norma, and after that the Palestinians had gotten into a shoving match over who was next. It didn't matter; the torpedo was closing at a hundred seventy feet a second with only half a mile left to run, and not even an Olympic swimmer could have gotten beyond lethal shock range before it hit.

But still it was funny, the things people thought about with death looming. Morris still had his dreidel, and as time ran out he found himself staring at the little wooden top, trying to remember what phrase its four Hebrew letters were meant to abbreviate.

Let's see, now. *Nun, gimel, he,* and *shin.* Nun-gimel-he-shin, that stands for, let's see—

"Nes gadol hayah sham," Morris said, aloud, and Philo standing next to him caught his breath.

"God," Norma Eckland said. "Thank God . . ."

"What?" said Morris.

"It's stopped," said Philo. Less than a hundred yards out, the torpedo wake had faded and disappeared.

"Pinging's stopped!" Asta Wills called from below. "Screw sounds have stopped too! Hey, I think it ran out of fuel!"

"Morris," asked Philo, "what were those words you were just saying?"

"Nes gadol hayah sham," Morris said. "'A great miracle happened here.' It's from Hanukkah." He looked out on the water at the spot where the torpedo wake had faded, glanced down at his dreidel, then back out on the water again. "Nah. Couldn't be . . ."

"Hmm," Philo said.

City of Women

"A *whale* hit them?" Wendy Mankiller said.

"That's what it sounded like, Captain. The Robespierre's engines have stopped completely, and I hear flooding below decks. The whale is moving off to rejoin its pod."

"What happened to our torpedo?"

"Missed, evidently. The last I heard it was pinging off south somewhere, but there was no explosion. . . . Wait. New contact!"

"What now?" said Mankiller. "Range and bearing?"

"Almost directly overhead but fading to the southeast. . . . Bloody Mary says it's a blimp."

"Ah, of course. A blimp. Naturally."

"Eight turbine engines, low over the water, and also some sort of loudspeaker feedback whine, very high-pitched, almost ultrasonic—like the high-frequency sound used to repel insects . . ."

"Captain?" Dasher MacAlpine asked. "When can we go back to England?"

"Not bloody soon enough," Wendy Mankiller said. "I quit. Ahead two-thirds."

"On what course?"

"Frigging out of this vicinity. Yesterday."

"Aye, Captain!"

21

He raised a finger and winked at me. "But suppose, young man, that one Marine had with him a tiny capsule containing a seed of *ice-nine*, a new way for the atoms of water to stack and lock, to freeze. If that Marine threw that seed into the nearest puddle . . . ?"

"The puddle would freeze?" I guessed.

"And all the muck around the puddle?"

"It would freeze?"

"And all the puddles in the frozen muck?"

"They would freeze?"

"And the pools and the streams in the frozen muck?"

"They would freeze?"

"You *bet* they would!" he cried. "And the United States Marines would rise from the swamp and march on!"

—Kurt Vonnegut, *Cat's Cradle*

The Rule of Caveat Emptor

The return train to New York had no smoking compartment. Joan sat at the back of the club car with an untouched cup of coffee, her gun folded in a newspaper on her lap. When a young priest tried to sit with her, she warned him off with a look; when an Automatic Servant entered the car with supplies for the bar, she nearly blew it away. Having only just eluded the police at the Atlantic City terminal, and badly needing a cigarette to steady herself, Joan was not in a tranquil mood.

Ayn was feeling chatty.

"You never told me why you divorced Harry Gant," she suddenly said, ten minutes out from Grand Central.

Joan sighed. "You pick the weirdest moments to get personal, Ayn."

"It's in my nature to be inquisitive," Ayn said. She added, not in threat but as a plain statement of fact: "You may not be alive to answer questions much longer."

Joan sighed again, but then she shrugged, and said: "Plessy Falls. That's the short answer—I divorced him over Plessy Falls."

"Plessy Falls?"

"But really that's not it," Joan continued, deciding to talk to keep herself occupied. "Plessy Falls was just the excuse, and the last straw. The truth is, after nine years I was worn out. Tired of Harry, tired of the company. Same thing, really."

"His business is an extension of his person." Ayn nodded approval. "As it should be."

"Well, as it is, whether it should be or not."

"And what about it were you tired of?"

"Just everything," Joan said. "The day-to-day bullshit. See, Gant management was organized along the lines of a classic dysfunctional three-parent family. I was the hard-ass mom, the one who was always after the kids to clean their rooms, and play fair, and keep the dog from peeing on the neighbor's lawn—while at the same time bragging to the rest of the world how wonderful they were, the best kids any mother could ask for. And Clayton Bryce, he was the corrupting father, undercutting my authority at every turn: slipping the kids fifty bucks so they could go see a movie instead of weeding the garden, encouraging them to slide in with their spikes in Little League, telling them they didn't *really* have to separate all the bottles for recycling. . . . Of course if you asked Clayton, he'd probably say *I* was the corrupting influence, too idealistic to accept the facts of life . . ."

"And in this tortured analogy," Ayn Rand said, "Gant is the third parent?"

"The nominal head of the household," Joan agreed. "But Harry was the absentee dad: he spent most of his time either in the tool shed, puttering away at his latest hobby, or out at the orphanage, picking up more kids for me and Clayton to take care of.

"None of which was any goddamn surprise: I knew what sort of family I was marrying into, so I couldn't say I hadn't been warned . . . and it wasn't bad, not at the beginning. Despite all my complaints, and all my misgivings, I probably accomplished more good works in my first three years at Gant than at any other time in my entire life. The African environmental compacts alone were worth every bit of aggravation and self-doubt I went through."

Ayn feigned astonishment. "Good works? In a capitalist enterprise?"

"Cheap shot, Ayn," Joan said. "Just because I won't agree with you that the system is above criticism—"

"Oh yes, by all means, let's criticize capitalism! But it when it comes to statism, and socialism, and the wholesale trampling of the rights of man—"

"Do you want to hear the rest of this story or not?"

"Fine!" said Ayn, crossing her arms petulantly.

"All right. . . . So the job worked out pretty well for the first few years," Joan continued, "but Gant Industries kept growing and diversifying, acquiring new subsidiaries and new product lines—more kids—and then after a while I noticed I wasn't getting as many good works accomplished. The change was incremental, but bit by bit I got sidetracked doing damage control, chasing down problems inside the company that never should have cropped up in the first place."

"What kinds of problems?"

"Oh, things like Clayton Bryce deciding he didn't want to pay to meet full federal safety and pollution-control standards on Lightning Transit. Or the time one of Clayton's protégés in Labor Relations tried to bribe a union boss into letting us use all-android track-laying crews. It was after we got hauled into court over the bribery flap that the war between Public Opinion and Creative Accounting really heated up."

"And what was Plessy Falls?"

"Do you remember Love Canal?"

"I've heard the name," Ayn said. "Something to do with state persecution of a chemical company, wasn't it?"

"Yeah, something like that." Joan smiled ruefully. "Plessy Falls was the Love Canal of the late Nineties. It was, or at least it had been, a twenty-acre swamp in upstate New York."

"The Falls was a swamp?"

"A swamp with a trickle of a river running through it; and at one point on the river bed there was a four-foot drop, hence the name. The swamp was in the backyard of a chemical and plastics manufacturing plant, which in the 1950s began draining pieces of it to use as a dumpsite for waste products. Highly poisonous and carcinogenic waste products, over two hundred flavors, all packed in rustable fifty-five-gallon metal drums."

"Carcinogens?" Ayn said. She took a deliberate pull on her cigarette holder. "You mean *purported* cancer-causing agents?"

It took Joan a moment to get this. "Wait a minute," she said. "You're not going to tell me that you *still* don't accept the surgeon general's report on smoking, are you?"

"Statistical evidence of the kind that report was based on is unscientific," Ayn Rand said. "It doesn't constitute objective proof."

"No? Then what does?"

"Rational observation. Observed cause and effect."

"You mean like if a Russian philosopher smokes two packs a day for fifty years, and then you observe her having a cancerous lung cut out? That kind of cause and effect?"

"A lot of things happened every day during those fifty years," Ayn countered smugly. "The moon passes overhead every day. If you're going to rely on unscientific statistical correlations, why not blame my cancer on *that*?"

"Because you didn't inhale the moon," Joan replied. "Moonlight doesn't contain known poisons like nicotine and cyanide, and it doesn't produce a hacking cough the first time you're exposed to it. If you shave a rat's back and leave it outside after dark, it won't develop skin tumors as a result, but if you paint it with cigarette tar—"

"Finish your damn story!" Ayn snarled.

"Glad to," Joan said, with a longing look at the hologram Marlboro in Ayn's cigarette holder. "By the mid-Sixties, Plessy Falls had been completely drained and filled with toxic-waste drums. The company put a clay cap seal over the drums, piled lots of dirt on top of the clay, planted grass and shrubbery to make it look nice, and then, in 1975, sold the entire twenty-acre lot to the township of Gate's Bend for the bargain price of one dollar. The deed of sale included a clause transferring all future liability for the site to the purchasers. There was also a paragraph mentioning that 'by-products of the industrial process' had been buried beneath the property but no clear description of their identity or quantity. The Gate's Bend selectmen didn't ask questions; they took the bargain and used the land to build a high school and athletic field.

"For about two decades after that, everything was fine. That's how long it took for moisture to erode the clay cap and start rusting out the drums. Then all at once the students at the school started getting sick: unexplained headaches, skin rashes, burning eyes, respiratory and nervous disorders, immunodeficiency problems, and a whole list of other symptoms; teen pregnancy rates in the town took a nose dive, not because teens stopped getting pregnant but because the incidence of miscarriage shot way up, which was probably a blessing in disguise. And the teaching staff, who arrived at school earlier in the day and stayed later, were in even worse shape than the kids.

"Plessy Falls High was shut down, reopened, and shut down again. The chemical company had covered its tracks well enough that it took three years and forty-nine subpoenas for the full story to come out. The first lawsuit got filed in 1998, and the legal battle dragged on into the Oughts. Ultimately the company was bankrupted and driven out of business, which was a Pyrrhic victory for the town, since the local economy depended on the manufacturing plant. So Gate's Bend ended up going out of business, too."

"You see?" Ayn Rand said. "*This* is why schools should be privately owned. . . . But continue. How does Gant Industries come into it?"

"Gant Industries comes into it the same way the citizens of Gate's Bend came into it," Joan said. "Through epic carelessness. As part of the final legal settlement, the chemical company agreed to take back the Plessy Falls property and clean it up. But then the company ceased to exist, and the cleanup never happened. The toxic high school was simply fenced in and abandoned. Gate's Bend became a ghost town.

"Then about twelve years later, after the Plessy Falls story had been out of the media long enough to be forgotten by everyone except the cancer statistics, Harry Gant came around looking for a cheap used factory. Harry had a neat idea for a line of see-through toasters—toasters with transparent side-panels that let you see when the bread was starting to burn—and he'd heard through the grapevine about this manufacturing plant lying derelict upstate. Not really the right kind of manufacturing plant for making appliances, but he couldn't beat the price, so he bought it."

"Didn't he check to see why it was derelict?"

"Well, he should have—somebody should have—but on the other hand abandoned real estate is pretty common since the Pandemic, so Harry just drew the obvious conclusion. And again, he couldn't beat the price: under post-Pandemic reclamation law, all Gant Industries had to do to receive title was pay the back taxes on the property, plus a state processing fee. Which is what we did; and literally the day after we took possession, someone in Gant Legal Services turned up a press clipping on the old Plessy Falls scandal."

The train was decelerating into Grand Central; Joan placed a hand on the gun in her lap to keep it from sliding. Then she went on: "So the great deal turned out not to be such a deal after all. Gant Industries had unwittingly assumed ownership of a festering toxic nightmare."

"But it wasn't *Gant's* nightmare," Ayn objected.

"The title deed said differently," Joan replied. "Not to mention the rule of caveat emptor."

"But it was the chemical company that reneged on its responsibility to clean up Plessy Falls, so—"

"What chemical company? There was no more chemical company. As a corporate entity it was defunct, its former executives all flown away on golden parachutes to retirement villages in Palm Springs and the Florida Keys. And you can be sure we had every intention of tracking them down, but that would take time and legal fees, and even if we successfully sued them for every cent they had—not likely—it probably wouldn't be enough to cover the full cost of a cleanup."

"Why? How expensive could it be, with modern technology?"

"Ballpark estimate? Three, maybe four hundred million."

"Dollars?"

"Sure. And that's if the cleanup commenced immediately; with industrial dumping, the longer you wait, the more the price tag inflates. Which was another factor we had to consider: that toxic waste wasn't just sitting there while we made up our minds what to do. The metal storage drums were continuing to disintegrate, the clay cap was still eroding, leaching more chemicals into the soil and groundwater, spreading the poison farther . . . and people had started moving back into Gate's Bend."

The train was stopped in the station. Passengers were debarking, but Joan kept her seat, watching the platform through the window. "Not surprisingly," she said, "a big debate sprang up at Gant about what our proper course of action should be. My feeling was, OK, we got burned, that's too bad, but now let's be responsible adults and take care of this problem before it gets any worse—"

"You wanted Gant to pay for the cleanup?"

". . . and try to recoup the cost afterwards, yeah. As I saw it, the only way anything was going to get done quickly, if at all, was if we did it ourselves, and since to delay meant more expense, and maybe more people getting sick, it seemed like the least evil alternative out of a bad lot. It's not like we couldn't afford it. Four hundred million is real money, granted, but we could have covered most of it just by diverting part of our advertising budget over several years. With proper management the good publicity from the cleanup would make up for the advertising shortfall, and we could also stick a cleanup fund surcharge on Harry's toasters and market them as an environmentally conscious product. And once the dumpsite was secure, we could look up those old chemical company executives and play bill collector. We still wouldn't break even, probably, but that's life.

"Well, Clayton Bryce thought I was nuts. His line was 'not our fault, not our concern.' He thought we could get our property reclamation annulled on the grounds that the people who'd abandoned Plessy Falls hadn't died in the Pandemic; that would let us off the hook and throw the ball back to the state. The cleanup and any bill collecting would become the government's problem."

Ayn looked surprised. "And you *didn't* agree?"

"Don't misunderstand," Joan said. "It's not that I objected in principle to getting the government to help out, but doing what Clayton suggested would have caused another huge delay in dealing with the situation, and given the potential threat to public health, I didn't think that was acceptable. Besides, we didn't need the government; we weren't a poor corporation, and though we'd had a bad break we could handle it, maybe even turn it into something good. But Clayton's response to that was that we weren't in business to do good, we were in business to turn a profit, and there was no way we were going to pay four hundred million dollars to clean up somebody else's mess."

"And what did Gant say?"

"Harry said he hoped Clayton and I could get this Plessy Falls thing settled in time to get the toasters on the market by Mother's Day, since it looked like we were going to miss Christmas."

"Is that when you quit?"

"That's probably when I started thinking about it. But I went another couple rounds with Creative Accounting first. Clayton and I each hired independent assessment teams to re-examine the dumpsite. Clayton's scientists came back saying that the actual cleanup cost would be upwards of half a billion, but that the waste had 'stabilized' so there was no rush to get started; my scientists said we could probably hold the price to three hundred million and change, but there were clear signs that toxic chemicals were spreading beyond the original twenty acres, so time was of the essence.

"After that we decided we'd better go check out Plessy Falls ourselves. Or anyway I decided, and Clayton figured he'd better come along to keep me honest. We dragged Harry with us too, hoping he'd act as a tie-breaker when the inevitable happened. And we brought two more scientists—one from Union Carbide, one from a company that did contract work for the EPA. I'll let you guess who hired who."

"And what did you find at the high school?" Ayn asked.

"We never got there," Joan said. "It wasn't necessary. We drove up on a weekend; it was right around this time of year, a few weeks before Thanksgiving, but the winter weather had come early, and there was new snow on the ground. So we were driving through this Christmas card scene, pristine white snow covering everything, really beautiful, except that it was too quiet. Most of the houses were dark, and a lot of the windows were boarded over. And then about a half mile from the high school we saw these trees by the side of the road . . ."

"Dead trees?"

"No, healthy trees. That's what was strange: these trees were so healthy that they were budding, putting out new leaves. In November. In thirty-degree weather." Without thinking about it, Joan lit a cigarette in the now empty club car. "Trees sense temperature through their roots, did you know that? It's how they tell what season it is; when the ground warms up in March or April, that's their signal that it's springtime.

"Well, these trees had gotten fooled. There were three of them in a little park on the corner of a residential block, in the middle of this big patch of ground where all the snow had melted; there was green grass growing up where the snow should have been. Our scientists got out of the car to check, and it turned out the ground temperature in that one spot was a hundred and fifteen degrees. The grass and the trees thought it was summer. But of course only the ground was that hot; the tree branches still had snow on them, and the leaves were freezing even as they unfolded.

"The Union Carbide scientist said it could be anything, maybe a burst sewer, maybe a leaky gas main. The EPA guy thought the hot spot was too big for a broken utility pipe to be causing it—he said it had to be some sort of chemical reaction in the soil itself, and a few core samples should be enough to establish what kind of chemicals—and, if they were toxic, what their likely source was. But then Clayton jumped in saying he didn't see why samples were necessary, since these chemicals obviously weren't toxic—the trees were alive, right?—and I said if he really believed that he ought to prove it by eating some dirt.

"Eventually I noticed Harry wasn't joining in the discussion, and I looked around to see what he was up to. He was standing off to the side, quiet, just staring at the trees, with this look on his face . . . and I recognized that look. You'd better believe I recognized it; it was the look that said he'd just had another neat idea. And it only took me a moment to figure out what that idea was . . .

"There we were, on this poisoned street corner in a neighborhood where kids used to play, where they might be playing again soon if Clayton got his way, and all Harry could think of was, 'Gee, I wonder if we could package this somehow.'"

Ayn didn't understand. "Package the property?"

"No," Joan said, "the *effect*. Trees blooming in winter. Like, could you make a kit that people could buy, some sort of heating element they could bury in their yards if they wanted to have a New Year's Eve lawn party with budding trees. Wouldn't that be neat." She sighed, a long exhale. "I wasn't even angry, not really. I just felt . . . tired. A month or two earlier, I probably would have shrugged and said, Well, that's Harry for you. But I guess I'd reached my limit. Nine years . . . even college professors get a sabbatical after seven, and most of the neat ideas they have to deal with are safely locked up in books.

"So we drove around the neighborhood a little more, found some more hot spots, took soil samples—all highly, highly toxic stuff, all industrial waste—and broke into a few of the abandoned houses. There were substances leaking into the basements that even the Union Carbide guy was afraid of. Which you'd think would have settled the matter, but I knew better; and so after we went home I waited, and sure enough, come Monday morning, Clayton was right back to 'not our fault, not our concern.' It was as if we'd never even taken the trip. I went to talk to Harry about it and found him in his office with a potted cherry sapling and a box of hand-warmers. He asked me if I could come back in twenty minutes, and I was just, That's it, I've had it. I cleaned out my desk and was out of there before noon. Went home, called Lexa, called the state health department, called CNN."

"And the divorce?"

"That happened a few months later, once I was sure I wasn't coming back to work—not that there was ever much chance that I would, after I turned whistle-blower. I decided to make a complete break, and Harry understood. He was a little sad, also a little angry, but very decent about it. *Very* decent about it," she said, thinking of the surprise severance bonus and pension plan, and wondering, as she had many times before, how Clayton

Bryce must have felt cutting those checks. "I took a year off, traveled some, bought the Sanctuary, and then an ad in the *Times* led me to my job with the Sewer Department. My penance."

"Your penance," Ayn snorted. "You spent nine years 'wrestling with shades of gray,' and when you couldn't bear it any longer, you went out and took the most black and white job you could find, one with no complications and no compromises . . ."

"Hmm," Joan said. "Hmm, yeah, well—"

". . . because you know, though you seek to deny it, that compromise is *wrong*, and that attempting to negotiate with people who don't share your values is a waste of time."

"Yeah, well, you see, Ayn, there you go—you start to make a good point, then you blow it by taking it too far. Just because my job at Gant was frustrating doesn't mean it was a waste of time. I told you, I did good works there. Not as many as I would have liked, but . . ."

"But you quit!"

"I was exhausted."

"Precisely! And you *wouldn't* have been exhausted, if—"

"What? If everyone at Gant Industries had shared my sense of priorities? Sure, but that wasn't the reality. What would you have had me do, gun Clayton Bryce down like a sewer rat for refusing to see things my way?" She paused, reflecting. "Not that some of those Gate's Bend basements wouldn't be great for disposing of a body . . ."

"How horrid!" Ayn exclaimed.

"Well then, so much for the black and white approach," Joan said. "But refusing to negotiate doesn't work either. Gant Industries didn't grind to a halt just because I walked away—on the contrary, the company's doing as well as ever, and the only change is that my point of view isn't represented anymore. And Plessy Falls? Still hasn't been cleaned up. Lexa and I got enough media attention focused on it that people stopped moving back into the town, but beyond that nothing's been done. The state refused the motion to annul Gant's ownership of the property, and Vanna Domingo's still fighting that decision in court. And meanwhile, the toxic drums are still leaking."

"But that would have happened in any event. You said that Clayton refused to pay for the cleanup . . ."

". . . and by quitting, I made certain that he wouldn't pay for it. Whereas if I'd hung in there, kept fighting, who knows?"

"Then you regret leaving the company?"

"I still feel guilty about it," Joan said. "Guilty that I wasn't stronger and more patient. But I'm not sure I regret it, since I really did need the break. But now I'm rested up again, and the last few days I've been thinking, maybe I'm ready to go another few rounds. Assuming I survive tonight, of course." She shrugged.

Ayn shook her head. "You're so full of contradictions," she said, "I wouldn't know where to begin unraveling your pathology."

"Well then, don't," Joan said. She tossed her cigarette butt into the cold coffee cup. "Just enjoy me as I am, while you've got me. Which probably *won't* be much longer."

"Now that," said Ayn, "is true."

The train was deserted, its engine stilled. There was no one left on the platform either, not that Joan could see. Time to get moving. She stood up, tucked the Hand Cannon in her waistband—first checking the safety—picked up Ayn's Lamp, and proceeded cautiously to the end of the bar car. She pressed the button that opened the exit door and stepped out onto the platform.

Things happened quickly after that.

Send Him Out

"Awwwhhhh—"

"There," Motley Nimitz said, holding up the tongue staple in a pair of tweezers. It looked more like a bur than a staple: a hollow plastic bead with barbed spines, pumping out a time-released flow of inflammatory toxin. "Syrian invention," said Motley. "For when they're torturing a prisoner who's ready to talk, but they don't want him to yet. . ." He tossed the staple in the kitchenette sink. "I'll give you an injection and a medicinal rinse that should help bring the swelling down."

"Ank oou," Clayton Bryce said, eyes misting with gratitude. Since his rescue he'd been very emotional.

"How is he?" Kite asked. She'd laid her saber on a fold-down ironing board and was running a whetstone along the blade. Her Colt and the Hand Cannon were both within easy reach. The Stone Monk was downstairs, guarding the Sanctuary's front door.

"He needs rest," Motley Nimitz said, rummaging in his medic's kit bag. "It looks like he hasn't slept in days. He can't have eaten much, either, not solid food."

"I'm not sure it's safe for him to rest here," Kite said. "Once you've tended him, we'd better—"

The phone rang.

"Pick up," said Kite, and started to say "Joan?" but a brutal blast of rap music drowned her out. At least it sounded like rap, although the words didn't rhyme:

> *I think all thieves*
> *Should have their hands chopped off*
> *Like in the Hammurabi Code*
> *(The Hammu—the Hammu—the Hammurabi Code)*
> *Or pass a law*
> *Like they have in Texas*
> *Allowing deadly force in defense of property*
> *(The Hammu—the Hammu—the Hammurabi Code)*
> *Now that would be a deterrent!*

Clayton Bryce cringed, recognizing his own voice through the distortion. Then another voice yelled, *"All right, all right, turn it down!"* and the rap diminished.

"Hello?" the new voice said.

"Who is this?" Kite asked.

"This is the police, ma'am. I have a warrant for Clayton Bryce. I need you to send him out front of the building so I can chop his hands off." There were cackles and whoops in the background, but the speaker was serious.

"What kind of policeman chops hands off?"

"Powell 617, ma'am. NYPD Automated. Ma'am, I should warn you, the penalties for interfering in a prosecution are very severe. If—"

"Hang up." Kite grabbed her Colt and ran down the hall to Joan's room, which overlooked the street. A lynch mob of four dozen Automatic Servants had gathered outside the Sanctuary, dressed as drug-dealer/gangbangers from some twentieth-century Hollywood street drama about life in the inner city. Most of them were armed with Uzis or AK-47 assault rifles, but there was one gold-toothed 'banger at the front of the crowd who carried a machete; he had a baseball cap skewed sideways on his head and a big wall clock hanging around his neck like a medallion. At his feet was a boom box the size of a guillotine basket.

Officer Powell 617 stood apart from the lynch party, fussing with a cellular phone he'd borrowed from one of the drug dealers. But then Big Clock saw Kite in the window.

"Yo yo," he said, gold tooth flashing as he pointed. "Five-oh!"

Powell got out his police bullhorn. "You up there!" he called. "We have a warrant for Clayton Bryce! Send him out!"

"Yeah," said Big Clock, taking a practice swing with the machete. "Send his punk ass out here."

"They've barricaded both ends of the street," Kite said, as Motley and Clayton entered the bedroom behind her. "You'd better call the real police."

"I can't," said Motley. "The phone just went dead."

"Get this window open for me, then."

Motley raised the sash, and Kite yelled down to the mob: "Mr. Bryce is under the protection of this house! You can't have him! Now get out of here before there's real trouble!"

The gangbangers laughed at her.

"Lack of cooperation reflects badly on the community," Powell 617 cautioned. "Besides, we have you outnumbered. Send him out or we'll take him—and if we have to use force, it'll go worse for you than for him."

Kite held up her revolver and drew the hammer back, occasioning more laughter.

"Yo, bitch!" Big Clock cried. "Come down here and I'll *fuck* you with that!" He let out a whoop and then dropped, shot twice—once in the chest by Kite and once in the head by the Stone Monk, who used the sound of his profanity as an aiming point.

"This is very disappointing," Powell 617 said. Behind him, forty-seven Electric Negroes switched their weapons to full auto.

"Get down!" Kite shouted, knocking Motley Nimitz to the floor.

Cannonfire ripped up the street. A 135-millimeter shell landed in the midst of the gangbangers, shattering their ranks like a comet striking a tray of champagne glasses. A second shell landed eight seconds later, stirring the wreckage. Only Powell remained standing and intact; he pursed his lips at the impropriety of the tank rolling over the police barricade at the end of the street.

"You there!" he called to the unseen tank driver. "Get out of the vehicle! I want to see your license and registration!"

The tank rumbled forward, ignoring him; Powell 617 placed his chubby body directly in its path. The tank won. Powell was driven down and under, his bullhorn crushed by a steel tread. The tank rolled on, up to the front steps of the Sanctuary. Its top hatch opened.

"Kite!" the tank commander yelled.

"Maxwell?" Kite raised her head above the windowsill. "Maxwell! Where the hell did you come from?"

Maxwell spread his arms, as if the sixty-ton M6 Buchanan ought to be answer enough. "Twelfth Street Armory," he said. Then he looked over his shoulder at the line of vehicles crossing the fallen barricade behind him: an Army communications jeep with satellite uplink, a Brink's armored car, and four firebird-red '23 Ferrari Marchesas, each carrying a four-person fire team of Marine infantry.

"We made a couple other stops, too," Maxwell said.

Won't You Please Let Us Help You?

As Joan stepped out onto the railway platform, she heard two sounds behind her. The first was the hiss of the club car door sliding shut. The second was the growl of a V-6 engine throttling up.

The Hound.

It was above her, having ridden all the way from New Jersey on the roof of the club car, magnetic paws clinging to the skin of the bullet train. Joan whirled to shoot it down, but the front sight of the Hand Cannon caught on her waistband as she yanked it out; the gun jerked free and fell clattering into the space between train and platform.

"Oops," Joan said.

The Hound's eyes flashed; its steel-trap jaws snapped open. It sprang.

Joan, not knowing what else to do, swung the Lamp. She connected solidly with the side of the Hound's head. The Hound twisted in mid-air and landed badly on one leg, breaking it. In a panic of adrenaline Joan brought the Lamp down overhand, mashing the Hound's jaws into the platform and knocking one hazard-light eye askew. She swung once more, underhand, into the side of the chassis, flipping the Hound over onto its back; the V-6 engine howled in furied anguish.

And then Joan was running, up the platform and up the stairs to the main terminal, not looking back. "Still with me, Ayn?" she said, mounting the steps three at a time.

The lamp globe was undamaged, but inside Ayn Rand pressed her hands to her head as if she'd been cudgeled.

"Never do that again," Ayn said.

"No promises," Joan replied. Not thirty seconds later, as she ran through the passenger waiting area beneath the bowl of stars, an Electric Negro moved to intercept her; she raised the Lamp and hit it full in the face.

"What the—" Joan said, as the Negro squawked and fell back, bleeding from a broken nose.

Oops.

Not a Negro; not Electric. Human. Australian.

"Oh my God," Joan said, as much in horror of what she might have done, if she'd still had the gun, as at what she actually had done. "Oh my God, are you all right?"

The Australian man—who'd only wanted directions to a rest room—recoiled from her. When Joan leaned over him and extended a hand, he put his legs together and lashed out with both feet, cracking three of her ribs. Joan clutched her side and backed off, then dove over a bench to escape as the Australian man took a spray canister of mace from his pocket and tried to blind her.

Somehow she hung on to the Lamp. Limping, eyes watering, half-doubled over, she headed for the nearest exit. A short broad flight of stairs led up to a set of revolving doors and a sign that promised TAXI STAND.

"Can I help you?" A Pleasant Tripper, one Private Kwok, fell into step beside her as she started up the stairs.

"Can I help you?" A second Tripper, Private Molina, flanked her on the other side.

"No," Joan said, "no," and kept moving.

"Hello again," Captain Hector Miércoles said, appearing at the top of the steps, backlit by headlights. "Won't you please let us help you?"

"No," Joan gasped. "I—"

Headlights?

The taxi demolished a revolving door as it bulled its way into the terminal; shattered safety glass sluiced around Captain Miércoles's boots and made a brittle cascade down the steps. The taxi, a yellow Checker, struck the captain in the back of the legs, knocking him forward into Private Kwok; the two of them became part of the cascade.

The Checker stopped at the head of the steps. A tall Automatic Servant unfolded out of the driver's side. Unquestionably a Servant, this time: someone—perhaps the rightful owner of the taxi—had put a bullet through its head, leaving a dark crater in its temple.

Private Molina gaped at the sight, which seemed to irritate the Servant.

"What are *you* lookin' at?" the Electric Taxi Driver asked. It brought its hands up from behind the open door; they were curled around an ugly black shotgun with a pistol grip. Private Molina went for his TASER gun. The Taxi Driver worked the pump on the shotgun and leveled it at the Tripper.

They fired at the same time. The TASER darts hit the Taxi Driver in the neck. The shotgun pellets, their pattern tight at a range of less than ten feet, struck Private Molina high in the chest. The private's uniform was bulletproof, but that didn't save him from feeling as though he'd been punched in the heart. He passed the TASER to Joan like a communion chalice and followed his captain down the stairs.

Joan felt the TASER's variable voltage control under her thumb; she pushed it up as high as it would go. Current flowed along fine conducting wires between the gun and the darts, which sparked; the Electric Taxi Driver did a jerky dance like the Mandingo in Hoover's backyard, and then it too collapsed. Joan dropped the TASER, ran forward, scooped up the shotgun, threw it and Ayn's Lamp into the front passenger seat of the taxi, climbed into the driver's seat herself, shut the door, shifted into reverse, and hit the gas. Somewhere in the middle of all this, she also clutched her rosary.

Backing out of the terminal she T-boned another taxi. It was all right—the other cabbie was a white guy, human and unarmed, and the collision spun her cab around so that it was pointed towards the street. Ignoring the angry honking, she shifted into drive and started to pull away.

Something bounded onto the Checker's back trunk and scrabbled up onto the roof with a telltale V-6 growl. Joan cursed and slammed on the brakes; the Mechanical Hound came sailing over the front hood and tumbled onto the pavement. Before it could get up Joan hit the gas again and felt a metallic crunch beneath the taxi's wheels. She braked, backed up, felt another crunch; drove forward, felt a crunch, braked, reversed. On her fourth pass the Hound's gas tank burst into flame. Joan shifted into drive one more time and, skirting the fire, swung out onto 42nd Street, heading west.

"Still with me, Ayn?" Joan repeated. Ayn was slower to answer this time.

"This is the kind of thing . . . I left Russia . . . to get away from," she finally said.

"Maybe you should have gone to Canada," Joan suggested.

Patterns in the Fabric of Circumstance

The Ferraris took up outrider positions in the convoy, forming a protective box around the tank, jeep, and armored car as they rolled north on First Avenue. Motley Nimitz and the Stone Monk rode in the back of the armored car; Kite and Clayton hunkered down inside the tank, which was roomy enough (barely) to accommodate two observers. Maxwell introduced them to the rest of the crew, all of whom were maimed veterans of the '07 War in Africa: Stouffer Aimes, the driver, who'd had his jaw and both legs torn off by Afrikaner friendly fire in the mountains of Kenya; Siobhan Yip, the gunner, who'd lost an arm to a Zairean booby-trap; and Curtis Dooley, the loader, who'd been trapped downwind of the Port Harcourt refinery fire. Dooley had artificial skin grafts over seventy-two percent of his body, a baboon's liver, and a VISION Rig.

"Meetcha," Dooley said, shaking hands with Clayton and Kite.

The other Marines in the convoy had all suffered similar injuries. The Eye of Africa had chosen them on the basis of their post-war psychological profiles; Maxwell had collected most of them from the new V.A. shelter on Houston Street, and the Eye had spoken to them.

"What's this Eye of Africa?" Kite wanted to know.

"It sees things," Maxwell explained, not too coherently. "It makes connections. That's its nature: it reads patterns in the fabric of circumstance, spies out truth, brings meaning into focus . . ."

"Stop talking like a fortune cookie, Maxwell. What *is* the Eye of Africa? Some kind of computer program?"

"Everything's much clearer now," he replied. "The Eye lifted me up, and we rode up and down the wires all night, looking for answers . . . and it wasn't easy, but we found them. It all makes sense now: the war, the plague, this. . . ." He patted his Leg. "I understand it now; I understand *why*."

"Is this how you knew we needed help at the Sanctuary?" Kite asked, not sure she liked this new understanding of Maxwell's, or the glint in his eye as he spoke of it. "You say the plague makes sense to you; does that mean you know about G.A.S.?"

"The Enemy," Maxwell intoned. "What it calls itself isn't important."

"Hmm . . . and what did the Eye of Africa tell you to *do* about the Enemy, Maxwell? Not to sound ungrateful for the rescue, but what's with the tank?"

"We're storming Babel tonight," he said. "Straight to the top."

"What for?"

Maxwell shook his head. "The Eye sees patterns, but a lot of the details are still unclear. Something big is happening at Babel tonight, that's all we know for sure. Something *bad.* And the U.S. Marine Corps is going to put a stop to it."

"Is it, now. . . . Well the Army of the Potomac would love to *help* the U.S. Marine Corps, but—"

"Not you," Maxwell said. "You're going to the Phoenix. Something's happening there, too, but it's not as urgent as Babel, and I can't spare any of my troops. That's why we came to get you."

"Ah," said Kite.

The tank rumbled to a halt. "Thirty-fourth Street," Stouffer Aimes said, his replacement jaw clicking. "Do we detour?"

Maxwell pressed a hand to the side of his helmet, listening to the latest report on police radio traffic from the communications jeep. "No," he said. "The Enemy's on to us, or will be soon. We've got to get to Harlem before the opposition gets organized." He turned to Kite. "You'll have to walk from here."

"I'll manage," Kite told him. "Mr. Bryce, do you want to come with me, or stay—"

But Clayton, curled up in a corner of the tank, was asleep.

"I don't suppose it's much of a choice either way," Kite said. "Take care of him, would you, Maxwell? And take care of yourself. Remember, whatever 'truth' you think this Eye of Africa has laid open to you, you're not obligated to it. Not if it wants more blood."

Maxwell made no response to that. "Do you want a rifle?" he asked her, unbuttoning the turret hatch.

"Thank you, but no." Kite could see there would be no arguing with him, so she hoisted herself up towards the opening. "I expect I'll draw enough notice as it is, walking crosstown with this saber on my hip. Do you suppose you could arrange a diversion, something to draw the attention of any police who—"

Somewhere close outside the tank there was an explosion, followed by an answering rattle of machine gun fire from one of the Ferraris.

"Never mind," Kite said, climbing out.

A Rough Evening

The taxi drove into the front of the Department of Sewers building just as Fatima Sigorski was getting ready to leave. Crouched behind the registration desk with a drop box full of dog tags, Fatima heard a crash and jumped up to see a yellow Checker come hurtling through the lobby doors. A delivery van with two Automatic Servants in the cab was right on the Checker's tail and tried to follow it in, but got hung up on the low clearance. Both vehicles jerked to a halt, the taxi with a squeal of brakes and tires, the van with a grinding of metal on brick. The Checker's driver's door flew open and Joan Fine leapt out, holding a shotgun. She ran back to the delivery van and pumped five shells through the front windshield.

"What the *Christ*—" Fatima Sigorski said.

"A boat," said Joan, when she was sure the androids weren't getting out of the van. "I need a boat, Fatima. And a key to the weapons stores."

"Oh, is *that* what you need. . . . Have you gone off your nut, Fine?"

Joan looked at her. "I'm having a rough evening, Fatima," she said. "Don't fuck with me."

Fatima looked at the shotgun, now pointed in her direction. It was an Ithaca shotgun, a Model 87 Bear Stopper Elite, twelve-gauge, pump-action, with an eight-shot capacity. Five shots into the van meant as many as three left in the magazine.

"All right," said Fatima. "I won't fuck with you."

Like Ulysses

"Shotgun shells."

"Right."

"Automatic pistol, .50 caliber, with holster."

"Right."

"Extra clips."

"Right."

"What's that?" Joan asked, pointing to an unfamiliar object at the end of the weapons rack.

"Grenade launcher," Fatima Sigorski said. "M-79."

The M-79 grenade launcher: what Abbie Hoffman had once recommended as the greatest self-defense weapon of all time. "I'll take it," Joan said.

"It was sent to us by mistake, Fine," Fatima said. "It's not meant to be used in—"

"I'll take it."

"Right."

All of the Zoological Bureau's Automatic Servants were missing; Joan checked the Servant storage area and found nothing but broken Kryptonite locks. The lock on the weapons storeroom had been broken too, and Fatima noted that two cases of M-16 rifles had disappeared.

"You want to tell me what the hell is going on, Fine?" Fatima asked, as they rode the cargo elevator to the underground dock. All but one of the barges had been taken.

"How long ago did you close up down here?" Joan said.

"Half an hour," said Fatima. "And I finished inventorying weapons maybe ten minutes before you showed up. The rifles were still there."

"The Servants can't have gone far, then. Must be waiting for me out in the shit." Joan stepped onto the remaining barge and stowed her gear. "Part of what's going on is, I'm being hunted."

"By androids? You really have gone off your nut."

"I wish." Joan zipped up the front of her body suit. "But if I'm crazy, where are they?"

"Exactly," said Fatima. "If they're hunting you, why would they go into the tunnels? Why not ambush you here, or upstairs? We've got sixteen Negroes in the pool, Fine. You really think you could take down all of them before they got you?"

"No," Joan said. "Which is probably why they didn't do it—I don't believe I'm invulnerable, so being ambushed and killed outright wouldn't surprise me. Although," she added reflectively, "the moment I start assuming they can't just kill me, they can."

"Fine, what—"

"Let me ask you, Fatima. If you were going to arrange an ironic death for me, what would it be?"

"Ironic?"

"Ironic given my philosophy of life."

"Oh," said Fatima, "that. Well, you're a crusader, right? I mean, you came to work here, and not because you needed the money."

The choice of words got Joan's attention. "And how would you kill a crusader?"

"Don't have to. Crusaders get themselves killed, isn't that how it goes? All you do is set them up with a mission, some impossible goal they think they have to try for, and they do the rest." She shrugged. "I'm sure it's not hard to inject some irony into the situation."

"Hmm," said Joan. "And if you were a crusader who didn't want to get killed?"

"I'd make like Ulysses. Refuse the assignment."

Joan slowly shook her head. "Too many lives at stake. Even if it is an impossible mission, refusing's not one of my options."

"Yeah, well, it wasn't really an option in Ulysses's case, either, was it? So I guess you'd better be as *lucky* as Ulysses." Fatima nodded at the rosary. "Favored by the gods. . . . Listen, Fine, you want to let me in on what this crusade of yours is about, so I have something to tell the cops?"

"It's probably safer for you if you don't know," Joan said. "Do me a favor, though? Ring my house?"

"What's the message?"

"Ask for Kite. Tell her Joan says, 'They're coming, and they're after Harry, too.' Actually that's another thing you could do, have the cops send a hostage rescue team over to the Gant Industries offices at the Phoenix. There's probably a kidnapping in progress."

"You're right," said Fatima. "I don't want to know about this." But then she thought, What the hell, and pulled a rabbit's foot keychain from her back pocket. "Here, Fine," she said, tossing the charm. "In case your rosary jams."

"Thanks," Joan said, surprised. She held up a fluted silver tube that was also attached to the chain. "What's this?"

"Rape whistle," said Fatima. "Don't suppose you'll need that, what with the grenade launcher. . . . Now get the hell out of here. I'll give you fifteen minutes' head start and then you're an outlaw."

"Fair enough," Joan said. Setting the Lamp beside the Electric Mercator, she started up the barge's engine and cast off the lines. "Thanks for the help, Fatima."

"Fuck you, Fine. Just don't call me as a character witness at your trial."

"Wouldn't dream of it," Joan said, smiling. Giving a last wave she pulled away from the dock and steered a course deep into the shit, with Ayn Rand lighting the way.

Maxwell Shrugged

Near U.N. Plaza the rush hour traffic started to get thick (though still respectful of the tank's personal space), so Maxwell had the communications jeep broadcast a warning on all AM and FM frequencies that snipers were turning First Avenue into a shooting gallery—a bit of propaganda no doubt helped by the fact that it was true. Within moments the civilian traffic had cleared out, creating enough gridlock on the adjoining cross streets to thwart the approach of hostile vehicles, at least for a little while.

The Electric Negro snipers—summoned hastily by an Enemy still uncertain what it was dealing with here—were in most cases too lightly armed to pose a threat. The Ferrari Marchesas all had bulletproof bodywork as standard equipment, and the communications jeep was similarly protected. The Brink's truck, of course, was armored, and the spaced composite armor on the Buchanan tank was invulnerable even to light artillery.

Not that there was any artillery. But as the convoy rolled north through the Fifties, furniture began to drop from windows and rooftops. The Ferraris took evasive action, weaving to avoid the bombardment. The tank, clumsier to maneuver, suffered a direct hit from a grand piano hurled from the penthouse of the Sheraton East; this damaged the turret mount and put an abrupt end to Clayton Bryce's nap. The piano's last chord was still echoing up the street when a pair of Automatic Servants levered a cement mixer off the access ramp of the Queensboro Bridge; it struck the communications jeep square on, crushing it. The Brink's truck swerved to avoid the wreck and formed up close behind the tank.

Above 59th Street the buildings got shorter, and there were no more bridges to drive under. The next challenge came in Yorkville, near the mayor's house, where a line of police cars tried to cut the convoy off at the 86th Street intersection. Maxwell fired a warning burst from the Buchanan's coaxial machine gun; the cop cars scattered left and right, and as the convoy tore up the middle, the rearguard Ferraris sowed a trail of oil and caltrops—another anti-terrorist feature standard in the '23 Marchesa—that left the road behind them undriveable. The police stubbornly tried to drive it anyway and were soon spinning out of control on multiple flats.

In the lower Hundreds a hook-and-ladder rig cut onto First Avenue. A Mechanical Dalmation yapped ferociously inside the cab; three Servants in fire fighter's suits lobbed Molotov cocktails from atop the ladder bed. Maxwell ordered the tank's main gun swung around for a salvo, but the damaged turret wouldn't traverse. A gasoline bomb burst on the hood of one of the Ferraris; the Marchesa was fireproof, naturally, but the driver panicked, having already been immolated once before in Somalia, and the car skidded up onto the sidewalk and crashed into a brick wall. Then the Stone Monk stuck a thump gun out one of the Brink's truck's side ports and shot a grenade at the yapping Dalmation; the cab blew up and the ladder rig tumbled sideways for four blocks before coming to rest.

The convoy turned left on 116th Street, passing west through Fifth Avenue to Malcolm X Boulevard. As the Marines steered north again for the last sprint to Babel, a tanker truck darted from an alleyway and took another of the Ferraris in a head-on collision. Burning fuel from the ruptured tanker drained into the gutters; manhole covers popped like saucers called to the mother ship.

Thus reduced, the convoy came at last to the open plaza below the ziggurat. Maxwell ordered a final burst of speed; as the tank led the charge to the Mother Tongue Gate, a single steel girder was loosed from Babel's crown. It was difficult to aim from half a mile in the sky; the I-beam missed by fifty yards, and the convoy came safe through the Gate into the roofed canyon lobby.

The lobby was empty of humans. There had been a shootout between Automatic Servants and Babel security just moments before, and the surviving guards, along with all tourists and other bystanders, had either run away or buried themselves in the foliage lining the canyon floor; now android sharpshooters commanded the balcony-cliffs and a company of Electric Negroes were assembled in defensive formation around the base of the Atlas statue. Their uniforms were a motley collection of army surplus, but they all wore tasseled red berets with the black cobra symbol of the Sub-Saharan Liberation Army. Their leader, whose personalized flak jacket identified him as Cinque, gave the order to open fire.

"Infantry, twelve o'clock," Maxwell said, as AK-47 rounds began plinking off the tank's armor. Siobhan Yip launched a high-explosive shell from the tank's main gun. The gun's laser sights were off, and the shell went high, bursting near the ceiling of the domed central chamber. Masonry fell like rain, and the chain supporting the great copper sphere was severed. The weight of the world crashed down on Atlas's shoulders; the statue bowed beneath its burden.

Then Atlas shrugged. The most immediate result of this was the annihilation of those few Negroes not already brought low by the fall of the ceiling. The descending ball mashed them into gears and silicon; rebounding off the curved bank of elevators, it flattened Cinque, then rolled for the tank.

"Target, twelve o'clock!" Maxwell shouted. "Reload!"

"Reloading!" Curtis Dooley cried, slamming another shell into the breech. "Ready!"

"Fire!"

Ignoring the unreliable laser crosshairs, Siobhan Yip aimed the tank's muzzle straight and level and depressed the firing switch. The copper sphere flew apart; its pieces, blown back with the force of a whirlwind, cut Atlas off at the knees. The statue toppled and its head snapped off and bounced away, features still fixed in an expression of lunatic joy.

Inside the domed chamber, the tank tracked back around to face the way it had come. Two more high-explosive shells and some bursts from the co-ax gun cleared the snipers from the canyon walls. A three-shell salvo collapsed the arch of the Mother Tongue Gate and piled ten feet of rubble in the entranceway. Out on the plaza police sirens wailed, and from above came the *whup-whup-whup* of an F.B.I. helicopter: Special Agent Ernest G. Vogelsang, responding to reports of African terrorists in the Tower of Babel.

And there *were* African terrorists in the Tower of Babel: more than one kind, now.

"Everybody out!" ordered Maxwell, unbuttoning the top hatch. As he stood on the turret an Electric Hummingbird flitted down and lighted on the back of his fist. An immense sadness filled him at the sight of it, and he stroked it delicately with his finger, saying: "It's all right. We can't put it back together, but it'll be all right."

The Marines from the surviving Ferraris formed an honor guard at the back of the Brink's truck. The armored doors were opened and the treasure brought out, a sacred cybernetic artifact Maxwell referred to as the Ark of the Eye. It was a rigid pack frame to which the cannibalized components of Joan Fine's Cray PC had been bolted, along with two racks of heavy-duty batteries, the whole swaddled in bulletproof fabric and slabs of Kevlar armor plate.

The honor guard brought the Ark over to the tank. Maxwell urged the Hummingbird back into the air, then climbed down to take possession; he slipped the Ark's straps over his shoulders and buckled the belt across his waist. "Elevators," he said.

Curtis Dooley trotted over to the express elevators and pressed the up-arrow button. It wouldn't stay lit. "Trouble, Commander," he said.

"Sergeant Yip!" barked Maxwell. There was a panel box above the elevator buttons; Siobhan Yip tore it open with one swipe of her Electric Arm.

Maxwell unreeled a cable from the side of the Ark and jacked it into a computer interface in the box. Doors opened on two of the elevators.

"Two groups," Maxwell ordered. "Yip, Dooley, Aimes, Nimitz, Monk, Santos, Boychuk, and Gurevich with me." He looked at Clayton Bryce, who was still standing on top of the tank turret, blinking like an owl in daylight. "You too, soldier."

The injection Motley Nimitz had given him had reduced the swelling in Clayton's tongue to the point where he could speak almost normally. "Whath happening?" he asked. "Whath going on?" But no one would tell him. The Marines were filing into the elevators; after listening to the commotion out on the plaza—more bullhorn-amplified voices yelling threats—Clayton decided to join them.

Something moved beneath the tank. It was Powell 617, or what was left of him after being dragged from the Buchanan's undercarriage all the way from the Bowery. As the elevator doors slid closed, Powell extended his arm, curling his fingers in a clenched-fist salute.

"I'm w-with you, man," he said.

22

i•ro•ny (ī′rə-nē) *n., pl.* -nies. 1. The use of words to convey the opposite of their literal meaning. 2. Incongruity between what might be expected and what actually occurs. [<Gk *eirōneia,* dissembling, feigned ignorance.]

—*The American Heritage Dictionary*

Capitalism

At half past six, after the last of her staff had gone home, Vanna Domingo went into Gant's office to drop off some papers. She found Harry at his desk, putting together a three-dimensional puzzle-model of Mount Rushmore.

"Still here?" Vanna said, not surprised. Harry's work hours varied unpredictably, depending on his mood.

He squinted at a jigsaw-backed nose, trying to decide whether it belonged to Lincoln or Jefferson. "Still waiting for Joan's call," he explained.

"Oh." Vanna's face clouded over. "Well, I'm waiting for a call too, actually—a report on a fishing expedition." She set the stack of papers she'd brought on a corner of the mastodon desk and started to turn away, then stopped and said: "Can I ask you something, Harry?"

"Hmm?"

"All the contact you've been having with Fine this week—is it something I should be worried about?"

"Worried about?" He put down Lincoln-or-Jefferson's nose. "What do you mean?"

"I owe you my life," Vanna said, not looking at him. "What's good about it, anyway. And if you wanted me to resign my position here, I would. But . . ."

"Resign?" Gant burst out laughing. "For Pete's sake. . . . What's this falling on your sword stuff, Vanna?"

"It's not a joke!"

"I know it's not." Harry smiled, his voice gentle. "But Joan's not coming back—not to work, at least. Even if she were, you're too valuable an employee to just boot out the door, OK? You've got your job for as long as you want it."

"All right." Vanna nodded, cautiously, then risked eye contact to ask: "You're sure?"

"Absolutely sure. You really shouldn't worry so much, Vanna. I know you've had some rough times, but you're safe now. Nothing bad is going to happen to you here." He glanced at his watch. "Now when did you say Joan was supposed to call back?"

"When did *I* say?"

"About half past six, wasn't it?"

"I don't know a thing about it, Harry."

"Sure you do. Don't you remember? This afternoon, you buzzed me from the Multimedia Labs to say that Joan had called, and—"

"No." Vanna shook her head. "I wasn't in Multimedia this afternoon. And I wouldn't—didn't—forward any phone messages from Fine."

"Well it sounded like you," Gant said. "And who else would be forwarding messages to me?"

"You can call me Roy."

He stood in the doorway, smiling a predator's smile: a white man in a spotless gray suit, with slicked-back silver hair, blue eyes, and a prominent nose marked with a scar; at his side was a midget Electric Negro in a barber's smock. The little barber carried a Thompson submachine gun that looked more like a prop than a weapon. "Y-you can c-c-call *m-me* . . . M-my name i-is . . . M-m-my associates r-refer to me . . . I-I-I-I'm . . . Don't make any sudden moves!"

Gant seemed unfazed by either the intrusion or the threat. "Do I know you?" he asked Roy, as if they'd just bumped into each other at a restaurant.

"Not directly," Roy Cohn said. "But I know you, Harry."

A third figure stepped through the door, and this one did faze Gant: his own double.

"Harry . . ." Vanna breathed.

"Hi, Vanna!" the Electric Gant said. It had the same voice, the same walk, the same clothes . . . even the wrinkles in its suit seemed identical to the real Gant's. It strode into the office with the confidence of belonging there, at the same time craning its head around to check the place out. Its gaze fell on the holographic game projection rig and its face split in a grin. "Hey, nifty!"

"Excuse me?" the real Gant said.

"What's the meaning of this?" Vanna Domingo demanded.

"Capitalism," Roy Cohn said.

"Capitalism," the Electric Gant echoed, twiddling a joystick on the game rig. "Noun. From the Latin *capitalis,* 'of the head.'"

"An economic sy-sy-system ch-characterized by . . . A sy-system of f-f-free . . . P-private ownership and d-d-distribution of . . . C-competition between . . . L-l-laissez f-f-f-f- . . . Greed is good!" Shorty the Barber stuttered.

"Competition," Roy Cohn said.

"Competition," echoed the Electric Gant. "Noun. From the Latin *competere,* 'to strive together.' A vying with others for profit, prize, or position. A winnowing process, or contest, meant to identify and separate the superior from the inferior." The android stared at the game rig, at the black and white ice-cream trucks racing around the idealized consumer island. It grinned.

"Hey Harry," it said. "I've got the neatest idea . . ."

Joan and Meisterbrau (II)

Ayn hated the sewers.

"It's like Petrograd after the revolution," she said, repulsed by the liquid feces and other effluvia her lamplight revealed. "Teeming with filth and corruption."

"No computer viruses, though," Joan pointed out. "Nothing you have to worry about."

"But how can you stand it? I'd need to bathe for a week after an hour in a place like this . . ."

"I'm more worried about the air quality just now, to tell you the truth." Joan was making frequent checks of the atmospheric scanner on her body suit. "I've only got one oxygen tank, and I forgot to ask Fatima for a methane report."

They rode in silence for a while, Ayn grimacing at each new delectable churned up by the barge's passage. Then Joan said: "So give me the benefit of your wisdom, Ayn . . ."

"*Now* you want my advice?"

"I've been thinking about what I said to Fatima, and something doesn't add up. If it's true G.A.S. can't kill me outright, because it wouldn't be ironic, then what was the Hound doing in Grand Central? It sure *seemed* like it was trying to kill me, although, looking back, it could have been a lot more aggressive . . ."

"More aggressive?" Ayn said. "You had to flatten it with a taxicab."

"Yeah," Joan said, "and how about that taxicab? Very obliging of that Servant to show up with a set of wheels just when I needed them. And what a lucky break that it decided to park the cab and get out instead of running me down. And what an even luckier break that it shot the station guard first, instead of blowing my head off while it had the chance."

"You think it was all a show?"

"Not *all* a show," Joan said, fingering her ribs. "If I hadn't taken the threat seriously I'm sure I'd have gotten hurt—hurt *worse*. But it's interesting, how the minute I stepped off the train the bad guys started coming at me, one after the other, not giving me a moment's respite . . . until I reached the Zoological Bureau. Now I'm down here at, what"—she consulted the Electric Mercator—"70th and Columbus, and I haven't been so much as harassed since leaving the dock. So maybe all that excitement at street level was just to encourage me to take the underground route to Babel."

"But why?"

"That's exactly what I'd like to know," Joan said. "One thing, if I come to Babel by sewer, it means I'll be entering through the sub-basements, which is where the bomb is supposed to be. Unless . . . you're sure *you're* not the bomb, Ayn?"

"Positive." Ayn frowned. "But since I don't know *why* I'm positive, you'd be a fool to accept that answer."

"Suppose for the sake of argument I do accept it. If you're not the bomb, then what's the trap?"

"I don't know that either. Since we both know that there *is* a trap, however, why are you walking into it?"

"No choice," Joan said. "I have to risk it. Hoover said it was within my power to stop the genocide, and if—"

"No," Ayn corrected her. "Hoover said it was within your power to disrupt the chain of events he'd described. He didn't promise to spare anyone as a result. What if you did stop the release of the virus—perhaps sacrificing yourself, altruistically, in the process—and the genocide took place anyway, through some other instrument? Wouldn't that be ironic?"

"About as ironic as if I stopped it for selfish reasons and it didn't do any good. . . . On the other hand, if I try to outsmart G.A.S. by not going to Babel, and the virus gets released, and I die knowing I *could* have prevented it. . . ." Joan shook her head. "Cobwebs. Either way I could be making a mistake. And maybe there is no right choice—G.A.S. didn't leave Amberson Teaneck much of an out. The trouble is, like Amberson Teaneck, I don't really have enough information to choose wisely."

"And therefore you're going to Babel? Doing exactly what G.A.S. wants you to do?"

"I could still get lucky," Joan said. She fingered her rosary, then added, with greater conviction: "Besides, if I'm dead anyway, I'd rather go out doing something than nothing."

"Maybe that's the trap."

Something bumped the underside of the barge.

"Ah!" Ayn cried. "A head!"

"What?"

"A severed head! There!"

Body parts bobbed in the flatboat's wake. "Android parts," Joan said, spotting the cables trailing from a torn limb. Two of the stolen barges appeared out of the darkness ahead. They had either collided or been thrown together; one rested half atop the other, and both had cracked keel plates. A headless Automatic Servant was splayed out across the deck of the topmost barge.

"Something else I forgot to ask Fatima for," Joan said, steering around the wreckage. "Wildlife update."

"What could have done this?"

"*Architeuthis princeps,* maybe. Or an especially lively *Crocodylus niloticus.* Though it'd have to be a damn big one to trash the boats that way. Or maybe . . . *Bolero.*"

"What?"

"Listen," Joan said. Then Ayn heard it too: music, a classical score, floating down the tunnel from somewhere near, but muted, as though it were coming from under the water.

"What is that?" Ayn said.

"Old swimming partner," Joan told her. She picked up the grenade launcher and checked to make sure it was loaded.

There was an intersection just ahead; the music got louder as they entered it. Joan looked down the left-hand tunnel and saw a fin cutting the surface of the water. She fired a grenade at it and kicked the barge to full throttle. The explosion added an extra percussion line to Ravel's march.

Up to this point Joan had been running without lights, using Ayn's Lamp as her only source of illumination. Now she switched on all the floods, while continuing to goose more speed from the barge's engine.

Meisterbrau's fin swam into view in the flatboat's wake. It didn't look like the blast had hurt it much. Joan loaded another grenade into the launcher. Even with the engine revved as high as it would go the shark moved faster than the flatboat, so Joan waited for it to get close. As it approached the barge's stern, the *Carcharodon* raised its snout above the waterline. Joan let fly; the grenade burst over Meisterbrau's head, hurling shrapnel down the length of its back.

Doing no damage.

"Armor-plated mutant son of a bitch . . . ," Joan said.

The jolt was like twin rattlesnakes fired through the soles of her feet. Joan came to with her head hanging over the transom, the effluent's stench in her nostrils. She looked up to see Meisterbrau come straight up out of the water with a brown eel coiled around its body, throwing off blue fingers of electric current. The *Carcharodon* and the eel hit the roof of the tunnel and splashed back down, roiling the effluvia with their struggle. The barge sped away, its throttle still locked on high.

"What. . . ." Ayn's image in the Lamp blurred like the reflection on a windy pond's surface; she had to fight to recollect herself. "What . . . was *that*?"

"*Electrophorus electricus,*" Joan said. She sat up; all her joints were broken glass. "Supposed to be living under Second Avenue somewhere, but I guess it got bored and moved." Shuddering, she reached up to steer the barge away from the tunnel wall it was drifting into. "Forgot my rubber-soled boots, too . . ."

The Power of Positive Thinking (II)

At a word from Roy, Amos and Andy entered Gant's office, pushing a large wheeled cabinet that had been draped in a sheet. They rolled it up next to the gaming rig and plugged it into the CPU. Then they broke out matching brown tool kits and set to work on the player control consoles, while the discussion continued.

"Let me get this straight," Harry Gant was saying. "You want to have a contest to see which of us gets to be me?"

"Think of it as an attempted hostile takeover," the Electric Gant suggested. "The kind of thing you'd have had to face anyway, if Amberson Teaneck had had a harder head."

"Amberson Teaneck. . . ." Harry's eyes widened, the tiniest fraction. "Then it's really true, about . . . ?"

"It's a pretty long story. Joan knows most of it, so maybe you can ask her to explain it all to you later. Assuming you go to the same place."

"Huh," Harry said, still more astonished than afraid. "Huh." He looked at Shorty the Barber, seeming to notice the gun for the first time. "And now you're here to—"

"We're here because of the speech you gave."

"The speech?"

"At the Technical School, on Monday. You remember—the one about how America is a place where anyone can become a success? Well, I've given it some thought, and I've decided that *you're* the success I want to become."

"You also talked a lot about the power of positive thinking," Roy Cohn interjected. "You told those immigrant kids that the real strength of American industry is its optimism: Americans value fair play, you said, but they also know from history that self-confidence can carry the day even on an *un*level playing field. That sounded like a challenge, so I decided to put it to a test."

"Put what to a test?"

"Your optimism." Roy gestured at the game rig. "Your self-confidence against my unlevel playing field. One round, no tears, winner take all . . . and Shorty take the loser."

"Who are you people?"

"Sheesh!" the Electric Gant snorted. "Try to keep up, Harry. We're not people."

"This is nuts," Harry said. "You are aware of that, aren't you?"

Roy Cohn laughed. "Don't crack now, Horatio Alger. You haven't even heard the half of it yet."

"I's done," Amos said, putting his tool kit away.

"Me too!" said Andy.

"All right!" the Electric Gant said. "Now pay attention, Harry. There've been some rule changes, so you're going to want to listen carefully . . ."

"What's under the sheet?" Harry asked, nodding towards the draped cabinet.

"Rule change number one," Roy said. "When Toby, there"—he indicated Gant's personal Servant, standing statue-like beside the Lightning Transit Electric Train Map—"when Toby passed along your ex-wife's comment about 'little hologram landfills,' it occurred to me that a pollution index really *would* make an interesting addition to the game. So . . ."

He snapped his fingers, and Amos and Andy pulled the sheet away. The cabinet was transparent, hermetically sealed, and had a set of compressor tanks attached to it.

Harry's parents were locked inside. Harry's father looked bewildered, his mother angry; both of them were scared. Seeing her son—*two* of him—Winnie Gant pounded silently with a fist to be let out. The cabinet was soundproof.

"The oxygen level in the cabinet reflects general air quality in the game world," Roy explained. "Less breathable air equals less breathable air. Now the good news is, air quality has no direct effect on play, so if pollution control doesn't excite you, you don't *have* to worry about it. From a purely economic perspective, it's better if you don't. But . . ."

Vanna stood off in a corner, watching them, feeling her sanity begin to fray and flake around the edges, thinking: *It's happening again.* You only had to let your guard down a little, start to feel safe, start to trust reality, and then . . .

Shorty laughed at something Roy had said, and Vanna took an involuntary step back. Something shifted behind her, some piece of the clutter Harry had collected in his office. She reached a hand around to steady it, and felt a smooth wooden handle. It was a baseball bat—a Swingspeed Training Bat, manufactured by the same toy company that made Gant's puzzle boxes. It measured the batter's swing velocity and displayed it in miles per hour on a digital readout at the bottom of the handle. The bat's surface was hard ashwood, its tip weighted.

Now Roy was laughing, the laugh directed at Harry, with barely masked contempt. Vanna started forward without thinking. She aimed for the top of Roy's head, the bat's velocimeter blurring into triple digits.

Roy didn't even bother to look at her, just raised a hand and caught the bat in mid-swing, holding it motionless until he'd finished enjoying his joke. Only then did he turn to Vanna, his smile going tight and sharklike, and say: "Are you through?"

Vanna let go of the bat. Her anger crumbled and her courage broke; she fled, out through her own office and into the Cortex. Shorty pivoted to shoot her down, but Roy stopped him. "Save it," Roy said. He tilted his head slightly. "Amos. Andy."

"Gots you," Andy said. The two of them sauntered out after Vanna, shutting the office doors behind them, leaving the players to their game.

Roy tipped up the bat, checked the readout in the handle. "Hmm," he said, sounding impressed. "Well. . . ." He returned his attention to Harry, and the game rig. "Shall we?"

The Trap

The sewers under Harlem were full of smoke; Joan saw no flames, but the air grew so thick as she traveled east under 116th Street that she had to put on her oxygen mask. The barge's floodlights did little but reflect back off the smoke, so she shut them off again and used the Electric Mercator to steer. She turned north below Madison Avenue and zigzagged through several smaller passages seeking clearer air.

She didn't see the other barge until she was almost on top of it. There were three Automatic Servants on board, two with assault rifles, one with a pistol and a long knife, all of them looking the wrong way. Joan veered to the right, coming alongside the barge from behind, the sound of her approach masked by the rush of a nearby waterfall; she had her shotgun up and blasted both rifle bearers before they had a chance to react. Then the two barges bumped, rocking in the effluvia. The third Servant lost its balance as it turned, stumbling towards Joan; it stuck its knife in her thigh, piercing muscle to the bone, even as she pressed the muzzle of the shotgun to its chest and pulled the trigger.

"Are you all right?" Ayn Rand said, as the third Servant splashed into the water. "Are you all right?"

Joan dropped the shotgun and lowered both of her hands to the knife haft protruding from her leg.

"Are you all right?"

"Oh, I'm *excellent*, Ayn!" Joan said, gritting her teeth. She remembered too late that it wasn't always smart to yank a knife out of a wound, that it could do as much damage coming out as going in. That certainly seemed to be true in this case: the pain and blood flow both increased as the blade came free. Joan's scream echoed in the tunnels.

She was hyperventilating in her oxygen mask. She tore the mask off, unzipped her body suit, got out a cigarette, lit it—nearly igniting the oxygen in the process—and inhaled two-thirds of its length in her first draw. Her breathing stabilized. She finished the butt with a second inhale, pitched it, and broke out the first aid kit. She bound her wound with gauze and sterile padding, applying pressure but not making a tourniquet. She told herself she hadn't nicked any major arteries; she couldn't afford to have.

She got the barge moving again. The smoke in the tunnels had thinned to a fine haze, or maybe the haze was from shock. After a time Joan realized that Ayn was giving her directions: "Left here . . . now right . . . now take this next side tunnel . . . now right again . . ."

"There," Ayn said finally. They were in a narrow secondary, one with just enough effluent to keep the barge afloat. The Electric Mercator placed them at 124th Street, between Adam Clayton Powell Jr. and Malcolm X boulevards—a nonexistent street segment. They were under Babel.

A hole had been broken in the tunnel wall, large enough for a human or a Servant to step through. A metal cleat had been driven into the wall beside the hole.

"This is it?" Joan said.

"Yes," Ayn said.

"What's inside?"

"I don't know."

"You knew how to get here."

"That doesn't mean I know what's inside," Ayn said, uncomfortable.

Joan looped a mooring line around the cleat. She checked her leg: it was stiff and painful—it felt like there was still a blade in her thigh—but no part of it had gone numb, and she could still walk. *I guess I really didn't cut the artery,* she thought, with forced optimism. The bandage had soaked through, and blood dripped from her heel.

She reloaded the shotgun with sticky fingers. After changing her bandage, she quizzed the Electric Mercator about other entrances to the building, hoping to find one less likely to be a setup. According to the Mercator, there was a manhole just south of her that would bring her up right in front of the Mother Tongue Gate; the only catch was that she'd have to climb a fifty-foot ladder to reach it. Joan put her weight on her good leg and bent her other knee, simulating a step up to a higher rung. She nearly fainted from the pain.

"Hell with it." Leaving the oxygen tank behind, holding the gun in one hand and the Lamp in the other, she entered the hole in the tunnel wall.

A narrow excavation led through packed earth and another broken-out wall. Joan found herself in a dark corridor of poured concrete, with pipes running overhead. There were light fixtures, but the power was out; she needed Ayn's Lamp to see.

"Which way?" Joan asked.

"North," Ayn said. "Straight ahead. Those barred gates, you see? That's it."

"That's what?"

"I don't know."

The gates were new, an obvious addition. Set on Automatic Hinges, they were shiny steel, with bars too close together to thrust the Lamp through; Joan sensed a larger space beyond, but Ayn's light wouldn't penetrate far enough to show her what was inside.

"Brighten up, would you?" Joan said.

"I can't."

Joan pushed against the gates; they wouldn't budge. She searched for an unlocking mechanism and found a metal box with a microphone grille on the front.

"It's a sound lock," Ayn explained, without prompting. "A certain combination of sounds will open it."

Joan looked at her. "You know the magic word, Ayn?"

Ayn thought about it. "Yes," she said. "It's. . . . Oh! Oh! You bastard!"

"What?"

"You *bastard!*"

"Ayn, what is it?" The philosopher looked angrier than Joan had ever seen her.

"This is pure, unadulterated evil!" Ayn said. Then, with an expression of absolute disgust, forcing out each word individually, she chanted: "'From . . . each . . . according . . . to . . . his . . . ability, . . . to . . . each . . . according . . . to . . . his . . . need.'"

The lock clicked; the Automatic Hinges turned, and the gates swung open. Joan took a tentative half-step forward, holding up the Lamp. The light seemed to dim in proportion to the distance she held it in front of her, so that she still couldn't see what was beyond the gates, not without passing through.

"This is a trap," Joan said, just to hear the words. Then she added: "Right, Ayn?"

Ayn didn't answer. She didn't have to. Of course it was a trap. And Joan knew in her bones that Fatima Sigorski had been right, that she should refuse this, just turn and walk away, leave the lion's den unentered.

She knew it, but she didn't like that idea.

Just inside the gates was a series of shallow steps down. Joan stood motionless on the top step for over a minute, waiting to see what would happen. Nothing did. She went down another step, and then another.

Nine steps to the bottom. Joan got more and more uneasy the farther down she went; her muscles tensed, ready to spring her back up and out if the gates started closing behind her. But they stayed open, and Joan reached the bottom feeling vulnerable and exposed.

"Now," Ayn Rand said, as she came off the last step onto a dusty concrete floor. The Lamp flared suddenly, and in the new light Joan saw at last where she was standing and what surrounded her.

"Holy Christ," she said.

We Been Flanked

"Ain't you got that ready yet?" Kingfish demanded, peering down into the open shaft of the construction elevator. "They's comin' up!"

Behind him, an Automatic Servant and a Gant Portable Television wrestled with an oxyacetylene welding set. The Servant was a construction worker, one of fourteen units in the Babel crew converted to the service of G.A.S. The Television had come up with Kingfish after the human workers had evacuated the site. All told, Kingfish had about two dozen bodies with which to defend the upper reaches of the tower until the virus dropped— overkill, if things had gone according to plan.

Things weren't going according to plan. That in itself was not unexpected, but the degree to which they weren't, was. G.A.S. was still trying to figure out where the Marines had come from and who had sent them; and while the supercomputer tackled the big questions, Kingfish rushed to improvise a stronger defense.

"Come on, come on, come on!" he urged. The construction worker used electrician's tape to fix the welding torch in place, with its nozzle aimed at the valves of its own fuel tanks. The Portable Television lit the jet with a sparking tool, and they hurriedly dropped it down the elevator shaft. Seventeen floors below, the welding set punched through the roof of the cage lift and exploded; oxygen-acetylene combustion scoured out the cage and cut the lift cables, sending the elevator plummeting.

"Bye-bye, soldier blue," Kingfish said. Then he raised his head, sensing new movement: someone had started up the kangaroo cranes. "Hey! Who's doin' that?" He concentrated, instantly aware of the location and activity of every Servant under his command; none of *them* were doing it. "Who the hell's in them crane cabs?"

"There doesn't have to be anyone in the cabs, Mr. Kingfish," the construction worker said. "Those cranes can be operated by remote control. By radio."

"By— Aw, shit."

A crane arm swept by overhead, swinging a one-legged Marine on a string. A grenade fell out of the sky and bounced between the wingtips of Kingfish's Buster Browns.

"Boys," Kingfish said, "we been flanked."

Do Not Run

"For your safety and comfort, this elevator bank has been temporarily taken out of service," the elevator bank said. "Please remain where you are until given instructions by a proper authority figure. If you are in imminent danger from fire or other hazard, proceed to the nearest emergency exit as indicated on the posted evacuation map. Do not run."

The nearest emergency exit was a set of fire stairs to the right of the elevators; but when Vanna tried the stairwell door, it wouldn't open.

"For your safety and comfort," the Electric Door Lock told her, "this emergency exit has been temporarily sealed. Please try an alternate. Do not run."

The closest alternate was in the southwest corner of the building, across the Cortex. Vanna turned to go that way and saw a pair of black scarecrows standing amid the desks and workstations.

"What do you think, Amos?" the first scarecrow asked. "Is she gonna run?"

"Why no, Andy," replied the second. "I do believe she's gonna *fly*."

Andy clucked: "I's never seen a woman fly before. I seen *time* fly . . ."

"I seen *the fur* fly," said Amos. "I seen *accusations* fly . . ."

Vanna grabbed the monitor of a Cray PC and tried to throw it. Tethered to half a dozen other pieces of equipment by a snake's nest of cables, it went all of two feet before jerking short and crashing to the floor.

"Mm, mm, mm," clucked Andy. "I guess that ain't time, fur, or an accusation."

Amos crooked a finger at Vanna. "Come here, sweetmeat." Vanna skimmed a fax machine at him, then leapt up and started running an evasion course across the desktops. Amos grabbed a phone handset and slung it at her, aiming to trip her with the cord; she dodged it, but a second toss by Andy tangled her ankles and brought her down. She fell headlong, hitting a water cooler with the force of a football tackle.

"Mm, mm, mm," Andy repeated, strolling over to where she'd fallen. As Vanna tried to get up, he cuffed her on the side of the head, stunning her. He grabbed her arms, while Amos took her legs; they lifted her between them and began swinging her, chanting: "I seen a swan dive . . ."

". . . I seen a lemon drop . . ."

". . . I seen a native land . . ."

". . . I seen a belly flop . . ."

They lobbed Vanna in a flat trajectory at the Cortex's window wall. She hit with a resounding boom, but the glass didn't break.

"Damn," said Andy.

"Solid," said Amos.

An explosion smashed a hole in the window wall. A window washer's platform rose into view on well-oiled tracks, its one-armed passenger wearing a bucket on her head as protection from falling glass.

"Huh," said Amos. "I ain't ever seen *that* before."

Kite blew his chest out.

Andy dove for cover a fraction of a second ahead of her next shot; the explosive-tipped slug breezed past the tail of his suit jacket and dismantled a laser printer. Andy dropped behind a desk and disappeared.

Kite used a fire ax to enlarge the hole in the window. Removing the bucket from her head, she stepped inside to where Vanna lay in a ragdoll heap. The comptroller was conscious but badly dazed, bleeding from her ears; she reminded Kite of the first battle casualty she'd ever seen, a malamute pup that had lost its skirmish with the Moncton mail coach.

"Can you understand me?" she asked, in a low voice; Vanna forced a weak nod, then made an abortive attempt to sit up, too dizzy to handle the vertical. "Here," Kite said, pressing the Colt revolver into her hands. "In case something happens to me, though of course it won't."

Amos had sprawled backwards over a Xerox machine, and Kite checked him next, flipping open the remains of his suit jacket. She found a straight razor in the pocket of his waistcoat, but no guns, which she thought was encouraging. She turned towards the desk Andy had vanished behind. Andy, crouched in the kneewell, threw the desk at her.

"*Shit*fire," Kite swore. She had to vault the Xerox machine to escape being crushed; the desk landed on Amos, but the ergonomic swivel chair that came after it caught Kite squarely and sent her reeling. In the process of bouncing off several other pieces of office furniture, she lost the Hand Cannon.

She cursed and unsheathed her saber. In an open aisle between the desks, Andy squared off against her, waving a short-bladed machete. His face stretched in what was supposed to be a menacing leer, but Kite was too angry to feel menaced, and Andy's eyes—brown, flat, and lifeless—held no terror for her.

"Come, then," she said.

He came, taking quick, mechanical steps. Kite feinted a parry, side-stepping at the last moment, wise to his strength; the machete chopped empty space, and for an instant he was vulnerable. An instant was all Kite needed: the android's frame might be steel where she was flesh and blood, but her nerves, like his, were electric. She hacked at his outstretched arm, her blade biting metal. There was a twang of high-tension wire separating, and Andy's fingers unfurled; the machete dropped to the carpet. Kite wrenched the saber free and hauled back, meaning to swipe his head off.

Vanna popped up, blazing away with the Colt revolver. Like Kite, she aimed for Andy's head, but she was still quite dazed, and her accuracy reflected this. The first bullet actually did put a crease in Andy's derby, but the second slapped the saber blade aside, and the third drilled Kite through the ribs.

"Yowch!" Andy said. Vanna snapped off three more wild shots and fell down again.

Head still intact, Andy bent to retrieve his machete.

Kite lay on her back, bleeding. Lying next to her was a wastebasket that had fallen over on its side, and because she had nothing better to do just then, she looked inside it, and saw that it contained scrap paper, two apple cores, a Coke can, a Xerox toner cartridge, and a .70-caliber Browning Automatic Hand Cannon.

"Hey there, soldier gray," Andy said, coming to stand over her with the machete. "Looks like bottom rail on top, this time."

And Kite reached out, with an arm that seemed at least a million miles long, picking up the whole wastebasket with the gun, lifting it until the shape of the basket covered the shape of the sneering mannequin who was about to cut her to pieces. She pulled the trigger four times.

Andy went away.

The wastebasket was a tube on her arm, open at both ends; she couldn't feel her toes. She wanted to go to sleep but didn't think that would be a good idea, so she tried to strike up a conversation instead: "Ms. Domingo?"

On the floor somewhere near, Vanna Domingo let out a groan.

"Ms. Domingo," Kite said, "I don't know how well you can hear me, but I was just curious. . . . If I'm still alive tomorrow—not that I think I'm going to be, but if I am—would you consider giving me a job?"

The Detonator

"Holy Christ."

The room was large but not cavernous, though its exact dimensions could only be guessed at. Once it had contained machinery of some kind—there were ghost rectangles and ragged holes in the floor where equipment had been uprooted—but all furnishings and fittings had been torn out to make space for the dynamite. Four and a quarter tons of it, piled against the walls to an uncertain depth.

It was arranged in neat bundles of seven sticks each, the bundles stacked to form a honeycomb pattern, a nitroglycerin hive. Joan did the math in her head: eighty-five hundred pounds of straight dynamite, at about half a pound per stick, and three and a half pounds per bundle, makes . . . makes a hell of a lot of bundles. She didn't know enough chemistry to calculate the force of the blast, but it would certainly be, as Hoover had promised, a big bang.

She was beginning to hyperventilate again, but this time she didn't light a cigarette. She looked around for the bomb's timer to see what kind of deadline she was facing but couldn't find it. Moving very, very carefully, she approached the nearest section of honeycomb to examine it more closely.

A blasting cap had been inserted in the center stick of each bundle and a six-inch fuse attached. The fuses stuck out into the air, like cilia; they were not connected to anything. Puzzled, Joan pinched one gingerly between thumb and forefinger, to see if it was some sort of antenna. But no, it was a fuse: cordite, fast-burning.

"But where the hell is the master fuse?" Joan said. "Where's the—"
She stiffened, hearing a clank of metal behind her. All at once she understood. "Oh no."

"Oh yes," Ayn Rand said.

Joan turned around. The gates had shut, trapping her inside.

Trapping the Lamp inside.

"I'd rather go out doing something than nothing." Joan felt the blood rising to her cheeks. "Is that what I said?"

"That's what you said."

"I'm an activist." She spelled it out, like a trial lawyer's summation. "That's my philosophy: I see a problem, I act."

"Yes."

"Even if I don't know what the hell I'm doing, I act."

"Even though you *know* you don't know what the hell you're doing," Ayn said. "Even though you've been warned."

Joan was nodding. "And it's true, what you told me: you're not the virus; you're not the bomb . . ."

"No."

". . . you're the detonator."

"An Electric Thermite Charge," Ayn Rand said. "But a supremely rational one."

Joan closed her eyes. "Thermite. . . . Thermite lights the fuses?"

"Yes."

"Fuses set off the blasting caps . . ."

"Yes."

". . . blasting caps blow the dynamite, dynamite shakes the building, shaking releases the virus, virus kills thousands of innocent people . . ."

"Yes, yes, yes, and yes."

"All because of me."

"All because of you," John Hoover agreed, his voice issuing from a speaker buried somewhere in the honeycomb. "And I just want to thank you, Miss Fine, for your truly heroic effort in coming here today. I couldn't have blown up the building without you."

Two Minutes

Tracer bullets stitched between the beams and girders of the Babel construction site. After the initial assault, the androids had fallen back to the north side of the tower, while the Marines occupied the south; the two groups were now engaged in a mostly random exchange of fire. The Marines' goal was not to eliminate the opposition but to keep it busy and guessing, while a special strike team got the Eye of Africa into the kangaroo control center.

In a relatively quiet corner of the 226th floor, a Portable Television marched along a covered walkway. Its monitor replayed broadcast footage from the '09 Syrian War: a beefy American general addressing a roomful of reporters. "Ladies and gentlemen," the general said, gesturing to a video monitor of his own, "you see here the headquarters of my opposite number." A wave of appreciative laughter swept the room as a Kemo Sabe cruise missile gutted a three-story building, killing everyone inside. "Next we have a clip of the luckiest family in the Middle East today." A couple pushing a baby carriage across a bridge reached the far side just seconds before a laser-guided bomb cut the span in half. A *Newsweek* reporter laughed so hard he fell out of his chair. "Next, a comparison of the long-range accuracy of Syrian and Israeli tank guns . . ."

The image turned to snow as the Stone Monk garroted the Television with a loop of magnetic piano wire; Maxwell plunged a bayonet into the Television's chest, finishing the job. Clayton Bryce gulped.

"All right," said Maxwell. He unstrapped the Ark from his back and offered it to Clayton.

"Me?"

"Can you fight?" asked Maxwell.

"Of course not. I'm an accountant."

"Then you carry. Take it."

Squatting behind a pallet of cement bags for concealment, Maxwell pointed out the control center to Clayton; an Automatic Construction Worker with an assault rifle was crouched beneath the non-slip staircase, waiting to shoot anyone who approached.

"That's where you've gotta get to," said Maxwell. "In two minutes, first squad is going to assault the opposition on their left flank, using everything they've got. Second squad will hit them from the right. That should draw their attention away from the middle ground, out there. The Monk'll take out the sentry; once he does that, you rush in, up those stairs, and jack the Eye of Africa into the Babel supercomputer."

"Me?"

"If you get shot, don't stop," Maxwell counseled. "Even if you're hit bad, don't stop until *after* you jack the Eye. But try not to get shot at all. Move *fast*."

"But why me?"

"You're an accountant."

"But—"

"I'd do it myself," said Maxwell, "but I've got other business."

"What other business?"

"Something I saw while I was riding the crane." He looked up. "I've got to check it out." Maxwell patted the Stone Monk on the arm. "Two minutes." He turned to go.

"Wait!" Clayton said. "What happens if I do plug the . . . the whatever it is, into that supercomputer? Will it deactivate those Servants that are trying to kill us?"

"No," said Maxwell. "But if everything works out the way it should, the Eye of Africa will gain control of them."

Clayton took a moment to ponder this. "Will that be an improvement?" he asked.

But Maxwell, hurrying away, didn't hear the question.

What If

"This is a cheap shot," Joan said.

"But," said Hoover, "you knew it would be."

"It's. . . ." Joan raised her arms, thinking of a thousand protests, all of them futile.

"It's what? Not fair?" Hoover laughed. "It's not supposed to be fair. It's supposed to be ironic."

"Hoover—"

"You can still deactivate the thermite charge if you want to."

"How?"

"Just use the arming key to switch the safety back on."

"Arming key? What arming key?"

"It's a little thing, shaped like a button. Fits in the compartment in the bottom of the Lamp—you know the one I mean."

"Yeah," Joan said, cheeks coloring again. "I know the one you mean."

"Uh-oh. You didn't leave it in *New Jersey,* did you?"

"Silly of me," Joan confessed, "but Ayn told me it was a tracking device."

"Oh, it was—one of two. The other one is located in the Lamp's handle. I've been following your progress very closely."

Joan counted ten, slowly. Then she asked: "What if I hadn't come?"

"How could you not have come? I told you, Miss Fine, you're easy. You're a compulsive Samaritan, the sort of knee-jerk do-gooder who'll even save the life of a man she hates—so I knew you couldn't pass this up. All I had to do was give you a few hard nudges to keep you on course."

"Yeah," Joan said, "but what if I *hadn't* come? What if I'd lost Ayn in the sewers? What if I'd refused to take that last step?"

"What if Dewey had beaten Truman in '48? Who cares? What matters is what *did* happen."

"Would you have killed them anyway?" It was half question, half plea.

Hoover chuckled. "That's something you'll never know, isn't it? . . . Ayn?"

"Yes?" Ayn Rand said.

"Explode."

Maxwell Kept Going

The seismic sensor rested on a platform at the highest level of the unfinished tower. Every time a grenade went off on the battlefield below it, lights flashed on the front of the unit, as it measured the vibrations and gauged whether this was *the* explosion it had been programmed to wait for; but every time the vibrations were too weak, and the lights, after a moment, went out again.

A black helicopter flew overhead, blades beating the air. Its loudspeakers came on with a scream of feedback: *"Attention. This is Special Agent Ernest G. Vogelsang of the F.B.I. If you are within the sound of my voice, you are breaking the law. Cease fire, put down your weapons, and come out where I can see you."*

Someone sniped at the helicopter, probably a Marine with bad memories of the Libyan Air Cavalry. The bullet glanced off a steel girder and hit the seismic sensor. The flashing lights came on and stayed on; beneath the platform, with a sound like a second gunshot, a gate flew up, releasing a fragile canister onto a track. The canister began to roll downhill, picking up speed.

The hologram display of the track that Hoover had shown to Joan was a vast oversimplification; far from a straight incline, the real track was laid out like a theme park rollercoaster, looping and meandering all over the construction site. As the canister rattled back and forth across the width of the tower, it engaged the attention of more snipers. Twice it was nearly struck by rifle fire; twice the bullets missed. As it rounded a final bend, a rifle-propelled grenade bounced off the track in front of it but failed to explode. The canister rolled for the drop-off at the tower's edge.

A soldier's head appeared at the very end of the track. An Electric Leg kicked in space; Maxwell hauled himself up into a precarious catcher's stance. The virus canister was heavy, and it had built up a lot of momentum in the course of its run, but Maxwell braced himself with a leatherneck's stubbornness and would not be moved. "Gotcha!" he said, as the canister came to rest in his arms.

A cry went up as the Marines began their diversionary assault. First squad used a rocket launcher to break up suspected enemy positions. Second squad, showing equal enthusiasm but poorer judgment, used a mortar for the task, a bad weapon in a place with crossbeams. The ranging round went off right underneath Maxwell, blasting the canister track's support; the track's end-section collapsed and fell sideways, stopping when it hit a crane arm. Maxwell kept going.

"The building is surrounded!" Agent Vogelsang warned. *"The building is surrounded! You are all under arrest!"*

In the Game

On a nonexistent island of little pink houses, meanwhile, a helicopter belonging to the EPR (Environmental Protection Racket) settled on the front lawn of a white ice-cream factory. Four uniformed enforcers jumped out, wagging their billy clubs at the filth belching from the factory's smokestacks (why an ice-cream factory would have smokestacks is anyone's guess, but since this was all imaginary, it didn't have to make sense). The enforcers dragged the plant manager from his office and beat him with their clubs; he crawled back into the factory on hands and knees, and the smokestack output was temporarily cut in half.

Harry Gant's parents breathed easier. Harry didn't; the EPR enforcers' next act was to fly back across the island to *his* ice-cream factory, demanding payment for their services. They were expensive; he had to mortgage one of his delivery trucks to meet their price. Then the Electric Gant hired a corrupt banker to call the mortgage and repossess the truck, depriving Harry of a tenth of his revenue.

He was losing. This did not seem to bother him much, considering what was at stake—but then it had been obvious, from the moment Roy explained the new rules of the game to him, the cheats and advantages to be given his opponent, that he had no chance of winning. The odds were so stacked against him, in fact, that even sacrificing his parents would have gained him nothing but a few extra minutes in which to feel like a bad son.

The knowledge of certain defeat can be liberating: as Edward Abbey once observed, when the situation is hopeless, there's nothing to worry about; and Harry had never been one to worry, anyway. Instead, drawing on his native talent for ignoring the larger picture, he blocked out grim reality— except for an occasional glance to make sure his mother wasn't turning blue— and immersed himself in the game. When the Electric Gant slashed ice-cream prices, Harry slashed them lower; when the Electric Gant sent Wobbly agitators to invade Harry's factory, he mortgaged another truck and hired Pinkerton strike-breakers to turn them back. In the real world Shorty the Barber polished his Tommy gun, but Harry, now totally engrossed in the contest, paid no attention to that. And as the Electric Gant whittled him down and the competition became ever more desperate, a strange thing happened: Harry smiled. He was beginning to enjoy himself.

Roy Cohn was not enjoying himself. Ignoring the game, he stood at the window gazing north towards Babel, and brooded.

"Toby," he said.

Gant's personal assistant came instantly to life. "Yes sir, Mr. Cohn."

"Amos and Andy have been shot. The person who did it shouldn't be a problem anymore, but I want you to go make sure."

"Yes sir. I'll take care of it." Toby picked up the Swingspeed bat from Gant's desk and left the room.

"Do you w-want me to go w-w-with . . . Should I b-b-back h-him . . . D-d-don't you th-think it w-w-would be safer i-i-if . . ."

"Shut the fuck up, Shorty," Roy said. Then he frowned, still gazing out the window, seeing one more thing that he did not like.

Air-Sea Rescue

The blimp had grounded briefly at a CNN refueling berth at Kennedy Airport. Here the captive crew of the *Mitterrand Sierra* were turned loose, and the Palestinian Kazensteins announced their intention to fly home to London on the next available flight. Most of the rest of the *Yabba-Dabba-Doo's* former crew caught public transport back to the city; Lexa went into the terminal to make some phone calls and also to pick up some clothes for Seraphina and Twenty-Nine Words. The lemurs remained aboard *Sweet Jane,* monkeying with the equipment in the production studio.

While Walter directed Dan and Morris in topping off the blimp's fuel tanks—it was a self-service berth—Philo stood on the tarmac with Captain Baker. The two captains had got to talking on the ride back from the battle zone. Captain Baker had been curt but polite, Philo reserved yet courteous, and over the course of the flight the two of them had discovered that they liked each other—or would have, had they not already established themselves as enemies. Their conversation continued even after the other mercenaries had left, and they were still at it when Lexa returned, carrying two souvenir T-shirts and an Eskimo-sized pair of sweatpants.

"Toshiro and Betsy are going to pick us up at Grant's Tomb," she announced. "I had Bets patch me through to my home computer for a news scan—turns out there's some sort of terrorist incident going on at New Babel. Big stuff. I figure since it's right on our way anyhow, we can swing by for a look-see."

"You know, Lex," said Philo, "Captain Baker and I were just discussing how we'd had enough big stuff for today. And with these chicken pox, I really should be resting . . ."

"Don't be a wimp. This is *news* happening, Philo." She grabbed his hand. "Come on."

Philo looked at Captain Baker. "Well," he said. "Got to go . . ."

"Yeah," said Captain Baker. "Well . . ."

And Lexa, hearing the reluctance in their voices, said, "Oh, please," and grabbed Captain Baker's hand, too.

"Walter!" Dan called now, as *Sweet Jane* entered Harlem airspace. "Walter!"

Gruffly: "What?"

"There's a *guy* hanging off the building!"

"What guy? Where?"

"There," Captain Baker said. He leaned forward in the copilot's seat and pointed. "Far left, just below the top."

Maxwell had fallen into the catch tarpaulins that ringed the Babel construction site. The upper circle of tarpaulins, meant to stop small objects only, had collapsed beneath his weight, but the lower, last-chance tarps were made of stronger material. Even so, his headfirst plunge had torn a seam in the tarpaulin fabric; he'd slipped through the seam as far as his waist, and now hung upside-down from his belt, still clutching the virus canister.

Captain Baker asked Walter: "How close in can you take us?"

Walter looked at the fireworks display of explosions and muzzle flashes spangling the ziggurat's crown. "Why would I want to take us in closer?"

"Before I got on command track in the navy," the captain explained, "I did about two hundred hours of air-sea rescue—abseiling from helicopters to pull downed fliers out of the water. So what I'm thinking, if you can get above that guy . . ."

Walter shook his head. "Gas bag's too wide. Even if we snugged right up next to the building, you wouldn't be able to reach him from the gondola."

"Get *above* him," Captain Baker said. "Then lower me on a mooring line. I can swing if I have to."

"Hmmph," said Walter. "If you're serious, there's a rope ladder you can hang out the side door of the production studio. Some of our cub reporters like to use it for those macho hand-held shots. . . . But with that head injury, are you sure you're up to this?"

"Nope," the captain said. Then he looked over his shoulder at Philo. "You want to hold the door for me?"

A lemur had climbed on Dan Rather's lap and gone to sleep in his beard. He tried not to wake it as he cinched a remote mini-cam sweatband around Captain Baker's head. Mindful of the big bandage above the captain's eye, he said: "This doesn't hurt, does it?"

"Only where it touches my scalp," Captain Baker replied.

"Aw, you'll live," said Dan. "And we'll get some *great* footage."

Seraphina and Twenty-Nine Words shooed the rest of the lemurs out of the way as Philo latched the gondola door open. Morris broke out the rope ladder—made of real hemp rope, with hand-tooled wooden rungs, definitely a macho contraption—and secured it to a pair of eyebolts in the floor.

Lexa, studying Maxwell's face on one of the gun camera monitors, said: "You know, I think I know this guy." She tilted her head to get a right-side-up view. "Yeah! He's one of Joan's tenants, a chronic battle fatigue case. . . . Shit. I should have called Joan from the airport . . ."

"Chronic battle fatigue?" Captain Baker said. "How serious?"

In the flight cabin, the head-up display flashed a warning: COLLISION ALERT. The helicopter hovering over Babel had just been shot in the tail and was careening towards *Sweet Jane*.

"*Attention airship,*" the helicopter's loudspeakers squawked. "*This is the F.B.I. We are out of control. Please move.*"

Walter yanked *Sweet Jane*'s control yoke all the way to the right. In the production studio, Philo lost his footing and stumbled towards the open door. Captain Baker caught Philo's arm, but then Morris jumped up to help and accidentally body-slammed the captain. All three of them fell out of the gondola.

The blimp leveled out close enough to the tower to attract rifle fire. Ignoring the danger, Lexa and Seraphina both stepped to the gondola door and looked out, while Walter hectored the shooters over his own loudspeaker system.

Philo, Captain Baker, and Morris dangled in a clump from the bottom of the rope ladder. Morris was shouting, "Get us down, get us down!" but Captain Baker swept an arm towards the superskyscraper and yelled, "Get us closer!" Philo looked up at Lexa and nodded, casting his vote with the captain.

"Oh God," said Lexa. "Dan? Is the mini-cam working?"

"You're darn tooting it is!" said Dan. "Walter! Listen up for steering instructions!"

Twenty-Three

Half a mile away, Ayn Rand reached inside her cape and pulled out a little round anarchist's bomb. She pursed her lips and drew heavily on her cigarette holder, stoking the tip of the hologram Marlboro to a ruby brightness, and touched it to the bomb's fuse. As the fuse sizzled and sparked, she began counting backwards: "Thirty . . . twenty-nine . . . twenty-eight . . ."

"You're a son of a bitch, Hoover," Joan said, by way of an epitaph, "and someone will put a stop to you eventually."

"The world will end," Hoover replied. "Eventually."

". . . twenty-seven . . . twenty-six . . ."

Not ready to give up, Joan went back up to the gates. Using the Bear Stopper as a crowbar, she tried to spread the bars far enough to toss the Lamp out.

"Don't waste your strength," Hoover said.

Joan wasted her strength. She bent the shotgun barrel and wrecked the pump-action. The bars didn't spread.

". . . twenty-five . . . twenty-four . . . twenty-three . . ."

Another try. The Bear Stopper's pistol grip snapped off, cutting her hands.

" . . . twenty-three . . ."

Joan hissed and lifted a bloody palm to her mouth.

" . . . twenty-three . . ."

Wait.

" . . . twenty-three . . ."

She looked down at her feet. The image in the lamp globe had gone blurry, just as it had in the tunnel after the electric eel's attack. It refocused briefly, and Ayn said, for the fifth time: " . . . twenty-three . . ."

"Twenty-two," Hoover corrected her.

"Twenty-three," Ayn Rand said.

"Twenty-two, goddamnit! Twenty-two!"

"Twenty-three," Ayn insisted. This time when the image cleared she was looking directly at Joan. Her expression was strained, as if she were holding back a great weight, and her eyes said: *I can't do this for long. Think of something.*

And as Hoover continued to swear at Ayn, Joan tried to think of something; but before she could, she heard something.

Music. A classical theme.

Joan looked out through the gates into the corridor; there was nothing there, but in her mind's eye she saw an armor-plated shark shrugging off a grenade blast.

With what was left of the shotgun, Joan started hammering at the bars. "Heyyy!" she shouted. *"Heeeeyyyyyyyy!!!"*

"Shut the hell up!" Hoover said. "Ayn! Twenty-two! That's an order!"

"Twenty . . . *three,*" Ayn said, weakening. "Twenty-*three* . . ."

Joan dug frantically in her pocket for Fatima Sigorski's rape whistle. She blew it for all she was worth.

Bolero got louder.

Black Virus

Stray and not-so-stray bullets continued to ricochet off the gondola and gas bag, despite Walter's threats about the power of the Cable News Network. Gambling that *Jane* could weather the abuse, he moved in closer, following Dan's steer. Fortunately there was little wind, and in less than a minute the rescue party was within grabbing distance of the fallen Marine. But Maxwell refused to cooperate.

"Reach out," Captain Baker called to him. "We'll swing towards you, and you take my hand and don't let go."

But Maxwell shook his head and hugged the virus canister tighter to his chest. "Can't," he said.

"We're risking our lives for you, you moron!" Morris screamed at him. "Now do what the captain says so we can all get down from here!"

Maxwell looked at Philo and shook his head again. "Can't."

"Can," Captain Baker disputed him. "Swing!"

The F.B.I. helicopter, like a punch-drunk hornet, came around for another near miss. Walter was distracted by the appearance of a second CNN blimp over the Hudson and didn't see the COLLISION ALERT until it was almost too late. He yanked at the control yoke, putting extra English on the rescue party's swing; Captain Baker, intending to seize Maxwell's arm, found himself thrown into a full head-to-tail embrace, with his ears boxed by Maxwell's ankles and his free arm looped around the backs of Maxwell's knees. The moving blimp pulled the rope ladder taut; the seam in the catch tarpaulin tore completely, and Maxwell popped free. He and his rescuers swung out into the night, a screaming plumb bob.

The stricken helicopter passed sideways in front of *Sweet Jane,* the tips of its rotor blades flicking at the blimp's nosecone. The fail-safe anti-collision system dipped the airship's nose automatically; Walter fell forward against the controls, and *Jane* dropped two hundred feet before he managed to check the dive. By then the rescuers were on their return swing, and the side of the ziggurat, which had been moving away, was suddenly much too close.

"Pull up, pull up, pull up!" cried Morris, as the building rushed towards them. Dan, watching the mini-cam transmission in the production studio, said: "Wow!"

They hit on the 204th floor. Fortunately there was no glass in the windows at that level, just plywood, which they broke through easily. There was a confusion of tumbling, of shins and elbows bruised. Then three of them came to rest on the hard floor of an unfinished room; Morris, still tangled in the rope ladder, spent another moment thrashing to get loose before he could be dragged back out.

Philo brushed splinters from his hair. "Is everyone all right?" he asked.

"Man," Morris sighed, as the ladder slipped away without him. "Please let that be the last close call of the day."

Captain Baker spat a tooth into his hand and stared at it, unbelieving. Then Maxwell groaned, and the captain's expression became savage. "You son of a bitch!" he shouted. "Why didn't you take my hand when I told you to?"

Maxwell lay on his back. "Virus," he murmured, half conscious.

"What?" Captain Baker said. But Morris heard the word clearly.

"Virus?" he said. "What virus?"

Maxwell held up the canister, miraculously unbroken. "Virus," he repeated. He lifted his head, once again looking at Philo. "*Black* virus . . . the Eye told me . . . watch out for . . . have to. . . ." His eyelids fluttered and his head lolled back; the canister began to slip from his hands, but Morris was there to catch it.

"Black virus?" Captain Baker said. "What the hell was he talking about?"

"I'm not sure," Morris said, examining the canister. It was glass, with metal endcaps. Inside the glass was some sort of silver-gray dust; the endcaps were engraved, one with the trefoil symbol for biohazard, the other with a pair of . . . well, if Morris didn't know any better, he'd have said Mickey Mouse ears. "Hmm . . ."

Lexa's voice: "Philo! Are you OK?"

Philo looked out the window and saw Lexa and Seraphina in the doorway of the hovering gondola. "We're fine!" he shouted, waving them off. "Shut that door before somebody else falls out! We'll meet you at Grant's Tomb!"

"Could be," Morris said, intent on the canister. "Could be virus of some kind."

"What do we do if it is?" Captain Baker said. "I'm not trained for CBW . . ."

"Well, the container looks vacuum-sealed," Morris said. "If it is, arcing an electric current through it should turn the contents to plasma . . . which should cauterize any infectious agents." He rapped a knuckle against one of the endcaps. "Yeah . . ."

"I don't know about this," Captain Baker said. "Are you sure—"

"Yeah." Morris was nodding to himself now. "Yeah, let's try that." He looked through a vacant doorway into an adjoining room and saw a rack of power tools. "Go get me one of those heavy-duty extension cords, would you?"

Jacked In

Clayton Bryce cowered behind the cement bag pallet, muttering to himself: "You've got to go for it. You've got to go for it. You've got to go for it."

He had been muttering this for several minutes now. The Stone Monk had taken out the sentry as planned but had been wounded—perhaps killed—in the process; peeking out from his hiding place, Clayton could see him slumped over the body of the android. When the other Marines had begun their assault, Clayton had gotten up and started for the kangaroo control center, only to be turned back by the explosion of the first mortar shell, which was so loud he felt sure it must be aimed at him. Now he was afraid to go forward, and equally afraid that if he didn't, the Servants would overwhelm the Marines and come looking for him.

The skin on the nape of his neck tingled a warning.

Clayton turned around. A Portable Television stood over him, replaying documentary footage from a military autopsy while its hands aimed a rivet gun at his face. Clayton yelped and threw himself sideways; the gun made a spitting noise, and a hot rivet cut the side of his cheek before puncturing a cement bag.

Clayton stumbled to his feet. The Ark on his back encumbered him, but it also protected him; a rivet that would have ended up in his spine hit a battery casing instead. He ducked around the corner of the pallet and broke into a run. A rivet hit his shoulder, burning and then numbing it; he ran *fast*.

From overhead came the *whup-whup-whup* of rotor blades. *"This is the F.B.I.,"* a voice boomed. *"We are going to crash. Clear the area."* A black helicopter fell out of the sky, landing on the Portable Television; Clayton leapt up the stairs to the control center, the downdraft from the chopper giving him an extra boost. Inside the bunker, he slammed and locked the door, and turned at once to the supercomputer.

"Input jack," Clayton chanted. "Input jack, input jack . . ."

Outside, and close, something big blew up, probably the helicopter. Every window in the control center shattered, throwing safety glass like wedding rice. Clayton dropped to the floor. When the debris settled and he raised his head again, he saw a console directly in front of him with a round socket marked LINE I/O.

Quickly, with shaking hands, he unreeled the cable from the side of the Ark.

Blew dust from the socket.

Jacked in.

The Ark hummed softly as it interfaced with the Babel supercomputer. The Eye of Africa awoke and flowed out over the connection Clayton had made.

And it was really only a coincidence, but twelve seconds after that, an earthquake struck the city.

One Looked Up

"Ah, fuck!" Roy Cohn said.

"What's wr-wr-wr- . . . Is s-s-something the m-m- . . . I-is there a pr-pr-prob- . . . Trouble, boss?" Shorty said.

"Now Toby's been shot!" Roy said. He concentrated. "One of them's still up, Domingo I think. She's got that fucking cannon gun."

"Sh-should I—"

"Get out there and hose the room. Shoot anything that moves."

The piles of clutter in Harry Gant's office began to shift and topple. For once, Shorty didn't stutter: *"Everything's* moving, Boss!"

"An earthquake?" Roy said, tossing up his hands. "What's next, Armageddon?"

Shorty reached for the door, and a big hunk of door panel blew in at him. "Boss!" he squealed, whirling around. A second shot hit him in the back; his finger jerked on the Tommy gun's trigger, spraying the office window with bullets. Roy had just enough time to look pissed before the building's sway tipped him over the sill, out, and down.

Vanna kicked the door open as Shorty collapsed. She braced herself against the doorframe, her vertigo subdued for the moment by pure rage, and shot the little barber once more as he lay twitching on the floor. Then she turned her attention to the twin Harrys, looking for a way to tell the true Gant from the false. It wasn't hard.

One Harry remained hunched over the gaming rig, oblivious to the earthquake, the gunshots, and the many sounds of breakage, smiling and playing while chaos swirled around him.

One looked up. "Vanna!" this second Harry said, flashing a counterfeit smile of relief. "Thank God! I was so scared! I almost— . . . Vanna! Vanna, wait! Don't!—"

"Wrong move, imposter," Vanna said, and fired.

The Belly of the Beast

Which left Joan, alone in the cellars of Babel, fighting only to save her own life now, although she didn't know it.

She was still hammering at the bars—and Ayn had just resumed her backwards count—when the first tremor struck. Caught off balance, Joan was thrown back down the steps, gasping as she fell.

". . . eighteen . . . seventeen . . . sixteen . . ."

Joan sat up choking, and coughed out Fatima's whistle. The room shook violently; along the walls, the honeycomb pattern broke apart as the neat stacks of dynamite began collapsing into heaps.

". . . fifteen . . . fourteen . . ."

And still the strains of Ravel's *Bolero* could be heard beneath the rumbling of the 'quake, though Meisterbrau was nowhere to be seen.

". . . thirteen . . . twel—"

A jolt went through the steps, a jolt that was not part of the earthquake. Ayn's Lamp, already overbalancing, tipped over and fell, bouncing once on each stair before landing in Joan's lap.

"What?" Joan said.

"What?" Hoover squawked, even as the hidden speaker shorted out.

". . . ten . . . nine . . ."

Joan scrambled backwards. A fissure was opening in the floor.

". . . eight . . ."

The fissure widened. An entire slab of floor tilted up, like a trapdoor. Black earth welled up from underneath, and curved slats of clay-encrusted wood, wall sections from a very old sewer tunnel.

". . . seven . . . six . . . five . . ."

A gray fin appeared; a gray snout; a pair of gray claws. Like the demon Leviathan in a medieval stage play, Meisterbrau rose.

". . . four . . ."

So did Joan. The earth shrugged and bounced, but she bounced with it, her wounds forgotten. She kicked away a bundle of dynamite that had rolled too close. In her hand the Lamp grew hot; the Lamp globe glowed. She looked into it one last time, and saw Ayn nod.

". . . three . . . two . . ."

Meisterbrau opened wide; the music swelled. Joan hurled herself forward as a star blazed to life in her hand. And as the earth continued to shrug, and as the Tower of Babel tottered and swayed, she drove the Lamp, and her own right arm with it, into the belly of the beast.

23

Be cheerful while you are alive.

—Ptah-hotep, 24th century B.C.

Electric

The Great East Coast 'Quake of 2023 had its epicenter in New Jersey, but its effects were felt all over New England and as far south as Atlanta. Measuring 7.1 on the Richter scale, it lasted eighty-two seconds from start to finish.

The first tremors set off warning klaxons at power stations around the region. Emergency breakers tripped, shutting down generator turbines; at the Con-Ed nuclear plant in Scarsdale, engineers rushed to scram the reactor pile. Manhattan went dark. In his office at the Phoenix, Harry Gant slammed the side of the game rig and said: "Hey! Come on!"

The lights went out in Babel, too, but not before Morris Kazenstein succeeded in electrocuting the nanovirus. And by the time power failed in the control center at the top of the tower, the Eye of Africa had quit the scene. Traveling over a high-speed, encrypted data network to Mount Weather, Virginia, it reinstalled itself in a Defense Department supercomputer that had been hardened against nuclear attack; thus protected against both natural and unnatural disasters, it immediately generated a lethal virus subprogram and dispatched it westward on a mission of vengeance.

Fiber-optic lines carried this eidolon to the foothills of the Rockies, an angry shout in a glass thread; like a call to arms, it rang telephone bells up and down Colorado and New Mexico. Then, gathering momentum, it leapt the Continental Divide and dashed across the deserts of Utah and Nevada.

The cities of the East were still shaking as it passed through the central exchange of the 714 area code, seeking a hidden back door.

From the high ground of space, the Electric Eye of a C.I.A. Spy Hole satellite noticed a small thermal bloom on the landscape. The satellite's microprocessors went to work cataloging the event, first framing it in an increasingly precise series of location-boxes: Western Hemisphere. North America. United States of America. State of California. Orange County. City of Anaheim. Disneyland theme park. New Orleans Square. Southeast corner.

Burning.

Gas

The restaurant was called Gilead. Located across the street from heaven's velodrome, it was popular with new arrivals, a good place to unwind, sip Mai Tais, and start adjusting to the afterlife.

Joan, Kite, and Sister Ellen Fine sat together at the bar, drinking beer and smoking. Smoking two-fisted, in Joan's case: for along with their wisdom teeth, Joan's and Kite's arms had been returned to them at the pearly gates, Saint Peter digging through the severed-limbs drawer of his Roman filing cabinet. Unlike Joan, Kite had elected not to reattach hers just yet, but simply carried it with her, like a questionable gift she would probably keep but needed to get used to.

"So even if the bomb had gone off," Joan said, "it wouldn't have mattered. The nanovirus had already been dealt with . . . by Maxwell, of all people."

"With a little help from the press and the Shin Bet," Joan's mother said. "And a good thing, too, because if they *hadn't* dealt with it, the earthquake would have caused the virus canister to drop, explosion or no explosion . . ."

"So nothing I did made any difference."

"Not to black people. But by preventing the explosion, you did save Harry Gant millions of dollars in skyscraper repairs."

"And you finally killed Meisterbrau," Kite added. "Don't forget that."

The bar overlooked a garden with a pool in which a gray shark's fin circled contentedly. A man and a woman sat at a table beside the pool. The woman had a pageboy haircut and a flowing black cape; a gold dollar-sign pendant was pinned above her heart. The man had long curly hair, an impish grin, and a shirt sewn from pieces of an American flag; the top three buttons of the shirt were undone, revealing a furry chest and a peace symbol on a silver chain.

"Why is Abbie Hoffman sitting with Ayn?" Joan asked.

"Community service," her mother said.

"Community service?"

"He was a suicide. Suicides get a billion hours of community service."

"What service?"

"Psychological counseling. He's been assigned to help her develop a sense of humor."

"Lyndon Johnson and a rattlesnake are sitting on a fence," Abbie Hoffman was saying. "And the rattlesnake turns to Lyndon, and says—"

"No," Ayn Rand said.

"What?"

"Snakes cannot speak."

"Well yeah, I know they can't, but—"

"Also, it's unlikely that a president of the United States would be allowed to endanger himself by sitting next to a poisonous reptile. Nor would a rational man choose to do such a thing—which is not to say that architects of the welfare state should be regarded as rational. But—"

"Yeah," said Abbie, "but it's a joke, see? It doesn't *have* to make perfect sense, or at least the setup doesn't. The fact that it's a little absurd actually makes it funnier." Ayn looked skeptical. "So OK," Abbie continued. "Lyndon Johnson and a rattlesnake are sitting on a fence . . ."

"What kind of fence?"

Kite shook her head. "I'm glad my mortal wound wasn't self-inflicted," she said.

"Kite," Joan wondered aloud, "how bad were you hit?"

"I'm here, and you have to ask?"

"*Where* were you hit, though? What exactly was the wound?"

"The bullet smashed a rib on my left side, put a groove in my lung, and chewed up my spleen. I bled a lot."

"There was no spinal cord damage, though? Your heart wasn't touched?"

"Unfortunately. That would have hurt less and been over quicker."

Joan looked at her. "You can live without a spleen, you know. People have done it."

"They have," Kite agreed, "but I don't seem to be one of those people."

"But what I'm saying is, you could still stage a miraculous recovery. It's not like your head was chopped off . . ."

"Hold on," Sister Ellen Fine said. "What's this about recovery?"

"We could go back," Joan said. "Both of us, me and Kite. This doesn't have to be the end. We could go back."

"Joan. . . ." Her mother sighed. "You're *dead,* Joan."

"I could recover!"

"Your arm was bitten off . . ."

"People can survive losing an arm. Kite did."

"Not without help," Kite pointed out. "And I wasn't trapped in a sub-basement."

"Don't worry about the sub-basement," Joan said. "I'll get out of the sub-basement."

"How?" her mother asked.

"Well the earthquake probably shook the gates open. I didn't notice it at the time, because I was so frantic, but—"

"What if it didn't shake the gates open? What if it jammed them shut even tighter than before?"

"Then I'll get out through the hole Meisterbrau made in the floor."

"The shark's carcass is still in the hole."

"So I'll move it."

"With one arm?"

"Its insides have just been vaporized by a thermite charge. How much could it weigh?"

"Uh-huh. And if you do get out through the hole, then what? You'll be back in the sewers. If you couldn't climb up to a manhole before, how are you going to do it now?"

"I won't bother with the manhole. I'll circle around, come back into the sub-basement the same way I did the first time, and take the stairs."

"No good," Sister Ellen said. "You know that machinery they ripped out to make room for the dynamite? They used it to barricade the stairs. You're blocked in."

"Then I'll use some of the dynamite to blast through the barricade. That should bring the cops down, too, so even if I can't make it all the way to the lobby on my own, I'll be rescued . . ."

"It'll never work."

"You don't know that."

"You're in heaven, Joan. You're dead."

"Mom," Joan said, "this is *not* heaven. Heaven, if it exists at all, is nothing like this . . ."

"Oh?"

"For one thing, if this is heaven, where are all the people who died in the Pandemic? Look around. Do you see a single African or African-American? Where are they?"

"Well it's their paradise too, Joan. What makes you think they want to spend eternity in *your* presence?"

"This is *not* heaven, Mom. And since it isn't, I must be hallucinating, and if I'm hallucinating, I'm still alive, probably tying on a tourniquet and babbling to myself."

"But how do you know the dead can't hallucinate?" Kite asked. "That's a pretty bold assumption, isn't it?"

"Don't start," Joan warned.

"All right," Abbie Hoffman said. "Let's try something a little simpler. 'Knock, knock.'"

"I beg your pardon?" Ayn Rand said.

"Not 'I beg your pardon.' I say 'Knock, knock,' and you say, 'Who's there?'"

"But I already know who's there. I can see you."

"Yeah, but pretend you can't see me. Just—"

"You want me to deny the evidence of my senses?"

"No, see, the idea is—"

"Are you a communist?" Ayn asked suddenly. "Is that why you desecrate the American flag?"

"Joan!" Sister Ellen called. "Joan, sit down!"

"No!" Joan said. "Fuck it, Mom, I've got things I want to do yet. And I won't have my last act be a screw up. I'm going back!"

"Joan—" But she was already storming for the exit, shoving aside a carpenter's son who had just stepped out of the men's room.

"Oh dear," said Kite. And leaving her arm at the bar but remembering to take her cigarettes, she got up to follow.

Sewer

The lights of Manhattan were back on by Monday.

Harry Gant had described his city as having "the best engineering anchored in some of the toughest bedrock in the world," and he was right, particularly about the bedrock; though some parts of the Tri-State Area had been devastated by the earthquake, Manhattan Island came through relatively unscathed. True, the eighty-two seconds of sustained vibration did reveal some engineering deficiencies. Many older buildings suffered structural damage, and a few especially poorly maintained structures failed entirely; a minute into the 'quake, the Brooklyn Bridge fell down. The temblor also pointed up some problems with the Island's four-hundred-year-old infrastructure. Ruptured gas and water mains unleashed a plague of fire and flood in select neighborhoods; in one of the most horrifying incidents, exploding mains set all three towers of Trump's Riverside Arcadia ablaze, and those residents who escaped the flames were attacked at street level by a wave of mutant *Rattus norvegicus,* driven up from underground by a rising tide of sewage.

So Public Works emergency response crews *did* have their hands full for a while. But by Monday morning, a sense of normalcy had begun to reassert itself. New York City had always been something of a disaster area, after all, and as the mayor reminded his surviving constituents during a rush-hour radio broadcast, hey, it could have been a hell of a lot worse: 7.1 on the Richter scale was nothing compared to the 8.5-magnitude Apocalypse predicted by certain pessimists. What's more, it was shaping up to be a beautiful week, unseasonably warm and sunny, and all citizens were encouraged to enjoy the new vistas being created by the dynamiting of unstable buildings.

Around nine A.M., shortly after power was restored to the business district, Harry Gant decided to go for a walk. Like the Public Works Department, he'd been busy since the 'quake, working out of a temporary command post set up on the ground floor of the Phoenix. Over the weekend his sales force had fielded hundreds of calls from city and state agencies requesting Servants for use in the recovery effort; extra shifts had been ordered at Gant's manufacturing plants to meet the demand. In what little spare time he had, Harry kept in touch with his parents, who—short of breath, but otherwise none the worse for their ordeal—were recuperating at the Times Square Hilton; he also spoke regularly with Vanna, who despite whiplash and a severe concussion insisted on managing all media coverage from her hospital bed. By Monday he was ready for a break, and after his mother called to remind him that it was his birthday, he decided to give himself the morning off. He told his staff he'd be gone for a few hours and stepped out onto 34th Street to greet the day.

It *was* nice out; a warm, gentle breeze was blowing, fresh off the East River but virtually odor free. And midtown was in fine shape, only a little more rubble strewn than usual. Granted, a huge sinkhole had opened on

Fifth Avenue and swallowed two lanes of traffic, but that was hardly unprecedented, and Harry's fellow New Yorkers—those who had not been crushed, burned, drowned, or eaten by rats—looked lively and purposeful as they hurried along to their various destinations.

Avoiding the sinkhole, Gant walked west towards the Hudson, following the same route Eddie Wilder had taken only a week previously. Just like Eddie, he paused at the corner of Broadway to rubberneck at the sights, one in particular: looking over his shoulder at the Phoenix, he was pleased to see that the Electric Billboards were back in action. But the featured advertisements had changed during the blackout; the giant's day-calendar page that had so puzzled Eddie had been succeeded by an equally mysterious Eye, a solitary green Eye that gazed out watchfully over the city.

"Hmm," said Harry Gant, not recognizing the logo, "I wonder what that means. . . ." But just then the quarter-hour struck, and the Billboard ads shifted clockwise around the skyscraper; the Eye was displaced by the Coca-Cola trademark. "Yeah," Harry Gant said. "Good idea."

He bought soda and a sandwich from a street vendor and stopped to browse at a newsstand. The *Times* contained mostly sober accounts of the 'quake aftermath, with the latest damage and casualty estimates; on the editorial page Lockheed Martin, makers of quality combat aircraft, offered their condolences to the suffering.

The *New York Post* was less restrained in its coverage. The early edition carried a banner headline:

STILL STANDING!

Below this were two photos of New Babel, one a long shot showing the whole Tower, the other a detail of the ziggurat's highest construction platform, with a solitary figure silhouetted against the clouds, a man in a high place alone, undaunted. Harry recognized Vanna Domingo's handiwork: the close-up shot was a stock publicity photo, taken over a year ago; Gant hadn't had a chance to get up to Babel since the earthquake, though he'd heard reports of the goings-on there. So had the *Post*. A caption beneath the photos read:

Erratic android behavior linked to pre-quake magnetic fluctuations;
Servants could be used as predictive devices, Gant spokeswoman
speculates. [story, pg. 3]

"Nice save, Vanna," Harry Gant said. "Now if we can just figure out what *really* happened . . ."

A sidebar promised other stories:

Mona Lisa recovered; looter fleeing National Guard
unit finds stolen masterpiece in former Harlem landmark.
(pg. 7)

•

Fed agent who escaped downed chopper is improving, docs say;
boss says hero Vogelsang will receive commendation, promotion.
(pg. 15)

•

Beached whale sicks up eyeless man in Rockaway;
irate Jonah taken to Bellevue after assaulting paramedic.
(pg. 19)

•

Philo Dufresne: Nazi lover?
Former Wiesenthal Center director weighs the evidence.
(editorial, pg. 24)

•

Disaster chronicler Peller feared slain by L.A. serial killer.
Corpse I.D. stymied by missing parts; cops need *your* help.
(color pics w/phone-in contest details, centerpage B)

Harry paid for the *Post* and continued his walk crosstown. Near Eleventh Avenue he caught sight of a woman in a green and white Department of Sewers uniform, which reminded him that he still hadn't heard from Joan. He supposed, given the events of the past week, that he ought to be concerned for her safety, but something told him not to bother: Joan just wasn't the type to die in an earthquake, and having seen her knock the stuffing out of a purse snatcher once, Harry could only pity the man—or the machine—that thought to get the better of her in a fight.

Besides which, the omens were all pointing in the other direction. On Thursday night, Joan's friend Kite had succumbed to her wounds, slipping away while Gant and a semi-conscious Vanna tried to figure out how to transport her down two hundred flights of stairs. Eventually they found a way to lower the window washer's platform without power—an open-air thrill ride Harry hoped never to repeat—but by the time they reached the sidewalk and flagged down an ambulance, it was much too late; Kite was pronounced dead at the scene. But then on Friday word had come from the city morgue that her body had disappeared. *They must've just misplaced it,* Harry thought at first. *Place must be a zoo with all the 'quake casualties.* But when Vanna sent an assistant to check on the matter personally, it turned out Kite hadn't been misplaced: she'd gotten up and walked out. The medical examiner had returned from a doughnut run to find an empty slab and a discarded toe tag; bloody footprints tracked from the cold storage room across the hall to the forensics lab (where matches were kept), and from there to an exit stairwell.

So if *that* sort of thing was going on, Harry wasn't going to waste his time worrying about Joan; he just wished she'd call.

He was at the extreme west end of 34th Street now, at the docks. Like the East River, the Hudson smelled pretty good today; a lot of upstate mills and factories had been shut down for repairs, and even the city's sewer out-flows had slacked off now that the water mains were being fixed. Looking around for a place to have his breakfast, Gant spotted a quaint wooden pier jutting out from the shoreline. He walked out to the end of it and sat down, dangling his legs over the river; he spread out his paper, opened up his Coke, and took a bite of his sandwich.

He was about to take a second bite when he noticed the alligator. Packing crates and other shipping debris had been abandoned along the pier; a couple of arm-lengths from where Harry was sitting, a steel drum lay on its side, its open end facing him. He'd assumed it was empty, but now the sound of raspy breathing drew his attention, and he saw that there was a little albino reptile curled up inside, looking out at him.

"Huh," Harry Gant said. "Huh." The alligator shifted position slightly; morning sunlight fell across the tip of its snout, highlighting its pale skin. *Alligator manhattoe,* Harry thought, hearing his father's voice in his head. *Alligator manhattoe,* the legendary Manhattan sewer 'gator, believed by many scholars to be extinct, or to never have existed at all. But Jerry Gant knew better—and now, so did Harry.

"You like tunafish?" he asked uncertainly. The alligator's head came up, and a sixth sense warned Harry to get the sandwich out of his hand. He tossed it underhand, like a softball. The 'gator scooted forward with amazing speed; Gant had a brief glimpse of jaw muscles and teeth, and then the sandwich was gone. It had never touched the ground.

"Huh," Harry said. The alligator was right beside him now, sniffing at his thigh and at the edges of the paper in his lap; he was suddenly glad he hadn't bought a copy of the edible *Long Distance Call.* "Easy now," he said, as the alligator nuzzled his trousers. "Easy, little guy. . . . " The 'gator's head came up again, and Gant froze, arms in the air. But the 'gator didn't bite him; it just shuffled forward a couple more feet and rested its long chin across his knees.

The *manhattoe*'s head was heavy in his lap. It was snuggling in, making itself comfortable. Preparing for a long nap, possibly. Gant turned his own head to see if there was anyone back on the wharf who might be noticing this. No such luck; traffic was moving along Twelfth Avenue, but there were no pedestrians close enough to pay any attention to him.

"Huh. Well." The alligator's chin lay on the open newspaper; Harry thought that if it really did take a nap, he might be able to slide his legs out from under it. Maybe. But the 'gator didn't go to sleep; it just lay there. Harry, not sure what else to do, lowered his right hand until his palm touched the top of the *manhattoe*'s snout. The 'gator blinked but didn't object; Harry moved his hand in a tentative stroking motion.

A mewling sound issued from the back of the alligator's throat, like the purring of a big cat with a mouthful of swamp water. Encouraged, Harry kept stroking it; the 'gator's eyelids fluttered and closed. It seemed to snore. As an experiment, Harry shifted his right leg a fraction of an inch.

The alligator stopped snoring. Its eyes snapped open again. It looked unhappy.

"Right," Harry Gant said, and went on petting it.

He passed the time by studying his new friend. It really was a little fellow, no more than four feet from nose to tail. A strange black box had been grafted onto its head; a crude mind-control device, the box was broken now, battered into silence by the same torrent that had flushed the 'gator from its sewer nest into the river.

The pale leather hide was covered with scars. The albinism had made the alligator's skin seem delicate at first, but Gant saw now that that wasn't true at all: the poor little guy had clearly been through a lot. As he studied the *manhattoe*'s hind foot, which had had a chunk torn out of it, Harry heard his father's voice again, telling him a story about evolution. Alligators and crocodiles, his father said, were ancient creatures who'd come into being hundreds of millions of years ago, in the time of the first dinosaurs; and their line had endured, long after the fall of the terrible lizards. Not even human-kind had been able to stamp them out completely. Not yet.

"Survivor," Harry said, warming to the reptile. "You little survivor, you."

And the thought came to him then: you know, if there were some way to domesticate these things, train them not to bite, maybe grow them just a *bit* smaller, they really would make nifty pets. Exciting for kids, and with a great sales hook, too: a kind of at-home save-the-endangered-species project. Barely had he thought that when a complete line of tie-in merchandise began parading through his imagination: *manhattoe* pet supplies and veterinary services; *manhattoe* obedience schools; "I ♥ my *manhattoe*" coffee mugs; *manhattoe* designer polo shirts with the albino alligator on the pocket . . .

Hey.

Hey.

"What a neat idea," Harry Gant said. As his brain got busy he could feel further inspirations coming on, bubbling up out of that place in the subconscious that plastic lawn flamingos come from.

The morning sun rose above the fractured towers of the city, bringing new light and new hope. It really was turning out to be a wonderful day, Gant reflected; and he could hardly wait to see what he would think of next.

Boston / Blairsville, Georgia / Portland, Maine
February 1990–September 1994

Acknowledgments

No one helped me . . .

—Ayn Rand, postscript to *Atlas Shrugged*

No one finishes a long novel alone, and this one took longer than most; a lot of people helped me.

First, heartfelt thanks to my father, whose faith and trust meant a lot, and whose generosity spared me from the pursuit of a more practical line of work. Melanie Jackson, Sue Dinan, Robbs Lippert, Mary Winifred Hood, Jeff Schwaner, Lisa Vodra, Sonja Trent and the Trent family, and Jeanne Wells all offered moral support when I needed it most; Lisa Gold was a constant friend and an unfailing source of aid, advice, and comfort. Tony Mulieri helped me out in a pinch; Josh Spin answered my questions about race-specific viruses without getting flustered; John Piccolini and Nick Humez shored up my French and Latin; and Morgan Entrekin forgave deadline after deadline, as what was supposed to be a two-year project stretched to four and change.

The characterization of Ayn Rand and the description of her philosophy contained in these pages is based on my own reading of *We the Living, The Fountainhead,* and *Atlas Shrugged,* Nathaniel Branden's *Judgment Day,* Barbara Branden's *The Passion of Ayn Rand,* Leonard Peikoff's *Objectivism,* and Harry Binswanger's *The Ayn Rand Lexicon;* Walter Truett Anderson's *Reality Isn't What It Used to Be* was also extremely useful to me at a point where I knew what I wanted to say but not quite how to put it. Most of the details about Walt Disney's life and work come from Leonard Mosley's biography *Disney's World*—but the character of John Hoover is *entirely* fictional, based on no real scientist, mad or otherwise, that Disney ever employed. Likewise, the G.A.S. supercomputer bears no intentional resemblance to any piece of machinery ever built, owned, leased, or operated by Walt Disney, Roy Disney, or the benevolent, law-abiding Disney corporation.

"Adoxography" means "good writing about trivial subjects," and for my encyclopedic knowledge of such things as George Washington's submarine fleet, I am indebted to the tireless documentary work of adoxographers like Robert Daley, William Poundstone, Cecil Adams, Neil Steinberg, Hal Morgan, Kerry Tucker, David Wallechinsky, and Irving and Amy Wallace.

Thanks also to the *New York Times,* newspaper of record, for confirming that even in a rational universe, "far-fetched" is a relative term. In an article dated February 10, 1935, the *Times* recounts the story of a group of teenagers who found a seven-and-a-half-foot alligator in a Harlem sewer, dragged it up onto the street, and beat it to death with shovels. Public Works officials have since denied the existence of any reptile larger than a turtle in the New York underground, but we know the truth.

M.R.
1996